Rage

WILBUR SMITH

HEINEMANN : LONDON

William Heinemann Ltd
10 Upper Grosvenor Street, London W1X 9PA
LONDON   MELBOURNE
JOHANNESBURG   AUCKLAND

First published 1987
© Wilbur Smith 1987

0 434 71418 6

Printed in Great Britain by
Richard Clay Ltd, Bungay, Suffolk

I dedicate this book to my wife, Danielle

Hand in hand we have crossed the continents of this earth,
But none of them was as broad as my love for you.

Together we have voyaged on all the oceans,
But none was as deep as my love for you.

Tara Courtney had not worn white since her wedding day. Green was her favourite colour, for it best set off her thick chestnut hair.

However, the white dress she wore today made her feel like a bride again, tremulous and a little afraid but with a sense of joy and deep commitment. She had a touch of ivory lace at the cuffs and the high neckline, and had brushed her hair until it crackled with ruby lights in the bright Cape sunshine. Excitement had rouged her cheeks and although she had carried four children, her waist was slim as a virgin's. So the wide sash of funereal black that she wore over one shoulder was all the more incongruous: youth and beauty decked in the trappings of mourning. Despite her emotional turmoil, she stood with her hands clasped in front of her and her head bowed, silent and still.

She was only one of almost fifty women, all dressed in white, all draped with the black sashes, all in the same attitude of mourning, who stood at carefully spaced intervals along the pavement opposite the main entrance of the parliament buildings of the Union of South Africa.

Nearly all of the women were young matrons from Tara's own set, wealthy, privileged and bored by the undemanding tenor of their lives. Many of them had joined the protest for the excitement of defying established authority and outraging their peers. Some were seeking to regain the attentions of their husbands which after the first decade or so of marriage were jaded by familiarity and fixed more on business or golf and other extra marital activity. There was, however, a hard nucleus to the movement consisting mostly of the older women, but including a few of the younger ones like Tara and Molly Broadhurst. These were moved only by revulsion at injustice. Tara had tried to express her feelings at the press conference that morning when a woman reporter from the *Cape Argus* had demanded of her, 'Why are you doing this, Mrs Courtney?' and she had replied, 'Because I don't like bullies, and I don't like cheats.' For her that attitude was partially vindicated now.

'Here comes the big bad wolf,' the woman who stood five paces on Tara's right said softly. 'Brace up, girls!' Molly Broadhurst was one of the founders of the Black Sash, a small determined woman in her early thirties whom Tara greatly admired and strove to emulate.

1

A black Chevrolet with government licence plates had drawn up at the corner of Parliament Square and four men climbed out on to the pavement. One was a police photographer and he went to work immediately, moving quickly down the line of white-clad, black-draped women with his Hasselblad camera, photographing each of them. He was followed by two of the others brandishing notebooks. Though they were dressed in dark, ill-cut business suits, their clumpy black shoes were regulation police issue and their actions were brusque and businesslike as they passed down the ranks demanding and noting the names and addresses of each of the protesters. Tara, who was fast becoming something of an expert, guessed that they probably ranked as sergeants in the special branch, but the fourth man she knew by name and by sight, as did most of the others.

He was dressed in a light grey summer suit with brown brogues, a plain maroon tie and a grey fedora hat. Though of average height and unremarkable features, his mouth was wide and friendly, his smile easy as he lifted his hat to Molly.

'Good morning, Mrs Broadhurst. You are early. The procession won't arrive for another hour yet.'

'Are you going to arrest us all again today, Inspector?' Molly demanded tartly.

'Perish the thought.' The inspector raised an eyebrow. 'It's a free country, you know.'

'You could have fooled me.'

'Naughty Mrs Broadhurst!' He shook his head. 'You are trying to provoke me.' His English was excellent, with only a faint trace of an Afrikaans accent.

'No, Inspector. We are protesting the blatant gerrymandering of this perverse government, the erosion of the rule of law, and the abrogation of the basic human rights of the majority of our fellow South Africans merely on the grounds of the colour of their skins.'

'I think, Mrs Broadhurst, you are repeating yourself. You told me all this last time we met.' The inspector chuckled. 'Next you'll actually be demanding that I arrest you again. Let's not spoil this grand occasion —'

'The opening of this parliament, dedicated as it is to injustice and oppression, is a cause for lament not celebration.'

The inspector tipped the brim of his hat, but beneath his flippant attitude was a real respect and perhaps even a little admiration.

'Carry on, Mrs Broadhurst,' he murmured. 'I'm sure we'll meet again soon,' and he sauntered on until he came opposite Tara.

'Good morning to you, Mrs Courtney.' He paused, and this time his admiration was unconcealed. 'What does your illustrious husband think of your treasonable behaviour?'

'Is it treason to oppose the excesses of the National Party and its legislation based on race and colour, Inspector?'

His gaze dropped for a moment to her bosom, large and yet finely shaped beneath the white lace, and then returned to her face.

'You are much too pretty for this nonsense,' he said. 'Leave it to the grey-headed old prunes. Go home where you belong and look after your babies.'

'Your masculine arrogance is insufferable, Inspector.' She flushed with anger, unaware that it heightened the looks he had just complimented.

'I wish all traitoresses looked the way you do. It would make my job a great deal more congenial. Thank you, Mrs Courtney.' He smiled infuriatingly and moved on.

'Don't let him rattle you, my dear,' Molly called softly. 'He's an expert at it. We are protesting passively. Remember Mahatma Gandhi.'

With an effort Tara controlled her anger, and reassumed the attitude of the penitent. On the pavement behind her the crowds of spectators began to gather. The rank of white-clad women became the object of curiosity and amusement, of some approbation and a great deal of hostility.

'Goddamn commies,' a middle-aged man growled at Tara. 'You want to hand the country over to a bunch of savages. You should be locked up, the whole lot of you.' He was well dressed, and his speech cultivated. He even wore the small brass tin hat insignia in his lapel to signify that he had served with the volunteer forces during the war against fascism. His attitude was a reminder of just how much tacit support the ruling National party enjoyed even amongst the English-speaking white community.

Tara bit her lip and forced herself to remain silent, head bowed, even when the outburst earned a ragged ironical cheer from some of the coloured people in the growing crowd.

It was getting hot now, the sunshine had a flat Mediterranean brilliance, and though the mattress of cloud was building up above the great flat-topped bastion of Table Mountain, heralding the rise of the south-easter, the wind had not yet reached the city that crouched below it. By now the crowd was dense and noisy, and Tara was jostled, she suspected deliberately. She kept her composure and concentrated on the building across the road from where she stood.

Designed by Sir Herbert Baker, that paragon of Imperial architects, it was massive and imposing, red brick colonnaded in shimmering white – far from Tara's own modern taste, which inclined to uncluttered space and lines, to glass and light Scandinavian pine furnishing. The building seemed to epitomize all that was inflexible

3

and out-dated from the past, all that Tara wanted to see torn down and discarded.

Her thoughts were broken by the rising hum of expectation from the crowd around her.

'Here they come,' Molly called, and the crowd surged and swayed and broke into cheers. There was the clatter of hooves on the hard-metalled roadway and the mounted police escort trotted up the avenue, pennants fluttering gaily at the tips of their lances, expert horsemen on matched chargers whose hides gleamed like burnished metal in the sunlight.

The open coaches rumbled along behind them. In the first of these rode the governor-general and the prime minister. There he was, Daniel Malan, champion of the Afrikaners, with his forbidding almost froglike features, a man whose only consideration and declared intent was to keep his *Volk* supreme in Africa for a thousand years, and no price was for him too high.

Tara stared at him with palpable hatred, for he embodied all that she found repellent in the government which now held sway over the land and the peoples which she loved so dearly. As the coach swept past where she stood, their eyes met for a fleeting moment and she tried to convey the strength of her feelings, but he glanced at her without a flicker of acknowledgement, not even a shadow of annoyance, in his brooding gaze. He had looked at her and had not seen her, and now her anger was tinged with despair.

'What must be done to make these people even listen?' she wondered, but now the dignitaries had dismounted from the carriages and were standing to attention during the playing of the national anthems. And though Tara did not know it then, it was the last time 'The King' would be played at the opening of a South African Parliament.

The band ended with a fanfare of trumpets and the cabinet ministers followed the governor-general and the prime minister through the massive front entrance doors. They were followed in turn by the opposition front-benchers. This was the moment Tara had been dreading, for her own close family now formed part of the procession. Next behind the leader of the opposition came Tara's own father with her stepmother on his arm. They made the most striking couple in the long procession, her father tall and dignified as a patriarchal lion, while on his arm Centaine de Thiry Courtney-Malcomess was slim and graceful in a yellow silk dress that was perfect for the occasion, a jaunty brimless hat on her small neat head with a veil over one eye; she seemed not a year older than Tara herself, though everybody knew she had been named Centaine because she had been born on the first day of the twentieth century.

4

Tara thought she had escaped unnoticed, for none of them had known she intended joining the protest, but at the top of the broad staircase the procession was held up for a moment and before she entered the doorway Centaine turned deliberately and looked back. From her vantage point she could see over the heads of the escort and the other dignitaries in the procession, and from across the road she caught Tara's eye and held it for a moment. Although her expression did not alter, the strength of her disapproval was even at that range like a slap in Tara's face. For Centaine the honour, dignity and good name of the family were of paramount importance. She had warned Tara repeatedly about making a public spectacle of herself and flouting Centaine was a perilous business, for she was not only Tara's stepmother but her mother-in-law as well, and the doyenne of the Courtney family and fortune.

Halfway up the staircase behind her Shasa Courtney saw the direction and force of his mother's gaze, and turning quickly to follow it saw Tara, his wife, in the rank of black-sashed protesters. When she had told him that morning at breakfast that she would not be joining him at the opening ceremony, Shasa had barely looked up from the financial pages of the morning newspaper.

'Suit yourself, my dear. It will be a bit of a bore,' he had murmured. 'But I would like another cup of coffee, when you have a moment.'

Now when he recognized her, he smiled slightly and shook his head in mock despair, as though she were a child discovered in some naughty prank, and then he turned away as the procession moved forward once again.

He was almost impossibly handsome, and the black eye-patch gave him a debonair piratical look that most women found intriguing and challenging. Together they were renowned as the handsomest young couple in Cape Town society. Yet it was strange how the passage of a few short years had caused the flames of their love to sink into a puddle of grey ash.

'Suit yourself, my dear,' he had said, as he did so often these days.

The last back-benchers in the procession disappeared into the House, the mounted escort and empty carriages trotted away and the crowds began to break up. The demonstration was over.

'Are you coming, Tara?' Molly called, but Tara shook her head.

'Have to meet Shasa,' she said. 'See you on Friday afternoon.' Tara slipped the wide black sash off over her head, folded it and placed it in her handbag as she threaded her way through the dispersing crowd. She crossed the road.

She saw no irony in now presenting her parliamentary pass to the doorman at the visitors' entrance and entering the institution against

5

whose actions she had been so vigorously protesting. She climbed the side staircase and looked into the visitors' gallery. It was packed with wives and important guests, and she looked over their heads down into the panelled chamber below to the rows of sombre-suited members on their green leather-covered benches, all involved in the impressive ritual of parliament. However, she knew that the speeches would be trivial, platitudinous and boring to the point of pain, and she had been standing in the street since early morning. She needed to visit the ladies room as a matter of extreme urgency.

She smiled at the usher and withdrew surreptitiously, then turned and hurried away down the wide panelled corridor. When she had finished in the ladies room, she headed for her father's office, which she used as her own.

As she turned the corner she almost collided with a man coming in the opposite direction. She checked only just in time, and saw that he was a tall black man dressed in the uniform of a parliamentary servant. She would have passed on with a nod and a smile, when it occurred to her that a servant should not have been in this section of the building during the time when the House was in session, for the offices of the prime minister and the leader of the opposition were at the end of the corridor. Then again, although the servant carried a mop and pail, there was something about him that was neither menial nor servile and she looked sharply at his face.

She felt an electric tingle of recognition. It had been many years, but she could never forget that face – the features of an Egyptian pharaoh, noble and fierce, the dark eyes alive with intelligence. He was still one of the finest-looking men she had ever seen, and she remembered his voice, deep and thrilling so that the memory of it made her shiver slightly. She even remembered his words: 'There is a generation, whose teeth are as swords . . . to devour the poor from the earth.'

It was this man who had given her the first glimmer of understanding as to what it was like to be born black in South Africa. Her true commitment dated from that distant meeting. This man had changed her life with a few words.

She stopped, blocking his path, and tried to find some way to convey her feelings to him, but her throat had closed and she found she was trembling from the shock. The instant he knew he had been recognized, he changed, like a leopard coming on guard as it becomes aware of the hunters. Tara sensed she was in danger, for a sense of African cruelty invested him, but she was unafraid.

'I am a friend,' she said softly, and stood aside to let him pass. 'Our cause is the same.'

He did not move for a moment, but stared at her. She knew that

6

he would never forget her again, his scrutiny seemed to set her skin on fire, and then he nodded.

'I know you,' he acknowledged, and once again his voice made her shiver, deep and melodious, filled with the rhythm and cadence of Africa. 'We will meet again.'

Then he passed on and without a backward glance disappeared around the corner of the panelled corridor. She stood staring after him, and her heart was pounding, her breath burned the back of her throat.

'Moses Gama,' she whispered his name aloud. 'Messiah and warrior of Africa —' then she paused and shook her head. 'What are you doing here, in this of all places?'

The possibilities intrigued and stirred her, for now she knew with a deep instinct that the crusade was afoot, and she longed to be part of it. She wanted to do more than merely stand on a street corner with a black sash draped over her shoulder. She knew Moses Gama had only to crook his finger and she would follow him, she and ten million others.

'We will meet again,' he had promised, and she believed him.

Light with joy she went on down the passageway. She had her own key to her father's office and as she fitted it to the lock, her eyes were on a level with the brass plate:

COLONEL BLAINE MALCOMESS
DEPUTY LEADER OF THE OPPOSITION

With surprise she found that the lock was already opened, and she pushed the door wide and went in.

Centaine Courtney-Malcomess turned from the window beyond the desk to confront her. 'I have been waiting for you, young lady.' Centaine's French accent was an affectation that annoyed Tara. She has been back to France just once in thirty-five years, she thought, and lifted her chin defiantly.

'Don't toss your head at me, Tara *chérie*,' Centaine went on. 'When you act like a child, you must expect to be treated as a child.'

'No, Mater, you are wrong. I do not expect you to treat me as a child, not now or ever. I am a married woman of thirty-three years of age, the mother of four children and the mistress of my own establishment.'

Centaine sighed. 'All right,' she nodded. 'My concern made me ill-mannered, and I apologize. Let's not make this discussion any more difficult for each other than it already is.'

'I was not aware that we needed to discuss anything.'

'Sit down, Tara,' Centaine ordered, and Tara obeyed instinctively

7

and then was annoyed with herself for doing so. Centaine took her father's chair behind the desk, and Tara resented that also – it was Daddy's chair and this woman had no right to it.

'You have just told me that you are a wife with four children,' Centaine spoke quietly. 'Would you not agree that you have a duty —'

'My children are well cared for,' Tara flared at her. 'You cannot accuse me of that.'

'And what about your husband and your marriage?'

'What about Shasa?' Tara was immediately defensive.

'You tell me,' Centaine invited.

'It's none of your business.'

'Oh, but it is,' Centaine contradicted her. 'I have devoted my entire life to Shasa. I plan for him to be one of the leaders of this nation.' She paused and a dreamy glaze covered her eyes for a moment, and she seemed to squint slightly. Tara had noticed that expression before, whenever Centaine was in deep thought, and now she wanted to break in upon it as brutally as she could.

'That's impossible and you know it.'

Centaine's eyes snapped back into focus and she glared at Tara. 'Nothing is impossible – not for me, not for us.'

'Oh yes it is,' Tara gloated. 'You know as well as I do that the Nationalists have gerrymandered the electorate, that they have even loaded the Senate with their own appointees. They are in power for ever. Never again will anyone who is not one of them, an Afrikaner Nationalist, ever be this country's leader, not until the revolution – and when that is over, the leader will be a black man,' Tara broke off and thought for an instant of Moses Gama.

'You are naïve,' Centaine snapped. 'You do not understand these things. Your talk of revolution is childish and irresponsible.'

'Have it your own way, Mater. But deep down you know it's so. Your darling Shasa will never fulfil your dream. Even he is beginning to sense the futility of being in opposition for ever. He is losing interest in the impossible. I wouldn't be surprised if he decides not to contest the next election, gives up the political aspirations that you have foisted on him and simply goes off to make himself another trillion pounds.'

'No,' Centaine shook her head. 'He won't give up. He is a fighter like I am.'

'He'll never be even a cabinet minister, let alone prime minister,' Tara stated flatly.

'If you believe that, then you are no wife for my son,' Centaine said.

'You said it,' Tara said softly. 'You said it, not me.'

'Oh, Tara, my dear, I am sorry.' Centaine reached across the desk

8

but it was too broad for her to touch Tara's hand. 'Forgive me. I lost my temper. All this is so desperately important to me. I feel it so deeply, but I did not mean to antagonize you. I want only to help you – I am so worried about you and Shasa. I want to help, Tara. Won't you let me help you?'

'I don't see that we need help,' Tara lied sweetly. 'Shasa and I are perfectly happy. We have four lovely children —'

Centaine made an impatient gesture. 'Tara, you and I haven't always seen eye to eye. But I am your friend, I truly am. I want the best for you and Shasa and the little ones. Won't you let me help you?'

'How, Mater? By giving us money – you have already given us ten or twenty million – or is it thirty million pounds? I lose track sometimes.'

'Won't you let me share my experience with you? Won't you listen to my advice?'

'Yes, Mater, I'll listen. I don't promise to take it, but I'll listen to it.'

'Firstly, Tara dear, you must give up these crazy left-wing activities. You bring the whole family into disrepute. You make a spectacle of yourself, and therefore of us, by dressing up and standing on street corners. Apart from that, it is positively dangerous. The Suppression of Communism Act is now law. You could be declared a communist, and placed under a banning order. Just consider that, you would become a non-person, deprived of all human rights and dignity. Then there is Shasa's political career. What you do reflects on him.'

'Mater, I promised to listen,' Tara said stonily. 'But now I withdraw that promise. I know what I am doing.' She stood up and moved to the door where she paused and looked back. 'Did you ever think, Centaine Courtney-Malcomess, that my mother died of a broken heart, and it was your blatant adultery with my father that broke it for her? Yet you can sit there smugly and advise me how to conduct my life, so as not to disgrace you and your precious son.' She went out and closed the heavy teak door softly behind her.

* * *

Shasa Courtney lolled on the opposition front bench with his hands pushed deeply into his pockets, his legs thrust out and crossed at the ankles, and listened intently to the minister of police outlining the legislation which he intended bringing before the House during the current session.

The minister of police was the youngest member of the cabinet, a

9

man of approximately the same age as Shasa, which was extraordinary. The Afrikaner revered age and mistrusted the inexperience and impetuosity of youth. The average age of the other members of the Nationalist cabinet could not be less than sixty-five years, Shasa reflected, and yet here was Manfred De La Rey standing before them, a mere stripling of less than forty years, setting out the general contents of the Criminal Law Amendment Bill which he would be proposing and shepherding through its various stages.

'He is asking for the right to declare a state of emergency which will put the police above the law, without appeal to the courts,' Blaine Malcomess grunted beside him, and Shasa nodded without looking at his father-in-law. Instead he was watching the man across the floor.

Manfred De La Rey was speaking in Afrikaans, as he usually did. His English was heavily accented and laboured, and he spoke it unwillingly, making only the barest gesture towards the bilingualism of the House. On the other hand, when speaking in his mother tongue, he was eloquent and persuasive, his oratorial attitudes and devices were so skilled as to seem entirely natural and more than once he raised a chuckle of exasperated admiration from the opposition benches and a chorus of *'Hoor, hoor!'* from his own party.

'The fellow has a damned cheek.' Blaine Malcomess shook his head. 'He is asking for the right to suspend the rule of law and impose a police state at the whim of the ruling party. We'll have to fight that tooth and nail.'

'My word!' Shasa agreed mildly, but he found himself envying the other man, and yet mysteriously drawn to him. It was strange how their two destinies seemed to be inexorably linked.

He had first met Manfred De La Rey twenty years ago, and for no apparent reason the two of them had flown at each other on the spot like young game cocks and fought a bloody bout of fisticuffs. Shasa grimaced at the way it had ended, the drubbing he had received still rankled even after all that time. Since then their paths had crossed and recrossed.

In 1936 they had both been on the national team that went to Adolf Hitler's Olympic Games in Berlin, but it had been Manfred De La Rey in the boxing ring who collected the only gold medal the team had won, while Shasa returned empty-handed. They had hotly and acrimoniously contested the same seat in the 1948 elections that had seen the National Party come sweeping to power, and again it was Manfred De La Rey who had won the seat and taken his place in parliament, while Shasa had to wait for a by-election in a safe United Party constituency to secure his own place on the opposition benches from which to confront his rival once again. Now Manfred

10

was a minister, a position that Shasa coveted with all his heart, and with his undoubted brilliance and oratorical skills together with growing political acumen and a solid power base within the party, Manfred De La Rey's future must be unbounded.

Envy, admiration and furious antagonism – that was what Shasa Courtney felt as he listened to the man across the floor from him, and he studied him intently.

Manfred De La Rey still had a boxer's physique, wide shoulders and powerful neck, but he was thickening around the waist and his jawline was beginning to blur with flesh. He wasn't keeping himself in shape and hard muscle was turning flabby. Shasa glanced down at his own lean hips and greyhound belly with self-satisfaction and then concentrated again on his adversary.

Manfred De La Rey's nose was twisted and there was a gleaming white scar through one of his dark eyebrows, injuries he had received in the boxing ring. However, his eyes were a strange pale colour, like yellow topaz, implacable as the eyes of a cat and yet with the fire of his fine intellect in their depths. Like all the Nationalist cabinet ministers, with the exception of the prime minister himself, he was a highly educated and brilliant man, devout and dedicated, totally convinced of the divine right of his party and his *Volk*.

'They truly believe they are God's instruments on earth. That's what makes them so damned dangerous.' Shasa smiled grimly as Manfred finished speaking and sat down to the roar of approval from his own side of the House. They were waving order papers, and the prime minister leaned across to pat Manfred's shoulder, while a dozen congratulatory notes were passed to him from the back benches.

Shasa used this distraction to murmur an excuse to his father-in-law. 'You won't need me for the rest of the day, but if you do, you'll know where to find me.' Then he stood up, bowed to the Speaker and, as unobtrusively as possible, headed for the exit. However, Shasa was six foot one inch tall and with the black patch over one eye and his dark waving hair and good looks, he drew more than a few speculative glances from the younger women in the visitors' gallery, and a hostile appraisal from the government benches.

Manfred De La Rey glanced up from the note he was reading as Shasa passed, and the look they exchanged was intent but enigmatic. Then Shasa was out of the chamber and he shrugged off his jacket and slung it over his shoulder, as he acknowledged the salute of the doorman and went out into the sunshine.

Shasa did not keep an office in the parliament building, for the seven-storied Centaine House, the headquarters of the Courtney Mining and Finance Co. Ltd., was just two minutes' walk across the

11

gardens. As he strode along under the oaks he mentally changed hats, doffing his political topper for the businessman's Homburg. Shasa kept his life in separate compartments, and he had trained himself to concentrate on each in its turn, without ever allowing his energy to dissipate by spreading it too thinly.

By the time he crossed the road in front of St George's cathedral and went into the revolving glass front door of Centaine House, he was thinking of finance and mining, juggling figures and choices, weighing factual reports against his own instincts, and enjoying the game of money as hugely as he had the rituals and confrontations on the floor of the houses of parliament.

The two pretty girls at the reception desk in the entrance lobby with its marbled floors and columns burst into radiant smiles.

'Good afternoon, Mr Courtney,' they chorused, and he devastated them with his smile as he crossed to the lifts. His reaction to them was instinctive; he liked pretty females around him, although he would never touch one of his own people. Somehow that would have been incestuous, and unsporting for they would not have been able to refuse him, too much like shooting a sitting bird. Still the two young females at the desk sighed and rolled their eyes as the lift doors closed on him.

Janet, his secretary, had heard the lift and was waiting as the doors opened. She was more Shasa's type – mature and poised, groomed and efficient, and though she made little attempt to conceal her adoration, Shasa's self-imposed rules prevailed here also.

'What have we got, Janet?' he demanded, and as she followed him across the ante-chamber to his own office, she read off his appointments for the rest of the afternoon.

He went first to the ticker-tape in the corner and ran the closing prices through his fingers. Anglos had dropped two shillings, it was almost time to buy again.

'Ring Allen and put him off. I'm not ready for him yet,' he told Janet and went to his desk. 'Give me fifteen minutes and then get David Abrahams on the phone.'

As she left the room Shasa settled to the pile of telex sheets and urgent messages that she had left on his blotter. He worked swiftly through them, undistracted by the magnificent view of Table Mountain through the window on the opposite wall, and when one of the phones rang he was ready for David.

'Hello, Davie, what's happening in Jo'burg?' It was a rhetorical question, he knew what was happening and what he was going to do about it. The daily reports and estimates were amongst the pile on his desk, but he listened carefully to David's résumé.

David was group managing-director. He had been with Shasa since varsity days and he was as close to Shasa as no other person, with the exception of Centaine, had come.

Although the H'ani diamond mine near Windhoek in the north was still the fountainhead of the company's prosperity, and had been for the thirty-two years since Centaine Courtney had discovered it, under Shasa's direction the company had expanded and diversified until he had been forced to move the executive headquarters from Windhoek to Johannesburg. Johannesburg was the commercial centre of the country and the move was inevitable, but Johannesburg was also a bleak, heartless and unattractive city. Centaine Courtney-Malcomess refused to leave the beautiful Cape of Good Hope to live there, so the company's financial and administrative headquarters remained in Cape Town. It was a clumsy and costly duplication, but Centaine always got her way. Moreover, it was convenient for Shasa to be so close to parliament and as he loved the Cape as much as she did, he did not try to change her mind.

Shasa and David spoke for ten minutes before Shasa said, 'Right, we can't decide on this on the phone. I'll come up to you.'

'When?'

'Tomorrow afternoon. Sean has a rugby match at ten in the morning. I can't miss it. I promised him.'

David was silent a moment as he considered the relative importance of a schoolboy's sporting achievement against the possible investment of something over ten million pounds in the development of the company's options on the new Orange Free State goldfields.

'Give me a ring before you take off,' David agreed with resignation. 'I'll meet you at the airfield myself.'

Shasa hung up and checked his wristwatch. He wanted to get back to Weltevreden in time to spend an hour with the children before their bath and dinner. He could finish his work after his own dinner. He began to pack the remaining papers on his desk into his black crocodile-skin Hermès briefcase, when Janet tapped on the interleading door and came into his office.

'I'm sorry, sir. This has just been delivered by hand. A parliamentary messenger, and he said it was very urgent.'

Shasa took the heavy-quality envelope from her. It was the type of expensive stationery reserved for use by members of the cabinet and the flap was embossed with the coat of arms of the Union, the quartered shield and rampant antelopes supporting it with the motto in the ribbon beneath *Ex Unitate Vires* – Strength through Unity.

'Thank you, Janet.' He broke the flap with his thumb and took out a single sheet of notepaper. It was headed: 'Office of the Minister of Police', and the message was handwritten in Afrikaans.

Dear Mr Courtney,

Knowing of your interest in hunting, an important personage has asked me to invite you to a springbok hunt on his ranch over the coming weekend. There is an airstrip on the property and the coordinates are as follows: 28°32′S 26°16′E.

I can assure you of good sport and interesting company. Please let me know if you are able to attend.

Sincerely,
Manfred De La Rey.

Shasa grinned and whistled softly through his teeth as he went to the large-scale map on the wall and checked the coordinates. The note amounted to a summons, and he could guess at the identity of the important personage. He saw that the ranch was in the Orange Free State just south of the goldfields at Welkom, and it would mean only a minor detour off his return course from Johannesburg to reach it.

'I wonder what they are up to now,' he mused, and he felt a prickle of anticipation. It was the kind of mystery he thoroughly enjoyed, and he scribbled a reply on a sheet of his personal notepaper.

Thank you for your kind invitation to hunt with you this weekend. Please convey my acceptance to our host and I look forward to the hunting.

As he sealed the envelope he muttered, 'In fact, you'd have to nail both my feet to the ground to keep me away.'

*　　*　　*

In his green Jaguar SS sports car, Shasa drove through the massive white-painted gateway of Weltevreden. The pediment had been designed and executed in 1790 by Anton Anreith, the Dutch East India Company's architect and sculptor, and such an exquisite work of art was a fitting entrance to the estate.

Since Centaine had handed the estate over to him and gone to live with Blaine Malcomess on the far side of the Constantia Berg mountains, Shasa had lavished the same love and care upon Weltevreden as she had before. The name translated from the Dutch as 'Well Satisfied' and that was how Shasa felt as he slowed the Jaguar to a walking-pace, so as not to blow dust over the vineyards that flanked the road.

The harvest was in full swing, and the headscarves of the women working down the rows of shoulder-high vines were bright spots of colour that vied with the leaves of red and gold. They straightened

14

up to smile and wave as Shasa passed, and the men, doubled under the overflowing baskets of red grapes, grinned at him also.

Young Sean was on one of the wagons in the centre of the field, walking the draught horses slowly, keeping pace with the harvest. The wagon was piled high with ripe grapes that glowed like rubies where the powdery bloom had been rubbed from their skin.

When he saw his father, Sean tossed the reins to the driver who had been tactfully supervising him, and leapt over the side of the wagon and raced down the rows of vines to intercept the green Jaguar. He was only eleven years old, but big for his age. He had inherited his mother's clear shining skin and Shasa's looks, and although his limbs were sturdy, he ran like an antelope, springy and quick on his feet. Watching him Shasa felt that his heart might burst with pride.

Sean flung open the passenger door of the Jag and tumbled into the seat, where he abruptly recovered his dignity.

'Good evening, Papa,' he said, and Shasa put an arm around his shoulders and hugged him.

'Hello, sport. How did it go today?'

They drove down past the winery and the stables and Shasa parked in the converted barn where he kept his collection of a dozen vintage cars. The Jaguar had been a gift from Centaine and he favoured it even over the 1928 Phantom I Rolls Royce with Hooper coachwork beside which he parked it.

The other children had witnessed his arrival from the nursery windows and came pelting down across the lawns to meet him. Michael, the youngest boy was leading, with Garrick, his middle son, a good five lengths back. Less than a year separated each of the boys. Michael was the dreamer of the family, a fey child who at nine years of age could lose himself for hours in *Treasure Island* or spend an afternoon with his box of water-colours, lost to all else in the world. Shasa embraced him as affectionately as he had his eldest, and then Garrick came up, wheezing with asthma, pale-faced and skinny, with wispy hair that stuck up in spikes.

'Good afternoon, Papa,' he stuttered. He really was an ugly little brat, Shasa thought, and where the hell did he get them from, the asthma and the stutter?

'Hello, Garrick.' Shasa never called him 'son' or 'my boy' or 'sport' as he did the other two. It was always simply 'Garrick' and he patted the top of his head lightly. It never occurred to him to embrace the child, the little beggar still peed his bed and he was ten years old.

Shasa turned with relief to meet his daughter.

'Come on, my angel, come to your daddy!' And she flew into his arms and shrieked with rapture as he swung her high, then wrapped

15

both arms around his neck and showered warm wet kisses on his face.

'What does my angel want to do now?' Shasa asked, without lowering her to earth.

'I wanna wide,' Isabella declared, and she was already wearing her new jodhpurs.

'Then wide we shall,' Shasa agreed. Whenever Tara accused him of encouraging her lisp, he protested, 'She's only a baby.'

'She's a calculating little vixen who knows exactly how to twist you around her little finger – and you let her do it.'

Now he swung her up on to his shoulders, and she sat astride his neck and took a handful of his hair to steady herself while she bounced up and down chanting, 'I love my daddy.'

'Come on, everybody,' Shasa ordered. 'We are going for a wide before dinner.'

Sean was too big and grown up to hold hands, but he kept jealously close to Shasa's right side; Michael was on his left clinging unashamedly to Shasa's hand, while Garrick trailed five paces behind looking up adoringly at his father.

'I came first in arithmetic today, Daddy,' Garrick said softly, but in all the shouting and laughter Shasa didn't hear him.

The grooms had the horses saddled up already, for the evening ride was a family ritual. In the saddle room Shasa slipped off his city shoes and changed them for old well-polished riding boots, before he lifted Isabella on to the back of her plump little piebald Shetland. Then he went up into the saddle of his own stallion and took Isabella's lead rein from the groom.

'Company, forward – walk, march, trot!' He gave the cavalry command and pumped his hand over his head, a gesture which always reduced Isabella to squeals of delight, and they clattered out of the stableyard.

They made the familiar circuit of the estate, stopping to talk with any of the coloured boss-boys they met, and exchanging shouted greetings with the gangs of labourers trudging home from the vineyards. Sean discussed the harvest with his father in adult terms, sitting straight and important in the saddle, until Isabella, feeling left out, intervened and immediately Shasa leaned over to listen deferentially to what she had to tell him.

The boys ended the ride as always with a mad gallop across the polo fields and up the hill to the stables. Sean, riding like a centaur, was far ahead of the rest of them, Michael was too gentle to use the whip and Garrick bounced awkwardly in the saddle. Despite Shasa's drilling, his seat was atrocious with toes and elbows sticking out at odd angles.

16

'He rides like a sack of potatoes,' Shasa thought with irritation, following them at the sedate pace set by Isabella's portly Shetland on the lead rein. Shasa was an international polo player, and he took his middle son's maladroit seat as a personal affront.

Tara was in the kitchens overseeing the last-minute details for dinner, when they came trooping in. She looked up and greeted Shasa casually.

'Good day?' She was wearing those appalling trousers in faded blue denim which Shasa detested. He liked feminine women.

'Not bad,' he answered, trying to divest himself of Isabella who was still wrapped around his neck. He dislodged her and handed her over to Nanny.

'We are twelve for dinner.' Tara turned her attention back to the Malay chef who was standing by dutifully.

'Twelve?' Shasa asked sharply.

'I invited the Broadhursts at the last moment.'

'Oh God,' Shasa groaned.

'I wanted some stimulating conversation at the table for a change, not just horses and shooting and business.'

'Last time she came to dinner your and Molly's stimulating conversation broke the party up before nine o'clock.' Shasa glanced at his wristwatch. 'I'd better think about dressing.'

'Daddy, will you feed me?' Isabella called from the children's dining-room beyond the kitchen.

'You are a big girl, angel,' he answered. 'You must learn to feed yourself.'

'I can feed myself – I just like it better when you do it. Please, Daddy, pretty please a trillion times.'

'A trillion?' Shasa asked. 'I am bid one trillion – any advance on a trillion?' but he went to her summons.

'You spoil her,' Tara said. 'She's becoming impossible.'

'I know,' said Shasa. 'You keep telling me.'

Shasa shaved quickly while his coloured valet laid out his dinner-jacket in the dressing-room and put the platinum and sapphire studs into his dress shirt. Despite Tara's vehement protests he always insisted on black tie for dinner.

'It's so stuffy and old-fashioned and snobby.'

'It's civilized,' he contradicted her.

When he was dressed, he crossed the wide corridor strewn with oriental carpets, the walls hung with a gallery of Thomas Baines water-colours, tapped on Tara's door and went in to her invitation.

Tara had moved into this suite while she was carrying Isabella, and had stayed here. Last year she had redecorated it, removing the

17

velvet drapes and George II and Louis XIV furniture, the Qum silk carpets and the magnificent oils by De Jong and Naudé, stripping the flocked wallpaper and sanding the golden patina off the yellow-wood floor until it looked like plain deal.

Now the walls were stark white with only a single enormous painting facing the bed; it was a monstrosity of geometrical shapes in primary colours in the style of Miró, but executed by an unknown art student at the Cape Town University Art School and of no value. To Shasa's mind paintings should be pleasing decorations but at the same time good long-term investments. This thing was neither.

The furniture Tara had chosen for her boudoir was made of angular stainless steel and glass, and there was very little of it. The bed was almost flat on the bare boards of the floor.

'It's Swedish decor,' she had explained.

'Send it back to Sweden,' he had advised her.

Now he perched on one of the steel chairs and lit a cigarette. She frowned at him in the mirror.

'Forgive me.' He stood up and went to flick the cigarette out of the window. 'I'll be working late after dinner,' he turned back to her, 'and I wanted to warn you before I forget that I'm flying up to Jo'burg tomorrow afternoon and I'll be away for a few days, maybe five or six.'

'Fine.' She pursed her lips as she applied her lipstick, a pale mauve shade that he disliked intensely.

'One other thing, Tara. Lord Littleton's bank is preparing to underwrite the share issue for our possible new development on the Orange Free State goldfields. I would take it as a personal favour if you and Molly could refrain from waving your black sashes in his face and from regaling him with merry tales of white injustice and bloody black revolution.'

'I can't speak for Molly, but I promise to be good.'

'Why don't you wear your diamonds tonight?' he changed the subject. 'They look so good on you.'

She hadn't worn the suite of yellow diamonds from the H'ani Mine since she had joined the Sash movement. They made her feel like Marie Antoinette.

'Not tonight,' she said. 'They are a little garish, it's really just a family dinner party.' She dusted her nose with the puff and looked at him in the mirror.

'Why don't you go down, dear. Your precious Lord Littleton will be arriving at any moment.'

'I just want to tuck Bella up first.' He came to stand behind her.

They stared at each other in the mirror, seriously.

'What happened to us, Tara?' he asked softly.

18

'I don't know what you mean, dear,' she replied, but she looked down and adjusted the front of her dress carefully.

'I'll see you downstairs,' he said. 'Don't be too long, and do make a fuss of Littleton. He's important, and he likes the girlies.'

After he had closed the door Tara stared at it for a moment, then she repeated his question aloud. 'What happened to us, Shasa? It's quite simple really. I just grew up and lost patience with the trivialities with which you fill your life.'

On the way down she looked in on the children. Isabella was asleep with teddy on top of her face. Tara saved her daughter from suffocation and went to the boys' rooms. Only Michael was still awake. He was reading.

'Lights out!' she ordered.

'Oh, Mater, just to the end of the chapter.'

'Out!'

'Just this page.'

'Out, I said!' And she kissed him lovingly.

At the head of the staircase she drew a deep breath like a diver on the high board, smiled brightly and went down into the blue drawing-room where the first guests were already sipping sherry.

Lord Littleton was much better value than she had expected – tall, silver-haired and benign.

'Do you shoot?' she asked at the first opportunity.

'Can't stand the sight of blood, me dear.'

'Do you ride?'

'Horses?' he snorted. 'Stupid bloody animals.'

'I think you and I are going to be good friends,' she said.

There were many rooms in Weltevreden that Tara disliked; the dining-room she actively hated with all those heads of long-dead animals that Shasa had massacred staring down from the walls with glass eyes. Tonight she took a chance and seated Molly on the other side of Littleton and within minutes Molly had him hooting with delighted laughter.

When they left the men with the port and Hauptmanns and went through to the ladies room, Molly pulled Tara aside, bubbling over with excitement.

'I've been dying to get you alone all evening,' she whispered. 'You'll never guess who is in the Cape at this very moment.'

'Tell me.'

'The secretary of the African National Congress – that's who. Moses Gama, that's who.'

Tara went very still and pale and stared at her.

'He's coming to our home to talk to a small group of us, Tara. I invited him, and he especially asked for you to be present. I didn't know you knew him.'

19

'I met him only once —' she corrected herself, 'twice.'

'Can you come?' Molly insisted. 'It'll be best if Shasa does not know about it, you understand.'

'When?'

'Saturday evening, eight o'clock.'

'Shasa will be away and I'll be there,' Tara said. 'I wouldn't miss it for the world.'

*   *   *

Sean Courtney was the stalwart of the Western Province Preparatory School first fifteen, or Wet Pups, as the school was known. Quick and strong, he ran in four tries against the Rondebosch juniors and converted them himself, while his father and two younger brothers stood on the touchline and yelled encouragement.

After the final whistle blew Shasa lingered just long enough to congratulate his son, with an effort restraining himself from hugging the sweaty grinning youngster with grass stains on his white shorts and a graze on one knee. A display like that in front of Sean's peers would have mortified him horribly. Instead they shook hands.

'Well played, sport. I'm proud of you,' he said. 'Sorry about this weekend, but I'll make it up to you.' And although the expression of regret was sincere, Shasa felt a buoyancy of his spirits as he drove out to the airfield at Youngsfield. Dicky, his erk, had the aircraft out of the hangar and ready for him on the hardstand.

Shasa climbed out of the Jaguar and stood with his hands in his pockets and the cigarette in the corner of his mouth, staring at the sleek machine with rapture.

It was a DH 98 Mosquito fighter bomber. Shasa had bought it at one of the RAF disposal sales at Biggin Hill and had it completely stripped and overhauled by De Havilland trained riggers. He had even had them re-glue the sandwich construction of the wooden bodywork with the new Araldite wonder glue. The original Rodux adhesives had proves unreliable under tropical conditions. Stripped of all armaments and military fittings, the Mosquito's already formidable performance had been considerably enhanced. Not even Courtney Mining could afford one of the new civilian jet-engined aircraft, but this was the next best thing.

The beautiful machine crouched on the hardstand like a falcon at bate, the twin Rolls Royce Merlin engines ready to roar into life and hurtle her into the blue. Blue was her colour, sky blue and silver; she shone in the bright Cape sunlight and on her fuselage where once the RAF roundel had been was now emblazoned the Courtney Company

20

logo, a stylized silver diamond, its facets entwined with the Company's initials.

'How is the port number two magneto?' Shasa demanded of Dicky as he sauntered across in his oily overalls. The little man bridled.

'Ticking over like a sewing machine,' he answered. He loved the machine even more than Shasa did, and any imperfection, no matter how minor, wounded him deeply. When Shasa reported one, he took it very badly. He helped Shasa load his briefcase, overnight bag and guncase into the bomb bay which had been converted into a luggage compartment.

'All tanks are full,' he said, and stood aside looking superior as Shasa insisted on checking them visually, and then made a fuss of his walk-around inspection.

'She'll do,' Shasa agreed at last and could not resist stroking the wing, as though it were the limb of a lovely woman.

Shasa switched to oxygen at eleven thousand feet and levelled out at Angels twenty, grinning into his oxygen mask at the old airforce slang. He tuned her for cruise, carefully watching the exhaust gas temperatures and engine revs and then settled back to enjoy it.

Enjoy was too mild a term for it. Flying was an exultation of spirit and a fever in his blood. The immense lion-tawny continent drifted by beneath him, washed by a million suns and burned by the hot herb-scented Karoo winds, its ancient hide riven and wrinkled and scarred with donga and canyon and dried riverbed. Only up here, high above it, did Shasa truly realize how much he was a part of it, how deep was his love for it. Yet it was a hard land and cruel, and it bred hard men, black and white, and he knew that he was one of them. There is no place for weaklings here, he thought, only the strong can flourish.

Perhaps it was the pure oxygen he breathed, enhanced by the ecstasy of flight, but his mind seemed clearer up here. Issues that had been obscure became lucid, uncertainties resolved, and the hours sped away as swiftly as the lovely machine streaked across the blue so that when he landed at Johannesburg's civilian airport, he knew with certainty what had to be done. David Abrahams was waiting for him, lanky and skinny as ever, but he was balding a little and he had taken to wearing gold-rimmed spectacles which gave him a perpetually startled expression. Shasa jumped down off the wing of the Mosquito and they embraced happily. They were closer than brothers. Then David patted the aircraft's wing.

'When do I get to fly her again?' he asked wistfully. David had got a DFC in the western desert and a bar to it in Italy. He had been credited with nine kills and ended the war as a wing commander, while Shasa had been a mere squadron leader when he had lost his eye in Abyssinia and been invalided home.

'She's too good for you,' Shasa told him and slung his luggage into the back seat of David's Cadillac.

As David drove out through the airfield gates they exchanged family news. David was married to Mathilda Janine, Tara Courtney's younger sister, so David and Shasa were brothers-in-law. Shasa boasted about Sean and Isabella without mentioning his other two sons and then they went on to the real objects of their meeting.

These, in order of importance, were, first, the decision whether or not to exercise the option on the new Silver River mining prospect in the Orange Free State. Then there was the trouble with the company's chemical factory on the Natal coast. A local pressure group was kicking up a rumpus about poisoning the sea bed and reefs in the area where the factory was discharging effluent into the sea. And finally, there was David's crazy fixation, from which Shasa was finding it difficult to dislodge him, that they should spend something over a quarter of a million pounds on one of those new elephantine electric calculators.

'The Yanks did all the calculations for the atomic bomb with one of them,' David argued. 'And they call them computers, not calculators,' he corrected Shasa.

'Come on, Davie, what are we going to blow up?' Shasa protested. 'I'm not designing an A-bomb.'

'Anglo-American have one. It's the wave of the future, Shasa. We'd better be on it.'

'It's a quarter-million-pound wave, old son,' Shasa pointed out. 'Just when we need every penny for Silver River.'

'If we'd had one of these computers to analyse the geological drilling reports from Silver River, we'd have already saved ourselves almost the entire cost of the thing, and we'd be a lot more certain of our final decision than we are now.'

'How can a machine be better than a human brain?'

'Just come and have a look at it,' David pleaded. 'The university has just installed an IBM 701. I have arranged a demonstration for you this afternoon.'

'Okay, Davie,' Shasa capitulated. 'I'll look, but that doesn't mean I'm buying.'

The IBM supervisor in the basement of the engineering faculty building was no more than twenty-six years of age.

'They're all kids,' David explained. 'It's a young people's science.'

The supervisor shook hands with Shasa, and then removed her horn-rimmed spectacles. Suddenly Shasa's interest in electronic computers burgeoned. Her eyes were clear bright green and her hair

22

was the colour of wild honey made from mimosa blossom. She wore a green sweater of tight-fitting angora wool, and a tartan skirt which left her smooth tanned calves bare. It was immediately obvious that she was an expert, and she answered all Shasa's questions without hesitation in a tantalizing southern drawl.

'Marylee has a master's in electrical engineering from MIT,' David murmured, and Shasa's initial attraction was spiced with respect.

'It's so damned big,' he protested. 'It fills the entire basement. The ruddy thing is the size of a four-bedroomed house.'

'Cooling,' Marylee explained. 'The heat build-up is enormous. 'Most of the bulk is oil cooling baffles.'

'What are you processing at the moment?'

'Professor Dart's archaeological material from the Sterkfontein caves. We are correlating about two hundred thousand observations of his against over a million from the sites in East Africa.'

'How long will that take you?'

'We started the run twenty minutes ago, we'll finish it before we shut down at five o'clock.'

'That's in fifteen minutes,' Shasa chuckled. 'You're having me on!'

'I wouldn't mind,' she murmured speculatively, and when she smiled her mouth was wide and moist and kissable.

'You say you shut down at five?' he asked. 'When do you start up again?'

'Eight tomorrow morning.'

'And the machine stands idle overnight?'

Marylee glanced down the length of the basement. David was at the other end watching the print-out and the hum of the computer covered their voices.

'That's right. It will stand idle all tonight. Just like me.' Clearly she was a lady who knew exactly what she wanted, and how to get it. She looked at him directly, challengingly.

'We can't have that,' Shasa shook his head seriously. 'One thing my mummy taught me was 'Waste not, want not'. I know a place called the Stardust. The band is far beyond belief. I will wager a pound to a weekend in Paris that I can dance you until you plead for mercy.'

'It's a bet,' she agreed as seriously. 'But do you cheat?'

'Of course,' he answered. David was coming back and Shasa went on smoothly and professionally. 'What about running costs?'

'All in, including insurance and depreciation, a little under four thousand pounds a month,' she told him with a matching businesslike expression.

As they said goodbye and shook hands, she slipped a card into Shasa's palm. 'My address,' she murmured.

23

'Eight o'clock?' he asked.

'I'll be there,' she agreed.

In the Cadillac, Shasa lit a cigarette and blew a perfect smoke ring that exploded silently against the windscreen.

'Okay, Davie, contact the dean of engineering first thing tomorrow. Offer to hire that monster all its down time from five o'clock in the evening until eight the next morning, and weekends also. Offer him four thousand a month and point out that he'll get the use of it for free. We'll be paying all his costs.'

David turned to him with a startled expression and almost drove up on to the pavement, then corrected with a wild swing of the wheel.

'Why didn't I think of that?' he wondered when he had the Cadillac under control.

'You have to get up earlier,' Shasa grinned and then went on, 'Once we know how much time we will need on the thing, we'll sublet the surplus time to a couple of other non-competitor companies who must be thinking about buying a computer themselves. That way we'll get our own usage free, and when IBM have improved the design and made the damned thing smaller, then we will buy our own.'

'Son of a gun.' David shook his head in awe. 'Son of a gun.' Then with sudden inspiration, 'I'll get young Marylee on our payroll —'

'No,' said Shasa sharply. 'Get someone else.'

David glanced at him again and his excitement faded. He knew his brother-in-law too well.

'You won't be taking up Matty's invitation to dinner this evening, will you?' he asked morosely.

'Not this evening,' Shasa agreed. 'Give her my love and apologies.'

'Just be careful. It's a small town and you are a marked man,' David warned as he dropped Shasa off at the Carlton Hotel where the company kept a permanent suite. 'Do you think you will be fit for work tomorrow?'

'Eight o'clock,' Shasa told him. 'Sharp!'

By mutual agreement the dance competition at the Stardust was declared a draw, and Shasa and Marylee got back to his Carlton suite a little after midnight.

Her body was young and smooth and hard and just before she drifted off to sleep with her thick honey-coloured hair spread on his bare chest, she whispered drowsily, 'Well, I guess that's about the only thing my IBM 701 can't do for me.'

Shasa was in the Courtney mining offices fifteen minutes before David the next morning. He liked to keep everybody on their toes.

Their offices occupied the entire third floor of the Standard Bank building in Commissioner Street. Although Shasa owned a prime piece of real estate on the corner of Diagonal Street opposite the stock exchange and within yelling distance of Anglo American Corporation's head office, he hadn't yet got around to building on it; any spare money in the company always seemed to be earmarked for mining options or extensions or other income-producing enterprises.

The young blood on the Courtney executive board was judicially leavened with a few grey heads. Doctor Twentyman-Jones was still there, in an old-fashioned black alpaca jacket and string tie, hiding his affection for Shasa behind a mournful expression. He had run the very first prospect on the H'ani diamond mine for Centaine back in the early twenties and was one of the three most experienced and gifted mining consultants in southern Africa, which meant the world.

David's father Abraham Abrahams was still head of the legal section, perched up beside his son, bright and chirpy as a little silver sparrow. His files were piled high on the table in front of him, but he seldom had to refer to them. With half a dozen other newcomers whom Centaine and Shasa between them had hand-picked, it was a balanced and functional team.

'Let's talk about the Courtney chemical plant at Chaka's Bay first.' Shasa brought the meeting to order. 'How much meat is there in the beef against us, Abe?'

'We are running hot sulphuric acid into the sea at a rate of between eleven and sixteen tons per day at a concentration of one in ten thousand,' Abe Abrahams told him matter-of-factly. 'I've had an independent marine biologist do a report on it for us.' He tapped the document. 'It isn't good. We have altered the pH for five miles along the coastline.'

'You haven't circulated this report?' Shasa asked sharply.

'What do you think?' Abe shook his head.

'All right, David. What will it cost us to modify the manufacturing procedure on the fertilizer division to dispose of the acid waste some other way?'

'There are two possible modifications,' David told him. 'The simplest and cheapest is trucking the effluent in tankers, but then we have to find another dumping ground. The ideal solution is recycling the acid.'

'Costs?'

'One hundred thousand pounds per annum for the tankers – one shot of almost three times that for the other way.'

'A year's profits down the drain,' Shasa said. 'That's not acceptable.

25

Who is this Pearson woman that is heading up the protest? Can we reason with her?'

Abe shook his head. 'We have tried. She is holding the whole committee together. Without her they would crumble.'

'What is her position?'

'Her husband owns the local bakery.'

'Buy it,' said Shasa. 'If he won't sell, let him know discreetly that we will open another bakery in competition and subsidize its product. I want this Pearson woman far away and long ago. Any questions?' He looked down the table. Everybody was busy making notes, nobody looked at him and he wanted to ask them reasonably, 'All right, gentlemen, are you prepared to spend three hundred thousand pounds to give a good home to the oysters and the sea urchins of Chaka's Bay?'

'No questions!' he nodded instead. 'All right, let's take on the big one now. Silver River.'

They all shifted in their seats, and there was simultaneous and nervous exhalation of breath.

'Gentlemen, we have all read and studied Dr Twentyman-Jones's geological report based on his drilling on the property. It is a superb piece of work, and I don't have to tell you that it's the best opinion you'll get on Harley Street. Now I want to hear from each of you your own opinions as departmental heads. Can we start with you, Rupert?'

Rupert Horn was the junior member of the executive team. As treasurer and chief accountant he filled in the financial background.

'If we let the option lapse, we shall be writing off the two point three million that we have spent on exploration over the last eighteen months. If we take up the option it will mean an initial payment of four million on signature.'

'We can cover that from the rainy-day account,' Shasa intervened.

'We are holding four point three million in the provisional fund,' Rupert Horn agreed. 'We have it invested in Escom 7% Stock at present, but once we utilize that fund we will be in an extremely exposed position.'

One after the other, in ascending order of seniority, Shasa's managers gave their views as seen from their own departments, and David put it all together at the end.

'So it seems that we have twenty-six days remaining on the option, and four million to pay if we take it up. That is going to leave us bare-bummed, and facing development costs of three million pounds for the main shaft alone, plus another five million for plant, interest and running costs to see us into the production phase, four years from now in 1956.' He stopped and they all watched intently while

Shasa selected a cigarette and tapped it lightly on the lid of his gold case.

Shasa's expression was deadly serious. He knew better than any of them that the decision could destroy the company or take it up onto a new high plateau, and nobody could make that decision for him. He was up on the lonely pinnacle of command.

'We know there is gold down there,' he spoke at last. 'A thick rich reef of it. If we reach it, it will go on producing for the next fifty years. However, gold is standing at thirty-five dollars an ounce. The Americans have pegged it, they have threatened to keep the price there for all time. Thirty-five dollars an ounce – and it will cost us between twenty and twenty-five an ounce to go down that deep and bring it to the surface. A slim margin, gentlemen, much too slim.'

He lit the cigarette, and they all sighed and relaxed, at the same time disappointed and relieved. It would have been glorious to make the charge, but disastrous to have failed. Now they would never know. But Shasa hadn't finished. He blew a spinning smoke-ring down the length of the table, and went on.

'However, I don't think the Americans are going to be able to keep the lid on the gold price much longer. Their hatred of gold is emotional, not based on economic reality. I know, deep down in my guts, that the day is not far off when we will see gold at sixty dollars and one day, sooner than any of us think, it will be a hundred and fifty dollars – perhaps even two hundred!' They stirred with disbelief, and Twentyman-Jones looked as though he might break down and weep in the face of such wild optimism, but Shasa ignored him and turned to Abe Abrahams.

'Abe, at noon on the eighteenth of next month, twelve hours before the option expires, you will hand over a cheque for four million to the owners of Silver River farms, and take possession of the property in the name of a company to be formed.' Shasa turned to David. 'At the same time we will simultaneously open subscription lists on the Johannesburg and London stock exchanges for ten million £1 shares in the Silver River gold-mining property. You and Doctor Twentyman-Jones will start today drawing up the prospectus. Courtney Mining will register the property in the name of the new company in return for the balance of five million shares transferred into our name. We will also be responsible for the management and development.' Quickly, succinctly, Shasa laid out the structure, financing and management of the new company, and more than once these wily seasoned campaigners glanced up from their notepads in blatant admiration of some deft and unusual touch he added to the scheme.

'Is there anything I have left out?' Shasa asked at the end, and

27

when they shook their heads, he grinned. David was reminded strongly of the movie he and Matty had taken the children to see the previous Saturday afternoon, *The Sea Hawk*, though the eye-patch made Shasa look even more piratical than Errol Flynn had done in the title role.

'The founder of our company, Madame Centaine de Thiry Courtney-Malcomess, has never approved of the consumption of alcohol in the boardroom. However —' Still grinning, Shasa nodded at David, who went to open the main doors of the boardroom and a secretary wheeled in a trolley on which the rows of glasses clinked and the green bottles of Dom Perignon swished in their silver ice-buckets. 'Old customs give way to new,' Shasa said, and drew the first cork with a discreet pop.

* * *

Shasa throttled back the Rolls Royce engines and the Mosquito sank down through the ribbons of scattered cirrus cloud, and the endless golden plains of the high African shield came up to meet her. Off to the west Shasa could just make out the clustered buildings of the mining town of Welkom, centre of the Orange Free State goldfields. Founded only a few years previously, when the vast Anglo American Corporation began opening up these fields, it was already a model town of over a hundred thousand persons.

Shasa unclipped his oxygen mask and let it dangle on his chest, as he leaned forward on his straps and peered ahead through the windshield ahead of the Mosquito's blue nose.

He picked out the tiny steel tower of the drilling rig almost lost in the immensity of the dusty plain, and using it as a landmark traced the gossamer thread of fences that enclosed the Silver River farms – eleven thousand acres, most of it bare and undeveloped. It was amazing that the geologists of the big mining houses had overlooked this little pocket, but then nobody could have reasonably expected the gold reef to spur off like that – that is, nobody but Twentyman-Jones and Shasa Courtney.

Yet the reef was as far beneath the earth as the Mosquito now circled above it. It seemed impossible that any human endeavour would be able to burrow down that deep, but already Shasa could see in his imagination the tall headgear of the Silver River main towering two hundred feet above the bleak plain, with its shaft stabbing down a mile and more into the underground river of precious metal.

'And the Yanks can't hold out for ever – they will have to let gold go free,' he told himself.

28

He stood the Mosquito on one wing and on the instrument panel the gyro compass revolved smoothly. Shasa lifted the wing and she was precisely on her new heading of 125°.

'Fifteen minutes, with these winds,' he grunted, as he marked the large-scale map on his knee, and the fine exaltation of spirit stayed with him for the remainder of the flight until he saw the dark pencil-line of smoke rising into the still air dead ahead. They had put up a smoke beacon to guide him in.

There was a Dakota parked in front of the lonely galvanized iron-clad hangar at the end of the strip. The big aircraft had airforce markings. The runway was of rolled yellow clay, hard and smooth and the Mosquito settled to it with barely a jolt. It had taken endless practice to develop that sort of distance judgement after he had lost the eye.

Shasa slid back the canopy and taxied towards the hangar. There was a green Ford pick-up near the mast of the windsock, and a lone figure dressed in khaki shorts and shirt stood beside the smoke pot, fists clenched on his hips, watching Shasa taxi up and cut the engines. Then as Shasa jumped down, he stepped forward and offered his right hand, but his expression, solemn and reserved, was at odds with the welcoming gesture.

'Good afternoon, Minister.' Shasa was as unsmiling and their grip was hard but brief. Then as Shasa looked deeply into Manfred De La Rey's pale eyes, he had a strange feeling of *déjà vu*, of having stared into those same eyes in desperate circumstances before. He had to shake his head slightly to be rid of it.

'I am glad for both our sakes that you were able to come. Can I help you with your bags?' Manfred De La Rey asked.

'Don't worry. I can manage.' Shasa went back to tie down and secure the Mosquito and fetch his luggage from the bomb bay, while Manfred doused the smoke pot.

'You brought your own rifle,' Manfred remarked. 'What is it?'

'Seven mm Remington magnum.' Shasa swung the luggage into the back of the truck and stepped up into the passenger door of the Ford.

'Perfect for this type of shooting,' Manfred approved as he started the truck. 'Long shots over flat ground.' He swung on to the track and they drove for a few minutes in silence.

'The prime minister could not come,' he said. 'He intended to be here, but he sent a letter for you. It confirms that I speak with his authority.'

'I'll accept that.' Shasa kept a straight face.

'The minister of finance is here, and the minister of agriculture is our host – this is his farm. One of the biggest in the Free State.'

29

'I am impressed.'

'Yes,' Manfred nodded. 'I think you will be.' He stared hard at Shasa. 'Is it not strange how you and I seem doomed always to confront each other?'

'It had crossed my mind,' Shasa admitted.

'Do you think there is some reason for it – something of which we are unaware?' Manfred insisted, and Shasa shrugged.

'I shouldn't think so – coincidence only.' The reply seemed to disappoint Manfred.

'Has your mother never spoken about me?'

Shasa looked startled. 'My mother! Good Lord, I don't think so. She may have mentioned you casually – why do you ask?'

Manfred seemed not to have heard, he looked ahead. 'There is the homestead,' he said, with a finality that closed the subject.

The track breasted the rim of a shallow valley and the homestead nestled below them. Here the water must be near the surface for the pasturage was lush and green and the skeletal steel towers of a dozen windmills were scattered down the valley. A plantation of eucalyptus trees surrounded the homestead, and beyond it stood substantial outbuildings, all freshly painted and in good repair. Twenty or more brand new tractors were lined up before one of the long garages, and there were flocks of fat sheep on the pastures. The plain beyond the homestead reaching almost to the horizon was already ploughed, thousands of acres of chocolate loam ready for sowing with maize seed. This was the heart land of Afrikanerdom, this was where the support of the National Party was solid and unwavering, and it was the reason why under the Nationalists the electoral areas had been re-demarcated to swing the centres of power away from the urban concentrations of population to favour these rural constituencies. That was why the Nationalists would stay in power for ever, and Shasa grimaced sourly. Immediately Manfred glanced at him, but Shasa offered no explanation and they drove down to the homestead and parked in the farm yard.

There were a dozen men sitting at the long yellow-wood kitchen table, smoking and drinking coffee and chatting while the women hovered in attendance. The men rose to welcome Shasa and he went down the table shaking hands with each of them and exchanging polite, if not effusive greetings.

Shasa knew every one of them. He had faced all of them across the floor of the house and had lashed most of them with his tongue, and in return had been attacked and vilified by each of them, but now they made room for him at the table and the hostess poured strong black coffee for him and placed a dish of sweet cakes and hard-baked rusks in front of him. They all treated him with that innate

30

courtesy and hospitality that is the hallmark of the Afrikaner. Though they were dressed in rough hunting clothing and pretended to be bluff and simple farmers, they were in reality a group of shrewd and adroit politicians, amongst the richest and most powerful men in the land.

Shasa spoke their language perfectly, understood the most heavily veiled references and laughed at their private jokes, but he was not one of them. He was the *rooinek*, the traditional enemy, and subtly they had closed their ranks against him.

When he had drunk his coffee his host, the minister of agriculture, told him, 'I will show you to your room. You will want to change and unpack your rifle. We will hunt as soon as it is cooler.'

A little after four o'clock, they set out in a procession of pick-up trucks, the elder more important men riding in the cabs while the others stood in the open backs of the trucks. The cavalcade climbed out of the valley, skirted the ploughed lands and then sped out across the plains towards a line of low hills on the horizon.

They saw game now, small herds of springbok far out on the plain like a fine dusting of cinnamon powder on the pale earth, but the trucks raced on, slowing only as they reached the foot of the rocky hills. The lead truck stopped for a moment and two of the hunters jumped down and scrambled into a shallow donga.

'Good luck! Shoot straight,' they called to them as they passed and a few hundred yards farther the convoy stopped again to let another pair take up their positions.

Within half an hour all of the huntsmen had been hidden in an irregular extended line below the ragged range of hills. Manfred De La Rey and Shasa had been placed together in a cluster of broken grey rock, and they squatted down to wait with their rifles across their laps, staring out across the flats that were speckled with darker scrub.

The trucks, driven by the teenage sons of their host, headed out in a wide circle until they were merely specks against the pale glare of the horizon, each marked by the ostrich feather of dust it drew behind it. Then they turned back towards the hills, travelling more slowly, not much above walking pace, as they began to move the scattered herds of antelope ahead of them.

Shasa and Manfred had almost an hour to wait for the driven game to come within rifle shot, and they chatted in a desultory, seemingly aimless manner, at first touching only lightly on politics, but rather discussing their host, the minister of agriculture, and the other guests. Then quite subtly Manfred changed the direction of their talk and remarked on how little real difference existed between the policies and aspirations of the governing National Party and Shasa's own opposition United Party.

31

'If you examine it carefully, our differences are only those of style and degree. We both want to keep South Africa safe for the white man and for European civilization. We both know that for all of us *apartheid* is a matter of life and death. Without it we will all drown in the black sea. Since the death of Smuts, your party has moved sharply towards our own thinking, and the leftists and liberals have begun to split away from you.'

Shasa was noncommittal, but the point was apt and painful. There were deep cracks appearing in his own party, and every day it became more apparent that they would never again form the government of this land. However, he was intrigued to know where Manfred De La Rey was leading. He had learned never to underestimate this adversary, and he sensed that he was being artfully prepared for the true purpose of this invitation. It was quite obvious that their host had manoeuvred to place them together, and that every other member of the party was privy to the business afoot. Shasa spoke little, conceding nothing, and waited with rising anticipation for the lurking beast to reveal its shape.

'You know that we have entrenched the language and culture of the English-speaking South Africans. There will never be any attempt to erode those rights – we look upon all English speakers of good will who consider themselves South Africans first as our brothers. Our destinies are linked with chains of steel —' Manfred broke off, and lifted his binoculars to his eyes. 'They are moving in closer now,' he murmured. 'We had better get ready.' He lowered the binoculars and smiled carefully at Shasa. 'I have heard that you shoot well. I look forward to a demonstration.'

Shasa was disappointed. He had wanted to know where the carefully rehearsed recital had been heading, but now he hid his impatience behind that easy smile of his and opened the breech of the rifle across his lap.

'You are right in one thing, Minister,' he said. 'We are linked together with chains of steel. Let us hope the weight of them doesn't draw us all under.' He saw a strange flash in those topaz yellow eyes, of anger or triumph, he was not certain, and it lasted only an instant.

'I will fire only on a line from dead ahead towards the right,' Manfred said. 'You only in an arc to the left. Agreed?'

'Agreed,' Shasa nodded, although he felt a prickle of irritation at being out-manoeuvred so soon and so easily. Manfred had carefully placed himself to cover the right flank, the natural side for a right-handed marksman to swing.

'You will need the advantage,' Shasa thought grimly and asked aloud. 'I hear you also are a fine shot. What about a small wager on the bag?'

32

'I do not gamble,' Manfred replied easily. 'That is a device of the devil, but I will count the bag with interest,' and Shasa was reminded of just how puritanical was the extreme Calvinism that Manfred De La Rey practised.

Carefully Shasa loaded his rifle. He had hand-loaded his own cartridges for he never trusted mass-produced factory ammunition. The shiny brass cases were filled with a charge of Norma powder that would drive the Nosler Partition bullet at well over three thousand feet a second. The special construction of the bullet would ensure that it mushroomed perfectly on impact.

He worked the bolt and then raised the weapon to his shoulder and used the telescopic sight to scan the plain. The pick-up trucks were less than a mile away, gently weaving back and forth, to prevent the herds breaking back, keeping them moving slowly down towards the line of hills and the hunters hidden below them. Shasa blinked his eye rapidly to clear his vision, and he could make out each individual animal in the herds of antelope trotting ahead of the vehicles.

They were light as smoke, and they rippled like cloud shadow across the plain. Trotting daintily with heads held high and with their horns shaped like perfect miniature lyres, they were graceful and indescribably lovely.

Without stereoscopic vision, Shasa had difficulty in judging distance, but he had developed the knack of defining relative size and added to this a kind of sixth sense that enabled him to pilot an aircraft, strike a polo ball, or shoot as well as any fully sighted person.

The nearest of the approaching antelope were almost at extreme range, when there was a crackle of rifle fire from farther down the line and immediately the herds exploded into silent airy flight. Each tiny creature danced and bounced on long legs no thicker than a man's thumb. Seeming no longer bounded by the dictates of gravity, every fluid leap blurring against the matching background of parched earth, they tumbled and shot into the mirage-quivering air in the spectacular display of aerobatics that gave them their name, and down each of their backs a frosty mane came erect and shone with their alarm.

It was more difficult than trying to bring down a rocketing grouse with a spreading pattern of shot, impossible to hold the darting ethereal shapes in the cross-hairs of the lens, fruitless to aim directly at the swift creatures – necessary rather to aim at the empty space where they would be a micro second later when the supersonic bullet reached them.

With some men shooting well is skill learned with much practice and concentration. With Shasa it was a talent that he had been born with. As he turned his upper body, the long barrel pointed exactly where he was looking and the cross hairs of the telescopic sight moved smoothly in the centre of his vision and settled on the nimble body of a racing antelope as it went bounding high in the air. Shasa was not conscious of squeezing the trigger, the rifle seemed to fire of its own accord and the recoil drove into his shoulder at precisely the correct instant.

The ram died in the air, turned over by the bullet so his snowy belly flashed in the sunlight, somersaulting to the impetus of the tiny metal capsule as it lanced his heart, and he fell and rolled horned head over dainty hooves as he hit the earth and lay still.

Shasa worked the bolt and picked up another running creature and the rifle fired again and the sharp stink of burned powder prickled his nostrils. He kept shooting until the barrel was hot enough to raise blisters and his eardrums ached to the crackle of shot.

Then the last of the herds were gone past them and over the hills behind them, and the gunfire died away. Shasa unloaded the cartridges that remained in his rifle and looked at Manfred De La Rey.

'Eight,' Manfred said, 'and two wounded.' It was amazing how those tiny creatures could carry away a misplaced bullet. They would have to follow them up. It was unthinkable to allow a wounded animal to suffer unnecessarily.

'Eight is a good score,' Shasa told him. 'You can be pleased with your shooting.'

'And you?' Manfred asked. 'How many?'

'Twelve,' Shasa answered expressionlessly.

'How many wounded?' Manfred hid his chagrin well enough.

'Oh.' Shasa smiled at last. 'I don't wound animals – I shoot where I aim.' That was enough. He did not have to rub in salt.

Shasa left him and walked out to the nearest carcass. The springbok lay on its side and in death the deep fold of skin along its back had opened and from it the snowy plume started erect. Shasa went down on one knee and stroked the lovely plume. From the glands in the fold of skin had exuded reddish-brown musk, and Shasa parted the long plume and rubbed the secretion with his forefinger, then raised it to his face and inhaled the honey-scented aroma. It smelled more like a flower than an animal. Then the hunter's melancholy came upon him, and he mourned the beautiful little creature he had killed.

'Thank you for dying for me,' he whispered the ancient Bushman prayer that Centaine had taught him so long ago, and yet the sadness was pleasure, and deep inside him the atavistic urge of the hunter was for the moment replete.

*   *   *

34

In the cool of the evening the men gathered around the pits of glowing embers in front of the homestead. The *braaivleis*, or meat bake, was a ritual that followed the hunt; the men did the cooking while the women were relegated to the preparation of salads and pudding at the long trestle tables on the stoep. The game had been marinated or larded or made into spiced sausage. and the livers, kidneys and tripes were treated to jealously guarded recipes before they were laid upon the coals in the grilling pit, while the self-appointed chefs kept the heat of the fires from becoming oppressive with liberal draughts of *mampoer*, the pungent peach brandy.

A scratch band of coloured farm labourers belted out traditional country airs on banjo and concertina and some of the guests danced on the wide front stoep. A few of the younger women were very interesting, and Shasa eyed them thoughtfully. They were tanned and glowing with health and an unsophisticated sensuality that was made all the more appealing by the fact of their Calvinist upbringing. Their untouchability and probable virginity made them even more attractive to Shasa who enjoyed the chase as much as the kill.

However, there was too much at stake here to risk giving the slightest offence. He avoided the shy but calculating glances that some of them cast in his direction, and avoided just as scrupulously the savage peach brandy and filled his glass with ginger ale. He knew he would need all his wits before the night was ended.

When their appetites, sharpened on the hunting veld, had been blunted by the steaming platters piled with grilled venison, and the leftovers had been carried away delightedly to the servants' quarters, Shasa found himself sitting at the end of the long stoep farthest from the band. Manfred De La Rey was sitting opposite him, and the two other ministers of the government sprawled contentedly in their deep lounging chairs flanking him. Despite their relaxed attitudes, they watched him warily from the corners of their eyes.

'The main business is about to begin,' Shasa decided, and almost immediately Manfred stirred.

'I was telling Meneer Courtney that in many ways we are very close,' Manfred started quietly, and his colleagues nodded sagely. 'We all want to protect this land and preserve all that is fine and worthwhile in it.'

'God has chosen us as guardians – it is our duty to protect all its peoples, and make certain that the identity of each group and each separate culture is kept intact, and apart from the others.'

It was the party line, this notion of divine selection, and Shasa had heard it all a hundred times before; so although he nodded and made

35

small noncommittal sounds, he was becoming restless.

'There is still much to be done,' Manfred told him. 'After the next election we will have great labours ahead of us, we are the masons building a social edifice that will stand for a thousand years. A model society in which each group will have its place, and will not intrude upon the space of others, a broad and stable pyramid forming a unique society.' They were all silent then for a while, contemplating the beauty of the vision, and though Shasa kept his expression neutral, still he smiled inwardly at the apt metaphor of a pyramid. There was no doubt in any of their minds as to which group was divinely ordained to occupy the pinnacle.

'And yet there are enemies?' the minister of agriculture cued Manfred.

'There are enemies, within and without. They will become more vociferous and dangerous as the work goes ahead. The closer we come to success, the more avid they become to prevent us achieving it.'

'Already they are gathering.'

'Yes,' Manfred agreed. 'And even old and traditional friends are warning and threatening us. America, who should know better, racked by her own racial problems, the unnatural aspirations of the negroes they brought as slaves from Africa. Even Britain with her Mau Mau troubles in Kenya and the disintegration of her Indian Empire wishes to dictate to us and divert us from the course we know is right.'

'They believe us to be weak and vulnerable.'

'They already hint at an arms embargo, denying us the weapons to defend ourselves against the dark enemy that is gathering in the shadows.'

'They are right,' Manfred cut in brusquely. 'We are weak and militarily disorganized. We are at the mercy of their threats —'

'We have to change this,' the finance minister spoke harshly. 'We must make ourselves strong.'

'At the next budget the defence allocation will be fifty million pounds, while by the end of the decade it will be a billion.'

'We must put ourselves above their threats of sanction and boycott and embargo.'

'Strength through Unity, *Ex Unitate Vires*,' said Manfred De La Rey. 'And yet by tradition and preference, the Afrikaner people have been farmers and country folk. Because of the discrimination which was practised against us for a hundred years and more, we have been excluded from the marketplace of commerce and industry and we have not learned the skills which come so readily to our English-speaking countrymen.' Manfred paused, glanced at the other two, as

36

if for approval, and then went on. 'What this country needs desperately is the wealth to make our vision come true. It is a massive undertaking for which we lack the skills. We need a special type of man.' They were all looking keenly at Shasa now. 'We need a man with the vigour of youth but the experience of age, a man with proven genius for finance and organization. We can find no member of our own party with those attributes.'

Shasa stared at them. What they were suggesting was outrageous. He had grown up in the shadow of Jan Christian Smuts and had a natural and unshakable allegiance to the party that Smuts, that great and good man, had founded. He opened his mouth to answer angrily, but Manfred De La Rey raised his hand to stop him.

'Hear me out,' he said. 'The person chosen for this patriotic work would be immediately given a senior cabinet appointment which the prime minister would create specifically for him. He would become minister of mines and industry.'

Shasa closed his mouth slowly. How carefully they must have studied him, and how accurately they had analysed him and arrived at his price. The very foundations of his political beliefs and principles were shaken, and the walls cracked through. They had led him up into a high place and shown him the prize that was his for the taking.

*   *   *

At twenty thousand feet Shasa levelled the Mosquito and trimmed for cruise. He increased the flow of oxygen into his mask to sharpen his brain. He had four hours' flying time to Youngsfield, four hours to think it all out carefully, and he tried to divorce himself from the passions and emotions which still swept him along and attempt instead to reach his decision logically – but the excitement intruded upon his meditations. The prospect of wielding vast powers, building up an arsenal that would make his country supreme in Africa and a force in the world was awe-inspiring. That was power. The thought of it all made him slightly light-headed, for it was all there at last, everything he had ever dreamed of. He had only to reach out his hand and seize the moment. Yet what would be the cost in honour and pride – how would he explain to men who trusted him?

Then abruptly he thought of Blaine Malcomess, his mentor and adviser, the man who had stood in the place of his own father all these years. What would he think of this dreadful betrayal that Shasa was contemplating?

'I can do more good by joining them, Blaine,' he whispered into

37

his mask. 'I can help change and moderate them from within more effectively than in opposition, for now I will have the power —' but he knew he was prevaricating, and all else was dross.

It all came down to that one thing in the end, the power – and he knew that although Blaine Malcomess would never condone what he would see as treachery, there was one person who would understand and give him support and encouragement. For after all it was Centaine Courtney-Malcomess who had so carefully schooled her son in the acquisition and use of wealth and power.

'It could all come true, Mater. It could still happen, not exactly as we planned it, but it could still happen all the same.' Then a thought struck him, and a shadow passed across the bright light of his triumph.

He glanced down at the red folder that Manfred De La Rey, minister of police, had given him at the airstrip, just as he was about to climb up into the Mosquito, and which now lay on the co-pilot's seat beside him.

'There is only one problem we will have to deal with, if you accept our offer,' Manfred had said as he handed it over, 'and it is a serious problem. This is it.'

The folder contained a police special branch security report, and the name on the cover was:

TARA ISABELLA COURTNEY née MALCOMESS

*　　*　　*

Tara Courtney made her round of the children's wing, calling in at each of the bedrooms. Nanny was just tucking Isabella under her pink satin eiderdown, and the child let out a cry of delight when she saw Tara.

'Mummy, Mummy, teddy has been naughty. I'm going to make him sleep on the shelf with my other dolls.'

Tara sat on her daughter's bed and hugged her while they discussed teddy's misdemeanours. Isabella was pink and warm and smelled of soap. Her hair was silky against Tara's cheek and it took an effort for Tara to kiss her and stand up.

'Time to go to sleep, Bella baby.'

The moment the lights went out Isabella let out such a shriek that Tara was stricken with alarm.

'What is it, baby?' She snapped on the lights again and rushed back to the bed.

'I've forgiven teddy. He can sleep with me after all.'

The teddy-bear was ceremoniously reinstated in Isabella's favour

38

and she took him in a loving half-nelson and stuck her other thumb in her mouth.

'When is my Daddy coming home?' she demanded drowsily around the thumb, but her eyes were closed and she was asleep before Tara reached the door.

Sean was sitting on Garrick's chest in the middle of the bedroom floor, tweaking the hair at his brother's temples with sadistic finesse. Tara separated them.

'Sean, you get back to your own room this instant, do you hear me? I have warned you a thousand times about bullying your brothers. Your father is going to hear all about this when he gets home.'

Garrick snuffled up his tears and came wheezing to his elder brother's defence.

'We were only playing, Mater. He wasn't bullying me.' But she could hear that he was on the verge of another asthma attack. She wavered. She really should not go out, not with an attack threatening, but tonight was so important.

'I'll prepare his inhaler and tell Nanny to look in on him every hour until I get back,' she compromised.

Michael was reading, and barely looked up to receive her kiss. 'Lights out at nine o'clock. Promise me, darling.' She tried never to let it show, but he was always her favourite.

'I promise, Mater,' he murmured and under cover of the eiderdown carefully crossed his fingers.

On the way down the stairs she glanced at her wristwatch. It was five minutes before eight. She was going to be late, and she stifled her maternal feelings of guilt and fled out to her old Packard.

Shasa detested the Packard, taking its blotched sun-faded paint-work and its shabby stained upholstery as an affront to the family dignity. He had given her a new Aston Martin on her last birthday, but she left it in the garage. The Packard suited her Spartan image of herself as a caring liberal, and it blew a streamer of dirty smoke as she accelerated down the long driveway, taking a perverse pleasure in sending a pall of fine dust over Shasa's meticulously groomed vineyards. It was strange how even after all these years she felt herself a stranger at Weltevreden, and alien amongst its treasures and stuffy old-fashioned furnishings. If she lived here another fifty years it would never be her home, it was Centaine Courtney-Malcomess' home, the other woman's touch and memory lingered in every room that Shasa would never allow her to redecorate.

She escaped through the great ostentatious Anreith gateway into the real world of suffering and injustice, where the oppressed masses wept and struggled and cried out for succour and where she felt useful and relevant, where in the company of other pilgrims she could march forward to meet a future full of challenge and change.

The Broadhursts' home was in the middle-class suburb of Pinelands, a modern ranch-type home with a flat roof and large picture windows, with ordinary functional mass-produced furniture and nylon wall-to-wall carpets. There were dog hairs on the chairs, well thumbed intellectual books piled in odd corners or left open on the dining-room table, children's toys abandoned in the passageways, and cheap reproductions of Picasso and Modigliani hanging askew on the walls marked with grubby little fingerprints. Tara felt comfortable and welcome here, mercifully released from the fastidious splendour of Weltevreden.

Molly Broadhurst rushed out to meet her as she parked the Packard. She was dressed in a marvellously flamboyant caftan.

'You're late!' She kissed Tara heartily and dragged her through the disorder of the lounge to the music room at the rear.

The music room was an afterthought stuck on to the end of the house without any aesthetic considerations and was filled now with Molly's guests who had been invited to hear Moses Gama. Tara's spirits soared as she looked around her, they were all vibrant creative people, all of them spirited and articulate, filled with the excitement of living and a fine sense of justice and outrage and rebellion.

This was the type of gathering that Weltevreden would never see. Firstly, black people were included, students from the black University of Fort Hare and the fledgling University of the Western Cape, teachers and lawyers and even a black doctor, all of them political activists who, although denied a voice or a vote in the white parliament, were beginning to cry out with a passion that must be heard. There was the editor of the black magazine *Drum* and the local correspondent of the *Sowetan*, named after that sprawling black township.

Just to mingle socially with blacks made her feel breathlessly daring.

The whites in the room were no less extraordinary. Some of them had been members of the Communist Party of South Africa before that organization had been disbanded a few years previously. There was a man called Harris who she had met before at Molly's house. He had fought with the Irgun in Israel against the British and the Arabs, a tall fierce man who inspired a delicious fear in Tara. Molly hinted that he was an expert in guerrilla warfare and sabotage, and certainly he was always travelling secretly around the country or slipping across the border into neighbouring states on mysterious business.

Talking earnestly to Molly's husband was another lawyer from

40

Johannesburg, Bram Fischer, who specialized in defending black clients charged under the myriad laws that were designed to muzzle and disarm them and restrict their movements. Molly said that Bram was reorganizing the old Communist Party into underground cells, and Tara fantasized that she might one day be invited to join one of these cells.

In the same group was Marcus Archer, another ex-communist and an industrial psychologist from the Witwatersrand. He was responsible for the training of thousands of black workers for the gold-mining industry, and Molly said that he had helped to organize the black mineworkers' union. Molly had also whispered that he was a homosexual, and she had used an odd term for it that Tara had never heard before. 'He's gay, gay as a lark.' And because it was totally unacceptable to polite society, Tara found it fascinating.

'Oh God, Molly,' Tara whispered. 'This is so exciting. These are all real people, they make me feel as though I am truly living at last.'

'There he is.' Molly smiled at this outburst and dragged Tara with her through the press of bodies.

Moses Gama leaned against the far wall faced by a half circle of admirers, yet standing head and shoulders above them, and Molly pushed her way into the front row.

Tara found herself staring up at Moses Gama, and she thought that even in this brilliant company he stood out like a black panther in a pack of mangy alley cats. Though his head seemed carved from a block of black onyx, and his handsome Nilotic features were impassive, yet there was a force within him that seemed to fill all the room. It was like standing on the high slopes of a dark Vesuvius, knowing that at any instant it could boil over into cataclysmic eruption.

Moses Gama turned his head and looked at Tara. He did not smile, but a shadowy thing moved in the depths of his dark gaze.

'Mrs Courtney – I asked Molly to invite you.'

'Please don't call me that. My name is Tara.'

'We must talk later, Tara. Will you stay?'

She could not answer, she was too overcome at being singled out, but she nodded dumbly.

'If you are ready, Moses, we can begin,' Molly suggested, and taking him out of the group led him to the raised dais on which the piano stood.

'People! People! Your attention, please!' Molly clapped her hands, and the animated chatter died away. Everybody turned towards the dais. 'Moses Gama is one of the most talented and revered of the new generation of young black African leaders. He has been a member of the African National Congress since before the war, and

41

a prime mover in the formation of the African Mineworkers' Union. Although the black trade unions are not officially recognized by the government of the day, yet the secret union of mineworkers is one of the most representative and powerful of all black associations, with more than a hundred thousand paid-up members. In 1950 Moses Gama was elected Secretary of the ANC, and he has worked tirelessly, selflessly and highly effectively in making the heart cry of our black citizens heard, even though they are denied a voice in their own destiny. For a short while Moses Gama was an appointed member of the government's Natives' Representative Council, that infamous attempt to appease black political aspirations, but it was he who resigned with the now celebrated remark, 'I have been speaking into a toy telephone, with nobody listening at the other end.'

There was a burst of laughter and applause from the room, and then Molly turned to Moses Gama.

'I know that you have nothing to tell us that will comfort and soothe us – but, Moses Gama, in this room there are many hearts that beat with yours and are prepared to bleed with yours.'

Tara applauded until the palms of her hands were numb, and then leaned forward to listen eagerly as Moses Gama moved to the front of the dais.

He was dressed in a neat blue suit and a dark blue tie with a white shirt. Strangely, he was the most formally dressed man in a room full of baggy woollen sweaters and old tweed sports coats with leather patches on the elbows and gravy stains on the lapels. His suit was severely cut, draped elegantly from wide athletic shoulders, but he imparted to it a panache that made it seem that he wore the leopard-skin cloak of royalty and the blue heron feathers in his close-cropped mat of hair. His voice was deep and thrilling.

'My friends, there is one single ideal to which I cling with all my heart, and which I will defend with my very life, and that is that every African has a primary, inherent and inalienable right to the Africa which is his continent and his only motherland,' Moses Gama began, and Tara listened, enchanted, as he detailed how that inherent right had been denied the black man for three hundred years, and how in these last few years since the Nationalist government had come to power, those denials were becoming formally entrenched in a monumental edifice of laws and ordinances and proclamations which was the policy of *apartheid* in practice.

'We have all heard it said that the whole concept of *apartheid* is so grotesque, so obviously lunatic, that it can never work. But I warn you, my friends, that the men who have conceived this crazy scheme are so fanatical, so obdurate, so convinced of their divine guidance,

42

that they will force it to work. Already they have created a vast army of petty civil servants to administer this madness, and they have behind them the full resources of a land rich in gold and minerals. I warn you that they will not hesitate to squander that wealth in building up this ideological Frankenstein of theirs. There is no price in material wealth and human suffering that is too high for them to contemplate.'

Moses Gama paused and looked down upon them, and it seemed to Tara that he personally felt every last agony of his people, and was filled with suffering beyond that which mortal men could bear.

'Unless they are opposed, my friends, they will create of this lovely land a desolation and an abomination; a land devoid of compassion, of justice, a land materially and spiritually bankrupt.'

Moses Gama spread his arms. 'These men call those of us who defy them traitors. Well, my friends, I call any man who does not oppose them a traitor – a traitor to Africa.'

He was silent then, glaring this accusation at them, and they were struck dumb for a moment, before they began to cheer him. Only Tara remained still in the uproar, staring up at him; she had no voice, and she was shivering as though there was malaria in her blood.

Moses' head sank until his chin was on his chest, and they thought he had finished. Then he raised that magnificent head again and spread his arms.

'Oppose them? How do we oppose them? I reply to you – we oppose them with all our strength and all our resolve and with all our hearts. If no price is too high for them to pay, then no price is too high for us. I tell you, my friends, there is nothing —' He paused for emphasis '—*nothing* I would not do to further the struggle. I am prepared both to die and to kill for it.'

The room was silent in the face of such deadly resolve. For those of them who were practitioners of elegant, socialist dialectic, the effete intellectuals, such a declaration was menacing and disquieting, it had the sound of breaking bones in it and the stench of fresh-spilled blood.

'We are ready to make a beginning, my friends, and already our plans are far advanced. Starting in a few months' time we will conduct a nationwide campaign of defiance against these monstrous *apartheid* laws. We will burn the passes which we are ordered by act of parliament to carry, the hated *dompas* which is akin to the star that the Jews were forced to wear, the document that marks us as racial inferiors. We will make a bonfire of them and the smoke of their burning will sting and offend the nostrils of the civilized world. We will sit in the whites-only restaurants and cinemas, we will ride in the whites-only coaches of the railways, and swim from the whites-only beaches. We will cry out to the fascist police, 'Come! Arrest us.' And in our thousands we will overflow the white man's jails and block his law courts with our multitudes until the whole giant apparatus of *apartheid* breaks down under the strain.'

Tara lingered afterwards as he had asked her to, and when Molly had seen most of her guests leave, she came and took Tara's arm. 'Will you risk my spaghetti Bolognaise, Tara dear? As you know, I'm the worst cook in Africa, but you are a brave girl.'

Only a half dozen of the guests had been invited to remain for a late dinner and they sat out on the patio. The mosquitoes whined around their heads and every once in a while a shift of the wind brought a sulphurous whiff from the sewerage works across the Black River. It did not seem to spoil their appetites and they tucked into Molly's notorious spaghetti Bolognaise and washed it down with tumblers of cheap red wine. Tara found it a relief from the elaborate meals that were served at Weltevreden, accompanied always by the quasi-religious ceremony of tasting wines that cost a working man's monthly wage for the bottle. Here food and wine were merely fuel to power the mind and tongue, not for gloating over.

Tara sat beside Moses Gama. Although his appetite was hearty, he hardly touched the tumbler of wine. His table manners were African. He ate noisily with an open mouth, but strangely this did not offend Tara in the least. Somehow it confirmed his differentness, marked him as a man of his own people.

At first Moses gave most of his attention to the other guests, replying to the questions and comments that were called down the table to him. Then gradually he concentrated on Tara, at first including her in his general conversation, and at last, when he had finished eating, turning in his chair to face her fully and lowering his voice to exclude the others.

'I know your family,' he told her. 'Know them well, Mrs Centaine Courtney and more especially your husband, Shasa Courtney.'

Tara was startled. 'I have never heard them speak of you.'

'Why would they do so? In their eyes I was never important. They would have forgotten me long ago.'

'Where did you know them and when?'

'Twenty years ago. Your husband was still a child. I was a boss-boy, a supervisor on the H'ani diamond mine in South West Africa.'

'The H'ani,' Tara nodded. 'Yes, the fountainhead of the Courtney fortune.'

'Shasa Courtney was sent by his mother to learn the workings of the mine. He and I were together for a few weeks, working side by

44

side —' Moses broke off and smiled. 'We got along well, as well as a black man and a little white *baas* ever could, I suppose. We talked a great deal, and he gave me a book. Macaulay's *History of England*. I still have it. I recall how some of the things I said puzzled and disturbed him. He told me once, "Moses, that is politics. Blacks don't take part in politics. That's white men's business."' Moses chuckled at the memory, but Tara frowned.

'I can hear him say it,' she agreed. 'He hasn't changed much in twenty years,' and Moses stopped laughing.

'Your husband has become a powerful man. He has great wealth and influence.'

Tara shrugged. 'What good is power and wealth unless it is used with wisdom and compassion.'

'You have compassion, Tara,' he said softly. 'Even if I did not know of the work that you do for my people, I would sense it in you.'

Tara lowered her eyes from his smouldering regard.

'Wisdom.' His voice sank even lower. 'I think you have that also. It was wise not to speak of our last meeting in front of others.'

Tara's head came up and she stared at him. In the evening's excitement she had almost forgotten their encounter in the forbidden corridors of parliament.

'Why?' she whispered. 'Why were you there?'

'One day I may tell you,' he replied. 'When we have become friends.'

'We are friends,' she said, and he nodded.

'Yes, I think we are friends, but friendships have to be tried and proven. Now, tell me about your work, Tara.'

'It's so very little that I am able to do —' and she told him about the clinic and the feeding scheme for the children and the old people, unconscious of her own enthusiasm and animation until he smiled again.

'I was right, you do have compassion, Tara, enormous compassion. I would like to see this work. Is it possible?'

'Oh, would you come – that would be marvellous!'

Molly brought him out to the clinic the following afternoon.

The clinic was on the southern edge of the black township of Nyanga – the name meant 'dawn' in the Xhosa language, but was hardly apt. Like most black townships it comprised row upon row of identical brick cottages with asbestos sheet roofs separated by dusty lanes; although aesthetically ugly and uninspiring, the accommodation was adequate and offered reticulated water, mains sewerage and electricity. However, beyond the township proper, in the bushy dune country of the Cape Flats, had sprung up a shanty town that housed

45

the overflow of black migrants from the impoverished rural areas, and Tara's clinic found its main clientele amongst these wretches.

Proudly Tara led Moses and Molly around the small building.

'Being the weekend, none of our volunteer doctors are here today,' she explained and Moses stopped to chat with the black nurses and with some of the mothers waiting patiently with their small children in the yard.

Afterwards she made coffee for all three of them in her tiny office and when Moses asked how the clinic was financed, Tara told him vaguely.

'Oh, we get a grant from the local provincial government —' but Molly Blackhurst cut in.

'Don't let her fool you – most of the running costs come out of her own pocket.'

'I cheat my husband on the housekeeping,' Tara laughed, dismissing it lightly.

'Would it be possible for us to drive around the squatter slums? I'd like to see them.' Moses looked at Molly, but she bit her lip and glanced at her wristwatch.

'Oh, damn, I have to get back,' and Tara intervened quickly.

'Don't worry, Molly. I can drive Moses around. You get on back and I will drop him off at your house later this evening.'

In the old Packard they bumped over the sandy tracks amongst the overgrown dunes, where the Port Jackson willow had been cleared to make way for hutments of rusty corrugated iron and cardboard and tattered plastic sheeting. Now and then they stopped and walked amongst the shanties. The south-easter was roaring in off the bay, filling the air with a mist of dust. They leaned against it as they walked.

The people knew Tara and smiled and called greetings to her as she passed, and the children ran to meet her and danced around her begging for the cheap boiled sweets she kept in her pocket.

'Where do they get water?' Moses asked, and she showed him how the older children had banded old oil drums with discarded car tyres. They filled the drums at a communal water tap at the boundary of the official township a mile away, and rolled the drums back to their hovels.

'They cut the Port Jackson willow for fuel,' Tara told him. 'but in winter the children are always full of colds and flu and pneumonia. You don't have to ask about about sewerage —' she sniffed at the thick odour of the shallow toilet pits, screened with strips of old burlap.

It was half dark when Tara parked the Packard at the back door of the clinic and switched off the engine. They sat quietly for a few minutes.

'What we have seen is no worse than a hundred other shanty towns, places where I have lived most of my life,' Moses said.

'I am sorry.'

'Why do you apologize?' Moses asked.

'I don't know, I just feel guilty.' She knew how inadequate it sounded and she opened the door of the Packard.

'There are some papers I must get from my office. I won't be a minute, and then I will drive you back to Molly's house.'

The clinic was deserted. The two nurses had locked up and gone home an hour before. Tara let herself in with her own key and went through the single consulting room to her own office. She glanced at herself in the mirror above the washstand in the corner as she washed her hands. She was flushed and her eyes sparkled. She was so accustomed to the squalor of the squatter camps that it had not depressed her as it once had; instead she felt tingling alive and strangely elated.

She stuffed the folder of correspondence and bills into her leather sling bag and locked the drawer of her desk, made sure the plug of the electric kettle was pulled out of the wall-socket and that the windows were closed, then switched off the lights and hurried out into the consulting room. She stopped with surprise. Moses Gama had followed her into the building and was sitting on the white draped examination bed against the far wall.

'Oh,' she recovered. 'Sorry I took so long —'

He shook his head, then stood up and crossed the tiled floor. He stopped, facing her. She felt awkward and uncertain as he studied her face solemnly.

'You are a remarkable woman,' he said in a deep quiet voice that she had not heard him use before. 'I have never met another white woman like you.'

She could think of no reply, and he went on softly, 'You are rich and privileged. You are gifted with everything that your life can offer you, and yet you come here. To this poverty and misery.'

He reached out and touched her arm. His palm and the inside of his fingers were a pale rose colour, contrasting vividly with the back of his hand and his dark muscular forearm, and his skin felt cool. She wondered if it were really so, or if her own skin was hot. She felt hot, she felt a furnace glow deep within her. She looked down at his hand on her smooth pale arm. She had never been touched by a black man before, not deliberately, not lingeringly like this.

She let the strap of the sling bag slide off her shoulder and it fell to the tiled floor with a thud. She had been holding her own hands clasped in front of her hips in an instinctively defensive gesture but

47

now she let them fall to her sides, and almost without conscious volition arched her back and pushed her lower body towards him. At the same time she raised her head and looked squarely into his eyes. Her lips parted and her breathing quickened. She saw it reflected in his own eyes and she said,

'Yes.'

He stroked her arm, up from the elbow to the shoulder, and she shuddered and closed her eyes. He touched her left breast and she did not pull away. His hand closed around her, she felt it fill his grip, and her flesh hardened, her nipple swelled and thrust out into his palm and he squeezed her. The feeling was so intense it was almost painful and she gasped as it rippled down her spine spreading like wavelets when a stone is thrown into a quiet pool.

Her arousal was so abrupt that she was unprepared. She had never considered herself a sensual person. Shasa was the only man she had ever known and it took all his skill and patience to quicken her body, but now at a touch her bones went soft with desire and her loins melted like wax in the flame and she could not breathe, so strong was her need of this man.

'The door,' she blurted. 'Lock the door.'

Then she saw that he had already barred the door, and she was grateful for it, for she felt that she could not have brooked the delay. He picked her up quickly and carried her to the bed. The sheet that covered it was spotless and so crisply starched that it crackled softly under her weight.

He was so huge that he terrified her, and though she had borne four children, she felt as though she was being split asunder as his blackness filled her, and then the terror passed to be replaced by a strange sense of sanctity. She was the sacrificial lamb, with this act she was redeeming all the sins of her own race, all the trespasses that they had committed against his people down the centuries; she was wiping away the guilt that had been her stigmata since as far back as she could remember.

When at the end he lay heavy upon her with his breathing roaring in her ears and the last wild convulsions racking his great black muscles, she clung to him with a joyous gratitude. For he had, at one and the same time, set her free from guilt and made her his slave for ever.

*　　*　　*

Subdued by the sadness of after love, and by the certain knowledge that her world was for ever altered, Tara was silent on the drive back to Molly's home. She parked a block before she reached it, and

48

keeping the engine running she turned to examine his face in the reflection of the street lights.

'When will I see you again?' she asked the question that countless women in her position had asked before her.

'Do you wish to see me again?'

'More than anything else in my life.' She did not at that moment even think of her children. He was the only thing in her existence.

'It will be dangerous.'

'I know.'

'The penalties if we are discovered – disgrace, ostracism, imprisonment. Your life would be destroyed.'

'My life was a sham,' she said softly. 'Its destruction would be no great loss.'

He studied her features carefully, searching for insincerity. At last he was satisfied.

'I will send for you, when it is safe.'

'I will come immediately, whenever you call.'

'I must leave you now. Take me back.'

She parked at the side of Molly's house, in the shadow where they could not be observed from the road.

'Now the subterfuge and dissembling begins,' she thought calmly. 'I was right. It will never be the same again.'

He made no attempt to embrace her, it was not the African way. He stared at her, the whites of his eyes gleaming like ivory in the half dark.

'You realize that when you choose me you choose the struggle?' he asked.

'Yes, I know that.'

'You have become a warrior and you and your wants, even your life, are of no consequence. If you have to die for the struggle, I will not lift my hand to save you.'

She nodded. 'Yes, I know that.' The nobility of the concept filled her chest and made it difficult for her to breathe so her voice was laboured as she whispered, 'Greater love hath no man – I will make any sacrifice you ask of me.'

* * *

Moses went to the guest bedroom which Molly had allocated to him, and as he washed his face in the basin Marcus Archer slipped into the room without knocking, closed the door and leaned against it, watching Moses in the mirror.

'Well?' he asked at last, as though he was reluctant to hear the answer.

'Just as we planned it.' Moses dried his face on a clean towel.

'I hate the silly little bitch,' Marcus said softly.

'We agreed it was necessary.' Moses selected a fresh shirt from the valise on his bed.

'I know we agreed,' Marcus said. 'It was my suggestion, if you remember, but I do not have to like her for it.'

'She is an instrument. It is folly to let your personal feelings intrude.'

Marcus Archer nodded. In the end he hoped he could act like a true revolutionary, one of the steely hard men which the struggle needed, but his feelings for this man, Moses Gama, were stronger than all his political convictions.

He knew that it was completely one-sided. Over the years Moses Gama had used him as cynically and as calculatingly as he now planned to use the Courtney woman. His vast sexual appeal was to Moses Gama merely another weapon in his arsenal, another means of manipulating people. He could use it on men or women, young or old, no matter how attractive or unappealing, and Marcus admired him for the ability, and at the same time was devastated by it.

'We leave for the Witwatersrand tomorrow,' he said, as he pushed himself away from the door, for the moment controlling his jealousy. 'I have made the arrangements.'

'So soon?' Moses asked.

'I have made the arrangements. We will travel by car.'

It was one of the problems which dogged their work. It was difficult for a black man to travel about the huge sub-continent, liable as he was at any time to demands to show his *dompas* and to interrogation when the authority realized that he was far from the domicile shown on the pass without apparent reason, or that the pass had not been stamped by an employer.

Moses' association with Marcus and the nominal employment he provided with the Chamber of Mines gave him valuable cover when it was necessary to travel, but they always needed couriers. That was one of the functions that Tara Courtney would perform. In addition she was by birth and by marriage highly placed, and the information she could provide would be of the greatest value in the planning. Later, after she had proved herself, there would be other, more dangerous work.

*   *   *

In the end, Shasa Courtney realized, it was his mother's advice which would tip the fine balance and decide whether he accepted or rejected the offer that had been made to him during the springbok hunt on the open plains of the Orange Free State.

50

Shasa would have been the first to despise any other man of his age who was still firmly enmeshed in the maternal apron strings, but he never considered that this applied to him. The fact that Centaine Courtney-Malcomess was his mother was merely incidental. What influenced him was that she was the shrewdest financial and political brain he had access to; she was also his business partner and his only true confidante. To make such an important decision without consulting her never even occurred to him.

He waited a week after his return to Cape Town to let his own feelings distil out, and for an opportunity to have Centaine alone, for he was in no doubt as to what his stepfather's reaction would be to the proposal. Blaine Malcomess was the opposition representative on the parliamentary sub-committee examining the proposed establishment of an oil-from-coal project, part of the government's long-term plan to reduce the country's reliance on imported crude oil. The committee was going to take evidence on site, and for once Centaine was not accompanying her husband. That was the opportunity Shasa needed.

It was less than half an hour's drive from Weltevreden, across the Constantia Nek pass and down the other side of the mountains to the Atlantic seaboard where the home that Centaine had made for Blaine stood on five hundred acres of wild protea-covered mountainside that dropped steeply down to rocky headlands and white beaches. The original house, Rhodes Hill, had been built during Queen Victoria's reign by one of the old mining magnates from the Rand, but Centaine had stripped the interior and refurbished it completely.

She was waiting for Shasa on the verandah when he parked the Jaguar, and ran up the steps to embrace her.

'You're getting too thin,' she scolded him fondly. She had guessed from his telephone call that he wanted a serious discussion, and they had their own traditions. Centaine was dressed in an open-neck cotton blouse and slacks with comfortable hiking boots, and without discussing it she took his arm and they set out along the path that skirted her rose gardens and climbed the untended hillside.

The last part of the ascent was steep and the path rough, but Centaine took it without pause and came out on the summit ahead of him. Her breathing was hardly altered, and within a minute had returned to normal. 'She keeps herself in wonderful condition, Heaven alone knows what she spends on health cures and potions, and she exercises like a professional athlete,' Shasa thought as he grinned down at her proudly. He placed an arm around her small firm waist.

'Isn't it beautiful?' Centaine leaned lightly against him and looked

51

out over the cold green Benguela current, as it swirled, decked in lacy foam, around Africa's heel, which like a medieval knight was spurred and armoured with black rock. 'This is one of my favourite places.'

'Whoever would have guessed it,' Shasa murmured, and led her to the flat lichen-covered rock that was her seat.

She perched up on it, hugging her knees and he sprawled on the bed of moss below her. They were both silent for a few moments, and Shasa wondered how often they had sat like this at this special place of hers, and how many heavy decisions they had taken here.

'Do you remember Manfred De La Rey?' he asked suddenly, but he was unprepared for her reaction. She started and looked down at him, colour draining from her cheeks, with an expression he could not fathom.

'Is something wrong, Mater?' He began to rise, but she gestured at him to remain seated.

'Why do you ask about him?' she demanded, but he did not reply directly.

'Isn't it strange how our paths seem to cross with his family? Ever since his father rescued us, when I was an infant and we were castaways living with the Bushmen in the Kalahari.'

'We needn't go over all that again,' Centaine stopped him, and her tone was brusque. Shasa realized he had been tactless. Manfred's father had robbed the H'ani Mine of almost a million pounds' worth of diamonds, an act of vengeance for fancied wrongs that he had convinced himself Centaine had inflicted on him. For that crime he had served almost fifteen years of a life sentence for robbery, and had been pardoned only when the Nationalist government had come to power in 1948. At the same time the Nationalists had pardoned many other Afrikaners serving sentences for treason and sabotage and armed robbery, convicted by the Smuts' government when they had attempted to disrupt the country's war effort against Nazi Germany. However, the stolen diamonds had never been recovered, and their loss had almost destroyed the fortune that Centaine Courtney had built up with so much labour, sacrifice and heartache.

'Why do you mention Manfred De La Rey?' she repeated her question.

'I had an invitation from him to a meeting. A clandestine meeting – all very cloak and dagger.'

'Did you go?'

He nodded slowly. 'We met at a farm in the Free State, and there were two other cabinet ministers present.'

'Did you speak to Manfred alone?' she asked, and the tone of the question, the fact that she used his Christian name, caught Shasa's attention. Then he remembered the unexpected question that Manfred De La Rey had put to him.

'Has your mother ever spoken about me?' he had asked, and faced by Centaine's present reaction to his name, the question took on a new significance.

'Yes, Mater, I spoke to him alone.'

'Did he mention me?' Centaine demanded, and Shasa gave a little chuckle of puzzlement.

'He asked the same question – whether you ever spoke about him. Why are the two of you so interested in each other?'

Centaine's expression turned bleak, and he saw her close her mind to him. It was a mystery he would not solve by pursuing it openly, he would have to stalk it.

'They made me a proposition.' And he saw her interest reawaken.

'Manfred? A proposition? Tell me.'

'They want me to cross the floor.'

She nodded slowly, showing little surprise and not immediately rejecting the idea. He knew that if Blaine were here it would have been different. Blaine's sense of honour, his rigid principles, would have left no room for manoeuvre. Blaine was a Smuts man, heart and blood, and even though the old field-marshal had died of a broken heart soon after the Nationalists unseated him and took over the reins of power, still Blaine was for ever true to the old man's memory.

'I can guess why they want you,' Centaine said slowly. 'They need a top financial brain, an organizer and a businessman. It's the one thing they lack in their cabinet.'

He nodded. She had seen it instantly, and his enormous respect for her was confirmed yet again.

'What price are they willing to pay?' she demanded.

'A cabinet appointment – minister of mines and industry.'

He saw her eyes go out of focus, and cross in a myopic stare as she gazed out to sea. He knew what that expression meant. Centaine was calculating, juggling with the future, and he waited patiently until her eyes snapped back into focus.

'Can you see any reason for refusing?' she asked.

'How about my political principles?'

'How do they differ from theirs?'

'I am not an Afrikaner.'

'That might be to your advantage. You will be their token English-man. That will give you a special status. You will have a freer rein. They will be more reluctant to fire you than if you were one of their own.'

53

'I don't agree with their native policy, this *apartheid* thing of theirs, it's just financially unsound.'

'Good Lord, Shasa. You don't believe in equal political rights for blacks, do you? Not even Jannie Smuts wanted that. You don't want another Chaka ruling us, black judges and a black police force working for a black dictator?' She shuddered. 'We'd get pretty short shrift from them.'

'No, Mater, of course not. But this *apartheid* thing is merely a device for grabbing the whole pie. We have to give them a slice of it, we can't hog it all. That's a certain recipe for eventual bloody revolution.'

'Very well, *chéri*. If you are in the cabinet, you can see to it that they get a fair crack of the whip.'

He looked dubious, and made a side-show of selecting a cigarette from his gold case and lighting it.

'You have a special talent, Shasa,' Centaine went on persuasively. 'It's your duty to use it for the good of all.'

Still he hesitated, he wanted her to declare herself fully. He had to know if she wanted this as much as he did.

'We can be honest with each other, *chéri*. This is what we have worked towards since you were a child. Take this job and do it well, after that who knows what else may follow.'

They were both silent then, they knew what they hoped would follow. They could not help themselves, it was their nature always to strive towards the highest pinnacle.

'What about Blaine?' Shasa said at last. 'How will he take it? I don't look forward to telling him.'

'I'll do that,' she promised. 'But you will have to tell Tara.'

'Tara,' he sighed. 'Now that will be a problem.'

They were silent again, until Centaine asked, 'How will you do it? If you cross the floor it will expose you to a blaze of hostile publicity.'

So it was agreed without further words, only the means remained to be discussed.

'At the next general election I will simply campaign in different colours,' Shasa said. 'They will give me a safe seat.'

'So we have a little time to arrange the details then.'

They discussed them for another hour, planning with all the meticulous attention that had made them such a formidably successful team over the years, until Shasa looked up at her.

'Thank you,' he said simply. 'What would I ever do without you! You are tougher and cleverer than any man I know.'

'Get away with you,' she smiled. 'You know how I hate praise.'

They both laughed at that absurdity.

'I'll walk you down, Mater.' But she shook her head.

'I've still got some thinking to do. Leave me here.'

She watched him go down the hill and her love and pride was so intense as to almost suffocate her.

'He is everything I ever wanted in a son, and he has fulfilled all my expectations, a thousand times over. Thank you, my son, thank you for the joy you have always given me.'

Then abruptly the words 'my son' triggered another reaction, and her mind darted back to the earlier part of their conversation.

'Do you remember Manfred De La Rey?' Shasa had asked her, but he could never know what the answer to that must be.

'Can a woman ever forget the child she bears?' she whispered the reply aloud, but her words were lost on the wind and on the sound of the green surf breaking on the rocky shore below the hill.

*　　*　　*

Every pew of the church was filled. The women's bonnets were colourful as a field of wild Namaqua daisies in the springtime, while the men's suits were sombre and severe. All their faces were upturned towards the magnificent carved pulpit of polished black stinkwood in which stood the most reverend Tromp Bierman, moderator of the Dutch Reformed Church of South Africa.

Manfred De La Rey considered once again how much Uncle Tromp had aged in the years since the war. He had never fully recovered from the pneumonia he had contracted in the concentration camp at Koffiefontein, where that English-lover Jannie Smuts had incarcerated him with hundreds of other patriotic Afrikaners for the duration of the English war with Germany.

Uncle Tromp's beard was snow white now, even more spectacular than the curly black bush it once had been. The hair on his head, also white, had been close cropped to conceal its sparsity and it glittered like powdered glass on the high-domed pate, but his eyes were full of fire as he glowered at his congregation, and his voice that had earned him the sobriquet 'The Trumpet of God' had lost none of its power and rolled like a cannonade against the high-arched ceiling of the nave.

Uncle Tromp could still pack the pews, and Manfred nodded soberly but proudly as the thunderous outpouring burst over his head. He was not really listening to the words, merely enjoying the sense of continuity that filled him; the world was a safe good place when Uncle Tromp was in his pulpit. Then a man could trust in the God of the *Volk* which he evoked with so much certainty, and believe in the divine intervention which directed his life.

55

Manfred De La Rey sat in the front pew at the right side of the nave nearest the aisle. It was the most prestigious position in the congregation, and rightly so for Manfred was the most powerful and important man in the church. The pew was reserved for him and his family, and their names were gold-leafed on the hymn books that lay beside each seat.

Heidi, his wife, was a magnificent woman, tall and strong, her bare forearms below the puff sleeves were smooth and firm, her bosom large and shapely, her neck long and her thick golden hair plaited into ropes that were twisted up under the wide-brimmed black hat. Manfred had met her in Berlin when he had been the gold medallist light heavyweight boxer at the Olympic Games in 1936, and Adolf Hitler himself had attended their wedding. They had been separated during the war years, but afterwards Manfred had brought her out to Africa with their son, little Lothar.

Lothar was almost twelve years old now, a fine strong boy, blond as his mother, and upright as his father. He sat very straight in the family pew, his hair neatly slicked down with Brylcreem and the stiff white collar biting into his neck. Like his father, he would be an athlete, but he had chosen the game of rugby at which to excel. His three younger sisters, blond and pretty in a fresh-faced healthy way, sat beyond him, their faces framed by the hoods of their traditional *voortrekker* bonnets and full-length skirts reaching to their ankles. Manfred liked them to wear national dress on Sundays.

Uncle Tromp ended with a salvo that thrilled his flock with the threat of hell-fire, and they rose to sing the final hymn. Sharing the hymn book with Heidi, Manfred examined her handsome Germanic features. She was a wife to be proud of, a good housekeeper and mother, a fine companion whom he could trust and confide in, and a glittering ornament to his political career. A woman like this could stand beside any man, even the prime minister of a powerful and prosperous nation. He let himself dwell on that secret thought. Yet everything was possible, he was a young man, the youngest by far in the cabinet, and he had never made a political mistake. Even his wartime activities gave him credit and prestige with his peers, although few people outside the inner circle knew of the full role he had played in the militant anti-British pro-Nazi secret army of the *Ossewa Brandwag.*

Already they were whispering that he was the coming man, and it was evident in the huge respect that was shown him as the service ended and the congregation left the church. Manfred stood, with Heidi beside him, on the lawns outside the church while one after another important and influential men came up to deliver social invitations, to ask a favour, to congratulate him on his speech introducing the new Criminal Law Amendment Bill in the House, or simply to pay their respects. It was almost twenty minutes before he was able to leave the church grounds.

The family walked home. It was only two blocks under the green oaks that lined the streets of Stellenbosch, the small university town which was the citadel of Afrikaner intellectualism and culture. The three girls walked ahead, Lothar followed them and Manfred with Heidi on his arm brought up the rear, stopping every few paces to acknowledge a greeting or exchange a few words with a neighbour or a friend or one of Manfred's constituents.

Manfred had purchased the house when they had arrived back from Germany after the war. Although it stood in a small garden, almost facing on to the street, it was a large house with spacious high-ceilinged rooms that suited the family well. Manfred had never seen any reason to change it, and he felt comfortable with Heidi's formal Teutonic furnishings. Now Heidi and the girls rushed through to help the servants in the kitchen, and Manfred went around the side of the house to the garage. He never used his official chauffeur-driven limousine at weekends, and he brought out his personal Chevrolet sedan and drove to fetch his father for the family Sunday luncheon.

The old man seldom attended church, especially when the Reverend Tromp Bierman was preaching. Lothar De La Rey lived alone on the smallholding that Manfred had bought for him on the outskirts of the town at the foot of the Helshoogte Pass. He was out in the peach orchard pottering with his beehives and Manfred paused by the gate to watch him with a mixture of pity and deep affection.

Lothar De La Rey had once been tall and straight as the grandson who now bore his name, but the arthritis he had contracted during the years in Pretoria Central Prison had bowed and twisted his body and turned his single remaining hand to a grotesque claw. His left arm was amputated above the elbow, too high to fit an artificial limb. He had lost it during the robbery that led to his imprisonment. He was dressed in dirty blue dungarees, with a stained brown hat on his head, the brim drooped over his eyes. One sleeve of the dungaree was pinned back.

Manfred opened the gate and went down into the peach orchard where the old man was stooping over one of the wooden hives.

'Good morning, Pa,' Manfred said softly. 'You aren't ready yet.'

His father straightened up and stared at him vaguely, and then started with surprise.

'Manie! Is it Sunday again already?'

'Come along, Pa. Let's get you tidied up. Heidi is cooking a roast of pork – you know how you love pork.'

57

He took the old man's hand, and led him unprotestingly up to the cottage.

'It's a mess, Pa.' Manfred looked around the tiny bedroom with distaste. The bed had obviously been slept in repeatedly without being remade, soiled clothing was strewn on the floor and used plates and mugs stood on the bedside table. 'What happened to the new maid Heidi found for you?'

'I didn't like her, cheeky brown devil,' Lothar muttered. 'Stealing the sugar, drinking my brandy. I fired her.'

Manfred went to the cupboard and found a clean white shirt. He helped the old man undress.

'When did you last bath, Pa?' he asked gently.

'Hey?' Lothar peered at him.

'It doesn't matter.' Manfred buttoned his father's shirt. 'Heidi will find another maid for you. You must try and keep her longer than a week this time.'

It wasn't the old man's fault, Manfred reminded himself. It was the prison that had affected his mind. He had been a proud free man, a soldier and a huntsman, a creature of the wild Kalahari Desert. You cannot cage a wild animal. Heidi had wanted to have the old man to live with them, and Manfred felt guilty that he had refused. It would have meant buying a larger home, but that was the least of it. Manfred could not afford to have Lothar dressed like a coloured labourer wandering vaguely around the house, coming into his study uninvited when he had important visitors with him, slobbering his food and making inane statements at the dinner table when he was entertaining. No, it was better for all of them, the old man especially, that he lived apart. Heidi would find another maid to take care of him, but he felt corrosive guilt as he took Lothar's arm and led him out to the Chevrolet.

He drove slowly, almost at a walking pace, steeling himself to do what he had been unable to do during the years since Lothar had been pardoned and freed from prison at Manfred's instigation.

'Do you remember how it was in the old days, Pa? When we fished together at Walvis Bay?' he asked, and the old man's eyes shone. The distant past was more real to him than the present, and he reminisced happily, without hesitation recalling incidents and the names of people and places from long ago.

'Tell me about my mother, Pa,' Manfred invited at last, and he hated himself for leading the old man into such a carefully prepared trap.

'Your mother was a beautiful woman,' Lothar nodded happily, repeating what he had told Manfred so many times since childhood. 'She had hair the colour of the desert dunes, with the early sun shining on them. A fine woman of noble German birth.'

'Pa,' Manfred said softly. 'You aren't telling me the truth, are you?' He spoke as though to a naughty child. 'The woman you call my mother, the woman who was your wife, died years before I was born. I have a copy of the death certificate signed by the English doctor in the concentration camp. She died of diphtheria, the white sore throat.'

He could not look at his father as he said it, but stared ahead through the windscreen, until he heard a soft choking sound beside him and with alarm turned quickly. Lothar was weeping, tears slid down his withered old cheeks.

'I'm sorry, Pa.' Manfred pulled the Chevrolet off the road and switched off the engine. 'I shouldn't have said that.' He pulled the white handkerchief from his pocket and handed it to his father.

Lothar wiped his face slowly, but his hand was steady, and his wandering mind seemed to have been concentrated by the shock.

'How long have you known that she was your real mother?' he asked, and his voice was firm and sure. Manfred's soul quailed, he had hoped to hear his father deny it.

'She came to see me when first I stood for parliament. She blackmailed me, for her other son's sake. I had him in my power. She threatened to expose the fact that I was her bastard son and destroy my candidacy if I acted against her other son. She dared me to ask you if it was not true, but I could not bring myself to do it.'

'It's true,' Lothar nodded. 'I'm sorry, my son. I lied to you only to protect you.'

'I know.' Manfred reached across and took the bony hand as the old man went on.

'When I found her in the desert, she was so young and helpless – and beautiful. I was young and lonely – it was just the two of us, and her infant, alone together in the desert. We fell in love.'

'You don't have to explain,' Manfred told him, but Lothar seemed not to hear him.

'One night two wild Bushmen came into our camp. I thought they were marauders, come to steal our horses and oxen. I followed them, and caught up with them at dawn. I shot them down before I was within range of their poison arrows. It was the way we dealt with those dangerous little yellow animals in those days.'

'Yes, Pa, I know.' Manfred had read the history of his people's conflict with and extermination of the Bushmen tribes.

'I did not know it then, but she had lived with these same two little Bushmen before I found her. They had helped her survive the desert and tended her when she gave birth to her first child. She had come to love them, she even called them "old grandfather" and "old grandmother".' He shook his head wonderingly, still unable to

59

comprehend this relationship of a white woman with savages. 'I did not know it, and I shot them without realizing what they meant to her. Her love for me changed to bitter hatred. I know now that her love could not have been very deep, perhaps it was only loneliness and gratitude and not love at all. After that she hated me, and the hatred extended to my child that she was carrying in her womb. To you, Manie. She made me take you away the moment you were born. She hated us both so deeply that she wanted never to set eyes on you. I cared for you after that.'

'You were my father and my mother.' Manfred bowed his head, ashamed and angry that he had forced the old man to relive those tragically cruel events. 'What you have told me explains so much that I could never understand.'

'*Ja.*' Lothar wiped fresh tears away with the white handkerchief. 'She hated me, but you see I still loved her. No matter how cruelly she treated me, I was obsessed with her. That was the reason why I committed the folly of the robbery. It was a madness and it cost me this arm.' He held up the empty sleeve. 'And my freedom. She is a hard woman. A woman without mercy. She will not hesitate to destroy anything or anybody who stands in her way. She is your mother, but be careful of her, Manie. Her hatred is a terrible thing.' The old man reached across and seized his son's arm, shaking it in his agitation. 'You must have nothing to do with her, Manie. She will destroy you as she has destroyed me. Promise me you will never have anything to do with her or her family.'

'I'm sorry, Pa,' Manfred shook his head. 'I am already tied to her through her son,' he hesitated to give voice to the next words, 'to my brother, to my half-brother, Shasa Courtney. It seems, Papa, that our bloodlines and our destinies are so closely tangled together that we can never be free of each other.'

'Oh, my son, my son,' Lothar De La Rey lamented. 'Be careful – please be careful.'

Manfred reached for the ignition key to start the engine, but paused before he touched it.

'Tell me, Pa. How do you feel for this woman now – for my mother?'

Lothar was silent for a moment before he answered. 'I hate her almost as much as I still love her.'

'It is strange that we can love and hate at the same time.' Manfred shook his head slightly with wonder. 'I hate her for what she has done to you. I hate her for all the things she stands for, and yet her blood calls to mine. At the end, when all else is put aside, Centaine Courtney is my mother and Shasa Courtney is my brother. Love or hatred – which will prevail, Papa?'

'I wish I could tell you, my son,' Lothar whispered miserably. 'I can only repeat what I have already told you. Be careful of them, Manie. Mother and son, they are dangerous adversaries.'

*   *   *

For almost twenty years Marcus Archer had owned the old farmhouse at Rivonia. He had purchased the five-acre smallholding before the area became fashionable. Now the fairways and greens of the Johannesburg Country Club, the most exclusive private club on the Witwatersrand, backed right up against Marcus' boundary. The trustees of the Country Club had offered him fifteen times his original purchase price, over £100,000, but Marcus steadfastly refused to sell.

On all the other large plots that comprised the Rivonia Estate, the prosperous new owners – entrepreneurs and stockbrokers and successful doctors – had built large pretentious homes, most of them in the low sprawling ranch house style which was the rage, or with pink clay tile roofs, imaginative copies of Mexican *haciendas* or Mediterranean villas, and they had surrounded the main buildings with paddocks and stables, with tennis courts and swimming-pools and wide lawns that the winter highveld frosts burned the colour of cured tobacco leaves.

Marcus Archer had re-thatched the roof of the old farmhouse, whitewashed the walls, and planted frangipani and bougainvillaea and other flowering shrubs and let the grounds grow wild and unkempt, so that even from its own boundary fence the house was completely screened.

Although the area was now very much a bastion of the wealthy white elite, the Country Club employed a large staff of waiters and kitchen helpers and groundsmen and golf caddies, so black faces were not remarkable, as they might have been on the streets of some of the other wealthy white suburbs. Marcus's friends and political allies could come and go without arousing unwelcome interest. So Puck's Hill, as Marcus had recently renamed his farmhouse, gradually became the rallying ground for some of the most active of the African Nationalist movements, the leaders of black consciousness and their white compatriots, the remnants of the defunct Communist Party.

It was only natural, therefore, that Puck's Hill was chosen as the headquarters for the final planning and co-ordination of the black disobedience campaign that was about to begin. However, it was not a unified group that came together under Marcus Archer's roof, for although their stated final objective was the same, their separate visions of the future differed widely.

Firstly, there was the old guard of the African National Congress

61

headed by Dr Xuma. They were the conservatives, committed to plodding negotiation with white civil servants within the unyielding established system.

'You people have been doing that since 1912 when the ANC was formed,' Nelson Mandela glared at him. 'It is time to move on to confrontation, to force our will upon the Boers.'

Nelson Mandela was a young lawyer, practising on the Witwatersrand in partnership with another activist named Oliver Tambo. Together they were making a strong challenge for the leadership of the young Turks in the Congress hierarchy.

'It is time for us to move on to direct action.' Nelson Mandela leaned forward in his chair and looked down the long kitchen table. The kitchen was the largest room in Puck's Hill, and all their meetings were held in it. 'We have drawn up a programme of boycott and strike and civil disobedience.' Mandela was speaking in English, and Moses Gama sitting near the end of the table watched him impassively, but all the time his mind was racing ahead of the speaker, assessing and evaluating. He as much as any of them present was aware of the undertones in the room. There was not a single black man present who did not cherish, somewhere in his soul, the dream of one day leading all the others, of one day being hailed as the paramount chief of all southern Africa.

Yet the fact that Mandela spoke in English pointed up the single most poignant fact that they had to face: they were all different. Mandela was a Tembu, Xuma was a Zulu, Moses Gama himself was an Ovambo, and there were half a dozen other tribes represented in the room.

'It would be a hundred times easier if we blacks were all one people,' Moses thought, and then despite himself he glanced uneasily at the Zulus, sitting together as a group across the table. They were the majority, not only in this room, but in the country as a whole. What if they somehow formed an alliance with the whites? – It was a disquieting thought, but he put it firmly aside. The Zulus were the proudest, most independent of the warrior tribes. Before the white man came, they had conquered all their neighbouring peoples and held them subjugated. The Zulu King Chaka had called them his dogs. Because of their multitudes and their warrior tradition, it was almost certain that the first black president of South Africa would be a Zulu, or someone with very close ties to the Zulu nation. Ties of marriage – not for the first time, Moses thought about that possibility with narrowed eyes, it was time he married anyway. He was almost forty-five years of age. A Zulu maiden of royal blood? He stored the idea for future consideration, and concentrated once again on what Nelson Mandela was saying.

The man had charisma and a presence, and he was articulate and persuasive, a rival – a very dangerous rival. Moses recognized that fact as he had often before. They were all rivals. However, the Youth League of the ANC was Nelson Mandela's power base, the hotheads, young men burning for action, and even now Mandela was proposing caution, tempering his call for action with reservations.

'There must be no gratuitous violence,' he was saying. 'No damage to private property, no danger to human life —' and although Moses Gama nodded wisely, he wondered how much appeal that would have with the rank and file of the Youth League. Would they not prefer the offer of a bloody and glorious victory? That was something else to be considered.

'We must show our people the way, we must demonstrate that we are all one in this enterprise,' Mandela was saying now, and Moses Gama smiled inwardly. The total membership of the ANC was seven thousand, while his secret union of mineworkers numbered almost ten times that figure. It would be as well to remind Mandela and the rest of them of his overwhelming support amongst the best paid and most strategically placed of all the black population. Moses turned slightly and looked at the man who sat beside him, and felt an untoward pang of affection. Hendrick Tabaka had been beside him like this for twenty years.

Swart Hendrick was a big man, as tall as Moses but wider across the shoulder, and heavier around the middle, with thick muscled limbs. His head was round and bald as a cannonball and laced with scars from ancient fights and battles. His front teeth were missing, and Moses remembered how the white man who had done that to him had died.

He was Moses' half-brother, son of the same father, a chief of the Ovambo, but of a different mother. He was the one man in all the world whom Moses trusted, a trust not lightly given but earned over all of those twenty years. He was the only black man in this room who was not a rival, but was instead both comrade and loyal servant. Swart Hendrick nodded at him unsmilingly and Moses realized that Nelson Mandela had finished speaking and that they were all watching him, waiting for him to reply. He rose slowly to his feet, aware of the impression he was making, and he could see the respect in their expressions. Even his enemies in the room could not entirely conceal the awe which he inspired.

'Comrades,' he began. 'My brothers. I have listened to what my good brother Nelson Mandela has said and I agree with every word of it. There are just a few points which I feel I must add —' and he spoke for nearly an hour.

Firstly he proposed to them a detailed plan to call a series of wildcat strikes in the mines where the labour force was controlled by his unions.

'The strikes will be in sympathy with the defiance campaign, but we will not call a general strike which would give the Boers an excuse for heavy-handed action. We will bring out only a few mines at any one time, and then only for a limited period, before going back to work, just enough to thoroughly disrupt gold production and to exasperate management. We will nip at their heels like a terrier harassing a lion, ready to spring away the instant he turns. But it will be a warning. It will let them realize our strength, and what would happen if we called a general strike.'

He saw how they were impressed with his planning, and when he asked for a vote to confirm his proposal, he was given unanimous approval. It was another small victory, another addition to his prestige and influence within the group.

'In addition to the strike action, I would like to propose a boycott of all white-owned business on the Witwatersrand for the duration of the defiance campaign. The people will be allowed to buy their necessities of life from shops owned and run by black businessmen only.'

Hendrick Tabaka owned over fifty large general dealer stores in the black townships along the gold reef, and Moses Gama was his sleeping partner. He saw the others at the table baulk at the suggestion, and Mandela objected.

'It will cause undue hardship amongst our people,' he said. 'Many of them live in areas where they can trade only with white stores.'

'Then they must travel to areas where there are black-owned businesses, and it will do our people no harm to learn that the struggle demands sacrifices from all of us,' Moses answered him quietly.

'A boycott such as you propose would be impossible to enforce,' Mandela insisted, and this time Hendrick Tabaka replied to the objection.

'We will use the Buffaloes to make sure the people obey,' he growled, and now the more conservative members of the Council looked positively unhappy.

The Buffaloes were the union enforcers. Hendrick Tabaka was their commander and they had a reputation for swift, ruthless action. They were too close to being a private political army for the peace of mind of some of the other men in the room, and Moses Gama frowned slightly. It had been a mistake for Hendrick to mention his Buffaloes at all. Moses hid his chagrin when the vote to declare a boycott of white dealers on the Witwatersrand and enforce it strictly was defeated. It was a victory for Mandela and his moderates. So far the score was even, but Moses was not finished yet.

'There is one other matter I would like to bring up before we adjourn. I would like to consider what lies beyond the defiance campaign. What action do we take if the campaign is crushed by ruthless white police action, and followed by an onslaught on the black leaders and the promulgation of even more draconian laws of domination?' he asked. 'Will our response always be mild and sub-servient, will we always take off our caps and mutter "Yes, my white *baas*! No, my white *baas*"?'

He paused, and studied the others, seeing the disquiet he had expected in the faces of old Xuma and the conservatives, but he had not spoken for them. At the far end of the table there were two young men, still in their early twenties. They were observers from the executive of the Youth League of the ANC and Moses knew them both to be militants longing for fierce action. What he was about to say now was for them, and he knew they would take his words back to the other young warriors. It could begin the erosion of Nelson Mandela's support amongst the youth, and the transfer-ence of that support to a leader who was prepared to give them the blood and fire for which they hungered.

'I propose the formation of a military wing of the ANC,' Moses said, 'a fighting force of trained men, ready to die for the struggle. Let us call this army *Umkhonto we Sizwe*, the Spear of the Nation. Let us forge the spear secretly. Let us hone its edge to razor-sharpness, keeping it hidden, but always ready to strike.' He used that deep thrilling tone of his, and he saw the two young men at the end of the table stir eagerly and their faces begin to glow with expectation. 'Let us choose our brightest and fiercest young men, and from them form the impis as our forefathers did.' He paused, and his expression became scornful. 'There are old men amongst us, and they are wise. I respect their grey hairs and their experience. But remember, comrades, the future belongs to the young. There is a time for fine words, and we have heard them spoken at our councils – often, too often. There is a time also for action, bold action and that is the world of the young.'

When at last Moses Gama sat down again he saw that he had moved them all deeply, each in his separate way. Old Xuma was shaking his grey pate, and his lips quivered. He knew his day had passed. Nelson Mandela and Oliver Tambo watched him impassively, but he saw the fury in their hearts beamed through their eyes. The battle lines had been drawn, and they had recognized their enemy. Yet, most important of all, he saw the expressions on the faces of the two Youth Leaguers. It was the look of men who had found a new star to follow.

*   *   *

65

'Since when have you conceived such a burning interest in arch-aeological anthropology?' Shasa Courtney asked as he shook out the pages of the *Cape Times*, and turned from the financial section to the sports pages at the rear.

'It was one of my majors,' Tara pointed out reasonably. 'May I pour you another cup of coffee?'

'Thank you, my dear.' He sipped the coffee before he spoke again. 'How long do you intend being away?'

'Professor Dart will be giving a series of four lectures on successive evenings, covering all the excavations from his original discovery of the Taung skull, right up to the present time. He has been able to correlate the whole mass of material with one of these new electronic computers.'

Behind his newspaper Shasa smiled reflectively as he remembered Marylee from MIT and her IBM 701. He wouldn't mind another visit to Johannesburg himself in the near future.

'It's absolutely riveting stuff,' Tara was saying, 'and it all fits in with the new discoveries at Sterkfontein and Makapansgat. It really does seem that southern Africa was the true cradle of mankind, and that *Australopithecus* is our direct ancestor.'

'So you will be away for at least four days?' Shasa interrupted. 'What about the children?'

'I have spoken to your mother. She will be happy to come across and stay at Weltevreden while I am away.'

'I won't be able to join you,' Shasa pointed out. 'The third reading of the new Criminal Law Amendment Bill is coming up, and all hands are needed in the House. I could have flown you up in the Mosquito – now you'll have to take the commercial flight on the Viscount.'

'What a pity,' Tara sighed. 'You would have enjoyed it. Professor Dart is a fascinating speaker.'

'You'll stay at the Carlton suite, of course. It's standing empty.'

'Molly has arranged for me to stay with a friend of hers at Rivonia.'

'One of her Bolshies, I presume.' Shasa frowned slightly. 'Try not to get yourself arrested again.' He had been waiting for an opportunity to talk about her political activities and he lowered the newspaper and looked at her thoughtfully, then realized it was not the correct moment and merely nodded. 'Your grass orphans and your widower will try to bumble along without you for a few days.'

'With your mother and sixteen servants at hand, I have no doubt you will survive,' she told him crisply, letting her irritation show through for an instant.

Marcus Archer met her at the airport. He was affable and amusing

66

and while they listened to a Mozart programme on the car radio as they drove out to Rivonia, Marcus discussed the composer's life and works. He knew much more about music than she did, but although she listened to his dissertation with pleasure and attention, she was nevertheless aware of his enmity. It was well concealed, but flashed out in a barbed remark or a spiced glance. He never mentioned Moses Gama's name, and nor did she. Molly had said he was a homosexual, the first she had ever encountered to her certain knowledge, and she wondered if they all hated women.

Puck's Hill was a delight, with its shaggy thatch and unkempt grounds, so different from Weltevreden's carefully manicured splendour.

'You'll find him at the end of the front stoep,' Marcus said, as he parked under one of the bluegums at the rear of the house. It was the first time he had referred to Moses, but even then he did not use his name. He wandered away and left her standing.

She had not known how to dress, though she imagined that he would not approve of slacks. So she had chosen a long loose skirt made of cheap but colourful trade print that she had purchased in Swaziland, and with it wore a simple green cotton blouse with sandals on her feet. Again, she had not been sure whether she should wear make-up, and she had compromised with a pale pink lipstick and just a touch of mascara. She thought she looked well enough in the mirror of the women's room at the airport as she combed her dense chestnut curls, but was suddenly stricken by the thought that he would find her pale skin insipid and unattractive.

Now standing alone in the sunshine, she was once again attacked by doubts and that terrible sense of inadequacy. If Marcus had been there, she would have begged him to drive her back to the airport, but he had disappeared and so she summoned up all her courage and walked slowly around the side of the whitewashed house.

She paused at the corner and looked down the long covered verandah. Moses Gama was sitting at a table at the far end with his back to her. The table was piled with books and writing materials. He was wearing a casual white shirt with open neck that contrasted with the marvellous anthracite of his skin. His head was bowed and he was writing rapidly on a block of notepaper.

Timidly she stepped up on to the verandah and although her approach was noiseless, he sensed her presence and turned abruptly when she was half-way down the verandah. He did not smile, but she thought she saw pleasure in his gaze as he stood up and came to meet her. He did not attempt to embrace her, or kiss her, and she was pleased, for it confirmed his differentness. Instead he led her to the second chair placed beside his table, and seated her in it.

'Are you well?' he asked. 'Are your children well?' The innate African courtesy, always the enquiry and then the offer of refreshment, 'Let me give you a cup of tea.' He poured from the tray already set on his cluttered desk, and she sipped with pleasure.

'Thank you for coming,' he said.

'I came as soon as I received your message from Molly, as I promised I would.'

'Will you always keep your promises to me?'

'Always,' she answered with simple sincerity, and he studied her face.

'Yes,' he nodded. 'I think you will.'

She could hold his gaze no longer, for it seemed to sear her soul and lay it bare. She looked down at the table top, at the closely written sheets of his handwriting.

'A manifesto,' he said, following her gaze. 'A blueprint for the future.'

He selected half a dozen sheets and handed them to her. She set aside her tea cup and took them from his hand, shivering slightly as their fingers touched. His skin was cool – that was one of the things that she remembered.

She read the sheets, her attention becoming fastened upon them more firmly the more she read, and when she finished them, she lifted her eyes to his face again.

'You have a poetry in your choice of words that makes the truth shine more luminously,' she whispered.

They sat on the cool verandah, while outside the brilliant high-veld sun threw shadows black and crisp as paper cut-outs beneath the trees and the noonday swooned in the heat, and they talked.

There were no trivialities in their discussion, everything he said was thrilling and cogent, and he seemed to inspire her for her replies and her own observations she knew were measured and lucid and she saw she had aroused and held his interest. She no longer was aware of her small vanities of dress and cosmetics, all that mattered now were the words that they exchanged and the cocoon they wove out of them. With a start she realized that the day had slipped away unnoticed and the short African twilight was upon them. Marcus came to fetch her and show her to her sparsely furnished bedroom.

'We will leave for the museum in twenty minutes,' he told her.

In the lecture theatre of the Transvaal museum the three of them sat near the back. There were half a dozen other blacks in the crowded audience, but Marcus sat between the two of them. A black man beside a white woman would have excited interest, and certain hostility. Tara found it difficult to concentrate on the eminent professor's address, and though she glanced in his direction only once or twice, it was Moses Gama who occupied all her thoughts.

Back at Puck's Hill they sat late in the cavernous kitchen, while Marcus hovered over the Aga stove, joining in their conversation while he produced a meal that even in her preoccupation Tara realized was as good as anything that had ever come out of the kitchens of Weltevreden.

It was after midnight when Marcus stood up abruptly.

'I will see you in the morning,' he said, and the look he gave Tara was once again spiced with venom. She could not understand how she had offended him, but soon it did not matter for Moses took her hand.

'Come,' he said softly, and she thought her legs might not support her weight.

Long afterwards she lay pressed to him, her body bathed in sweat and her nerves still spasming and twitching uncontrollably.

'Never,' she whispered, when she could speak again. 'I have never known anyone like you. You teach me things about myself that I never suspected. You are a magician, Moses Gama. How do you know so much about a woman?'

He chuckled softly. 'You know we are entitled to many wives. If a man cannot keep them all happy at the same time, then his life becomes a torment. He has to learn.'

'Do you have many wives?' she asked.

'Not yet,' he answered. 'But one day —'

'I will hate every one of them.'

'You disappoint me,' he said. 'Sexual jealousy is a silly European emotion. If I were to detect it in you, I would despise you.'

'Please,' she said quietly, 'never despise me.'

'Then never give me reason, woman,' he commanded, and she knew she was his to command.

*   *   *

She realized that the first day and night with him, spent alone and uninterrupted, was exceptional. She realized also that he must have set the time aside for her, and it must have been difficult to do so for there were others, hundreds of others, demanding his attention.

He was like one of the ancient African kings holding tribal court on the verandah of the old house. There were always men and women waiting patiently under the bluegum trees in the yard for their turn to speak to him. They were of all types and ages, from simple uneducated folk newly arrived from the reserves in the country to sophisticated lawyers and businessmen in dark suits arriving at Puck's Hill in their own automobiles.

They had one thing in common only – the deference and respect they showed Moses Gama. Some of them clapped their hands in the traditional greeting and called him *Baba* or *Nkosi*, father or lord, others shook his hand in the European manner, but Moses greeted each of them in their own dialect. 'He must speak twenty languages,' Tara wondered.

Mostly he allowed Tara to sit quietly beside his table and he explained her presence with a quiet word.

'She is a friend – you may speak.'

However, twice he asked her to leave while he spoke to his more important visitors and once when a great black bull of a man, bald and scarred and gap-toothed, arrived in a shiny new Ford sedan, he excused them.

'This is Hendrick Tabaka, my brother,' he said, and the two of them left the verandah and strolled side by side in the sunlit garden just out of earshot of where Tara sat.

What she saw during those days impressed her immensely and confirmed her feelings of reverence for this man. Everything he did, every word he uttered marked him as different, and the respect and adulation showered upon him by his fellow Africans proved that they also recognized that he was the giant of the future.

Tara felt awed that he had selected her for special attention, and yet already saddened by the certain knowledge that she could never have for herself alone any part of him. He belonged to his people, and she must be grateful for the precious grains of his time which she could glean for herself.

Even the evenings that followed, unlike that first evening, were crowded with people and events. Until long after midnight they sat at the table in the kitchen, sometimes as many as twenty of them at one time, smoking and laughing and eating and talking. Such talk, such ideas that lit the gloomy room and shimmered like angels' wings in the air around their heads. Then later, in the quiet dark hours, they made love and she felt as though her body no longer belonged to her but that he had taken it for his own, and devoured it like some darkly beloved predator.

She must have met a hundred new faces in those three short days and nights, and though some of them were hazy and made little lasting impression, it seemed as though she had become a member of a large diffuse new family, and because of the patronage of Moses Gama, she was immediately accepted and accorded complete unquestioning trust by both black and white.

On the last evening before her return to the dream world at Weltevreden, there was a guest beside her at the kitchen table to whom Tara took an instant unqualified liking. She was a young woman, at

70

least ten years junior to Tara, barely into her twenties, but with an unusual maturity for one so young.

'My name is Victoria Dinizulu,' she introduced herself. 'My friends call me Vicky. I know you are Mrs Courtney.'

'Tara,' Tara corrected her quickly. Nobody had used her surname since she had left Cape Town and it sounded a jarring note in her own ears.

The girl smiled shyly in acknowledgement. She had the serene beauty of a black madonna, the classic moon face of the high-bred Zulu with huge almond eyes and full lips, her skin the colour of dark amber, her hair plaited into an intricate pattern of tiny curls over her skull.

'Are you related to the Courtneys of Zululand?' she asked Tara. 'Old General Sean Courtney and Sir Garrick Courtney of Theuniskraal, near Ladyburg?'

'Yes.' Tara tried not to show the shock she felt at the mention of those names. 'Sir Garrick was my husband's grandfather. My own sons are named Sean and Garrick after them. Why do you ask, Vicky? Do you know the family well?'

'Oh yes, Mrs Courtney – Tara.' When she smiled, the Zulu girl's face seemed to glow like a dark moon. 'Long ago, during the last century, my grandfather fought at General Sean Courtney's side in the Zulu wars against Cetewayo who stole the kingship of Zululand from my family. It was my grandfather, Mbejane, who should have been king. Instead he became General Courtney's servant.

'Mbejane!' Tara cried. 'Oh yes. Sir Garrick Courtney wrote about him in his *History of Zululand*. He was Sean Courtney's faithful retainer until his death. I remember they came up here to the gold-fields of the reef together and later went on to what is now Rhodesia, hunting ivory.'

'You know all about that!' Vicky laughed with pleasure. 'My father used to tell me the same stories when I was a little girl. My father still lives near Theuniskraal. After my grandfather, Mbejane Dinizulu, died my father took his place as the old general's body servant. He even went to France with the general in 1916 and worked for him until the general was murdered. In his will the general left him a section of Theuniskraal for his lifetime and a pension of a thousand pounds a year. They are a fine family, the Courtneys. My old father still weeps whenever he mentions the general's name —' Vicky broke off and shook her head, suddenly perplexed and saddened. 'Life must have been so simple in those days, my grandfather and my father were hereditary chieftains and yet they were satisfied to spend their lives subservient to a white man, and strangely they loved that man and he, in his way,

71

seemed to love them. I wonder sometimes if theirs was not the better way —'

'Do not even think that,' Tara almost hissed at her. 'The Courtneys have always been heartless robber barons, plundering and exploiting your people. Right and justice are on the side of your struggle. Never entertain the slightest doubt of that.'

'You are right,' Vicky agreed firmly. 'But sometimes it's nice to think of the friendship of the general and my grandfather. Perhaps one day we could be friends again, equal friends, both sides stronger for the friendship.'

'With every new oppression, with every new law passed, the prospect fades,' Tara said grimly, 'and I become more ashamed of my race.'

'I don't want to be sad and intense tonight, Tara. Let's talk about happy things. You said you have sons, Sean and Garrick, named after their ancestors. Tell me about them, please.'

However, the thought of the children and Shasa and Weltevreden made Tara feel guilty and uncomfortable, and as soon as she could she changed the subject again.

'Now tell me about yourself, Vicky,' she insisted. 'What are you doing in Johannesburg, so far from Zululand?'

'I work at Baragwanath Hospital,' Vicky told her.

Tara knew that was one of the largest hospitals in the world, certainly the largest in the southern hemisphere, with 2400 beds and over 2000 nurses and doctors, most of them black, for the hospital catered exclusively for black patients. All hospitals, like schools and transport and most other public facilities, were strictly segregated by law, true to the grand concept of *apartheid*.

Vicky Dinizulu was so modest about her own achievements that Tara had to draw out of her the fact that she was a qualified theatre sister.

'But you are so young, Vicky,' she protested.

'There are others younger,' the Zulu girl laughed. Her laughter had a pleasing musical lilt.

'She really is a lovely child,' Tara thought, smiling in sympathy, and then corrected herself. 'No, not a child – a clever and competent young woman.'

So Tara told her about her clinic at Nyanga, and the problems of malnutrition and ignorance and poverty they encountered, and Vicky related some of her experiences and the solutions they had found to the terrible challenges that faced them in caring for the physical wellbeing of a peasant population trying to adapt to an urban existence.

'Oh, I have enjoyed talking to you,' Vicky blurted out at last. 'I don't know when I have ever spoken to a white woman like this before. So natural and relaxed and,' she hesitated, 'just like an elder sister or a dear friend.'

'A dear friend. Yes, I like that,' Tara agreed. 'And Puck's Hill is probably one of the few places in the whole of this country where we could meet and talk like this.'

Involuntarily both of them looked up towards the head of the long kitchen table. Moses Gama was watching them intently, and Tara felt her stomach flop over like a stranded fish. For a few moments there, she had been totally engrossed with the Zulu girl, but now her feelings for Moses Gama flooded back at full ebb. She forgot Vicky, until the girl spoke quietly beside her.

'He is a great man – our hope for the future.'

Tara glanced at her sideways. Vicky Dinizulu's face glowed with hero worship as she smiled shyly at Moses Gama, and jealousy struck Tara such a sickening blow in the pit of her stomach, that for a moment she believed she was going to be physically ill.

The jealousy and terror of imminent separation persisted even after Tara was alone with Moses that night. When he made love to her she wanted to hold him within her for all eternity, knowing that this was the only time that he truly belonged to her. Too soon she felt the great dam burst and flood her and she cried out, pleading for it never to end, but her cry was incoherent and without sense, and then he was gone from within her and she was desolated.

She thought he had fallen asleep, and she lay and listened to his quiet breathing, holding him in the circle of her arms, but he was awake and he spoke suddenly, startling her.

'You were speaking to Victoria Dinizulu,' he said, and it took an effort for her to cast her mind back to the early part of the evening. 'What did you think of her?' he persisted.

'She is a lovely young woman. Intelligent and obviously dedicated. I like her very much.' She tried to be objective, but the sick jealous feeling was there deep in her belly.

'I had her invited,' Moses said. 'It was the first time I have met her.'

Tara wanted to ask, 'Why? – Why did you invite her?' But she remained silent, dreading the reply. She knew her instincts had been correct.

'She is of the royal house of Zulu,' he said softly.

'Yes. She told me,' Tara whispered.

'She is well favoured, as I was told she was, and her mother had many sons. They breed many sons in the Dinizulu line. She will make a good wife.'

'Wife?' Tara breathed. She had not expected that.

'I need the alliance with the Zulus, they are the largest and most

73

powerful tribe. I will begin the negotiations with her family immediately. I will send Hendrick to Ladyburg to see her father and make the arrangements. It will be difficult, he is one of the old school, dead set against mixed tribal marriages. It must be a wedding that will impress the tribe, and Hendrick will convince the old man of the wisdom of it.'

'But, but,' Tara found she was stuttering. 'You hardly know the girl. You spoke barely a dozen words to her all evening.'

'What does that have to do with it?' His tone was genuinely puzzled, and he rolled away from her and switched on the bedside light, dazzling her.

'Look at me!' he commanded, taking her by the chin and lifting her face to the light, studying it for a moment and then removing his fingers as though he had touched something loathsome. 'I have misjudged you,' he said scornfully. 'I believed that you were an exceptional person. A true revolutionary, a dedicated friend of the black people of this land, ready to make any sacrifice. Instead I find a weak, jealous woman, riddled with bourgeois white prejudices.'

The mattress tipped under her as Moses stood up. He towered over the bed.

'I have been wasting my time,' he said, gathered his clothing, and still naked turned towards the door.

Tara threw herself across the room and clung to him, barring his way to the door.

'I'm sorry. I didn't mean it. Forgive me. Please forgive me,' she pleaded with him, and he stood cold and aloof and silent. She began to weep, her tears muffling her voice, until she was no longer making sense.

Slowly she slid down with her arms still encircling him, until she was on her knees hugging his legs.

'Please,' she sobbed. 'I will do anything. Just don't leave me. I will do anything, everything you tell me to do – only just don't send me away like this.'

'Get up,' he said at last, and when she stood before him like a penitent, he said softly, 'You have one more chance. Just one. Do you understand?' and she nodded wildly, still choking on her sobs, unable to answer him. She reached out hesitantly and when he did not pull away, took his hand and led him back to the bed.

As he mounted her again, he knew that at last she was ready, completely prepared. She would do anything and everything he commanded.

*　　*　　*

74

In the dawn she came awake to find him leaning over her staring into her face and immediately she relived the night's terror, the dreadful fear of his scorn and rejection. She felt weak and trembly, her tears very close, but he took her calmly and made love to her with a gentle consideration that reassured her and left her feeling whole and vital again. Then he spoke to her quietly.

'I am going to put my trust in you,' he told her, and her gratitude was so strong it left her breathless. 'I am going to accept you as one of us, one of the inner circle.'

She nodded, but could not speak, staring into his fierce black eyes.

'You know how we have conducted the struggle thus far,' he said, 'we have played by the white man's rules, but he made those rules, and he designed them so we could never win. Petitions and delegations, commissions of enquiry and representations – but in the end there are always more laws made against us, governing every facet of our lives, how we work, where we live, where we are allowed to travel, or eat or sleep or love —' he broke off with an exclamation of scorn. 'The time is coming when we will rewrite the rule book. First, the defiance campaign when we will deliberately flout the mass of laws which bind us, and after that —' Now his expression was savage. 'And after that the struggle will go on and become a great battle.'

She was silent beside him, studying his face.

'I believe there comes a time when a man confronted by great evil must take up the spear and become a warrior. He must rise up and strike it down.' He was watching her, waiting for a reply.

'Yes,' she nodded. 'You are right.'

'These are words, ideas, Tara,' he told her. 'But what of action? Are you ready for action?'

She nodded. 'I am ready.'

'Blood, Tara, not words. Killing and maiming and burning. Tearing down and destroying. Can you face that, Tara?'

She was appalled, facing the reality at last, not merely the dizzy rhetoric. In her imagination she saw the flames roaring up through the great roof of Weltevreden and blood splashed on the walls shining wetly in the sunlight, while in the courtyard lay the broken bodies of children, of her own children, and she was on the very point of rejecting the images when he spoke again.

'Destroying what is evil, Tara, so that we may rebuild a good and just society.' His voice was low and compelling, it thrilled like a drug through her veins and the cruel images faded, she looked beyond them to the paradise, the earthly paradise they would build together.

'I am ready,' she said, and there was not a trace of a quaver in her voice.

There was an hour before Marcus would take her to the airport to catch the Viscount flight back to Cape Town. They sat at his table on the verandah, just the two of them, and Moses explained to her in detail what must be done.

'*Umkhonto we Sizwe,*' he told her. 'The Spear of the Nation.' The name shimmered and rang like polished steel in her brain.

'Firstly, you must withdraw from all overt liberal activities. You must abandon your clinic —'

'My clinic!' she exclaimed. 'Oh Moses, my poor little ones, what will they do —' she broke off as she saw his expression.

'You care for the physical needs of a hundred,' he said. 'I'm concerned for the welfare of twenty million. Tell me which is more important.'

'You are right,' she whispered. 'Forgive me.'

'You will use the excuse of the defiance campaign to make a statement of your disillusion with the freedom movement and to announce your resignation from the Black Sash.'

'Oh dear, what will Molly say?'

'Molly knows,' he assured her. 'Molly knows why you are doing it. She will help you in every way. Of course, the police special branch will continue to keep you under observation for a while, but when you give them nothing more for their files, they will lose interest and drop you.'

She nodded. 'I understand.'

'You must take more interest in your husband's political activities, cultivate his parliamentary associates. Your own father is the deputy leader of the opposition, with access to the government ministers. You must become our eyes and our ears.'

'Yes, I can do all that.'

'Later, there will be other tasks for you. Many difficult and some even dangerous. Would you risk your life for the struggle, Tara?'

'For you, Moses Gama, I would do more. I would willingly lay down that life for you,' she replied, and when he saw that she meant it, he nodded with deep satisfaction.

'We will meet whenever we can,' he promised her. 'Whenever it is safe to do so.' And then he gave her the salute which would become the rallying cry of the defiance campaign, '*Mayibuye! Afrika!*'

And she replied, '*Mayibuye! Afrika!* Africa, let it persist!'

* * *

'I am an adulteress,' Tara thought, as she had each morning as she sat at the breakfast table during all the weeks that had passed since she had arrived back from Johannesburg. 'I am an adulteress.' And she thought it must show, like a brand upon her forehead for all the

76

world to see. Yet Shasa had greeted her cheerfully on her return, apologizing for sending a driver to meet her at the airport and not coming in person, asking her if she had enjoyed her illicit interlude with *Australopithecus*. 'Thought you might have gone for someone a little younger. I mean a million years old is just a little long in the tooth, isn't it?' And since then their relationship had continued unaltered.

The children, with the exception of Michael, seemed not to have missed her at all. Centaine had run the household in her absence with her usual iron fist in a candy-flavoured glove and after they had greeted Tara with dutiful but offhand kisses, the children were full of what Nana had done and said, and Tara was painfully aware that she had neglected to bring any presents for them.

Only Michael was different. For the first few days he would not let her out of his sight, but traipsed around behind her, even insisting on spending his precious Saturday afternoon with her at the clinic while his two brothers went off to Newlands Rugby Ground with Shasa to watch Western Province playing the visiting All Blacks team from New Zealand.

Michael's company helped alleviate a little of the pain of making the first arrangements to close down the clinic. She had to ask her three black nursing sisters to start looking for other jobs. 'Of course, you'll be paid your salaries until you find other positions, and I will help you all I can —' But still she had to suffer the reproach in their eyes.

Now, almost a month later, she sat at Weltevreden's laden breakfast table on a Sunday morning in the dappled shade beneath the trellised vines of the terrace, while the servants in crisp white uniform fussed about them. Shasa read aloud extracts from the *Sunday Times* to which none of them listened, Sean and Garrick wrangled acrimoniously over who was the best full-back in the world, and Isabella clamoured for her daddy's attention. Michael was giving her a detailed account of the plot of the book he was reading, and she felt like an impostor, an actress playing a role for which she had not rehearsed her lines.

Shasa finally crumpled his newspaper and dropped it beside his chair, acceding to Isabella's request to 'Take me on your lap, Daddy!', ignoring Tara's ritual protest and demanded:

'All right, everybody, this meeting will come to order and address the serious question of what we are all going to do with this Sunday.' This precipitated a near riot which Isabella punctuated with shrill cries of 'Picnic! Picnic!' and finally picnic it was, after Shasa had used his casting vote in his daughter's favour.

Tara tried to excuse herself, but Michael was so close to tears that

77

she relented and they all rode out together, with the servants and the picnic baskets following them in the little two-wheeled dog cart. Of course they could have gone by car, but the ride was half the fun.

Shasa had had the pool below the waterfall bricked out to make a natural swimming-pool and had built a thatched summer house on the bank. The great attraction was the long slide down the glassy smooth rock of the waterfall on a red rubber inner tube, and the plunge over the final sheer drop into the green pool below, the entire journey accompanied by howls and shrieks of glee. It was sport that never palled and it kept the children busy all morning.

Shasa and Tara, in their bathing-suits, lolled on the grassy bank, basking in the hot bright sunlight. They used to come here often in the first days of their marriage, even before the pool was bricked and the summer house built. In fact Tara was certain that more than one of the children had been conceived on this grassy bank. Some of the warm feelings from those days persisted. Shasa opened a bottle of Riesling, and they were both more relaxed and friendly towards each other than they had been for years.

Shasa sensed his opportunity, fished the wine bottle out of the ice bucket and refilled Tara's glass before he said, 'My dear, I have something to tell you that is of great importance to both of us and may quite substantially change our lives.'

'He has found another woman,' she thought, half in dread, half in relief, so that she did not at first understand what he was telling her. Then suddenly the enormity of it crashed in upon her. Shasa was going to join them, he was going across to the Boers. He was throwing in his lot with the band of the most evil men that Africa had ever spawned. Those supreme architects of misery and suffering and oppression.

'I believe that I am being offered the opportunity to use my talents and my financial gift for the greater good of this land and its people,' he was saying, and she twirled the stem of the wineglass between her fingers and stared down into the pale golden liquid, not daring to lift her eyes and look at him in case he saw what she was thinking.

'I have considered it from every angle, and I have discussed it with Mater. I think I have a duty to the country, to the family and to myself. I believe that I have to do it, Tara.'

It was a terrible thing to feel the last blighted fruits of her love for him shrivel and fall away, and then almost instantly she felt free and light, the burden was gone and in its place came a rush of contrary emotion. It was so powerful that she could not put a name to it for a moment, and then she knew it was hatred.

She wondered that she had ever felt guilty on his account, she wondered even that she could ever have loved him. His voice droned

78

on justifying himself, attempting to excuse the inexcusable, and still she knew she dared not look up at him lest he see it in her eyes. She felt an almost irresistible need to scream at him, 'You are callous, selfish, evil, as they are!' and physically to attack him, to claw at his single eye with her nails, and it took all her will power to sit still and quiet. She remembered what Moses had told her, and she clung to his words. They seemed the only sane things in all this madness.

Shasa finished the explanation that he had so carefully prepared for her, and then waited for her reply. She sat on the plaid rug in the sun with her legs curled up under her, staring into the glass in her hands, and he looked at her as he had not done for years and saw that she was still beautiful. Her body was smooth and lightly tanned, her hair sparkled with ruby lights in the sun, and her big breasts that had always enchanted him, seemed to have filled out again. He found himself attracted by her and excited as he had not been for a long time and he reached out gently and touched her cheek.

'Talk to me,' he invited. 'Tell me what you think about it.' And she lifted her chin and stared at him. For an instant he was chilled by her gaze, for it was as inscrutable and merciless as the stare of a lioness, but then Tara smiled slightly and shrugged, and he thought that he had been mistaken, it was not hatred he had seen in her eyes.

'You have decided already, Shasa. Why do you need my approval? I have never been able to prevent you doing anything you wanted to do before. Why would I presume to do that now?'

He was amazed and relieved, he had anticipated a bitter battle.

'I wanted you to know why,' he said. 'I want you to know that we both want the same thing – prosperity and dignity for everybody in this land. That we have different ways of trying to achieve it, and I believe that my way is more effective.'

'I repeat, why do you need my approval?'

'I need your co-operation,' he corrected her. 'For in a way this opportunity depends on you.'

'How?' she asked, and looked away from him to where the children were splashing and cavorting. Only Garrick was not in the water. Sean had ducked him, and now he sat shivering on the edge of the pool. His thin weedy body was blue with cold. He was fighting for breath, the rack of his ribs sticking out of his chest as he coughed and wheezed.

'Garry,' she called sharply. 'That's enough. Dry yourself and put on your jersey.'

'Oh, Ma,' he gasped a protest, and she flared at him.

'Do it this instant.' And when he went reluctantly to the summer-house she turned back to Shasa.

'You want my co-operation?' She felt totally in control of herself.

79

She would not let him see how she felt towards him and his monstrous intention. 'Tell me what you want me to do.'

'It will come as no surprise to you to hear that BOSS, the Bureau of State Security, has quite an extensive file on you.'

'In view of the fact that they have arrested me three times,' Tara smiled again, a tight humourless grimace, 'you are right, I'm not surprised.'

'Well, my dear, what it boils down to is that it would be impossible for me to hold cabinet rank while you were still raising Cain and committing mayhem with your sisters in the Black Sash.'

'You want me to give up my political work? But what about my record? I mean, I am an old hardened jailbird, you know.'

'Fortunately the security police regard you with a certain amused indulgence. I have seen a copy of your file. The assessment is that you are a dilettante, naïve and impressionable, and easily swayed by your more vicious associates.'

That insult was difficult to bear. Tara jumped to her feet and strode around the edge of the pool, seized Isabella by the wrist and dragged her from the pool.

'That's enough for you also, young lady.' She ignored Isabella's howls of protest and stripped off her bathing costume.

'You're hurting me,' Isabella wailed as Tara scrubbed her sodden hair with a rough dry towel and then wrapped her in it.

Isabella ran to her father, still snivelling and tripping over the tails of the towel.

'Mommy won't let me swim.' She crawled into his lap.

'Life is full of injustice.' Shasa hugged her, and she gave one last convulsive sob and then cuddled her damp curls against his shoulder.

'All right, I am an ineffectual dilettante.' Tara flopped down on the rug again. She had regained her composure and sat cross-legged facing him. 'But what if I refuse to give up? What if I continue to follow the dictates of my conscience?'

'Tara, don't try and force a confrontation,' he said softly.

'You always get what you want, don't you, Shasa?' She was goading him, but he shook his head, refusing the challenge.

'I want to discuss this logically and calmly,' he said, but she could not prevent herself flouting him, for the insult rankled.

'I would get the children – you must know that, your clever lawyers must have warned you of that.'

'God damn it, Tara, you know that's not what I had in mind,' Shasa said coldly, but he hugged the child closer and Isabella reached up and touched his chin.

'You are all scratchy,' she murmured happily, unaware of the tension. 'But I still love you, my daddy.'

'Yes, my angel, I love you also,' he said, and then to Tara, 'I wasn't threatening you.'

'Not yet,' she qualified. 'But that comes next, if I know you – and I should.'

'Can't we discuss this sensibly?'

'It's not necessary,' Tara capitulated suddenly. 'I had already made up my mind. I had already seen the futility of our little protests. I have known for some time that it was a waste of my life. I know I have neglected the children and during this last visit to Johannesburg I decided that I should take up my studies again and leave politics to the professionals. I had already decided to resign from the Sash and close down the clinic or hand it over to somebody else.'

He stared at her in amazement. He distrusted any victory too easily won.

'What do you want in return?' he asked.

'I want to go back to university and take a Ph.D. in archaeology,' she said crisply. 'And I want complete freedom to travel and pursue my studies.'

'You have a bargain,' he agreed readily, not even attempting to conceal his relief. 'You keep your nose clean politically, and you can go where and when you want.' And then despite himself his eyes dropped back to her breasts. He was right, they had filled out beautifully and bulged from the thin silken cups of her bikini. He felt a quick hot need of her.

She saw that look on his face. She knew it so well, and she was revolted by it. After what he had just told her, after the insults he casually offered her, after his betrayal of that which she held sacred and dear, she knew she could never take him again. She pulled up the top of her bikini and reached for her robe.

Shasa was delighted with their bargain, and though he seldom drank more than a glassful, this afternoon he finished the rest of the Riesling while he and the boys cooked their lunch on the barbecue pit.

Sean took his duties as assistant chef seriously. Only one or two of the chops landed up in the dirt, but as Sean explained to his younger brothers, 'Those are yours, and if you don't let your teeth touch, then you won't even feel the grit.'

At the table in the summer-house Isabella helped Tara prepare the salads, dousing herself liberally with French dressing in the process, and when they sat down to eat Shasa had the children shrieking with laughter at his stories. Only Tara sat aloof from the general hilarity.

When the children were given permission to leave the table with the injunction not to swim again for an hour while their food digested,

Tara asked him quietly, 'What time are you leaving tomorrow?'

'Early,' he replied. 'I have to be in Johannesburg before lunch. Lord Littleton is arriving on the Comet from London. I want to be there to meet him.'

'How long will you be away this time?'

'After the launching David and I will be going on tour,' he replied. He had wanted her to attend the launching party which would celebrate and publicize the opening of the subscription lists for shares in the new Silver River mine. She had found an excuse but she noticed that he did not repeat the invitation now.

'So you'll be gone about ten days?' Every quarter Shasa and David made a tour of all the company's operations, from the new chemical factory at Chaka's Bay, and the paper pulp mills in the eastern Transvaal to the H'ani Diamond Mine in the Kalahari Desert, which was the company's flagship.

'Perhaps a little longer,' Shasa demurred. 'I'll be in Johannesburg at least four days,' and he thought happily of Marylee from MIT and her IBM 701.

*   *   *

David Abrahams had persuaded Shasa to hand the Silver River launching over to one of those public relations consultants, a breed that had recently sprung up but which Shasa viewed with suspicion. Despite his original misgiving he was now reluctantly prepared to concede that it wasn't such a bad idea as he had first believed, even though it was going to cost over five thousand pounds.

They had flown out the editors of the London *Financial Times* and the *Wall Street Journal*, with their wives, and afterwards would be taking them on for five days in the Kruger National Park with all expenses paid. All the local press and radio journalists were invited and as an unexpected bonus the television team that had come out from New York to do a series called 'Focus on Africa' for North American Broadcasting Studios had also accepted an invitation to attend the launching party.

In the entrance lobby of the Courtney Mining Co. offices they had set up a twenty-five-foot-high working replica of the mine headgear that would be erected above the Silver River main, and had surrounded it with an enormous display of wild proteas designed and executed by the same team which had won a gold medal at the Chelsea Flower Show in London the previous year. Appreciating that journalism is thirsty work, David had laid in one hundred cases of Moët & Chandon, although Shasa had vetoed the idea of a vintage *cru*.

'Even non-vintage is too damn good for them.' Shasa did not have a lofty view of the profession of journalism.

David had also hired the chorus line from the Royal Swazi Spa to provide a floor-show. The promise of a flash of bared bosom would be almost as big a draw as the champagne; to the South African censors the female nipple was every bit as dangerous as Karl Marx's Communist Manifesto.

On arrival every guest was handed a presentation pack which contained a glossy colour brochure, a certificate made out in his or her name for one £1 share in the Silver River Mining Co. and a genuine miniature bar of twenty-two carat South African gold, stamped with the company logo. David had sought Reserve Bank authority to have these bars struck by the South African mint, and at almost thirty dollars each they had been a major part of the advertising budget, but the excitement they created and the subsequent publicity fully justified the expense.

Shasa made his address before the Moët & Chandon could soften the wits of his guests or the floor-show distract them. Speaking in public was something that Shasa had always enjoyed. Neither the fusillade of camera flashes nor the sultry brilliance of the arc lights set up by the NABS television camera team detracted from his enjoyment this evening.

Silver River was one of the major achievements of his career to date. He alone had recognized the chance that the gold reef spurred at depth from the main run of the Orange Free State series, and personally he had negotiated the drilling options. Only when the diamond drills had finally intercepted the narrow black band of the gold-bearing carbon leader almost a mile and a half below the surface of the arid plain had Shasa's decision been vindicated. The strike was rich beyond even his expectations, running at over twenty-six penny-weights of pure gold to the ton of reef.

Tonight was Shasa's night. It was his particular gift that he was able to extract from everything he did the last ounce of enjoyment, and he stood in the arc lights tall and debonair in his immaculately tailored evening dress, the black eye-patch giving him a rakish and dangerous air, so obviously at ease and in control of himself and the company he commanded, that he carried them all along with him effortlessly.

They laughed and applauded at the right places, and they listened with fascinated attention as he explained the scale of the investment that was called for and how it would help to strengthen the bonds of kinship that tied South Africa so securely to England and the British Commonwealth of Nations, and set up new lines of friendship with the investors of the United States of America from

83

where he hoped almost thirty per cent of the necessary capital for the project would come.

When he ended to prolonged applause, Lord Littleton, as head of the underwriting bank, stood up to reply. He was lean and silver-haired, his evening dress just that touch archaic in cut, with wide cuffs to the trousers, as if to underline his aristocratic scorn of fashion. He told them of his bank's strong relationship with Courtney Mining and the intense interest that this new company had aroused in the City of London.

'From the very beginning we at Littleton Bank were pretty damned certain that we were going to earn our underwriting fees very easily. We knew that there would be very few unsubscribed shares for us to take up. So it gives me a deal of pleasure to stand before you here this evening and say, I told you so.' There was a buzz of comment and speculation which he raised a hand to silence. 'I am going to tell you something that not even Mr Shasa Courtney knows yet, and which I only learned myself an hour ago.' He reached into his pocket and brought out a telex flimsy which he waved at them.

'As you are aware, the subscription lists for shares in Silver River Mining opened this morning at 10 a.m. London time, two hours behind South African time. When my bank closed a few hours ago, they sent me this telex.' He placed gold-rimmed reading glasses on his nose. 'I quote: "Please convey congratulations to Mr Courtney and Courtney Mining and Finance as promoters of Silver River Gold-Mining Co. Stop as of 4 pm London time today the Silver River issue was oversubscribed by four times Ends Littleton Bank."'

David Abrahams seized Shasa's hand, the first to congratulate him. In the roar of applause they grinned at each other happily, until Shasa broke away and jumped down off the dais.

Centaine Courtney-Malcomess was in the first row of his audience and she sprang lightly to her feet to meet him. She was dressed in a sheath of gold lamé and wearing her full suite of diamonds, each stone carefully picked from thirty years' production of the H'ani Mine. Slim and glittering and lovely, she went to meet her son.

'Now we have it all, Mater,' he whispered as he hugged her.

No, *chéri*, we'll never have it all,' she whispered back. 'That would be dull. There is always something more to strive for.'

Blaine Malcomess was waiting to congratulate him, and Shasa turned to him with an arm still around Centaine's waist.

'Big night, Shasa.' Blaine took his hand. 'You deserve it all.'

'Thank you, sir.'

What a pity Tara couldn't be here,' Blaine went on.

'I wanted her to come.' Shasa was immediately defensive. 'But as you know she decided she couldn't leave the children again so soon.'

The crowd surged around them, and they were laughing and replying to congratulations, but Shasa saw the public relations director hovering and eased his way through to her.

'Well, Mrs Anstey, you have done us proud.' He smiled at her with all his charm. She was tall and rather bony but with silky blond hair that hung in a thick curtain over her bare shoulders.

'I always try to give full satisfaction.' Jill Anstey hooded her eyes and pouted slightly to give the remark an ambiguous slant. They had been teasing each other ever since they had met the previous day. 'But I'm afraid I have some more work for you, Mr Courtney. Will you bear with me just once more?'

'As often as you wish, Mrs Anstey.' Shasa played the game out, and she placed her hand on his forearm to lead him away, squeezing just a little more than was necessary.

'The television people from NABS want to do a five-minute interview with you, for inclusion in their "Africa in Focus" series. It could be a wonderful chance to speak directly to fifty million Americans.'

The TV team was setting up their equipment in the boardroom; the lights and cameras were being trained on the far end of the long room, where Centaine's portrait by Annigoni, hung on the stinkwood panelling. There were three men in the camera crew, all young and casually dressed but clearly highly professional and competent, and with them was a girl.

'Who will do the interview?' Shasa asked, glancing around curiously.

'That's the director,' Jill Anstey said. 'And she'll talk to you.' It took him a moment to realize that she meant the girl, then he saw that without seeming to do so, the girl was directing the set-up, indicating a camera angle or a lighting change with a word or a gesture.

'She's just a child,' Shasa protested.

'Twenty-five and smart as a bunch of monkeys,' Jill Anstey warned him. 'Don't let the little-girl look fool you. She's a professional and a strong comer with a big following in the States. She did that incredible series of interviews with Jomo Kenyatta, the Mau Mau terrorist, not to mention the "Heartbreak Ridge" story in Korea. They say she'll get an Emmy for it.'

South Africa did not have a TV network, but Shasa had seen 'Heartbreak Ridge' on BBC television during his last stay in London. It was a gritty, totally absorbing commentary on the Korean war, and Shasa found it hard to believe that this child had done that. She turned now and came directly to him, holding out her hand, frank and friendly, a fresh-faced *ingénue*.

'Hello, Mr Courtney, I'm Kitty Godolphin.' She had an enchanting southern accent and there were fine golden freckles across her cheeks and her small pert nose, but then he saw that she had good bone structure and interesting planes to her face that would render her highly photogenic.

'Mr Courtney,' she said. 'You speak so well, I couldn't resist trying to get a little more of you on film. I hope I haven't put you out too much.' She smiled at him, a sweet engaging smile, but he looked beyond it into eyes as hard as any diamonds from the H'ani Mine, eyes that were bright with a sharp cynical intelligence and ruthless ambition. That was unexpected and intriguing.

'Here's a show that will be worth the entrance fee,' he thought and glanced down. Her breasts were small, smaller than he usually chose, but they were unsupported and he could see their shape beneath her blouse. They were exquisite.

She led him to the leather chairs she had arranged to face each other under the lights.

'If you would sit on this side we'll get right into it. I'll do my introduction later. I don't want to keep you any longer than I have to.'

'As long as you like.'

'Oh, I know that you have a room full of important guests.' She glanced at her crew and one of them gave her a thumbs-up. She looked back at Shasa. 'The American public knows very little about South Africa,' she explained. 'What I am trying to do is capture a cross-section of your society and figure out how it all works. I will introduce you as a politician, mining tycoon and financier, and tell them about this fabulous new gold-mine of yours. Then we'll cut to you. Okay?'

'Okay!' He smiled easily. 'Let her roll.'

The clapper loader snapped the board in front of Shasa's face, somebody said 'Sound?' and somebody else replied 'Rolling' and then 'Action'.

'Mr Shasa Courtney, you have just told a meeting of your shareholders that your new gold-mine will probably be one of the five richest in South Africa, which makes it one of the richest in the world. Can you tell our viewers just how much of that fabulous wealth will be going back to people from which it was stolen in the first place?' she asked with breathtaking candour. 'And I am, of course, referring to the black tribes who once owned the land.'

Shasa was off-balance for only the moment that it took him to realize that he was in a fight. Then he responded easily.

'The black tribes who once owned the land on which the Silver River mine is situated were slaughtered, to the last man, woman

86

and child, back in the 1820s by the impis of Kings Chaka and Mzi-likazi, those two benevolent Zulu monarchs who between them managed to reduce the population of southern Africa by fifty per cent,' he told her. 'When the white settlers moved northwards, they came upon a land denuded of all human life. The land they staked was open, they stole it from nobody. I bought the mineral rights from people who had clear undisputed title to it.' He saw a glint of respect in her eyes, but she was as quick as he had been. She had lost a point but she was ready to play the next.

'Historical facts are interesting, of course, but let's return to the present. Tell me, if you had been a man of colour, Mr Courtney, say black or an Asiatic businessman, would you have been allowed to purchase the concessions to the Silver River mine?'

'That's a hypothetical question, Miss Godolphin.'

'I don't think so —' she cut off his escape. 'Am I wrong in thinking that the Group Areas Act recently promulgated by the parliament of which you are a sitting member, prevents non-white individuals and companies owned by blacks from purchasing land or mineral rights anywhere in their own land?'

'I voted against that legislation,' Shasa said grimly. 'But yes, the Group Areas Act would have prevented a coloured person acquiring the rights in the Silver River mine,' he conceded. Too clever to labour a point well taken, she moved on swiftly.

'How many black people does the Courtney Mining and Finance Company employ in its numerous enterprises?' she asked with that sweet open smile.

'Altogether through eighteen subsidiary companies, we provide work for some two thousand whites and thirty thousand blacks.'

'That is a marvellous achievement, and must make you very proud, Mr Courtney.' She was breathlessly girlish. 'And how many blacks do you have sitting on the boards of those eighteen companies?'

Again he had been wrong-footed, and he avoided the question. 'We make a point of paying well above the going rate for the job, and the other benefits we provide to our employees —' Kitty nodded brightly, letting him finish, quite happy that she could edit out all this extraneous material, but the moment he paused, she came in again:

'So there are no black directors on the Courtney companies' boards. Can you tell us how many black departmental managers you have appointed?'

Once long ago, hunting buffalo in the forests along the Zambezi river, Shasa had been attacked by a heat-maddened swarm of the big black African honey-bees. There had been no defence against them, and he had only escaped at last by diving into the crocodile-infested Zambezi river. He felt that same sense of angry helplessness now, as she buzzed around his head, effortlessly avoiding his attempts to swat her down and darting out to sting painfully almost at will.

'Thirty thousand black men working for you, and not a single director or manager amongst them!' she marvelled ingenuously. 'Can you suggest why that might be?'

'We have a predominantly tribal rural black society in this country and they come to the cities unskilled and untrained —'

'Oh, don't you have training programmes?'

Shasa accepted the opening. 'The Courtney group has a massive training programme. Last year alone we spent two and a half million pounds on employee education and job training.'

'How long has this programme been in operation, Mr Courtney?'

'Seven years, ever since I became chairman.'

'And in seven years, after all that money spent on education, not one black of all those thousands has been promoted to managerial status? Is that because you have not found a single capable black, or is it because your job reservation policy and your strict colour bar prevent any black, no matter how good —'

He was driven back inexorably until in anger he went on the offensive. 'If you are looking for racial discrimination, why didn't you stay in America?' he asked her, smiling icily. 'I'm sure your own Martin Luther King would be able to help you more than I can.'

'There is bigotry in my country,' she nodded. 'We understand that, and we are changing it, educating our people and outlawing its practice, but from what I have seen, you are indoctrinating your children in this policy you call *apartheid* and enshrining it in a monumental fortress of laws like your Group Areas Act and your Population Registration Act which seeks to classify all men by the colour of their skin alone.'

'We differentiate,' Shasa conceded, 'but that does not mean that we discriminate.'

'That's a catchy slogan, Mr Courtney, but not original. I have already heard it from your minister of Bantu affairs, Dr Hendrik Frensch Verwoerd. However, I suggest to you that you do discriminate. If a man is denied the right to vote or to own land merely because his skin is dark, that in my book is discrimination.'

And before he could respond, she had switched again.

'How many black people do you number amongst your personal friends?' she asked engagingly, and the question transported Shasa instantly back across the years. He remembered as a lad standing his first shifts on the H'ani Mine and the man who had been his friend. The black boss-boy in charge of the weathering grounds on which

88

the newly mined blue ore from the pit was laid out to soften and crumble to the point at which it could be carted to the mill.

He hadn't thought about him for years, yet he remembered his name without effort, Moses Gama, and he saw him in his mind's eye, tall and broad-shouldered, handsome as a young pharaoh with skin that glowed like old amber in the sunlight as they toiled side by side. He remembered their long rambling discussions, how they had read and argued together, drawn together by some unusual bond of the spirit. Shasa had lent him Macaulay's *History of England*, and when Moses Gama was fired from the H'ani Mine on the instigation of Centaine Courtney as a direct result of the unacceptably intimate friendly relationship between them, Shasa had asked him to keep the book. Now he felt again a faint echo of the sense of deprivation he had experienced at the time of their enforced parting.

'I have only a handful of personal friends,' he told her now. 'Ten thousand acquaintances, but only a very few friends —' He held up the fingers of his right hand. 'No more than that, and none of them happen to be black. Though once I had a black man as a friend, and I grieved when our ways parted.'

With the sure instinct which made her supreme in her craft, Kitty Godolphin recognized that he had given her a perfect peg on which to hang the interview.

'Once I had a black man as a friend,' she repeated softly. 'And I grieved when our ways parted. Thank you, Mr Courtney.' She turned to her camera man. 'Okay, Hank, cut it and get the studio to print it tonight.'

She stood up quickly and Shasa towered over her.

'That was excellent. There is a great deal of material there we can use,' she enthused. 'I am really grateful for your co-operation.'

Smiling urbanely Shasa leaned close to her. 'You are a devious little bitch, aren't you?' he said softly. 'A face like an angel and a heart of hell. You know it isn't like you made it sound, and you don't care. As long as you get a good story, you don't give a damn whether it's true or not or who it hurts, do you?'

Shasa turned from her and strode out of the boardroom. The floor-show had started and he went to the table at which Centaine and Blaine Malcomess were sitting, but the night had been spoiled for him.

He sat and glowered at the swirling dancers, not really seeing their long naked limbs and gleaming flesh but thinking furiously of Kitty Godolphin instead. Danger excited him, that was why he hunted lion and buffalo and flew his own Tiger Moth and played polo. Kitty Godolphin was dangerous. He was always attracted to intelligent and competent women, with strong personalities – and this one was devastatingly competent and made of pure silk and steel.

He thought about that lovely innocent face and childlike smile and the hard gleam of her eyes, and his fury was compounded by his desire to subjugate her, emotionally and physically, and the fact that he knew it would be difficult made the thought all the more obsessive. He found that he was physically aroused and that increased his anger.

He glanced up suddenly, and from across the room Jill Anstey, the public relations director, was watching him. The coloured lights played on the Slavic planes of her face and glinted on the platinum sheet of her hair. She slanted her eyes at him and ran the tip of her tongue over her lower lip.

'All right,' he thought. 'I have to take it out on somebody and you will do.' He inclined his head slightly, and Jill Anstey nodded and slipped out of the door behind her. Shasa murmured an apology to Centaine, then stood up and moved through the pounding music and semi-darkness towards the door through which Jill Anstey had disappeared.

Shasa got back to the Carlton Hotel at nine o'clock in the morning. Still in black tie and dinner jacket, he avoided the lobby and went up the back stairs from the underground garage. Centaine and Blaine were in the company suite, and Shasa had the smaller suite across the passage. He dreaded meeting either of them dressed as he was at this time in the morning, but he was lucky and got into his lounge uninterrupted.

Somebody had slipped an envelope under his door and he picked it up without particular interest, until he saw the Killarney Film Studios crest on the flap. Kitty Godolphin was working out of that studio and he grinned and split the flap with his thumbnail.

Dear Mr Courtney,
    The rushes are just great – you look better than Errol Flynn on film. If you want to see them, call me at the studio.

Kitty Godolphin

His anger had cooled and he was amused by her cheek, and though he had a full day ahead – lunch with Lord Littleton and meetings all afternoon – he phoned the studio.

'You just caught me,' Kitty told him. 'I was on my way out. You want to see the rushes? Okay, can you get up here at six this evening?'

She was smiling that sweet childlike smile and mocking him with a malicious green sparkle in her eyes as she came down to the reception desk of the studio to shake his hand and lead him to her hired projection room in the complex.

'I knew I could rely on your masculine vanity to get you up here,' she assured him.

Her film crew were sprawled untidily over the front row of seats in the projection room, smoking Camels and drinking Cokes, but Hank, the camera man, had the film clip in the projector ready to run, and they watched it through in silence.

When the lights went up again, Shasa turned to Kitty and conceded.

'You are good – you made me look a real prick most of the time. And, of course, you can always lose the parts where I held my own on the cutting-room floor.'

'You don't like it?' she grinned, wrinkling her small nose so the freckles on it gleamed like tiny gold coins.

'You are a bushwhacker, shooting from cover, and I'm out there with my back wide open.'

'If you accuse me of faking it,' she challenged him, 'how about you taking me and showing me the way it really is. Show me the Courtney mines and factories and let me film them!'

So that was why she had called him. He smiled to himself, but asked, 'Have you got ten days?'

'I've got as long as it takes,' she assured him.

'All right, let's start with dinner tonight.'

'Great!' she enthused, and then turned to her crew. '*Mazeltov*, boys, Mr Courtney is standing us all dinner.'

'That's not exactly what I had in mind,' he murmured.

'Do tell?' She gave him her innocent little girl look.

Kitty Godolphin was a rewarding companion. Her interest in everything he said or showed her was flattering and unfeigned. She watched his eyes or his lips as he spoke, and often leaned so close to listen that he could feel her breath on his face, but she never actually touched him.

For Shasa her appeal was heightened by her personal cleanliness. In the days they spent together, hot dusty days in the desert of the far west or in the eastern forests, tramping through pulp mills or fertilizer factories, watching the bulldozers strip the overburden from the coal deposits in billowing clouds of dust, or baking in the depths of the great excavation of the H'ani Mine, Kitty was always fresh-faced and cool-looking. Even in the dust her eyes were clear and her small even teeth sparkled. When or where she had an opportunity to rinse her clothes he could never decide, but they were always clean and crisp and her breath when she leaned close to him was always sweet.

She was a professional. That impressed Shasa also. She would go to any lengths to get the film footage she wanted, taking no account of fatigue or personal danger. He had to forbid her riding on the outside of the mine cage on the H'ani main incline shaft to film the drop into the pit, but she went back later, while he was in a meeting with his mine manager, and got exactly the shot she wanted and then smiled away his fury when he found out. Her crew treated her wth an ambivalence that amused Shasa. They held her in fond affection and were immensely protective of her, as though they were her elder brothers, and their pride in her achievements was unconcealed. However, at the same time they were much in awe of her ruthless search for excellence, to which they knew she would sacrifice them and anything else that got in her way. Her temper, although not often displayed, was merciless and vitriolic and when she gave an order, no matter how quietly or how sweet the smile that accompanied it, they jumped.

Shasa was also affected by the deep feelings which she had conceived for Africa, its land and its people.

'I thought America was the most beautiful country in all the world,' she said quietly one evening as they watched the sun set behind the great desolate mountains of the western deserts. 'But when I look at this, I have to wonder.'

Her curiosity took her into the compounds where the Courtney Company employees were housed, and she spent hours talking to the workers and their wives, filming it all, the questions and answers of black miners and white overseers and shift bosses, their homes and the food they ate, their recreations and their worship, and at the end Shasa asked her, 'So how do you like the way I oppress them?'

'They live well,' she conceded.

'And they are happy,' he pushed her. 'Admit it. I hid nothing from you. They are happy.'

'They are happy like children,' she agreed. 'As long as they look up to you like big daddy. But just how long do you think you can keep fooling them? How long is it going to be before they look at you in your beautiful airplane flying back to parliament to make a few more laws for them to obey and say to themselves, "Hey man! I'd like to try that also"?'

'For three hundred years under white government the people of this land have woven a social fabric which has held us all together. It works, and I would hate to see it torn asunder without knowing what will replace it.'

'How about democracy for a start?' she suggested. 'That's not a bad thing to replace it with – you know, *the will of the majority must prevail*!'

'You left out the best bit,' he flashed back at her. '*The interests of the minority must be safeguarded*. That doesn't work in Africa. The

African knows and understands one principle: winner takes all –
and let the minority go to the wall. That's what will happen to the
white settlers in Kenya if the British capitulate to the Mau Mau
killers.'

So they wrangled and sparred during the long hours of flying
which took them over the enormous distances of the African continent. From one destination to the next, Shasa and Kitty went ahead
in the Mosquito, and the helmet and oxygen mask were too large for
her and made her appear even younger and more girlish. David
Abrahams piloted the slower and more commodious company De
Havilland Dove, the camera equipment and the crew flying with
him, and even though most of Shasa's time on the ground was spent
in meetings with his managers and administrative staff, there was
still much time that he could devote to the seduction of Kitty
Godolphin.

Shasa was not accustomed to prolonged resistance from any female
who warranted his concentrated attention. There might be a token
flight, but always with coy glances over the shoulder, and usually
they chose to hide from him in the nearest bedroom, absentmindedly
forgetting to turn the key in the lock, and he expected it to go very
much the same way with Kitty Godolphin.

Getting into her blue jeans was his first priority; convincing her
that Africa was different from America and that they were doing the
best job they could came second by a long way. At the end of the ten
days he had succeeded in neither endeavour. Both Kitty's political
convictions and her virtue remained intact.

Kitty's interest in him, however wide-eyed and intense, was totally
impersonal and professional, and she gave the same attention to an
Ovambo witchdoctor demonstrating how he cured abdominal cancer
with a poultice of porcupine dung, or a muscled and tattooed white
shift-boss explaining to her that a black worker should never be
punched in the stomach as their spleens were always enlarged from
malaria and could easily rupture – hitting them in the head was all
right, he explained, because the African skull was solid bone anyway
and you couldn't inflict serious damage that way.

'Mary Maria!' Kitty breathed. 'That was worth the trip in itself!'

So on the eleventh day of their odyssey, they flew out of the
vastness of the Kalahari Desert from the remote H'ani Diamond
Mine on its mystic and brooding range of hills, into the town of
Windhoek, capital of the old German colony of South West Africa
which had been mandated to South Africa at the Treaty of Versailles.
It was a quaint little town, the German influence still very obvious in
the architecture and the way of life of the inhabitants. Set in the hilly
uplands above the arid littoral, the climate was pleasant and the

Kaiserhof Hotel, where Shasa kept another permanent suite, offered many of the creature comforts that they had lacked during the previous ten days.

Shasa and David spent the afternoon with their senior staff in the local office of the Courtney Company, which before its move to Johannesburg had been the head office, but which was still responsible for the logistics of the H'ani Mine. Kitty and her team, never wasting a moment, filmed the German colonial buildings and monuments and the picturesque Herero women on the streets. In 1904 this tribe of warriors had engaged the German administration in their worst colonial war which finally left eighty thousand Hereroes dead of famine and battle out of a total population of a hundred thousand. They were tall and magnificent-looking people and the women wore full-length Victorian skirts in butterfly colours and tall matching headdresses. Kitty was delighted with them, and late that afternoon came back to the hotel in ebullient mood.

Shasa had planned carefully, and had left David at the Courtney Company offices to finish the meeting. He was waiting to invite Kitty and her team through to the beer garden of the hotel where a traditional oom-pa-pa band in Lederhosen and alpine hats was belting out a medley of German drinking songs. The locally brewed Hansa Pilsner was every bit as good as the original of the Munich beerhalls, with a clear golden colour and thick creamy head. Shasa ordered the largest tankards, and Kitty drank level with her crew.

The mood turned festive until Shasa drew Kitty aside and under cover of the band told her quietly, 'I don't quite know how to break this to you, Kitty, but this will be our last evening together. I had my secretary book seats on the commercial flight for you and your boys to fly back to Johannesburg tomorrow morning.'

Kitty stared at him aghast. 'I don't understand. I thought we were flying down to your diamond concessions in the *Sperrgebiet*.' She pronounced it 'Spear Beat' in her enchanting accent. 'That was going to be the main act.'

'*Sperrgebiet* means "Forbidden Area",' Shasa told her sadly. 'And it means just that, Kitty, forbidden. Nobody goes in there without a permit from the government inspector of mines.

'But I thought you had arranged a permit for us,' she protested.

'I tried. I telexed our local office to arrange it. The application was denied. The government doesn't want you in there, I'm afraid.'

'But why not?'

'There must be something going on in there that they don't want you to see or film,' he shrugged, and she was silent but he saw the play of fierce emotion across her innocent features and her eyes

94

blazed green with anger and determination. He had early on discovered that the infallible means of making anything irresistibly attractive was to deny it to Kitty Godolphin. He knew that now she would lie, cheat or sell her soul to get into the *Sperrgebiet*.

'You could smuggle us in,' she suggested.

He shook his head. 'Not worth the risk. We might get away with it, but if I were caught it could mean a fine of £100,000 or five years in the slammer.'

She laid her hand on his arm, the first time she had deliberately touched him. 'Please, Shasa. I want so badly to film it.'

He shook his head sorrowfully. 'I'm sorry, Kitty, can't be done, I'm afraid,' and he stood up. 'Got to go up and change for dinner. You can break it to your crew while I'm away. Your flight back to Jo'burg leaves ten o'clock tomorrow.'

It was obvious at the dinner-table that she hadn't warned her crew of the change of plans, for they were still jovial and garrulous with good German beer.

For once Kitty took no part in the conversation, and she sat morosely at the end of the table, nibbling without interest at the hearty Teutonic fare and occasionally darting a sulky glance at Shasa. David skipped coffee to go and make his nightly phone call to Matty and the children, and Hank and his crew had been told of a local night spot with hot music and even hotter hostesses.

'Ten days with no feminine company except the boss,' Hank complained. 'My nerves need soothing.'

'Remember where you are,' Shasa warned him. 'In this country black velvet is royal game.'

'Some of the poontang I've seen today would be worth five years' hard labour,' Hank leered.

'Did you know that we have a South African version of Russian roulette?' Shasa asked him. 'What you do is take a coloured girl into a telephone booth. Then you phone the police flying squad and see who comes first.'

Kitty was the only one who didn't laugh, and Shasa stood up. 'I've got some papers to go over. We'll save the farewells until breakfast.'

In his suite he shaved and showered quickly, then slipped on a silk dressing-gown. As he went through to check that there was ice in the bar, there was a light tap on the door of the suite.

Kitty stood on the threshold looking tragic.

'Am I disturbing you?'

'No, of course not.' He held the door open and she crossed the lounge and stood staring out of the window.

'Can I get you a night-cap?' Shasa asked.

95

'What are you drinking?' she asked.

'A rusty nail.'

'I'll have one also – whatever it is.'

While he mixed Drambuie and malt whisky, she said, 'I came to thank you for everything you've done for me these last ten days. It's going to be hard to say goodbye.'

He carried the glasses across to where she stood in the middle of the floor, but when he reached her she took both glasses from him and placed them on the coffee table. Then she stood on tiptoe, slid both arms around his neck and turned her face up for his kiss.

Her lips were soft and sweet as warm chocolate, and slowly she pushed her tongue deeply into his mouth. When at last their mouths parted with a little wet sucking sound, he stooped and hooked an arm around the back of her knees and lifted her against his chest. She clung to him, pressing her face against his throat as he carried her through to the bedroom.

She had the lean hips and flat belly of a boy, and her buttocks were white and round and hard as a pair of ostrich eggs. Like her face, her body seemed childlike and immature except for those tight little pear-shaped breasts and the startling burst of thick dark hair at the base of her belly, but when he touched her there he found to his surprise that it was fine as silk and soft as smoke.

Her love-making was so artful as to seem totally uncontrived and spontaneous. She had the trick of telling him exactly what he was doing to her in the coarsest barnyard terms, and the obscenities on that soft innocent-looking mouth were shockingly erotic. She took him to those heights that he had seldom scaled before, and left him completely satiated.

In the dawn glow she snuggled against him and whispered, 'I don't know how I am going to be able to bear being parted from you after this.'

He could see her face in the wall mirror across the room, although she was unaware of his scrutiny. 'Damn it – I can't let you go,' he whispered back. 'I don't care what it costs I'm taking you down to the *Sperrgebiet* with me.'

In the mirror he watched her smile, a complacent and smug little smile. He had been correct, Kitty Godolphin used her sexual favours like trumps in a game of bridge.

At the airport her crew were packing their equipment into the Dove under David Abrahams' supervision when Shasa and Kitty drove up in the second company car, and Kitty jumped out and went to David.

'How are you going to work it, Davie?' she asked, and he looked puzzled.

'I don't understand the question.'

'You'll have to fake the flight plan, won't you?' Kitty insisted. Still mystified, David glanced at Shasa. Shasa shrugged and Kitty became exasperated.

'You know very well what I mean. How are you going to cover the fact that we are going into the *Sperrgebiet* without permits?'

'Without permits?' David echoed, and fished a handful of documents out of the zip pocket of his leather flying-jacket. 'Here are the permits. They were issued a week ago – all kosher and correct.'

Kitty wheeled and glared speechlessly at Shasa, but he refused to meet her eyes and instead ambled off to make his walk-around check of the Mosquito.

They didn't speak to each other again until Shasa had the Mosquito at twenty thousand feet, flying straight and level, then Kitty said into his earphones, 'You son of a bitch.' Her voice shook with fury.

'Kitty, my darling.' He turned and smiled at her over the oxygen mask, his single eye glinting happily. 'We both got what we wanted, and had a lot of fun in the process. What are you so mad about?'

She turned her face away and stared down at the magnificent lion-coloured mountains of the *Khama's Hochtland*. He left her to sulk. Some minutes later he heard an unusual stuttering sound in his headset, and he frowned and leaned forward to adjust the radio. Then, from the corner of his eye he saw that Kitty was hunched up in the seat shaking uncontrollably and that the stuttering sound was coming from her.

He touched her shoulder and she turned her face to him, it was swollen and crimson with suppressed laughter and tears of mirth were squeezing out of the corners of her eyes with the pressure. She couldn't hold it any longer, and she let out a snort.

'You crafty bastard,' she sobbed. 'Oh, you tricky monster —' and then she became incoherent as laughter overwhelmed her.

A long time later she wiped away her tears. 'We are going to get on just fine together, you and me,' she declared. 'Our minds work the same way.'

'Our bodies don't do too badly either,' he pointed out, and she unclipped her oxygen mask and leaned across to offer him her mouth again. Her tongue was sinuous and slippery as an eel.

*　　*　　*

Their time in the desert together passed too swiftly for Shasa, for since they had become lovers he found her a constant joy to be with.

Her quick and curious mind stimulated his own, and through her observant eyes he saw old familiar things afresh.

Together they watched and filmed the elephantine yellow caterpillar tractors ripping the elevated terraces that had once been the ocean bed. He explained to Kitty how in the time when the crust of the earth was soft and the molten magma still burst through to the surface, the diamonds, conceived at great depth and heat and pressure, were carried up with this sulphurous outpouring.

In the endless rains of those ancient times the great rivers scoured the earth, running down to the sea, washing the diamonds down with them, until they collected in the pockets and irregularities of the seabed closest to the river mouth. As the emerging continent shrugged and shifted, so the old seabed was lifted above the surface. The rivers had long ago dried up or been diverted, and sediment covered the elevated terraces, concealing the diamond-bearing pockets. It had taken the genius of Twentyman-Jones to work out the old river courses. Using aerial photography and an inherent sixth sense, he had pinpointed the ancient terraces.

Kitty and her team filmed the process by which the sand and rubble churned up by the dozer blades was screened and sieved, and finally dry-blown with great multi-bladed fans, until only the precious stones – one part in tens of millions – remained.

In the desert nights the mine hutments, lacking air-conditioning, were too hot for sleep. Shasa made a nest of blankets out amongst the dunes, and with the faint peppery smell of the desert in their nostrils, they made love under a blaze of stars.

On their last day Shasa commandeered one of the company jeeps and they drove out into a land of red dunes, the highest in all the world, sculptured by the incessant winds off the cold Benguela Current, their ridges crested like living reptiles as they writhed high against the pale desert sky.

Shasa pointed out to Kitty a herd of gemsbok, each antelope large as a pony, but with a marvellously patterned face mask of black and white and slender horns, straight and long as they were tall, that were the original unicorn of the fable. They were beautiful beasts, so adapted to their harsh country that they need never drink from surface water, but could survive only on the moisture they obtained from the silvery sun-scorched grasses. They watched them dissolve magically into the heat mirage, turning to squirming black tadpoles on the horizon before they disappeared.

'I was born here. Somewhere in these deserts,' Shasa told her as they stood hand in hand on the crest of one of the dunes and looked down a thousand feet to where they had left the jeep in the gut of the sand mountains.

He told her how Centaine had carried him in her womb through this terrible terrain, lost and abandoned, with only two little Bushmen as her guides and companions, and how the Bushwoman, for whom the H'ani Mine was named, acted as midwife at his birth and named him Shasa – 'Good Water' – after the most precious substance in her world.

The beauty and the grandeur affected them both so they drew close together in the solitude, and by the end of that day Shasa was sure that he truly loved her and that he wanted to spend the rest of his life with her.

Together they watched the sun sink towards the red dunes and the sky turned to a screen of hot hammered bronze, dented with flecks of blue cloud as though by blows from a celestial blacksmith's hammer. As the sky cooled, the colours chameleoned into puce and orange and lofty purples until the sun sank behind the dunes – and at the instant it disappeared, a miracle occurred.

They both gasped in wonder as in a silent explosion the entire heavens flared into electric green. It lasted only as long as they held their breath, but in that time the sky was as green as the ocean depths or the ice in the gaping cracks of a high mountain glacier. Then it faded swiftly into the drab gun-metal of dusk, and Kitty turned to him with a silent question in her eyes.

'We saw it together,' Shasa said softly. 'The Bushmen call it the Green Python. A man can live a lifetime in the desert without seeing it. I have never witnessed it, not until this moment.'

'What does it mean?' Kitty asked.

'The Bushmen say it is the most fortuitous of all good omens.' He reached out and took her hand. 'They say that those who see the Green Python will be specially blessed – and we saw it together.'

In the fading light they went down the slip face of the dune to where Shasa had parked the jeep. They sank almost knee-deep in the fluffy sun-warm sand, and laughing they clung to each other for support.

When they reached the jeep, Shasa took her by the shoulders, turned her to face him and told her, 'I don't want it to end, Kitty. Come with me. Marry me. I'll give you everything that life has to offer.'

She threw back her head to laugh in his face. 'Don't be daft, Shasa Courtney. What I want from life isn't yours to give,' she told him. 'This was fun, but it wasn't reality. We can be good friends for as long as you want, but our feet are set on different paths, and we aren't going in the same direction.'

The next day when they landed at Windhoek airport, a telegram addressed to her was pinned to the board in the crew room. Kitty read it swiftly. When she looked up she wasn't seeing Shasa any longer.

'There is another story breaking,' she said. 'I have to go.'

'When will I see you again?' Shasa asked, and she looked at him as though he were a complete stranger.

'I don't know,' she said, and she and her crew were on the commercial flight that left for Johannesburg an hour later.

*　　*　　*

Shasa was angry and humiliated. He had never offered to divorce Tara for any other woman – had never even contemplated it – and Kitty had laughed at him.

There were well-explored avenues down which he knew he could cure his anger, one was the hunt. For Shasa nothing else existed in the world when the hunter's passion thrilled in his blood, when a bull buffalo, big as a mountain and black as hell, came thundering down upon him, bloody saliva drooling from its raised muzzle, the polished points of its curved horns glinting, and murder in its small piglike eyes. However, this was the rainy season and the hunting grounds in the north would be muggy wet and malarial, and the grass high above a man's head. He could not hunt so he turned to his other sure panacea, the pursuit of wealth.

Money held endless fascination for Shasa. Without that obsessive attraction he could not have accumulated such a vast store of it, for that required a devotion and dedication that few men are capable of. Those that lack it console themselves with old platitudes about it not buying happiness and being the root of all evil. As an adept, Shasa knew that money was neither good nor evil, but simply amoral. He knew that money had no conscience, but that it contained the most powerful potential for both good and evil. It was the man who possessed it who made the ultimate choice between them, and that choice was called power.

Even when he had believed himself to be totally absorbed with Kitty Godolphin, his instinct had been in play. Almost subconsciously he had noticed those tiny white specks way out on the green Benguela Current of the Atlantic. Kitty Godolphin had not been gone from his life for an hour before he stormed into the offices of Courtney Mining and Finance in Windhoek's main street and started demanding figures and documents, making telephone calls, summoning lawyers and accountants, calling in favours from men in high places in government, despatching his minions to search the archives of the registrar and the local newspapers, assembling the tools of his trade, facts, figures and influence, and then losing himself happily in them, like an opium-eater with his pipe.

It was another five days before he was ready to bring it all together, and make the final weighing up. He had kept David Abrahams with him, for David was an excellent sounding-board in a situation like this one, and Shasa liked to bounce ideas off him and catch the returns.

'So this is what it looks like,' Shasa began the summing up. There were five of them in the boardroom, sitting under the magnificent Pierneef murals that Centaine had commissioned when the artist was in his prime, Shasa and David, the local manager and secretary of Courtney Mining, and the German lawyer based in Windhoek whom Shasa kept on permanent retainer.

'It looks like we have been asleep on our feet. In the last three years an industry has sprung up under our noses, an industry that last year alone netted twenty million pounds, four times the profits of the H'ani Mine, and we have let it happen.'

He glowered cyclops-eyed at his local manager for an explanation.

'We were aware of the recommencement of the fishing industry at Walvis Bay,' that unfortunate gentleman sought to explain. 'The application for pilchard trawling licences was gazetted, but I didn't think that fishing would match up with our other activities.'

'With due respect, Frank, that's the kind of decision I like to make myself. It's your job to pass on all information, of whatever nature, to me.' It was said quietly, but the three local men had no illusions as to the severity of the reprimand and they bowed their heads over their notepads. There was silence for ten seconds while Shasa let them suffer.

'Right, Frank,' Shasa ordered him. 'Tell us now what you should have told us four or five years ago.'

'Well, Mr Courtney, the pilchard-fishing industry was started in the early 1930s at Walvis Bay and although initially successful, it was overtaken by the depression, and with the primitive trawling methods of those days was unable to survive. The factories closed down and became derelict.'

As Frank spoke, Shasa's mind went back to his childhood. He remembered his first visit to Walvis Bay and blinked with the realization that it had been twenty years ago. He and Centaine had driven down in her daffodil-coloured Daimler to call in the loan she had made to De La Rey's canning and fishing company and to close down the factory. Those were the desperate years of the depression when the Courtney companies had survived only through his mother's pluck and determination – and ruthlessness.

He remembered how Lothar De La Rey, Manfred's father, had pleaded with his mother for an extension of the loan. When his trawlers lay against the wharf, loaded to the gunwales with their

101

catch of silver pilchards, and the sheriff of the court, on Centaine's orders, had put his seals on the factory doors.

That was the day he had first met Manfred De La Rey. Manfred had been a bare-footed, cropped-head hulk of a lad, bigger and stronger than Shasa, burned dark by the sun, dressed in a navy-blue fisherman's jersey and khaki shorts that were smeared with dried fish-slime, while Shasa had worn immaculate grey slacks, white open neck shirt and a college sweater with polished black shoes on his feet.

Two boys from different worlds, they had come face to face on the main fish wharf and their hostility had been instantaneous, their hackles rising like dogs, and within minutes, gibes and insults had turned to blows and they had flown at each other furiously, punching and wrestling down the wharf while the coloured trawlermen had egged them on delightedly. He remembered clearly even after all this time Manfred De La Rey's pale ferocious eyes glaring into his as they fell from the wharf on to the slippery, stinking cargo of dead pilchards, and he felt again the dreadful humiliation as Manfred had forced his head deeply into the quagmire of cold dead fish and he had begun to drown in their slime.

He jerked his mind back to the present, to hear his manager saying, 'So the position is now that the government has issued four factory licences to catch and process pilchards at Walvis Bay. The department of fisheries allocates an annual quota to each of the licensees, which is presently two hundred thousand tons.' Shasa contemplated the enormous profit potential of those quantities of fish. According to their published accounts, each of those four factories had averaged two million pounds profit in the last fiscal year. He knew he could improve on that, probably double it, but it didn't look as though he was going to get the chance.

'Approaches to both the Fisheries Department, and to higher authority —' Shasa had taken the administrator of the territory himself to dinner, 'have elicited the firm fact that no further licences will be issued. The only way to enter the industry would be to buy out one of the licensees.' Shasa smiled sardonically for he had already sounded out two of the companies. The owner of the first one had told Shasa in movingly eloquent terms to commit an unnatural sexual act on himself and the other had quoted a figure at which he might be prepared to negotiate which ended with a string of zeros that reached to the horizon. Despite his gloomy expression, it was the kind of situation in which Shasa revelled, seemingly hopeless, and yet with the promise of enormous rewards if he could find his way around the obstacles.

'I want a detailed breakdown of balance sheets on all four companies,' he ordered. 'Does anybody know the director of fisheries?'

102

'Yes, but he's straight up and down,' Frank warned him, knowing how Shasa's mind worked. 'His fists are tight closed, and if we try to slip him a little gifty, he'll raise a stink they'll smell in the high court in Bloemfontein.'

'Besides which the issue of licences is outside his jurisdiction,' the company secretary agreed with him. 'They are granted exclusively by the ministry in Pretoria, and there won't be any more. Four is the limit. That is the decision of the minister himself.'

Five more days Shasa remained in Windhoek, covering every possible lead or chance with a total dedication to detail that was one of his strengths, but at the end of that time he was no closer to owning a factory licence at Walvis Bay than he had been when he had first spotted the little white trawlers out on the green ocean. The only thing he had achieved was to forget that malignant little sprite, Kitty Godolphin, for ten whole days.

However, when at last he admitted to himself that there was nothing more to be gained by staying on in Windhoek and he climbed into the pilot's seat of the Mosquito, Kitty Godolphin's memory mocked him from the empty seat beside him. On impulse, instead of laying a course direct to Cape Town, he detoured westwards, heading for the coast and Walvis Bay, determined to have one long look at the site before finally abandoning the idea.

There was something else besides Kitty's memory that plagued him as the Mosquito dropped down the escarpment towards the sea. It was a burr of doubt, a prickle of discomfort that he had overlooked something important in his investigations.

He saw the ocean ahead, wreathed in tendrils of fog where the cold current brushed the land. The high dunes writhed together like a nest of razor-backed vipers, the colour of ripe wheat and copper, and he banked the Mosquito and followed the endless beaches upon which the surf broke in regular snowy lines until he saw the horn of the bay spike into the restless ocean and the lighthouse on Pelican Point winked at him through the fog banks.

He throttled back the Rolls Royce Merlins and went down, brushing the tops of the scattered fog banks and in the gaps he saw the trawler fleet at work. They were close in to the land, on the edge of the current line. Some of the boats had their nets full, and he saw the silver treasure glittering through the water as the trawlermen raised it slowly to the surface, while over them hung a shimmering white panoply of seabirds, greedy for the feast.

Then a mile away he picked out another boat hunting, cutting a foaming arabesque with its wake as it stalked yet another pilchard shoal.

Shasa pulled on flap and banked the Mosquito steeply, turning above the trawler to watch the hunt develop. He saw the shoal, a dark shadow as though a thousand gallons of ink had been spilled into the green waters, and he was amazed by its size, a hundred acres of solid fish, each individual no longer than his hand, but in their multitudes dwarfing leviathan.

'Millions of tons in one shoal,' he whispered. As he translated it into terms of wealth, the acquisitive passion flared up in him again. He watched the trawler beneath him throw its net around a tiny part of the gigantic shoal, and then he levelled out and flew at a hundred feet, skimming the fog banks, towards the maw of the bay. There were the four factory buildings, standing on the edge of the water, each with its own jetty thrusting out into the shallow waters, and black smoke billowing from the chimney stacks of the furnaces.

'Which one belonged to old De La Rey?' he wondered. On which of those flimsy structures had he fought with Manfred and ended with his ears and nose and mouth filled with fish slime? He grinned ruefully at the memory.

'But surely it was farther north,' he puzzled, trying to cast his mind back twenty years. 'It wasn't down here so close to the hook of the bay.' He banked the Mosquito and flew back parallel to the beach, and then a mile ahead he saw the line of palings, rotted and black, running in an irregular line out into the waters of the bay, and on the beach the roofless old ruins of the factory.

'It's still there,' he realized, and instantly his skin prickled with excitement. 'It's still there, deserted and forgotten all these years.' He knew then what he had overlooked.

He made two more passes, so low that the blast of his propellers raised a miniature sandstorm from the tops of the dunes. On the seaward wall of the derelict factory whose corrugated iron covering was gnawed and streaked with red rust, he could still make out the faded lettering: SOUTH WEST AFRICAN CANNING AND FISHING CO. LTD.

He pushed on throttle and lifted the Mosquito's nose into a gentle climbing turn, bringing her out of the turn on course for Windhoek. Cape Town and his promise to his sons and Isabella to be home before the weekend were forgotten. David Abrahams had flown the Dove back to Johannesburg, leaving a few minutes before Shasa that morning, so there was nobody in Windhoek whom Shasa would trust to conduct the search. He went down to the registrar of deeds himself and an hour before the deed office closed for the weekend he found what he was looking for.

The licence to capture and process pilchards and all other pelagic fish was dated 20 September 1929 and signed by the administrator of the territory. It was made out in favour of one Lothar De La Rey of

Windhoek, and there was no term of expiry. It was good now and for all time.

Shasa stroked the crackling, yellowing document, smoothing out the crumples in it lovingly, admiring the crimson revenue stamps and the administrator's fading signature. Here in these musty drawers it had lain for over twenty years – and he tried to put a value on this scrap of paper. A million pounds, certainly – five million pounds, perhaps. He chuckled triumphantly and took it to the deeds clerk to have a notorized copy made.

'It will cost you a pretty penny, sir,' the clerk sniffed. 'Ten and six for the copy and two pounds for the attestation.'

'It's a high price,' Shasa agreed, 'but I can just afford it.'

*   *   *

Lothar De La Rey came bounding up the wet black rocks, surefooted as a mountain goat, dressed only in a pair of black woollen bathing trunks. In one hand he carried a light fishing rod and in the other he held the trace on the end of which a small silver fish fluttered.

'I've got one, Pa,' he called excitedly, and Manfred De La Rey roused himself. He had been lost in thought; even on this, one of his rare vacations, his mind was still concentrated on the work of his ministry.

'Well done, Lothie.' He stood up and picked up the heavy bamboo surf rod that lay beside him. He watched his son gently unhook the small bait fish and hand it to him. He took it from him. It was cold and firm and slippery, and when he pressed the sharp point of his large hook through its flesh, the tiny dorsal fin along its back came erect and its struggles were frantic.

'Man, no old kob will be able to resist that.' Manfred held the live bait up for his son to admire. 'It looks so good, I could eat it myself.' He picked up the heavy rod.

For a minute he watched the surf break on the rocks below them, and then timing his moment he ran down to the edge, moving lightly for such a big man. The foam sucked at his ankles as he poised, and then swung the bamboo rod in a full whipping action. The cast was long and high, the live bait sparkled as it spun a parabola in the sunlight and then hit the green water a hundred yards out, beyond the first line of breakers.

Manfred ran back as the next wave dashed head-high at him. With the rod over his shoulder and line still streaming from the big Scarborough reel he beat the angry white surf and regained his seat high up on the rocks.

He thrust the butt of the rod into a crack in the rocks and jammed his old stained felt hat against the reel to hold it. Then he settled down on his cushion with his back to the rock and his son beside him.

'Good kob water,' he grunted. The sea was discoloured and cloudy, like home-made ginger beer, the perfect conditions for the quarry they were seeking.

'I promised Ma we would bring her a fish for pickling,' Lothar said.

'Never count your kob before it's in the pickle barrel,' Manfred counselled, and the boy laughed.

Manfred never touched him in front of others, not even in front of his mother and the girls, but he remembered the enormous pleasure it had given him when he was Lothar's age to have his own father's embrace, and so at times when they were alone together like this he would let his true feelings show. He let his arm slip down off the rock and fall around the boy's shoulders and Lothar froze with joy and for a minute did not dare to breathe. Then slowly he leaned closer to his father and in silence they watched the tip of the long rod nod in rhythm to the ocean.

'And so, Lothie, have you decided what you want to do with your life when you leave Paul Roos?' Paul Roos was the leading Afrikaans medium school in the Cape Province, the South African equivalent of Eton or Harrow for Afrikaners.

'Pa, I've been thinking.' Lothar was serious. 'I don't want to do law like you did, and I think medicine will be too difficult.'

Manfred nodded resignedly. He had come to terms with the fact that Lothar was not academically brilliant, but just a good average student. It was in all the other fields that he excelled. Already it was clear that his powers of leadership, his determination and courage, and his athletic prowess were all exceptional.

'I want to join the police,' the boy said hesitantly. 'When I finish at Paul Roos, I want to go to the police academy in Pretoria.'

Manfred sat quietly, trying to hide his surprise. It was probably the last thing he would have thought of himself.

At last he said. '*Ja*, why not! You'd do well there.' He nodded. 'It's a good life, a life of service to your country and your *Volk*.' The more he thought about it, the more he realized that Lothar was making a perfect choice – and of course, the fact that his father was minister of police wouldn't hurt the boy's career either. He hoped he would stick to it. '*Ja*,' he repeated, 'I like it.'

'Pa, I wanted to ask you —' Lothar started, and the tip of the rod jerked, bounced straight, and then arced over boldly. Manfred's old hat was thrown clear of the spinning reel as the line hissed from it in a blur.

106

Father and son leapt to their feet and Manfred seized the heavy bamboo and leaned back against it to set the hook.

'It's a monster,' he shouted, as he felt the weight of the fish, and the flow of line never checked, even when he thrust the palm of the leather mitten he wore against the flange of the reel to brake it. Within seconds blue smoke burned from the friction of reel and leather glove.

When it seemed that the last few turns of line would be stripped from the spindle of the reel, the fish stopped, and two hundred yards out there under the smoky grey waters it shook its head doggedly so the rod butt kicked against Manfred's belly.

With Lothar dancing at his side, howling encouragement and advice, Manfred winched in the fish, pumping the rod to recover a few turns of line at a time, until the reel was almost full again and he expected to see the quarry thrashing in the surf below the rocks. Then suddenly the fish made another long heavy run, and he had to begin the laborious back-straining task all over again.

At last they saw it, deep in the water below the rocks, its side shining like a great mirror as it caught the sun. With the rod bent taut as a longbow, Manfred forced it up until it flapped ponderously, washing back and forth in the suck and thrust of the waves, gleaming in marvellous iridescent shades of rose and pearl, its great jaws gaping with exhaustion.

'The gaff!' Manfred shouted. 'Now, Lothie, now!' and the boy sprang down to the water's edge with the long pole in his hands and buried the point of the gaff hook into the fish's shoulder, just behind the gills. A flush of blood stained the waters pink, and then Manfred threw down his rod and jumped down to help Lothar with the gaff pole.

Between them they dragged the fish, flapping and thumping, up the rocks above the high-water mark.

'He's a hundred pounds if he's an ounce,' Lothar exulted. 'Ma and the girls will be up till midnight pickling this one.'

Lothar carried the rods and the fishing box while Manfred slung the fish over his shoulder, a short loop of rope through its gills, and they trudged back around the curve of white beach. On the rocks of the next headland, Manfred lowered the fish for a few minutes to rest. Once he had been Olympic light heavyweight champion, but he had fleshed out since those days, his belly was softening and spreading and his breath was short.

'Too much time behind my desk,' he thought ruefully, and sank down on a black boulder. As he mopped his face he looked around him.

This place always gave him pleasure. It grieved him that he could

107

find so little time in his busy life to come here. In their old student days he and Roelf Stander, his best friend, had fished and hunted on this wild unspoiled stretch of coast. It had belonged to Roelf's family for a hundred years, and Roelf would never have sold the smallest piece of it to anybody but Manfred.

In the end he had sold Manfred a hundred acres for one pound. 'I don't want to get rich on an old friend,' he had laughed away Manfred's offer of a thousand. 'Just let us have a clause in the contract of sale that I have a right of first option to buy it back at the same price at your death or whenever you want to sell.'

There beyond the headland on which they sat was the cottage that he and Heidi had built, white stucco walls and thatch, the only sign of human habitation. Roelf's own holiday house was hidden beyond the next headland, but within easy walking distance so they could be together whenever both families were on holiday at the same time.

There were so many memories here. He looked out to sea. That was where the German U-boat had surfaced when it had brought him back in the early days of the war. Roelf had been on the beach, waiting for him, and had rowed out in the darkness to fetch him and his equipment ashore. What mad exciting days those had been, the danger and the fighting, as they had struggled to raise the Afrikaner *Volk* in rebellion against the English-lover Jan Christian Smuts, and to declare South Africa a republic under the protection of Nazi Germany – and how very close they had come to success.

He smiled and his eyes glowed at the memory. He wished he could tell the boy about it. Lothie would understand. Young as he was, he would understand the Afrikaner dream of republic and he would be proud. However that was a story that could never be told. Manfred's attempt to assassinate Jan Smuts and precipitate the rebellion had failed. He had been forced to fly the country, and to languish for the rest of the war in a far-off land, while Roelf and the other patriots had been branded traitors and hustled into Jannie Smuts' internment camps, humiliated and reviled until the war ended.

How it had all changed. Now they were the lords of this land, although nobody outside the inner circle knew the part that Manfred De La Rey had played in those dangerous years. They were the overlords, and once again the dream of republic burned brightly, like a flame on the altar of Afrikaner aspirations.

His thoughts were broken up by the roar of a low-flying aircraft overhead, and Manfred looked up. It was a sleek blue and silver machine, turning away steeply to line up for the airstrip that lay just beyond the first line of hills. The airstrip had been built by the public works department when Manfred had achieved full ministerial rank. It was essential that he was in close contact with his department at

108

all times, and from that landing-field an airforce plane could fetch him within hours if he were needed in an emergency.

Manfred recognized this machine and knew who was flying it, but frowned with annoyance as he stood up and hefted the huge carcass of the fish again. He treasured the isolation of this place, and fiercely resented any unwarranted intrusion. He and Lothar set off on the last leg of the long haul back to the cottage.

Heidi and the girls saw them coming, and ran down the dunes to meet them and then surrounded Manfred, laughing and squealing their congratulations. He plodded up the soft dunes, with the girls skipping beside him, and hung the fish on the scaffold outside the kitchen door. While Heidi went to fetch her Kodak camera, Manfred stripped off his shirt which was stained with fish blood and stooped to the tap of the rainwater tank and washed the blood from his hand and the salt from his face.

As he straightened up again, with water dripping from his hair and running down his bare chest, he was abruptly aware of the presence of a stranger.

'Get me a towel, Ruda,' he snapped, and his eldest daughter ran to his bidding.

'I was not expecting you.' Manfred glowered at Shasa Courtney. 'My family and I like to be alone here.'

'Forgive me. I know I am intruding.' Shasa's shoes were floury with dust. It was a mile walk from the airstrip. 'I am sure you will understand when I explain that my business is urgent and private.'

Manfred scrubbed his face with the towel while he mastered his annoyance, and then, when Heidi came out with the camera in her hand, he introduced her gruffly.

Within minutes Shasa had charmed both Heidi and the girls into smiles, but Lothar stood behind his father and only came forward reluctantly to shake hands. He had learned from his father to be suspicious of Englishmen.

'What a tremendous kob,' Shasa admired the fish on the scaffold. 'One of the biggest I have seen in years. You don't often get them that size any more. Where did you catch it?'

Shasa insisted on taking the photographs of the whole family grouped around the fish. Manfred was still bare-chested, and Shasa noticed the old bluish puckered scar in the side of his chest. It looked like a gunshot wound, but there had been a war and many men bore scars of that nature now. Thinking of war wounds, he adjusted his own eye-patch self-consciously as he handed the camera back to Heidi.

'You will stay to lunch, *Meneer*?' she asked demurely.

'I don't want to be a nuisance.'

109

'You are welcome.' She was a handsome woman, with a large high bosom and wide fruitful hips. Her hair was dense and golden blond, and she wore it in a thick plaited rope that hung almost to her waist, but Shasa saw Manfred De La Rey's expression and quickly transferred all his attention back to him.

'My wife is right. You are welcome.' Manfred's natural Afrikaner duty of hospitality left him no choice. 'Come, we will go to the front stoep until the women call for us to eat.'

Manfred fetched two bottles of beer from the ice-chest and they sat in deckchairs, side by side, and looked out over the dunes to the wind-flecked blue of the Indian Ocean.

'Do you remember where we first met, you and I?' Shasa broke the silence.

'*Ja,*' Manfred nodded. 'I remember very well.'

'I was back there two days ago.'

'Walvis Bay?'

'Yes. To the canning factory, the jetty where we fought,' Shasa hesitated, 'where you thumped me, and pushed my head into a mess of dead fish.'

Manfred smiled with satisfaction at the memory. '*Ja*, I remember.'

Shasa had to control his temper carefully. It still rankled and the man's smugness infuriated him, but the memory of his childhood victory had softened Manfred's mood as Shasa had intended it should.

'Strange how we were enemies then, and now we are allies,' Shasa persisted, and let him think about that for a while before he went on. 'I have most carefully considered the offer you made to me. Although it is difficult for a man to change sides, and many people will put the worst construction on my motives, I now see that it is my duty to my country to do what you suggest and to employ what talent I have for the good of the nation.'

'So you will accept the prime minister's offer?'

'Yes, you may tell the prime minister that I will join the government, but in my own time and my own way. I will not cross the floor of the House, but as soon as parliament is dissolved for the coming elections, I will resign from the United Party to stand for the National Party.'

'Good,' Manfred nodded. 'That is the honourable way.'

But there was no honourable way, Shasa realized, and was silent for a moment before he went on.

'I am grateful for your part in this, *Meneer*. I know that you have been instrumental in affording me this opportunity. In view of what has happened between our families, it is an extraordinary gesture you have made.'

'There was nothing personal in my decision.' Manfred shook his head. 'It was simply a case of the best man for the job. I have not forgotten what your family has done to mine – and I never will.'

'I will not forget either,' Shasa said softly. 'I have inherited guilt – rightly or wrongly, I will never be sure. However, I would like to make some reparation to your father.'

'How would you do that, *Meneer*?' Manfred asked stiffly. 'How would you compensate a man for the loss of his arm and for all those years spent in prison? How will you pay a man for the damage to his soul that captivity has inflicted?'

'I can never full compensate him,' Shasa agreed. 'However, suddenly and unexpectedly I have been given the opportunity to restore to your father a large part of that which was taken from him.'

'Go on,' Manfred invited. 'I am listening.'

'Your father was issued a fishing licence in 1929. I have searched the records. That licence is still valid.'

'What would the old man do with a fishing licence now? You don't understand – he is physically and mentally ruined.'

'The fishing industry out of Walvis Bay has revived and is booming. The number of licences has been severely limited. Your father's licence is worth a great deal of money.'

He saw the shift in Manfred's eyes, the little sparks of interest swiftly screened.

'You think my father should sell it?' he asked heavily. 'And by any chance would you be interested in buying it?' He smiled sarcastically.

Shasa nodded. 'Yes, of course I'd like to buy it, but that might not be best for your father.' Manfred's smile withered, he hadn't expected that.

'What else could he do with it?'

'We could re-open the factory and work the licence together as partners. Your father puts up the licence, and I put up the capital and my business skills. Within a year or two, your father's share will almost certainly be worth a million pounds.'

Shasa watched him carefully as he said it. This was more, much more than a business offer. It was a testing. Shasa wanted to reach beyond the man's granite crust, that monumental armour of puritanical righteousness. He wanted to probe for weaknesses, to find any chinks that he could exploit later.

'A million pounds,' he repeated. 'Perhaps even a great deal more.' And he saw the sparks in the other man's fierce pale eyes again, just for an instant, the little yellow sparks of greed. The man was human after all. 'I can deal with him now,' Shasa thought, and to cover his

111

relief he lifted his briefcase from the floor beside his deckchair and opened it on his lap.

'I have worked out a rough agreement —' he took out a sheaf of typed blue foolscap sheets '— you could show it to your father, discuss it with him.'

Manfred took the sheets from him. '*Ja*, I will see him when I return home next week.'

'There is one small problem,' Shasa admitted. 'This licence was issued a long time ago. The government department may wish to repudiate it. It is their policy to allow only four licences —'

Manfred looked up from the contract. 'That will be no problem,' Manfred said, and Shasa lifted his beer tankard to hide his smile. They had just shared their first secret. Manfred De La Rey was going to use his influence for personal gain. Like a lost virginity, the next time would be easier.

Shasa had realized from the beginning that he would be an outsider in a cabinet of Afrikaner Nationalists. He desperately needed a trustworthy ally amongst them, and if that ally could be linked to him by shared financial blessings and a few off-colour secrets, then his loyalty would be secured. Shasa had just achieved this, with the promise of vast profits to himself to sweeten the bargain. A good day's work, he thought, as he closed the briefcase with a snap.

'Very good, *Meneer*. I'm grateful to you for having given me your time. Now I will leave you to enjoy what remains of your holiday undisturbed.'

Manfred look up. '*Meneer*, my wife is preparing lunch for us. She will be very unhappy if you leave so soon.' At last his smile was genial. 'And this evening I will have a few good friends visit me for a *braaivleis*, a barbecue. There are plenty of spare beds. Stay the night. You can leave early tomorrow morning.'

'You are very kind.' Shasa sank back in his chair. The feeling between them had changed, but Shasa's intuition warned him there were hidden depths in their relationship which still had to be plumbed, and as he smiled into Manfred De La Rey's topaz-coloured eyes, he felt a sudden small chill, a cold wind through a chink in his memory. Those eyes haunted him. He was trying to remember something. It remained obscure but somehow strangely menacing. Could it have been from their childhood fight? he wondered. But he did not think so. The memory was closer than that, and more threatening. He almost grasped it, and then Manfred looked down at the contract again, almost as though he had sensed what Shasa was searching for, and the shape of the memory slipped away beyond Shasa's grasp.

Heidi De La Rey came out on to the verandah in her apron, but

112

she had changed out of her faded old skirt and twisted her plaited hair up on top of her head.

'Lunch is ready – and I do hope you eat fish, Meneer Courtney.'

Shasa set out to charm the family during lunch. Heidi and the girls were easy. The boy Lothar was different, suspicious and withdrawn. However, Shasa had three sons of his own, and he drew him out with stories of flying and hunting big game, until despite himself the boy's eyes shone with interest and admiration.

When they rose from the table, Manfred nodded grudgingly. '*Ja, Meneer*, I must remember never to underestimate you.'

That evening a small group comprising a man and woman and four children came straggling over the dunes from the south, and Manfred's children rushed out to meet them and lead them up on to the verandah of the cottage.

Shasa stayed in the background throughout the noisy greetings of the two families. Theirs was obviously a close relationship of long standing.

Of course, Shasa recognized the head of the other family. He was a big man, even heavier in build than Manfred De La Rey. Like him, he had also been a member of the boxing team that had participated in the Berlin Olympic Games of 1936. He had been a senior lecturer in law at Stellenbosch University, but had recently resigned to become a junior partner in the firm of Van Schoor, De La Rey and Stander, the firm in which Manfred De La Rey had become the senior partner after the death of old Van Schoor some years before.

Apart from his law practice, Roelf Stander acted as Manfred's chief party organizer and had managed Manfred's 1948 campaign for him. Although not himself a member of parliament, he was a leg man of the National Party and Shasa knew that he was almost certainly a member of the *Broederbond*, the Brotherhood, that clandestine society of elite Afrikaners.

When Manfred De La Rey began to introduce them, Shasa saw that Roelf Stander recognized him and looked a little sheepish.

'I hope you aren't going to throw eggs at me again, Meneer Stander,' Shasa challenged him, and Roelf chuckled.

'Only if you make another bad speech, Meneer Courtney.'

During the 1948 election, in which Shasa had been defeated by Manfred De La Rey, this man had organized the gang of bully boys who had broken up Shasa's election meetings. Though Shasa was smiling now, his resentment was almost as fierce as it had been at the time. It had always been standard Nationalist tactics to break up the meetings of their opponents. Manfred De La Rey sensed the hostile feelings between them.

'We will soon be on the same side,' he said, as he stepped between

113

them placatingly and placed a hand on each of their arms. 'Let me find a beer for both of you and we'll drink to letting bygones be bygones.'

The two of them turned away and quickly Shasa scrutinized Roelf Stander's wife. She was thin, almost to the point of starvation, and there was an air of resignation and weariness about her, so it took a moment for even Shasa's trained eye to see how pretty she must once have been, and how attractive she still was. She was returning his scrutiny, but dropped her eyes the moment they met Shasa's single eye.

Heidi De La Rey had not missed the exchange and now she took the woman's arm and led her forward.

'Meneer Courtney, this is my dear friend Sarah Stander.'

'*Aangename kennis,*' Shasa bowed slightly. 'Pleasant meeting, *Mevrou.*'

'How do you do, Squadron Leader,' the woman replied quietly, and Shasa blinked. He had not used his rank since the war. It was, of course, poor form to do so.

'Have we met?' he asked, for once off-balance and the woman shook her head quickly and turned to Heidi to speak about the children. Shasa was unable to pursue the matter, for at that moment Manfred handed him a beer and the three men carried their tankards down off the stoep to watch Lothar and the Standers' eldest boy, Jakobus, build the fire for the barbecue. Though the masculine conversation was informed and their views interesting – both Manfred and Roelf Stander were educated and highly intelligent men – Shasa found his thoughts returning to the thin pale woman who had used his airforce rank. He wished for the opportunity to speak to her alone, but realized that was unlikely and dangerous. He knew very well how protective and jealous the Afrikaners were of their women, and how easy it would be to precipitate an ugly and damaging incident. So he kept away from Sarah Stander, but for the rest of the evening observed her carefully, and so gradually became aware of undercurrents of emotion in the relationships of the two families. The two men seemed very close and it was obvious that their friendship was of long standing, but with the women it was different. They were just too kind and considerate and appreciative of each other, the certain indications of deep-seated female antagonism. Shasa stored that revelation, for human relationships and weaknesses were essential tools of his trade, but it was only later in the evening that he made two other important discoveries.

He intercepted an unguarded look that Sarah Stander directed at Manfred De La Rey while he was laughing with her husband, and Shasa recognized it instantly as a look of hatred, but that particularly corrosive type of hatred that a woman can conceive for a man whom she once loved. That hatred explained for Shasa the weariness and resignation that had almost ruined Sarah Stander's beauty. It explained also the resentment that the two women felt for each other. Heidi De La Rey must realize that Sarah had once loved her husband, and that beneath the hatred she probably still did. The play of feelings and emotions fascinated Shasa, he had learned so much of value and had achieved so much in a single day that he was well satisfied by the time that Roelf Stander called his family together.

'It's almost midnight, come on, everybody. We have a long walk home.'

Each of them had brought a flashlight, and there was a flurry of farewells, the girls and women exchanging kisses, while first Roelf Stander and then his son Jakobus came to shake Shasa's hand.

'Goodbye,' Jakobus said, with the innate good manners and respect for elders that every Afrikaner child is taught from birth. 'I would also like to hunt a black-maned lion one day.'

He was a tall well-favoured lad, two or three years older than Lothar; he had been as fascinated as Lothar by Shasa's hunting stories but there was something familiar about him that had niggled Shasa all evening. Lothar stood beside his friend, smiling politely, and suddenly it dawned on Shasa. The boys had the same eyes, the pale cat-eyes of the De La Reys. For a moment he was at a loss to explain it, and then it all fell into place. The hatred he had observed in Sarah Stander was explained. Manfred De La Rey was the father of her son.

Shasa stood beside Manfred on the top stair of the stoep and they watched the Stander family climb the dunes, the beams of their flashlights darting about erratically and the shrill voices of the children dwindling into the night, and he wondered if he could ever piece together the clues he had gleaned this evening and discover the full extent of Manfred De La Rey's vulnerability. One day it might be vital to do so.

It would be easy enough discreetly to search the records for the marriage date of Sarah Stander and compare it to the birth date of her eldest son, but how would he ever coax from her the true significance of her use of his military rank. She had called him 'Squadron Leader'. She knew him, that was certain, but how and where? Shasa smiled. He enjoyed a good mystery, Agatha Christie was one of his favourite authors. He would work on it.

*　　*　　*

Shasa woke with the grey of dawn lining the curtains over his bed, and a pair of bokmakierie shrikes singing one of their complicated duets from the scrub of the dunes. He stripped off the pyjamas Manfred had lent him and shrugged on the bathrobe, before he crept from the silent cottage and went down to the beach.

He swam naked, slashing over-arm through the cold green water and ducking under the successive lines of breaking white surf until he was clear; then he swam slowly parallel to the beach but five hundred yards off. The chances of shark attack were remote, but the possibility spiced his enjoyment. When it was time to go in he caught a breaking wave and rode it into the beach, and waded ashore, laughing with exhilaration and the joy of life.

He mounted quietly to the stoep of the cottage, not wanting to disturb the family, but a movement from the far end stopped him. Manfred sat in one of the deckchairs with a book in his hands. He was already shaved and dressed.

'Good morning, *Meneer*,' Shasa greeted him. 'Are you going fishing again today?'

'It's Sunday,' Manfred reminded him. 'I don't fish on a Sunday.'

'Ah, yes.' Shasa wondered why he felt guilty for having enjoyed his swim, then he recognized the antique leather-covered black book that Manfred was holding.

'The Bible,' he remarked, and Manfred nodded.

'*Ja*, I read a few pages before I begin each day, but on Sunday or when I have a particular problem to face, I like to read a full chapter.'

'I wonder how many chapters you read before you screwed your best friend's wife,' Shasa thought, but said aloud, 'Yes, the Book is a great comfort,' and tried not to feel a hypocrite as he went through to dress.

Heidi laid an enormous breakfast, everything from steak to pickled fish, but Shasa ate an apple and drank a cup of coffee before he excused himself.

'The forecast on the radio is for rain later. I want to get back to Cape Town before the weather closes in.'

'I will walk up to the airstrip with you.' Manfred stood up quickly.

Neither of them spoke until the track reached the ridge, and then Manfred asked suddenly, 'Your mother – how is she?'

'She is well. She always is, and she never seems to age.' Shasa watched his face, as he went on, 'You always ask about her. When last did you see her?'

'She is a remarkable woman,' Manfred said stolidly, avoiding the question.

'I have tried to make up in some way for the damage she has done

116

your family,' Shasa persisted, and Manfred seemed not to have heard. Instead he stopped in the middle of the track, as if to admire the view, but his breathing was ragged. Shasa had set a fast pace up the hill.

'He's out of condition,' Shasa gloated. His own breathing was unruffled, and his body lean and hard.

'It's beautiful,' Manfred said, and only when he made a gesture that swept the wide horizon, did Shasa realize that he was talking about the land. He looked and saw that from the ocean to the blue mountains of the Langeberge inland, it was indeed beautiful.

'And the Lord said unto him, "This is the land which I sware unto Abraham, unto Isaac and unto Jacob, saying, I will give it unto thy seed",' Manfred quoted softly. 'The Lord has given it to us, and it is our sacred duty to keep it for our children. Nothing else is important compared to that duty.'

Shasa was silent. He had no argument with that sentiment, although the expression of it was embarrassingly theatrical.

'We have been given a paradise. We must resist with our lives all efforts to despoil it, or to change it,' Manfred went on. 'And there are many who will attempt just that. They are gathering against us already. In the days ahead we will need strong men.'

Again Shasa was silent, but now his agreement was tinged with scepticism. Manfred turned to him.

'I see you smile,' he said seriously. 'You see no threat to what we have built up here on the tip of Africa?'

'As you have said, this land is a paradise. Who would want to change it?' Shasa asked.

'How many Africans to do you employ, *Meneer*?' Manfred seemed to change course.

'Almost thirty thousand altogether,' Shasa frowned with puzzlement.

'Then you will soon learn the poignancy of my warning,' Manfred grunted. 'There is a new generation of trouble-makers who have grown up amongst the native people. These are the bringers of darkness. They have no respect for the old orders of society which our forefathers so carefully built up and which have served us so faithfully for so long. No, they want to tear all that down. As the Marxist monsters destroyed the social fabric of Russia, so they seek to destroy all that the white man has built up in Africa.'

Shasa's tone was disparaging as he replied. 'The vast bulk of our black peoples are happy and law-abiding. They are disciplined and accustomed to authority, their own tribal laws are every bit as strict and circumscribing as the laws we impose. How many agitators are there amongst them, and how great is their influence? Not many and not much, would be my guess.'

117

'The world has changed more in the short time since the end of the war than it ever did in the hundred years before that.' Manfred had recovered his breath now, and he spoke forcefully and eloquently in his own language. 'The tribal laws which governed our black peoples are eroded as they leave the rural areas and flock to the cities in search of the sweet life. There they learn all the white man's vices, and they are ripened for the heresies of the bringers of darkness. The respect that they have for the white man and his government could easily turn to contempt, especially if they detect any weakness in us. The black man respects strength and despises weakness, and it is the plan of this new breed of black agitators to test our weaknesses and expose them.'

'How do you know this?' Shasa asked and then immediately was angry with himself. He did not usually deal in banal questions, but Manfred answered seriously.

'We have a comprehensive system of informers amongst the blacks, it is the only way a police force can do its job efficiently. We know that they are planning a massive campaign of defiance of the law, especially those laws that have been introduced in the last few years –the Group Areas Act and the Population Registration Act and the pass laws, the laws necessary to protect our complicated society from the evils of racial integration and miscegenation.'

'What form will this campaign take?'

'Deliberate disobedience, flouting of the law, boycotts of white businesses and wild-cat strikes in mining and industry.'

Shasa frowned as he made his calculation. The campaign would directly threaten his companies. 'Sabotage?' he asked. 'Destruction of property – are they planning that?'

Manfred shook his head. 'It seems not. The agitators are divided amongst themselves. They even include some whites, some of the old comrades from the communist party. There are a few amongst them who favour violent action and sabotage, but apparently the majority are prepared to go only as far as peaceful protest – for the moment.'

Shasa sighed with relief, and Manfred shook his head. 'Do not be too complacent, *Meneer*. If we fail to prevent them, if we show weakness now, then it will escalate against us. Look what is happening in Kenya and Malaya.'

'Why do you not simply round up the ringleaders now, before it happens?'

'We do not have such powers,' Manfred pointed out.

'Then you should damned well be given them.'

'*Ja*, we need them to do our job, and soon we will have them. But in the meantime we must let the snake put its head out of the hole before we chop it off.'

'When will the trouble begin?' Shasa demanded. 'I must make my arrangements to deal with the strikes and disturbances —'

'That is one thing we are not certain of, we do not think the ANC itself has as yet decided —'

'The ANC,' Shasa interjected. 'But surely they aren't behind this? They have been around for forty years or so, and they are dedicated to peaceful negotiations. The leaders are decent men.'

'They were,' Manfred corrected him. 'But the old leaders have been superseded by younger more dangerous men. Men like Mandela and Tambo and others even more evil. As I said before, times change – we must change with them.'

'I had not realized that the threat was so real.'

'Few people do,' Manfred agreed. 'But I assure you *Meneer*, that there is a nest of snakes breeding in our little paradise.'

They walked on in silence, down to the clay-surfaced airstrip where Shasa's blue and silver Mosquito stood. While Shasa climbed into the cockpit and readied the machine for flight, Manfred stood quietly at the wingtip watching him. After Shasa had completed all his checks, he came back to Manfred.

'There is one certain way to defeat this enemy,' Shasa said. 'This new militant ANC.'

'What is that, *Meneer*?'

'To pre-empt their position. Take away from our black people the cause of complaint,' Shasa said.

Manfred was silent, but he stared at Shasa with those implacable yellow eyes. Then Manfred asked, picking his words carefully, 'Are you suggesting that we give the natives political rights, *Meneer*? Do you think that we should give in to the parrot cry of "One man, one vote" – is that what you believe, *Meneer*?' On Shasa's reply rested all Manfred's plans. He wondered if he could have been so wrong in his selection. Any man who believed that could never be a member of the National Party, let alone bear the responsibility of cabinet rank. His relief was intense as Shasa dismissed the idea contemptuously.

'Good Lord, no! That would be the end of us and white civilization in the land. Blacks don't need votes, they need a slice of the pie. We must encourage the emergence of a black middle class, they will be our buffer against the revolutionaries. I never saw a man yet with a full belly and a full wallet who wanted to change things.'

Manfred chuckled. 'That's good, I like it. You are correct, *Meneer*. We need massive wealth to pay for our concept of *apartheid*. It will be expensive, we accept that. That is why we have chosen you. We look to you to find the money to pay for our future.'

Shasa held out his hand and Manfred took it. 'On a personal level, *Meneer*, I am pleased to hear that your wife has taken notice of

119

whatever you said to her. Reports from my special branch indicate that she has given up her liberal left wing associations and is no longer taking any part in political protests.'

'I convinced her how futile they were,' Shasa smiled. 'She has decided to become an archaeologist instead of a Bolshevik.'

They laughed together, and Shasa climbed back into the cockpit. The engines started with a stuttering roar and a mist of blue smoke blew from the exhaust ports, clearing quickly. Shasa lifted a hand in salute and closed the canopy.

Manfred watched him taxi down to the end of the strip then come thundering back, and hurtle aloft in a flash of silver and blue. He shaded his eyes to watch the Mosquito bank away towards the south, and he felt again that strange almost mystic bond of blood and destiny to the man under the perspex canopy as Shasa waved in farewell. Though they had fought and hated each other, their separate people were bound together by a similar bond and at the same time held apart by religion and language and political beliefs.

'We are brothers, you and I,' he thought. 'And beyond the hatred lie the dictates of survival. If you join us, then other Englishmen may follow you, and neither of us can survive alone. Afrikaner and Englishman, we are so bound together that if one goes down, we both drown in the black ocean.'

*　　*　　*

'Garrick has to wear glasses,' Tara said, and poured fresh coffee into Shasa's cup.

'Glasses?' He looked up from his newspaper. 'What do you mean glasses?'

'I mean eye glasses – spectacles. I took him to the optician while you were away. He is shortsighted.'

'But nobody in our family has ever worn glasses.' Shasa looked down the breakfast table at his son, and Garrick lowered his head guiltily. Until that moment he had not realized that he had disgraced the entire family. He had believed the humiliation of spectacles was his alone.

'Glasses.' Shasa's scorn was undisguised. 'While you are having him fitted with glasses, you might as well get them to fit a cork in the end of his whistle to stop him wetting his bed also.'

Sean let out a guffaw and dug an elbow into his brother's ribs, and Garrick was stung into self-defence. 'Gee, Dad, I haven't wet my bed since last Easter,' he declared furiously, red-faced with embarrassment and close to tears of humiliation.

120

Sean made circles with his thumbs and forefingers and peered through them at his brother.

'We will have to call you "Owly Wet Sheets",' he suggested, and as usual Michael came to his brother's defence.

'Owls are wise,' he pointed out reasonably. 'That's why Garry came top in his class this term. Where did you come in yours, Sean?' and Sean glared at him wordlessly. Michael always had a mild but stinging retort.

'All right, gentlemen.' Shasa returned to his newspaper. 'No bloodshed at the breakfast table, please.'

Isabella had been out of the limelight for long enough. Her father had given far too much of his attention to her brothers, and she hadn't yet received her dues. Her father had arrived home late the previous evening, long after she was in bed, and the traditional ceremony of home-coming had not been fully enacted. Certainly he had kissed and pampered her and told her how beautiful she was, but one vital aspect had been neglected, and though she knew it was bad manners to ask, she had contained herself long enough.

'Didn't you even bwing me a pwesent?' she piped, and Shasa lowered his newspaper again.

'A pwesent? Now what on earth is a pwesent?'

'Don't be a silly-billy, Daddy – you know what it is.'

'Bella, you know you mustn't beg for presents,' Tara chided.

'If I don't tell him, Daddy might just forget,' Isabella pointed out reasonably, and made her special angel face at Shasa.

'My goodness gracious me.' Shasa snapped his fingers. 'I did almost forget!' And Isabella hopped her lace-clad bottom up and down on her high stool with excitement.

'You did! You did bring me one!'

'Finish your porridge first,' Tara insisted, and Isabella's spoon clanked industriously on china as she devoured the last of it and scraped the plate clean.

They all trooped though from the breakfast room to Shasa's study.

'I'm the likklest one. I get my pwesent first.' Isabella made up the rules of life as she went along.

'All right, likklest one. Step to the front of the line, please.'

Her face a masterpiece of concentration, Isabella stripped away the wrappings from her gift.

'A doll!' she squeaked and showered kisses upon its bland china face. 'Her name is Oleander, and I love her already.' Isabella was the owner of what was probably one of the world's definitive collections of dolls, but all additions were rapturously received.

When Sean and Garry were handed their long packages, they went

121

still with awe. They knew what they were – they had both of them pleaded long and eloquently for this moment and now that it had arrived, they were reluctant to touch their gifts in case they disappeared in a puff of smoke. Michael hid his disappointment bravely; he had hoped for a book, so secretly he empathized with his mother when she cried with exasperation, 'Oh, Shasa, you haven't given them guns?'

All three rifles were identical. They were Winchester repeaters in .22 calibre, light enough for the boys to handle.

'This is the best present anybody ever gave me.' Sean lifted his weapon out of the cardboard box and stroked the walnut stock lovingly.

'Me too.' Garrick still couldn't bring himself to touch his. He knelt over the open package in the middle of the study floor, staring raptly at the weapon it contained.

'It's super, Dad,' said Michael, holding his rifle awkwardly and his smile was unconvincing.

'Don't use that word, Mickey,' Tara snapped. 'It's so American and vulgar.' But she was angry with Shasa, not Michael.

'Look.' Garry touched his rifle for the first time. 'My name – it's got my own name on it.' He stroked the engraving on the barrel with his fingertip, then looked up at his father with myopic adoration.

'I wish you'd brought them anything but guns,' Tara burst out. 'I asked you not to, Shasa. I hate them.'

'Well, my dear, they must have rifles if they are coming on a hunting safari with me.'

'A safari!' Sean shouted gleefully. 'When?'

'It's time you learned about the bush and the animals.' Shasa put his arm around Sean's shoulders. 'You can't live in Africa without knowing the difference between a scaly anteater and a chacma baboon.'

Garry snatched up his new rifle and went to stand as close to his father's side as he could, so that Shasa could also put his other arm around his shoulders – if he wanted to. However, Shasa was talking to Sean.

'We'll go up to south west in the June hols, take a couple of trucks from the H'ani Mine and drive through the desert until we reach the Okavango Swamps.'

'Shasa, I don't know how you can teach your own children to kill those beautiful animals. I really don't understand it,' Tara said bitterly.

'Hunting is a man's thing,' Shasa agreed. 'You don't have to understand – you don't even have to watch.'

'Can I come, Dad?' Garry asked diffidently, and Shasa glanced at him.

'You'll have to polish up your new specs, so you can see what you're shooting at.' Then he relented. 'Of course you are coming, Garry,' and then he looked across at Michael, standing beside his mother. 'What about you, Mickey? Are you interested?'

Michael glanced apologetically at his mother before he replied softly. 'Gee, thanks Dad. It should be fun.'

'Your enthusiasm is touching,' Shasa grunted and then, 'Very well, gentlemen, all the rifles locked in the gun room, please. Nobody touches them again without my permission and my supervision. We'll have our first shooting practice this evening when I get back home.'

Shasa made a point of getting back to Weltevreden with two hours of daylight in hand, and he took the boys down to the range he had built over which to sight in his own hunting rifles. It was beyond the vineyards and far enough from the stables not to disturb the horses or any of the other livestock.

Sean with the co-ordination of a born athlete, was a natural shot. The light rifle seemed immediately an extension of his body, and within minutes he had mastered the art of controlling his breathing and letting the shot squeeze away without effort. Michael was nearly as good, but his interest wasn't really in it and he lost concentration quickly.

Garry tried so hard that he was trembling, and his face was screwed up with effort. The horn-rimmed spectacles which Tara had fetched from the optician that morning kept sliding down his nose and misting over as he aimed, and it took ten shots for him finally to get one on the target.

'You don't have to pull the trigger so hard, Garry,' Shasa told him with resignation. 'It won't make the bullet go any farther or any faster, I assure you.'

It was almost dark when the four of them got back to the house, and Shasa led them down to the gun room and showed them how to clean their weapons before locking them away.

'Sean and Mickey are ready to have a crack at the pigeons,' Shasa announced, as they trooped upstairs to change for dinner. 'Garry, you will need a little more practice, a pigeon is more likely to die of old age than one of your bullets.'

Sean shouted with laughter. 'Kill them with old age, Garry.'

Michael did not join in. He was imagining one of the lovely blue and pink rock pigeons that nested on the ledge outside his bedroom window, dying in a drift of loose feathers, splattering ruby drops as it fluttered to earth. It made him feel physically sick, but he knew his father expected it of him.

That evening as usual the children came one at a time to say

123

goodnight to Shasa as he was tying his black bow tie. Isabella was first.

'I'm not going to sleep a wink until you come home tonight, Daddy,' she warned him. 'I'm just going to lie all by myself in the dark.'

Sean came next. 'You are the best Dad in the world,' he said as they shook hands. Kissing was for sissies.

'Will you let me have that in writing?' Shasa asked solemnly.

It was Michael who was always the most difficult to answer. 'Dad, do animals and birds hurt a lot when you shoot them?'

'Not if you learn to shoot straight,' Shasa assured him. 'But, Mickey, you have too much imagination. You can't go through life worrying about animals and other people all the time.'

'Why not, Dad?' Michael asked softly, and Shasa glanced at his wristwatch to cover his exasperation.

'We have to be at Kelvin Grove by eight. Do you mind if we go into that some other time, Mickey?'

Garrick came last. He stood shyly in the doorway of Shasa's dressing-room, but his voice shook with determination as he announced, 'I'm going to learn to be a crack shot, like Sean. You'll be proud of me one day, Dad. I promise you.'

Garrick left his parents' wing and crossed to the nursery. Nanny stopped him at Isabella's door.

'She's asleep already, Master Garry.'

In Michael's room they discussed the promised safari, but Mickey's attention kept wandering back to the book in his hands, and after a few minutes Garry left him to it.

He looked into Sean's room cautiously, ready to take flight if his elder brother showed any signs of becoming playful. One of Sean's favourite expressions of fraternal affection was known as a chestnut and consisted of a painful knuckling of Garry's prominent ribcage. However, this evening Sean was hanging backwards over his bed, heels propped on the wall and the back of his head almost touching the floor, a Superman comic book held at arm's length above his face.

'Goodnight, Sean,' Garry said.

'Shazam!' said Sean without lowering the comic book.

Garrick retreated thankfully to his own room and locked the door. Then he went to stand before the mirror and regard the reflection of his new horn-rimmed spectacles.

'I hate them,' he whispered bitterly, and when he removed them they left red indentations on the bridge of his nose. He went down on his knees, removed the skirting board under the built-in wardrobe and reached into the secret recess beyond. Nobody, not even Sean, had discovered this hiding place.

Carefully he withdrew the precious package. It had cost him eight

124

weeks of his accumulated pocket money, but was worth every penny. It had arrived in a plain wrapper with a personal letter from Mr Charles Atlas himself. 'Dear Garrick,' the letter had begun, and Garry had been overcome with the great man's condescension.

He laid out the course on his bed and stripped to his pyjama pants as he revised the lessons.

'Dynamic tension,' he whispered aloud, and he took up his stance before the mirror. As he began the sequence of exercises he kept time with the soft chant of, 'More and more in every way, I'm getting better every day.'

When he finished he was sweating heavily but he made an arm and studied it minutely.

'They *are* bigger,' he tried to put aside his doubts as he poked the little walnut of muscle that popped out of his straining biceps, 'they really are!'

He stowed the course back in its hidy-hole and replaced the skirting board. Then he took his raincoat from the wardrobe and spread it on the bare boards.

Garrick had read with admiration how Frederick Selous, the famous African hunter, had toughened himself as a boy by sleeping uncovered on the floor in winter. He switched out the light and settled down on the raincoat. It was going to be a long uncomfortable night, he knew from experience, already the floor boards were like iron, but the raincoat would prevent Sean detecting any nocturnal spillage when he made his morning inspection, and Garrick was certain that his asthma had improved since he had stopped sleeping on a soft mattress with a warm eiderdown over him.

'I'm getting better every day,' he whispered, closing his eyes tightly and willing himself to ignore the cold and the hardness of the floor. 'And then one day Dad will be proud of me – just like he is of Sean.'

*　　*　　*

'I thought your speech this evening was very good, even for you,' Tara told him, and Shasa glanced at her with surprise. She had not paid him a compliment for a long time now.

'Thank you, my dear.'

'I sometimes forget what a gifted person you are,' she went on. 'It's just that you make it seem so easy and natural.' He was so moved that he might have reached across to caress her, but she was leaning away from him and the Hooper coachwork of the Rolls was too wide for him to reach her.

'I must say, you look absolutely stunning this evening,' he compromised with a matching compliment, but as he had expected, she dismissed it with a grimace.

'Are you really going to take the boys on safari?'

'My dear, we have to let them make up their own minds about life. Sean will love it, but I'm not too sure about Mickey.' Shasa replied, and she noticed that he hadn't mentioned Garrick.

'Well, if you are determined, then I'm going to take advantage of the boys' absence. I have been invited to join the archaeological dig at the Sundi caves.'

'But you are a novice,' he was surprised. 'That's an important site. Why would they invite you?'

'Because I offered to contribute two thousand pounds to the cost of the dig, that's why.'

'I see, this is straight blackmail.' He chuckled sardonically as he saw the reason for her flattery. 'All right, it's a deal. I'll give you a cheque tomorrow. How long will you be away?'

'I'm not sure.' But she thought, 'as long as I can be close to Moses Gama.'

The site at Sundi Caves was only an hour's drive from the house at Rivonia. She reached under the fur coat and touched her stomach. It would begin to show soon – she had to find excuses to keep away from the eyes of the family. Her father and Shasa would not notice, she was sure of that, but Centaine de Thiry Courtney-Malcomess had eyes like a hawk.

'I presume that my mother has agreed to care for Isabella while you are away,' Shasa was saying, and while she nodded, her heart was singing.

'Moses, I'm coming back to you – both of us are coming back, to you, my darling.'

*   *   *

Whenever Moses Gama came to Drake's Farm it was like a king returning to his own realm after a successful crusade. Within minutes of his arrival, the word was flashed almost telepathically through the vast sprawling black township, and a sense of expectancy hung over it, as palpable as the smoke from ten thousand cooking fires.

Moses usually arrived with his half brother, Hendrick Tabaka, in the butcher's delivery van. Hendrick owned a chain of a dozen butcher shops in the black townships along the Witwatersrand, so the signwriting on the side of the van was authentic. In sky blue and crimson, it declared:

PHUZA MUHLE BUTCHERY
BEST MEAT AT BEST PRICES

From the vernacular 'Phuza Muhle' translated as 'Eat Well' and

126

the van provided a perfect cover for Hendrick Tabaka wherever he went. Whether he was genuinely delivering slaughtered carcasses to his butcheries or goods to his general dealer stores, or was engaged in less conventional business: the distribution of illicitly brewed liquor, the notorious *skokiaan* or township dynamite, or ferrying his girls to their places of business nearer the compounds that housed the thousands of black contract workers of the gold-mines so that they could briefly assist them in relieving their monastic existence, or whether he was on the business of the African Mineworkers Union, that close-knit and powerful brotherhood whose existence the white government refused to acknowledge – the blue and red van was the perfect vehicle. When he was at the wheel, Hendrick wore a peaked driver's cap and a khaki tunic with cheap brass buttons. He drove sedately and with meticulous attention to all the rules of the road, so that in twenty years he had never been stopped by the police.

When he drove the van into Drake's Farm, with Moses Gama sitting in the passenger seat beside him, they were entering their own stronghold. This was where they had established themselves when together they had arrived from the wastelands of the Kalahari twenty years before. Although they were sons of the same father, they had been different in almost every way. Moses had been young and tall and marvellously handsome, while Hendrick was years older, a great bull of a man with a bald, scarred head and gapped and broken teeth.

Moses was clever and quick, self-educated to a high standard, charismatic and a leader of men, while Hendrick was the faithful lieutenant, accepting his younger brother's authority and carrying out his orders swiftly and ruthlessly. Though Moses Gama had conceived the idea of building up a business empire, it was Hendrick who had made the dream a reality. Once he was shown what to do, Hendrick Tabaka was as much a bulldog in tenacity as he was in appearance.

For Hendrick, what they had built between them, the business enterprises both illicit and legitimate, the trade union and its private army of enforcers known and dreaded throughout the compounds where the mineworkers lived and through the black townships as 'The Buffaloes', all these were an end in themselves. But for Moses Gama it was different. What they had achieved thus far was only the first stage on his quest for something so much greater that although he had explained it many times to Hendrick, his brother could not truly grasp the enormity of Moses Gama's vision.

In the twenty years since they had arrived here, Drake's Farm had changed entirely. In those early days it had been a small squatters' encampment, hanging like a parasite tick on the body of the huge

127

complex of gold-mines that made up the central Witwatersrand. It had been a collection of squalid hovels, built of scrap lumber and wattle poles and old iron sheets, flattened paraffin cans and tarpaper on the bleak open veld, a place of open drains and cesspools, lacking reticulated water or electricity, without schools or clinics or police protection, not even recognized as human habitation by the white city fathers in Johannesburg's town hall.

It was only after the war that the Transvaal Divisional Council had decided to recognize reality and to expropriate the land from the absentee landowners. They had declared the entire three thousand acres an official township set aside for black occupation under the Group Areas Act. They had retained the original name, Drake's Farm, for its picturesque connotations to old Johannesburg, unlike the more mundane origin of the nearby Soweto, which was merely an acronym for South Western Townships. Soweto already housed over half a million blacks, while Drake's Farm was home to less than half that number.

The authorities had fenced off the new township and covered the greater part of it with monotonous lines of small three-roomed cottages, each identical except for the number stencilled on the cement brick front wall. Crowded close together and separated by narrow lanes with dusty untarred surfaces, the flat roofs in galvanized corrugated iron shone like ten thousand mirrors in the brilliant highveld sunlight.

In the centre of the township were the administrative buildings where, under a handful of white municipal supervisors, the black clerks collected the rents and regulated the basic services of reticulated water and refuse removal. Beyond this Orwellian vision of bleak and soulless order, lay the original section of Drake's Farm, its hovels and shebeens and whorehouses – and it was here that Hendrick Tabaka still lived.

As he drove the delivery van slowly through the new section of the township, the people came out of their cottages to watch them pass. They were mostly women and children, for the men left each morning early, commuting to their employment in the city and returning only after nightfall. When they recognized Moses, the women clapped and ululated shrilly, the greeting for a tribal chief, and the children ran beside the van, dancing and laughing with excitement at being so close to the great man.

They drove slowly past the cemetery where the untidy mounds of earth were like a vast mole run. On some of the mounds crudely wrought crosses had been set while on the others raggedy flags fluttered in the wind and offerings of food and broken household utensils and weirdly carved totems had been placed to placate the

128

spirits, Christian symbols side by side with those of the animists and witch-worshippers. They went down into the old township, into the higgledy-piggledy lanes, where the stalls of the witchdoctors stood side by side with those offering food and trade cloth and used clothes and stolen radios. Where the chickens and pigs rooted in the muddy ruts of the road and naked toddlers with only a string of beads around their fat little tummies defecated between the stalls and the young whores strutted their wares and the stink and the noise were wondrous.

This was a world no white men ever entered, and where even the black municipal police came only on invitation and under sufferance. It was Hendrick Tabaka's world, where his wives kept nine houses for him in the centre of the old quarter. They were sturdy well-built houses of burned brick, but the exteriors were left deliberately shabby and uncared for, so they blended into the general squalor. Hendrick had learned long ago not to draw attention to himself and his material possessions. Each of his nine wives had her own home, built in a circle around Hendrick's slightly more imposing house, and he had not limited himself to women of his own Ovambo tribe. His wives were Pondo and Xhosa and Fingo and Basuto, but not Zulu. Hendrick would never trust a Zulu in his bed.

They all came out to greet him and his famous brother as Hendrick parked the van in the lean-to at the back of his own house. The obeisances of the women and their soft clapping of respect ushered the men into the living-room of Hendrick's house where two plush chairs covered with tanned leopard skins were set like thrones at the far end. When the brothers were seated the two youngest wives brought pitchers of millet beer, freshly brewed, thick as gruel, tart and effervescent and cold from the paraffin refrigerator, and when they had refreshed themselves, Hendrick's sons came in to greet their father and pay their respects to their uncle.

The sons were many, for Hendrick Tabaka was a lusty man and bred all his wives regularly each year. However, not all his elder sons were present today. Those of them whom Hendrick considered unworthy had been sent back to the country to tend the herds of cattle and goats that were part of Hendrick's wealth. The more promising boys worked in the butchery shops, the general dealers or the shebeens, while two of them, those especially gifted with intelligence, were law students at Fort Hare, the black university in the little town of Alice in the eastern Cape.

Only Hendrick's younger boys were here to kneel respectfully before him, and of these there were two whom Moses Gama looked upon with particular pleasure. They were the twin sons of one of Hendrick's Xhosa wives, a woman of unusual accomplishments.

Apart from being a dutiful wife and a breeder of sons, she was an accomplished dancer and singer, an amusing story-teller, a person of shrewd common sense and intelligence, and a noted *sangoma*, a healer and occult doctor with sometimes uncanny powers of pre-science and divination. Her twins had inherited most of her gifts together with their father's robust physique and some of their uncle Moses' fine features.

At their birth, Hendrick had asked Moses to name them, and he had chosen their names from his treasured copy of Macaulay's *History of England*. Of all his nephews they were his favourites, and he smiled now as they knelt before him. They were already thirteen years old, Moses realized.

'I see you, Wellington Tabaka,' he greeted first the one and then the other. 'I see you, Raleigh Tabaka.'

They were not identical twins. Wellington was the taller lad, lighter-skinned, toffee-coloured against Raleigh's mulberry-stain black. His features had the same Nilotic cast as Moses' own, while Raleigh was more negroid, flat-nosed and thick-lipped, his body heavier and squatter.

'What books have you read since we last met?' Moses changed into English, forcing them to reply in the same language. 'Words are spears, they are weapons with which to defend yourself and with which to attack your enemies. English words have the sharpest blades, without them you will be warriors disarmed,' he had explained to them, and now he listened attentively to their halting replies in that language.

However, he noted the improvements in their command of the language and remarked on it. 'It is still not good enough, but you will learn to speak it better at Waterford,' and both boys looked uncomfortable. Moses had arranged for them to write the entrance examination for this elite multi-racial school across the border in the independent black kingdom of Swaziland, and the twins had both passed and been accepted and now were dreading the day not far away when they would be uprooted from this comfortable familiar world of theirs and packed off into the unknown. In South Africa all education was strictly segregated, and it was the declared policy of the minister of Bantu affairs, Dr Hendrik Verwoerd, not to educate black children to the point of discontentment. He had told parliament quite frankly that education for blacks should not conflict with the government policy of *apartheid* and should not be of such a standard as to evoke in the black pupil expectations which could never be fulfilled. The annual expenditure by the state on each white pupil was £60 while that on a black student was £9 per annum. Those black parents who could afford it, the chiefs and small businessmen,

130

sent their children out of the country to be educated, and Waterford was a favourite choice.

The twins escaped from the daunting presence of their father and uncle with relief, but their mother was waiting for them in the yard beside the blue and crimson van, and with a sharp inclination of her head ordered them into her own parlour.

The room was a sorceress's lair from which the twins were usually barred, and now they crept in with even more trepidation than they had entered their father's house. Against the far wall stood their mother's gods and goddesses carved in native woods and dressed in feathers and skins and beads, with eyes of ivory and mother-of-pearl, and bared teeth of dog and baboon. They were a terrifying assembly, and the twins shivered and dared not look directly upon them.

Before the family idols were arranged offerings of food and small coins, and from the other walls hung all the gruesome accoutrements of their mother's craft, gourds and clay pots of ointments and medicines, bundles of dried herbs, snake skins and mummified iguana lizards, bones and baboon skulls, glass jars of hippopotamus and lion fat, musk of crocodile, and other nameless substances which festered and bubbled and stank so foully that it made the teeth ache in their jaws.

'You wore the charms I gave you?' Kuzawa, their mother, asked. She was incongruously handsome in the midst of her unholy and hideous tools and medicines, full-faced and glossy-skinned with very white teeth and liquid gazelle eyes. Her limbs were long and gleamed with secret and magical ointments and her breasts under the necklaces of ivory beads and charms were big and firm as wild Kalahari melons.

In response to her question, the twins nodded vehemently, too overcome to speak, and unbuttoned their shirts. The charms were hung around their necks, each on a thin leather thong. They were the horns of the little grey duiker, the open ends sealed with gum arabic, and Kuzawa had taken all the twelve years of their lives to assemble the magical potion that was contained in each of them. It was made up of samples of all the bodily excretions of Hendrick Tabaka, the father of the twins, his faeces and urine, his spittle and nasal mucus, his sweat and his semen, the wax from his ears and the blood from his veins, his tears and his vomit. With these, Kuzawa had mixed the dried skin from the soles of his feet, the clippings of his nails, the shavings of his beard and his pate and pubes, the lashes of his eyes plucked in his sleep, and the crusted scabs and pus from his wounds. Then she had added herbs and fats of wonderful efficacy, and spoken the words of power over them and finally, to make the charm infallible, she had paid a vast sum to one of the grave-robbers

131

who specialized in such procurements to bring her the liver of an infant drowned at birth by its own mother.

All these ingredients she had sealed in the two little duiker horns, and the twins were never allowed into their father's presence except that they wore them hung around their necks. Now Kuzawa retrieved the two charms from her sons. They were far too precious to leave in the children's possession. She smiled as she weighed them in the smooth pink palms of her delicately shaped hands. They had been worth all the expense and the patience and the meticulous application of her skills to create.

'Did your father smile when he saw you?' she asked.

'He smiled like the rise of the sun,' Raleigh replied, and Kuzawa nodded happily.

'And were his words kind, did he make enquiry of you fondly?' she insisted.

'When he spoke to us he purred like a lion at meat,' Wellington whispered, still intimidated by his surroundings. 'And he asked us how we fared at school, and he commended us when we told him.'

'It is the charms that have ensured his favour,' Kuzawa smiled contentedly. 'As long as you wear them, your father will prefer you over all his other children.'

She took the two little buckhorns and went to kneel before the central carved figure in the array of idols, a fearsome image with a headdress of lion's mane that housed the spirit of her dead grandfather.

'Guard them well, oh venerable ancestor,' she whispered, as she hung them around the neck of the image. 'Keep their powers strong until they are needed once again.'

They were safer there than in the deepest vault of the white man's banks. No human being, and only the most powerful of the dark ones, would dare challenge her grandfather's spirit for possession of the charms, for he was the ultimate guardian.

Now she turned back to the twins, took their hands and led them out of her lair into the family kitchen next door, putting aside the mantle of the witch and assuming that of the loving mother as she passed through the door and closed it behind her.

She fed the twins, bowls piled with fluffy white maize meal and butter beans and stew swimming with delicious fat, food that befitted the family of a rich and powerful man. And while they ate, she tended them lovingly, questioning and chaffing them, pressing more food upon them, her dark eyes glowing with pride, and finally reluctantly letting them go.

They fled from her, delirious with excitement, into the narrow fetid lanes of the old quarter. Here they were entirely at their ease.

132

The men and women smiled and called greetings and pleasantries as they passed and laughed delightedly at their repartee for they were the favourites of all, and their father was Hendrick Tabaka.

Old Mama Nginga, fat and silver-haired, sitting at the front door of the shebeen that she ran for Hendrick, shouted after them, 'Where are you going, my little ones?'

'On secret business we cannot discuss,' Wellington shouted back, and Raleigh added:

'But next year our secret business will be with you, old mama. We will drink all your *skokiaan* and stab all your girls.'

Mama Nginga wobbled with delight, and the girls sitting in the windows shrieked with laughter. 'He is the cub of the lion, that one,' they told each other.

As they scurried through the lanes, they called out and from the hovels and the shanties of the old quarter and from the new brick cottages that the white government had built, their comrades hurried out to join them, until there were fifty or more lads of their own age following them. Some of them carried long bundles, carefully wrapped and bound up with rawhide thongs.

At the far end of the township the high fence had been cut, the gap concealed from casual scrutiny by a clump of scrub. The boys climbed through the gap and in the plantation of bluegums beyond, they gathered in an excited jabbering cluster and stripped off the shabby western European clothing they wore. They were un-circumcised, their penises although beginning to develop were still surmounted by the little wrinkled caps of skin. In a few years' time they would all of them go into the initiation class and endure the ordeal of the isolation and hardship, and the agony of the blade together. This, even more than their tribal blood, bound them to-gether; all their lives they would be comrades of the circumcision knife.

They set aside their clothing carefully – any losses would have to be accounted for to angry parents – and then naked, they gathered around the precious rolls and watched impatiently as they were opened by their acknowledged captains Wellington and Raleigh Tabaka, and each of them were issued with the uniform of the Xhosa warrior – not the true regalia, the cow-tails and rattles and headdress – those were for circumcised *amadoda* only. These were childish re-plicas, merely skins of dogs and cats, the strays and pariahs of the township, but they donned them as proudly as if they were genuine, and bound their upper arms and thighs and foreheads with strips of fur, and then took up their weapons.

Again these were not the warriors' long-bladed assegais, but were merely the traditional fighting-sticks. However, even in the hands of

133

these children the long limber staves were formidable weapons. With a stick in each hand they were immediately transformed into shrieking demons. They brandished and swung the staves, using a practised wrist action that made them hiss and sing and whistle, they rattled them together, crossing them to form a guard against which the blows of their peers clattered, and they leapt and cavorted and danced, aiming blows at each other, until Raleigh Tabaka blew a sharp fluting command on his buckhorn whistle, and they fell in behind him in a compact, disciplined column.

He led them away. In a swaying stylized trot, fighting-sticks held high, singing and humming the battle chants of their tribe, they left the plantation and went out into the open undulating veld. The grass was knee-high and brown, and the chocolate red earth showed through it in raw patches. The ground fell away gently to a narrow stream, its rocky bed enclosed by steep banks and then climbed again to meet the pale sapphire of the highveld sky.

Even as they started down the slope, the clean sweep of the far skyline was interrupted, a long line of waving headdresses showed above it, and then another band of lads appeared, clad like them in loincloths of skin, legs and arms and torsos bare. Carrying their fighting-sticks high, they paused along the crest, and as they saw each other, both bands gave tongue like hounds taking the scent.

'Zulu jackals,' howled Raleigh Tabaka, and his hatred was so intense that a fine sheen of sweat burst out upon his brow. For as long and as far back as his tribal memory reached, this had been the enemy; his hatred was in his blood, deep and atavistic. History did not record how often this scene had been repeated, how many thousands of times over the centuries armed impis of Xhosa and Zulu had faced each other thus; all that was remembered was the heat of the battle and the blood and the hatred.

Raleigh Tabaka leapt as high as the shoulder of his brother beside him, and screamed wildly, his treacherous voice breaking into a girlish squeak at the end.

'I am thirsty. Give me Zulu blood to drink!' and his warriors leapt and screamed.

'Give us Zulu blood!'

The threats and insults and challenges were flung back at them from the opposite ridge, carried to them on the wind. Then spontaneously both impis started down, singing and prancing into the shallow valley, until from the steep red banks they faced each other across the narrow streambed, and their captains strode forward to exchange more insults.

The Zulu *induna* was a lad the same age as the twins. He attended the same class as they did in the government secondary school in the

134

township. His name was Joseph Dinizulu, and he was as tall as Wellington and as broad across the chest as Raleigh. His name and his strutting arrogance reminding the world that he was a princeling of the royal house of Zulu.

'Hey, you eaters of hyena dung,' he called. 'We smelt you from a thousand paces against the wind. The smell of Xhosa makes even the vultures puke.'

Raleigh leapt high, turning in the air and lifting the skirts of his loincloth to expose his buttocks. 'I cleanse the air of the Zulu stench with a good clean fart!' he shouted. 'Sniff that, you jackal-lovers,' and he blew a raspberry so loud and long that the Zulus facing him hissed murderously and rattled their fighting-sticks.

'Your fathers were women, your mothers were monkeys,' Joseph Dinizulu cried, scratching his own armpits. 'Your grandfathers were baboons,' he imitated a simian lollop, 'and your grandmothers were —' Raleigh interrupted this recital of his ancestral line with a blast on the buckhorn whistle and leapt from the bank into the streambed. He landed on his feet, light as a cat, and with a bound was across. He went up the far bank so fast that Joseph Dinizulu, who had expected the exchange of pleasantries to last a little longer, fell back before his onslaught.

A dozen of the other Xhosa lads had responded to his whistle and followed him across, and Raleigh's furious attack had won a bridgehead for them on the far bank. They bunched up behind him with sticks hissing and singing, and drove into the centre of the opposing impi. The battle lust was on Raleigh Tabaka. He was invincible, his arms tireless, his hands and wrists so cunning that his sticks seemed to have separate life, finding the weak places in the guards of the Zulus who opposed him, thudding on flesh, cracking on bone, cutting open skin so that soon their sticks shone wet with blood and little droplets of it flew in the sunlight.

It seemed nothing could touch him, until abruptly something crashed into his ribs just below his raised right arm, and he gasped with pain and the sudden awareness of his own humanity. For a minute there he had been a warrior god, but suddenly he was a small boy, almost at the end of his strength, hurting very badly, and so tired that he could not mouth another challenge while before him danced Joseph Dinizulu, who seemed to have grown six inches in as many seconds. Again his fighting-stick whistled in, aimed at Raleigh's head, and only with a desperate defence he deflected it. Raleigh fell back a pace and looked around him.

He should have known better than to attack a Zulu so boldly. They were the most treacherous and sly of all adversaries, and the stratagem of encirclement was always their master-stroke. Chaka

135

Zulu, the mad dog who had founded this tribe of wolves, had called the manoeuvre 'the Horns of the Bull'. The horns surrounded the enemy while the chest crushed him to death.

Joseph Dinizulu had not fallen back out of fear or surprise, it was his instinctive cunning, and Raleigh had led his dozen stalwarts into the Zulu trap. They were alone, none of the others had followed them across the stream. Over the heads of the encircling Zulus he could see them on the far bank, and Wellington Tabaka, his twin brother, stood at their head, silent and immobile.

'Wellington!' he screamed, his voice breaking with exhaustion and terror. 'Help us! We have the Zulu dog by the testicles. Come across and stab him in the chest!'

That was all he had time for. Joseph Dinizulu was on him again and each stroke of his seemed more powerful than the last. Raleigh's chest was agony, and then another blow crashed through his guard and caught him across the shoulder, paralysing his right arm to the fingertips, and the stick flew from his grasp.

'Wellington!' he screamed again. 'Help us!' and all around him his men were going down, some of them beaten to their knees, others simply dropping their sticks and cowering in the dust, screaming for mercy while the Zulu boys crowded in with their sticks rising and falling, the blows flogging into soft flesh, the Zulu war cries rising in jubilant chorus like hounds crowding in to rend the hares.

'Wellington!' He had one last glimpse of his brother across the stream and then a blow caught him on the forehead just above his eye, and he felt the skin split as warm blood poured down his face. Just before it blinded him he caught a last glimpse of Joseph Dinizulu's face, crazy with blood lust, and then his legs collapsed under him and he flopped face-first into the dirt, while the blows still thudded across his back and shoulders.

He must have lost consciousness for a moment, for when he rolled on to his side and wiped the blood from his eyes with the back of his hand, he saw that the Zulus had crossed the stream in a phalanx and that the remnants of his impi were racing away in wild panic towards the bluegum plantation pursued by Dinizulu's men.

He tried to push himself upright, but his senses reeled and darkness filled his head, as he toppled once again. When next he came to, he was surrounded by Zulus, jeering and mocking, covering him with insults. This time he managed to sit up, but then the tumult around him quieted and was replaced by an expectant hush. He looked up and Joseph Dinizulu pushed his way through the ranks and sneered down at him.

'Bark, Xhosa dog,' he ordered. 'Let us hear you bark and whine for mercy.'

136

Groggy, but defiant, Raleigh shook his head, and pain flared under his skull at the movement.

Joseph Dinizulu placed a bare foot on his chest and shoved hard. He was too weak to resist and he toppled over on his back. Joseph Dinizulu stood over him, and lifted the front of his loincloth. With his other hand he drew back his foreskin exposing the pink glans, and he directed a hissing stream of urine into Raleigh's face.

'Drink that, you Xhosa dog,' he laughed. It was hot and ammoniacal and burned like acid in the open wound on his scalp – and Raleigh's rage and humiliation and hatred filled all his soul.

* * *

'My brother, it is only very seldom that I try to dissuade you from something on which you have set your mind.' Hendrick Tabaka sat on the leopard-skin covering of his chair, leaning forward earnestly with his elbows on his knees. 'It is not the marriage in itself, you know how I have always urged you to take a wife, many wives, and get yourself sons – it is not the idea of a wife I disapprove of, it is this Zulu baggage that makes me lie awake at night. There are ten million other nubile young women in this land – why must you choose a Zulu? I would rather you took a black mamba into your bed.'

Moses Gama chuckled softly. 'Your concern for me proves your love.' Then he became serious. 'Zulu is the largest tribe in southern Africa. Numbers alone would make them important, but add to that their aggressive and warlike spirit, and you will see that nothing will change in this land without Zulu. If I can form an alliance with that tribe, then all the dreams I have dreamed need not be in vain.'

Hendrick sighed, and grunted and shook his head.

'Come Hendrick, you have spoken with them. Have you not?' Moses insisted, and reluctantly Hendrick nodded.

'I sat four days at the kraal of Sangane Dinizulu, son of Mbejane who was the son of Gubi, who was the son of Dingaan, who was the brother of Chaka Zulu himself. He deems himself a prince of Zulu, which he is at pains to point out means "The Heavens" and he lives in grand style on the land that his old master, General Sean Courtney, left him on the hills above Ladyburg, where he keeps many wives and three hundred head of fat cattle.'

'All this I know, my brother,' Moses interrupted. 'Tell me about the girl.'

Hendrick frowned. He liked to begin a story at the beginning and work through it, sparing no detail, until he reached the end.

'The girl,' he repeated. 'That old Zulu rogue whines that she is the moon of his night and the sun of his day, no daughter has ever been

137

loved as he loves her – and he could never allow her to marry any man but a Zulu chief.' Hendrick sighed. 'Day after day I heard the virtues of this Zulu she-jackal recounted, how beautiful she is, how talented, how she is a nurse at the government hospital, how she comes from a long line of son-bearing wives —' Hendrick broke off and spat with disgust. 'It took three days before he mentioned what had been on his mind from the first minute – the *lobola*, the bride price,' and Hendrick threw up his hands in a gesture of exasperation. 'All Zulus are thieves and dung-eaters.'

'How much?' Moses asked with a smile. 'How much did he need to compensate him for a marriage outside the tribe?'

'Five hundred head of prime cattle, all cows in calf, none older than three years,' Hendrick scowled with outrage. 'All Zulus are thieves and he claims to be a prince, which makes him a prince of thieves.'

'Naturally you agreed to his first price?' Moses asked.

'Naturally I argued for two more days.'

'The final price?'

'Two hundred head,' Hendrick sighed. 'Forgive me, my brother. I tried, but the old dog of a Zulu was like a rock. It was his very lowest price for the moon of his night.'

Moses Gama leaned back in his chair, and thought about it. It was an enormous price. Prime cattle were worth £50 the head, but unlike his brother, Moses Gama had no yen for money other than as a means to procure an end.

'Ten thousand pounds?' he asked softly. 'Do we have that much?'

'It will hurt. I will ache for a year as though I have been whipped with a sjambok,' Hendrick grumbled. 'Do you realize just how much else a man could buy with ten thousand pounds, my brother? I could get you at least ten Xhosa maidens, pretty as sugar birds and plump as guinea fowl, each with her maidenhead attested by the most reliable midwife —'

'Ten Xhosa maidens would not bring the Zulu people within my reach,' Moses cut him off. 'I need Victoria Dinizulu.'

'The *lobola* is not the only price demanded,' Hendrick told him. 'There is more.'

'What else?'

'The girl is a Christian. If you take her, there will be no others. She will be your only wife, my brother, and listen to a man who has paid for wisdom in the heavy coin of experience. Three wives are the very minimum a man needs for contentment. Three wives are so busy competing with one another for their husband's favour, that a man can relax. Two wives are better than one. However, a single wife, a one and only wife, can sour the food in your belly and frost

138

your hair with silver. Let this Zulu wench go to someone who deserves her, another Zulu.'

'Tell her father that we will pay the price he asks and that we agree to his terms. Tell him also that if he is a prince, then we expect him to provide a marriage feast that befits a princess. We expect a marriage that will be the talk of Zululand from the Drakensberg Mountains to the ocean. I want every chieftain and elder of the tribe there to see me wed, I want every counseller and *induna*, I want the king of the Zulus himself to come and when they are all assembled, I will speak to them.'

'You might as well talk to a troop of baboons. A Zulu is too proud and too full of hatred to listen to sense.'

'You are wrong, Hendrick Tabaka.' Moses laid his hand on his brother's arm. 'We are not proud enough, nor do we hate enough. What pride we do have, the little hatred that we do have, is misspent and ill-directed. We waste it on each other, on other black men. If all the tribes of this land took all their pride and all their hatred and turned it on the white oppressor – then how could he resist us? This is what I will talk about when I speak at my wedding feast. This is what I have to teach the people. It is for this that we are forging *Umkhonto we Sizwe*, the Spear of the Nation'.

They were silent awhile. The depth of his brother's vision, the terrible power of his commitment, always awed Hendrick.

'It will be as you wish,' he agreed at last. 'When do you wish the wedding to take place?'

'On the full moon of mid-winter.' Moses did not hesitate. 'That will be the week before our campaign of defiance begins.'

Again they were silent, until Moses roused himself. 'It is settled then. Is there anything else we should discuss before we take the evening meal?'

'Nothing.' Hendrick rose to his feet and was about to call his women to bring their food, when he remembered. 'Ah. There is one other thing. The white woman, the woman who was with you at Rivonia – do you know the one?'

Moses nodded. 'Yes, the Courtney woman.'

'That is the one. She has sent a message. She wishes to see you again.'

'Where is she?'

'She is close by, at a place called Sundi Caves. She has left a telephone number for you. She says it is an important matter.'

Moses Gama was clearly annoyed. 'I told her not to try and contact me,' he said. 'I warned her of the dangers.' He stood up and paced the floor. 'Unless she learns discipline and self-control, she will be of no value to the struggle. White women are like that, spoiled and disobedient and self-indulgent. She must be trained —'

Moses broke off and went to the window. Something in the yard had caught his attention, and he called out sharply.

'Wellington! Raleigh! Come here, both of you.'

A few seconds later the two boys shuffled self-consciously into the room, and stood just inside the door, hanging their heads guiltily.

'Raleigh, what has happened to you?' Hendrick demanded angrily. The twins had changed their furs and loincloths for their ordinary clothing, but the gash in Raleigh's forehead was still weeping through the wad of grubby rags he had strapped on it. There were speckles of blood on his shirt, and the swelling had closed one eye.

'*Baba!*' Wellington started to explain. 'It was not our fault. We were set upon by the Zulus.' And Raleigh darted a look of contempt at him before he contradicted his twin.

'We arranged a faction fight with them. It went well, until some of us ran away and left the others,' Raleigh raised his hand to his injured head. 'There are cowards even amongst the Xhosa,' he said, and again glanced at his twin. Wellington stood silent.

'Next time fight harder and show more cunning,' Hendrick Tabaka dismissed them and when they scurried from the room he turned to Moses. 'Do you see, my brother. Even with the children, what hope do you have of changing it?'

'The hope is with the children,' Moses told him. 'Like monkeys, you can train them to do anything. It is the old ones who are difficult to change.'

*   *   *

Tara Courtney parked her shabby old Packard on the edge of the mountain drive and stood for a few seconds looking down on the city of Cape Town spread below her. The south-easter was whipping the waters of Table Bay to cream.

She left the car and walked slowly along the verge, pretending to admire the flush of wild flowers which painted the rocky slope above her. At the head of the slope the grey rock bastion of the mountain rose sheer to the heavens, and she stopped walking and tilted her head back to look up at it. The clouds were driving over the top, creating the illusion that the wall of rock was falling.

Once again she darted a glance along the road up which she had driven. It was still empty. She was not being followed. The police must have finally lost interest in her. It was weeks since last she had been aware of being tailed.

Her aimless behaviour altered and she returned to the Packard and took a small picnic basket from the boot, then she walked quickly back to the concrete building that housed the lower cable

140

station. She ran up the stairs and paid for a return ticket just as the attendant opened the doors at the end of the waiting room, and the small party of other passengers trooped out to the gondola and crowded into it.

The crimson car started with a jerk and they rose swiftly, dangling below the silvery thread of the cable. The other passengers were exclaiming with delight as the spreading panorama of ocean and rock and city opened below them, and Tara inspected them surreptitiously. Within a few minutes she was convinced that none of them were plain-clothes members of the special branch and she relaxed and turned her attention to the magnificent view.

The gondola was climbing steeply, rising almost vertically up the face of the cliff. The rock had weathered into almost geometrical cubes, so that they seemed to be the ancient building blocks of a giant's castle. They passed a party of rock-climbers roped together inching their way hand over hand up the sheer face. Tara imagined being out there, clinging to the rock with the empty drop sucking at her heels, and vertigo made her sway dizzily. She had to clutch the handrail to steady herself, and when the gondola docked at the top station on the brink of the thousand-foot-high cliff, she escaped from it thankfully.

In the little tearoom, built to resemble an alpine chalet, Molly was waiting for her at one of the tables and she jumped up when she saw her friend.

Tara rushed to her and embraced her. 'Oh Molly, my dear dear Molly, I have missed you so.'

After a few moments they drew apart, slightly embarrassed by their own display and the smiles of the other teashop customers.

'I don't want to sit still,' Tara told her. 'I'm just bursting with excitement. Come on, let's walk. I've brought some sandwiches and a Thermos.'

They left the tearoom and wandered along the path that skirted the precipice. In mid-week there were very few hikers on the mountain, and before they had gone a hundred yards they were alone.

'Tell me about all my old friends in the Black Sash,' Tara ordered. 'I want to know everything you have been doing. How is Derek and how are the children? Who is running my clinic now? Have you been there recently? Oh, I so miss it all, all of you.'

'Steady on,' Molly laughed. 'One question at a time —' and she began to give Tara all the news. It took time, and while they chatted, they found a picnic spot and sat with their legs dangling over the cliff, drinking hot tea from the Thermos, and with scraps of bread feeding the fluffy little hyrax, the rock rabbits that crept out of the crevices and cracks of the cliff.

At last they exhausted their stocks of news and gossip, and sat in companionable silence. Tara broke it at last.

'Molly, I'm going to have another baby.'

'Ah ha!' Molly giggled. 'So that's what has been keeping you busy.' She glanced at Tara's stomach.

'It doesn't show yet. Are you certain?'

'Oh, for Pete's sake, Molly. I'm hardly the simpering virgin, you know. Give me credit for the four I have already! Of course I'm certain.'

'When is it due?'

'January next year.'

'Shasa will be pleased. He dotes on the kids. In fact, apart from money, they are the only things I've ever seen Shasa Courtney sentimental about. Have you told him yet?'

Tara shook her head. 'No. You are the only one I've told. I came to you first.'

'I'm flattered. I wish you both joy.' Then she paused as she noticed Tara's expression and studied her more seriously.

'For Shasa there will be little joy in it, I'm afraid,' Tara said softly. 'It's not Shasa's baby.'

'Good Lord, Tara! You of all people —' then she broke off, and thought about it. 'I'm going to ask another silly question, Tara darling, but how do you know it isn't Shasa's effort?'

'Shasa and I – we haven't – well, you know – we haven't been man and wife since – oh, not for ages.'

'I see.' Despite her affection and friendship, Molly's eyes sparkled with interest. This was intriguing. 'But, Tara love, that isn't the end of the world. Rush home now and get Shasa's pants off. Men are such clots, dates don't mean much to them, and if he does start counting, you can always bribe the doctor to tell him it's a prem.'

'No, Molly, listen to me. If ever he saw the infant, he would know.'

'I don't understand.'

'Molly, I am carrying Moses Gama's baby.'

'Sweet Christ!' Molly whispered.

The strength of Molly's reaction brought home to Tara the full gravity of the predicament in which she found herself.

Molly was a militant liberal, as colour-blind as Tara was herself, and yet Molly was stunned by the idea of a white woman bearing a black man's infant. In this country miscegenation was an offence punishable by imprisonment, but that penalty was as nothing compared to the social outrage it would engender. She would become an outcast and a pariah.

142

'Oh dear,' Molly moderated her language. 'Oh dear, oh dear! My poor Tara, what a mess you are in. Does Moses know?'

'Not yet, but I hope to see him soon and I'll tell him.'

'You will have to get rid of it, of course. I have an address in Lourenço Marques. There is a Portuguese doctor there. We sent one of our girls from the orphanage to him. He's expensive, but clean and good, not like some dirty old crone in a back room with a knitting needle.'

'Oh Molly, how could you think that of me? How could you believe I would murder my own baby?'

'You are going to keep it?' Molly gaped at her.

'Of course.'

'But, my dear, it will be —'

'Coloured,' Tara finished for her. 'Yes, I know, probably *café au lait* in colour and with crispy black hair and I will love it with all my heart. Just as I love the father.'

'I don't see how —'

'That's why I came to you.'

'I'll do whatever you want – just tell me what that is.'

'I want you to find me a coloured couple. Good decent people, preferably with children of their own, who will take care of the infant for me until I can arrange to take it myself. Of course, they will have all the money they need and more —' her voiced trailed off and she stared at Molly imploringly.

Molly considered for a minute. 'I think I know the right couple. They are both school-teachers and they have four of their own, all girls. They'll do it for me – but, Tara, how are you going to hide it? It will begin to show soon, you were huge with Isabella. Shasa might not notice, he's so busy looking into his cheque book, but your mother-in-law is an absolute tartar. You couldn't get anything by her.'

'I've already made plans to cover that. I have convinced Shasa that I have conceived a burning interest in archaeology to replace my political activities and I've got a job on the dig at Sundi Caves with the American archaeologist, Professor Marion Hurst, you know.'

'Yes, I've read two of her books.'

'I've told Shasa that I will only be away for two months, but once I'm out of his sight I'll just keep postponing my return. Centaine will look after the children, I've arranged that also, she loves doing it and, the Lord knows, the kids will benefit from it. She's a much better disciplinarian than I am. They'll be perfectly behaved angels by the time my beloved mother-in-law is finished with them.'

'You'll miss them,' Molly stated, and Tara nodded.

'Yes, of course, I shall miss them, but it's only another six months to go.'

'Where will you have the child?' Molly persisted.

'I don't know. I can't go to a recognized hospital or nursing home. Oh God, could you imagine the fuss if I produced a little brown bundle on their clean whites-only sheets, in their lovely clean whites-only maternity hospital. Anyway, there is plenty of time to arrange all that later. The first thing is to get away to Sundi, away from Centaine Courtney-Malcomess' malevolent eye.'

'Why Sundi, Tara, what made you choose Sundi?'

'Because I will be near to Moses.'

'Is it that important?' Molly stared at her mercilessly. 'Do you feel like that about him? It wasn't just a little experiment, just a little kinky fun to find out what it is really like with one of them?'

Tara shook her head.

'Are you sure, Tara? I mean I've had the same urge occasionally. I suppose it's natural to be curious, but I've never been caught at it.'

'Molly, I love him. If he asked me, I would lay down my life for him without a qualm.'

'My poor sweet Tara.' Tears started in Molly's eyes, and she reached out with both arms. They hugged desperately and Molly whispered, 'He is far beyond your reach, my darling. You can never, never have him.'

'If I can have a little piece of him, for even a little while. That will be enough for me.'

* * *

Moses Gama parked the crimson and blue butchery van in one of the visitors' bays and switched off the engine. In front of him stretched lawns on which a single small sprinkler was trying to atone for all the frosts and drought of the highveld winter, but the Kikuyu grass was seared and lifeless. Beyond the lawn was the long double-storied block of the Baragwanath nurses' home.

A small group of black nurses came up the pathway from the main hospital. They were in crisp white uniform, neat and efficient-looking, but when they drew level with the van and saw Moses at the wheel, they dissolved into giggles, hiding their mouths with their hands in the instinctive gesture of subservience to the male.

'Young woman, I wish to speak to you.' Moses leaned out of the window of the van. 'Yes, you!' The chosen nurse was almost overcome with shyness. Her friends teased her as she approached Moses and paused timidly five paces from him.

'Do you know Sister Victoria Dinizulu?'

144

'Eh he!' the nurse affirmed.

'Where is she?'

'She is coming now. She is on the day shift with me.' The nurse looked around for escape, and instead picked out Victoria in the middle of the second group of white-clad figures coming up the path. 'There she is. Victoria! Come quickly!' the girl cried, and then fled, taking the steps up into the nurses' home two at a time. Victoria recognized him, and with a word to her friends, left them and cut across the dry brown lawns, coming directly to him. Moses climbed out of the van, and she looked up at him.

'I'm sorry. There was a terrible bus accident, we were working in theatre until the last case was attended to. I have kept you waiting.'

Moses nodded. 'It's not important. We have plenty of time still.'

'It will take me only a few minutes to change into street clothes,' she smiled up at him. Her teeth were perfect, so white that they seemed almost translucent and her skin had the lustre of health and youth. 'I am so pleased to see you again – but I do have a very big bone to pick with you.' They were speaking English, and although hers was accented, she seemed confident in the language with a choice of words which matched his own fluency.

'Good,' he smiled gravely. 'We will have your bone for dinner – which will save me money.'

She laughed, a fine throaty chuckle. 'Don't go away, I will be back.' She turned and went into the nurses' home, and he watched her with pleasure as she climbed the steps. Her waist was so narrow that it accentuated the swell of her buttocks under the white uniform. Although her bosom was small, she was full-bottomed and broad-hipped; she would carry a child with ease. That kind of body was the model of Nguni beauty, and Moses was strongly reminded of the photographs he had seen of the Venus de Milo. Her carriage was erect, her neck long and straight, and although her hips swayed as though she danced to a distant music, her head and shoulders never moved. It was obvious that as a child she had taken her turn with the other young girls at carrying the brimming clay pots up from the water-hole, balancing the pot on her head without spilling a drop. That was how the Zulu girls acquired that marvellously regal posture.

With her round madonna face and huge dark eyes, she was one of the handsomest women he had ever seen, and while he waited, leaning against the bonnet of the van, he pondered how each race had its ideal of feminine beauty, and how widely they differed. That led him on to think of Tara Courtney, with her huge round breasts and narrow boyish hips, her long chestnut hair and soft insipid white skin. Moses grimaced, faintly repelled by the image, and yet both women were crucial to his ambitions, and his sensual response to them – attraction or revulsion – was completely irrelevant. All that mattered was their utility.

Victoria came back down the steps ten minutes later. She was wearing a vivid crimson dress. Bright colours suited her, they set off that glossy dark skin. She slid into the passenger's seat of the van beside him, and glanced at the cheap gold-plated watch on her wrist. 'Eleven minutes sixteen seconds. You cannot really complain,' she announced, and he smiled and started the engine.

'Now let us pick your thighbone of a dinosaur,' he suggested.

'Tyrannosaurus Rex,' she corrected him. 'The most ferocious of the dinosaurs. But, no, we'll keep that for dinner as you suggested.'

Her banter amused him. It was unusual for an unmarried black girl to be so forthcoming and self-assured. Then he remembered her training and her life here at one of the world's largest and busiest hospitals. This wasn't a little country girl, empty-headed and giggling, and as if to make the point, Victoria fell into an easy discussion of General Dwight Eisenhower's prospects for election to the White House, and how that would affect the American civil rights struggle – and ultimately their own struggle here in Africa.

While they talked, the sun began to set and the city, with all its fine buildings and parks, fell behind them, until abruptly they entered the half world of Soweto township where half a million black people lived. The dusk was thick with the smell of wood-smoke from the cooking fires, and it turned the sunset a diabolical red, the colour of blood and oranges. The narrow unmade sidewalks were crowded with black commuters, each of them carrying a parcel or a shopping bag, all hurrying in the same direction, back to their homes after a long day that had begun before the sun with a tortuous journey by bus or train to their places of work in the outer world, and that now ended in darkness with the reverse journey which fatigue made even longer and more tedious.

The van slowed as the streets became more crowded, and then some of them recognized Moses and ran ahead of them, clearing the way.

'Moses Gama! It's Moses Gama, let him pass!' And as they went by, some of them shouted greetings.

'I see you, *Nkosi*.'

'I see you, *Baba*!' They called him father and lord.

When they reached the community centre which abutted the administration buildings, the huge hall was overflowing, and they were forced to leave the van and go on foot for the last hundred yards.

However, the Buffaloes were there to escort them. Hendrick

Tabaka's enforcers pushed a way through the solid pack of humanity, tempering this show of force with smiles and jokes so the crowd made way for them without resentment.

'It is Moses Gama, let him pass,' and Victoria hung on to his arm and laughed with the excitement of it.

As they went in through the main doors of the hall, she glanced up and saw the name above the door: H. F. VERWOERD COMMUNITY HALL.

It was fast becoming a custom for the Nationalist government to name all state buildings, airports, dams and other public works after political luminaries and mediocrities, but there was an unusual irony in naming the community hall of the largest black township after the white architect of the laws which they had gathered here to protest. Hendrik Frensch Verwoerd was the minister of Bantu affairs, and the principal architect of *apartheid*.

Inside the hall, the noise was thunderous. A permit to use the hall for a political rally would have been denied by the township administration, so officially this had been billed and advertised as a rock 'n' roll concert by a band that gloried in the name of 'The Marmalade Mambas'.

They were on the stage now, four of them dressed in tight-fitting sequined suits that glittered in the flashing coloured lights. A bank of amplifiers sent the music crashing over the packed audience, like an aerial bombardment, and the dancers screamed back at them, swaying and writhing to the rhythm like a single monstrous organism.

The Buffaloes opened a path for them across the dance floor and the dancers recognized Moses and shouted greetings, trying to touch him as he passed. Then the band became aware of his presence and broke off in the middle of the wild driving beat to give him a trumpet fanfare and a roll of drums.

Dozens of willing hands helped Moses up on to the stage, while Victoria remained below with her head at the level of his knees, trapped in the press of bodies that pressed forward to see and to hear Moses Gama. The band leader attempted to introduce him but even the power of the electronic amplifiers could not lift his voice above the tumultuous welcome that they gave Moses. From four thousand throats a savage sustained roar rose and went on and on without diminution. It broke over Moses Gama like a wild sea driven by a winter gale, and like a rock he stood unmoved by it.

Then he lifted his arms, and the sound died away swiftly until a suppressed and aching silence hung over that great press of humanity, and into that silence Moses Gama roared.

'*Amandla!* Power!'

147

As a single voice they roared back at him, *'Amandla!'*

He shouted again, in that deep thrilling voice that rang against the rafters and reached into the depths of their hearts.

'Mayibuye!'

They bellowed the reply back at him

'Afrika! Let Africa persist.'

And then they were silent again, expectant and wound up with excitement and tension, as Moses Gama began to speak.

'Let us talk of Africa,' he said.

'Let us talk of a rich and fruitful land with tiny barren pockets on which our people are forced to live.

'Let us speak of the children without schools and the mothers without hope.

'Let us speak of taxes and passes.

'Let us speak of famine and sickness.

'Let us speak of those who labour in the harsh sunlight, and in the depths of the dark earth.

'Let us speak of those who live in the compounds far from their families.

'Let us speak of hunger and tears and the hard laws of the Boers.'

For an hour he held them in his hands, and they listened in silence except for the groans and involuntary gasps of anguish, and the occasional growl of anger, and at the end Victoria found she was weeping. The tears flowed freely and unashamedly down her beautiful upturned moon face.

When Moses finished, he dropped his arms and lowered his chin upon his chest, exhausted and shaken by his own passion and a vast silence fell upon them. They were too moved to shout or to applaud.

In the silence Victoria suddenly flung herself on to the stage and faced them.

'Nkosi sikelel' iAfrika,' she sang.

'God save Africa,' and immediately the band picked up the refrain, while from the body of the hall their magnificent African voices soared in haunting chorus. Moses Gama stepped up beside her and took her hand in his, and their voices blended.

At the end it took them almost twenty minutes to escape from the hall, their way was blocked by the thousands who wanted the experience to last, to touch them and to hear their voices and to be a part of the struggle.

In the course of one short evening the beautiful Zulu girl in the flaming crimson dress had become part of the almost mystic legend that surrounded Moses Gama. Those who were fortunate enough to be there that evening would tell those who had not, how she had looked like a queen as she stood and sang before them, a queen that befitted the tall black emperor at her side.

'I have never experienced anything like that,' Vicky told him, when at last they were alone again, and the little blue and crimson van was humming back along the main highway towards Johannesburg. 'The love they bear you is so powerful —' she broke off. 'I just can't describe it.'

'Sometimes it frightens me,' he agreed. 'They place such a heavy responsibility upon me.'

'I don't believe you know what fear is,' she said.

'I do.' He shook his head. 'I know it better than most.' And then he changed the subject. 'What time is it? We must find something to eat before curfew.'

'It's only nine o'clock.' Victoria looked surprised as she turned the dial of her wristwatch to catch the light of a street lamp. 'I thought it would be much later. I seem to have lived a lifetime in one short evening.'

Ahead of them a neon sign flickered: 'DOLLS' HOUSE DRIVE-IN. Tasty Eats.' Moses slowed and turned the van into the parking lot. He left Vicky for a few minutes to go to the counter of the replica dolls' house, then he returned with hamburgers and coffee in two paper mugs.

'Ah, that's good!' she mumbled through a mouthful of hamburger. 'I didn't realize I was so hungry.'

'Now what about this bone you threaten me with?' Moses asked, and he spoke in fluent Zulu.

'You speak Zulu!' She was amazed. 'I didn't know. When did you learn?' she demanded in the same language.

'I speak many languages,' he told her. 'If I want to reach all the people, there is no other way.' And he smiled. 'However, young woman, you don't change the subject so easily. Tell me about this bone.'

'Oh, I feel so stupid talking about it now, after all we have shared this evening —' she hesitated. 'I was going to ask you why you sent your brother to speak to my father before you had said anything to me. I'm not a country girl of the kraals, you know. I am a modern woman with a mind of my own.'

'Victoria, we should not discard the old traditions in our struggle for liberation. What I did was out of respect for you and for your father. I am sorry if it offended you.'

'I was a little ruffled,' she admitted.

'Will it help at all if I ask you now?' he smiled. 'You can still refuse. Before we go any further, think very deeply. If you marry me, you marry the cause. Our marriage will be part of the struggle of our

149

people, and the road before us will be hard and dangerous, with never an end in sight.'

'I do not need to think,' she said softly. 'Tonight when I stood there before our people with your hand in mine, I knew that was the reason why I was born.'

He took both her hands in his and drew her gently towards him, but before their mouths could touch, the harsh white beam of a powerful spotlight shone into their faces. Startled, they drew apart, shielding their eyes with raised hands.

'Hey, what is this?' Moses exclaimed.

'Police!' a voice answered from the darkness beyond the open side window. 'Get out both of you!'

They climbed out of the van, and Moses went around the bonnet to stand beside Victoria. He saw that while they had been engrossed with each other, a police pick-up had entered the parking lot and parked beside the restaurant building. Now four blue-uniformed constables with flashlights were checking the occupants of all the parked vehicles in the lot.

'Let me see your passes, both of you.' The constable in front of him was still shining the light in his eyes, but beyond it Moses could make out that he was very young.

Moses reached into his inner pocket, while Victoria searched in her purse, and they handed their pass booklets to the constable. He turned the beam of the flashlight on them and studied them minutely.

'It's almost curfew,' he said in Afrikaans, as he handed them back. 'You Bantu should be in your own locations at this time of night.'

'There is still an hour and a half until curfew,' Victoria replied sharply, and the constable's expression hardened.

'Don't take that tone with me, maid.' That term of address was insulting and again he shone the flashlight in her face. 'Just because you've got shoes on your feet and rouge on your face, doesn't mean you are a white woman. Just remember that.'

Moses took Victoria's arm and firmly steered her back to the van. 'We are leaving right away, officer,' he said placatingly, and once they were both in the van, he told Victoria, 'You will accomplish nothing by getting us both arrested. That is not the level at which we should conduct the struggle. That is just a callow little white boy with more authority than he knows how to carry.'

'Forgive me,' she said. 'I just get so angry. What were they looking for anyway?'

'They were looking for white men with black girls, their Immorality Act to keep their precious white blood pure. Half their police force

150

spends its time trying to peer into other people's bedrooms.' He started the van and turned into the highway.

Neither of them spoke again until he parked in front of the Baragwanath nurses' home.'

'I hope we will not be interrupted again,' Moses said quietly, and placing an arm around her shoulders turned her gently to face him.

Although she had seen how it was done on the cinema screen, and although the other girls in the hostel endlessly discussed what they referred to as 'Hollywood style', Victoria had never kissed a man. It was not part of Zulu custom or tradition. So she lifted her face to him with a mixture of trepidation and breathless expectation, and was amazed at the warmth and softness of his mouth. Swiftly the stiffness and tension went out of her neck and shoulders and she seemed to mould herself to him.

*   *   *

The work at Sundi Caves was even more interesting than Tara Courtney had expected it to be, and she adapted rapidly to the leisurely pace and life and intellectually stimulating companionship of the small specialist team of which she was now a part.

Tara shared a tent with two young students from the University of the Witwatersrand, and she found with mild surprise that the close proximity of other women in such spartan accommodation did not bother her. They were up long before dawn to escape the heat in the middle of the day, and after a quick and frugal breakfast, Professor Hurst led them up to the site and allocated the day's labours. They rested and ate the main meal at noon, and then as the day cooled, they returned to the site and worked on until the light failed. After that they had only enough energy for a hot shower, a light meal and the narrow camp beds.

The site was in a deep kloof. The rocky sides dropped steeply two hundred feet to the narrow riverbed in the gut. The vegetation in the protected and sun-warmed valley was tropical, quite alien to that on the exposed grasslands that were scoured by wind and winter frosts. Tall candelabra aloes grew on the upper slopes, while farther down it became even denser, and there were tree ferns and cycads, and huge strangler figs with bark like elephant hide, grey and wrinkled.

The caves themselves were a series of commodious open galleries that ran with the exposed strata. They were ideal for habitation by primitive man, located high up the slope and protected from the prevailing winds yet with a wide view out across the plain on to which the kloof debouched. They were close to water and readily

151

defensible against all marauders, and the depth of the midden and accumulated detritus on the floor of the caves attested to the ages over which they had been occupied.

The roofs of the caves were darkened with the smoke of countless cooking fires and the inner walls were decorated with the engravings and childlike paintings of the ancient San peoples and their predecessors. All the signs of a major site with the presence of very early hominids were evident, and although the dig was still in its early stages and they had penetrated only the upper levels, spirits and optimism were high and the whole feeling on the dig was of a close-knit community of persons bound by a common interest cooperating selflessly on a project of outstanding importance.

Tara particularly liked Marion Hurst, the American professor in charge of the excavations. She was a woman in her early fifties, with cropped grey hair, and a skin burned to the colour and consistency of saddle-leather by the suns of Arabia and Africa. They had become firm friends even before Tara discovered that she was married to a negro professor of anthropology at Cornell. That knowledge made their relationship secure, and relieved Tara of the necessity of any subterfuge.

One night she sat late with Marion in the shed they were using as a laboratory, and suddenly Tara found herself telling her about Moses Gama and her impossible love, even about the child she was carrying. The elder woman's sympathy was immediate and sincere.

'What iniquitous social order can keep people from loving others – of course, I knew all about these laws before I came here. That is why Tom stayed at home. Despite my personal feelings, the work here was just too important to pass up. However, you have my promise that I will do anything in my power to help the two of you.'

Yet Tara had been on the dig for five weeks without having heard from Moses Gama. She had written him a dozen letters and telephoned the Rivonia number, and the other number in Drake's Farm township. Moses was never there, and never responded to her urgent messages.

At last she could stand it no longer, and she borrowed Marion's pick-up truck and went into the city, almost an hour's drive with the first half of the journey over clay roads that were rutted and bumpy, and finally over wide black-top highways in a solid stream of heavy traffic, coming up from the coalfields at Witbank.

She parked the pick-up under the bluegum trees at the back of Puck's Hill and was suddenly afraid to see him again, terrified that it had all changed and he would send her away. It took all her courage to leave the cab of the pick-up and go around the big unkempt house to the front verandah.

At the far end there was a man sitting at the desk and her heart soared and then as swiftly plunged as he turned and saw her and stood up. It was Marcus Archer. He came down the long verandah towards her, and his smile was spiteful and vinegary.

'Surprise!' he said. 'The last person I expected to see.'

'Hello, Marcus. I was looking for Moses.'

'I know who you are looking for, dearie.'

'Is he here?'

Marcus shook his head. 'I haven't seen him for almost two weeks.'

'I have written and telephoned – he doesn't reply. I was worried.'

'Perhaps he doesn't reply, because he doesn't want to see you.'

'Why do you dislike me so, Marcus?'

'Oh my dear, whatever gave you that idea?' Marcus smiled archly.

'I'm sorry to have bothered you.' She began to turn away and then paused. Her expression hardened. 'Will you give him a message, when you see him?'

Marcus inclined his head, and for the first time she noticed the grey hairs in his ginger sideburns and the wrinkles in the corners of his eyes. He was much older than she had thought.

'Will you tell Moses that I came to find him, and that nothing has changed. That I meant every word I said.'

'Very well, dearie. I'll tell him.'

Tara went down the steps, but when she reached the bottom, he called after her.

'Tara.' And she looked up. He leaned on the railing of the verandah. 'You'll never have him. You know that, don't you? He will keep you only as long as he needs you. Then he will cast you aside. He will never belong to you.'

'Nor to you either, Marcus Archer,' she said softly, and he recoiled from her. 'He belongs to neither of us. He belongs to Africa and his people.' And she saw the desolation in his eyes. It gave her no satisfaction, and she went slowly back to the pick-up and drove away.

*　　*　　*

At Level Six in the main gallery of the Sundi Caves they exposed an extensive deposit of clay pottery fragments. There were no intact artefacts, and it was obviously a dumping site for the ancient potters. Nevertheless, the discovery was of crucial importance in dating the levels for the pottery was of a very early type.

Marion Hurst was excited by the find, and transmitted her excitement to all of them. By this time Tara had been promoted from the heavy work of grubbing in the dirt at the bottom of the trenches. She had displayed a natural aptitude for the puzzle game of fitting the fragments of bone and pottery together in their original form, and she now worked in the long prefabricated shed under Marion Hurst's direct supervision and was making herself an invaluable member of the team.

Tara found that while she was absorbed with the fragments, she could suppress the ache of longing and the turmoil of uncertainty and guilt. She knew that her neglect of her children and her family was unforgivable. Once a week she telephoned Rhodes Hill and spoke to her father and Centaine and to Isabella. The child seemed quite content, and in a strangely selfish way Tara resented the fact that she seemed not to pine for her mother but was accepting her grandmother as a happy substitute. Centaine was friendly and made no criticism of her continued absence, but Blaine Malcomess, her beloved father, was as usual bluntly outspoken.

'I don't know what you are trying to run away from, Tara, but believe me it never works. Your place is here with your husband and your children. Enough of this nonsense now. You know your duty, however unpleasant you may find it – it's still your duty.'

Of course, Shasa and the boys would soon be returning from their grand safari, and then she could procrastinate no longer. She would have to make a decision, and she was not even certain of the alternatives. Sometimes in the night, in those silent small hours when human energy and spirits are at their lowest ebb, she even considered following Molly's advice and aborting the child from her womb and turning her back on Moses, going back to the seductive and destructively soft life of Weltevreden.

'Oh, Moses, if only I could see you again. Just to speak to you for a few hours – then I would know what to do.'

She found herself withdrawing from the company of the other workers on the excavation. The cheerful carefree attitude of the two university students she shared her tent with began to irritate her. Their conversation was so naïve and childlike, even the music they played endlessly on a portable tape recorder was so loud and uncouth that it rasped her nerves.

With Marion's blessing she purchased a small bell tent of her own and erected it near the laboratory where she worked, so that when the others took their noonday siesta, she could slip back to her work bench and forget all her insoluble problems in the totally absorbing task of fitting together the shattered scraps. Their antiquity seemed to soothe her and make the problems of the present seem trivial and unimportant.

It was here, at her bench, in the middle of a hot somnolent highveld afternoon, that the light from the open doorway was blocked suddenly, and she looked up frowning, wiping back the sweaty wisps

154

of hair from her forehead with the back of her hand, and then her mouth went dry and her heart seemed to freeze for a long moment and then race wildly.

The sunlight was behind him, so his was a tall silhouette, broad-shouldered, slim-hipped and regal. She sobbed and sprang up from the bench and flew to him, wrapping her arms around his chest and pressing her face to his heart so that she could feel it beat against her cheek. She could not speak, and his voice was deep and gentle above her.

'I have been cruel to you. I should have come to you sooner.'

'No,' she whispered. 'It doesn't matter. Now that you are here, nothing else matters.'

He stayed only one night, and Marion Hurst protected them from the other members of the expedition so that they were alone in her small tent, isolated from the world and its turmoil. Tara did not sleep that night, each moment was far too precious to waste.

In the dawn he said to her. 'I must go again soon. There is something that you must do for me.'

'Anything!' she whispered.

'Our campaign of defiance begins soon. There will be terrible risk and sacrifice by thousands of our people, but for their sacrifice to be worth while it must be brought to the attention of the world.'

'What can I do?' she asked.

'By a most fortunate coincidence, there is an American television team in the country at this very moment. They are making a series called "Africa on Focus".'

'Yes, I know about them. They interviewed —' she broke off. She didn't want to mention Shasa, not now, not during this treasured interlude.

'They interviewed your husband,' he finished for her. 'Yes, I know. However, they have almost finished filming and I have heard that they plan to return to the United States within the next few days. We need them here. We need them to film and record our struggle. They must show it to the world – the spirit of our people, the indomitable will to rise above oppression and inhumanity.'

'How can I help?'

'I cannot reach the producer of this series on my own. I need a go-between. We have to prevent them leaving. We have to make certain they are here to film the defiance when it begins. You must speak to the woman in charge of the filming. Her name is Godolphin, Kitty Godolphin, and she will be staying at the Sunnyside Hotel in Johannesburg for the next three days.'

'I will go to her today.'

'Tell her that the time is not yet agreed – but when it is, I will let her know, and she must be there with her camera.'

155

'I will see that she is,' Tara promised, and he rolled her gently on to her back and made love to her again. It seemed impossible, but for Tara every time was better than the last, and when he left her and rose from the campbed, she felt weak and soft and warm as molten wax.

'Moses,' she said softly, and he paused in buttoning the pale blue open-neck shirt.

'What is it?' he asked softly.

She had to tell him about the child she was carrying. She sat up, letting the rumpled sheet fall to her waist and her breasts, already heavy with her pregnancy, were dappled with tiny blue veins beneath the ivory smooth skin.

'Moses,' she repeated stupidly, trying to find the courage to say it, and he came to her.

'Tell me,' he commanded, and her courage failed her. She could not tell him, the risk that it would drive him away was too great.

'I just wanted to tell you how grateful I am that you have given me this opportunity to be of service to the struggle.'

* * *

It was much easier to contact Kitty Godolphin than she had expected it to be. She borrowed Marion's pick-up and drove five miles to the nearest village, and she telephoned from the public booth in the little single-roomed post office. The operator in the Sunnyside Hotel put her through to the room, and a firm young voice with a Louisiana lilt said, 'Kitty Godolphin. Who is this please?'

'I'd rather not give my name, Miss Godolphin. But I would like to meet you as soon as possible. I have a story for you, an important and dramatic story.'

'When and where do you want to meet?'

'It will take me two hours to reach your hotel.'

'I'll be waiting for you,' said Kitty Godolphin, and it was as easy as that.

Tara checked with Reception and the girl at the desk phoned through to Miss Godolphin's suite and then told her to go up.

A young girl, slim and pretty, in a tartan shirt and blue jeans opened the door to Tara's ring.

'Hello, is Miss Godolphin in? She's expecting me.'

The girl looked her over carefully, taking in her khaki bush skirt and mosquito boots, her tanned arms and face and the scarf tied around her thick auburn hair.

'I'm Kitty Godolphin,' said the girl, and Tara could not hide her surprise.

156

'Okay, don't tell me. You expected an old bag. Come on in and tell me who you are.'

In the lounge Tara removed her sunglasses and faced her.

'My name is Tara Courtney. I understand you know my husband. Shasa Courtney, Chairman of Courtney Mining and Finance.'

She saw the shift in the other woman's expression, and the sudden hard gleam in those eyes that she had thought were frank and innocent.

'I meet a lot of people in my business, Mrs Courtney.'

Tara had not expected the hostility, and hurriedly she tried to forestall it.

'I'm sure you do —'

'Did you want to talk to me about your husband, lady? I don't have a lot of time to waste.' Kitty looked pointedly at her wristwatch. It was a man's Rolex and she wore it on the inside of her wrist like a soldier.

'No, I'm sorry. I didn't mean to give you that impression. I have come here on behalf of someone else, someone who is unable to come to you himself.'

'Why not?' Kitty asked sharply, and Tara readjusted her early estimate of her. Despite her childlike appearance, she was as tough and sharp as any man Tara had ever met.

'Because he is being watched by the police special branch, and because what he is planning is dangerous and illegal.' Tara saw instantly that she had said the right things and had aroused the newswoman's instinct.

'Sit down, Mrs Courtney. Do you want some coffee?' She picked up the house phone and ordered from room service, then turned back to Tara.

'Now tell me. Who is this mysterious person?'

'You probably have never heard of him, but soon the whole world will know his name,' Tara said. 'It's Moses Gama.'

'Moses Gama, hell!' Kitty Godolphin exclaimed. 'For six weeks now I've been trying to catch up with him. I was beginning to think he was just a rumour, and that he didn't really exist. A scarlet pimpernel.'

'He exists,' Tara assured her.

'Can you get me an interview with him?' Kitty demanded, so anxious that she leaned across and grasped Tara's wrist impulsively. 'He's an Emmy score, that one. He is the one person in South Africa I really want to talk to.'

'I can do a whole lot better than that,' Tara promised her.

*   *   *

157

Shasa Courtney was determined that his sons would not grow up believing that the affluent white suburbs of Cape Town and Johannesburg were all of Africa. This safari was to show them the old Africa, primeval and eternal, and to establish for them a firm link with their history and their ancestors, to engender in them a sense of pride in what they were and in those who had gone before them.

He had set aside six whole weeks, the full period of the boys' school holidays, for this venture, and that had taken a great deal of planning and considerable heart-searching. The affairs of the company were so many-faceted and complex that he did not like leaving them, even in such capable hands as those of David Abrahams. The shaft-sinking at Silver River was going ahead apace, and they were down almost a thousand feet already while work on the plant was also far advanced. Apart from that, the first six pilchard trawlers for the factory at Walvis Bay were due for delivery in three weeks' time, and the canning plant was on the water from the suppliers in the United Kingdom. There was so much happening, so many problems that could demand his immediate decision.

Centaine was, of course, always on hand for David to consult with, but of late she had withdrawn more and more from the running of the company, and there were many eventualities that might arise that could only be dealt with by Shasa personally. Shasa weighed up the chances of this happening against what was necessary, in his view, for his sons' education and understanding of their place in Africa and their inherited duties and responsibilities, and decided he had to risk it. As a last resort he arranged a strict itinerary for the safari, of which both Centaine and David had a copy, so that they would know exactly where he was during every day of his absence, and a radio contact would be maintained with the H'ani Mine so that an aircraft could reach any of his camps in the deep bush within four or five hours.

'If you do call me out, then the reason had better be ironclad,' Shasa warned David grimly. 'This is probably the only time in our lives that the boys and I will be able to do this.'

They left from the H'ani Mine the last week in May. Shasa had taken the boys out of school a few days early, which in itself was enough to put everybody in the right mood and ensure a splendid beginning. He had commandeered four of the mine's trucks and made up a full team of safari boys, including drivers, camp servants, skinners, trackers, gunbearers and the chef from the H'ani Mine Club. Of course, Shasa's own personal hunting vehicle was always kept in the mine workshops, tuned to perfection and ready to go at any time. It was an ex-army jeep which had been customized and modified by the mine engineers without regard to expense. It had everything from long-range fuel tanks and gun racks to a shortwave radio set, and the seats were upholstered in genuine zebra skin while the paintwork was an artistic creation in bush camouflage. Proudly the boys clipped their Winchester .22 repeaters into the gun rack beside Shasa's big .375 Holland and Holland magnum, and dressed in their new khaki bush jackets, scrambled into their seats in the jeep. As was the right of the eldest, Sean sat up front beside his father, with Michael and Garry in the open back.

'Anybody want to change his mind and stay at home?' Shasa asked as he started the jeep, and they took the question seriously, shaking their heads in unison, eyes shining and faces pale with excitement, too overcome to speak.

'Here we go then,' Shasa said and they drove down the hill from the mine offices with the convoy of four trucks following them.

The uniformed mine guards opened the main gates and gave them a flashy salute, grinning widely as the jeep passed, and behind them the camp boys on the backs of the open trucks started to sing one of the traditional safari songs.

> Weep, oh you women, tonight you sleep alone
> The long road calls us and we must go —

Their voices rose and fell to the eternal rhythm of Africa, full of its promise and mystery, echoing its grandeur and its savagery, setting the mood for the magical adventure into which Shasa took his sons.

They drove hard those first two days to get beyond the areas which had been spoiled by men's too frequent intrusions with rifle and four-wheel drive vehicle, where the veld was almost bare of large game and those animals that they did see were in small herds that were running as soon as they heard the first hum of the jeep engine and were merely tiny specks in their own dust by the time they spotted them.

Sadly Shasa realized how much had changed since his earliest memory of this country. He had been Sean's age then and the herds of springbok and gemsbok had been on every side, great herds, trusting and confiding. There had been giraffe and lion, and small bands of Bushmen, those fascinating little yellow pygmies of the desert. Now, however, wild men and beast had all retreated before the inexorable advance of civilization deeper and deeper into the wilderness. Even now, Shasa could look ahead to the day when there would be no more wilderness, no more retreat for the wild things, when the roads and the railway lines would criss-cross the land and the endless villages and kraals would stand in the desolation they had created. The time when the trees were all cut down for firewood, and the grass was eaten to the roots by the goats and the top soil turned to dust and blew on the wind. The vision filled him with sadness and a sense of despair, and he had to make a conscious effort to throw it off so as not to spoil the experience for his sons.

'I owe them this glimpse of the past. They must know a little of the Africa that once was, before it has all gone, so that they will understand something of its glory.' And he smiled and told them the stories, reaching back in his memory to bring out for them all his own experiences, and then going back farther, to what he had learned from his own mother, and from his grandfather, trying to make clear to them the extent and depth of their family's involvement with this land, and they sat late around the camp fire that first night, listening avidly until, despite themselves, their eyelids drooped and their heads began to nod.

On they went, driving hard all day over rutted tracks, through desert scrub and grassland and then through mopani forest, not yet stopping to hunt, eating the food they had brought with them from the mine, though that night the servants muttered about fresh meat.

On the third day they left the rudimentary road they had been following since dawn. It was nothing more than a double track of tyres that had last been used months before, but now Shasa let it swing away towards the east and they went on northwards, breaking fresh ground, weaving through the open forest until abruptly they came out on the banks of a river, not one of the great African rivers like the Kavango, but one of its tributaries. Still, it was fifty feet wide, but green and deep, a formidable barrier that would have turned back any hunting safari before them that had come this far north.

Two weeks previously Shasa had reconnoitred this entire area from the air, flying the Mosquito low over the tree tops so that he could count the animals in each herd of game, and judge the size of the ivory tusks that each elephant carried. He had marked this branch of the river on his large-scale map, and had navigated the convoy back to this exact spot. He recognized it by the oxbow bend of the banks and the giant makuyu trees on the opposite side, with a fish eagle nest in the upper branches.

They camped another two days on the southern river bank while every member of the safari, including the three boys and the fat Herero chef, helped to build the bridge. They cut the mopani poles in the forest, thick as a fat woman's thigh and forty feet long, and dragged them up with the jeep. Shasa kept guard against crocodiles, standing high on the bank with the .375 magnum under his arm while his naked gangs floated the poles out into the centre of the river and set them into the mud of the bottom. Then they lashed the cross-ties to them with ropes of mopani bark that still wept glutinous sap, red as blood.

When at last the bridge was complete, they unloaded the vehicles to lighten them, and one at a time Shasa drove them out on to the rickety structure. It swayed and creaked and rocked under them, but at last he had the jeep and all four trucks on the far bank.

'Now the safari truly begins,' he told the boys. They had entered a pocket of country, protected by its remoteness and its natural barriers of forest and river from men's over-exploitation, and from the air Shasa had seen the herds of buffalo thick as domestic cattle and the clouds of white egrets hovering over them.

That night he told the boys stories about the old elephant hunters – 'Karamojo' Bell, and Frederick Selous and Sean Courtney their own ancestor, Shasa's great-uncle and the namesake of his eldest son.

'They were tough men, all of them, incredible shots and natural athletes. They had to be to survive the hardships and the tropical disease. When he was a young man, Sean Courtney hunted on foot in the tsetse-fly belt of the Zambezi valley where the temperature reaches 115° at noon, and he could run forty miles in a day after the big tuskers. His eye was so sharp he could actually see the flight of his bullet.' The boys listened with total fascination, pleading with him to continue whenever he paused, until at last he told them, 'That's enough. You have to be up early tomorrow. Five o'clock in the morning. We are going to hunt for the first time.'

In the dark they drove slowly along the northern bank of the river in the open jeep, all of them bundled up against the cold for the frost lay thick in the open vleis and crunched under the jeep's tyres. In the first feeble light of dawn they found where a herd of buffalo had drunk during the night and then gone back into the heavy bush.

They left the jeep on the river bank, and stripped off their padded anoraks. Then Shasa put his two Ovambo trackers to the spoor and they followed the herd on foot. As they moved silently and swiftly through the dense second-growth mopani thickets, Shasa explained it all to the boys, speaking in a whisper and relying on hand signals to point out the different hoof prints of old bull and cow and calf, or to draw their attention to other smaller but equally fascinating animals and birds and insects in the forest around them.

A little before noon they finally came up with the herd. Over a hundred of the huge cow-like beasts, with their trumpet-shaped ears and the drooping horns that gave them such a lugubrious air. Most of them were lying in the mopani shade, ruminating quietly, although one or two of the herd bulls were dozing on their feet. The only

161

movement was the lazy flick of their tails as the stinging flies swarmed over their flanks.

Shasa showed the boys how to work in close. Using the breeze and every stick of cover, freezing whenever one of the great horned heads swung in their direction, he took them within thirty feet of the biggest of the bulls. They could smell him, the hot rank bovine reek of him, and they could hear his breathing puffing through his wet drooling muzzle, hear his teeth grinding on his cud, so close they could see the bald patches of age on his shoulders and rump and the balls of dried mud from the wallow that clung in the stiff black hairs of his back and belly.

While they held their breaths in delicious terror and watched in total fascination, Shasa slowly raised the heavy rifle and aimed into the bull's thick neck, just forward of his massive shoulder.

'Bang!' he shouted, and the great bull plunged forward wildly, crashing into the screen of thick mopani, and Shasa gathered his sons and drew them into the shelter of one of the grey tree trunks, keeping his arms around them while on all sides the panicking herd galloped, huge black shapes thundering by, the calves bawling and the old bulls grunting.

The sounds of their flight dwindled away into the forest though the dust of their passage hung misty in the air around them, and Shasa was laughing with the joy of it as he let his arms fall from their shoulders.

'Why did you do that?' Sean demanded furiously, turning his face up to his father. 'You could have shot him easily – why didn't you kill him?'

'We didn't come out here to kill,' Shasa explained. 'We came here to hunt.'

'But —' Sean's outrage turned to bewilderment '— but what's the difference?'

'Ah! That's what you have to learn. That bull was a big one, but not big enough, and we have all the meat we need, so I let him go. That's lesson number one. Now, for lesson number two – none of you is going to kill anything until you know all about that animal, understand its habits and life cycle, and learn to respect it and hold it in high esteem. Then and only then.'

In camp that evening he gave them each two books, which he had had bound in leather with their own names on the cover: Roberts' *Mammals of South Africa* and his *Birds of South Africa*.

'I brought these especially for you, and I want you to study them,' he ordered. Sean looked appalled, he hated books and studying, but both Garry and Mickey hurried to their tent to begin the task.

Over the days that followed he questioned them on every animal and bird they saw. At first the questions were elementary, but he made them progressively more difficult and soon they could quote the biological names and give him full details of sizes and body weights of males and females, their calls and behaviour patterns, distribution and breeding, down to the smallest detail. Set an example by his younger brothers, even Sean mastered the difficult Latin names.

However, it was ten days before they were allowed to fire a shot – and then it was only bird-hunting. Under strict supervision, they were allowed to hunt the fat brown francolin and speckled guinea fowl with their strange waxen yellow helmets in the scrub along the river. Then they had to clean and dress their kill and help the Herero chef to prepare and cook it.

'It's the best meal I've ever eaten,' Sean declared, and his brothers agreed with him enthusiastically through full mouths.

The next morning Shasa told them, 'We need fresh meat for the men.' In camp there were thirty mouths to feed, all with an enormous appetite for fresh meat. 'All right, Sean, what is the scientific name for impala?'

'*Aepyceros Melampus*,' Sean gabbled eagerly. 'The Afrikaners call it *rooibok* and it weighs between 130 and 160 pounds.'

'That will do,' Shasa laughed. 'Go and get your rifle.'

In a patch of whistling thorn near the river, they found a solitary old ram, an outcast from the breeding herd. He had been mauled by a leopard and was limping badly on one foreleg, but he had a fine pair of lyre-shaped horns. Sean stalked the lovely red brown antelope just as Shasa had taught him, using the river bank and the wind to get within easy shot, even with the light rifle. However, when the boy knelt and raised the Winchester to his shoulder, Shasa slipped the safety-catch of his heavy weapon, ready to render the *coup de grâce*, if it was needed.

The impala dropped instantly, shot through the neck, dead before it heard the shot, and Shasa went to join his son at the kill.

As they shook hands, Shasa recognized in Sean the deep atavistic passion of the hunter. In some contemporary men that urge had cooled or been suppressed – in others it still burned brightly. Shasa and his eldest son were of that ilk, and now Shasa stooped and dipped his forefinger in the bright warm blood that trickled from the tiny wound in the ram's neck and then he traced his finger across Sean's forehead and down each cheek.

'Now you are blooded,' he said, and he wondered when that ceremony had first been performed, when the first man had painted his son's face with the blood of his first kill, and he knew instinctively that it had been back before recorded time, back when they still dressed in skins and lived in caves.

163

'Now you are a hunter,' he said, and his heart warmed to his son's proud and solemn expression. This was not a moment for laughter and chatter, it was something deep and significant, something beyond mere words. Sean had sensed that and Shasa was proud of him.

The following day they drew lots and it was Michael's turn to kill. Again Shasa wanted a solitary impala ram, so as not to alarm the breeding herd, but an animal with a good pair of horns as a trophy for the boy. It took them almost all that day of hunting before they found the right one.

Shasa and his two brothers watched from a distance as Michael made his stalk. It was a more difficult situation than Sean had been presented with, open grassland and a few scattered flat-top acacia thorns, but Michael made a stealthy approach on hands and knees, until he reached a low ant heap from which to make his shot.

Michael rose slowly and lifted the light rifle. The ram was still unaware, grazing head down thirty paces off, broadside on and offering the perfect shot for either spine or heart. Shasa was ready with the Holland and Holland to back him, should he wound the impala. Michael held his aim, and the seconds drew out. The ram raised its head and looked around warily, but Michael was absolutely still, the rifle to his shoulder, and the ram looked past him, not seeing him. Then it moved away unhurriedly, stopping once to crop a few mouthfuls. It disappeared into a clump of taller grass and without having fired, Michael slowly lowered his rifle.

Sean jumped to his feet, ready to rush out and challenge his brother, but Shasa restrained him with a hand on his shoulder. 'You and Garry go and wait for us back at the jeep,' he said.

Shasa walked out to where Michael was sitting on the ant heap with the unfired Winchester held across his lap. He sat down beside Michael and lit a cigarette. Neither of them said anything for almost ten minutes and then Michael whispered, 'He looked straight at me – and he had the most beautiful eyes.'

Shasa dropped the butt of his cigarette and ground it out under his heel. They were silent again, and then Michael blurted, 'Do I really *have* to kill something, Dad? Please don't make me.'

'No, Mickey,' Shasa put his arm around his shoulders. 'You don't have to kill anything. And in a different sort of way, I'm just as proud of you as I am of Sean.'

*   *   *

Then it was Garrick's turn. Again it was a solitary ram with a beautiful head of wide-curved horns and the stalk was through scattered bush and waist-high grass.

164

His spectacles glinting determinedly, Garry began his stalk under Shasa's patient supervision. However, he was still a long way out of range of the ram, when there was a squawk and Garry disappeared into the earth. Only a small cloud of dust marked the spot where he had been. The impala raced away into the forest, and Shasa and the two boys ran out to where Garry had last been seen. They were guided by muffled cries of distress, and a disturbance in the grass. Only Garry's legs were still above ground, kicking helplessly in the air. Shasa seized them and heaved Garry out of the deep round hole in which he was wedged from the waist.

It was the entrance to an antbear burrow. Intent on his stalk, Garry had tripped over his own bootlace and tumbled headlong into the hole. The lenses of his spectacles were thick with dust and he had skinned his cheek and torn his bushjacket. These injuries were insignificant when compared to the damage to his pride. In the next three days Garry made as many attempts to stalk. All of these were detected by his intended victim, long before he was within gunshot. Each time as he watched the antelope dash away, Garry's dejection was more abject and Sean's derision more raucous.

'Next time we will do it together,' Shasa consoled him, and the following day he coached Garry quietly through the stalk, carrying the rifle for him, pointing out the obstacles over which Garry would have tripped, and leading him the last ten yards by the hand until they were in a good position for the shot. Then he handed him the loaded rifle.

'In the neck,' he whispered. 'You can't miss.'

The ram had the best trophy horns they had seen yet, and he was twenty-five yards away. Garry lifted the rifle and peered through spectacles that were misted with the heat of excitement and his hands began to shake uncontrollably.

Watching Garry's face screwed up with tension, and seeing the erratic circles that the rifle barrel was describing, Shasa recognized the classic symptoms of 'buck fever' and reached out to prevent Garry firing. He was too late, and the ram jumped at the sharp crack of the shot, and then looked around with a puzzled expression. Neither Shasa nor the animal, and least of all Garry, knew where the bullet had gone.

'Garry!' Shasa tried to prevent him, but he fired again as wildly, and a puff of dust flicked from the earth half-way between them and the ram.

The impala went up into the air in a fluid and graceful leap, a flash of silken cinnamon-coloured skin and a glint of sweeping horns and then it was bounding away on those long delicate legs, so lightly it seemed not to touch the earth.

They walked back to the jeep in silence, Garry trailing a few paces behind his father, and his elder brother greeted him with a peal of merry laughter.

'Next time throw your specs at him, Garry.'

'I think you need a little more practice before you have another go at it,' Shasa told him tactfully. 'But don't worry. Buck fever is something that can attack anyone – even the oldest and most experienced.'

*　　*　　*

They moved camp, going deeper into the little Eden they had discovered. Now every day they came across elephant droppings, knee-high piles of fibrous yellow lumps the size of tennis balls, full of chewed bark and twigs and the stones of wild fruit in which the baboons and red-cheeked francolin delved delightedly for titbits.

Shasa showed the boys how to thrust a finger into the pile of dung to test for body heat and judge its freshness, and how to read the huge round pad-marks in the dust. To differentiate between bull and cow, between front and rear foot, to tell the direction of travel and to estimate the age of the animal. 'The tread is worn off the feet of the old ones – smooth as an old car tyre.'

Then, at last, they picked up the spoor of a huge old bull elephant, with smooth pad-marks the size of garbage-bin lids, and they left the jeep and followed him on foot for two days, sleeping on the spoor, eating the hard rations they carried. In the late afternoon of the second day, they caught up with the bull. He was in almost impenetrable jess bush through which they crept on hands and knees, and they were almost within touching distance when they made out the loom of the colossal grey body through the interlaced branches. Eleven foot high at the shoulder, he was grey as a storm cloud, and his belly rumbled like distant thunder. One at a time Shasa took the boys up closer to have a good look at him, and then they retreated out of the jess bush and left the outcast to his eternal wanderings.

'Why didn't you shoot him, Dad?' Garry stuttered. 'After following all that way?'

'Didn't you see? One tusk was broken off at the tip and despite his bulk, the other tusk was pretty small.'

They limped back over the miles on feet that were covered in blisters, and it took two rest days in camp for the boys to recover from a march that had been beyond their strength.

Often during the nights they were awakened and lay in their narrow camp beds, thrilling to the shrieking cries of the hyena scavenging the garbage dump beside the lean-to kitchen. They were

166

accompanied by the soprano yelping bark of the little dog-like jackals. The boys learned to recognize all these and the other sounds of the night – the birds such as the night jar and the dikkop, the smaller mammals, the night ape, the genet and the civet, and the insects and reptiles that squealed and hummed and croaked in the reeds of the waterhole.

They bathed infrequently, in matters of hygiene Shasa was more easy-going than their mother and a thousand times more so than their grandmother, and they ate the delicious concoctions that the Herero chef dreamed up for them with plenty of sugar and condensed milk. School was far away and they were happy as they had ever been with their father's complete and undivided attention and his wonderful stories and instruction.

'We haven't seen any signs of lions yet,' Shasa remarked at breakfast one morning. 'That's unusual. There are plenty of buffalo about, and the big cats usually keep close to the herds.'

Mention of lions gave the boys delightful cold shivers, and it was as though Shasa's words had conjured up the beast.

That afternoon as the jeep bumped and weaved slowly through the long grass avoiding antbear holes and fallen logs, they came out on the edge of a long dry vlei, one of those grassy depressions of the African bush that during the rainy season become shallow lakes and at other times are treacherous swamps where a vehicle can easily bog down, or in the driest months are smooth treeless expanses resembling a well-kept polo ground. Shasa stopped the jeep in the tree line and searched the far side of the vlei, panning his binoculars slowly to pick up any game standing amongst the shadows of the tall grey mopani trees on the far side.

'Only a couple of bat-eared foxes,' he remarked, and passed the binoculars to the boys. They laughed at the antics of these quaint little animals, as they hunted grasshoppers in the short green grass in the centre of the vlei.

'Hey, Dad!' Sean's tone changed. 'There is a big old baboon in the top of that tree.' He passed the binoculars back to his father.

'No,' Shasa said, without lowering the glasses. 'That's not a baboon. It's a human being!'

He spoke in the vernacular to the two Ovambo trackers in the back of the jeep, and there was a quick but heated discussion, everybody taking differing views.

'All right, let's go and take a look.' He drove the jeep out into the open vlei, and before they were half-way across there was no longer any doubt. In the top branches of a high mopani crouched a child, a little black girl dressed only in a loin cloth of cheap blue trade cotton.

167

'She's all alone,' Shasa exclaimed. 'Out here, fifty miles from the nearest village.'

Shasa sent the jeep roaring across the last few hundred yards then pulled up in a rolling cloud of dust and ran to the base of the mopani. He shouted up at the almost naked child. 'Come down!' and gestured to reinforce the command that she would certainly not understand. She neither moved nor raised her head from the branch on which she lay.

Shasa looked around him quickly. At the base of the tree lay a blanket roll which had been ripped open, the threadbare blankets had been shredded and torn. A skin bag had also been ripped and the dry maize meal it contained had poured into the dust, there was a black three-legged pot lying on its side, a crude axe with the blade rough forged from a piece of scrap mild steel, and the shaft of a spear snapped off at the back of the head, but the point was missing.

A little farther off were scattered a few rags on which blood stains had dried black as tar, and some other objects which were covered by a living cloak of big shimmering iridescent flies. As Shasa approached, the flies rose in a buzzing cloud, revealing the pathetic remains on which they had been feasting. There were two pairs of human hands and feet, gnawed off at the wrists and ankles, and then – horribly – the heads. A man and a woman, their necks chewed through and the exposed vertebrae crushed by great fangs. Both heads were intact, although the mouths and nostrils and empty eye-sockets were filled with the white rice pudding of eggs laid by the swarming flies. The grass was flattened over a wide area, crusted with dried blood, and the trodden dust was patterned with the un-mistakable pug-marks of a fully grown male lion.

'The lion always leaves the head and hands and feet,' his Ovambo tracker said in a matter-of-fact voice, and Shasa nodded and turned to warn the boys to stay in the car. He was too late. They had followed him and were studying the grisly relics with varied expressions – Sean with ghoulish relish, Michael with nauseated horror and Garry with intense clinical interest.

Swiftly Shasa covered the severed heads with the torn blankets. He smelt that they were already in an advanced state of de-composition: they must have lain here many days. Then once again he turned his attention to the child in the branches high above them, calling urgently to her.

'She is dead,' said his tracker. 'These people have been dead four days at least. The little one has been in the tree all that time. She is surely dead.'

Shasa would not accept that. He removed his boots and safari jacket and climbed into the mopani. He went up cautiously, testing

168

each hand-hold and every branch before committing his weight to it. To a height of ten feet above the ground the bark of the tree had been lacerated by claws. When the child was directly above him, almost within reach, Shasa called to her softly in Ovambo and then in Zulu.

'Hey, little one, can you hear me?'

There was no movement and he saw that her limbs were thin as sticks, and her skin ash-grey with that peculiar dusty look that in the African presages death. Shasa eased himself up the last few feet and reached up to touch her leg. The skin was warm, and he felt an unaccountable rush of relief. He had expected the soft cold touch of death. However, the child was unconscious and her dehydrated body was light as a bird as Shasa gently loosened her grip on the branch and lifted her against his chest. He climbed down slowly, shielding her from any jarring or rough movement and when he reached the ground carried her to the jeep and laid her in the shade.

The first-aid kit contained a comprehensive collection of medical equipment. Long ago, Shasa had been forced to minister to one of his gunbearers mauled by a wounded buffalo and after that he never hunted without the kit, and he had learned to use all of it.

Swiftly he prepared a drip set and probed for the vein in the child's arm. The vein had collapsed, her pulse was weak and erratic, and he had to try again in the foot. This time he got the canula in and administered a full bag of Ringers lactate, and while it was flowing he added ten ccs of glucose solution to it. Only then did he attempt to make the child take water orally, and her swallowing reflex was still evident. A few drops at a time he got a full cup down her throat, and she showed the first signs of life, whimpering and stirring restlessly.

As he worked, he gave orders to his trackers over his shoulder. 'Take the spade, bury those people deep. It is strange that the hyena haven't found them yet, but make sure they don't do so later.'

One of the trackers held the child on his lap during the rough journey back to camp, protecting her from the jolts and heavy bumps. As soon as they arrived, Shasa strung the aerial of the short-wave radio to the highest tree in the grove, and after an hour of frustration finally made contact, not with the H'ani Mine, but with one of the Courtney Company's geological exploration units that was a hundred miles closer. Even then the contact was faint and scratchy and intermittent, but with many repetitions he got them to relay a message to the mine. They were to send an aircraft, with the mine doctor, to the landing strip at the police post at Rundu as soon as possible.

By this time, the little girl was conscious and talking to the Ovambo trackers in a weak piping voice that reminded Shasa of the chirping of a nestling sparrow. She was speaking an obscure dialect

169

of one of the river people from Angola in the north, but the Ovambo was married to a woman of her tribe and could translate for Shasa. The story she told was harrowing.

She and her parents had been on a journey to see her grand-parents at the river village of Shakawe in the south, a trek on foot of hundreds of miles. Carrying all their worldly possessions, they had taken a short cut through this remote and deserted country when they had become aware that a lion was dogging them, fol-lowing them through the forest – at first keeping its distance and then closing in.

Her father, an intrepid hunter, had realized the futility of stopping and trying to build some sort of shelter or of taking to the trees where the beast would besiege them. Instead he had tried to keep the lion off by shouting and clapping while he hurried to reach the river and the sanctuary of one of the fishing villages.

The child described the final attack when the animal, its thick ruff of black mane erect, had rushed in at the family, grunting and roaring. Her mother had only time enough to push the girl into the lowest branch of the mopani before the lion was on them. Her father had stood gallantly to meet it, and thrust his long spear into its chest, but the spear had snapped and the lion leapt upon him and tore out his bowels with a single swipe of curved yellow claws. Then it had sprung at the mother as she was attempting to climb into the mopani and hooked its claws into her back and dragged her down.

In her small birdlike voice the child described how the lion had eaten the corpses of her parents, down to the heads and feet and hands, while she watched from the upper branches. It had taken two days over the grisly feast, at intervals pausing to lick the spear wound in its shoulder. On the third day it had attempted to reach the child, ripping at the trunk of the mopani and roaring horribly. At last it had given up and wandered away into the forest, limping heavily with the wound. Even then the child had been too terrified to leave her perch and she had clung there until at last she had passed out with exhaustion and grief, exposure and fear.

While she was relating all this, the camp servants were refuelling the jeep and preparing supplies for the journey to Rundu. Shasa left as soon as this was done, taking the boys with him. He would not leave them in the camp while there was a wounded man-eating lion roaming in the vicinity.

They drove through the night, recrossing their jerry-built bridge and retracing their tracks until the following morning they intersected the main Rundu road, and that afternoon they finally arrived, dusty and exhausted, at the airstrip. The blue and silver Mosquito that Shasa had left at H'ani Mine was parked in the shade of the trees at

170

the edge of the strip and the company pilot and the doctor were squatting under the wing, waiting patiently.

Shasa gave the child into the doctor's care, and went quickly through the pile of urgent documents and messages that the pilot had brought with him. He scribbled out orders and replies to these, and a long letter of instruction to David Abrahams. When the Mosquito took off again, the sick girl went with them. She would receive first-rate medical attention at the mine hospital, and Shasa would decide what to do with the little orphan once she was fully recovered.

The return to the safari camp was more leisurely than the outward journey, and over the next few days the excitement of the lion adventure was forgotten in the other absorbing concerns of safari life, not least of which was the business of Garry's first kill. Bad luck now combined with his lack of coordination and poor marksmanship to cheat him of this experience that he hungered for more than any other, while on the other hand Sean succeeded in providing meat for the camp at every attempt.

'What we are going to do is practise a little more on the pigeons,' Shasa decided, after one of Garry's least successful outings. In the evenings the flocks of fat green pigeons came flighting in to feast on the wild figs in the grove beside the waterhole.

Shasa took the boys down as soon as the sun lost its heat, and placed them in the hides they had built of saplings and dried grass, each hide far enough from the next and carefully sited so that there was no danger of a careless shot causing an accident. This afternoon Shasa put Sean into a hide at the near end of the glade, with Michael, who had once again declined to take an active part in the sport, to keep him company and pick up the fallen birds for him.

Then Shasa and Garry set off together for the far side of the grove. Shasa was leading with Garry following him as the game path twisted between the thick yellow trunks of the figs. Their bark was yellow and scaly as the skin of a giant reptile, and the bunches of figs grew directly on the trunks rather than on the tips of the branches. Beneath the trees the undergrowth was tangled and thick, and the game path was so twisted that they could see only a short distance ahead, The light was poor this late in the afternoon, with the branches meeting overhead.

Shasa came around another turn and the lion was in the game path, walking straight towards him only fifty paces away. In the instant he saw it, Shasa realized that it was the man-eater. It was a huge beast, the biggest he had ever seen in a lifetime of hunting. It stood higher than his waist, and its mane was coal-black, long and shaggy and dense, shading to blue grey down the beast's flanks and back.

171

It was an old lion, its flat face criss-crossed with scars. Its mouth was gaping, panting with pain as it limped towards him, and he saw that the spear wound in the shoulder had mortified, the raw flesh crimson as a rose petal and the fur around the wound wet and slicked down where the lion had been licking it. The flies swarmed to the wound, irritating and stinging, and the lion was in a vicious mood, sick with age and pain. It lifted its dark and shaggy head and Shasa looked into the pale yellow eyes and saw the agony and blind rage they contained.

'Garry!' he said urgently. 'Walk backwards! Don't run, but get out of here,' and without looking around he swung the sling of the rifle off his shoulder.

The lion dropped into a crouch, its long tail with the black bush of hair at the tip lashed back and forth like a metronome, as it gathered itself for the charge, and its yellow eyes fastened on Shasa, a focus for all its rage.

Shasa knew there would be time for only a single shot, for it would cover the ground between them in a blazing blur of speed. The light was too bad and the range was too far for that single shot to be conclusive, he would let it come in to where there could be no doubt, and the big 300-grain soft-nosed bullet from the Holland and Holland would shatter its skull and blow its brains to a mush.

The lion launched into its charge, keeping low to the earth, snaking in and grunting as it came, gut-shaking bursts of sound through the gaping jaws lined with long yellow fangs. Shasa braced himself and brought up the rifle, but before he could fire, there was the sharp crack of the little Winchester beside him and the lion collapsed in the middle of his charge, going down head first and cartwheeling, flopping over on its back to expose the soft butter-yellow fur of its belly, its limbs stretching and relaxing, the long curved talons in its huge paws slowly retracting into the pads, the pink tongue lolling out of its open jaws, and the rage dying out of those pale yellow eyes. From the tiny bullet hole between its eyes a thin serpent of blood crawled down to dribble from its brow into the dirt beneath it.

In astonishment Shasa lowered his rifle and looked round. Beside him stood Garry, his head at the level of Shasa's lowest rib, the little Winchester still at his shoulder, his face set and deadly pale, and his spectacles glinting in the gloom beneath the trees.

'You killed it,' Shasa said stupidly. 'You stood your ground and killed it.'

Shasa walked forward slowly and stooped over the carcass of the man-eater. He shook his head in amazement, and then looked back at his son. Garry had not yet lowered the rifle, but he was beginning now to tremble with delayed terror. Shasa dipped his finger into the

172

blood that dribbled from the wound in the man-eater's forehead, then walked back to where Garry stood. He painted the ritual stripes on the boy's forehead and cheeks.

'Now you are a man and I'm proud of you,' he said. Slowly the colour flushed back into Garry's cheeks and his lips stopped trembling, and then his face began to glow. It was an expression of such pride and unutterable joy that Shasa felt his throat close up and tears sting his eyelids.

Every servant came from the camp to view the man-eater and to hear Shasa describe the details of the hunt. Then, by the light of the lanterns, they carried the carcass back. While the skinners went to work, the men sang the song of the hunter in Garry's honour.

Sean was torn between incredulous admiration and deepest envy of his brother, while Michael was fulsome in his praises. Garry refused to wash the dried lion's blood from his face when at last, well after midnight, Shasa finally ordered them to bed. At breakfast he still wore the crusted stripes of blood on his beaming grubby face and Michael read aloud the heroic poem he had written in Garry's honour. It began:

With lungs to blast the skies with sound
And breath hot as the blacksmith's forge
Eyes as yellow as the moon's full round
And the lust on human flesh to gorge –

Shasa hid a smile at the laboured rhyming, and at the end applauded as loudly as the rest of them. After breakfast they all trooped out to watch the skinners dressing out the lion-skin, pegging it fur side down in the shade, scraping away the yellow subcutaneous fat and rubbing in coarse salt and alum.

'Well, I still think it died of a heart attack,' Sean could suppress his envy no longer, and Garry rounded on him furiously.

'We all know what a clever dick you are. But when you shoot *your* first lion, then you can come and talk to me, smarty pants. All you are good for is a few little old impala!'

It was a long speech, delivered in white heat, and Garry never stumbled nor stuttered once. It was the first time Shasa had seen him stand up to Sean's casual bullying, and he waited for Sean to assert his authority. For seconds it hung in the balance, he could see Sean weighing it up, deciding whether to tweak the spikes of hair at Garry's temple or to give him a chestnut down the ribs. He could see also that Garry was ready for it, his fists clenched and his lips set in a pale determined line. Suddenly Sean grinned that charming smile.

'Only kidding,' he announced airily, and turned back to admire

173

the tiny bullet-hole in the skull. 'Wow! Right between the eyes!' It was a peace offering.

Garry looked bemused and uncertain. It was the first time that he had forced Sean to back down, and he wasn't able immediately to grasp that he had succeeded.

Shasa stepped up and put his arm around Garry's shoulders. 'Do you know what I'm going to do, champ? I'm going to have the head fully mounted for the wall in your room, with eyes and everything,' he said.

For the first time, Shasa was aware that Garry had developed hard little muscles in his shoulders and upper arm. He had always thought him a runt. Perhaps he had never truly looked at the child before.

*   *   *

Then suddenly it was over, and the servants were breaking camp and packing the tents and beds on to the trucks, and appallingly the prospect of the return to Weltevreden and school loomed ahead of them. Shasa tried to keep their spirits jaunty with stories and songs on the long drive back to H'ani Mine but with every mile the boys were more dejected.

On the last day when the hills which the Bushmen call the 'Place of All Life' floated on the horizon ahead of them, detached from the earth by the shimmering heat mirage, Shasa asked, 'Have you gentlemen decided what you are going to do when you leave school?' It was an attempt to cheer them up, more than a serious enquiry. 'What about you, Sean?'

'I want to do what we have been doing. I want to be a hunter, an elephant hunter like great-grand-uncle Sean.'

'Splendid!' Shasa agreed. 'Only problem I can see is that you are at least sixty years too late.'

'Well then,' said Sean, 'I'll be a soldier – I like shooting things.'

A shadow passed behind Shasa's eyes before he looked at Michael.

'What about you, Mickey?'

'I want to be a writer. I will work as a newspaper reporter and in my spare time I'll write poetry and great books.'

'You'll starve to death, Mickey,' Shasa laughed, and then he swivelled around to Garry who was leaning over the back of the driving seat.

'What about you, champ?'

'I'm going to do what you do, Dad.'

'And what is it I do?' Shasa demanded with interest.

'You are the chairman of Courtney Mining and Finance, and you tell everybody else what to do. That's what I want to be one day, chairman of Courtney Mining and Finance.'

Shasa stopped smiling and was silent for a moment, studying the child's determined expression, then he said lightly, 'Well then, it looks as though it's up to you and me to support the elephant hunter and the poet.' And he ran his hand over Garry's already unruly hair. It no longer required any effort to make an affectionate gesture towards his ugly duckling.

*　　*　　*

They came singing across the rolling grasslands of Zululand, and they were one hundred strong. All of them were members of the Buffaloes and Hendrick Tabaka had carefully picked them for this special honour guard. They were the best, and all of them were dressed in tribal regalia, feathers and furs and monkey-skin capes, kilts of cow-tails. They carried only fighting-sticks, for the strictest tradition forbade metal weapons of any kind on this day.

At the head of the column Moses Gama and Hendrick Tabaka trotted. They also had set aside their European clothing for the occasion, and of all their men they alone wore leopard-skin cloaks, as was their noble right. Half a mile behind them rose the dust of the cattle herd. This was the *lobola*, the marriage price, two hundred head of prime beasts, as had been agreed. The herd-boys were all of them sons of the leading warriors who had ridden in the cattle trucks with their charges during the three-hundred-mile journey from the Witwatersrand. In charge of the herd-boys were Wellington and Raleigh Tabaka and they had detrained the herd at Ladyburg railway station. Like their father, they had discarded their western-style clothing for the occasion and were dressed in loincloths, and armed with their fighting-sticks, and they danced and called to the cattle, keeping them in a tight bunch, both of them excited and filled with self-importance by the task they had been allotted.

Ahead of them rose the high escarpment beyond the little town of Ladyburg. The slopes were covered with dark forests of black wattle and all of it was Courtney land, from where the waterfall smoked with spray in the sunlight around the great curve of hills. All ten thousand acres of it belonged to Lady Anna Courtney, the relict of Sir Garrick Courtney and to Storm Anders, who was the daughter of General Sean Courtney. However, beyond the waterfall lay a hundred choice acres of land which had been left to Sangane Dinizulu in terms of the will of General Sean Courtney, for he had been a

175

faithful and beloved retainer of the Courtney family as had his father Mbejane Dinizulu before him.

The road descended the escarpment in a series of hairpin bends, and when Moses Gama shaded his eyes and stared ahead, he saw another band of warriors coming down it to meet them. They were many more in number, perhaps five hundred strong. Like Moses' party they were dressed in full regimentals, with plumes of fur and feathers on their heads and war rattles on their wrists and ankles. The two parties halted at the foot of the escarpment, and from a hundred paces faced each other, though still they sang and stamped and brandished their weapons.

The shields of the Zulus were matched, selected from dappled cowhides of white and chocolate brown, and the brows of the warriors that carried them were bound with strips of the same dappled hide while their kilts and their plumes were cow-tails of purest white. They made a daunting and warlike show, all big men, their bodies gleaming with sweat in the sunlight, their eyes bloodshot with dust and excitement and the pots of millet beer they had already downed.

Facing them Moses felt his nerves crawl with a trace of the terror that these men had for two hundred years inspired in all the other tribes of Africa, and to suppress it he stamped and sang as loudly as his Buffaloes who pressed closely around him. On this his wedding day, Moses Gama had put aside all the manners and mores of the west, and slipped back easily into his African origins and his heart pumped and thrilled to the rhythms and the pulse of this harsh continent.

From the Zulu ranks opposite him sprang a champion, a magnificent figure of a man with the strip of leopard skin around his brow that declared his royal origins. He was one of Victoria Dinizulu's elder brothers, and Moses knew he was a qualified lawyer with a large practice at Eshowe, the Zululand capital, but today he was all African, fierce and threatening as he swirled in the *giya*, the challenge dance.

He leapt and spun and shouted his own praises and those of his family, daring the world, challenging the men who faced him, while behind him his comrades drummed with their sticks on the rawhide shields, and the sound was like distant thunder, the last sound that a million victims had ever heard, the death-knell of Swazi and Xhosa, of Boer and Briton in the days when the impis of Chaka and Dingaan and Cetewayo had swept across the land, from Isandhlawana, the Hill of the Little Hand, where seven hundred British infantry were cut down in one of the worst military reverses that England had ever suffered in Africa, to the 'Place of Weeping' which the Boers named 'Weenen' for their grief for the women and children who died to that

176

same dreadful drum roll when the impis came swarming down across the Tugela river, to a thousand other nameless and forgotten killing grounds where the lesser tribes had perished before the men of Zulu.

At last the Zulu champion staggered back into the ranks, streaked with sweat and dust, his chest heaving and froth upon his lips, and now it was Moses' turn to *giya*, and he danced out from amongst his Buffaloes, and leapt shoulder-high with his leopard-skins swirling around him. His limbs shone like coal freshly cut from the face, and his eyes and teeth were white as mirrors flashing in the sunlight. His voice rang from the escarpment, magnified by the echoes, and though the men facing him could not understand the words, the force and meaning of them was clear, his haughty disdain evident in every gesture. They growled and pressed forward, while his own Buffaloes were goaded by his example, their blood coming to the boil, ready to rush forward and join battle with their traditional foe, ready to perpetuate the bloody vendetta that had already run a hundred years.

At the very last moment, when violence and inevitable death were only a heartbeat away, and rage was as thick in the air as the static electricity of the wildest summer thunderstorm, Moses Gama stopped dancing abruptly, posing like a heroic statue before them – and so great was the force of his personality, so striking his presence, that the drumming of shields and the growl of battle rage died away.

Into the silence Moses Gama called in the Zulu language. 'I bring the marriage price!' and he held his stick aloft, a signal to the herd-boys who followed the marriage party.

Lowing and bawling, adding their dust to the dust of the dancers, the herd was driven forward and immediately the mood of the Zulus changed. For a thousand years, since they had come down from the far north, following the tsetse-fly-free corridors down the continent with their herds, the Nguni peoples from which the Zulu tribe would emerge under the black emperor Chaka, had been cattle men. Their animals were their wealth and their treasure. They loved cattle as other men love women and children. Almost from the day they could walk unaided, the boys tended the herds, living with them in the veld from dawn to dusk of every day, establishing with them a bond and almost mystic communion, protecting them from predators with their very lives, talking to them and handling them and coming to know them completely. It was said that King Chaka knew every individual beast in his royal herds, and that out of a hundred thousand head he would know immediately if one were missing and would ask for it with a complete description, and not hesitate to order his executioners with their knobkerries to dash out the brains of even the youngest herd-boy if there was even a suspicion of his negligence.

177

So it was a committee of strict and expert judges who put aside the dancing and posturing and boasting, and instead applied themselves to the serious business of appraising the bride price. Each animal was dragged from the herd, and amid a buzz of comment and speculation and argument, was minutely examined. Its limbs and trunk were palpated by dozens of hands simultaneously, its jaws were forced open to expose the teeth and tongue, its head twisted so that its ears and nostrils could be peered into, its udders stroked and weighed in the palm, its tail lifted to estimate its calf-bearing history and potential. Then finally, almost reluctantly, each animal was declared acceptable by old Sangane Dinizulu himself, the father of the bride. No matter how hard they tried, they could find no grounds for rejecting a single animal. The Ovambo and the Xhosa love their cattle every bit as much as the Zulu, and are as expert in their judgement. Moses and Hendrick had exercised all their skills in making their selection, for pride and honour were at stake.

It took many hours for every one of the two hundred animals to be examined while the bridegroom's party, still keeping aloof from the Zulus, squatted in the short grass on the side of the road, pretending indifference to the proceedings. The sun was hot and the dust aggravated the men's thirst, but no refreshment was offered while the scrutiny went on.

Then at last Sangane Dinizulu, his silver pate shining in the sun, but his body still upright and regal, called his herd-boys. Joseph Dinizulu came forward. As the senior herdsman, the old man gave the herd into his care. Although his exhortations were severe and he scowled most ferociously, the old man's affection for his youngest son was ill-concealed, as was his delight at the quality of the stock which made up the marriage price. So when he turned and for the first time greeted his future son-in-law, he was having great difficulty in suppressing his smiles, they kept shooting out like beams of sunlight through cloud holes and were just as swiftly extinguished.

With dignity he embraced Moses Gama, and though he was a tall man, he had to reach up to do so. Then he stepped back and clapped his hands, calling to the small party of young women who were sitting a little way off.

Now they rose and helped each other to settle the enormous clay pots of beer upon each other's heads. Then they formed a line and came forward, singing and undulating their hips, although their heads remained steady and not a drop slopped over the rims of the pots. They were all unmarried girls, none of them wore the high clay headdress or the matron's leather cloak, and above their short beaded skirts their bodies were oiled and stark naked so their pert young breasts joggled and bounced to the rhythm of the song of welcome

178

and the wedding guests murmured and smiled appreciatively. Although deep down old Sangane Dinizulu disapproved of marriage outside the tribe of Zulu, the *lobola* had been good and his future son-in-law was, by all accounts, a man of stature and importance. None could reasonably object to suitors of this calibre, and as there might be others like him in the bridegroom's party, Sangane was not loath to show off his wares.

The girls knelt in front of the guests, hanging their heads and averting their eyes shyly. Giggling in response to the knowing looks and sly sallies of the men, they proffered the brimming beer-pots, and then withdrew swinging their hips so their skirts swirled up and pert young buttocks peeked provocatively from beneath them.

The beer-pots were so heavy that they required both hands to lift, and when they were lowered, there were thick white moustaches on the upper lips of the guests. Noisily they licked them away and the laughter became more relaxed and friendly.

When the beer-pots were empty, Sangane Dinizulu stood before them and made a short speech of welcome. Then they formed up again and started up the road that climbed the escarpment, but now Zulu ran shoulder to shoulder with Ovambo and Xhosa. Moses Gama had never believed he would see that happen. It was a beginning, he thought, a fine beginning, but there remained to be scaled a range of endeavour as high as the peaks of the Drakensberg mountains which rose out of the blue distances before them as they topped the escarpment.

Sangane Dinizulu had set the pace up the slope, although he must be all of seventy years of age, and now he led the cavalcade of men and animals down to his kraal. It was sited on a grassy slope above the river. The huts of his many wives were arranged in a circle, beehives of smooth thatch each with an entrance so low that a man must stoop to enter. In the centre of the circle was the old man's hut. It also was a perfect beehive, but much grander than the others, and the thatch had been plaited into intricate patterns. It was the home of a chieftain of Zulu, a son of the heavens.

On the grassy slope was assembled a multitude, a thousand or more of the most important men of the tribe with all their senior wives. Many of them had travelled for days to be here, and they squatted in clumps and clusters down the slope, each chieftain surrounded by his own retainers.

When the bridegroom's party came over the crest, they rose as one man, shouting their greetings and drumming their shields, and Sangane Dinizulu led them down to the entrance of the kraal where he paused and spread his arms for silence. The wedding guests settled down again comfortably in the grass. Only the chieftains sat on their

179

carved stools of office, and while the young girls carried the beer-pots amongst them, Sangane Dinizulu made his wedding speech.

First he related the history of the tribe, and particularly of his own clan of Dinizulu. He recited their battle honours and the valiant deeds of his ancestors. These were many and it took a long time, but the guests were well content for the black beer-pots were replenished as swiftly as they were emptied, and although the old ones knew the history of the tribe as intimately as did Sangane Dinizulu, its repetition gave them endless satisfaction, as though it were an anchor in the restless sea of life. As long as the history and the customs persisted, the tribe was secure.

At last Sangane Dinizulu was done, and in a voice that was hoarse and scratchy, he ended, 'There are those amongst you who have queried the wisdom of a daughter of Zulu marrying with a man of another tribe. I respect these views, for I also have been consumed by doubts and have pondered long and seriously.'

Now the older heads in the congregation were nodding, and a few hostile glances were shot at the bridegroom's party, but Sangane Dinizulu went on.

'I had these same doubts when my daughter asked my permission to leave the hut of her mother and journey to *goldi*, the place of gold, and to work in the great hospital at Baragwanath. Now I am persuaded that what she has done was right and proper. She is a daughter of which an old man can be proud. She is a woman of the future.'

He faced his peers calmly and resolutely, seeing the doubt in their eyes, but ignoring it.

'The man who will be her husband is not of Zulu – but he also is a man of the future. Most of you have heard his name. You know him as a man of force and power. I am persuaded that by giving him my daughter in marriage I am once again doing what is right – for my daughter and for the tribe.'

When the old man sat down on his stool they were silent, serious and withdrawn, and they looked uneasily towards the bridegroom where he squatted at the head of his party.

Moses Gama rose to his feet, and strode up the slope from where he could look down upon them. He was silhouetted against the sky, his height was emphasized and the royal leopard skin declared his lineage.

'Oh people of Zulu, I greet you.' That deep thrilling voice reached to everyone of them, carrying clearly in the silence, and they stirred and murmured with surprise as they realized that he was speaking fluent Zulu.

'I have come to take one of the most comely daughters of your

180

tribe, but as part of the marriage price I bring you a dream and a promise,' he began, and they were attentive but puzzled. Slowly the mood changed as he went on to set out his vision for them, a unification of the tribes and a sloughing off of the white domination under which they had existed for three hundred years. The older men became more and more uneasy as they listened, they shook their heads and exchanged angry glances, some of them muttered aloud, an unusual discourtesy towards an important guest, but what he was suggesting was a destruction of the old ways, a denial of the customs and orders of society which had held together the fabric of their lives. In its place he was offering something strange and untested, a world turned upside down, a chaos in which old values and proven codes were discarded with nothing to replace them except wild words – and like all old men, they were afraid of change.

With the younger men it was different. They listened, and his words warmed them like the flames of the camp fire in the frosty winter night. One of them listened more intently than all the rest. Joseph Dinizulu was not yet fourteen years of age, but the blood of great Chaka charged his veins and pumped up his heart. These words, strange at first, began to sing in his head like one of the old fighting chants, and his breath came quicker as he heard Moses Gama end his bridal speech.

'So, people of Zulu, I come to give you back the land of your fathers. I come to give you the promise that once again a black man will rule in Africa, and that as surely as tomorrow's sun will rise, the future belongs to us.'

All of a sudden Joseph Dinizulu was struck by a sense of destiny.

'A black man will rule in Africa.'

For Joseph Dinizulu, as for many others there that day, the world would never be the same again.

*   *   *

Victoria Dinizulu waited in her mother's hut. She sat on the earthen floor with a tanned kaross of hyrax fur under her. She wore the traditional dress of a Zulu bride. The beadwork had been sewn by her mother and her sisters, intricate and beautiful, each pattern carrying a hidden message. There were strings of coloured beads around her wrists and her ankles, and necklaces of beads, while her short skirt of leather strips was beaded and strings of beads were plaited into her hair and draped around her waist. In one respect only did her costume differ from that of the traditional Zulu bride: her breasts were covered, as they had been since puberty when she had been baptized into the Anglican Church. She wore a blouse of

181

striped silk in gay colours which complemented the rest of her costume.

As she sat in the centre of the hut, she listened intently to the voice of her bridegroom from without. It carried clearly to her, though she had to shush the other girls when they whispered and giggled. Every word struck her with the force of an arrow, and she felt her love and duty for the man who uttered them swell until they threatened to choke her.

The interior of the hut was gloomy as an ancient cathedral for there were no windows, and the air was hazy with wood smoke that uncoiled lazily from the central fire and rose to the small hole in the summit of the belled roof. The cathedral atmosphere enhanced her mood of reverence, and when the voice of Moses Gama ceased, the silence seemed to enter her heart. No cheers or shouted agreement followed his speech. The men of Zulu were silent and disturbed by it. Victoria could feel it even where she sat in the darkened hut.

'It is time now,' her mother whispered, and lifted her to her feet. 'Go with God,' she whispered, for her mother was a Christian and had introduced her to that religion.

'Be a good wife to this man,' she instructed, and led her to the entrance of the hut.

She stepped outside, into the dazzling sunlight. This was the moment for which the guests had been waiting, and when they saw how beautiful she was, they roared like bulls and drummed their shields. Her father came to greet her and lead her to the carved ebony stool at the entrance of the kraal, so that the *cimeza* ceremony could begin.

The *cimeza* was the 'closing of the eyes' and Victoria sat with her eyes tightly closed as the representatives of the various clans came forward one at a time to place their gift before her. Only then was Victoria allowed to open her eyes and exclaim in wonder at the generosity of the givers. There were gifts of pots and blankets and ornaments, marvellously woven beadwork, and envelopes of money.

Shrewdly old Sangane calculated the value of each as he stood behind her stool, and he was grinning with satisfaction when at last he gave the signal to his son Joseph to drive in the feast. He had set aside twelve fat steers for the slaughter, a gesture that proved him to be even more generous than the bearers of the wedding gifts, but then he was a great man and head of a noble clan. The chosen warriors came forward to slaughter the steers, and their mournful death bellows and the rank smell of fresh blood in the dust soon gave way to the aroma from the cooking fires that drifted blue smoke across the hillside.

At a gesture from old Sangane Moses Gama strode up the slope

to the entrance of the kraal and Victoria rose to her feet to meet
him. They faced each other and once again a silence fell. The guests
were awed by this couple, the groom so tall and commanding, the
bride beautiful and nubile.

Involuntarily they craned forward as Victoria unclipped the *ucu*
string of beads from around her waist. This was the symbol of her
virginity, and she knelt before Moses and, with both hands cupped
in the formal and polite gesture, she offered him the beads. As he
accepted her and her gift, a great shout went up from the guests. It
was done, Moses Gama was her husband and her master at last.

Now the feasting and the beer-drinking could begin in earnest,
and the raw red meat was heaped upon the coals and snatched off
again barely singed, while the beer-pots passed from hand to hand
and the young girls went swinging down the slope bearing fresh pots
upon their heads.

Suddenly there was an uproar and a band of plumed warriors
came dashing up the slope towards where Victoria sat at the kraal
entrance. They were her brothers and half-brothers and nephews,
even Joseph Dinizulu was amongst them, and they shouted their war
cries as they came to rescue their sister from this stranger who would
take her from their midst.

However, the Buffaloes were ready for them, and with Hendrick
at their head and sticks whistling and hissing, they rushed in to
prevent the abduction. The women wailed and ululated and the
fighting-sticks clattered and whacked on flesh, and the warriors
howled and circled and charged at each other in a fine mist of
dust.

It was for this that all metal weapons were strictly banned from
the ceremony, for the fighting, which was at first playful, soon heated
up and blood dripped and bones cracked before the abductors
allowed themselves to be driven off. The blood was staunched with a
handful of dust clapped on the wound, and both victors and vanquished had worked up a fine thirst and shouted to the girls to bring
more beer. The uproar subsided for only a few minutes to be resumed
almost immediately as from the top of the slope came the rumble of
motor cars.

The children raced up the hill and began to clap and sing as two
big motor cars appeared over the brow and came bumping slowly
over the rough track that led to the kraal.

In the leading vehicle was a large white woman, with a red face as
lined and craggy as that of a bulldog, and a wide-brimmed old-
fashioned hat on her head from under which grey hair curled
untidily.

'Who is she?' Moses demanded.

'Lady Anna Courtney,' Victoria exclaimed. She was the one who encouraged me to leave here and go into the world.'

Impulsively Victoria ran forward to meet the vehicle, and when Lady Anna descended ponderously, she embraced her.

'So, my child, you have come back to us.' Lady Anna's accent was still thick, though she had lived thirty-five years in Africa.

'Not for long.' Victoria laughed and Lady Anna looked at her fondly. Once the child had served in the big house as one of her house maids, until her bright beauty and intelligence had convinced Lady Anna that she was superior to such menial work.

'Where is this man who is taking you away?' she demanded, and Victoria took her hand.

'First you must greet my father, then I will introduce you to my husband.'

From the second motor car a middle-aged couple climbed down to be enthusiastically greeted by the crowd that pressed forward around them. The man was tall and dapper, with the bearing of a soldier. He was tanned by the sun and his eyes had the far-away look of the outdoor man. He twirled his moustaches and took his wife on his arm. She was almost as tall and even slimmer than he was, and despite the streaks of grey in her hair, she was still an unusually handsome woman.

Sangane Dinizulu came to greet them.

'I see you, Jamela!' His dignity was somewhat tempered by a happy grin of welcome, and Colonel Mark Anders answered him in perfectly colloquial Zulu.

'I see you, old man.' The term was one of respect. 'May all your cattle and all your wives grow fat and sleek.'

Sangane turned to his wife Storm, who was the daughter of old General Sean Courtney. 'I see you, *Nkosikazi*, you bring honour to my kraal.' The bond between the two families was like steel. It went back to another century and had been tested a thousand times.

'Oh, Sangane, I am so happy for you this day – and for Victoria.' Storm left her husband and went quickly to embrace the Zulu girl.

'I wish you joy and many fine sons, Vicky,' she told her, and Victoria answered,

'I owe you and your family so much, *Nkosikazi*. I will never be able to repay you.'

'Don't ever try,' Storm told her with mock severity. 'I feel as though my own daughter is getting married today. Introduce us to your husband, Vicky.'

Now Moses Gama came towards them, and when Storm greeted him in Zulu, he replied gravely in English, 'How do you do, Mrs Anders. Victoria has spoken of you and your family very often.'

184

When at last he turned to Mark Anders, he proffered his right hand.

'How do you do, Colonel?' Moses asked, and a wry smile flitted across his lips as he saw the white man hesitate momentarily before accepting the handshake. It was unusual for men to greet each other thus across the dividing line of colour, and despite his fluency in the language and his pretended affection for the Zulu people, Moses recognized this man.

Colonel Mark Anders was an anachronism, a son of the English Queen Victoria, a soldier who had fought in two world wars, and the warden of Chaka's Gate National Park which he had saved from the poachers and despoilers by dedication and sheer bloody-mindedness, and made into one of Africa's most celebrated wild-life sanctuaries. He loved the wild animals of Africa with a kind of paternal passion, protecting and cherishing them, and to only a slightly less degree his attitude towards the black tribes, especially the Zulus, was the same, paternalistic and condescending. By this definition he was the mortal enemy of Moses Gama, and as they looked into each other's eyes, they both recognized this fact.

'I have heard the lion roar from afar,' Mark Anders said in Zulu. 'Now I meet the beast face to face.'

'I have heard of you as well, Colonel,' Moses replied, pointedly speaking English.

'Victoria is a gentle child,' Mark Anders persisted in his use of Zulu. 'We all hope you will not teach her your fierce ways.'

'She will be a dutiful wife,' Moses said in English. 'She will do what I ask of her, I am sure.'

Storm had been following the exchange, sensing the innate hostility between the two men and now she intervened smoothly.

'If you are ready, Moses, we can all go down to Theuniskraal for the ceremony.'

Victoria and her mother had insisted on a Christian ceremony to reinforce the traditional tribal wedding. Now Sangane and most of the other guests who were pagan and ancestor-worshippers, remained at the kraal, while the diminished bridal party crowded into the two motor vehicles.

Theuniskraal was the home of Lady Anna Courtney and the original seat of the Courtney family. It stood amongst its sprawling lawns and unruly gardens of palms and bourgainvillaea and pride of India trees at the foot of the Ladyburg escarpment. It was a rambling old building of oddly assorted architectual styles, and beyond the gardens stretched endless fields of sugar cane, that dipped and undulated to the breeze like the swells of the ocean.

The wedding party trooped into the house to change into garb more suitable than beads and furs and feathers for the second

185

ceremony while Lady Anna and the family went to greet the Anglican priest in the marquee that had been set up on the front lawn.

When the bridegroom and his attendants came out on to the lawns half an hour later, they wore dark lounge suits and Victoria's elder brother, who had pranced and swirled his plumes in the *giya* just a few hours before, now wore his Law Association tie in an impeccable Windsor knot and aviator-style dark glasses against the glare of Theuniskraal's whitewashed walls, as he chatted affably with the Courtney family, while they waited for the bride.

Victoria's mother was decked out in one of Lady Anna's cast-off caftans, for the two ladies were of similar build, and she was already sampling the fare that was laid out on the long trestle table in the marquee. Colonel Mark Anders and the Anglican priest stood a little aside from the main group; men of the same generation, they both found the proceedings disquieting and unnatural. It had taken all Storm's powers to persuade the priest to perform the ceremony, and then he had only agreed on condition that the wedding was not held in his own church in the village where his conservative white congregation might take offence.

'Damned if we weren't all a sight better off in the old days when everybody knew their place instead of trying to ape their betters,' Mark Anders grumbled, and the priest nodded.

'No sense in looking for trouble —' He broke off as Victoria came out on to the wide verandah. Storm Anders had helped her select her full-length white satin wedding dress with a wreath of tiny red tea roses holding the long veil in place around her brow. The contrast of red and white against her dark and glossy skin was striking and her joy was infectious. Even Mark Anders forgot his misgivings for the moment, as Lady Anna at the piano struck up the wedding march.

*   *   *

At her father's kraal, Victoria's family had built a magnificent new hut for her nuptial night. Her brothers and half-brothers had cut the wattle saplings and the trunk for the central post and plaited the stripped green branches into the shape of the beehive. Then her mother and sisters and half-sisters had done the women's work of thatching, carefully combing the long grass stems and lacing the crisp bundles on to the wattle framework, packing and trimming and weaving them until the finished structure was smooth and symmetrical and the brushed grass stems shone like polished brass.

Everything the hut contained was new, from the three-legged pot to the lamp and the blankets and the magnificent kaross of hyrax and monkeyskins which was the gift of Victoria's sisters, lovingly tanned and sewn by them into a veritable work of art.

At the cooking fire in the centre of the hut Victoria worked alone, preparing the first meal for her husband, while she listened to the shouted laughter of the guests outside in the night. The millet beer was mild. However, the women had brewed hundreds of gallons and the guests had been drinking since early morning.

Now she heard the bridegroom's party approaching the hut. There was singing and loud suggestive advice, cries of encouragement and rude exhortations to duty and then Moses Gama stooped through the entrance. He straightened and stood tall over her, his head brushing the curved roof and outside the voices of his comrades retreated and dwindled.

Still kneeling, Victoria sat back on her heels and looked up at him. Now at last she had discarded her western clothing and wore for the last time the short beaded skirt of the virgin. In the soft ruddy light of the fire her naked upper body had the dark patina of antique amber.

'You are very beautiful,' he said, for she was the very essence of Nguni womanhood. He came to her and took her hands and lifted her to her feet.

'I have prepared food for you,' she whispered huskily.

'There will be time later to eat.'

He led her to the piled kaross and she stood submissively while he untied the thong of her apron and then lifted her in his arms and laid her on the bed of soft fur.

As a girl she had played the games with the boys in the reed banks beside the waterhole, and out on the open grassy veld where she had gone with the other girls to gather firewood conveniently close to where the cattle were being herded. These games of touching and exploring, of rubbing and fondling, right up to the forbidden act of intromission, were sanctioned by tribal custom and smiled at by the elders, but none of them had fully prepared her for the power and skill of this man, or for the sheer magnificence of him. He reached deeply into her body and touched her very soul so that much later in the night she clung to him and whispered:

'Now I am more than just your wife, I am your slave to the end of my days.'

In the dawn her joy was blighted, and though her lovely moon face remained serene, she wept within when he told her, 'There will only be one more night – on the road back to Johannesburg. Then I must leave you.'

'For how long?' she asked.

'Until my work is done,' he replied, then his expression softened and he stroked her face. 'You knew that it must be so. I warned you that when you married me, you were marrying the struggle.'

'You warned me,' she agreed in a husky whisper. 'But there was no way that I could guess at the agony of your leaving.'

*   *   *

They rose early the following morning. Moses had acquired a second-hand Buick, old and shabby enough not to excite interest or envy, but one of Hendrick Tabaka's expert mechanics had overhauled the engine and tightened the suspension, leaving the exterior untouched. In it they would return to Johannesburg.

Though the sun had not yet risen, the entire kraal was astir, and Victoria's sisters had prepared breakfast for them. After they had eaten came the hard part of taking leave of her family. She knelt before her father.

'Go in peace, my daughter,' he told her fondly. 'We will think of you often. Bring your sons to visit us.'

Victoria's mother wept and keened as though it were a funeral, not a wedding, and Victoria could not comfort her although she embraced her and protested her love and duty until the other daughters took her away.

Then there were all her stepmothers and her half-brothers and half-sisters, and the uncles and aunts and cousins who had come from the farthest reaches of Zululand. Victoria had to make her farewells to all of them, though some partings were more poignant than others. One of these was her goodbye to Joseph Dinizulu, her favourite of all her relatives. Although he was a half-brother and seven years younger than she was, a special bond had always existed between them. The two of them were the brightest and most gifted of their generation in the family, and because Joseph lived at Drake's Farm with one of the elder brothers, they had been able to continue their friendship.

However, Joseph would not be returning to the Witwatersrand. He had written the entrance exams and been accepted by the exclusive multi-racial school, Waterford, in Swaziland, and Lady Anna Courtney would be paying his school fees. Ironically, this was the same school to which Hendrick Tabaka was sending his sons, Wellington and Raleigh. There would be opportunity for their rivalry to flourish.

'Promise me you will work hard, Joseph,' Vicky said. 'Learning makes a man strong.'

'I will be strong,' Joseph assured her. The elation that Moses Gama's speech had aroused in him still persisted. 'Can I come and visit you and your husband, Vicky? He is a man, the kind of man I will want to be one day.'

188

Vicky told Moses what the child had said. They were alone in the old Buick, all the wedding gifts and Vicky's possessions filling the boot and piled in the back seat, and they were leaving that great littoral amphitheatre of Natal, going up over the tail of the Drakensberg range on to the high veld of the Transvaal.

'The children are the future,' Moses nodded, staring ahead at the steep blue serpent of road that climbed the escarpment, past the green hill of Majuba where the Boers had thrashed the British in the first of many battles with them. 'The old men are beyond hope. You saw them at the wedding, how they kicked and baulked like unbroken oxen when I tried to show them the way – but the children, ah the children!' He smiled. 'They are like fresh clean sheets of paper. You can write on them what you will. The old men are stone-hard and impermeable, but the children are clay, eager clay waiting for the shaping hands of the potter.' He held up one of his hands. It was long and shapely, the hand of a surgeon or an artist and the palm was a delicate shade of pink, smooth and not calloused by labour. 'Children lack any sense of morality, they are without fear, and death is beyond their conception. These are all things they acquire later, by the teaching of their elders. They make perfect soldiers for they question nothing and it takes no great physical strength to pull a trigger. If an enemy strikes them down they become the perfect martyrs. The bleeding corpse of a child strikes horror and remorse into even the hardest heart. Yes, the children are our key to the future. Your Christ knew it when he said "Suffer the little children to come unto me".'

Victoria twisted on the leather bench seat of the Buick and stared at him.

'Your words are cruel and blasphemous,' she whispered, torn by her love for him and her instinctive rejection of what he had just said.

'And yet your reaction proves their truth,' he said.

'But —' she paused, reluctant to ask, and fearful to hear his reply, 'but are you saying that we should use our children —' She broke off, and an image of the paediatric section of the hospital came into her mind. She had spent the happiest months of all her training amongst the little ones. 'Are you suggesting that you would use the children in the front line of the struggle – as soldiers?'

'If a child cannot grow up a free man, then he might as well die as a child,' Moses Gama said. 'Victoria, you have heard me say this before. It is time now that you learn to believe it. There is nothing I would not do, no price I would not pay, for our victory. If I have to see a thousand little children dead so that a hundred thousand more may live to grow up free men, then for me the bargain is a fair one.'

189

Then, for the very first time in her life, Victoria Dinizulu was truly afraid.

*　　*　　*

That night they stayed at Hendrick Tabaka's house in Drake's Farm Township, and it was well after midnight before they could go to the small bedroom that had been set aside for them because there were many who demanded Moses' attention, men from the Buffaloes and the Mineworkers' Union, a messenger from the council of the ANC and a dozen petitioners and supplicants who came quietly as jackals to the lion when the word flashed through the township that Moses Gama had returned.

At all these meetings Victoria was present, although she never spoke and sat quietly in a corner of the room. At first the men were surprised and puzzled, darting quick glances across at her and reluctant to come to their business until Moses pressed them. None of them was accustomed to having women present when serious matters were discussed. However, none of them could bring themselves to protest, until the ANC messenger came into the room. He was invested with all the power and importance of the council he represented, and so he was the first to speak about Victoria's presence.

'There is a woman here,' he said.

'Yes,' Moses nodded. 'But not just a woman, she is my wife.'

'It is not fitting,' said the messenger. 'It is not the custom. This is men's business.'

'It is our purpose and our aim to tear down and burn the old customs and to build up the new. In that endeavour we will need the help of all our people. Not just the men, but the women and children also.'

There was a long silence while the messenger fidgeted under Moses' dark unrelenting stare.

'The woman can remain,' he capitulated at last.

'Yes,' Moses nodded. 'My wife will remain.'

Later in the darkness of their bedroom, in the narrowness of the single bed, Victoria pressed close to him, the soft plastic curves of her body conforming to his hardness and she said:

'You have honoured me by making me a part of your struggle. Like the children, I want to be a soldier. I have thought about it and I have discovered what I can do.'

'Tell me,' he invited.

'The women. I can organize the women. I can begin with the nurses of the hospital, and then the other women – all of them. We must take our part in the struggle beside the men.'

His arms tightened around her. 'You are a lioness,' he said. 'A beautiful Zulu lioness.'

'I can feel your heartbeat,' she whispered, 'and my own heart beats in exact time to it.'

In the morning Moses drove her to the nurses' home at the hospital. She stood at the top of the steps and did not go into the building. He watched her in the rear-view mirror as he drove away and she was still standing there when he turned into the traffic, heading back towards Johannesburg and the suburb of Rivonia.

He was one of the first to arrive at Puck's Hill that morning to attend the council meeting to which the previous night's messenger had summoned him.

Marcus Archer met Moses on the verandah, and his smile was vitriolic as he greeted him. 'They say a man is incomplete until he marries – and only then is he finished.'

There were two men already seated at the long table in the kitchen which had always been used as their council chamber. They were both white men.

Bram Fischer was the scion of an eminent Afrikaner family whose father had been a judge-president of the Orange Free State. Though he was an expert on mining law, and a QC at the Johannesburg bar, he had also been a member of the old Communist Party and was a member of the ANC, and lately his practice had become almost entirely the defence of those accused under the racial laws that the Nationalist government had enacted since 1948. Although he was a charming and erudite man with a real concern for his countrymen of all races, Moses was wary of him. He was a starry-eyed believer in the eventual miraculous triumph of good over evil, and firmly opposed the formation of *Umkhonto we Sizwe*, the military branch of the ANC. His pacifist influence on the rest of the Congress set a brake on Moses' aspirations.

The other white man was Joe Cicero, a Lithuanian immigrant. Moses could guess why he had come to Africa – and who had sent him. He was one of the eagles, fierce hearted as Moses was himself, and an ally when the need for direct and even violent action was discussed. Moses went to sit beside him, across the table from Fischer. He would need Joe Cicero's support this day.

Marcus Archer, who loved to cook, set a plate of devilled kidneys and *oeufs ranchero* in front of him, but before Moses had finished his breakfast, the others began to arrive. Nelson Mandela and his faithful ally Tambo, arrived together, followed quickly by Walter Sisulu and Mbeki and the others, until the long table was crowded and cluttered with papers and dirty plates, with coffee cups and ashtrays which were soon overflowing with crushed cigarette butts.

191

The air was thick with tobacco smoke and Marcus's cooking aromas, and the talk was charged and serious as they tried to decide and agree exactly what were the objects of the defiance campaign.

'We have to stir the awareness of our people, to shake them out of their dumb cowlike acceptance of oppression.' Mandela put the premier proposition, and across from him Moses leaned forward.

'More important, we must awaken the conscience of the rest of the world, for that is the direction from which our ultimate salvation will come.'

'Our own people —' Mandela began, but Moses interrupted him.

'Our own people are powerless without weapons and training. The forces of oppression ranged against us are too powerful. We cannot triumph without arms.'

'You reject the way of the peace then?' Mandela asked. 'You presuppose that freedom can only be won at the point of the gun?'

'The revolution must be tempered and made strong in the blood of the masses,' Moses affirmed. 'That is always the way.'

'Gentlemen! Gentlemen!' Bram Fischer held up his hand to stop them. 'Let us return to the main body of the discussion. We agree that by our campaign of defiance we hope to stir our own people out of their lethargy and to attract the attention of the rest of the world. Those are our two main objects. Let us now decide on our secondary objects.'

'To establish the ANC as the only true vehicle of liberation,' Moses suggested. 'At present we have less than seven thousand members, but by the end of the campaign we should aim to have enrolled one hundred thousand more.' To this there was general agreement, even Mandela and Tambo nodded and when the vote was taken it was unanimous and they could go on to discuss the details of the campaign.

It was a massive undertaking, for it was planned that the campaign should be nationwide and that it should be conducted simultaneously in every one of the main centres of the Union of South Africa so as to place the utmost strain on the resources of the government and to test the response of the forces of law and order.

'We must fill their gaols until they burst. We must offer ourselves up for arrest in our thousands until the machinery of tyranny breaks down under the strain,' Mandela told them.

For three more days they sat in the kitchen at Puck's Hill, working out and agreeing every minute detail, preparing the lists of names and places, putting together the timetable of action, the logistics of transport and communication, establishing the lines of control from the central committee down through the provincial headquarters of the movement, and ultimately to the regional cadres in every black township and location.

It was an onerous task but at last there was only one detail left to decide – the day on which it would begin. Now they all looked to Albert Luthuli at the head of the table and he did not hesitate.

'June the twenty-sixth,' he said, and when there was a murmur of agreement, he went on, 'So be it then. We all know our tasks.' And he gave them the salute of upraised thumbs. *'Amandla!* Power! *Ngawethu!'*

When Moses went out to where the old Buick was parked beneath the gum trees, the sunset was filling the western sky with furnace colours of hot orange and smouldering red, and Joe Cicero was waiting for him. He leaned against the silvery trunk of one of the bluegum trees, with his arms folded over his broad chest, a bearlike figure, short and squat and powerful.

He straightened up as Moses came towards him.

'Can you give me a lift in to Braamfontein, comrade?' he asked, and Moses opened the door of the Buick for him, and they drove in silence for ten minutes before Joe said quietly, 'It is strange that you and I have never spoken privately.' His accent was elusive, but the planes of his pale face above the short dark fringe of beard were flat and Slavic and his eyes were dark as tar pools.

'Why is it so strange?' Moses asked.

'We share common views,' Joe replied. 'We are both true sons of the revolution.'

'Are you certain of that?'

'I am certain,' Joe nodded. 'I have studied you and listened to you with approval and admiration. I believe that you are one of the steely men that the revolution needs, comrade.'

Moses did not reply. He kept his eyes on the road, and his expression impassive, letting the silence draw out, forcing the other man to break it.

'What are your feelings towards mother Russia?' Joe asked softly at last, and Moses considered the question.

'Russia has never had colonies in Africa,' Moses answered carefully. 'I know that she gives support to the struggle in Malaya and Algeria and Kenya. I believe she is a true ally of the oppressed peoples of this world.'

Joe smiled and lit another Springbok cigarette from the flat maroon and white pack. He was a chain-smoker and his stubby fingers were stained dark brown.

'The road to freedom is steep and rocky,' he murmured. 'And the revolution is never secure. The proletariat must be protected from itself by the revolutionary guards.'

'Yes,' Moses agreed. 'I have read the works of both Marx and Lenin.'

'Then I was correct,' Joe Cicero murmured. 'You are a believer.

We should be friends – good friends. There are difficult days ahead and there will be a need for steely men.' He reached over the back seat and picked up his attaché case. 'You can let me out at the central railway station, comrade,' he said.

*   *   *

It had been fully dark for two hours by the time Moses reached the camp in the gorge below the Sundi Caves and parked the Buick behind the Nissen hut that was the expedition's office and laboratory, and he went up the path to Tara Courtney's tent, stepping softly so as not alarm her. He saw her silhouette against the canvas side. She was lying on her stretcher bed reading by the light of the petromax lantern, and he saw her start as he scratched on the canvas.

'Don't be afraid,' he called softly. 'It's me.'

And her reply was low but quivering with joy. 'Oh God, I thought you'd never come.'

She was in a frenzy for him. Her other pregnancies had always left her feeling nauseous and bloated, and the thought of sexual contact during that time had been repugnant. But now, even though she was over three months pregnant, her wanting was a kind of madness. Moses seemed to sense her need, but did not try to match it. He lay naked upon his back on the stretcher, and he was like a pinnacle of black granite. Tara hurled herself upon him to impale herself. She was sobbing and uttering little cries and yelps. At once both clumsy and adroit, her body, not yet swollen by the child within her, thrashed and churned above him as he lay quiescent and unmoving, and she went on beyond physical endurance, beyond the limits of flesh, insatiable and desperate for him, until exhaustion at last overcame her and she rolled off him and lay panting weakly, her chestnut hair darkened by her own sweat and plastered to her forehead and neck, and there was a thin pink colouring of blood on the front of her thighs, so wild had been her passion.

Moses drew the sheet over her and held her until she had stopped shaking and her breathing had quietened, and then he said, 'It will begin soon – the date has been agreed.'

Tara was so transported that for a while she did not understand, and she shook her head stupidly.

'June the twenty-sixth,' Moses said. 'Across the land, in every city, all at the same time. Tomorrow I will be going to Port Elizabeth in the eastern Cape to command the campaign there.'

That was hundreds of miles from Johannesburg, and she had come to be near him. With the melancholy of after-love upon her, Tara felt cheated and abused. She wanted to protest but with an effort checked herself.

194

'How long will you be away?'

'Weeks.'

'Oh Moses!' she began, and then warned by his quick frown, she relapsed into silence.

'The American woman – the Godolphin woman. Have you contacted her? Without publicity the value of our efforts will be halved.'

'Yes.' Tara paused. She had been on the point of telling him that it was all arranged, that Kitty Godolphin would meet him any time he wanted, but she stopped herself. Instead of handing her over to Moses and standing aside, here was her chance to stay close to him.

'Yes, I have spoken to her. We met at her hotel, she is eager to meet you but she is out of town at the moment, in Swaziland.'

'That is no good,' Moses muttered. 'I had hoped to see her before I left.'

'I could bring her down to Port Elizabeth,' Tara cut in eagerly. 'She will be back in a day or two and I will bring her to you.'

'Can you get away from here?' he asked dubiously.

'Yes, of course. I will bring the television people down to you in my own car.'

Moses grunted uncertainly, and was silent while he thought about it, and then he nodded.

'Very well. I will explain how you will be able to contact me when you get there. I will be in the township of New Brighton, just outside the city.'

'Can I be with you, Moses? Can I stay with you?'

'You know that is impossible.' He was irritated by her persistence. 'No whites are allowed in the township without a pass.'

'The television team will not be able to help you much if we are kept out of the township,' Tara said quickly. 'We should be close to you to be of any use to the struggle.' Cunningly she had linked herself to Kitty Godolphin, and she held her breath as he thought about it.

'Perhaps,' he nodded, and she exhaled softly. He had accepted it. 'Yes. There might be a way. There is a mission hospital run by German nuns in the township. They are friends. You could stay there. I will arrange it.'

She tried not to let him see her triumph. She would be with him, that was all that was important. It was madness, but though her body was bruised and sore, already she wanted him again. It was not physical lust, it was more than that. It was the only way she could possess him, even for a few fleeting minutes. When she had him locked in her body, he belonged to her alone.

*　　*　　*

195

Tara was puzzled by Kitty Godolphin's attitude towards her. She was accustomed to people, both men and women, responding immediately to her own warm personality and good looks. Kitty was different, from the very beginning there had been a cold-eyed reserve and an innate hostility in her. Very swiftly Tara had seen beyond the angelic, little-girl image that Kitty so carefully projected, but even after she had recognized the tough and ruthless person beneath, she could find no logical reason for the woman's attitude. After all Tara was offering her an important assignment, and Kitty was examining the gift as though it were a live scorpion.

'I don't understand,' she protested, her voice and eyes snapping. 'You told me we could do the interview here in Johannesburg. Now you want me to traipse off into the deep sticks somewhere.'

'Moses Gama has to be there. Something important is about to take place —'

'What is so important?' Kitty demanded, fists on her lean denim-clad hips. 'What we agreed was important also.'

Most people, from leading politicians and international stars of sport and entertainment down to the lowest nonentity, were ready to risk slipping a spinal disc in their eagerness to appear for even the briefest moment on the little square screen. It was Kitty Godolphin's right, a semi-divine right, to decide who would be accorded that opportunity and who would be denied it. Moses Gama's cavalier behaviour was insulting. He had been chosen, and instead of displaying the gratitude which was Kitty Godolphin's due, he was setting conditions.

'Just what is so important that he cannot make the effort of common courtesy?' she repeated.

'I'm sorry, Miss Godolphin, I can't tell you that.'

'Well then, I'm sorry also, Mrs Courtney, but you tell Moses Gama from me that he can go straight to hell without passing GO and without collecting his two hundred dollars.'

'You aren't serious!' Tara hadn't expected that.

'I have never been more serious in my life.' Kitty rolled her wrist to look at her Rolex. 'Now, if you will excuse me, I have more important matters to attend to.'

'All right,' Tara gave in at once. 'I will risk it. I'll tell you what is going to happen —' Tara paused while she considered the consequences, and then asked, 'You will keep it to yourself, what I am about to tell you?'

'Darling, if there is a good story in it, they wouldn't get it out of me with thumbscrew and hot irons – that is, not until I splash it across the screen myself.'

Tara told her in a rush of words, getting it out quickly before she

196

could change her mind. 'It will be a chance to film him at work, to see him with his people, to watch him defying the forces of oppression and bigotry.'

She saw Kitty hesitating and knew that she had to think quickly.

'However, I should warn you, there may be danger. The confrontation could turn to violence and even bloodshed,' she said, and she had got it exactly right.

'Hank!' Kitty Godolphin shouted through to the lounge of her suite where the camera crew were strewn over the furniture like the survivors of a bomb blast, listening at full volume of the radio to the new rock 'n' roll sensation warning them to keep off his blue suede shoes.

'Hank!' Kitty raised her voice above Presley's. 'Get the cameras packed. We are going to a place called Port Elizabeth. If we can find where the hell it is.'

They drove through the night in Tara's Packard, and the suspension sagged under the weight of bodies and camera equipment. In his travels around the country Hank had discovered that cannabis grew as a weed around most of the villages in the reserves of Zululand and the Transkei. In an environment that the plant found agreeable, it reached the size of a small tree. Only a few of the older generation of black tribesmen smoked the dried leaves, and although it was proscribed as a noxious plant and listed as a dangerous drug, its use was so localized and restricted to the more primitive blacks in the remote areas – for no white person or educated African would lower himself to smoke it – that the authorities made little effort to prevent its cultivation and sale. Hank had found an endless supply of what he declared to be 'pure gold' for the payment of pennies.

'Man, a sack of this stuff on the streets of Los Angeles would fetch a hundred thousand dollars,' he murmured contentedly as he lit a hand-rolled cigarette and settled down on the back seat of the Packard. The heavy incense of the leaves filled the interior, and after a few draws Hank passed the cigarette to Kitty in the front seat. Kitty drew on the butt deeply and held the smoke in her lungs, as long as she was able, before blowing it out in a pale streamer against the windscreen. Then she offered the butt to Tara.

'I don't smoke tobacco,' Tara told her politely, and they all laughed.

'That ain't baccy, sweetheart,' Hank told her.

'What is it?'

'You call it *dagga* here.'

'Dagga.' Tara was shocked. She remembered that Centaine had

197

fired one of her houseboys who smoked it.

'He dropped my Rosenthal tureen, the one that belonged to Czar Nicholas,' Centaine had complained. 'Once they start on that stuff they become totally useless.'

'No thanks,' Tara said quickly, and thought how angry Shasa would be if he knew that she had been offered it. That thought gave her pause and she changed her mind. 'Oh, all right.' She took the butt, steering the Packard with one hand. 'What do I do?'

'Just suck it in and hold it down,' Kitty advised, 'and ride the glow.'

The smoke scratched her throat and burned her lungs, but the thought of Shasa's outrage gave her determination. She fought the urge to cough and held it down.

Slowly she felt herself relaxing, and a mild glow of euphoria made her body seem air-light and cleansed her mind. All the agonies of her soul became trivial and fell behind her.

'I feel good,' she murmured, and when they laughed, she laughed with them and drove on into the night.

In the early morning before it was fully light, they reached the coast, skirting the bay of Algoa where the Indian Ocean took a deep bite out of the continent, and the green waters were chopped to a white froth by the wind.

'Where do we go from here?' Kitty asked.

'The black township of New Brighton,' Tara told her. 'There is a mission run by German nuns, a teaching and nursing order, the Sisters of St Magdalene. They are expecting us. We aren't really allowed to stay in the township, but they have arranged it.'

Sister Nunziata was a handsome blond woman, not much older than forty years. She had a clear scrubbed-looking skin and her manner was brisk and efficient. She wore the light grey cotton habit of the order, and a white shoulder-length veil.

'Mrs Courtney, I have been expecting you. Our mutual friend will be here later this morning. You will want to bathe and rest.' She led them to the cells that had been set aside for them and apologized for the simple comforts they contained. Kitty and Tara shared a cell. The floor was bare cement, the only decoration was a crucifix on the whitewashed wall, and the springs of the iron bedsteads were covered with thin hard coir mattresses.

'She's just great,' Kitty enthused. 'I must get her on film. Nuns always make good footage.'

As soon as they had bathed and unpacked their equipment, Kitty had her crew out filming. She recorded a good interview with Sister Nunziata, her German accent lent interest to her statements, and then they filmed the black children in the schoolyard and the out-patients waiting outside the clinic.

Tara was awed by the girl's energy, her quick mind and glib tongue, and her eye for angle and subject as she directed the shooting. It made Tara feel superfluous, and her own lack of talent and creative skill irked her. She found herself resenting the other girl for having pointed up her inadequacies so graphically.

Then everything else was irrelevant. A nondescript old Buick sedan pulled into the mission yard and a tall figure climbed out and came towards them. Moses Gama wore a light blue open-neck shirt, the short sleeves exposed the sleek muscle in his upper arms and neck, and his tailored blue slacks were belted around his narrow waist. Tara didn't have to say anything, they all knew immediately who he was as Kitty Godolphin breathed softly beside her, 'My God, he is beautiful as a black panther.'

Tara's resentment of her flared into seething hatred. She wanted to rush to Moses and embrace him so that Kitty might know he was hers, but instead she stood dumbly while he stopped in front of Kitty and held out his right hand.

'Miss Godolphin? At last,' he said, and his voice brought out a rush of goose-bumps down Tara's arms.

The rest of the day was spent in reconnaisance and the filming of more background material, this time with Moses as the central figure in each shot. The New Brighton township was typical of the South African urban locations, rows of identical low-cost housing laid out in geometric squares of narrow roads, some of them paved and others rutted and filled with muddy puddles in which the pre-school children and toddlers, many of them naked or dressed only in ragged shorts, played raucously.

Kitty filmed Moses picking his way around the puddles, squatting to talk to the children, lifting a marvellously photogenic little black cherub in his arms and wiping his snotty nose.

'That's great stuff,' Kitty enthused. 'He's going to look magnificent on film.'

The children followed Moses, laughing and skipping behind him as though he were the Pied Piper, and the women attracted by the commotion came out of the squalid little cottages. When they recognized Moses and saw the cameras, they began to ululate and dance. They were natural actresses and completely without inhibition, and Kitty was everywhere, calling for shots and unusual camera angles, clearly delighted by the footage she was getting.

In the late afternoon the working men began to arrive back in the township by bus and train. Most of them were production-line workers in the vehicle assembly plants of Ford and General Motors, or factory-workers in the tyre companies of Goodyear and Firestone, for Port Elizabeth and its satellite town of Uitenhage formed the centre of the country's motor vehicle industry.

Moses walked the narrow streets with the camera following him, and he stopped to talk to the returning workers, while the camera recorded their complaints and problems, most of which were the practical everyday worries of making ends meet while remaining within the narrow lines demarcated by the forest of racial laws. Kitty could edit most of that out, but every one of them mentioned the 'show on demand' clause of the pass laws as the thing they hated and feared most. In every little vignette they filmed Moses Gama was the central heroic figure.

'By the time I've finished with him, he will be as famous as Martin Luther King,' Kitty enthused.

They joined the nuns for their frugal evening meal, and afterwards Kitty Godolphin was still not satisfied. Outside one of the cottages near the mission a family was cooking on an open fire, and Kitty had Moses join them, hunched over the fire in the night with the flames lighting his face, adding drama to his already massive presence as she filmed him while he spoke. In the background one of the women was singing a lullaby to the infant at her breast, and there were the murmurous sounds of the location, the soft cries of the children and the distant yapping of pariah dogs.

Moses Gama's words were poignant and moving, spoken in that deep thrilling voice, as he described the agony of his land and his people, so that Tara, listening to him in the darkness, found tears running down her face.

In the morning Kitty left her team at the mission, and without the camera the three of them, Kitty and Tara and Moses, drove in the Buick to the railway station that served the township and watched the black commuters swarm like hiving bees through the station entrance marked NON WHITES – NIE BLANKES, crowding on to the platform reserved for blacks, and as soon as the train pulled in, flooding into the coaches set aside for them.

Through the other entrance, marked WHITES ONLY – BLANKES ALLEENLIK, a few white officials and others who had business in the township sauntered and unhurriedly entered the first-class coaches at the rear of the train where they sat on green leather-covered seats and gazed out through glass at the black swarm on the opposite platform with detached expressions as though they were viewing creatures of another species.

'I've got to try and get that,' Kitty muttered. 'I've got to get that reaction on film.' She was busily scribbling notes in her pad, sketching rough maps of the station layout and marking in camera sites and angles.

Before noon Moses excused himself. 'I have to meet the local organizers and make the final plans for tomorrow,' and he drove away in the Buick.

Tara took Kitty and the team down to the seaside at St George's Strand, and they filmed the bathers on the beaches lying under the signboards BLANKES ALLEENLIK – WHITES ONLY. School was out and tanned young people, the girls in bikinis and the boys with short haircuts and frank open faces lolled on the white sand, or played beach games and surfed the rolling green waves.

When Kitty asked them, 'How would you feel if black people came to swim here?' some of them giggled nervously at a question they had never considered before:

'They aren't allowed to come here – they've got their own beaches.'

And at least one was indignant. 'They can't come here and look at our girls in bathing-costumes.' He was a beefy young man with sea-salt caked in his sun-streaked hair and skin peeling from his sun-burned nose.

'But wouldn't you look at the black girls in their bathing costumes?' Kitty asked innocently.

'*Sis*, man!' said the surfer, his handsome tanned features contorted with utter disgust at the suggestion.

'It's just too good to be true!' Kitty marvelled at her own fortune. 'I'll cut that in with some footage I've got of a beautiful black dancer in a Soweto night club.'

On the way back to the mission Kitty asked Tara to stop at the New Brighton railway station once again, for a final reconnaisance. They left the cameras in the Packard and two white-uniformed railway constables watched them with idle disinterest as they wandered around the almost deserted platforms that during the rush hours swarmed with thousands of black commuters. Quietly Kitty pointed out to her team the locations she had chosen earlier, and explained to them what shots she would be striving for.

That night Moses joined them for the evening meal in the mission refectory, and though the conversation was light and cheerful, there was a hint of tension in their laughter. When Moses left, Tara went out with him to where the Buick was parked in the darkness behind the mission clinic.

'I want to be with you tonight,' she told him pathetically. 'I feel so alone without you.'

'That is not possible.'

'It's dark – we could go for a drive to the beach,' she pleaded.

'The police patrols are looking for just that sort of thing,' Moses

201

told her. 'You would see yourself in the *Sunday Times* next week-end.'

'Make love to me here, please Moses,' and he was angry.

'Your selfishness is that of a spoilt child – you think only of your-self and your own desires, even now when we are on the threshold of great events, you would take risks that could bring us down.'

Tara lay awake most of the night and listened to Kitty's peaceful breathing in the iron bed across the cell.

She fell asleep just before dawn, and awoke feeling nauseous and heavy, when Kitty leapt gaily out of bed in her pink striped pyjamas, eager for the day.

'June twenty-sixth,' she cried. 'The big day at last!'

None of them took more than a cup of coffee for an early breakfast. Tara felt too sick and the others were too keyed up. Hank had checked his equipment the previous night, but now he went over it again before he loaded it into the Packard and they drove down to the railway station.

It was gloomy and the few street lights were still burning while under them the hordes of black commuters hurried. However, by the time they reached the station the first rays of the sun struck the entrance and the light was perfect for filming. Tara noticed that a pair of police Black Maria vans were parked outside the main en-trance and instead of the two young constables who had been on duty the previous day, there were eight railway policemen in a group under the station clock. They were in blue uniform with black peaked caps and holstered sidearms on their polished leather Sam Browne belts. They all carried riot batons.

'They have been warned,' Tara exclaimed, as she parked across the street from the two vans. 'They are expecting trouble – just look at them.'

Kitty had twisted around and was giving last-minute instructions to Hank in the back seat, but when Tara glanced at her to assess her reaction to the waiting police, something about Kitty's expression and her inability to meet Tara's eyes made her pause.

'Kitty?' she insisted. 'These policemen. You don't seem —' she broke off as she remembered something. The previous afternoon on the way to the beach, Kitty had asked her to stop outside the Humewood post office because she wanted to send a telegram. How-ever, from across the road looking through the post office window, Tara had seen her slip into one of the glass telephone booths. It had puzzled her at the time.

'You!' she gasped. 'It was you who warned the police!'

'Listen, darling,' Kitty snapped at her. 'These people want to get themselves arrested. That's the whole point. And I want film of them getting arrested. I did it for all our sakes —' she broke off and cocked her head. 'Listen!' she cried. 'Here they come!'

Faintly on the dawn there was the sound of singing, hundreds of voices together, and the group of policemen in the station entrance stirred and looked around apprehensively.

'Okay, Hank,' Kitty snapped. 'Let's go!'

They jumped out of the Packard, and hurried to the positions they had chosen, lugging their equipment.

The senior police officer with gold braid on his cap was a captain. Tara knew enough of police rank insignia from first-hand experience. He gave an order to his constables. Two of them began to cross the road towards the camera team.

'Shoot, Hank. Keep shooting!' Tara heard Kitty's voice, and the singing was louder now. The beautifully haunting refrain of *Nkosi Sikelel' iAfrika* carried by a thousand African voices made Tara shiver.

The two constables were halfway across the road when the first rank of protesters marched around the nearest row of shops and cottages and hurriedly the police captain called his constables back to his side.

They were twenty abreast, arms linked, filling the road from pavement to pavement, singing as they came on, and behind them followed a solid column of black humanity. Some of them were dressed in business suits, others in tattered cast-off clothing, some were silver-haired and others were in their teens. In the centre of the front rank, taller than the men around him, bare-headed and straight-backed as a soldier, marched Moses Gama.

Hank ran into the street with his sound technician following him. With the camera on his shoulder, he retreated in front of Moses, capturing him on film, the sound man recording his voice as it soared in the anthem, full and magnificent, the very voice of Africa and his features were lit with an almost religious fervour.

Hurriedly the police captain was drawing his men up across the whites-only entrance, and they were hefting their batons nervously, pale-faced in the early sunlight. The head of the column wheeled across the road and began to climb the steps, and the police captain stepped forward and spread his arms to halt them. Moses Gama held up one hand. The column came to a jerking shuffling halt, and the singing died away.

The police captain was a tall man with a pleasantly lined face. Tara could see him over their heads, and he was smiling. That was the thing that struck Tara. Faced with a thousand black protesters, he was still smiling.

'Come on now,' he raised his voice, like a schoolmaster addressing an unruly class. 'You know you can't do this, it's just nonsense, man. You are acting like a bunch of skollies, and I know you are good people.' He was still smiling as he picked a few of the leaders out of the front ranks. 'Mr Dhlovu and Mr Khandela – you are on the management committee, shame on you!' He waggled his finger, and the men he had spoken to hung their heads and grinned shamefacedly. The whole atmosphere of the march had begun to change. Here was the father figure, stern but benevolent, and they were the children, mischievous but at the bottom good-hearted and dutiful.

'Off you go, all of you. Go home and don't be silly now,' the captain called, and the column wavered. From the back ranks there was laughter, and a few of those who had been reluctant to join the march began to slip away. Behind the captain his constables were grinning with relief, and the crowd began to jostle as it broke up.

'Good Christ!' Kitty swore bitterly. 'It's all a goddamned anti-climax. I have wasted my time —'

Then on to the top steps of the railway station a tall figure stepped out of the ranks and his voice rang out over them, silencing them and freezing them where they stood. The laughter and the smiles died away.

'My people,' Moses Gama cried, 'this is your land. In it you have God's right to live in peace and dignity. This building belongs to all who live here – it is your right to enter, as much as any other person's that lives here. I am going in – who will follow me?'

A ragged, uncertain chorus of support came from the front ranks and Moses turned to face the police captain.

'We are going in, Captain. Arrest us or stand aside.'

At that moment a train, filled with black commuters, pulled into the platform and they hung out of the windows of the coaches and cheered and stamped.

'Nkosi Sikelel' iAfrika!' sang Moses Gama, and with his head held high he marched under the warning sign WHITES ONLY.

'You are breaking the law,' the captain raised his voice. 'Arrest that man.' And the thin rank of constables moved forward to obey.

Instantly a roar went up from the crowd behind him. 'Arrest me! Arrest me too!' And they surged forward, picking Moses up with them as though he were a surfer on a wave.

'Arrest me!' they chanted. 'Malan! Malan! Come and arrest us!'

The crowd burst through the entrance, and the white police constables were carried with them, struggling ineffectually in the press of bodies.

'Arrest me!' It had become a roar. *'Amandla! Amandla!'*

The captain was fighting to keep his feet, shouting to rally his men, but his voice was drowned out in the chant of, 'Power! Power!' The captain's cap was knocked over his eyes and he was shoved backwards on to the platform. Hank, the cameraman, was in the midst of it, holding his Arriflex high and shooting out of hand. Around him the white faces of the constables bobbed like flotsam in a wild torrent of humanity. From the coaches the black passengers swarmed out to meet and mingle with the mob, and a single voice called out.

'Jee!' the battle cry that can drive an Nguni warrior into the berserker's passion, and *'Jee!'* a hundred voices answered him and *'Jee!'* again. There was the crash of breaking glass, one of the coach windows exploded as a shoulder thrust into it and *'Jee!'* they sang.

One of the white constables lost his footing and went sprawling backwards. Immediately he was trampled under foot and he screamed like a rabbit in a snare.

'Jee!' sang the men, transformed into warriors, the veneer of western manners stripped away, and another window smashed. By now the platform was choked with a struggling mass of humanity. From the cab of the locomotive, the mob dragged the terrified engine-driver and his fireman. They jostled and pushed them, ringing them in.

'Jee!' they chanted, bouncing at the knees, working themselves up into the killing madness. Their eyes were glazing and engorging with blood, their faces turning into shining black masks.

'Jee!' they sang. *'Jee!'* and Moses Gama sang with them. Let the others call for restraint and passive resistance to the enemy, but all that was forgotten and now Moses Gama's blood seethed with all his pent-up hatred and *'Jee!'* he cried, and his skin crawled and itched with atavistic fury and his fighting heart swelled to fill his chest.

The police captain, still on his feet, had been driven back against the wall of the station-master's office. One epaulette had been torn from the shoulder of his uniform and he had lost his cap. There was a fleck of blood at the corner of his moustache where an elbow had struck him in the mouth, and he was struggling with the flap of the holster on his belt.

'Kill!' shouted a voice. *'Bulala!'* and it was taken up. Black hands clutched at the police captain's lapels, and he drew the service revolver from its holster and tried to raise it, but the crowd was packed too densely around him. He fired blindly from the hip.

The shot was a great blurt of sound, and somebody yelled with shock and pain, and the crowd around the captain backed away, leaving a young black man in an army surplus greatcoat kneeling at his feet, moaning and clutching his stomach.

205

The captain, white-faced and panting, lifted the revolver and fired again into the air.

'Form up on me!' he shouted in a voice hoarse and breaking with terror and exertion. Another of his men was down on his knees, submerged in the milling crowd, but he managed to clear his revolver from its holster and he fired point-blank, emptying the chamber into the press around him.

Then they were running, blocking the entrance, jamming in it as they sought to escape the gunfire, and all the police constables were firing, some on their knees, all of them dishevelled and terrified, and the bullets told in the mass of bodies with loud, meaty thumps, like a housewife beating the dust from a hanging carpet. The air was thick with the smell of gunsmoke and dust and blood, of sweat and unwashed bodies and terror.

They were screaming and pushing, fighting their way out into the street again, leaving their fallen comrades crumpled on the platform in seeping puddles of blood, or crawling desperately after them dragging bullet-shattered limbs.

And the little group of policemen were running to help each other to their feet, bruised and bloodied in torn uniforms. They gathered up the engine-driver and his fireman and, staggering, supporting each other, drawn revolvers still in their hands, they crossed the platform stepping over the bodies and the puddles of blood and hurried down the steps to the two parked vans.

Across the road the crowd had reassembled and they screamed and shook their fists and chanted as the policemen scrambled into the vehicles and drove away at speed, and then the crowd swarmed into the roadway and hurled stones and abuse at the departing vans.

Tara had watched it all from the parked Packard, and now she sat paralysed with horror, listening to the animal growl of the crowd penetrated by the cries and groans of the wounded.

Moses Gama ran to her and shouted into the open window, 'Go and fetch Sister Nunziata. Tell her we need all the help we can get.'

Tara nodded dumbly and started the engine. Across the road she could see Kitty and Hank still filming. Hank was kneeling beside a wounded man, shooting into his tortured face, panning down on to the pool of blood in which he lay.

Tara pulled away, and the crowd in the road tried to stop her. Black faces, swollen with anger, mouthed at her through the Packard's windows and they beat with their fists on the roof, but she sounded her horn and kept driving.

'I have to get a doctor,' she shouted at them. 'Let me pass, let me through.'

She got through them, and when she looked in the rear-view mirror, she saw that in frustration and fury they were stoning the railway station, ripping up the pavement and hurling the heavy slabs through the windows. She saw a white face at one of the windows, and felt a pang for the station-master and his staff. They had barricaded themselves in the ticket office.

The crowd outside the building was solid, and as she drove towards the mission she passed a flood of black men and women rushing to join it. The women were ululating wildly, a sound that maddened their menfolk. Some of them ran into the road to try and stop Tara, but she jammed her palm down on the horn ring and swerved around them. She glanced up into her driving-mirror and one of them picked up a rock from the side of the road and hurled it after the car. The rock crashed against the metal of the cab and bounced away.

At the mission hospital they had heard the sound of gunfire and the roar of the mob. Sister Nunziata, the white doctor, and her helpers, were anxiously waiting on the verandah and Tara shouted up at her.

'You must come quickly to the station, Sister, the police have shot and wounded people – I think some of them are dead.'

They must have been expecting the call, for they had their medical bags on the verandah with them. While Tara backed and turned the Packard, Sister Nunziata and the doctor ran down the steps, carrying their black bags. They clambered into the cab of the mission's small blue Ford pick-up and turned towards the gate, cutting in front of Tara's Packard. Tara followed them, but by the time she had turned the Packard and driven out through the gates, the little blue pick-up was a hundred yards ahead of her. It turned the corner into the station road and even above the engine-beat Tara heard the roar of the mob.

When she swung through the corner the Ford was stopped only fifty paces head of her. It was completely surrounded by the crowd. The road from side to side was packed with screaming black men and women. Tara could not hear the words, there was no sense to their fury, it was incoherent and deafening. They were concentraing on the Ford, and took no notice of Tara in the Packard.

Those nearest to the Ford were beating on the metal cab, and rocking the vehicle on its suspension. The side door opened and Sister Nunziata stood on the running board, a little higher than the heads of the howling mob that pushed closely around her. She was trying to speak to them, holding up her hands and pleading with them to let her through to take care of the wounded.

Suddenly a stone was thrown. It arced up out of the crowd and hit the nun on the side of her head. She reeled as she stood, and there was a bright flash of blood on her white veil. Stunned, she raised her hand to her cheek and it came away bloody.

The sight of blood enraged them. A forest of black arms reached up to Sister Nunziata and dragged her down from the vehicle. For a while they fought over her, dragging her in the road and worrying her like a pack of hounds with the fox. Then suddenly Tara saw the flash of a knife, and sitting in the Packard she screamed and thrust her fingers into her mouth to silence herself.

The old crone who wielded the knife was a *sangoma*, a witchdoctor, and around her neck she wore the necklace of bones and feathers and animal skulls that were her insignia. The knife in her right hand had a handle of rhino horn and the hand-forged blade was nine inches long and wickedly curved. Four men caught the nun and threw her across the engine bonnet of the Ford while the old woman hopped up beside her. The men held Sister Nunziata pinioned, face up, while the crowd began to chant wildly, and the *sangoma* stooped over her.

With a single stroke of the curved blade she cut through the nun's grey habit and split her belly open from groin to rib cage. While Sister Nunziata writhed in the grip of the men who held her, the crone thrust her hand and naked arm into the wound. Tara watched in disbelief as she brought out something wet and glistening and purple, a soft amorphous thing. It was done so swiftly, so expertly, that for seconds Tara did not realize that it was Sister Nunziata's liver that the crone held in her bloody hands.

With a slash of the curved blade, the *sangoma* cut a lump from the still living organ and hopped to her feet. Balancing on the curved bonnet of the Ford she faced the crowd.

'I eat our white enemy,' she screeched, 'and thus I take his strength.' And the mob roared, a terrible sound, as the old woman thrust the purple lump into her toothless mouth and chewed upon it. She hacked another piece off the liver, and still chewing with open mouth, she threw it to the crowd below her.

'Eat your enemy!' she shrilled, and they fought for the bloody scraps like dogs.

'Be strong! Eat the liver of the hated ones!'

She threw them more and Tara covered her eyes and heaved convulsively. Acid vomit shot up her throat and she swallowed it down painfully.

Abruptly the driver's door of the Packard beside her was jerked open and rough hands seized Tara. She was dragged out into the road. The blood roar of the crowd deafened her, but terror armed her with superhuman strength, and she tore herself free of the clutching hands.

She was at the edge of the mob, and the attention of most of them was entirely on the ghastly drama around the Ford. The crowd had set the vehicle alight. Sister Nunziata's mutilated body lay on the bonnet like a sacrifice on a burning altar, while trapped in the cab, the doctor thrashed around and beat at the flames with his bare hands, and the crowd chanted and danced around him like children around the bonfire on Guy Fawkes night.

For that instant Tara was free, but there were men around her, shouting and reaching for her, their faces bestial, their eyes glazed and insensate. No longer human, they were driven into that killing madness in which there was no reason nor mercy. Swift as a bird Tara ducked under the outstretched arms and darted away. She found that she had broken out of the mob, and in front of her was a plot of wasteland strewn with old rusted car bodies and rubbish. She fled across it and behind her she heard her pursuers baying like a pack of hunting dogs.

At the end of the open land a sagging barbed-wire fence blocked her way, and she glanced back over her shoulder. A group of men still followed her, and two of them had outdistanced the others. They were both big and powerful-looking, running strongly on bare feet, their faces contorted in a cruel rictus of excitement. They came on silently.

Tara stooped into the space between the strands of the wire. She was almost through when she felt the barbs catch in the flesh of her back, and pain arrested her. For a moment she struggled desperately, feeling her skin tear as she fought to free herself and blood trickled down her flanks – and then they seized her.

Now they shouted with wild laughter as they dragged her back through the fence, the barbs ripping at her clothing and her flesh. Her legs collapsed under her, and she pleaded with them.

'Please don't hurt me. I'm going to have a baby —'

They dragged her back across the waste plot, half on her knees, twisting and pleading in their grip – and then she saw the *sangoma* coming to meet them, hopping and capering like an ancient baboon, cackling through her toothless mouth, her bones and beads rattling around her scrawny neck and the curved knife in her blood-caked fingers.

Tara began to scream, and she felt her urine squirt uncontrollably down her legs. 'Please! Please don't!' she raved and terror was an icy blackness of her mind and body that crushed her to earth, and she closed her eyes and steeled herself to the stinging kiss of the blade.

Then in the mindless animal roar of the crowd, above the old crone's shrill laughter, there was another voice, a great lion's roar of anger and command that stilled all other sound. Tara opened her eyes and Moses Gama stood over her, a towering colossus, and his voice alone stopped them and drove them back. He lifted her in his arms and held her like a child. The crowd around the Packard opened before him as he carried her to it and placed her on the front seat and then slid behind the wheel.

As he started the engine and swung the Packard away in a hard U-turn, the black smoke from the burning van poured over them and obscured the windscreen for a moment, and Tara smelled Sister Nunziata's flesh roasting.

This time she could not control herself and she flopped forward, her head between her knees, and vomited on the floor of the Packard.

*   *   *

Manfred De La Rey had taken the chair at the top of the long table in the operations rooms in the basement of Marshall Square. He had come across from his own office suite in the Union Buildings in Pretoria to police headquarters at the centre of the storm, where he could be at hand to consider, with his senior officers, each fresh despatch as it came in from the police provincial HQs around the country.

The entire wall facing Manfred's seat was a large-scale map of the sub-continent. Working in front of it were two junior police officers. They were placing magnetic markers on the map. Each of the small black discs had a name printed upon it and represented one of the almost five hundred ANC officials and organizers that had been so far identified by the intelligence department.

The discs were clustered most thickly along the great crescent of the Witwatersrand in the centre of the continent, although others were scattered across the entire map as the physical whereabouts of each person was confirmed by the police reports that were coming in every few seconds.

Amongst the rash of black markers were a very few red discs, less than fifty in all. These represented the known members of the central committee of the African National Congress.

Some of the names were those of Europeans: Harris, Marks, Fischer, and some were Asians like Naicker and Nana Sita, but the majority were African. Tambo and Sisulu and Mandela – they were all there. Mandela's red disc was placed on the city of Johannesburg, while Moroka was in the Eastern Cape and Albert Luthuli was in Zululand.

Manfred De La Rey was stony-faced as he stared at the map, and the senior police officers seated around him studiously avoided catch-

210

ing his eye or even looking directly at him. Manfred had a reputation of being the strongman of the cabinet. His colleagues privately referred to him as 'Panga Man' after the heavy chopping knife that was used in the cane fields, and was the favourite weapon of the Mau Mau in Kenya.

Manfred looked the part. He was a big man. The hands that lay on the table before him were still, there was no fidgeting of nervousness or uncertainty, and they were big hard hands. His face was becoming craggy now, and his jowls and thick neck heightened the sense of power that emanated from him. His men were afraid of him.

'How many more?' he asked suddenly, and the colonel sitting opposite him, a man with the medal ribbons of valour on his chest, started like a schoolboy and quickly consulted his list.

'Four more to find – Mbeki, Mtolo, Mhlaba and Gama.' He read out the names on his list that remained unticked, and Manfred De La Rey relapsed into silence.

Despite his brooding stillness and forbidding expression, Manfred was pleased with the day's work. It was not yet noon on the first day and already they had pinpointed the whereabouts of most of the ringleaders. Altogether the ANC had planned the entire campaign with quite extraordinary precision and had exhibited unusual thoroughness and foresight in its execution, Manfred reflected. He had not expected them to be so efficient, the African was notoriously lackadaisical and happy-go-lucky – but then they had the advice and assistance of their white communist comrades. The protests and demonstrations and strikes were widespread and effective. Manfred grunted aloud and the officers at the table looked up apprehensively, but dropped their eyes hurriedly when he frowned.

Manfred returned to his thoughts. No, not bad for a bunch of kaffirs, even with a few white men to help them. Yet their naivety and amateurishness showed in their almost total lack of security and secrecy. They had blabbed as though they were at a beer-drink. Full of their own importance they had boasted of their plans and made little effort to conceal the identities of the leaders and cover their movements. The police informers had had little difficult in picking up the information.

There were, of course, exceptions and Manfred scowled as he considered the lists of leaders still unaccounted for. One name pricked like a burr, Moses Gama. He had made a study of the man's file. After Mandela, he was probably the most dangerous of them all.

'We must have him,' he told himself. 'We must get those two, Mandela and Gama.' And now he spoke aloud, barking the question: 'Where is Mandela?'

211

'At the moment he is addressing a meeting in the community hall at Drake's Farm township,' the colonel answered promptly, glancing up at the red marker on the map. 'He will be followed when he leaves, until we are ready to make the arrests.'

'No word of Gama yet?' Manfred asked impatiently, and the officer shook his head.

'Not yet, Minister, he was last seen here on the Witwatersrand nine days ago. He might have gone underground. We may have to move without him.'

'No,' Manfred snapped. 'I want him. I want Moses Gama.'

Manfred relapsed into silence, brooding and intense. He knew that he was caught in the cross-currents of history. He could feel the good winds blowing at his back, set fair to carry him away on his course. He knew also that at any moment those winds might drop, and the ebb of his tide might set in. It was dangerous – mortally dangerous but still he waited. His father and his ancestors had all been huntsmen. They had hunted the elephant and lion and he had heard them speak of the patience and the waiting that was part of the hunt. Now Manfred was a hunter as they had been, but his quarry, though every bit as dangerous, was infinitely more cunning.

He had set his snares with all the skill at his command. The banning orders, five hundred of them, were already made out. The men and women to whom they were addressed would be driven out from society into the wilderness. Prohibited from attending a gathering of more than three persons, physically confined to a single magisterial district, prohibited also from publishing a single written word and prevented from having their spoken word published by anyone else, their treacherous and treasonable voices would be effectively gagged. That was how he would deal with the lesser enemy, the smaller game of this hunt.

For the others, the fifty big game, the dangerous ones, he had other weapons ready. The warrants of arrest had been drawn up and the charges framed. Amongst them were high treason and furthering the aims of international communism, conspiracy to overthrow the government by violent revolution, incitement to public violence – and these, if proven, led directly to the gallows tree. Complete success was there, almost within his grasp, but at any moment it could be snatched away.

At that moment a voice was raised so loudly in the operations room beyond the cubicle windows that they all looked up. Even Manfred swung his head towards the sound and narrowed his pale eyes. The officer who had spoken was sitting with his back to the window holding the telephone receiver to his ear, and scribbling on the notepad on the desk in front of him. Now he slammed the receiver

212

back on to its bracket, ripped the top sheet off the pad and hurried into the map room.

'What is it?' demanded the super.

'We've got him, sir.' The man's voice was shrill with excitement. 'We've got Moses Gama. He is in Port Elizabeth. Less than two hours ago he was at the head of a riot at the New Brighton railway station. The police were attacked. and were forced to open fire in self-defence. At least seven people have been killed, one of them a nun. She was horribly mutilated – there is even an unconfirmed report that she was cannibalized – and her body has been burned.'

'Are they sure it was him?' Manfred asked.

'No doubt, Minister. He was positively identified by an informer who knows him personally and the police captain has identified him by file and photograph.'

'All right,' Manfred De La Rey said. 'Now we can move.' He looked down at the commissioner of police at the far end of the long table. 'Do it, please, Commissioner,' he said, and picked up his dark fedora hat from the table. 'Report to me the moment you have them all locked up.'

He rode up in the lift to ground level and his chauffeur-driven limousine was waiting to take him back to his office in the Union Buildings. As he settled back against the leather-padded rear seat and the limousine pulled away, he smiled for the first time that morning.

'A nun,' he said aloud. 'And they ate her!' He shook his head with satisfaction. 'Let the bleeding hearts of the world read that and know what kind of savages we are dealing with.'

He felt the good winds of his fortune freshen, bearing him away towards those places which only recently he had allowed himself to dream of.

*   *   *

When they got back to the mission, Moses helped Tara out of the Packard. She was still pale and shaking like a woman with malaria. Her clothing was ripped and soiled with blood and dirt, and she could hardly stand unaided.

Kitty Godolphin and her camera crew had escaped the wrath of the mob by running across the railway tracks and hiding in a storm-water drain, then working their way in a wide circle back to the mission.

'We've got to get out of here,' Kitty yelled at Tara as she came out on to the verandah and saw Moses helping her up the steps. 'I've got the most incredible footage of my life. I can't trust it to anybody

213

else. I want to get on the Pan Am flight from Jo'burg tomorrow morning and take the undeveloped cans to New York myself.' She was so excited that her voice shook wildly, and like Tara her denim jeans were torn and dusty. However, she was already packed and ready to leave, carrying the red canvas tote bag that was all her luggage.

'Did you film the nun?' Moses demanded. 'Did you film them killing Sister Nunziata?'

'Sure did, sweetheart!' Hank grinned. He was close behind Kitty. 'Got it all.'

'How many cans did you shoot?' Moses insisted.

'Four.' Hank was so excited he could not stand still. He was bouncing on his toes and snapping his fingers.

'Did you get the police shooting?'

'All of it, sweetheart, all of it.'

'Where is the film of the nun?' Moses demanded.

'Still in the camera.' Hank slapped the Arriflex that hung by his side. 'It's all here, baby. I had just changed film when they grabbed the nun and ripped her up.'

Moses left Tara leaning against the column of the verandah, and crossed to where Hank stood. He moved so casually that none of them realized what he was about to do. Kitty was still talking.

'If we leave right away, we can be in Jo'burg by tomorrow morning. The Pan Am flight leaves at 11.30 —'

Moses had reached Hank's side. He seized the heavy camera, twisting the carrying strap so that Hank was pulled up on his toes helplessly, and he unclipped the round magazine of film from its seat on top of the camera body. Then he turned and smashed the magazine against the brick column of the verandah.

Kitty realized what he was doing and she flew at him like an angry cat, clawing for his eyes with her nails. 'My film,' she screeched. 'God damn you to hell, that's my film.'

Moses shoved her so violently that she collided with Hank, taking him off balance and they fell over each other, sprawling together on the verandah floor.

Moses hit the magazine again and this time the can burst open. The ribbon of glistening celluloid spilled out and cascaded over the retaining wall.

'You've ruined it,' Kitty screamed, coming to her feet and charging at him.

Moses tossed the empty can away, and caught Kitty's wrists, lifting her bodily off the ground and holding her effortlessly, though she struggled and kicked at him.

'You have the film of police brutality, the murder of innocent blacks,' he said. 'The rest of it you were not meant to witness. I will not let you show that to the world.' He pushed her away. 'You may take the Packard.'

Kitty glared at him, massaging her wrists where the skin was red from his grip and she spat like a cat.

'I won't forget that – one day you will pay for that, Moses Gama.' Her malignancy was chilling.

'Go,' Moses commanded. 'You have a plane to catch.'

For a moment she hesitated, and then she whirled, picked up her tote bag.

'Come on, Hank,' she called, and she ran down the stairs to the Packard and sprang into the driver's seat.

'You cock-sucking bastard,' Hank hissed at Moses as he passed. 'That was the best stuff I ever scored.'

'You've still got three cans,' Moses said softly. 'Be grateful for that.'

Moses watched them drive away in the Packard and then turned to Tara.

'We must move very fast now – the police will act at once. We have to get out of the township before they cordon it off. I am a marked man – we have to get clear.'

'What do you want me to do?' Tara asked.

'Come, I'll explain later,' Moses said and hustled her towards the Buick. 'First, we must get clear.'

*   *   *

Tara gave the salesman a cheque and waited in the tiny cubicle of his office that stank of cheap cigar smoke while he phoned her bank in Cape Town.

There was a crumpled newspaper on the cluttered desk, and she picked it up and read it avidly.

SEVEN DEAD IN P.E. RIOTS
NATIONWIDE DISTURBANCES
500 ACTIVISTS BANNED
MANDELA ARRESTED

Almost the entire newspaper was devoted to the defiance campaign and its consequences. At the bottom of the page, under the lurid accounts of the killing and the cannibalization of Sister Nunziata, there were accounts of the action taken by the ANC in other sectors of the country. Thousands had been arrested, and there were photographs of protesters being loaded into police vans, grinning cheerfully and giving the thumbs-up sign that had become the protester's salute.

215

The inner page of the newspaper gave the lists of almost five hundred persons who had been banned, and explained the consequences of the banning orders – how they effectively terminated the public life of the victim.

There was also the much shorter list of persons who had been arrested for high treason and furthering the aims of the communist party, and Tara bit her lip when she saw Moses Gama's name. The police spokesman must have anticipated his arrest, but it was proof that the precautions Moses was taking were wise. High treason was a capital offence, and she had a mental picture of Moses, his head hooded, twisting and kicking from the gallows crossbeam. She shuddered and thrust the image aside, concentrating on the rest of the newspaper.

There were photographs, most of them murky and indistinct, of the leaders of the ANC, and she smiled humourlessly as she realized that these were the first fruits of the campaign. Up to this moment, not one in a hundred white South Africans had ever heard of Moses Gama, Nelson Mandela, or any of the other leaders, but now they had come bursting in on the national conscience. The world suddenly knew who they were.

The middle pages were mostly filled with public reaction to the campaign and to the government's counter measures. It was too soon for the foreign reactions, but local opinion seemed almost unanimous: condemnation of the barbaric murder of Sister Nunziata, and high praise for police courage and the swift action of the minister of police in crushing the communist-inspired plot.

The editor wrote:

We have not always been able to commend the actions and utterances of the Minister of Police. However, the need finds the man and we are thankful this day that a man of courage and strength stands between us and the forces of anarchy —

Tara's reading was interrupted by the used car salesman. He bustled back into the tiny office to fawn on Tara and to gush.

'My dear Mrs Courtney, you must forgive me. I had no idea who you were, or I would never have subjected you to the humiliation of querying your cheque.'

He ushered her out to the yard, bowing and grinning ingratiatingly, and held open the door of the 1951-model black Cadillac for which Tara had just given her cheque for almost a thousand pounds.

Tara drove down the hill and parked on the Donkin overlooking the sea. The military and naval outfitters were only half a block down the main street and from their stocks she picked out a chauffeur's cap with a glossy patent-leather peak and a dove-grey

216

tunic with brass buttons in Moses' size which the assistant packed in a brown paper bag.

Back in the new Cadillac she drove slowly down to the main railway station and parked opposite the entrance. She left the key in the ignition and slipped into the back seat. Within five minutes Moses came out. He was dressed in grubby blue overalls and the police constable at the railway entrance did not even glance at him. Moses sauntered down the sidewalk and as he drew level with the Cadillac, Tara passed the paper bag through the open window.

Within ten minutes Moses was back, the overalls discarded, wearing the chauffeur's cap and smart new tunic over his dark slacks and black shoes. He climbed into the driver's seat and started the engine.

'You were right. There is a warrant out for your arrest,' she said softly.

'How do you know?'

'There is a newspaper on the seat.' She had folded it open at the report on his arrest. He read it swiftly, and then eased the Cadillac out into the traffic stream.

'What are you going to do, Moses? Will you give yourself up and stand trial?'

'The courtroom would be a platform from which to speak to the world,' he mused.

'And if you were convicted, the gallows would be an even more riveting pulpit,' she pointed out acidly, and he smiled at her in the rear-view mirror.

'We need martyrs – every cause must have martyrs.'

'My God, Moses, how can you speak like that? Every cause needs a leader. There are many who would make fine martyrs, but very few who can lead.'

He drove in silence for a while and then he said firmly, 'We will go to Johannesburg. I must talk to the others before I decide.'

'Most of the others have been arrested,' Tara pointed out.

'Not all.' He shook his head. 'I must talk to those who have escaped. How much money do you have?'

She opened her handbag and counted the notes she had in her purse.

'Over a hundred pounds.'

'More than enough,' he nodded. 'Be prepared to play the grand lady when the police stop us.'

They ran into the first road-block on the outskirts of the city at the Swartkops bridge. There was a line of cars and heavy vehicles and they moved forward slowly, stopping and starting, until two police constables signalled them over and a young police warrant officer came to the passenger window.

217

'Good afternoon, *Mevrou*.' He touched his cap. 'May we look in the boot of your car?'

'What is this about, officer?'

'The troubles, madam. We are looking for the trouble-makers who killed the nun and ate her.'

Tara leaned forward and spoke sharply to Moses. 'Open the boot for the policeman, Stephen.' And Moses climbed out and held the lid open while the constables made a cursory search. Not one of them looked at his face, the chauffeur's uniform had rendered him miraculously invisible.

'Thank you, lady.'

The warrant officer waved them through and Moses murmured, 'That was most unflattering. I thought I was a celebrity now.'

It was a long and arduous drive from the coast, but Moses drove sedately, careful not to give anyone an excuse to stop them and question them more carefully.

As he drove he tuned the Cadillac's wireless for the South African Broadcasting Corporation's hourly news bulletin. The reception was intermittent as the terrain varied, but they picked up one exciting item.

The Soviet Union supported by her allies had demanded an urgent debate in the United Nations General Assembly on the situation in the country. This was the first time the UN had ever shown an interest in South Africa. For that alone all their sacrifice had been worthwhile. However, the rest of the news was disquieting. Over eight thousand protesters had been arrested and all the leaders banned or picked up, and a spokesman for the minister of police assured the country that the situation was firmly under control.

They drove on until after dark when they stopped at one of the small Orange Free State hotels that catered mainly for commercial travellers. When Tara asked for board and lodging for her chauffeur, the request was taken as matter of course because all the travellers employed coloured drivers and Moses was sent around the back to the servants' quarters in the hotel yard.

After the plain and unappetizing fare in the hotel dining-room, Tara telephoned Weltevreden, and Sean answered on the second ring. They had returned from their hunting safari with Shasa the previous day, and were garrulous and excited. Each of the boys spoke to her in turn, so she was treated to three separate accounts of how Garrick had shot a man-eating lion. Then Isabella came on the line, and her sweet childish lisp tugged at Tara's heart, making her feel dreadfully guilty at her lack of maternal duty. Yet none of the children, Isabella included, seemed to have missed her in the least. Isabella was just as long-winded as her brothers in recounting all the things that she and

218

Nana had done together, and the new dress that Nana had bought her and the doll that grandpa Blaine had brought back from England especially for her. None of them asked her how she was and when she was coming home to Weltevreden.

Shasa came on the line last, distant but friendly. 'We are all having a wonderful time – Garry shot a lion —'

'Oh God, Shasa, don't you tell me about it, I've already had three accounts of the poor beast's death.'

Within a few minutes they had run out of things to say to each other. 'Well then, old thing, take care of yourself. I see the uglies are cutting up rather rough on the Rand, but De La Rey has it well in hand,' Shasa ended. 'Don't get caught up in any unpleasantness.'

'I won't,' she promised. 'Now I'll let you go in to dinner.' Shasa liked to dine at eight o'clock sharp and it was four minutes before the hour. She knew he was already dressed and checking his watch. When she hung up she realized that he hadn't asked her where she was, what she was doing or when she was coming home.

'Saved me from having to lie,' she consoled herself.

From her bedroom she could look over the hotel yard, and the lights were on in the servants' quarters. Suddenly she was overwhelmed with loneliness. It was so chilling, that she seriously thought about creeping across the yard to be with him. It took an effort of will to thrust that madness aside, and instead she picked up the telephone again and asked the operator for the number at Puck's Hill.

A servant, with a marked African accent, answered and Tara's heart sank. It was vital that they find out whether the Rivonia house was still safe. They could be going into a police trap.

'Is Nkosi Marcus there?' she demanded.

'Nkosi Marcus no here, he go away, missus,' the servant told her. 'You Missus Tara?'

'Yes! Yes!' Although she did not remember a servant, he must have recognized her voice, and she was about to go on when Marcus Archer spoke in his normal voice.

'Forgive me, my dear, for the music-hall impression, but the sky has fallen in here. Everybody is in a panic – the pigs have moved much quicker than anybody expected. Joe and I are the only ones to survive, as far as I know. How is our good friend, have they got him?'

'He's safe. Can we come to Puck's Hill?'

'So far it seems as though they have overlooked us here, but do be careful, won't you? There are road-blocks everywhere.'

Tara slept very little and was up before dawn to begin the last leg of the journey. The hotel chef had made her a packet of corned beef sandwiches and a thermos of hot tea, so they breakfasted as they

219

drove. Any stop would increase their chances of discovery and arrest, and except to refuel, they kept going and crossed the Vaal river before noon.

Tara had been seeking the right moment to tell Moses ever since she had returned to the Transvaal to be near him, but now she knew that there would never be a right moment and that within hours they would be at Puck's Hill. After that nothing was certain except that there would be confusion and great danger for all of them.

'Moses,' she addressed the back of his head in a resolute voice, 'I can't keep it from you any longer. I have to tell you now. I am bearing your child.'

She saw his head flinch slightly and then those dark mesmeric eyes were glowering at her in the driver's mirror.

'What will you do?' he asked. He had not asked if she were certain nor had he queried his paternity of the child. That was typical of him – and yet he had accepted no responsibility either. 'What will you do?'

'I am not sure yet. I will find a way to have it.'

'You must get rid of it.'

'No,' she cried vehemently. 'Never. He's mine. I will take care of him.'

He did not remark on her choice of the masculine pronoun.

'The child will be half-caste,' he told her. 'Are you prepared for that?'

'I will find a way,' she insisted.

'I cannot help you – not at all,' he went on remorselessly. 'You understand that.'

'Yes, you can,' she answered. 'You can tell me that you are pleased that I am carrying your son – and that you will love him, as I love his father.'

'Love?' he said. 'That is not an African word. There is no word for love in my vocabulary.'

'Oh, Moses, that is not true. You love your people.'

'I love them as a people entire, not as individuals. I would sacrifice any one of them for the good of the whole.'

'But our son, Moses. Something precious that we have made between us – don't you feel anything at all for him?'

She watched his eyes in the mirror and saw the pain in them.

'Yes,' he admitted. 'Of course, I do. Yet I dare not acknowledge it. I must lock such feelings away lest they weaken my resolve and destroy us all.'

'Then I will love him for both of us,' she said softly.

As Marcus Archer had warned Tara, there were more road-blocks. As they drew closer to the great industrial and mining complex of

220

the Witwatersrand, they were stopped three times, the last at Halfway House, but each time the chauffeur's uniform and Tara's white face and haughty manner protected him.

Tara had expected Johannesburg to be like a city under siege, but the road-blocks and the news posters on the street corners were the only indications of something unusual afoot. The headgear wheels of the mines they passed were spinning busily, and beyond the perimeter fences they saw the black miners in gumboots and shiny hard hats flocking to the shaft heads.

When they passed through downtown Johannesburg, the city streets were crowded as usual with shoppers of all races and their faces were cheerful and relaxed. Tara was disappointed. She was not sure what she had expected, but at least she had hoped for some visible sign that the people were on the march.

'You cannot expect too much,' Moses told her when she lamented that nothing had changed. 'The forces against us are obdurate as granite, and the resources they command are limitless. Yet it is a beginning – our first faltering step on the road to liberation.'

They drove past Puck's Hill slowly. It seemed deserted, and at least there were no signs of police activity. Moses parked the Cadillac in the wattle plantation at the back of the Country Club and left Tara while he went back on foot to make absolutely certain they were not running into a police trap.

He was back within half an hour. 'It's safe. Marcus is there,' he told her as he started the Cadillac and drove back.

Marcus was waiting for them on the verandah. He looked tired and worn, and he had aged dramatically in the short time since Tara had last seen him.

He led them into the long kitchen, and went back to the stove on which he was preparing a meal for them, and while he worked he told them everything that had happened in their absence.

'The police reaction was so massive and immediate that it must have been carefully prepared. We expected a delay while they caught up with the situation and gathered themselves. We expected to be able to exploit that delay, and call upon the masses to join us in the defiance campaign until it gathered its own momentum and became irresistible, but they were ready for us. There are not more than a dozen of the leaders at large now, Moses is one of the lucky ones, and without leaders the campaign is already beginning to grind to a halt.'

He glanced at Tara with a vindictive sparkle in his eye before he went on.

'However, there are still some pockets of resistance – our little

221

Victoria is doing sterling work. She has organized the nurses at Baragwanath and brought them out as part of the campaign. She won't keep that up much longer – she'll be arrested or banned pretty damn soon, you can bet on that.'

'Vicky is a brave woman,' Moses agreed. 'She knows the risks, and she takes them willingly.'

He looked straight at Tara as he said it, as if daring her to voice her jealousy. She knew of his marriage, of course, but she had never spoken of it. She knew what the consequences would be, and now she dropped her eyes, unable to meet his challenge.

'We have underestimated this man De La Rey,' Moses said. 'He is a formidable opponent. We have achieved very little of what we hoped for.'

'Still, the United Nations is debating our plight,' Tara said quietly without looking up again.

'Debating,' Moses agreed scornfully. 'But it requires only a single veto from America or Britain or France, and no action will be taken. They will talk and talk while my people suffer.'

'Our people,' Marcus chided him. 'Our people, Moses.'

'My people,' Moses contradicted him harshly. 'The others are all in prison. I am the only leader who remains. They are my people.' There was silence in the kitchen, except for the scrape of utensils on the plates as they ate, but Marcus was frowning and it was he who broke the silence.

'So what happens now?' he asked. 'Where will you go? You cannot stay here, the police may swoop at any moment. Where will you go?'

'Drake's Farm?' Moses mused.

'No.' Marcus shook his head. 'They know you too well there. The moment you arrive the whole township will know and there are police informers everywhere. It will be the same as turning yourself in at the nearest police station.'

They were silent again until Moses asked, 'Where is Joe Cicero? Have they taken him?'

'No,' Marcus answered. 'He has gone underground.'

'Can you contact him?'

'We have an arrangement. He will ring me here – if not tonight, then tomorrow.'

Moses looked across the table at Tara. 'Can I come with you to the expedition base at Sundi Caves? It's the only safe place I can think of at the moment.' And Tara's spirits bounded. She would have him for a little longer still.

Tara explained to Marion Hurst, not attempting to conceal Moses' identity nor the fact that he was a fugitive, and she was not surprised by the American woman's response.

222

'It's like Martin Luther King coming and asking me for sanctuary,' she declared. 'Of course, I'll do whatever I can to help.'

As a cover, Marion gave Moses a job in the pottery section of the warehouse under the name of Stephen Khama, and he was absorbed immediately into the company of the expedition. Without asking questions the other members, both black and white, gathered around to shield him.

Despite Marcus Archer's assurances, it was almost a week before he was able to contact Joe Cicero, and another day before he could arrange for them to meet. The hardest possible way they had learned not to underestimate the vigilance of the police, while Joe Cicero had always been secretive and professional. Nobody was certain where he lived or how he maintained himself, his comings and goings were unannounced and unpredictable.

'I have always thought him to be theatrical and over-careful, but now I see the wisdom behind it,' Moses told Tara as they drove into the city. Moses was once more dressed in his chauffeur's uniform. 'From now on we must learn from the professionals, for those ranged against us are the hardest of professionals.'

Joe Cicero came out of the entrance of the Johannesburg railway station as Moses stopped the Cadillac for the red light at the pedestrian crossing, and he slipped unobtrusively into the back seat beside Tara. Moses pulled away, heading out in the direction of Doornfontein.

'I congratulate you on still being at large,' Joe told Moses wryly, as he lit a fresh cigarette from the butt of the last and glanced sideways at Tara. 'You are Tara Courtney,' and smiled at her surprise. 'What is your part in all this?'

'She is a friend,' Moses spoke for her. 'She is committed to us. You may speak freely in front of her.'

'I never speak freely,' Joe murmured. 'Only an idiot does that.' They were all silent then until Joe asked suddenly, 'And so, my friend, do you still believe that the revolution can be won without blood? Are you still one of the pacifists who would play the game by the rules that the oppressor makes and changes at will?'

'I have never been a pacifist,' Moses' voice rumbled. 'I have always been a warrior.'

'I rejoice to hear you say it, for it confirms what I have always believed.' Joe smiled a sly and inscrutable smile behind the fringe of dark beard. 'If I did not, I would not be sitting here now.' Then his tone altered. 'Make a U-turn here and take the Krugersdorp road!' he ordered.

The three of them were silent while Joe turned to scrutinize the following traffic. After a minute he seemed satisfied and relaxed in the back seat. Moses drove out of the built-up areas into the open grassy veld. The traffic around them thinned, and abruptly Joe Cicero leaned forward and pointed ahead to an empty lay-by on the side of the road.

'Pull in there,' he ordered, and as Moses parked the Cadillac he opened the door beside him. As he stepped out he jerked his head. 'Come!'

When Tara opened her own door to join them, Joe snapped. 'No, not you! Stay here!'

With Moses at his side he walked through the stand of scraggly black wattle into the open veld beyond, out of sight of the road.

'I told you the woman is trustworthy,' Moses said, and Joe shrugged.

'Perhaps. I do do not take chances until it is necessary to do so.' And then he changed direction. 'I asked you once what you thought of Mother Russia?'

'And I replied that she was a friend of the oppressed peoples of the world.'

'She wishes to be your friend also,' Joe said simply.

'Do you mean me personally – Moses Gama?'

'Yes, you personally – Moses Gama.'

'How do you know this?'

'There are men in Moscow who have watched you carefully for many years. What they have seen they approve of. They offer you the hand of friendship.'

'I ask you again. How do you know this?'

'I am a colonel in the Russian KGB. I have been ordered to tell you this.'

Moses stared at him. It was moving so fast that he needed a respite to catch up.

'What does the offer of friendship entail?' he asked cautiously, buying time in which to think, and Joe Cicero nodded approvingly.

'It is good you ask the terms of our friendship. It confirms our estimate of you. That you are a careful man. You will be given the answer to that in due course. In the meantime be content with the fact that we have singled you out above all others.'

'Very well,' Moses agreed. 'But tell me why I have been chosen. There are other good men – Mandela is one of them.'

'Mandela was considered, but we do not believe he has the steel. We detect a softness in him. Our psychologists believe that he will flinch from the hard and bloody work of the revolution. We know also that he does not have the same high regard for Mother Russia that you do. He has even called her the new oppressor, the colonialist of the twentieth century.'

'What about the others?' Moses asked.

'There are no others,' Joe told him flatly. 'It was either you or Mandela. It is you. That is the decision.'

'They want my answer now?' Moses stared into the tar pits of his eyes, but they had a strangely lifeless dullness in them and Joe Cicero shook his head.

'They want to meet you, talk to you, make sure you understand the bargain. Then you will be trained and groomed for the task ahead.'

'Where will this meeting take place?'

Joe smiled and shrugged. 'In Moscow – where else?' And Moses did not let his amazement show on his face, though his hands clenched into fists at his sides.

'Moscow! How will I get there?'

'It has been arranged,' Joe assured him, and Moses lifted his head and stared at the tall thunderheads that rose in silver and blue splendour along the horizon. He was lost in thought for many minutes.

He felt his spirits grow light and take wing up towards those soaring thunder clouds. It had come – the moment for which he had worked and waited a lifetime. Destiny had cleared the field of all his rivals, and he had been chosen.

Like a victor's laurel they were offering a land and a crown.

'I will go to meet them,' he agreed softly.

'You will leave in two days' time. It will take me that long to make the final arrangements. In the meantime keep out of sight, do not attempt to take leave of any friends, do not tell anybody you are going – not even the Courtney woman or your new wife. I will get a message to you through Marcus Archer and if he is arrested before then, I will contact you at the expedition base at Sundi Caves. Professor Hurst is a sympathizer.' Joe dropped the butt of his cigarette and while he ground it under his heel, he lit another. 'Now we will go back to the car.'

*   *   *

Victoria Gama stood at the top end of the sloping lawns of the Baragwanath nurses' home. She was still dressed in her uniform with the badges of a nursing sister sparkling on her tunic, but she looked very young and self-conscious as she faced the hundred or so off-duty nurses who were gathered on the lawns below her. The white matron had refused permission for them to meet in the dining-hall, so they were standing out under a sky full of towering thunderheads.

'My sisters!' She held out her hands towards them. 'We have a

225

duty to our patients – to those in pain, to those suffering and dying, to those who turn to us in trust. However, I believe that we have a higher duty and more sacred commitment to all our people who for three hundred years have suffered under a fierce and unrelenting oppression —'

Victoria seemed to gather confidence as she spoke, and her sweet young voice had a music and rhythm that caught their attention. She had always been popular with the other nurses, and her winning personality, her capacity for hard work and her unselfish attitude had seen her emerge, not only as one of the most senior nursing staff for her age, but also as an example and a trend-setter amongst the younger nurses. There were women ten and fifteen years older than she was, who listened now to her with attention and who applauded her when she paused for breath. Their applause and approval bolstered Victoria and her voice took on a sharper tone.

'Across the land our leaders, in actions rather than pale words, are showing the oppressors that we will no longer remain passive and acquiescent. They are crying to the world for justice and humanity. What kind of women will we be if we stand aside and refuse to join them? How can we ignore the fact that our leaders are being arrested and harassed by the infernal laws —'

There was a stir in the crowd of uniformed nurses, and the faces which had been lifted towards Victoria turned away and the expressions of rapt concentration changed to consternation. From the edges of the crowd one or two of the nurses broke away and scuttled back up the steps of the nurses' home.

Three police vans had driven up to the gates, and the white matron and two of her senior staff had hurried out to confer with the police captain in charge of the contingent as he alighted from the leading vehicle. The matron's white tunic and skirt contrasted with the blue of the police uniforms, and she was pointing at Victoria and talking animatedly to the captain.

Victoria's voice faltered, and despite her resolve, she was afraid. It was an instinctive and corrosive fear. From her earliest remembered childhood the blue police uniforms had been symbols of unquestionable might and authority. To defy them now went against all her instincts and the teaching of her father and all her elders.

'Do not challenge the white man,' they had taught her. 'For his wrath is more terrible than the summer fires that consume the veld. None can stand before it.'

Then she remembered Moses Gama, and her voice firmed; she beat down her fear and cried aloud, 'Look at yourselves, my sisters. See how you tremble and cast your eyes down at the sight of the

226

oppressor. He has not yet spoken nor raised a hand to you, but you have become little children!'

The police captain left the group at the gate and came to the edge of the lawn. There he paused and raised a bull-horn to his lips.

'This is an illegal gathering on state-owned property.' His voice was magnified and distorted. 'You have five minutes to disperse and return to your quarters.' He raised his arm and ostentatiously checked his wristwatch. 'If you have not done so in that time —'

The nurses were scattering already, scampering away, not waiting for the officer to complete his warning, and Victoria found herself alone on the wide lawn. She wanted to run and hide also, but she thought about Moses Gama and her pride would not let her move.

The police officer lowered his loud-hailer and turned back to the white matron. They conferred again, and the officer showed her a sheaf of paper which he took from his despatch case. The matron nodded and they both looked at Victoria again. Alone now, she still stood at the top of the lawn. Pride and fear held her rigid. She stood stiffly, unable to move as the police captain marched across to where she stood.

'Victoria Dinizulu? he asked her in a normal conversational voice, so different from the hoarse booming of the loud-hailer.

Victoria nodded, and then remembered. 'No,' she denied. 'I am Victoria Gama.' The police officer looked confused. He was very fair-skinned with a fine blond moustache. 'I was told you were Victoria Dinizulu – there has been a mess-up,' he muttered, and then he blushed with embarrassment and immediately Victoria felt sorry for him.

'I got married,' she explained. 'My maiden name was Victoria Dinizulu, but now I am Victoria Gama.'

'Oh, I see.' The captain looked relieved, and glanced down at the document in his hand. 'It's made out to Victoria Dinizulu. I suppose it's still all right though.' He was uncertain again.

'It's not your fault,' Victoria consoled him. 'The wrong name, I mean. They can't blame you. You couldn't have known.'

'No, you're right.' The captain perked up visibly. 'It's not my fault. I'll just serve it on you anyway. They can sort it out back at HQ.'

'What is it?' Victoria asked curiously.

'It's a banning order,' the captain explained. He showed it to her. 'It's signed by the minister of police. I have to read it to you, then you have to sign it,' he explained and then he looked contrite. 'I'm sorry, it's my duty.'

'That is all right.' Vicky smiled at him. 'You have to do your duty.'

He looked down at the document again and began to read aloud:

227

TO VICTORIA THANDELA DINIZULU

Notice in terms of Section 9(i) of the Internal Security Act 1950 (Act 44 of 1950). Whereas I, Manfred De La Rey, Minister of Police, am satisfied that you are engaged in activities which endanger or are calculated to endanger the maintenance of public order —

The captain stumbled over the more complicated legal phraseology and mispronounced some of the English words. Vicky corrected him helpfully. The banning document was four typewritten pages, and the policeman reached the end of it with patent relief.

'You have to sign here.' He offered her the document.

'I don't have a pen.'

'Here, use mine.'

'Thank you,' said Victoria. 'You are very kind.'

She signed her name in the space provided and as she handed him back his pen, she had ceased to be a complete person. Her banning order prohibited her from being in the company of more than two other persons at any one time, except in the course of her daily work, of addressing any gathering or preparing any written article for publication. It confined her physically to the magisterial area of Johannesburg and required that she remain under house arrest for twelve hours of the day and also that she report daily to her local police station.

'I'm sorry,' the police captain repeated, as he screwed the top back on his pen. 'You seem a decent girl.'

'It's your job,' Victoria smiled back at him. 'Don't feel bad about it.'

Over the following days Victoria retreated into the strange half-world of isolation. During working hours she found that her peers and superiors avoided her, as though she were a carrier of plague. The matron moved her out of the room that she shared with two other nursing sisters and she was given a small single room on the unpopular southern side of the hostel which never received the sun in winter. In this room her meals were served to her on a tray as she was prohibited from using the dining-hall when more than two other persons were present. Each evening after coming off shift she made the two-mile walk down to the police station to sign the register, but this soon became a pleasant outing rather than a penance. She was able to smile and greet the people she passed on the street for they did not know she was a non-person and she enjoyed even that fleeting human contact.

Alone in her room she listened to her portable radio and read the books that Moses had given her, and thought about him. More than once she heard his name on the radio. Apparently a controversial

228

film had been shown on the NABS television channel in the United States which had created a furore across the continent. It seemed that South Africa, which for most Americans was a territory remote as the moon and a thousand times less important, was suddenly a political topic. In the film Moses Gama had figured largely, and such was his presence and stature that he had been accepted abroad as the central figure in the African struggle. In the United Nations debate which had followed the television film, nearly every one of the speakers had referred to Moses Gama. Although the motion in the General Assembly calling for the condemnation of South Africa's racial discrimination had been vetoed in the Security Council by Great Britain, the debate had sent a ripple across the world and a cold shiver down the spine of the white government in the country.

South Africa had no television network, but on her portable radio Victoria listened to a pungent edition of 'Current Affairs' on the state-controlled South African Broadcasting Corporation in which the campaign of defiance was described as the action of a radical minority, and Moses Gama was vilified as a communist-inspired revolutionary criminal who was still at large, although a warrant had been issued for his arrest on a charge of high treason.

Cut off from all other sympathetic human contact, Victoria found herself pining for him with such desperate longing that she cried herself to sleep in her lonely room each night.

On the tenth day of her banning she was returning from her daily report to the police station, keeping to the edge of the pavement in that sensual gliding walk that the Nguni woman practises from childhood when she carries every load, from faggots of firewood to five-gallon clay pots of water, balanced upon her head. A light delivery van slowed down as it approached her from behind, and began to keep pace with her.

Victoria was accustomed to extravagant male attention, for she was the very essence of Nguni female beauty, and when the driver of the vehicle whistled softly, she did not glance in his direction but lifted her chin an inch and assumed a haughty expression.

The driver whistled again, more demandingly, and from the corner of her eye she saw the van was blue with the sign EXPRESS DRY CLEANERS – SIX HOUR SERVICE painted on the side. The driver was a big man, and although his cap was pulled low over his eyes, she sensed he was attractive and masterful. Despite herself her hips began to swing as she strode on, and her large perfectly round buttocks oscillated like the cheeks of a chipmunk chewing a nut.

'Victoria!' Her name was hissed, and the voice was unmistakable. She stopped dead and swung round to face him.

'You!' she whispered, and then glanced around her frantically.

For the moment the sidewalk was clear and only light traffic moved down the highway between rows of tall bluegum trees. Her eyes flashed back to his face, almost hungrily, and she whispered, 'Oh Moses, I didn't think you'd come.'

He leaned across the front seat of the van and opened the door nearest her, and she rushed across and threw herself into the moving van.

'Get down,' he ordered, and she crouched below the dashboard while he slammed the door closed and accelerated away.

'I couldn't believe it was you. I still don't – this van, where did you get it? Oh Moses, you'll never know how much – I heard your name on the radio, many times – so much has happened —' She found that she was gabbling almost hysterically. It had been so long since she had been able to talk freely, and it was as though the painful abscess of loneliness and longing had burst and all the poison was draining in the rush of words.

She began to tell him about the nurses' strike and the banning, and how Albertina Sisulu had contacted her and there was going to be a march by a hundred thousand women, to the government buildings at Pretoria, and she was going to defy her banning order to join the march.

'I want you to be proud of me. I want to be part of the struggle, for that is the only way I can truly be a part of you.'

Moses Gama drove in silence, smiling a little as he listened to her chatter. He wore blue overalls with the legend 'Express Dry Cleaners' embroidered across his back and the rear of the van was filled with racks of clothing that smelled strongly of cleaning solvent. She knew he had borrowed the van from Hendrick Tabaka.

After a few minutes Moses slowed the van and then turned off sharply on to a spur road which swiftly deteriorated into a rutted track, and then petered out entirely. He bumped the last few yards over tussocks of grass and then parked behind a ruined and roofless building, the windows from which the frames had been ripped out were like the eyes of a skull. Victoria straightened up from under the dashboard.

'I have heard about the nurses' strike and your banning,' he said softly as he switched off the engine. 'And yes, I am proud of you. Very proud. You are a wife fit for a chief.'

She hung her head shyly, and the pleasure his words gave her was almost unbearable. She had not truly realized how much she loved him while they had been separated, and now the full force of it rushed back upon her.

'And you are a chief,' she said. 'No, more than that – you are a king.'

230

'Victoria, I do not have much time,' he said. 'I should not have come here at all —'

'I would have shrivelled up if you had not – my soul was drought-stricken —' she burst out, but he laid his hand on her arm to still her.

'Listen to me, Victoria. I have come to tell you that I am going away. I have come to charge you to be strong while I am away.'

'Oh, my husband!' In her agitation she lapsed into Zulu. 'Where are you going?'

'I can tell you only that it is to a distant land.'

'Can I not journey by your side?' she pleaded.

'No.'

'Then I will send my heart to be your travelling companion, while the husk of me remains here to await your return. When will you come back, my husband?'

'I do not know, but it will be a long time.'

'For me every minute that you are gone will become a weary day,' she told him quietly, and he raised his hand and stroked her face gently.

'If there is anything you need you must go to Hendrick Tabaka. He is my brother, and I have placed you in his care.'

She nodded, unable to speak.

'There is only one thing I can tell you now. When I return I will take the world we know and turn it on its head. Nothing will ever be the same again.'

'I believe you,' she said simply.

'I must go now,' he told her. 'Our time together has come to an end.'

'My husband,' she murmured, casting down her eyes again. 'Let me be a wife to you one last time, for the nights are so long and cold when you are not beside me.'

He took a roll of canvas from the back of the van and spread it on the grass beside the parked van. Her naked body was set off by the white cloth as she lay upon it like a figure cast in dark bronze thrown down upon the snow.

At the end when he had spent and lay weak as a child upon her, she clasped his head tenderly to the soft warm swell of her bosom and she whispered to him, 'No matter how far and how long you travel, my love will burn away time and distance and I will be beside you, my husband.'

*   *   *

Tara was waiting for him, with the lantern lit, lying awake in the cottage tent when Moses returned to the camp. She sat up as he came through the fly. The blanket fell to her waist and she was naked. Her breasts were big and white and laced with tiny bluish veins around the swollen nipples – so different from those of the woman he had just left.

'Where have you been?' she demanded.

He ignored the question as he began to undress.

'You have been to see her, haven't you? Joe ordered you not to.'

Now he looked at her scornfully, and then deliberately re-buttoned the front of his overalls as he moved to leave the tent again.

'I'm sorry, Moses,' she cried, instantly terrified by the thought of his going. 'I didn't mean it, please stay. I won't talk like that again. I swear it, my darling. Please forgive me. I was upset, I have had such a terrible dream —' she threw aside the blanket and came up on her knees, reaching out both hands towards him. 'Please!' she entreated. 'Please come to me.'

For long seconds he stared at her and then began once more to unbutton his overalls. She clung to him desperately as he came into the bed.

'Oh Moses – I had such a dream. I dreamed of Sister Nunziata again. Oh God, the look on their faces as they ate her flesh. They were like wolves, their mouths red and running with her blood. It was the most horrific thing, beyond my imagination. It made me want to despair for all the world.'

'No,' he said. His voice was low but it reverberated through her body as though she were the sounding box of a violin trembling to the power of the strings. 'No!' he said. 'It was beauty – stark beauty, shorn of all but the truth. What you witnessed was the rage of the people, and it was a holy thing. Before that I merely hoped, but after witnessing that I could truly believe. It was a consecration of our victory. They ate the flesh and drank the blood as you Christians do to seal a pact with history. When you have seen that sacred rage you have to believe in our eventual triumph.'

He sighed, his great muscular chest heaved in the circle of her arms and then he went to sleep. It was something to which she could never grow accustomed, the way he could sleep as though he had closed a door in his mind. She was left bereft and afraid, for she knew what lay ahead for her.

Joe Cicero came for Moses in the night. Moses had dressed like one of a thousand other contract workers from the gold-mines in a surplus army greatcoat and woollen balaclava helmet that covered most of his face. He had no luggage, as Joe had instructed him, and when the ramshackle Ford pick-up parked across the road from them and flashed its lights once, Moses slipped out of the Cadillac and swiftly crossed to it. He did not say goodbye to Tara, they had taken their farewells long ago and he did not look back to where she sat forlornly behind the wheel of the Cadillac.

As soon as Moses climbed into the rear of the Ford, it pulled away. The tail lights dwindled and were lost around the first curve of the road, and Tara was smothered by such a crushing load of despair that she did not believe she could survive it.

*   *   *

François Afrika was the headmaster of the Mannenberg coloured school on the Cape Flats. He was a little over forty years old, a plump and serious man with a *café au lait* complexion and thick very curly hair which he parted in the middle and plastered flat with Vaseline.

His wife Miriam was plump also, but much shorter and younger than he. She had taught history and English at the Mannenberg junior school until the headmaster had married her, and she had given him four children, all daughters. Miriam was president of the local chapter of the Women's Institute which she used as a convenient cover for her political activities. She had been arrested during the defiance campaign, but when that petered out she had not been charged and had been released under a banning order. Three months later, when the furore had died away completely, her banning order had not been renewed.

Molly Broadhurst had known her since before she had married François, and the couple were frequent visitors at Molly's home. Behind her thick spectacles Miriam wore a perpetual chubby smile. Her home in the grounds of the junior school was clean as an operating theatre with crocheted antimacassars on the heavy maroon easy chairs, and a mirrorlike shine on the floors. Her daughters were always beautifully dressed with coloured ribbons in their pigtails and like Miriam were chubby and contented, a consequence of Miriam's cookery rather than her genes.

Tara met Miriam for the first time at Molly's home. Tara had come down by train from the expedition base at Sundi Caves two weeks before her baby was due. She had booked a private coupé compartment and kept the door locked the entire journey to avoid being recognized. Molly had met her at Paarl station, for she had not wanted to risk being seen at the main Cape Town terminus. Shasa and her family still believed that she was working with Professor Hurst.

Miriam was all that Tara had hoped for, all that Molly had promised her, although she was not prepared for the maternity dress.

233

'You are pregnant also?' she demanded as they shook hands, and Miriam patted her stomach shyly.

'It's a cushion, Miss Tara, I couldn't just pop a baby out of nowhere, could I? I started with just a small lump as soon as Molly told me, and I've built it up slowly.'

Tara realized what inconvenience she had put her to, and now she embraced her impulsively. 'Oh, I can never tell you how grateful I am. Please don't call me Miss Tara. I'm your friend and plain Tara will do very well.'

'I'll look after your baby like it's my own, I promise you,' Miriam told her, and then saw Tara's expression and hastily qualified her assurance. 'But he will always be yours, Tara. You can come and see him whenever, and one day if you are able to take him – well, François and I won't stand in your way.'

'You are even nicer than Molly told me!' Tara hugged her. 'Come, I want to show you the clothes I've brought for our baby.'

'Oh, they are all blue,' Miriam exclaimed. 'You are so sure you are going to have a boy?'

'No question about it – I'm sure.'

'So was I,' Miriam chuckled. 'And look at me now – all girls! Though it's not too bad, they are good girls and they are all expecting this one to be a boy,' she patted her padded abdomen, 'and I know they are going to spoil him something terrible.'

Tara's baby was born in Molly Broadhurst's guest room. Doctor Chetty Abrahamji who delivered it was an old friend of Molly's and had been a secret member of the Communist Party, one of its few Hindu members.

As soon as Tara went into labour, Molly telephoned Miriam Afrika, and she arrived with bag and bulging tummy and went in directly to see Tara.

'I'm so glad we have started at last,' she cried. 'I must admit that although it was a difficult pregnancy, it will be my quickest and easiest delivery.' She reached up under her own skirt and with a flourish produced the cushion. Tara laughed with her and then broke off as the next contraction seized her.

'Ouch!' she whispered. 'I wish mine was that easy. This one feels like a giant.'

Molly and Miriam took turns, sitting beside her and holding her hand when the contractions hit her, and the doctor stood at the foot of the bed exhorting her to, 'Push! Push!' By noon the following day Tara was exhausted, panting and racked, her hair sodden with sweat as though she had plunged into the sea.

'It's no good,' the doctor said softly. 'We'll have to move you into hospital and do a Caesar.'

234

'No! No!' Tara struggled up on an elbow, fierce with determination. 'Give me one more chance.'

When the next contraction came she bore down on it with such force that every muscle in her body locked and she thought the sinews in her loins must snap like rubber bands. Nothing happened, it was jammed solid, and she could feel the blockage like a great log stuck inside her.

'More!' Molly whispered in her ear. 'Harder – once more for the baby,' Tara bore down again with the strength of desperation and then screamed as she felt her flesh tear like tissue paper. There was a hot slippery rush between her thighs and relief so intense that her scream changed to a long drawn-out cry of joy, that joined with her infant's birth cry.

'Is it a boy?' she gasped, trying to sit up. 'Tell me – tell me quickly.'

'Yes,' Molly reassured her. 'It's a boy – just look at his whistle. Long as my finger. There's no doubt about that – he's a boy all right,' and Tara laughed out aloud.

He weighed nine and a half pounds with a head that was covered with pitch black hair, thick and curly as the fleece of an Astrakhan lamb. He was the colour of hot toffee, and he had Moses Gama's fine Nilotic features. Tara had never seen anything so beautiful in all her life, none of her other babies had been anything like this.

'Let me hold him,' she croaked, hoarse with the terrible effort of his birth, and they placed the child still wet and slippery in her arms.

'I want to feed him,' she whispered. 'I must give him his first suck – then he will be mine for ever.' She squeezed out her nipple and pressed it between his lips and he fastened on it, snuffling and kicking spasmodically with pleasure.

'What is his name, Tara?' Miriam Afrika asked.

'We'll call him Benjamin,' Tara said. 'Benjamin Afrika. I like that – he is truly of Africa.'

Tara stayed with the infant five days. When finally she had to relinquish him, and Miriam drove away with him in her little Morris Minor, Tara felt as though part of her soul had been hacked away by the crudest surgery. If Molly had not been there to help her through, Tara knew she could not have borne it. As it was Molly had something for her.

'I've been saving it until now,' she told Tara. 'I knew how you would feel when you had to give up your baby. This will cheer you up a little.' She handed Tara an envelope, and Tara examined the handwritten address. 'I don't recognize the writing.' She looked mystified.

'I received it by a special courier – open it up. Go on!' Molly ordered impatiently, and Tara obeyed. There were four sheets of cheap writing paper. Tara turned to the last sheet and as she read the signature her expression altered.

'Moses!' she cried. 'Oh I can't believe it – after all these months. I had given up hope. I didn't even recognize his handwriting.' Tara clutched the letter to her breast.

'He wasn't allowed to write, Tara dear. He has been in a very strict training camp. He disobeyed orders and took a grave risk to get this note out to you.' Molly went to the door. 'I'll leave you in peace to read it. I know it will make up a little for your loss.'

Even after Molly had left her alone, Tara was reluctant to begin reading. She wanted to savour the pleasure of anticipation, but at last she could deny herself no longer.

Tara, my dearest,
    I think of you every day in this place, where the work is very hard and demanding, and I wonder about you and our baby. Perhaps it has already been born, I do not know, and I wonder often if it is a boy or a little girl.
    Although what I am doing is of the greatest importance for all of us – for the people of Africa, as well as for you and me – yet I find myself longing for you. The thought of you comes to me unexpectedly in the night and in the day and it is like a knife in my chest.

Tara could not read on, her eyes were awash with tears.

'Oh Moses,' she bit her lip to prevent herself blubbering, 'I never knew you could feel like that for me.' She wiped her eyes with the back of her hand.

When I left you, I did not know where I was going, nor what awaited me here. Now everything is clear, and I know what the difficult tasks are that lie ahead of us. I know also that I will need your help. You will not refuse me, my wife? I call you 'wife' because that is how I feel towards you, now that you are carrying our child.

It was difficult for Tara to take it in. She had never expected him to give her this kind of recognition and now she felt humbled by it.

'There is nothing that I could ever refuse you,' she whispered aloud, and her eyes raced down the sheet. She turned it over quickly and Moses had written:

Once before I told you how valuable it would be if you used your family connections to keep us informed of affairs of state. Since then this has become more imperative. Your husband, Shasa Courtney, is going over to the side of the neo-fascist oppressors. Although this fills you with hatred and contempt for him, yet it is a boon we could not have expected or prayed for. Our information is that he has been promised a place in

236

the cabinet of that barbarous regime. If you were in his confidence, it would afford us a direct inside view and knowledge of all their plans and intentions. This would be so valuable that it would be impossible to put a price upon it.

'No,' she whispered, shaking her head, sensing what was coming, and it took courage for her to read on.

I ask you, for the sake of our land and our love, that when the child has been born and you are recovered from the birth, that you return to your husband's home at Weltevreden, ask his forgiveness for your absence, tell him that you cannot live without him and his children, and do all in your power to ingratiate yourself with him and to earn his confidence once more.

'I cannot do it,' Tara whispered, and then she thought of the children, and especially of Michael, and she felt herself wavering. 'Oh Moses, you don't know what you are asking of me.' She covered her eyes with her hand. 'Please don't make me do it. I have only just won my freedom – don't force me to give it up again.' But the letter went on remorselessly:

Every one of us will be called upon to make sacrifice in the struggle that lies ahead. Some of us may be required to lay down our very lives and I could well be one of those —

'No, not you, my darling, please not you!'

However, for the loyal and true comrades there will be rewards, immediate rewards in addition to the ultimate victory of the struggle and the final liberation. If you can bring yourself to do as I ask you, then my friends here will arrange for you and me to be together – not where we have to hide our love, but in a free and foreign land where, for a happy interlude, we can enjoy our love to the utmost. Can you imagine that, my darling? Being able to spend the days and nights together, to walk in the streets hand in hand, to dine together in public and laugh openly together, to stand up unafraid and say what we think aloud, to kiss and do all the silly adorable things that lovers do, and to hold the child of our love between us —

It was too painful, she could not go on. When Molly found her weeping bitterly, she sat on the bed beside her and took her in her arms.
'What is it, Tara dear, tell me, tell old Molly.'
'I have to go back to Weltevreden,' she sobbed. 'Oh God, Molly, I thought I was rid of that place for ever, and now I have to go back.'

* * *

237

Tara's request for a formal meeting to discuss their matrimonial arrangements threw Shasa into a state of utmost consternation. He had been well enough satisfied by the informal understanding between them, by which he had complete freedom of action and control of the children, together with the respectability and protection of the marriage form. He had been happy to pay without comment the bills that Tara forwarded to him, and to see that her generous allowance was paid into her bank account promptly on the first of each month. He had even made good the occasional shortfall when the bank manager telephoned him to report that Tara had overdrawn. On one occasion there was a cheque made out to a second-hand motor dealer, for almost a thousand pounds. Shasa did not query it. Whatever it was, it was a bargain as far as he was concerned.

Now it looked as if all this was coming to an end, and Shasa immediately called a meeting of his principal advisors in the boardroom of Centaine House. Centaine herself was in the chair and Abraham Abrahams had flown down from Johannesburg, bringing with him the senior partner of a firm of renowned but very expensive divorce lawyers.

Centaine took over immediately. 'Let us consider the worst possible case,' she told them crisply. 'Tara will want the children and she'll want a settlement, plus a living allowance for herself and each of the children.' She glanced at Abe who nodded his silver head, which set the rest of the legal counsel nodding like mandarin dolls, looking grave and learned, and secretly counting their fees, Shasa thought wryly.

'Damn it, the woman deserted me! I'll go to hell before I give her my children.'

'She will claim that you made it impossible for her to remain in the conjugal home,' Abe said, and then when he saw Shasa's thunderous expression, tried to soothe him. 'You must remember, Shasa, that she will probably be taking the best available legal advice herself.'

'Damned shyster lawyers!' said Shasa bitterly, and his counsel looked pained, but Shasa did not apologize nor qualify. 'I've already warned her I won't give her a divorce. My political career is at a very delicate stage. I cannot afford the scandal. Very soon I'll be contesting a general election.'

'You may not be able to refuse,' Abe murmured. 'Not if she has good grounds.'

'She hasn't any,' said Shasa virtuously. 'I've always been the considerate and generous husband.'

'Your generosity is famous,' Abe murmured drily. 'There is many an attractive young lady who could give you a testimonial on that score.'

'Really Abe,' Centaine intervened. 'Shasa has always kept out of trouble with women —'

'Centaine, my dear. We are dealing with facts here – not maternal illusions. I am not a private detective and Shasa's private life is none of my concern. However, completely disinterested as I am, I am able to cite you at least six occasions in the last few years when Shasa has given Tara ample grounds —'

Shasa was making frantic signals down the table to shut Abe up, but Centaine leaned forward with an interested expression.

'Go ahead, Abe,' she ordered. 'Start citing!'

'In January two years ago the leading lady in the touring production of the musical *Oklahoma*,' Abe began, and Shasa sank down in his chair and covered his eyes as though in prayer. 'A few weeks later the left-winger, ironically, in the visiting British women's hockey team.' So far Abe was avoiding mentioning names, but now he went on. 'Then there was the female TV producer from North American Broadcasting Studios, pert little vixen with a name like a fish – no a dolphin, that's it, Kitty Godolphin. Do you want me to go on? There are a few more, but as I have said already, I'm not a private investigator. You can be sure that Tara will get herself a good one, and Shasa makes very little effort to cover his tracks.'

'That will do, Abe,' Centaine stopped him, and considered her son with disapproval and a certain grudging admiration.

'It's the de Thiry blood,' she thought. 'The family curse. Poor Shasa.' But she said sternly, 'It looks as though we do have a problem after all,' and she turned to the divorce lawyer.

'Let us accept that Tara has grounds of infidelity. What is the worst judgement we might expect against us?'

'It's very difficult, Mrs Courtney —'

'I'm not going to hold you to it,' Centaine told him brusquely. 'You don't have to equivocate. Just give me the worst case.'

'She could get custody, especially of the two younger children, and a large settlement.'

'How much?' Shasa demanded.

'Considering your circumstances, it could be —' the lawyer hesitated delicately '— a million pounds, plus the trimmings, a house and allowance and a few other lesser items.'

Shasa sat up very straight in his chair. He whistled softly and then murmured 'That is really taking seriously something that was merely poked in fun,' he said, and nobody laughed.

So Shasa took pains preparing for the reunion with Tara. He studied the written advice which Abe and the other lawyers had drawn up for him, and had his tactics firmly established. He knew what to say and what to avoid. He was to make no admissions and no promises, particularly regarding the children.

For the venue he chose the pool at the foot of the Constantia Berg, hoping that Tara would associate it with the happy hours they had spent there. He had his chef prepare an exquisite picnic hamper which contained all Tara's favourite delicacies, and he chose half a dozen bottles of his best wines from the cellar.

He took especial care with his appearance. He had his hair trimmed and picked out a new black silk eye-patch from the drawer that he kept full of them. He wore the after-shave she had given him and the cream-coloured wild silk suit which she had once remarked on favourably, with his airforce scarf in the open neck of his blue shirt.

All the children were packed off to Rhodes Hill, into Centaine's care for the weekend, and he sent the chauffeur in the Rolls to fetch Tara from Molly Broadhurst's home where she was staying. The chauffeur brought her directly up to the pool and Shasa opened the door for her, and was surprised when she offered him her cheek for his kiss.

'You look so well, my dear,' he told her, and it was not entirely untrue. She had lost a lot of weight, her waist was once again wasped in and her bosom was magnificent. Despite the gravity of the moment Shasa felt his loins stir as he looked down that cleavage.

'Down boy!' he admonished himself silently and looked away, concentrating on her face. Her skin had cleared, the rings below her eyes were barely discernible and her hair had been washed and set. Obviously she had taken the same pains with her appearance as he had.

'Where are the children?' she demanded immediately.

'Mater has them – so we could talk without interruption.'

'How are they, Shasa?'

'They are all just fine. Couldn't be better.' He wanted there to be no special pleading on that score.

'I do miss them terribly,' she said. The remark was ominous, and he did not reply. Instead he led her to the summer-house and settled her on the couch facing the waterfall.

'It's so beautiful here.' She looked around her. 'It is my favourite spot on all of Weltevreden.' She took the wineglass he handed her.

'Better days!' He gave her the toast. They clinked glasses and drank.

Then she set her glass down on the marble table-top and Shasa steeled himself to receive the opening shot of the engagement.

'I want to come back home,' she said, and he spilled white wine down the front of his silk suit, and then dabbed at it with the handkerchief from his breast pocket to give himself time to recover his balance.

240

In a perverse way he had been looking forward to the bargaining. He was a businessman, supremely confident in his ability to get the best trade. Furthermore, he had already adjusted to the idea of becoming a bachelor once more, and was beginning to look forward to the delights of that state, even if it cost him a million pounds. He felt the prickle of disappointment.

'I don't understand,' he said carefully.

'I miss the children. I want to be with them – and yet I don't want to take them away from you. They need a father as much as a mother.'

It was too easy. There had to be more than that, Shasa's bargaining instincts were sure.

'I have tried living alone,' she went on. 'And I don't like it. I want to come back.'

'So we just pick it up again where we dropped it?' he asked carefully, but she shook her head.

'That's impossible, we both know that.' She prevented further questions with a raised hand. 'Let me tell you what I want. I want to have all the benefits of my old life, access to my children, the prestige that goes with the name Courtney and the money not to have to stint –'

'You were always scornful of the position and the money before.' He could not prevent the jibe, but she took no offence.

'I had never had to do without it before,' she said simply. 'However, I want to be able to go away for a while when it becomes too much for me here – but I will not embarrass you politically or in any other way.' She paused. 'That's all of it.'

'And what do I get in return?' he asked.

'A mother for your children, and a public wife. I will preside at your dinner-parties, and make myself agreeable to your associates, I will even help you with your political electioneering, I used to be very good at that.'

'I thought that my politics disgusted you.'

'They do – but I will never let it show.'

'What about my conjugal rights, as they are delicately referred to by the lawyers?'

'No.' She shook her head. 'That will only complicate our relationship.' She thought of Moses. She could never be unfaithful to him, even if he had ordered it. 'No, but I have no objection to you going elsewhere. You have always been reasonably discreet. I know you will continue to be.'

He looked at her bosom and felt a twinge of regret, but the bargain she was offering amazed him. He had everything he wanted, and had saved himself a million pounds into the bargain.

'Is that all?' he asked. 'Are you sure?'

'Unless you can think of anything else we should discuss.'

He shook his head. 'Shall we shake hands on it – and open a bottle of the Widow?'

She smiled at him over the rim of her glass to conceal what she truly felt for him and his world, and she made a vow as she sipped the tingling yellow wine.

'You will pay, Shasa Courtney, you will pay for your bargain much more than you ever dreamed.'

*   *   *

For over a decade Tara had been the mistress of Weltevreden, so there was nothing difficult or alien in taking up that role again, except that now more than ever she felt that she was acting a part in a tedious and unconvincing play.

There were some differences, however. The guest list had altered subtly, and now included most of the top Nationalist politicians and party organizers, and more often than before the conversation at the dinner-table was in Afrikaans rather than English. Tara's knowledge of Afrikaans was adequate, it was after all a very simple language with a grammar so uncomplicated that the verbs were not even conjugated and much of the vocabulary was taken directly from English. However, she had some difficulty with the guttural inflections, and most of the time smiled sweetly and remained silent. She found that by doing so her presence was soon overlooked and she heard much more than she would have had she joined in the conversation.

A frequent visitor to Weltevreden now was the minister of police, Manfred De La Rey, and Tara found it ironical that she was expected to feed and entertain the one man who to her epitomized all that was evil and cruel in the oppressive regime that she hated with all her being. It was like sitting down to a meal with a man-eating leopard, even his eyes were pale and cruel as those of a great predatory cat.

Strangely, she found that despite her loathing, the man fascinated her. It surprised her to find, once she had got over the initial shock of his presence, that he had a fine brain. Of course it was common knowledge that he had been a brilliant student in the law faculty of Stellenbosch University, and before standing for parliament, he had built up a highly successful law practice in his own right. She knew also that no man who was not essentially brilliant was included in the Nationalist cabinet, yet his intelligence was sinister and ominous. She found herself listening to the most heinous concepts expressed with such logic and eloquent conviction that she had to shake herself

242

out of his mesmeric influence, like a bird trying to break the spell of the cobra's swaying dance.

Manfred De La Rey's relationship to the Courtney family was another enigma to her. It was part of family lore how his father had robbed the H'ani Mine of a million pounds of diamonds, and how Blaine, her own father, and Centaine, before she was Blaine's wife, had pursued him into the desert and after a fierce battle captured him. Manfred's father had served fifteen years of a life sentence before being released under the amnesty that the Nationalists had granted to so many Afrikaner prisoners when they came to power in 1948.

The two families should have been bitter enemies, and indeed Tara detected definite traces of that hatred in the occasional tone of a remark and unguarded look that Manfred De La Rey and Shasa directed at each other, and there was a peculiarly brittle and artificial quality to the overtly friendly façade they showed, as though at any moment it might be stripped away and they would fly at each other's throats like fighting dogs.

On the other hand, Tara knew that Manfred was the one who had enticed Shasa into forsaking the ailing United Party and joining the Nationalists with the promise of ministerial rank, and that Shasa had made the De La Reys, father and son, major shareholders and directors in the new fish canning company at Walvis Bay, a company which looked set to turn half a million pounds of profit in its very first year of operation.

The mystery of their relationship was made even more intriguing by Centaine. On the second occasion that Shasa invited Manfred De La Rey and his wife to dine at Weltevreden, Centaine had telephoned her a few days beforehand, and asked her bluntly if she and Blaine might join the party.

Although Tara had determined to see as little of Centaine as possible, and to do all in her power to reduce Centaine's influence over the children and the general running of the estate, Tara had been so taken aback by the direct request that she had not been able to think of an excuse.

'Of course, Mater,' she had agreed with false enthusiasm. 'I would have invited you and Daddy anyway, but I thought you might have found the evening tedious, and I know Daddy cannot abide De La Rey —'

'Whatever gave you that idea, Tara?' Centaine asked tartly. 'They are on opposite sides of the house, but Blaine has a healthy respect for De La Rey, and he concedes that De La Rey certainly handled the troubles firmly enough. His police did a magnificent job in clamping down on the ringleaders and preventing serious disruptions and further loss of life.'

Furious words filled Tara's mouth and she wanted to hurl them at her mother-in-law, but she gritted her teeth and took a deep breath, before she said sweetly, 'Well then, Mater, both Shasa and I will be looking forward to Friday night. Half past seven for eight, and naturally the men will be wearing black tie.'

'Naturally,' said Centaine.

It had been a surprisingly mellow evening, when the explosive elements seated around the same table were considered, but it was a strict rule of Shasa's that shop party politics were never discussed in Weltevreden's palatial dining-room. The men's conversation ranged from the projected All Blacks rugby tour to the recent angling capture of a six hundred pound blue fin tunny in False Bay, the first of its kind. Manfred De La Rey and Blaine were both keen anglers and were excited by the prospect of such a magnificent prize.

Centaine was unusually quiet during the meal. Tara had placed her beside Manfred, but she listened attentively to everything that he said and when they went through to the blue drawing-room at the end of the meal, she stayed close to Manfred, and the two of them were soon oblivious of everyone else, lost in rapt but low-voiced discussion.

Manfred's statuesque blond German wife, Heidi, had failed to enthral Tara with a long-winded complaint about the laziness and dishonesty of her coloured servants, and Tara escaped as soon as she could and took another cognac to her father on the long blue velvet sofa, and then settled beside him.

'Centaine says that you admire De La Rey,' she said quietly, and they both looked across at the other couple on the far side of the room.

'He's a formidable piece of work,' Blaine grunted. 'Hard as iron and sharp as an axe. Do you know even his own colleagues call him "Panga Man"?'

'Why does he fascinate Centaine so much? She rang me and demanded an invitation when she knew he would be here. She seems to have some sort of obsession with him. Why is that, Daddy, do you know?'

Blaine dropped his eyes and considered the firm grey ash on his cigar. What could he tell her? he wondered. He was one of probably only four people in the world who knew Manfred De La Rey was Centaine's bastard son. He remembered his own shock and horror when she had told him. Not even Shasa knew that he and Manfred were half-brothers, though Manfred knew, of course. Centaine had told him, when she used it as blackmail to prevent Manfred destroying Shasa's political career back in 1948.

It was all so complicated, and Blaine found himself disturbed as

244

he had been so often over the years by the echoes of Centaine's follies and indiscretions before he had met her. Then he smiled ruefully. She was still a fiery and impetuous woman, and he wouldn't have had it any other way.

'I think she is interested in anything that affects Shasa's career. It's only natural she should be, De La Rey is Shasa's sponsor. It's as simple as that, my dear.'

'Yes, De La Rey is his sponsor,' Tara agreed. 'But what do you think, Daddy, about Shasa's turn of political coats?'

Despite her resolution to remain calm, she had raised her voice in agitation, and Shasa, who was in intimate conversation with the French ambassador's chic and bold-eyed young second wife, heard his name across the room and glanced up in her direction. Tara dropped her voice quickly.

'What do you think of it, Daddy? Weren't you simply appalled?'

'I was at first,' Blaine admitted. 'But then I discussed it with Centaine and Shasa came to see me. We thrashed it out between us, and I had my say – but in the end I came to see his point of view. I don't agree with it, but I respect it. He believes that he can do the greatest good —' Tara heard her own father repeating all Shasa's trite and glib justifications and the sense of outrage overwhelmed her all over again. She found herself trembling with suppressed passion, and she wanted to scream out at them, Shasa and Centaine and her own father, but then she thought of Moses and the struggle and with an effort she was able to retain her self-control.

'I must remember everything,' she told herself. 'Everything that they say or do. Even the smallest detail might be of inestimable value to the struggle.'

So, faithfully she reported it all to Molly Broadhurst. She slipped away from Weltevreden at least once a week on the pretence of visiting her dressmaker or her hairdresser. She and Molly met only after Tara had taken elaborate precautions to make sure she was not followed. Her instructions were to cut all her left-wing connections and to refrain at all times from political or socialistic comments in the presence of others. Molly was her only contact with the real world of the struggle, and she treasured every minute of their time together.

Miriam Afrika was always able to bring the baby to be with her during these interludes, and Tara held him in her arms and fed him his bottle as she made her report to Molly. Everything about little Benjamin fascinated her from the tight curls of crisp black hair that covered his scalp, through the exquisite softness and colour shading of his skin – honey and old ivory – down to the soles of his tiny feet which were the palest, clearest, coral pink.

245

Then on one of her visits Molly had another letter for her from Moses, and even the joy of holding baby Benjamin paled beside that of those written words.

The letter had been written in Addis Ababa, the capital of Ethiopia. Moses was there to address a meeting of the heads of the black African states at the express invitation of the Emperor Haile Selassie, and he described to her the warm welcome that he had been given, and the offers of support, moral, financial and military, that had been pledged to the struggle in Anzania – that was the new name for South Africa. It was the first time she had heard it, and when she repeated it aloud, the sound of it stirred a deep patriotic response in her that she had never felt before. She read the rest of Moses' letter:

From here I will travel on to Algeria, where I will meet with Colonel Boumedienne, who is at this moment struggling against French imperialism, and whose great valour will surely bring freedom and happiness to his tragically oppressed land.

After that I will fly to New York, and it seems certain that I will be allowed to put our case to the General Assembly of the United Nations. All this is exciting, but I have even better news that affects you and our baby Benjamin.

If you continue the important work you are doing for the cause, our powerful friends are determined to give you a special reward. Some day the three of us – you and me and Benjamin – will be together in London. I cannot tell you how greatly I look forward to holding my son and to greeting you again.

I will write to you as soon as I have more definite news. In the meantime I entreat you to continue your valuable work for the cause, in particular you should make every effort to see that your husband is elected to the government front benches at the elections next month. This will make your position and value to the struggle unique.

For days after receiving this letter Tara's mood was so light and gay that both Shasa and Centaine remarked on it, and took it as a sign that she had finally accepted her responsibilities as the mistress of Weltevreden, and was prepared to honour the agreement that she had made with Shasa.

*　　*　　*

When the prime minister announced the date of the general election, the country was immediately seized by the peculiar frenzy of excitement and intrigue which accompanies all major political activity in South Africa and the newspapers began their strident and partisan pronouncements.

Shasa's resignation from the United Party and his nomination as the Nationalist candidate for the constituency of South Boland was one of the highlights of the campaign. The English press castigated him, branding him a coward and a traitor, while the *Burger* and the *Transvaler*, those stalwarts of the Nationalist cause, hailed him as a far-seeing man of the future and looked forward to the day when all white South Africans, albeit under the firm hand of the National Party, marched shoulder to shoulder towards the golden republic which was the dream of all true South African patriots.

Kitty Godolphin had flown back from New York to cover the elections and to up-date her famous 'Focus on Africa' series that had won her another Emmy and had made her one of the highest paid of the new generation of young, pretty and waspish television commentators.

Shasa's political defection was the headline story when she landed at Jan Smuts airport, and she telephoned him from the airport on his private line and got him in his office just as the board meeting he had been chairing broke up, and he was about to leave Centaine House to fly up to the H'ani Mine for his monthly inspection.

'Hi!' she said gaily. 'It's me.'

'You bitch.' He recognized her voice instantly. 'After what you did to me, I should kick your bottom, wearing hobnailed boots and taking a full swing, at that.'

'Oh, did you see it? Wasn't it good? I thought I captured you perfectly.'

'Yes, I saw it last month on BBC while I was in London. You made me look like a cross between Captain Bligh and Simon Legree, although more pompous than either and a lot less lovable.'

'That's what I said – I got you perfectly.'

'I don't know why I am talking to you,' he chuckled despite himself.

'Because you are lusting after my miraculously beautiful body,' she suggested.

'I'd be wiser to make advances to a nest of hornets.'

'We aren't talking wisdom here, buddy boy, we are talking lust. The two are not compatible.' And Shasa had a poignant vision of her slim body and her perfect little breasts, and he felt slightly breathless.

'Where are you?' he asked.

'Johannesburg airport.'

'What are you doing this evening?' He made a quick calculation. He could postpone the H'ani Mine inspection, and it was four hours' flying time to Johannesburg in the Mosquito.

'I'm open to suggestions,' she told him, 'as long as the suggestions include an exclusive interview for NABS on your change of political

247

status and your view of the up-coming elections and what they mean to the ordinary people of this country.'

'I should know better,' he said. 'But I'll be there in five hours. Don't go away.'

Shasa placed the receiver back on its cradle and stood for a moment wondering at himself. His change of plans would throw the entire company into consternation, for he had a tight schedule laid out for the weeks ahead, including the opening of his election campaign, but the woman had woven some sort of spell around him. Like a malignant sprite her memory had danced at the edge of his mind all these months, and now the thought of being with her filled him with that quivering expectation he had not known since he was a lad embarking on his very first sexual explorations.

The Mosquito was fuelled and parked on the hardstand ready for the flight to H'ani Mine. It took him ten minutes to calculate his new flight plan and file it with air traffic control and then he climbed up into the cockpit and, grinning like a schoolboy playing hookey, he cranked the Rolls Royce Merlin engines.

It was dusk when he landed, but a company car was waiting for him and he drove directly to the Carlton Hotel in the centre of Johannesburg. Kitty was in the lobby as he came in through the revolving doors. She was fresh-faced as a teenager, long-legged and narrow-hipped in blue jeans, and she came to him with childlike enthusiasm and wrapped both arms around his neck to kiss him. Strangers in the lobby must have imagined Shasa was a father greeting his schoolgirl daughter, and they smiled indulgently.

'They let us into your suite,' she told him as she led him towards the elevator, skipping beside him to keep pace and hugging his arm in a pantomime of adoration. 'Hank had got his camera and lights set up already.'

'You aren't even giving me time to visit the heads,' Shasa protested, and she pulled a wry face.

'Let's get it over and done. Then we'll have more time for whatever you want to do afterwards.' She gave him a devilish grin, and he wagged his head in reluctant acquiescence.

It was deliberate, of course. Kitty was too professional to give him time to pull himself together and concentrate his mind. It was part of her technique to get her subject off-balance, while on the other hand, she had been carefully preparing her own notes and questions during the five hours since they had spoken on the telephone.

She had rearranged the furniture in his suite, making one corner into an intimate nook and Hank had lit it and was standing by with his Arriflex. Shasa shook hands with him and exchanged a friendly

248

greeting while Kitty poured him a massive whisky from the liquor cabinet.

'Take your jacket off,' she instructed as she handed it to him. 'I want you relaxed and casual. 'She led him to the two facing chairs and while he sipped his whisky she lulled him with an amusing account of the flight out which had been delayed by bad weather in London for eight hours. Then Hank gave her the signal and she said sweetly:

'Shasa Courtney, since the turn of this century your family has been a traditional ally of General Smuts. He was a personal friend of your grandfather, and your mother. He was a frequent guest in your house, and sponsored your own entry into the political arena. Now you have turned your back on the United Party which he led, and have deserted the fundamental principles of decency and fair play towards the coloured citizens of this country which were so much a part of General Smuts' philosophy. You have been called a deserter and a turncoat – and worse. Do you think that is a fair description, and if not, why not?'

The attack was so swift and savage that for a moment it checked him, but he had known what to expect, and he grinned. He knew he was going to enjoy this.

'General Smuts was a great man, but not quite as saintly towards the natives as you suppose. In all the time he was in power, their political status remained unchanged, and when they stepped out of line, he did not hesitate before sending in the troops and giving them a whiff of grape. Have you ever heard of the Bondelswart rebellion and the Bulhoek massacre?'

'You are suggesting that Smuts also oppressed the native people of this country?'

'No more than a strict headmaster oppresses his children. In the main, he never seriously addressed himself to the coloured question. He left that for a future generation to settle. We are that future generation.'

'All right, so what are you going to do about the black people of this country who outnumber you nearly four to one and have no political rights whatsoever in the land of their birth?'

'Firstly, we will try to avoid the trap of simplistic thinking.'

'Can you explain that?' Kitty frowned. She didn't want him to wriggle out of her grip by using vague terminology. 'Give us a concrete example of simplistic thinking.'

He nodded. 'You glibly use the terms black people and white people, dividing this population into two separate, if unequal, portions. That is dangerous. It might work in America. If all the American blacks were given white faces they would be simply Americans and think of themselves as that —'

'You are suggesting that this is not the case in Africa?'

'I am indeed,' Shasa agreed. 'If all the blacks in this country were given white faces, they would still think of themselves as Zulus and Xhosas and Vendas, and we would still be English and Afrikaners – very little would have altered.'

Kitty didn't like that, it was not what she wanted to tell her audiences.

'So, of course, you are ruling out the idea of a democracy in this country. You will never accept the policy of one man one vote, but will always aspire to white domination —'

Shasa cut in on her quickly. 'One man one vote would lead not to the black government you seem to foresee, but to a Zulu government, for the Zulus outnumber any other group. We would have a Zulu dictator, like good old King Chaka, and that would be a thrilling experience.'

'So what is your solution?' she demanded, hiding her irritation behind that little-girl smile. 'Is it white *baasskap*, white domination and savage oppression backed by an all-white army and police force —?'

'I don't know the solution,' he cut her off. 'It's something we have to work towards, but I expect it will be a system in which every tribal group, whether it be black, brown or white, can maintain its identity and its territorial integrity.'

'What a noble concept,' she agreed. 'But tell me when, in the history of mankind, any group who enjoyed supreme political power over all others ever gave up that power without an armed struggle. Do you truly believe the white South Africans will be the first?'

'We'll have to make our own history,' Shasa matched her honeyed smile. 'But in the meantime the material existence of the black people in this country is five or six times better than any other on the African continent. More is spent on black education, black hospitals and black housing, per capita, than in any other African country.'

'How does the expenditure per capita on black education compare with expenditure on white education?' Kitty shot back at him. 'My information is that five times more is spent on the education of a white child, than on a black.'

'We will strive to correct that imbalance, as we build up the wealth of our nation, as the black peasant becomes more productive and makes more of a contribution to the taxation that pays for that education. At the moment the white section of the population pays ninety-five per cent of the taxes —'

That wasn't the way the interview was meant to go and Kitty headed him off smoothly.

'And just how and when will the black people be consulted in these changes? Is it fair to say that nearly all blacks, and certainly all the educated and skilled blacks who are the natural leaders, totally reject the present political system which allows one sixth of the population to decide the fate of the rest?'

They were still sparring when Hank lifted his head from the camera lens, and rolled his eyes.

'Out of film, Kitty, you told me twenty minutes tops. We have forty-five minutes in the can.'

'Okay, Hank. My fault. I didn't realize we had such a garrulous bigot on the show.' She smiled at Shasa acidly. 'You can wrap it up, Hank, and I'll see you in the morning. Nine o'clock at the studio.' She turned back to Shasa and they didn't even look up as Hank left the suite. 'So what did we decide?' she asked Shasa.

'That the problem is more complex than anybody, perhaps even we in government, realize.'

'Insoluble?' Kitty asked.

'Certainly – without delicacy and the utmost good will of everybody in the country, and our friends abroad.'

'Russia?' she teased him, and he shuddered.

'Britain,' he said.

'What about America?'

'No. Britain understands. America is too wrapped up in her own racial problems. They aren't interested in the dissolution of the British Empire. However, we have always stood by Britain – and now Britain will stand by us.'

'Your confidence in the gratitude of great nations is refreshing. However, I think you will find that in the next decade there will be an enormous rip-tide of concern over human rights emanating from the United States. At least I hope so – and North American Broadcasting Studios will be doing all in its power to build it up into a tidal wave.'

'Your job is to report reality, not to attempt to re-structure it,' Shasa told her. 'You are a reporter, not the God of judgement.'

'If you believe that, you are naïve,' she smiled. 'We make and destroy kings.'

Shasa stared at her, as though he were seeing her for the first time. 'My God, you are in the power game, just like everybody else.'

'It's the only game in town, buddy boy.'

'You are amoral.'

'No more than you are.'

'Oh yes you are. We are prepared to make our decisions and live with the consequences. You wreak your destruction, then like a child with a broken toy, throw it aside and go on without a moment's remorse to some new cause that will sell more advertising time.'

251

He had made her angry. Her eyes slanted and narrowed into bright arrowheads and the freckles on her nose and cheeks glowed like specks of gold leaf. It roused him to see her come out from behind the screen, as hard and formidable as any adversary he had ever faced. He wanted to goad her further, to make her give way completely.

'You have made yourself the guru of southern Africa on US television for one reason only. Not for concern over the fate of the black masses, but quite simply because you smell blood and violence in the air. You have sensed that this is where the action will be next and you want to be the one who captures it on film —'

'You bastard,' she hissed at him. 'I want peace and justice.'

'Peace and justice don't make good footage, Kitty my love. You are here to record the killing and the screaming – and if it doesn't happen soon enough, well that is easily fixed – you'll give it a little shove.'

She was out of her chair now, facing him, and her lips were frosty with rage.

'For the last hour you have been spouting the most vicious racial poison, and now you accuse me of injustice. You call me an *agent provocateur* for the violence that is coming.'

He raised an eyebrow, giving her the taunting supercilious smile which had enraged his opponents across the floor of the House, and it was too much for her to bear. She sprang at him, white-lipped and shaking with fury, and she clawed for his single mocking eye with both hands.

Shasa caught her wrists, and lifted her feet clear of the floor. She was shocked by his strength, but she lifted her knee sharply, driving for his groin. He turned slightly and caught the knee on the hard muscle of his thigh.

'Where did a nice girl learn a trick like that?' he asked, and twisted her arms behind her, took both her wrists in his left hand and then bowed over her. She pressed her lips together, and tried to turn her face away, but he found her mouth and while he kissed her, he opened her blouse and with his free hand took out her small breasts. Her nipples were standing out like ripe mulberries, she was as aroused as he was, but kicking and spitting with fury.

He swung her round and threw her face down over the thick padded arm of the buttoned leather chair, pinning her with a hand between her shoulder blades, and her bottom in the air. That's how they had administered the cane at Shasa's school, and now while she screamed and kicked he jerked the leather belt out of the loops of her jeans, and pulled her trousers and panties down as far as her ankles and stepped in close behind her. Her buttocks were white and round and they maddened him.

Though she fought and struggled without let-up, at the same time she lifted her hips slightly and arched her back to make it easier for him, and only when it happened did she stop fighting and push back hard against him, sobbing with the effort of keeping pace with him.

It was over very quickly for both of them, and she rolled over and pulled him down on to the chair and whispered raggedly into his mouth, 'Well, that's one hell of a way to settle an argument, I'll give you that much.'

Shasa ordered dinner served in the suite, grilled crayfish with a sauce Mornay, followed by a Chateaubriand, baked baby potatoes and fresh young asparagus. He sent the waiter away and served it himself for Kitty was clad only in one of the hotel's long towelling dressing gowns.

As he drew the cork on the bottle of Chambertin, he told her, 'I've put four days aside for us. In the last few weeks I have been fortunate enough to get my hands on fifty thousand acres of land across the Sabi river from the Kruger National Park. I've been after it for fifteen years. It belonged to the widow of one of the old Randlords and I had to wait for the old biddy to cross the great divide before it came on the market. It's marvellous unspoilt bush country, teeming with wild game, perfect place for a lost weekend, we'll fly down after breakfast tomorrow – nobody will know where we are.'

She laughed at him. 'You are out of your little mind, lover. I'm a working girl. At eleven o'clock tomorrow I've got an interview with the leader of the opposition, De Villiers Graaff, and I'm certainly not breezing off into the boondocks with you to stare at lions and tigers.'

'No tigers in Africa – you are the African expert, you should know that.' He was angry again. 'It's a case of false pretences. You got me all the way up here for nothing,' he accused.

'Nothing?' she chuckled again. 'You call that *nothing*?'

'I expected four days of it.'

'You overestimate the going price for an interview. All you get is the rest of the night, and then tomorrow it's back to work – for both of us.'

She was getting under his guard too often, Shasa realized. Last time he had proposed marriage to her, and the idea still had its appeal. She had moved him the way no woman had since he had first met Tara. It was partly her unattainability that made her so desirable. Shasa was accustomed to getting what he wanted, even if it was a hard and heartless little vixen with a childlike face and body.

He watched her eat the rare steak with the same sensual gusto as she made love. She was sitting cross-legged on the front edge of her chair and the hem of her dressing-gown had ridden up high on her

253

thighs. She saw the direction of his gaze but made no effort to cover herself.

'Eat up,' she grinned at him. 'One thing at a time, lover.'

* * *

Shasa was chary of Tara's offer to assist his election campaign, and for the first two meetings left her at Weltevreden and drove out alone over Sir Lowry's Pass and the mountains.

South Boland, his new constituency, was an area of rich land, between the mountains and the sea, on the Cape's eastern littoral. The voters were almost entirely of Afrikaner extraction, and their families had held the land for three hundred years. They were wealthy farmers of wheat and sheep, Calvinist and conservative, but not as rabidly republican and anti-English as their cousins of the interior, the Free Staters and the Transvalers.

They received Shasa's first speeches with caution, and applauded him politely at the end. His opponent, the United Party candidate, was a blood Smuts man, like Blaine, who had been the incumbent until 1948 when he lost it to the Nationalists. Yet he still had a base of support in the district amongst the men who had known Smuts and had gone 'up north' to fight the Axis.

After Shasa's second meeting, the local Nationalist organizers were looking worried and scared.

'We are losing ground,' one of them told Shasa. 'The wives are suspicious of a man who campaigns without his own wife. They want to have a look at her.'

'You see, Meener Courtney, you are a bit too good-looking. It's okay for the younger women who think you look like Errol Flynn, but the older women don't like it, and the men don't like the way the young women look at you. We have to show them you are a family man.'

'I'll bring my wife,' Shasa promised, but his spirits sank. What kind of impression would Tara create in this dour God-fearing community where many of the women still wore the *voortrekker* bonnets and the men believed a woman's place was either in the bed or in the kitchen?

'Another thing,' the chief party organizer went on tactfully. 'We need one of the top men, one of the cabinet ministers to stand up on the platform with you. You see, Meneer Courtney, the people are having difficulty believing that you are a *ware* Nationalist. What with the English name and your family history.'

'We need somebody to make me look respectable, you mean?' Shasa hid his smile, and they all looked relieved.

254

'*Ja*, man! That's it!'

'What if I could get Minister De La Rey to come out for the meeting on Friday – and my wife, of course?'

'Hell, man!' they enthused. 'Minister De La Rey is perfect. The people like the way he handled the trouble. He is a good strong man. If you get him to come to talk to them, we'll have no more problems.'

Tara accepted the invitation without comment, and by an exercise in self-restraint Shasa refrained from giving her advice on how to dress or to conduct herself, and was delighted and grateful when she came on to the platform in the town hall of the little town of Caledon, dressed in a sober dark blue dress with her thick auburn hair neatly gathered into a bun behind her head.

Though pretty and smiling she was the picture of the good wife. Isabella sat up beside her with knee-length white socks and ribbons in her hair. A born actress, Isabella responded to the occasion by behaving like a candidate for holy orders. Shasa saw the organizers exchanging approving nods and relieved smiles.

Minister De La Rey, supported by his own blonde wife and large family, introduced Shasa with a fiery speech in which he made it very clear that the Nationalist government was not going to allow itself to be dictated to by foreign governments or communist agitators, especially not if these agitators were black as well as communist.

Manfred had a finely tuned style of oratory, and he thrust out his jaw and flashed those topaz-coloured eyes, he wagged his finger at them, and stood with arms defiantly akimbo when they stood up to applaud him at the end.

Shasa's style was different, relaxed and friendly, and when he tried his first joke, they responded with genuine amusement. He followed it with assurances that the government would increase the already generous subsidy for farm products, especially wool and wheat, and that they would at the same time foster local industry and explore new overseas markets for the country's raw materials, particularly wool and wheat. He ended by telling them that many English speakers were coming to realize that the salvation of the country lay in strong uncompromising government and predicted a substantial increase in the Nationalist majority.

This time there was no reservation in the tumultuous applause that followed his speech, and the votes of confidence in the government, the National Party and the Nationalist candidate for South Boland were all carried unanimously. The entire district, including the United Party supporters, turned up for the free barbecue on the local rugby grounds, to which Shasa invited them. Two whole oxen were roasted on the spit and were washed down with lakes of Castle beer and rivers of *mampoer*, the local peach brandy.

255

Tara sat with the women, looking meek and demure and speaking little, allowing the older women to develop pleasantly maternal feelings towards her, while Shasa circulated amongst their husbands, talking knowledgeably about such momentous subjects as scale on wheat and scab on sheep. The whole atmosphere was cosy and reassuring, and for the first time Shasa was able to appreciate the depth of planning by the party organizers, their dedication and commitment to the Nationalist cause, which resulted in this degree of mobilization of all its resources. The United Party could never match it, for the English speakers were complacent and lethargic when it came to politics. It was the old English fault of wanting never to appear to try too hard. Politics was a kind of sport and every gentleman knew that sport should be played only by amateurs.

'No wonder we lost control,' Shasa thought. 'These chaps are professionals, and we just couldn't match them' – and then he checked himself. These were his organizers now, no longer the enemy. He had become a part of this slick, highly tuned political machine, and the knowledge was a little daunting.

At last, with Tara at his side, Shasa made a round of goodnights with a party organizer steering him tactfully to each of the most important local dignitaries, making sure that none of these was slighted, and everybody agreed that the family made a charming group.

They stayed overnight with the most prosperous of the local farmers, and the following morning, which was Sunday, attended the Dutch Reformed Church in the village. Shasa had not been in a church since Isabella was christened. He was not looking forward to it. This was another grand show, for Manfred De La Rey had prevailed upon his uncle, the Reverend Tromp Bierman, moderator of the church, to deliver the sermon. Uncle Tromp's sermons were famous throughout the Cape, and families thought nothing of travelling a hundred miles to listen to them.

'I never thought I would ever speak for a cursed *rooinek*,' he told Manfred. 'It is either advancing senility, or a sign of my great love for you, that I do so now.' Then he climbed into the pulpit, and with his great silver beard flashing like the surf of a stormy sea, he lashed the congregation with such force and fury that they quivered and squirmed with delicious terror for their souls.

At the end of the sermon, Uncle Tromp reduced the volume to remind them that there was an election coming up, and that a vote for the United Party was a vote for Satan himself. No matter how some of them felt about Englishmen, they weren't voting for a man here, they were voting for the party upon which the Almighty had bestowed his blessing and into whose hands he had delivered the

256

destiny of the *Volk*. He stopped just short of closing the gates of Heaven in the face of any of them who did not put their cross opposite the name of Courtney, but when he glared at them threateningly, there were very few who felt inclined to take a chance on his continued forbearance.

'Well, my dear, I can't thank you enough for your help,' Shasa told Tara, as they drove home over the high mountain passes of the Hottentots Holland. 'From here on it looks like a cakewalk.'

'It was interesting to watch our political system in action,' Tara murmured. 'All the other jockeys got down off their mounts and shooed you in.'

Polling day in South Boland was merely an endorsement of certain victory, and when the votes were counted it appeared that Shasa had wooed across at least five hundred erstwhile United Party voters, and, much to the delight of the Nationalist hierarchy, increased the majority most handsomely. As the results came in from around the rest of the country, it became apparent that the trend was universal. For the first time ever, substantial numbers of English speakers were deserting Smuts' party. The Nationalists took 103 seats to the United Party's 53. The promise of strong uncompromising government was bearing good fruits.

At Rhodes Hill Centaine gave an elaborate dinner dance for 150 important guests to celebrate Shasa's appointment to the new cabinet.

As they swirled together around the dance floor to the strains of 'The Blue Danube', Centaine told Shasa, 'Once again we have done the right thing at the right time, *chéri*. It can still come true – all of it.' And she sang softly the praise song that the old Bushman had composed at Shasa's birth:

'His arrows will fly to the stars
And when men speak his name
It will be heard as far
And wherever he goes, he will find good water.'

The clicking sounds of the Bushman language, like snapping twigs and footsteps in mud, raised nostalgic memories from the distant time when they had been together in the Kalahari.

* * *

Shasa enjoyed the Houses of Parliament. They were like an exclusive men's club. He liked the grandeur of white columns and lofty halls, the exotic tiles on the floors, the panelling and the green leather-covered benches. He often paused in the labyrinth of corridors to

257

admire the paintings and the sculpted busts of famous men, Merriman and Louis Botha, Cecil Rhodes and Leander Starr Jameson, heroes and rogues, statesmen and adventurers. They had made this country's history – and then he reminded himself:

'History is a river that never ends. Today is history, and I am here at the fountainhead,' and he imagined his own portrait hanging there with the others one day. 'I'll have it commissioned at once,' he thought. 'While I am still in my prime. For the time being I'll hang it at Weltevreden, but I'll put a clause in my will.'

As a minister, he now had his own office in the House, the same suite of rooms that had been used by Cecil Rhodes when he was prime minister of the old Cape parliament before the House had been enlarged and extended. Shasa redecorated and furnished it at his own expense. Thesens, the timber firm from Knysna, installed the panelling. It was indigenous wild olive, marvellously grained and with a satiny lustre. He hung four of his finest Pierneef landscapes on the panelling, with a Van Wouw bronze of a Bushman hunter standing on the table beneath them. Although he was determined to keep the artwork authentically African, the carpet was the choicest green Wilton and his desk Louis XIV.

It felt strange to enter the chamber for the first time to take his place on the government front bench, a mirror image of his usual view. He ignored the hostile glances of his erstwhile colleagues, smiling only at Blaine's expressionless wink and while the Speaker of the House read the prayer, he measured the men to whom he had transferred his allegiance.

His reflections were interrupted as the Speaker of the House ended the prayer, and across the floor De Villiers Graaff, the tall handsome leader of the opposition, rose to propose the traditional vote of no confidence, while the government members, smug and cocksure, still revelling in their heady election triumph, mocked him noisily with cries of '*Skande!* Scandal!' and '*Siestog*, man! Shame on you, man!'

Two days later Shasa rose to deliver his first speech from the government front benches and pandemonium seized the House. His former comrades howled their contempt, and waved their order papers at him, stamping their feet and whistling with outrage, while his newly adopted party roared encouragement and support.

Tall and elegant, smiling with scorn, switching easily from English to Afrikaans, Shasa gradually quietened the benches opposite him with his low key but riveting oratorical style, and once he had their attention he made them squirm uneasily as he dissected their party with an insider's surgical skill, then held up their weaknesses and blemishes for them to contemplate.

258

When he sat down he left them severely discomforted, and the prime minister leaned forward in his seat to nod at him, an unprecedented public accolade, while most of the other ministers, even those northerners most hostile to his appointment, passed him notes of congratulation. Manfred De La Rey's note invited him to join a party of senior ministers for lunch in the member's dining-room. It was an auspicious beginning.

Blaine Malcomess and Centaine came out to Weltevreden for the weekend. As usual the family spent all of Saturday afternoon at the polo field. Blaine had recently resigned as captain of the South African team.

'It's obscene for a man over sixty to still be playing,' he had explained his decision to Shasa.

'You are better than most of us youngsters of forty, Blaine, and you know it.'

'Wouldn't it be pleasant to keep the captaincy in the family?' Blaine suggested.

'I've only got one eye.'

'Oh tush, man. You hit the ball as sweetly as you ever did. It's simply a matter of practice and more practice.'

'I don't have the time for that,' Shasa protested.

'There is time for everything in life that you really want.'

So Blaine forced him to practise, but deep down he knew that Shasa had lost interest in ball games and would never captain the national team. Oh, certainly he still rode like a centaur, his arm was strong and true and he had the courage of a lion when he was roused, but these days it needed stronger medicine to get his blood racing.

'It's a strange paradox that a man gifted with too many talents can fritter them all away without developing a single one to its full.' At that thought Blaine looked from Shasa to his sons.

As always Sean and Garrick had joined in the practice uninvited, and though they could not come close to matching the furious pace and skill of their elders, they were acting as pick-up men and passers for them.

Sean rode as his father had at that age and it gave Blaine a nostalgic pang to watch him. The horse was a part of him, the accord between rider and mount was total, his stick work was natural and unforced, but he lost interest quickly and made sloppy little errors, was more interested in teasing his brother and showing off and making eyes at the young girls in the stand than in perfecting his style.

Garrick was the opposite of his elder brother. He rode with enough sunlight shining between the saddle-leather and his bum to dazzle a blind man. However, his concentration was absolute, and he scowled murderously at the ball through his spectacles, using his stick with all the grace of a labourer digging a trench, but it was surprising how often he got a solid strike and how the bamboo root ball flew when he did. Then Blaine was amazed by the sudden change in his physique. From the skinny little runt he had been not long before, he was almost grotesquely overdeveloped in shoulder and chest and upper arms for a child of his age. Yet when they went in for tea and dismounted, his still skinny legs gave him an unfortunate anthropoid appearance. When he removed his riding cap, his hair stuck up in unruly dark spikes, and while Sean sauntered across to make the girls giggle and blush, Garrick stayed close to his father. Again Blaine was surprised at how often Shasa spoke directly to the child, even demonstrating a fine point of grip by rearranging his fingers on the handle of the stick, and when he perfected it, Shasa punched his arm lightly and told him:

'That's it, champ. We'll get you into a green and gold jersey one day.'

Garrick's glow of gratification was touching to watch, and Blaine exchanged a glance with Centaine. Not long before, they had discussed Shasa's total lack of interest in the child, and the detrimental effect that it might have on him. Their fears for Garrick seemed to have been unfounded, Blaine conceded, it was the other two they should have been worrying about.

Michael was not riding today. He had hurt his wrist, a mysterious injury which although excruciatingly painful, showed no bruising nor swelling. It was astonishing how often that wrist, or his ankle or his knee, plagued him whenever there was the prospect of hard physical exercise in the offing. Blaine frowned as he glanced at him now, sitting beside Tara at the tea table under the oaks, both their heads bowed over a book of poetry. Neither of them had looked up once during all the shouting and galloping and ribald exchanges on the field. Blaine was a firm believer in the old adage that a young man should have a disciplined mind in a healthy body, and should be able to join robustly in the rough and tumble of life. He had spoken to Tara about him, but though she had promised to encourage Michael's participation in sport and games, Blaine had not noticed any evidence that she had done so.

There was a chorus of muted shrieks and giggles behind him, and Blaine glanced over his shoulder. Wherever Sean was these days there seemed always to be a flock of females. He attracted them the way a tree full of fruit brings a swarm of noisy mousebirds to it. Blaine had no idea who all these girls belonged to, some of them were the daughters of the estate managers and of Shasa's German wine-maker, the pretty blond child was the American consul's daughter and the two little dark ones were the French ambassador's, but the others were unknown – probably the offspring of the half dozen politicians and other members of the diplomatic corps who made up the usual guest-list for Saturday high tea at Weltevreden.

'Shouldn't really interfere,' Blaine grumbled to himself. 'But I think I'll have a word with Shasa. No good speaking to Tara. She's too soft by a long chalk.' Blaine glanced around and saw that Shasa had left the group at the tea table under the oaks and had moved down the pony lines. He was squatting with one of the grooms to examine the fore hock of his favourite pony, a powerful stallion he had named Kenyatta, because he was black and dangerous.

'Good opportunity,' Blaine grunted and went to join Shasa. They discussed taping the pony's leg, his only weak point, and then stood up.

'How's Sean making out at Bishops?' Blaine asked casually, and Shasa looked surprised.

'Tara been talking to you?' he asked. Sean had gone up to the senior school at the beginning of the year, after ending as head boy and captain of sport at his preparatory school.

'Having trouble?' Blaine asked.

'Going through a phase,' Shasa shrugged. 'He'll be all right. He has too much talent not to make good in the end.'

'What happened?'

'Nothing to worry about. He's become a bit of a rebel, and his grades have gone to hell. I gave him the sweet end of the riding-crop. Only language he speaks fluently. He'll be all right, Blaine, don't worry.'

'For some people it's all too easy,' Blaine remarked. 'They get into the habit of free-wheeling through life.' He saw Shasa bridle slightly, and realized he was taking the remark personally. Good, he thought, let him – and he went on deliberately, 'You should know, Shasa. You have the same weakness.'

'I suppose you do have the right to speak to me like that. The only man in the world who does,' Shasa mused. 'But don't expect me to enjoy it, Blaine.'

'I expect young Sean cannot accept criticism either,' Blaine said. 'He's the one I wanted to talk about, not you. How did we end up discussing you? However, since we are, let an old dog give a few words of caution to both of you. Firstly, don't dismiss Sean's behaviour too lightly, you may just find yourself with a serious problem one day, if you don't check it now. Some people have to have constant stimulation or else they get bored. I think Sean might be one of those. They become addicted to excitement and danger. Watch him, Shasa.'

'Thank you, Blaine,' Shasa nodded, but he was not grateful.

'As for you, Shasa. You have been playing life like a game.'

'That's all it is, surely,' Shasa agreed.

'If you truly believe that, then you have no right to take on the responsibility of cabinet rank,' Blaine said softly. 'No, Shasa. You have made yourself responsible for the welfare of sixteen million souls. It's no longer a game, but a sacred trust.'

They had stopped walking and turned to face each other.

'Think about that, Shasa,' Blaine said. 'I believe that there are dark and difficult days ahead, and you won't be playing for an increase in company dividends – you will be playing for the survival of a nation, and if you fail, it will mean the end of the world you know. You will not suffer alone –'

Blaine turned to Isabella as she ran to him.

'Grandpapa! Grandpapa!' she cried. 'I want to show you the new pony daddy gave me,' and they both looked down at the beautiful child.

'No, Shasa, not you alone,' Blaine repeated, and took the child's hand.

'All right, Bella,' he said. 'Let's go down to the stables.'

*　　*　　*

Shasa had found that Blaine's words were like arrow-grass seeds. They scratched when they first attached themselves to your clothing, and then gradually worked themselves deeper until they penetrated the skin to cause real pain. Those words were still with him when he went into the cabinet room on Monday morning and took his place at the foot of the table, as befitted the most junior member of the gathering.

Before Blaine had spoken to him, Shasa had considered these meetings no more important than, say, a full board meeting of Courtney Mining and Finance. Naturally, he prepared himself as thoroughly, not only were his own notes exhaustive and cogent, but he had assembled full portfolios on every other member of the cabinet. Blaine had helped him with this work, and the results had been fed into the company computer and were kept up to the minute. After a lifetime in politics, Blaine was a skilled analyst and he had been able to trace in the tenuous and concealed lines of loyalty and commitment that bound this group of important men together.

At the broadest level every single one of them, apart from Shasa, was a member of the *Broederbond* – the Brotherhood – that invidious secret society of eminent Afrikaners whose single object was to advance the interest of the Afrikaner above all others at every

262

possible turn and at every level from that of national politics through business and the economy, on down to the levels of education and the civil service. No outsider could ever hope to fathom its ramifications, for it was protected by a curtain of silence which no Afrikaner dared to break. It united them all, no matter whether they were members of the Calvinist Dutch Reformed Church or of the even more extreme *Dopper* church, the Hervormde church which by Article No. 3 of its charter had ordained that heaven was reserved exclusively for members of the white race. The *Broederbond* united even the southerners, the Cape Nationalists, and those hard men from the north.

As Shasa rearranged his thick sheaf of notes, which he would not need since they were already committed to memory, he glanced down the table and saw how the two opposing forces in the cabinet had arranged themselves like the grouping of an army. Shasa was quite obviously arrayed with the southerners under Dr Theophilus Dönges, one of the most senior men, who had been a member of the cabinet since Dr Malan brought the party to power in 1948. He was leader of the party in the Cape, and Manfred De La Rey was one of his men. However, they were the smaller and least influential of the two groups. The northerners comprised both the Transvalers and the Orange Free Staters, and amongst them were the most formidable politicians in the land.

Strangely, in this assembly of impressive men. Shasa's attention went to a man who had been a member of the Senate as long as Shasa had himself been a member of the lower house. Before his appointment to the Senate in 1948, Verwoerd had been the editor of *Die Transvaler*, and before that he had been a Professor at Stellenbosch University. Shasa knew that he had lectured to Manfred De La Rey when he was a student, and had exerted enormous influence upon him. However, they were in different camps now, Verwoerd was of the north. Since 1950 he had been Minister of Bantu Affairs, with godlike powers over the black population and had made his name synonymous with the ideal of racial segregation at all levels of society.

For a man with such a monumental reputation for racial intolerance, the architect of the great edifice of *apartheid* which was being erected with intricate interlocking laws that dictated every aspect of the lives of the country's millions of black people, his appearance and manner were a pleasant surprise. His smile was kindly, almost benign, and he was quiet spoken but persuasive as he rose to address the cabinet and explain with the aid of a specially prepared map of South Africa his plans for the rearrangement of black population densities.

263

Tall and slightly round-shouldered, with his curly hair beginning to turn to silver, there could be little doubt of his utmost sincerity and belief in the absolute rightness of his conclusions. Shasa found himself being carried along on the plausible flood of his logic. Although his voice was pitched a little too high, and the tense note of his monologue grated on the ear, he carried them all on the strength, not only of his total conviction, but also of his personality. Even his opponents were filled with awe at his debating ability.

Only one small detail worried Shasa, Verwoerd's blue eyes were slitted, as though he were always looking into the sun, and though they were surrounded by a complex web of laughter lines, they were cold eyes, the eyes of a machine-gunner staring over the sights of his weapon.

Blaine's words came back to Shasa as he sat at the polished stinkwood table. 'No, Shasa, it's not a game. You have made yourself responsible for the welfare of sixteen million souls. It's no longer a game, but a sacred trust.'

But he remained expressionless as Verwoerd ended his presentation. 'Not one of us here today doubts that South Africa is a white man's country. My proposals will see to it that within the reserves the natives will have some measure of autonomy. However, as to the country as a whole, and the European areas in particular, we the white people, are and shall remain the masters.'

There was a general murmur of agreement and approbation, and two of the others asked for clarification on minor points. There was no call to vote or to make any joint decision, for Verwoerd's lecture had been in the form of a report back from his department.

'I think that Doctor Henk has covered this subject fully – unless anybody else has a question, we can go on to the next matter on the agenda.' The prime minister looked down the table at Shasa. The agenda read:

ITEM TWO: Projection by the Hon. Minister for Mines and Industry on the capital requirements of the private industrial sector over the next ten years and the proposal of means to satisfy such requirements.

This morning would be the first time Shasa would address the full cabinet, and he hoped he would muster only a small portion of Verwoerd's aplomb and persuasion.

His nervousness faded as soon as he rose to speak, for he had prepared in depth and detail. He began with an assessment of the foreign capital needs of the economy over the next decade, 'to carry us through to the end of the 1960s,' and then set out to estimate the amounts available to them from their traditional markets within the British Commonwealth.

'As you see, this leaves us with a considerable shortfall, particularly in mining, the new oil from coal industry and the armaments sector. This is how I propose that shortfall should be met: in the first instance we have to look to the United States of America. That country is a potential source of capital that has barely been tapped —'

He held their attention completely as he described his department's plans to advertise the country as a prosperous market amongst the American business leaders, and to entice as many of them as he could to visit South Africa at the expense of his department. He also intended establishing associations with sympathetic and influential politicians and businessmen in the United States and the United Kingdom to promote the country's image, and to this end he had already contacted Lord Littleton, head of Littleton merchant banks, who had agreed to act as chairman of the British South Africa Club. A similar association, the American South Africa Club, would be formed in the United States.

Shasa was encouraged by the obviously favourable reception of his presentation to continue with a matter he had not intended raising.

'We have just heard from Dr Verwoerd the proposal to build up self-governing black states within the country. I don't wish to tackle the political aspects of this scheme, but as a businessman I feel that I am competent to bring to your attention the final cost, in financial rather than human terms, of putting this into practice.'

Shasa went on swiftly to outline the massive obstacles in logistics and lost productivity that would result.

'We will have to duplicate a number of times the basic structures of the state in various parts of the country, and we must expect the bill for this to run into many billions of pounds. That money could more profitably be invested in wealth-producing undertakings —'

Across the table he saw Verwoerd's great charm ice over with a crust of hostility. Shasa knew he was autocratic and contemptuous of criticism, and he sensed that he was taking a risk by antagonizing a man who might one day wield ultimate power, but he went on doggedly.

'The proposal has another flaw. By decentralizing industry we will make it less effective and competitive. In a modern age when all countries are economically in competition with each other, we will be placing a handicap on ourselves.'

When he sat down he saw that though he might have convinced nobody, he had given them much to think about seriously and soberly, and when the meeting ended, one or two of the other ministers, most of them southerners, stayed to exchange a few words with him. Shasa sensed that he had enhanced his reputation and consolidated his place in the cabinet with that afternoon's work, and he drove back to Weltevreden feeling well pleased with himself.

He dropped his briefcase on the desk in his study and, hearing voices out on the terrace, went out into the late sunshine. The guest that Tara was entertaining was the headmaster of Bishops. Usually this worthy would summon the parents of recalcitrant pupils to appear before him as summarily as he did their offspring. This did not apply to the Courtney family. Centaine Courtney-Malcomess had been a governor of the school for almost thirty years, the only woman on the board. Her son had been head boy before the war and was now on the board with his mother, and both of them were major contributors to the College's coffers – amongst their gifts were the organ, the plate-glass windows in the new chapel, and the new kitchens to the main dining-hall. The headmaster had come to call upon Shasa, rather than the other way around. However, Tara was looking uneasy and stood up to greet Shasa with relief.

'Hello, Headmaster.' Shasa shook hands, but was not encouraged by the head's lugubrious expression.

'Headmaster wants to talk to you about Sean,' Tara explained. 'I think a man-to-man chat will be appropriate, so I will leave the two of you alone while I go and get a fresh pot of tea.'

She slipped away, and Shasa asked genially, 'Sun's over the yard arm. May I offer you a whisky, Headmaster?'

'No thank you, Mr Courtney.' That he had not used Shasa's Christian name was ominous, and Shasa adjusted his own expression to the correct degree of solemnity and took the chair beside him.

'Sean, hey? So what has that little hooligan been up to now?'

Tara opened the door to the dining-room quietly and crossed the floor to stand behind the drapes. She waited until the voices on the terrace were so intense and serious that she could be certain that Shasa would be there for the next hour at the least. She turned quickly and left the dining-room, closing the door behind her, and went swiftly down the wide marble-tiled passageway, past the library and the gun room. The door to Shasa's study was unlocked, the only doors ever locked at Weltevreden were those to the wine cellar.

Shasa's briefcase stood in the middle of his desk. She opened it and saw the blue folder embossed with the coat of arms of the state which contained the typed minutes of that day's cabinet meeting. She knew that numbered copies were made and distributed to each minister at the end of the weekly meetings, and she had expected to find it in his case.

She lifted it out, careful not to disarrange anything else in the crocodile-skin attaché case, and carried it to the table beside the french doors. The light was better here, and in addition, by glancing around the drapes, she could see down the terrace to where Shasa

266

and the headmaster were still deep in conversation under the trellis of vines.

Quickly she arranged the blue sheets on the table, and then focused the tiny camera that she took from the pocket of her skirt. It was the size of a cigarette-lighter. She was still unaccustomed to the mechanism, and her hands were shaking with nervousness. It was the first time she had done this.

Molly had given her the camera at their last meeting, and explained that their friends were so pleased by the quality of the information she was providing that they wanted to make her job easier for her. Her fingers felt like pork sausages as she manipulated the tiny knobs and snapped each of the sheets twice, to cover herself against possible mistakes of exposure or focus. Then she slipped the camera back into her pocket, before stacking the sheets in their folder and replacing it carefully in Shasa's briefcase in exactly the same way she had found it.

She was so nervous that her bladder felt as though it might burst and she had to run down the passage to the downstairs toilet. She only just reached it in time. Five minutes later she carried the silver Queen Anne teapot out on to the terrace. Usually this would have annoyed Shasa who did not like her to usurp the servants' work, especially in front of guests. However, he was too engrossed in his discussion with the headmaster to notice.

'I find it difficult to believe that it is anything more than robust boyish spirits, Headmaster.' He was frowning as he sat forward in his chair, hands on his knees, to confront the schoolmaster.

'I have tried to look upon it that way.' The headmaster shook his head regretfully. 'In view of the special relationship that your family has to the school, I have been as lenient as I can be. However,' he paused meaningfully, 'we are not dealing simply with an isolated instance. Not simply one or two boyish pranks, but a state of mind, an entire behaviour pattern which is most alarming.' The headmaster broke off to accept the cup of tea that Tara passed across the table to him. 'Forgive me, Mrs Courtney, this is as painful to me as it must be to you.'

Tara said quietly, 'I can believe that. I know you look upon each of your boys as one of your own sons.' And she glanced at Shasa. 'My husband has been reluctant to come to terms with the problem.' She hid her smug satisfaction behind a sorrowful but brave little smile. Sean had always been Shasa's child, strong-willed and thoughtless of others. She had never understood nor accepted that cruel streak in him. She recalled his selfishness and lack of gratitude even before he could talk. As an infant when he had gorged himself at her breast, he would let her know he was satiated by biting her nipple with sufficient force to bruise her painfully. She had loved him, of course, but had found it hard to like him. As soon as he had learned to walk, he headed straight for his father, staggering after him like a puppy, and his first word had been 'Dada'. That hurt her, after she had carried him big and heavy in her belly and given him birth and suck, 'Dada'. Well, he was Shasa's child now and she sat back and watched him grapple with the problem, feeling a spiteful pleasure at his discomfort.

'He's a natural sportsman,' Shasa was saying, 'and a born leader. He has a good mind – I am convinced that he will pull himself together. I gave him a good thrashing after his school report at the end of last term, and I'll give him another this evening to get him in the right frame of mind.'

'With some boys the cane has no effect, or rather it has the opposite to the desired effect. Your Sean looks upon corporal punishment the way a soldier looks on his battle wounds, as a mark of his courage and fortitude.'

'I have always been against my husband beating the children,' Tara said, and Shasa flashed her a warning look, but the headmaster went on.

'I have also tried the cane on Sean, Mrs Courtney. He seems positively to welcome that punishment as though it affords him some special distinction.'

'But he is a good athlete,' Shasa repeated rather lamely.

'I see you choose, as I would, the term "athlete" rather than "sportsman",' the headmaster nodded. 'Sean is precocious and mature for his age. He is stronger than the other boys in his group and has no qualms in using his strength to win, not always in accordance with the rules of the game.' The headmaster looked at Shasa pointedly. 'He does have a good brain, but his school marks indicate that he is not prepared to use it in the classroom. Instead he applies his mind to less commendable enterprises.' The headmaster paused, sensing that this was not the moment to give a doting father concrete examples. He went on: 'He is also, as you have noted, a born leader. Unfortunately, he gathers about him the least desirable elements in the school, which he has formed into a gang with which he terrorizes the other boys, even those senior to him are afraid of him.'

'I find this difficult to accept.' Shasa was grim-faced.

'To be blunt, Mr Courtney: Sean seems to have a vindictive and vicious streak in him. I am, of course, looking for an improvement in him. However, if that is not soon forthcoming, I will have to make a serious decision over Sean's future at Bishops.'

'I had set my heart on him being head boy, as I was,' Shasa admitted, and the headmaster shook his head.

268

'Far from becoming head boy, Mr Courtney, unless Sean has pulled up his socks by the end of the year, I am, with the greatest reluctance, going to have to ask you to remove him from Bishops altogether.'

'My God!' Shasa breathed. 'You don't really mean that?'

'I'm sorry to say that I do.'

*　　*　　*

It was quite remarkable that Clare East had ever been employed by the headmaster of Bishops. The explanation was that the appointment was a temporary one, a mere six-month contract, to fill in after the unexpected resignation of the previous art master on the grounds of ill-health. The salary offered was such that it had attracted only two other applications, both patently unsuitable.

Clare had come to the interview with the headmaster dressed in clothes she had not worn for six years, not since she was twenty-one years of age. She had exhumed them from a forgotten cabin trunk for the occasion, a high-buttoned dress in drab green that conformed closely to the head's own ideas of suitable apparel for a school-mistress. Her long black hair she had plaited and twisted up severely behind her head, and the portfolio of her painting she had chosen to show him, was composed of landscapes and seascapes and still lifes, subjects which had interested her at about the same time as she had bought the chaste woollen dress. At Bishops, art was not one of the main-stream subjects, but merely a catch-all for the pupils who showed little aptitude for the sciences.

Once Clare had charge of the art school, which was situated far enough from the main buildings as to offer her a certain freedom of behaviour, she reverted to her usual style of dress: wide loose skirts in vivid colours and flamboyant patterns, worn with Mexican-style blouses like those that Jane Russell had worn in *The Outlaw*. She had seen the movie five times while she was attending the London School of Arts, and modelled herself on Jane Russell, though of course Clare knew her own breasts were better than Russell's, just as big but higher and more pointed.

Her long hair she wore in a different style every day, and when she was teaching she always kicked off her sandals and strode around the art room barefooted, smoking thin black Portuguese cigarettes which one of her lovers brought her in packs of a thousand.

Sean had absolutely no interest in art. He had filtered down to this class by a process of natural rejection. Physics and chemistry demanded too much effort, and geography, the next lowest subject, was an even greater bore than paint-brushes.

269

Sean fell in love with Clare East the very moment that she walked into the art room. The first time she had paused at his easel to inspect the mess of colour he had smeared on his sheet of art paper, he realized that she was an inch shorter than he was, and when she reached up to correct one of his shaky outlines, he saw that she had not shaved her armpit. That bush of dark coarse hair glistening with sweat, induced the hardest and most painful erection he had ever experienced.

He tried to impress her with manly strutting behaviour, and when that failed, he used an oath in her presence that he usually reserved for one of his polo ponies. Clare East sent him to the head with a note and the head gave him four strokes of his heavy Malacca cane, accompanying the beating with a few words of counsel.

'You will have to learn, young man, WHACK, that I will not allow you to compound atrocious behaviour, WHACK, with foul language, WHACK, especially in the presence of a lady, WHACK.'

'Thank you very much, Headmaster.' It was traditional to express gratitude for these ministrations, and to refrain from rubbing the injured area in the great man's presence. When Sean returned to the art room, his ardour, far from being cooled by the Malacca cane, was rather inflamed to unbearable proportions, but he realized he had to change tactics.

He discussed it with his henchman, Snotty Arbuthnot, and was only mildly discouraged by Snotty's advice. 'Forget it, man. Every fellow in school is whacking away thinking about Marsh Mallows —' the nickname was a reference to Clare East's bosom, 'but Tug saw her at the movies with some chap at least thirty, with a moustache and his own car. They were smooching away like mad dogs in the back row. Why don't you go and see Poodle instead?'

Poodle was a sixteen-year-old from Rustenberg Girls' School, just across the railway line from Bishops. She was a young lady with a mission in life, to see as many boys across the borders of manhood as she could fit into her busy afternoons. Though Sean had never spoken to her, she had been a spectator at every one of his recent cricket matches and she had sent a message to him through a mutual friend suggesting a meeting in the pine forest on Rondebosch Common.

'She looks like a poodle,' Sean dismissed the suggestion scornfully, and resigned himself to distant adoration of Clare East, until one day he was searching her desk for those black Portuguese cigarettes for which he had developed a taste. Love did not mean he could not steal from her. In a locked drawer which he picked with a paper clip, he came across a stiff cardboard folder tied with green ribbons. The folder contained over twenty pencil drawings of nude male models,

270

all of them signed and dated by Clare East, and after the first jealous shock, Sean realized that each drawing was of a different subject with only one common feature. While the models' faces had been roughed in, their genitals had been depicted in minute and loving detail, and all of them were fully tumescent.

What Sean had discovered was Clare's collection of scalps, or an equivalent thereof. Clare East had strong tastes, but even more than garlic and red wine she needed men in her diet. This was so evident in the secret folder that all Sean's deflated hopes were once more revived, and that night he commissioned Michael, for the sum of five shillings, to paint a portrait of Clare East in Sean's art book.

Michael was in the junior art class and was able to make his studies for the portrait without the model's knowledge, and the completed work surpassed even Sean's expectations. He submitted the portrait and at the end of the following session Clare dismissed the class with a rider, 'Oh Sean, will you please remain behind?'

When the art room was cleared, she opened his art book at the painting of herself.

'Did you do this, Sean?' she asked. 'It really is very good.' The question was innocent enough, but the difference between the portrait and Sean's own murky compositions was so evident that even he saw the danger of claiming authorship.

'I was going to tell you I did it,' he admitted openly, 'but I can't lie to you, Miss East. I paid my brother to do it for me.'

'Why, Sean?'

'I suppose because I like you so much,' he mumbled, and to her surprise she saw that he was actually blushing. Clare was touched. Up to that time she had actively disliked this boy. He was brash and cocky and a disruptive influence in her class. She was certain that it was he who was stealing her cigarettes.

This unsuspected sensitivity surprised her, and suddenly she realized that his bumptious behaviour had been to attract her attention. She relented towards him, and over the following days and weeks she showed Sean that she had forgiven him, by giving him small largesse – from a special smile to an extra few minutes of her time tidying up his creative efforts.

In return Sean began leaving gifts in her desk, thereby confirming her suspicion that he had been into it before. However, the theft of cigarettes stopped and she accepted the offerings of fruit and flowers without comment, just a smile and a nod as she passed his easel.

Then one Friday afternoon she opened her drawer and there lay a blue enamel box with 'Garrards' in gold lettering on the lid. She opened it with her back turned to the class, and she started uncontrollably and almost dropped the box as she realized that it contained a

271

brooch of white gold. The centrepiece was a large star sapphire, and even Clare, who was no judge of gems, realized that it was an exquisite stone. It was surrounded by small diamonds set in a star pattern. Clare experienced a giddy rush of avarice. The brooch must certainly be worth many hundreds of pounds, more money than she had ever had in her hand at one time, more than a year's salary at her present parsimonious rate of pay.

Sean had taken the piece from his mother's dressing-table and hidden it in the thatch of the saddle room behind the stables until the furore had died down. All the house servants had been interrogated, first by Shasa, who was outraged by this breach of faith. Nothing, apart from liquor, had ever been stolen by his employees before. When his own investigations ran into a dead end, Shasa called in the police. Fortunately for Sean, it transpired that one of the junior maids had previously served a six-month sentence for theft from an employer. She was obviously guilty and the Wynberg magistrate gave her eighteen months, her offence compounded by her obstinate refusal to return the stolen brooch. Since she was now over twenty-one years, the maid was sent to the Pollsmoor Women's Prison.

Sean had waited another ten days for the incident to be forgotten before presenting the gift to the object of his passion. Clare East was mightily tempted. She realized that the brooch must have been stolen, but on the other hand she was, as usual for her, in serious financial difficulty. This was the only reason she had taken on her present employment. She looked back with nostalgic regret on the idle days of eating and drinking and painting and making love which had led her into her present embarrassed circumstances. The brooch would solve it all. She had no scruples of conscience, but a terror of being convicted of theft. She knew that her free and creative soul would wither behind the bars of a women's prison.

Surreptitiously she returned the brooch to her desk drawer and for the rest of that art period she was distracted and withdrawn. She chain-smoked cigarettes and kept well clear of the rear of the art room, where Sean made a fine picture of innocence as he applied himself with unusual industry to his easel. She did not have to tell him to remain behind when the bell rang at the end of the period. He came to where she sat at her desk.

'Did you like it?' he asked softly, and she opened the drawer and placed the enamel box in the centre of the desk between them.

'I cannot accept it, Sean,' she said. 'You know that very well.' She didn't want to ask him where he had obtained it. She didn't want to know, and involuntarily she reached out to touch the box for the last time. The enamel surface felt like a new-laid egg, smooth and warm to the touch.

'It's all right,' Sean said quietly. 'Nobody knows. They think somebody else took it. It's quite safe.'

Had the child seen through her so easily? She stared at him. Was it one amoral soul recognizing another? It made her angry to be found out, to have her greed so exposed. She took her hand off the box and placed it in her lap.

She drew a breath, and steeled herself to repeat her refusal, but Sean stilled her by opening his art book and taking out three loose leaves. He placed them beside the blue enamel box, and she drew a hissing breath. They were her own drawings from her fun folder, signed by herself.

'I took these – sort of fair exchange,' Sean said, and she looked at him and truly saw him for the very first time.

He was young in years only. In the museum in Athens she had been enchanted by a marble statue of the great god Pan in his manifestation as a young boy. A beautiful child, but about him an ancient evil as enthralling as sin itself. Clare East was not a teacher by vocation, she felt no innate revulsion at the corruption of the young. It was simply that she had not thought of it before. With her hearty sexual appetite she had experienced almost everything else, including partners of her own sex, although those had been unsuccessful experiments long ago put behind her. Men she had known, in the biblical sense, in every possible variation of size and shape and colour. She took and discarded them with a kind of compulsive fervour, seeking always an elusive fulfilment which seemed to dance for ever just beyond her grasp. Often she was afraid, truly terrified, that she had reached the point of satiety, when her pleasure was irreparably blunted and jaded.

Now she was presented with a new and titillating perversion, enough to reawaken the lusty response that she had thought lost for ever. This child's loveliness contained a wickedness that left her breathless as she discovered it.

She had never been paid before, and this mannikin was offering her a prostitute's fee that was princely enough for a royal courtesan. She had never been blackmailed before, and he was threatening her with those unwise sketches. She knew what would happen if they ever fell into the hands of the school governors, and she did not doubt that he would carry out the unspoken threat. He had already hinted that he had placed blame for the theft of the sapphire brooch on an innocent party. Most tantalizing, she had never had a child before. She let her eyes run over him curiously. His skin was clear and firm, with the sweet gloss of youth on it. The hair on his forearms was silky, but his cheeks were bare. He was using a razor already, and he was taller than she was, a man's outline emerging from

273

boyhood in his shoulders and narrow hips. His limbs were long and shapely, strange that she should never have noticed the muscle in his arms before. His eyes were green as emeralds, or of *crème de menthe* in a crystal glass and there were tiny flecks of brown and gold surrounding the pupils. She saw those pupils dilate sightly as she leaned forward, deliberately letting the top of her blouse gape open to expose the swell and cleavage of her breasts. Carefully she picked up the enamel box.

'Thank you, Sean,' she whispered hoarsely. 'It's a magnificent gift and I shall treasure it.'

Sean picked up the lewd sketches and slipped them into his art book, hostage to the unspoken pact between them.

'Thank you, Miss East.' His voice was as rough as hers. 'I am so glad you like it.'

It was so exciting to see his agitation that her own loins melted and she felt the familiar pressure build up swiftly in her lower body. With calculated cruelty she stood up, dismissing him to the exquisite torture of anticipation. Instinctively she knew that he had planned it all. No further effort would be required from her, the boy's genius would provide the means and the moment, and it was part of the excitement, waiting to see what he would do.

She did not have long to wait, and though she had expected something unusual, she was surprised by the note he left on her desk.

Dear Miss East,
    My son, Sean, tells me that you are having difficulty in procuring suitable lodgings. I do understand how difficult this can be, particularly in the summer when the whole world seems to descend upon our little peninsula.
    As it happens, I have a furnished cottage on the estate, which at the present time is standing empty. If you find it suitable, you are welcome to the use of it. The rental would be nominal. I should say a guinea a week would satisfy the estate bookkeeper, and you would find the cottage secluded and quiet with a lovely view over the Constantia Berg and False Bay, which will appeal to the artist.
    Sean speaks highly of your work, and I look forward to seeing examples of it.

Very sincerely,
Tara Courtney

Clare East was paying five guineas a week for a single squalid room beside the railway tracks at the back of Rondebosch station. When she sold the sapphire brooch for three hundred pounds, which she suspected was a fraction of its real value, Clare had been determined to pay off her accumulated debts. However, as with so many of her good intentions, she closed her mind to the impulse, and instead blew most of the money on a secondhand Morris Minor.

She drove out to Weltevreden the following Saturday morning. Some instinct warned her not to attempt to conceal her Bohemian inclinations, and she and Tara recognized kindred spirits at the very first meeting. Tara sent a driver and one of the estate lorries to fetch her few sticks of furniture and her pile of finished canvases, and personally helped her move into the cottage.

As they worked together, Clare showed Tara a few of the canvases, beginning with the landscapes and seascapes. Tara's response was noncommittal, so once again, following her instinct, Clare stripped the cover off one of her abstracts, a cubist arrangement of blues and fiery reds, and held it up for Tara.

'Oh God, it's magnificent!' Tara murmured. 'So fierce and un-compromising. I love it.'

A few evenings later Tara came down the path through the pines, carrying a small basket. Clare was on the stoep of the cottage, sitting bare-footed and cross-legged on a leather cushion with a sketch-pad on her lap.

She looked up and grinned, 'I hoped you'd come,' and Tara flopped down beside her and took a bottle of Shasa's best estate wine, the fifteen-year-old vintage, out of the basket.

They chatted easily while Clare sketched, drinking the wine and watching the sunset over the mountains.

'It's good to find a friend,' Tara said impulsively. 'You can't im-agine how lonely it is here sometimes.'

'With all the guests and visitors!' Clare chuckled at her.

'Those aren't real people,' Tara said. 'They are just talking dolls, stuffed with money and their own importance,' and she took a flat silver cigarette case out of the pocket of her skirt, and opened it. It contained rice papers and shredded yellow leaf.

'Do you?' she asked shyly.

'Darling, you have probably saved my life,' Clare exclaimed. 'Roll one for us this instant. I can't wait.'

They passed the joint back and forth, and in the course of their lazy conversation Clare remarked, 'I've been exploring. It's so beauti-ful here. A little earthly paradise.'

'Paradise can be an awful bore,' Tara smiled.

'I found a waterfall with a little summer-house.'

'That's the picnic spot. None of the servants are allowed there, so if you want to swim in the buff, you don't have to worry. Nobody is going to surprise you.'

Clare had not seen Sean on the estate since she moved into the cottage. She had expected him to come panting to the door on the very first day, and was slightly piqued when he did not. Then after a few more days she was amused by his restraint, he had an instinct far beyond his years, the touch of the born philanderer, and she waited with a rising sense of anticipation for him to approach her. Then the delay began to gall her. She was unaccustomed to extended periods of celibacy, and her sleep started to become fitful and disturbed by erotic dreams.

The spring evenings lengthened and became balmy, and Clare took up Tara's suggestion to visit the pool below the waterfall. Each afternoon she hurried back to Weltevreden after school, and pulled a pair of shorts and a sleeveless blouse over her bikini before taking the short cut through the vineyards to the foot of the hills. Tara's assurances were well founded. The pool was always deserted except for the sugar birds amongst the proteas on the bank, and soon she discarded the bikini.

On her third visit, as she was standing under the waterfall letting her long dark hair flow down her body, she was suddenly aware that she was being watched. She sank down quickly, the water up to her chin, and looked around her apprehensively.

Sean sat on one of the wet black rocks at the head of the pool, almost within touching distance. The roar of the waterfall had muffled any sound of his approach. He was regarding her solemnly, and the resemblance to the youthful Pan god was enhanced in this wild and beautiful place. He was barefoot and wore only shorts and a cotton shirt. His lips were slightly parted and his teeth were white and perfect, a lock of dark hair had fallen over one eye and he lifted his hand and brushed it aside.

Slowly she raised herself until the water dropped to her waist, the foam swirled around her, and her body shone with wetness. She saw his eyes go to her breasts, and his tongue flicked between his teeth and he winced as if in pain. Matching his solemn expression, she crooked her finger and beckoned him. The noise of the waterfall prevented all speech.

He stood up and began to unbutton his shirt, and then paused. She saw that at last he was uncertain, and his confusion amused and excited her. She nodded encouragement and beckoned again. His expression firmed and he stripped off his shirt and threw it aside, then he unbuckled his belt and let his shorts drop around his ankles.

She drew breath sharply and felt the muscles on the inside of her thighs tense. She was not sure what she had expected, but protruding from a smoky haze of pubic hair he was long and white and rigid. Here, as in so many other ways, he was almost fully matured, the lingering signs of childhood on his body were all the more titillating for this.

He stood naked for only an instant and then dived head first into the pool, to surface beside her, water streaming down his face, grinning like an imp. Immediately she ducked away, and he chased

276

her. He was a stronger swimmer than she was, moving in the water like a young otter, and he caught her in the middle of the pool.

They struggled together playfully, giggling and gasping, treading water, going under and bobbing up again. She was surprised by the hardness and strength of his body, and though she extended herself, he began to get the better of her. She was tiring and she slowed her movements and let him rub himself against her. Cold water and exertion had softened him, but she felt him grow again, his hips slipping over her belly, probing instinctively at her. She hooked an arm around his neck and pulled his face down between her breasts. His entire body arched and convulsed and for a moment she thought he had gone too far, and she reached down and squeezed him hard and painfully to stop him.

Then as he broke away, shocked by her assault, she turned and swam swiftly to the bank, dragged herself from the pool and ran wet and naked to the summer-house. She snatched up her towel, wiped her face dry and, holding the towel in front of her, turned back to face him as he reached the door of the summer-house behind her. He stood flushed and angry in the doorway, and they stared at each other, both of them panting heavily.

Then slowly she lowered the towel and tossed it over the couch. Swinging her hips deliberately she went to where he stood.

'All right, Master Sean. We know you are worse than useless with a paint brush. Let's see if there isn't anything else we can teach you.'

*   *   *

He was like a blank canvas on which she could trace her own designs, no matter how bizarre.

There were things from which her other lovers had recoiled, and other acts that she had only imagined and never had the courage to suggest to a partner. At last she felt free of all constraint. It was as though he could read her intentions. She had only to start some new experiment, guide him just part of the way, and he picked it up with a greedy relish that astonished her and carried it through to a conclusion that she had not always fully foreseen, and which sometimes left her stunned.

His strength and confidence increased with every one of their meetings. For the first time she had found something that did not swiftly pall. Gradually her existence seemed to centre around the summer-house beside the pool, and she could not wait to reach it each evening. It required all her self-discipline to keep her hands off him in the art room. She could not trust herself to stand close to him, or to look at him directly during her classes.

277

Then he initiated a new series of dangerous games. He would remain behind after class, for just a few minutes. It had to be very quick, but risk of discovery enhanced the thrill for both of them.

Once the janitor came in as they were busy and it was so close, so exciting, that she thought she had experienced heart failure at the climax. Sean was standing erect behind her desk, and she was kneeling in front of him. He had taken a handful of her hair and twisted it, holding her face against his lower body.

'I am looking for Miss East,' the janitor said from the doorway. He was a pensioner, almost seventy years of age but out of vanity he refused to wear spectacles. 'Is she here?' he demanded, peering at Sean myopically.

'Hello, Mr Brownlee. Miss East has gone up to the staff common room already,' Sean told him coolly, holding Clare by her hair so she could not pull away from him. The janitor muttered unintelligibly and turned to leave the art room, when to Clare's horror Sean called him back.

'Oh, Mr Brownlee, can I give her a message for you?' he asked, and he and the janitor talked for almost a minute that seemed like all the ages, while she, screened by the desk, was forced to continue.

She knew then, when she paused to think about it, that she was in over her head. She had seen glimpses of the cruelty and violence in him and as the months passed, his physical strength increased with all the sudden blooming of desert grass after rain. The last garlands of puppy fat around his torso were replaced by hard muscle and it seemed that before her eyes his chest broadened and took on a covering of springing dark curls.

Though sometimes she still challenged and fought him, each time he subdued her with greater ease, and then he would force her to perform one of the tricks to which she had originally introduced him, but which he had embroidered with little sadistic twists of his own.

She developed a taste for these humiliations, and she began deliberately to provoke him, until at last she succeeded beyond her expectations. It was in her cottage – the first time they had met there because there was always the danger that Tara would drop in unexpectedly, but by now both of them were reckless.

Clare waited until he was fully ripe, his eyes glazing and his lips pulled back in a rictus of ecstasy, then she twisted and bucked, throwing him off her and she knelt before him and jeered with laughter.

He was angry, but she calmed him down. Then a few minutes later she did it again, and this time she squeezed him painfully, just as she had done that first evening at the pool.

Seconds later she lay dazed, only semi-conscious, sprawled half off the bed, both her eyes rapidly closing with plum-coloured swellings, her lips broken against her teeth, and blood dripping from her nose. Sean stood over her. His face was white as ice, the knuckles of his clenched fists grazed raw, still shaking with fury. He caught her by the tresses of her dark hair and knelt over her while he forced her to take him through her split and bleeding lips. After that there was no question but that he was her master.

Clare missed three days of school, while the worst of the swelling subsided and the bruises faded, and then wore dark sunglasses to her art class. When she passed Sean at his easel, she brushed herself against him like a cat, and he waited behind again after class.

Sean had gone long enough without boasting of his conquest, but Snotty Arbuthnot refused to believe him.

'You've got a screw loose if you think I swallow that,' he taunted. 'You think I'm as green as I'm cabbage-looking, man? You and Marsh Mallows – in your dreams you mean!'

Sean had one alternative to beating him up. 'Okay then, I'll prove it to you.'

'Boy, it had better be good.'

'It will be,' Sean assured him grimly.

The following Saturday afternoon he placed Snotty amongst the protea bushes at the head of the waterfall, and for good measure, lent him the binoculars that his grandmother had given him for his fourteenth birthday.

'Let's take the cushions off the couch,' he suggested to Clare when she came into the summer-house. 'We'll put them on the lawn, there on the bank. It will be warmer in the sun.' She agreed with alacrity.

Snotty Arbuthnot was still almost inarticulate when they met at the school gates the next day.

'Hell, man, I never dreamed that people did that. I mean, *unbelievable*, man! When she – you know – when she actually – well, I thought I was going to die on the spot.'

'Did I tell the truth?' Sean demanded. 'Or did I lie to you?'

'Man, it was super titanic. Boy, Sean, I was painting maps of Africa over my sheets all last night, I kid you not. Will you let me watch again – please, Sean, please?'

'Next time will cost you money,' Sean said. Even though performing to an audience had filled an exhibitionist need, Sean meant it as a refusal, but when Snotty asked without hesitation, 'How much, Sean? Just name your price!' Sean looked at him appraisingly.

It was Shasa's policy to keep his sons on very modest pocket-money, a policy that he had inherited from his own mother. 'They must learn the value of money,' was the family maxim.

Even Snotty whose father was only a surgeon received four times the pittance that was Sean's allowance. The protection racket that

Sean ran amongst the juniors, an idea he had picked up from a George Raft movie at the Odeon, more than doubled his income. However, he was always lamentably short of hard cash, and Snotty could afford to pay.

'Two pounds,' Sean suggested. He knew that was exactly his weekly pocket money, but Snotty smiled radiantly. 'You're on, man!'

However, it was only when Snotty actually placed the two crumpled notes in Sean's fist the following Saturday morning that Sean realized the full financial potential.

There was very little chance of Clare realizing that she was on stage. The protea bushes were dense, the noise of the waterfall covered the sound of any involuntary gasps or sniggers, and anyway once she was started, Clare was deaf and blind to all else. Sean appointed Snotty his ticket salesman and organizer. The commission he received ensured Snotty's free admission to each Saturday performance. Reluctantly they decided to restrict admission to ten spectators at any one session, but even that meant a take of eighteen pounds every single week. It lasted almost three months, which was in itself a miracle, for after the first sell-out matinée, the entire senior school was agog.

The word-of-mouth publicity was so good that Snotty was able to demand cash with reservation, and even so his booking sheet was full as far ahead as the beginning of the hols and half the fellows were saving so frantically to try and come up with two pounds that sales at the school tuck shop fell off dramatically. Snotty was trying to get Sean to agree to a mid-week performance, or at least to an increase in the Saturday gate, when the first rumour reached the staff common room.

While passing the windows of one of the change rooms, the history teacher had overheard two satisfied customers discussing the previous Saturday's performance. The headmaster was unable to bring himself to take the report seriously. The whole idea was patently preposterous. Nevertheless, he knew it was his duty to have a discreet word with Miss East, if only to warn her of the revolting tittle-tattle that was circulating.

He went down to the art room after school, late on Friday afternoon, a most inopportune moment. Clare had by this time abandoned all sense of discretion, for her it had become almost a self-destructive frenzy. She and Sean were in the paint store at the back of the art school, and it was some seconds before either of them realized that the headmaster was in the room with them.

*   *   *

For Shasa everything seemed to happen at once. Sean's expulsion from Bishops was a bombshell that ripped through Weltevreden. When it happened, Shasa was in Johannesburg, and they had to call him out of a meeting with the representatives of the Chamber of Mines to receive the headmaster's telephone call. On the open line the headmaster would give no details, and Shasa flew back to Cape Town immediately and drove directly from the airfield to the school.

Flabbergasted and seething with anger at the stark details the headmaster gave him, Shasa sent the Jaguar roaring around the lower slopes of Table Mountain towards Weltevreden.

From the first he had not approved of the woman who Tara had installed in the cottage. She was all the things he despised, with her great sloppy breasts and silly pretensions which she thought made her *avant-garde* and artistic. Her paintings were atrocious, daubed primary colours and childish perspectives, and she tried to conceal her lack of talent and taste behind Portuguese cigarettes, sandals and skirts of blindingly vivid designs. He decided to deal with her first.

However, she had fled, leaving the cottage in slovenly disarray. Thwarted, Shasa took his anger unabated up to the big house and shouted at Tara as he stormed into the hall.

'Where is the little blighter – I'm going to skin his backside for him.'

The other children, all three of them, were peeking over the railing from the second-floor gallery, in a fine fever of vicarious terror. Isabella's eyes were as enormous as one of Walt Disney's fawns.

Shasa saw them and roared up the stair well. 'Back to your own rooms, this instant. That goes for you as well, young lady.' And they ducked and scampered. As an afterthought Shasa bellowed after them, 'And tell that brother of yours I want to see him in the gun room immediately.'

The three of them raced each other down the passage of the nursery wing, each of them determined to be the bearer of the dreaded summons. The gun room was the family equivalent of Tower Green where all executions took place.

Garrick got there first, and pounded on Sean's locked door.

'Pater wants you immediately,' he yelled.

'— in the gun room —' Michael joined in, and Isabella who had been left far behind at the start, piped up breathlessly, 'He's going to skin your backside!' She was flushed and trembling with eagerness, and she hoped desperately that Sean would show her his bottom after Daddy had carried out his threat. She couldn't imagine what it would look like, and she wondered if Daddy would have the skin made into a floor mat like the skins of the zebras and lions in the

281

gun room. It was probably the most exciting thing that had ever happened in her life.

In the entrance hall Tara was attempting to calm Shasa. She had seen him in a comparable rage only two or three times during their marriage, always when he fancied the family honour or reputation had been compromised. Her efforts were in vain, for he turned on her with his single eye glittering.

'Damn you, woman. This is mostly your fault. It was you who insisted on bringing that whore to live on Weltevreden.'

As Shasa stormed off to the gun room, his voice carried clearly up the stairwell to where Sean was bracing himself to come down and face retribution. Up to that moment Sean had been so confused by the speed of events that he hadn't been thinking clearly. Now, as he descended the stairs, his mind was racing as he prepared his defence. He passed his mother, still standing in the middle of the chessboard black and white marble squares of the entrance hall floor, and she gave him a strained smile of encouragement.

'I tried to help, darling,' she whispered. They had never been close, but now for once Shasa's rage made them allies.

'Thank you, Mater.'

He knocked on the gun-room door, and opened it cautiously when his father roared. He closed it carefully behind him and advanced to the centre of the lion skin where he halted and stood to attention.

Beatings at Weltevreden followed an established ritual. The riding crops were laid out on the baize gun table, five of them of various lengths, weights and stinging potential. He knew his father would make a show of selecting the correct one for the occasion, and that today it would almost certainly be the long whippy whalebone. Involuntarily he looked to the over-stuffed leather chair beside the fireplace over which he would be asked to drape himself, reaching over to grip the legs of the chair on the far side. His father was an international polo player with wrists like steel springs, his strokes made even the headmaster's seem like a powder puff.

Then deliberately Sean closed his mind against fear and lifted his chin to stare calmly at his father. Shasa was standing in front of the fireplace, hands clasped beside his back, rocking on the balls of his feet.

'You have been fired from Bishops,' he said.

Although the headmaster had not specifically mentioned this fact to Sean himself during his extended diatribe, the news did not come as a complete surprise.

'Yes, sir,' he said.

'I find it hard to believe what I have been told about you. It is true

282

that you were making a spectacle of yourself with this – this woman?'

'Yes, sir.'

'That you were letting your friends watch you?'

'Yes, sir.'

'And charging them money for the privilege?'

'Yes, sir.'

'A pound a head?'

'No, sir.'

'What do you mean – no sir?'

'Two pounds a head, sir.'

'You are a Courtney – what you do reflects directly on every member of this family. Do you realize that?'

'Yes, sir.'

'Don't keep saying that. In the name of all that is holy, how could you do it?'

'She started it, sir. I would have never even thought of it without her.'

Shasa stared at him, and suddenly his rage evaporated. He remembered himself at almost exactly the same age, standing chastened before Centaine. She had not beaten him, but had sent him to a lysol bath and a humiliating medical examination. He remembered the girl, a saucy little harlot only a year or two older than he was, with a shock of sunbleached hair and a sly smile – and he almost smiled himself. She had teased and provoked him, leading him on into folly, and yet he felt a strange nostalgic glow. His first real woman – he might forget a hundred others but never that one.

Sean had seen the anger fade out of his father's eye, and sensed that now was the moment to exploit the change of mood.

'I realize that I have brought scandal on the family, and I know that I have to take my medicine —' His father would like that, it was one of his sayings, 'Take your medicine like a man.' He saw the further softening of his father's regard. 'I know how stupid I have been, and before my punishment I would just like to say how sorry I am that I have made you ashamed of me.' This was not exactly true, and Sean instinctively knew it. His father was angry with him for being caught out, but deep down he was rather proud of his eldest son's now proven virility.

'The only excuse I have was that I couldn't help myself. She just drove me mad, sir. I couldn't think of anything else but – well, but what she wanted me to do with her.'

Shasa understood entirely. He was still having the same sort of problems at nearly forty – what was it that Centaine said? 'It's the de Thiry blood, we all have to live with it.' He coughed softly, moved by his son's honesty and openness. He was such a fine-looking boy, straight and tall and strong, so handsome and courageous, no wonder the woman had picked on him. He couldn't really be bad, Shasa thought, a bit of a devil perhaps, a little too cocksure, a little too eager for life – but not really bad. 'I mean, if boffing a pretty girl is mortal sin, there is no salvation for any of us,' he thought.

'I'm going to have to beat you, Sean,' he said aloud.

'Yes, sir, I know that.' Not a trace of fear, no whining. No, damn it, he was a good boy. A son to be proud of.

Shasa went to the gun table and picked up the long whalebone crop, the most formidable weapon in his arsenal, and without being ordered to do so, Sean marched to the armchair and adopted the prescribed position. The first stroke hissed in the air and cracked against his flesh, then suddenly Shasa grunted with disgust and threw the crop on to the gun table.

'The stick is for children – and you are no longer a child,' Shasa said. 'Stand up, man.'

Sean could hardly believe his luck. Although the single stroke had stung like a nest of scorpions, he kept an impassive face and made no effort to rub the seat of his pants.

'What are we going to do with you?' his father demanded, and Sean had the sense to remain silent.

'You have to finish matric,' Shasa stated flatly. 'We'll just have to find someone else to take you on.'

This was not as easy as Shasa had anticipated. He tried SACS and Rondebosch Boys and then Wynberg Boys. The headmasters all knew about Sean Courtney. He was, for a short while, the best-known schoolboy in the Cape of Good Hope.

In the end he was accepted by Costello's Academy, a cram school that operated out of a dilapidated Victorian mansion on the other side of Rondebosch common, and was not particular about its admissions. Sean arrived for the first day and was gratified to find he was already a celebrity. Unlike the exclusive boys school which he had recently left, there were girls in the classrooms and academic excellence and moral rectitude were not prerequisites for entrance to Costello's Academy.

Sean had found his spiritual home and he set about sorting out the most promising of his fellow scholars and organizing them into a gang which within a year was virtually running the cram school. His final selection included a half dozen of the most comely and accommodating young ladies on the academy's roll. As both his father and erstwhile headmaster had noted, Sean was a born leader.

*　　*　　*

284

Manfred De La Rey stood to attention on the reviewing stand. He wore a severe dark pinstripe suit and a black Homburg hat, with a small spray of carnations and green fern in his buttonhole. This was the uniform of a Nationalist cabinet minister.

The police band was playing a traditional country air *'Die Kaapse Nooi'* – 'The Cape Town girl', to a lively marching beat and the ranks of the police cadets stepped out vigorously, passing the stand with their FN rifles at the slope. As each platoon drew level with the dais, they gave Manfred the eyes right, and he returned the salute.

They made a grand show with their smart blue uniforms and sparkling brasswork catching the white highveld sunlight. These athletic young men, proud and eager, their perfect drill formations, their transparent dedication and patriotism filled Manfred De La Rey with a vast sense of pride.

Manfred stood to attention while the formations wheeled past him and then formed up in review order on the open parade ground facing the stand. The band played a final ruffle of drums and then fell silent. Resplendent in full dress uniform and decorations, the police general stepped to the microphone and in a few crisp sentences introduced the minister, then fell back relinquishing the microphone to Manfred.

Manfred had taken especial care with the preparation of his speech, but before he began he could not prevent himself from glancing aside to where Heidi sat in the front row of honoured guests. This was her day also, and she looked like a blond Valkyrie, her handsome Teutonic features set off by the wide-brimmed hat and its tall decoration of artificial roses. Few women would have the presence and stature to wear it without looking ridiculous, but on Heidi it was magnificent. She caught his eye and smiled at Manfred. 'What a woman,' he thought. 'She deserves to be First Lady in the land, and I will see that she is – one day. Perhaps sooner than she imagines.'

He turned back to the microphone and composed himself. He knew that he was a compelling orator, and he enjoyed the fact that thousands of eyes were concentrated upon him. He felt at ease up here on the dais, relaxed and in total control of himself and those below him.

'You have chosen a life of service to your *Volk* and to your country,' he began. He was speaking in Afrikaans and his reference to the *Volk* was quite natural. The intake of police recruits was almost exclusively from the Afrikaner section of the white community. Manfred De La Rey would not have had it any other way. It was desirable that control of the security forces should be vested solidly in the more responsible elements of the nation, those who

285

understood most clearly the dangers and threats that faced them in the years ahead. Now he began to warn this dedicated body of young men of those dangers.

'It will require all our courage and fortitude to resist the dark forces which are arrayed against us. We must thank our Maker, the Lord God of our fathers, that in the covenant he made with our ancestors on the battlefield of Blood river he has guaranteed us his protection and guidance. It needs only that we remain constant and true, trusting him, worshipping him, for the way always to be made smooth for our feet to follow.'

He ended his address with the act of faith that had lifted the Afrikaner out of poverty and oppression to his rightful place in the land:

Believe in your God.
Believe in your *Volk*.
Believe in yourself.

His voice, magnified a hundred times, boomed across the parade ground, and he truly felt the divine and benevolent presence very close to him as he looked out upon their shining faces.

Now came the presentation. Out on the field there were shouted orders and the blue ranks came to attention. A pair of officers stepped forward to flank Manfred and one of them carried a velvet-lined tray on which were laid out the medals and awards.

Reading from the list in his hands the second officer called the recipients forward. One at a time they left the ranks, marching briskly, to halt before the imposing figure of Manfred De La Rey. He shook hands with each of them, and then pinned the medals upon their chests.

Then came the moment, and Manfred felt his pride suffocating him. The last of the award-winners was marching towards him across the parade ground, and this one was the tallest and smartest and straightest of them all. In the front rank of guests, Heidi was weeping silently with joy, and she dabbed unashamedly at her tears with a lace handkerchief.

Lothar De La Rey came to a halt in front of his father and stood to rigid attention. Neither of them smiled, their expressions were stern; they stared into each other's eyes, but between them flowed such a current of feeling that made words or smiles redundant.

With an effort Manfred broke that silent rapport, and turned to the police colonel beside him. He offered the sword to Manfred, and the engraved scabbard glistened in silver and gold as Manfred took it from him and turned back to his son.

'The sword of honour,' he said. 'May you wear it with distinction,' and he stepped up to Lothar and attached the beautiful weapon to the blanched belt at his son's waist. They shook hands, both of them solemn still, but the brief grip they exchanged expressed a lifetime of love and pride and filial duty.

They stood to attention, holding the salute, as the band played the national anthem:

From the blue of our heavens
From the depths of our seas –

And then the parade was breaking up, and young men were swarming forward to find their families in the throng, and there were excited female cries and laughter and long fervent embraces as they met.

Lothar De La Rey stood between his parents, with the sword hanging at his side, and while he shook the hands of an endless procession of well-wishers and made modest responses to their fulsome congratulations, neither Manfred nor Heidi could any longer contain their proud and happy smiles.

'Well done, Lothie!' One of Lothar's fellow cadets got through to him at last, and the two lads grinned as they shook hands. 'No doubt about who was the best man.'

'I was lucky,' Lothar laughed self-deprecatingly, and changed the subject. 'Have you been told your posting yet, Hannes?'

'*Ja*, man. I'm being sent down to Natal, somewhere on the coast. How about you, perhaps we'll be together?'

'No such luck,' Lothar shook his head. 'They are sending me to some little station in the black townships near Vereeniging – a place called Sharpeville.'

'Sharpeville? Bad luck, man.' Hannes shook his head with mock sympathy. 'I've never heard of it.'

'Nor had I. Nobody has ever heard of it,' said Lothar with resignation. 'And nobody ever will.'

*   *   *

On 24 August 1958 the prime minister, Johannes Gerhardus Strijdom, 'Lion of the Waterberg', succumbed to heart disease. He had only been at the head of government for four years, but his passing left a wide gap in the granite cliffs of Afrikanerdom, and like termites whose nest has been damaged, they rushed to repair it.

Within hours of the announcement of the prime minister's death, Manfred De La Rey was in Shasa's office, accompanied by two of the senior Cape back-benchers of the National Party.

287

'We have to try and keep the northerners out,' he announced bluntly. 'We have to get our man in.'

Shasa nodded cautiously. He was still regarded by most of the party as an outsider in the cabinet. His influence in the coming election of a new leader would not be decisive, but he was ready to watch and learn as Manfred laid out their strategy for him.

'They have already made Verwoerd their candidate,' he said. 'All right, he has been in the Senate most of his career and has little experience as an MP, but his reputation is that of a strong man and a clever one. They like the way he has handled the blacks. He has made the name Verwoerd and the word *apartheid* mean the same thing. The people know that under him there will be no mixing of races, that South Africa will always belong to the white man.'

'*Ja*,' agreed one of the others. 'But he is so brutal. There are ways of doing things, ways of saying things that don't offend people. Our own man is strong also. Dönges introduced the Group Areas Bill and the Separate Representation of Voters bill – nobody can accuse him of being a *kafferboetie*, a nigger-lover. But he's got more style, more finesse.'

'The northerners don't want finesse. They don't want a genteel prime minister with sweet lips, they want a man of power, and Verwoerd is a talker, hell that man can talk and he's not afraid of work – and as we all know, anybody whom the English press hates so much can't be all bad.' They laughed, watching Shasa, waiting to see how he would take it. He was still an outsider, their tame *rooinek*, and he would not give them the satisfaction of seeing their raillery score. He smiled easily.

'Verwoerd is canny as an old bull baboon, and quick as a mamba. We'll have to work hard if we are to keep him out,' Shasa agreed.

They worked hard, all of them. Shasa was convinced that despite his record of introducing racially inspired legislation to the House, Dönges was the most moderate and altruistic of the three men who allowed themselves to be persuaded to stand as candidates for the highest office in the land.

As Dr Hendrik Verwoerd himself said, as he accepted nomination, 'When a man receives a desperate call from his people, he does not have the right to refuse.'

On 2 September 1958, the caucus of the National Party met to choose the new leader. The caucus was made up of 178 Nationalist members of parliament and Nationalist senators voting together, and Verwoerd's short term in parliament that had seemed at first to be a weakness, turned out to be an advantage. For years Hendrik Verwoerd had been the leader of the Senate, and had dominated the upper house by the strength of his personality and the powers of his oratory. The senators, docile and compliant, men whose ranks had been enlarged to enable the governing party to force through distasteful legislation, voted for Verwoerd as a block.

Dönges survived the first ballot in which 'Blackie' Swart, the Free State's candidate, was eliminated, but on the second ballot, a straight contest between Verwoerd and Dönges, the northerners closed their ranks and swept Verwoerd into the premiership by ninety-eight votes to seventy-five.

That evening when, as prime minister, Hendrik Frensch Verwoerd broadcast to the nation, he did not try to conceal the fact that his election had been the will of Almighty God. 'He it is who has ordained that I should lead the people of South Africa in this new period of their lives.'

Blaine and Centaine had driven across from Rhodes Hill. It was a family tradition to gather in this room to listen to important broadcasts. Here they had heard speeches and announcements that had shifted the world they knew on its axis: declarations of war and peace, the news of the evil mushroom clouds planted in the skies above Japanese cities, the death of kings and beloved rulers, the accession of a queen, to all these and others they had listened together in the blue drawing-room of Weltevreden.

Now they sat quietly as the high-pitched, nervously strained but articulate voice of the new prime minister came to them, jarring when he repeated platitudes and well-worn themes.

'No one need doubt for a single moment that it will always be my aim to uphold the democratic instutitions of our country, for they are the most treasured possessions of western civilization,' Verwoerd told them, 'and the right of people with other convictions to express their views will be maintained.'

'Just as long as those views are passed by the government board of censors, the synod of the Dutch Reformed Church and the caucus of the National Party,' Blaine murmured, a sarcastic qualification for him, and Centaine nudged him.

'Do be quiet, Blaine, I want to listen.'

Verwoerd had moved on to another familiar subject, how the country's enemies had deliberately misconstrued his racial policies. It was not he who had coined the word *apartheid*, but other dedicated and brilliant minds had foreseen the necessity of allowing all the races of a complicated and fragmented society to develop towards their own separate potential. 'As the minister of Bantu affairs, since 1950 it has been my duty to give cohesion and substance to this policy, the only policy which will allow full opportunity for each and every group within its own racial community. In the years ahead, we will not deviate one inch from this course.'

289

Tara had been tapping her foot restlessly as she listened, but now she sprang to her feet. 'I'm sorry,' she blurted. 'I'm feeling a little queasy. I must get a breath of fresh air on the terrace —' and she hurried from the room. Centaine glanced sharply at Shasa, but he smiled and shrugged, was about to make a light comment, when the voice on the radio riveted them all once more.

'I come now to one of the most, if not the most sacred ideal of our people,' the high-pitched voice filled the room, 'and that is the formation of the Republic. I know how many of the English-speaking South Africans listening to me tonight are filled with a sense of loyalty to the British Crown. I know also that this divided loyalty has prevented them from always dealing with the real issues on their merits. The ideal of monarchy has too often been a divisive factor in our midst, separating Afrikaners and English-speakers when they should have been united. In a de-colonizing world, the black man and his newly fledged nations are beginning to emerge as a threat to the South Africa we know and love. Afrikaner and Englishman can no longer afford to stand apart, but must now link arms as allies, secure and strong in the ideal of a new white republic.'

'My God,' Blaine breathed, 'that's a new line. It used always to be the Afrikaner Republic exclusively, and nobody took it seriously, least of all the Afrikaners. But this time he is serious, and he has started something that is going to raise a stink. I remember all too well the controversy over the flag, back in the 1920s. That will seem like a love feast compared to the idea of a republic —' he broke off to listen as Verwoerd ended:

'Thus I give you my assurance that from now on the sacred ideal of Republic will be passionately pursued.'

When the prime minister finished speaking, Shasa crossed the room and switched off the radio; then he turned and stood with his hands thrust deeply into his pockets, and his shoulders hunched as he studied their faces. They were all of them subdued and shaken. For one hundred and fifty years the country had been British, and there was a pride and a vast sense of security in that state. Now it was to change, and they were afraid. Even Shasa felt strangely bereft and uncertain.

'He doesn't mean it. It's just another sop for his own people. They are always ranting about the republic,' Centaine said hopefully, but Blaine shook his head.

'We don't know this man very well yet. We only know what he wrote when he was editor of *Transvaler*, and we know with what vigour and determination he has set about segregating our society. There is one other thing we have learned about him. He is a man who means exactly what he says, and who will let nothing stand in his way.' He reached across and took Centaine's hand. 'No, my heart. You are wrong. He means it.'

They both looked up at Shasa, and Centaine asked for both of them, 'What will you do, *chéri*?'

'I am not sure that I will have any choice. They say he brooks no opposition, and I opposed him. I lobbied for Dönges. I may not be on the list when he announces his cabinet on Monday.'

'It will be hard to move to the back bench again,' Blaine remarked.

'Too hard,' Shasa nodded. 'And I will not do it.'

'Oh *chéri*,' Centaine cried. 'You would not resign your seat – after all we have sacrificed, after all our hard work and hopes.'

'We'll know on Monday,' Shasa shrugged, trying not to let them see how bitterly disappointed he was. He had held true power for too short a time, just long enough to learn to enjoy the taste of it. He knew, furthermore, that there was so much he had to offer his country, so many of his efforts almost ready for harvesting. It would be hard to watch them wither and die with his own ambitions, before he had even tasted the first sweets, but Verwoerd would sack him from his cabinet. He could not doubt it for a moment.

'"If you can meet with triumph and disaster",' Centaine quoted, and then laughed gaily, with only the barest tremor in it. 'Now, *chéri*, let's open a bottle of champagne. It's the only way to treat those two impostors of Kipling's.'

Shasa entered his office in the House, and looked around it regretfully. It had been his for five years, and now he would have to pack up his books and paintings and furniture; the panelling and carpeting he would leave as a gift to the nation. He had hoped to make a larger bequest than that, and he grimaced and went to sit behind his desk for the last time and try to assess where he had erred and what he could have done if he had been allowed. The telephone on his desk rang, and he picked it up before his secretary in the outer office could reach it.

'This is the prime minister's secretary,' the voice told him, and for a moment he thought of the dead man and not his successor.

'The prime minister would like to see you as soon as is convenient.'

'I will come right away, of course,' Shasa replied, and as he replaced the receiver he thought, 'So he personally wants to have the pleasure of chopping me down.'

Verwoerd kept him waiting only ten minutes and then rose from behind his desk to apologize as Shasa entered his office. 'Forgive me. It has been a busy day,' and Shasa smiled at the understatement. His smile was not forced, for Verwoerd was displaying all his enormous charm, his voice soft and lulling, unlike the higher harsher tone of his public utterances, and he actually came around the desk and took Shasa's arm in an avuncular grip. 'But, of course, I had to speak to you, as I have spoken to all the members of my new cabinet.'

Shasa started so that he pulled his arm out of the other man's grip, and they turned to face each other.

'I am keeping the portfolio of Mines and Industry open, and of course there is no man better qualified for the job than you. I have liked your presentations to the old cabinet. You know what you are talking about.'

'I cannot pretend not to be surprised, Prime Minister,' Shasa told him quietly, and Verwoerd chuckled.

'It is good to be unpredictable at times.'

'Why?' Shasa asked. 'Why me?' Verwoerd cocked his head on the side, a characteristic gesture of interrogation, but Shasa insisted, 'I know you value straight talk, Prime Minister, so I will say it. You have no reason to like me or to consider me an ally.'

'That is true,' Verwoerd agreed. 'But I don't need sycophants. I have enough of those already. What I have considered is that the job you are doing is vital to the eventual well-being of our land, and that there is no one who could do it better. I am sure we will learn to work together.'

'Is that all, Prime Minister?'

'You have mentioned that I like to talk straight. Very well, that is not all. You probably heard me begin my premiership with an appeal for a drawing together of the two sections of our white population, an appeal to Boer and Briton to forget old worn-out antipathy and side by side to build the Republic. How would it look if with the next breath I fired the only Englishman in my government?'

They both laughed, and then Shasa shook his head. 'On the matter of the Republic I will oppose you,' he warned, and for a moment saw through a chink the cold and monolithic ego of a man who would never bow to the contrary view, and then the chink was closed and Verwoerd chuckled.

'Then I will have to convince you that you are wrong. In the meantime you will be my conscience – what is the name of the character in the Disney story?'

'Which one?'

'The story of the puppet – Pinocchio, is it? What was the name of the cricket?'

'Jiminy Cricket,' Shasa told him.

'Yes, in the meantime you will be my Jiminy Cricket. Do you accept the task?'

292

'We both know it is my duty, Prime Minister.' As Shasa said it, he thought cynically, 'Isn't it remarkable that once ambition has dictated, duty so readily concurs?'

*　　*　　*

They were dining out that night, but Shasa went to Tara's room to tell her the news as soon as he had dressed.

She watched him in the mirror as he explained his reasons for accepting the appointment. Her expression was solemn but her voice had a brittle edge of contempt in it as she said, 'I am delighted for you. I know that is what you want, and I know that you will be so busy you will not even notice that I am gone.'

'Gone?' he demanded.

'Our bargain, Shasa. We agreed that I could go away for a while when I felt the need. Of course, I will return – that was also part of our bargain.'

He looked relieved. 'Where will you go – and for how long?'

'London,' she replied. 'And I should be away several months. I want to attend a course on archaeology at London University.' She tried to hide it from him, but she was wildly, deliriously excited. She had only heard from Molly that afternoon, just after the new cabinet had been announced. Molly had a message. Moses had at last sent for her, and she had already booked passage for Benjamin, Miriam and herself on the *Pendennis Castle* to Southampton. She would take the child to meet his father.

The mailship sailing was an exciting event in which the citizens of the mother city, of whatever station in life, could join gaily. The deck was crowded and noisy. Paper streamers joined the tall ship to the quayside with a web of colour that fluttered in the south-easter. A coon band on the dock vied with the ship's band high up on the promenade deck, and the old Cape favourite 'Alabama' was answered by 'God be with you till we meet again'.

Shasa was not there. He had flown up to Walvis Bay to deal with some unforeseen problem at the canning factory. Nor was Sean, he was writing exams at Costello's Academy, but Blaine and Centaine brought the other three children down to the docks to see Tara off on her voyage.

They stood in a small family group, surrounded by the crowd, each of them holding a paper streamer and waving up at Tara on the first class 'A' deck. As the gap between the quay and the ship's side opened, the foghorns boomed, and the paper streamers parted and floated down to settle on the dark waters of the inner harbour. The tugs pushed the great bows around, until they lined up with the harbour entrance and under the stern the gigantic propeller chopped the water into foam and drove her out into Table Bay.

Tara ran lightly up the companionway to her stateroom. She had protested only mildly when Shasa had insisted that she cancel her original bookings in tourist and travel first class. 'My dear, there are bound to be people we know on board. What would they think of my wife travelling steerage?'

'Not steerage, Shasa – tourist.'

'Everything below "A" deck is steerage,' he had replied, and now she was glad of his snobbery for the stateroom was a private place where she could have Ben all to herself. It would have excited curiosity if she had been seen with a coloured child on the public deck. As Shasa had pointed out, there were watching eyes on board and the reports would have flown back to Shasa like homing pigeons. However, Miriam Afrika had good-naturedly agreed to wear a servant's livery and to act out the subterfuge of being Tara's maid during the voyage. Her husband had reluctantly let her go with Tara to England, despite the disruption to his own household. Tara had compensated him generously and Miriam had come aboard with the child registered as her own.

Tara hardly left her stateroom during the entire voyage, declining the captain's offer to join his table and shunning the cocktail parties and fancy-dress dance. She never tired of being with Moses' son, her love was a hunger that could never be appeased and even when, exhausted by her attentions, Benjamin fell asleep in his cot, Tara hovered over him constantly. 'I love you,' she whispered to him, 'best in the world after your Daddy,' and she did not think of the other children, not even Michael. She ordered all their meals to be sent up to her suite, and ate with Benjamin, almost jealously taking over his care from Miriam. Only late at night with the greatest reluctance did she let her carry the child away to the tourist cabin on the deck below.

The days sped by swiftly and, at last, holding Benjamin's hand she stepped off the gangplank to the boat train in Southampton docks for the ride up to London.

Again at Shasa's insistence, she had taken the suite at the Dorchester overlooking the park that the family always used, with a single room at the back for Miriam and the baby for which she requested a separate bill and paid in cash out of her own pocket so that Shasa would have no record of it on her bank statement.

There was a message from Moses waiting for her at the porter's desk when she registered. She recognized the handwriting. She opened the envelope the moment she entered the suite, and felt the cold slide of disappointment. He wrote very formally:

Dear Tara,
    I am sorry I was not able to meet you. However, it is necessary for me to attend important talks in Amsterdam with our friends. I will contact you immediately on my return.

                                                    Yours sincerely,
                                                    Moses Gama.

She was thrown into black despair by the tone of the letter and the dashing of her expectations. Without Miriam and the child she would have despaired. However, they passed the waiting days in the parks and zoos, and in long walks along the river bank and through London's fascinating alleys and convoluted streets. She shopped for Benjamin at Marks & Spencer and C & A, avoiding Harrods and Selfridges, for those were Shasa's haunts.

Tara registered at the university for the course in African archaeology. She did not trust Shasa not to check that she had done so. In accordance with Shasa's other expectations she even dressed in her most demure twin set and pearls and took a cab up to Trafalgar Square to make a courtesy call on the high commissioner at South Africa House. She could not avoid his invitation to lunch and had to show a bright face during a meal whose menu and wine-list and fellow guests could have been taken straight from a similar gathering at Weltevreden. She listened to the editor of the *Daily Telegraph*, who sat beside her, but kept glancing out of the windows at Nelson's tall column, and longed to be free as the cloud of pigeons that circled it. Her duty done, she escaped at last, only just in time to get back to the Dorchester and give Ben his bath.

She had bought him a plastic tugboat at Hamley's toy shop which was a great success, and Ben sat in the bath and chuckled with delight as the tugboat circled him.

Tara was laughing and drying her hands when Miriam came through from the lounge to the bathroom.

'There is somebody to see you, Tara.'

'Who is it?' Tara demanded without rising from where she knelt beside the bath.

'He wouldn't give his name.' Miriam kept a straight face. 'I will finish bathing Ben.'

Tara hesitated, she did not want to waste a minute away from her son. 'Oh all right,' she agreed, and with the towel in her hand she went through to the lounge, and stopped abruptly in the doorway.

The shock was so intense that her face drained of blood and she swayed giddily and had to snatch at the door jamb to steady herself.

'Moses,' she whispered, staring at him.

He wore a long tan-coloured trenchcoat, and the epauletted

shoulders were spattered with rain drops. The coat seemed to accentuate his height and the breadth of his shoulders. She had forgotten the grandeur of his presence. He did not smile, but regarded her with that steady heart-checking stare of his.

'Moses,' she said again, and took a faltering step towards him. 'Oh God, you'll never know how slowly the years have passed since last I saw you.'

'Tara.' His voice thrilled every fibre of her being. 'My wife,' and he held out his arms to her.

She flew to him and he enfolded her and held her close. She pressed her face to his chest and clung to him, inhaling the rich masculine smell of his body, as warm and exciting as the herby smell of the African noonday. For many seconds neither of them moved or spoke except for the involuntary tremors that shook Tara's body and the little moaning sound she made in her throat.

Then gently he held her off and took her face between his hands and lifted it to look into her eyes.

'I have thought about you every day,' he said, and suddenly she was weeping. The tears streamed down her cheeks, and into the corners of her mouth, so that when he kissed her, their metallic salt mingled with the slick taste of his saliva.

Miriam brought Benjamin out to them, clean and dry and dressed in his new blue pyjamas. He regarded his father solemnly.

'I greet you, my son,' Moses whispered. 'May you grow as strong and beautiful as the land of your birth,' and Tara thought that her heart might stop with the pride and sheer joy of seeing them together for the first time.

Though the colour of their skins differed, Benjamin was caramel and chocolate cream while Moses was amber and African bronze, Tara could see the resemblance in the shape of their heads and the set of jaw and brow. They had the same wide-spaced eyes, the same noses and lips, and to her they were the two most beautiful beings in her existence.

*   *   *

Tara kept the suite at the Dorchester, for she knew that Shasa would contact her there and that any invitations from South Africa House or correspondence from the university would be addressed to her at the hotel. But she moved into Moses' flat off the Bayswater Road.

The flat belonged to the Ethiopian emperor, and was kept for the use of his diplomatic staff. However, Haile Selassie had placed it at Moses Gama's disposal for as long as he needed it. It was a large rambling apartment, with dark rooms and a strange mixture of

296

furnishings, well-worn Western sofas and easy chairs, with hand-woven woollen Ethiopian rugs and wall hangings. The ornaments were African artefacts, carved ebony statuettes, crossed two-handed broadswords, bronze Somali shields and Coptic Christian crosses and icons, in native silver studded with semi-precious stones.

They slept on the floor, in the African manner, on thin hard mattresses filled with coir. Moses even used a small wooden head stool as a pillow, though Tara could not accustom herself to it. Benjamin slept with Miriam in the bedroom at the end of the passage.

Love-making was as naturally part of Moses Gama's life as eating or drinking or sleeping, and yet his skills and his consideration of her needs were an endless source of wonder and delight to her. She wanted more than anything else in life to bear him another child. She tried consciously to open the mouth of her womb, willing it to expand like a flower bud to accept his seed, and long after he had fallen asleep she lay with her thighs tightly crossed and her knees raised so as not to spill a precious drop, imagining herself a sponge for him, or a bellows to draw his substance up deeply into herself.

Yet the times they were alone were far too short for Tara, and it irked her that the flat seemed always filled with strangers. She hated to share Moses with them, wanting him all for herself. He understood this, and when she had been churlish and sulky in the presence of others, he reminded her sternly.

'I am the struggle, Tara. Nothing, nobody, comes ahead of that. Not even my own longings, not my life itself can come before my duty to the cause. If you take me, then you make that same sacrifice.'

To moderate the severity of his words, he lifted her in his arms and carried her to the mattress, and made love to her until she sobbed and rolled her head from side to side, delirious with the power and wonder of it, and then he told her, 'You have as much of me as any person will ever have. Accept that without complaint, and be grateful for it, for we never know when one of us may be called to sacrifice it all. Live now, Tara, live for our love this day, for there may never be a tomorrow.'

'Forgive me, Moses,' she whispered. 'I have been so small and petty. I will not disappoint you again.'

So she put aside her jealousy and joined in his work, and looked upon the men and women who came to the Bayswater Road no longer as strangers and interlopers, but as comrades – part of their life and the struggle. Then she could realize what a fascinating slice of humanity they represented. Most of them were Africans, tall Kikuyus from Kenya, Jomo Kenyatta's young men, the warriors of Mau Mau, once even the little man with a great heart and brain, Hastings Banda, spent an evening with them. There were Shonas and Shangaans from Rhodesia, Xhosas and Zulus from her own South Africa and even a few of Moses' own tribe from Ovamboland. They had formed a fledgling freedom association which they called South West African Peoples' Organization, and they wanted Moses' patronage, which he gave them willingly. Tara found it difficult to think of Moses as belonging to a single tribe, all of Africa was his fief, he spoke most of their separate languages and understood their specific fears and aspirations. If ever the word 'African' described one man, that man was Moses Gama.

There were others who came to the flat in Bayswater Road; Hindus and Moslems and men of the north lands, from Ethiopia and Sudan and Mediterranean Africa, some of them still living under colonial tyranny, others newly liberated and eager to help their suffering fellow Africans.

There were white men and women also, speaking in the accents of Liverpool and the north country, of the coal mines or the mills; and other white men and women whose English was halting and laboured, but whose hearts were fierce, patriots from Poland and East Germany and the Soviet bloc, some from Mother Russia herself. All had a common love of freedom and hatred of the oppressor.

From the unlimited letter of credit that Shasa had given her to his London bank, Tara filled the flat with good food and liquor, taking a vindictive pleasure in paying out Shasa's money for the very best fillet steak and choice lamb, for turbot and sole and lobster.

For the first time she derived pleasure from ordering Burgundies and clarets of the best vintages and noblest estates, about which she had listened to Shasa lecturing his dinner guests so pompously. She laughed delightedly when she watched the enemies of all Shasa stood for, the ones called the 'bringers of darkness', quaffing his wines as though they were Coca-Cola.

She had not prepared food for a long time, the chef at Weltevreden would have been mortified if she had attempted to do so, and now she enjoyed working with some of the other women in the kitchen. The Hindu wives showed her how to make wondrous curries and the Arab women prepared lamb in a dozen exciting ways, so that every meal was a feast and an adventure. From the impecunious students to the heads of revolutionary governments and the leaders in exile of captive nations, they came to talk and plan, to eat and drink and exchange ideas even more heady than the wines that Tara poured for them.

Always Moses Gama was at the centre of the excitement. His vast brooding presence seemed to inspire and direct their energies, and Tara realized that he was making bonds, forging loyalties and friendships to carry the struggle onwards to the next plateau. She

298

was immensely proud of him, and humbly proud of her own small part in the grand enterprise. For the very first time in her life she felt useful and important. Until the present time she had spent her life in trivial and meaningless activity. By making her a part of his work, Moses had made her a whole person at last. Impossible as it seemed, during those enchanted months her love for him was multiplied a hundredfold.

Sometimes they travelled together, when Moses was invited to speak to some important group, or to meet representatives of a foreign power. They went to Sheffield and Oxford to address elements from opposite ends of the political spectrum, the British Communist Party and the association of Conservative students. One weekend they flew to Paris to meet with officials from the French directorate of foreign affairs and a month later they even went to Moscow together. Tara travelled on her British passport and spent the days sightseeing with her Russian Intourist guide while Moses was closeted in secret talks in the offices of the fourth directorate overlooking the Gorky Prospekt.

When they returned to London, Moses and some of his exiled fellow South Africans organized a protest rally in Trafalgar Square directly opposite the imposing edifice of South Africa House, with its frieze of animal head sculptures and colonnaded front entrance. Tara could not join the demonstration, for Moses warned her that they would be photographed with telescopic lenses from the building, and forbade her to expose herself to the racist agents. She was far too valuable to the cause. Instead she struck upon a delightfully ironic twist, and telephoned the high commissioner. He invited her to lunch again. She watched from his own office, sitting in one of his easy chairs in the magnificent stinkwood-panelled room, while below her in the square Moses stood beneath a banner 'Apartheid is a crime against Humanity' and made a speech to five hundred demonstrators. Her only regret was that the wind and the traffic prevented her hearing his words. He repeated them to her that evening as they lay together on the hard mattress on the floor of their bedroom, and she thrilled to every single word.

One lovely English spring morning they walked arm in arm through Hyde Park, and Benjamin threw crumbs to the ducks in the Serpentine.

They watched the riders in Rotten Row, and admired the show of spring blooms in the gardens as they passed them on their way up to Speakers' Corner.

On the lawns the holiday crowds were taking advantage of the unseasonable sunshine, and many of the men were shirtless while the girls had pulled their skirts high on their thighs as they lolled on the grass. The lovers were entwined shamelessly, and Moses frowned. Public displays of this kind offended his African morality.

As they arrived at Speakers' Corner, they passed the militant homosexuals and Irish Republicans on their upturned milk crates and went to join the group of black speakers. Moses was instantly recognized, he had become a well-known figure in these circles, and half a dozen men and women hurried to meet him, all of them were coloured South African expatriates, and all of them were eager to give him the news.

'They have acquitted them —'

'They have set them all free —'

'Nokwe, Makgatho, Nelson Mandela – they are all free!'

'Judge Rumpff found every one of them not guilty of treason —'

Moses Gama stopped dead in his tracks and glowered at them as they surrounded him, dancing joyfully, and laughing in the pale English sunlight, these sons and daughters of Africa.

'I do not believe it,' Moses snarled angrily, and somebody shoved a crumpled copy of the *Observer* at him.

'Here! Read it! It's true.'

Moses snatched the newspaper fom him. He read swiftly, scanning the front-page article. His face was set and bleak, and then abruptly he thrust the paper into his pocket and shouldered his way out of the group. He strode away down the tarmac pathway, a tall brooding figure and Tara had to run with Benjamin to catch up with him.

'Moses, wait for us.'

He did not even glance at her, but his fury was evident in the set of his shoulders and the fixed snarl on his lips.

'What is it, Moses, what has made you so angry? We should rejoice that our friends are free. Please speak to me, Moses.'

'Don't you understand?' he demanded. 'Are you so witless that you do not see what has happened?'

'I don't – I'm sorry —'

'They have come out of this with enormous prestige, especially Mandela. I had thought that he would spend the rest of his life in prison, or better still, that they would have dropped him through the trap of the gallows.'

'Moses!' Tara was shocked. 'How can you speak like that? Nelson Mandela is your comrade.'

'Nelson Mandela is my rival to the death,' he told her flatly. 'There can only be one ruler in South Africa, either him or me.'

'I did not understand.'

'You understand very little, woman. It is not necessary that you should. All you must learn to do is obey me.'

300

She annoyed and irritated him with her perpetual moods and jealousies. He found it more difficult each day to accept her cloying adoration. Her soft pale flesh had begun to revolt him and each time it took more of an effort to feign passion. He longed for the day that he could be rid of her – but that day was not yet.

'I am sorry, Moses, if I have been stupid and made you angry.'

They walked on in silence, but when they came back to the Serpentine, Tara asked diffidently, 'What will you do now?'

'I have to lay claim to my rightful place as the leader of the people. I cannot allow Mandela to have a clear field.'

'What will you do?' she repeated.

'I must go back – back to South Africa.'

'Oh, no!' she gasped. 'You cannot do that. It is too dangerous, Moses. They will seize you the minute you set foot on South African soil.'

'No,' he shook his head. 'Not if I have your help. I will remain underground, but I will need you.'

'Of course. Whatever you want – but, my darling, what will you hope to achieve by taking such a dreadful risk?'

With an effort he put aside his anger, and looked down at her.

'Do you remember where we first met, the first time we spoke to each other?'

'In the corridors of the houses of parliament,' she answered promptly. 'I will never forget.'

He nodded. 'You asked me what I was doing there, and I replied that I would tell you one day. This is the day.'

He spoke for another hour, softly, persuasively, and as she listened her emotions rose and fell, alternating between a fierce joy and a pervading dread.

'Will you help me?' he asked at the end.

'Oh, I am so afraid for you.'

'Will you do it?'

'There is nothing I can deny you,' she whispered. 'Nothing.'

*   *   *

A week later Tara telephoned Centaine at Rhodes Hill and was surprised by the clarity of the connection. She spoke to each of the children in turn. Sean was monosyllabic and seemed relieved to surrender the telephone to Garry, who was solemn and pedantic, in his first year at business school. It was like talking to a little old man, and Garry's single topic of original news was the fact that his father had at last allowed him to start work part-time, as an office boy at Courtney Mining and Finance. 'Pater is paying me two

301

pounds ten shillings a day,' he announced proudly. 'And soon I am to have my own office with my name on the door.'

When his turn came to speak to her, Michael read her a poem of his own, about the sea and the gulls. It was really very good, so her enthusiasm was genuine. 'I love you so much,' he whispered. 'Please come home soon.'

Isabella was petulant. 'What present are you going to bring me?' she demanded. 'Daddy bought me a gold locket with a real diamond —' and Tara was guiltily relieved when her daughter passed the telephone back to Centaine.

'Don't worry about Bella,' Centaine soothed her. 'We've had a little confrontation and mademoiselle's feathers are a wee bit ruffled.'

'I want to buy a coming-home present for Shasa,' Tara told her. 'I have found the most gorgeous medieval altar that has been converted into a chest. I thought it would be just perfect for his cabinet office at the House. Won't you measure the length of the wall on the right of his desk, under the Pierneef paintings – I want to be certain it will fit in there.'

Centaine sounded a little puzzled. It was unusual for Tara to show any interest in antique furniture. 'Of course, I will measure it for you,' she agreed dubiously. 'But remember Shasa has very conservative tastes – I wouldn't choose anything too – ah —' she hesitated delicately, not wanting to denigrate her daughter-in-law's taste, 'too obvious or flamboyant.'

'I'll phone you tomorrow evening.' Tara did not acknowledge the advice. 'You can read me the measurements then.'

Two days later Moses accompanied her when she returned to the antique dealer in Kensington High Street. Together they made meticulous measurements of both the exterior and interior of the altar. It was truly a splendid piece of work. The lid was inlaid with mosaic of semi-precious stones while effigies of the apostles guarded the four corners. They were carved in ivory and rare woods and decorated with gold leaf. The panels depicted scenes of Christ's agony, from the scourging to the crucifixion. Only after careful examination did Moses nod with satisfaction.

'Yes, it will do very well.' Tara gave the dealer a bank draft for six thousand pounds.

'Price is Shasa's yardstick of artistic value,' she explained to Moses while they waited for his friends to come and collect the piece. 'At six thousand pounds he won't be able to refuse to have it in his office.'

The dealer was reluctant to hand the chest over to the three young black men who arrived in an old van in response to Moses' summons.

'It is a very fragile piece of craftsmanship,' he protested. 'I would feel a lot happier if you entrusted the packing and shipping to a firm of experts. I can recommend —'

'Please don't worry,' Tara reassured him. 'I accept full responsibility from now on.'

'It's such a beautiful thing,' the dealer said. 'I would simply curl up and die if it were even scratched.' He wrung his hands piteously as they carried it out and loaded it into the back of the van. A week later Tara flew back to Cape Town.

The day after the crate cleared Customs in Cape Town docks, Tara held a small, but select, surprise party in Shasa's cabinet office to present him with her gift. The prime minister was unable to attend, but three cabinet ministers came and with Blaine and Centaine and a dozen others crowded into Shasa's suite to drink Bollinger champagne and admire the gift.

Tara had removed the rosewood Georgian sofa table that had previously stood against the panelled wall, and replaced it with the chest. Shasa had some idea of what was in store. Centaine had dropped a discreet hint, and of course the charge had appeared on his latest statement from Lloyds Bank.

'Six thousand pounds!' Shasa had been appalled. 'That's the price of a new Rolls.' What on earth was the damned woman thinking of? It was ridiculous buying him extravagant gifts for which he paid himself; knowing Tara's tastes, he dreaded his first view of it.

It was covered by a Venetian lace cloth when Shasa entered his office, and he eyed it apprehensively as Tara said a few pretty words about how much she owed him, what a fine and generous husband and what a good father he was to her children.

Ceremoniously Tara lifted the lace cloth off the chest and there was an involuntary gasp of admiration from everyone in the room. The ivory figurines had mellowed to a soft buttery yellow and the gold leaf had the royal patina of age upon it. They crowded closer to examine it, and Shasa felt his unreasonable antipathy towards the gift cool swiftly. He would never have guessed that Tara could show such taste. Instead of the garish monstrosity he had expected, this was a truly great work of art, and if his instinct was correct, which it almost always was, it was also a first-class investment.

'I do hope you like it?' Tara asked him with unusual timidity.

'It's magnificent,' he told her heartily.

'You don't think it should be under the window?'

'I like it very well just where you put it,' he answered her, and then dropped his voice so nobody else could overhear. 'Sometimes you surprise me, my dear. I'm truly very touched by your thoughtfulness.'

'You too were kind and thoughtful to let me go to London,' she replied.

'I could skip the meeting this afternoon and get home early this evening,' he suggested, glancing down at her bosom.

'Oh, I wouldn't want you to do that,' she answered quickly, surprised by her own physical revulsion at the idea. 'I am certain to be exhausted by this afternoon. It's such a strain —'

'So our bargain still stands – to the letter?' he asked.

'I think that it is wiser that way,' she told him. 'Don't you?'

* * *

Moses flew from London directly to Delhi, and had a series of friendly meetings with Indira Gandhi, the president of the Indian Congress Party. She gave Moses the warmest encouragement and promises of help and recognition.

At Bombay he went on board a Liberian-registered tramp steamer with a Polish captain. Moses signed on as a deckhand for the voyage to Lourenço Marques in Portuguese Mozambique. The tramp called in at Victoria in the Seychelles Islands to discharge a cargo of rice and then sailed direct for Africa.

In the harbour of Lourenço Marques Moses said goodbye to the jovial Polish skipper and slipped ashore in the company of five members of the crew who were bound for the notorious red-light area of the seaport. His contact was waiting for him in a dingy night club. The man was a senior member of the underground freedom organization which was just beginning its armed struggle against Portuguese colonial rule.

They ate the huge juicy Mozambique prawns for which the club was famous, and drank the tart green wine of Portugal while they discussed the advancement of the struggle and promised each other the support and assistance of comrades.

When they had eaten, the agent nodded to one of the bar girls and she came to the table and after a few minutes of arch conversation took Moses' hand and led him through the rear door of the bar to her room at the end of the yard.

The agent joined them there after a few minutes and while the girl kept watch at the door, to warn them of a surprise raid by the colonial police, the man handed Moses the travel documents he had prepared for him, a small bundle of second-hand clothing, and sufficient escudos to see him across the border and as far as the Witwatersrand gold-mines.

The next afternoon Moses joined a group of a hundred or more labourers at the railway station. Mozambique was an important

304

source of labour for the gold-mines, and the wages earned by her citizens made a large contribution to the economy. Authentically dressed and in possession of genuine papers, Moses was indistinguishable from any other in the shuffling line of workers and he went aboard the third-class railway coach without even a glance from the uninterested white Portuguese official.

They left the coast in the late afternoon, climbed out of the muggy tropical heat and entered the hilly forests of the lowveld to approach the border post of Komatipoort early the following morning. As the coach rumbled slowly over the low iron bridge, it seemed to Moses that they were crossing not a river but a great ocean. He was filled with a strange blend of dismay and joy, of dread and anticipation. He was coming home – and yet home was a prison for him and his people.

It was strange to hear Afrikaans spoken again, guttural and harsh, but made even more ugly to Moses' ear because it was the language of oppression. The officials here were not the indolent and slovenly Portuguese. Dauntingly brisk and efficient, they examined his papers with sharp eyes, and questioned him brusquely in that hated language. However, Moses had already masked himself in the protective veneer of the African. His face was expressionless and his eyes blank, just a black face among millions of black faces, and they passed him through.

Swart Hendrick did not recognize him when he slouched into the general dealer's store in Drake's Farm township. He was dressed in ill-fitting hand-me-downs and wore an old golfing cap pulled down over his eyes. Only when he straightened up to his full height and lifted the cap did Swart Hendrick start and exclaim in amazement, then seized his arm and, casting nervous glances over his shoulder, hustled his brother through into the little cubicle at the back of the store that he used as an office.

'They are watching this place,' he whispered agitatedly 'Is your head full of fever, that you walk in here in plain daylight?' Only when they were safely in the locked office and he had recovered from the shock, did he embrace Moses. 'A part of my heart has been missing, but is now restored.'

He shouted over the rhino board partition wall of his office, 'Raleigh, come here immediately, boy!' and his son came to peer in astonishment at his famous uncle and then kneel before him, lift one of Moses's feet and place it on his own head in the obeisance to a great chief. Smiling, Moses lifted him to his feet and embraced him, questioned him about his schooling and his studies and then let him respond to Swart Hendrick's order.

'Go to your mother. Tell her to prepare food. A whole chicken

305

and plenty of maize meal porridge, and a gallon of strong tea with plenty of sugar. Your uncle is hungry.'

They stayed locked in Swart Hendrick's office until late that night, for there was much to discuss. Swart Hendrick made a full report of all their business enterprises, the state of the secret mineworkers' union, the organization of their Buffaloes, and then gave him all the news of their family and close friends.

When at last they left the office, and crossed to Swart Hendrick's house, he took Moses' arm and led him to the small bedroom which was always ready for his visits, and as he opened the door, Victoria rose from the low bed on which she had been sitting patiently. She came to him and, as the child had done, prostrated herself in front of him and placed his foot upon her head.

'You are my sun,' she whispered. 'Since you went away I have been in darkness.'

'I sent one of the Buffaloes to fetch her from the hospital,' Swart Hendrick explained.

'You did the right thing.' Moses stooped and lifted the Zulu girl to her feet, and she hung her head shyly.

'We will talk again in the morning.' Swart Hendrick closed the door quietly and Moses placed his forefinger under Vicky's chin and lifted it so he could look at her face.

She was even more beautiful than he remembered, an African madonna with a face like a dark moon. For a moment he thought of the woman he had left in London, and his senses cringed as he compared her humid white flesh, soft as putty, to this girl's glossy hide, firm and cool as polished onyx. His nostrils flared to her spicy African musk, so different from the other woman's thin sour odour which she tried to disguise with flowery perfumes. When Vicky looked up at him and smiled, the whites of her eyes and her perfect teeth were luminous and ivory bright in her lovely dark face.

When they had purged their first passion, they lay under the thick kaross of hyrax skins and talked the rest of the night away.

He listened to her boast of her exploits in his absence. She had marched to Pretoria with the other women to deliver a petition to the new minister of Bantu affairs, who had replaced Dr Verwoerd when he had become prime minister.

The march had never reached the Union Buildings. The police had intercepted it, and arrested the organizers. She had spent three days and nights in prison, and she related her humiliations with such humour, giggling as she repeated the *Alice in Wonderland* exchanges between the magistrate and herself, that Moses chuckled with her. In the end, the charges of attending an unlawful assembly and incitement to public violence had been dropped, and Vicky

306

and the other women had been released.

'But I am a battle-trained warrior now,' she laughed. 'I have bloodied my spear, like the Zulus of old King Chaka.'

'I am proud of you,' he told her. 'But the true battle is only just beginning —' and he told her a small part of what lay ahead for all of them, and in the yellow flickering light of the lantern, she watched his face avidly and her eyes shone.

Before they at last drifted off into sleep, the false dawn was framing the single small window, and Vicky murmured with her lips against his naked chest,

'How long will you stay this time, my lord?'

'Not as long as I wish I could.'

He stayed on three more days at Drake's Farm, and Vicky was with him every night.

Many visitors came when they heard that Moses Gama had returned and most of them were the fierce younger men of *Umkhonto we Sizwe*, the Spear of the Nation, the warriors eager for action.

Some of the older men of the Congress who came to talk with Moses left disturbed by what they had heard and even Swart Hendrick was worried. His brother had changed. He could not readily tell in what way he had changed, but the difference was there. Moses was more impatient and restless. The mundane details of business, and the day-to-day running of the Buffaloes and the trade union committees no longer seemed to hold his attention.

'It is as though he has fastened his eyes upon a distant hilltop, and cannot see anything in between. He speaks only of strange men in distant lands and what do they think or say that concerns us here?' he grumbled to the twins' mother, his only real confidante. 'He is scornful of the money we have made and saved, and says that after the revolution money will have no value. That everything will belong to the people —' Swart Hendrick broke off to think for a moment of his stores and his shebeens, the bakeries and herds of cattle in the reservations which belonged to him, the money in the post office savings book and in the white man's bank, and the cash that he kept hidden in many secret places – some of it even buried under the floor upon which he now sat and drank the good beer brewed by his favourite wife. 'I am not sure that I wish all things to belong to the people,' he muttered thoughtfully. 'The people are cattle, lazy and stupid, what have they done to deserve the things for which I have worked so long and hard?'

'Perhaps it is a fever. Perhaps your great brother has a worm in his bowel,' his favourite wife suggested. 'I will make a *muti* for him that will clear his guts and his skull.' Swart Hendrick shook his head sadly. He was not at all certain that even one of his wife's devastating laxatives would drive the dark schemes from his brother's head.

Of course, long ago he had talked and dreamed strange and wild things with his brother. Moses had been young and that was the way of young men, but now the frosts of wisdom were upon Hendrick's head, and his belly was round and full, and he had many sons and herds of cattle. He had not truly thought about it before, but he was a man contented. True he was not free – but then he was not sure what free really meant. He loved and feared his brother very much, but he was not sure that he wanted to risk all he had for a word of uncertain meaning.

'We must burn down and destroy the whole monstrous system,' his brother said, but it occurred to Swart Hendrick that in the burning down might be included his stores and bakeries.

'We must goad the land, we must make it wild and ungovernable, like a great stallion, so that the oppressor is hurled to earth from its back,' his brother said, but Hendrick had an uncomfortable image of himself and his cosy existence taking that same painful toss.

'The rage of the people is a beautiful and sacred thing, we must let it run free,' Moses said, and Hendrick thought of the people running freely through his well-stocked premises. He had also witnessed the rage of the people in Durban during the Zulu rioting, and the very first concern of every man had been to provide himself with a new suit of clothing and a radio from the looted Indian stores.

'The police are the enemies of the people, they too will perish in the flames,' Moses said, and Hendrick remembered that when the faction fighting between the Zulus and the Xhosas had swept through Drake's Farm the previous November, it was the police who had separated them and prevented many more than forty dead. They had also saved his stores from being looted in the uproar. Now Hendrick wondered just who would prevent them killing each other after the police had been burned, and just what day-to-day existence would be like in the townships when each man made his own laws.

However, Swart Hendrick was ashamed of his treacherous relief when three days later Moses left Drake's Farm, and moved to the house at Rivonia. Indeed it was Swart Hendrick who had gently pointed out to his brother the danger of remaining when almost everybody in the township knew he had returned, and all day long there was a crowd of idlers in the street hoping for a glimpse of Moses Gama, the beloved leader. It was only a matter of time before the police heard about it through their informers.

*   *   *

The young warriors of *Umkhonto we Sizwe* willingly acted as Moses' scouts in the weeks that followed. They arranged the meetings, the

308

small clandestine gatherings of the most fierce and bloody-minded amongst their own ranks. After Moses had spoken to them, the smouldering resentments which they felt towards the conservative and pacific leadership of the Congress was ready to burst into open rebellion.

Moses sought out and talked with some of the older members of Congress who, despite their age, were radical and impatient. He met secretly with the cell leaders of his own Buffaloes without the knowledge of Hendrick Tabaka for he had sensed the change in his brother, the cooling of his political passions which had never boiled at the same white heat as Moses' own. For the first time in all the years he no longer trusted him entirely. Like an axe too long in use, Hendrick had lost the keen bright edge, and Moses knew that he must find another sharper weapon to replace him.

'The young ones must carry the battle forward,' he told Vicky Dinizulu. 'Raleigh, and yes, you also, Vicky. The struggle is passing into your hands.'

At each meeting he listened as long as he spoke, picking up the subtle shifts in the balance of power which had taken place in the years that he had been in foreign lands. It was only then that he realized how much ground he had lost, how far he had fallen behind Mandela in the councils of the African National Congress and the imagination of the people.

'It was a serious error on my part to go underground and leave the country,' he mused. 'If only I had stayed to take my place in the dock beside Mandela and the others —'

'The risk was too great,' Vicky made excuse for him. 'If there had been another judgement – if any of the Boer judges other than Rumpff had tried them, they might have gone to the gallows and if you had gone with them the cause would have died upon the rope with all of you. You cannot die, my husband, for without you we are children without a father.'

Moses growled angrily. 'And yet, Mandela stood in the dock and made it a showcase for his own personality. Millions who had never heard his name before, saw his face daily in their newspapers and his words became part of the language.' Moses shook his head. 'Simple words: *Amandla* and *Ngawethu*, he said, and everyone in the land listened.'

'They know your name also, and your words, my lord.'

Moses glared at her. 'I do not want you to try to placate me, woman. We both know that while they were in prison during the trial – and I was in exile – they formally handed over the leadership to Mandela. Even old Luthuli gave his blessing, and since his acquittal Mandela has embarked on a new initiative. I know that he

309

has been travelling around the country, in fifty different disguises, consolidating that leadership. I must confront him, and wrest the leadership back from him very soon, or it will be too late and I will be forgotten and left behind.'

'What will you do, my lord? How will you unseat him? He is riding high now – what can we do?'

'Mandela has a weakness – he is too soft, too placatory towards the Boers. I must exploit that weakness.' He said it quietly, but there was such a fierce light in his eyes that Victoria shivered involuntarily, and then with an effort closed her mind against the dark images his words had conjured up.

'He is my husband,' she told herself, fervently. 'He is my lord, and whatever he says or does is the truth and the right.'

*   *   *

The confrontation took place in the kitchen at Puck's Hill. Outside the sky was pregnant with leaden thunder clouds, dark as bruises that cast an unnatural gloom across the room and Marcus Archer switched on the electric lights that hung above the long table in their pseudo-antique brass fittings.

The thunder crashed like artillery and rolled heavily back and forth through the heavens. Outside the lightning flared in brilliant crackling white light and the rain poured from the eaves in a rippling silver curtain across the windows. They raised their voices against tumultuous nature so they were shouting at each other. They were the high command of *Umkhonto we Sizwe*, twelve men in all, all of them black except Joe Cicero and Marcus Archer – but only two of them counted, Moses Gama and Nelson Mandela. All the others were silent, relegated to the role of observers, while these two, like dominant black-maned lions, battled for the leadership of the pride.

'If I accept what you propose,' Nelson Mandela was standing, leaning forward with clenched fists on the table top, 'we will forfeit the sympathy of the world.'

'You have already accepted the principle of armed revolt that I have urged upon you all these years.' Moses leaned back in the wooden kitchen chair, balancing on its two back legs with his arms folded across his chest. 'You have resisted my call to battle, and instead you have wasted our strength in feeble demonstrations of defiance which the Boers crush down contemptuously.'

'Our campaigns have united the people,' Mandela cried. He had grown a short dark beard since Moses had last seen him. It gave him the air of a true revolutionary, and Moses admitted to himself that

310

Mandela was a fine-looking man, tall and strong and brimming with confidence, a formidable adversary.

'They have also given you a good look at the inside of the white man's gaol,' Moses told him contemptuously. 'The time for those childish games has passed. It is time to strike ferociously at the enemy's heart.'

'You know we have agreed.' Mandela was still standing. 'You know we have reluctantly agreed to the use of force —'

Now Moses leapt to his feet so violently that his chair was flung crashing against the wall behind him.

'Reluctantly!' He leaned across the table until his eyes were inches from Mandela's dark eyes. 'Yes, you are as reluctant as an old woman and timid as a virgin. What kind of violence is this you propose – dynamiting a few telegraph poles, blowing up a telephone exchange?' Moses's tone was withering with scorn. 'Next you will blow up a public shit house and expect the Boers to come cringing to you for terms. You are naïve, my friend, your eyes are full of stars and your head full of sunny dreams. These are hard men you are taking on and there is only one way you will get their attention. Make them bleed and rub their noses in the blood.'

'We will attack only inanimate targets,' Mandela said. 'There will be no taking of human life. We are not murderers.'

'We are warriors.' Moses dropped his voice, but that did not reduce its power. His words seemed to shimmer in the gloomy room. 'We are fighting for the freedom of our people. We cannot afford the scruples with which you seek to shackle us.'

The younger men at the foot of the table stirred with a restless eagerness, and Joe Cicero smiled slightly, but his eyes were fathomless and his smile was thin and cruel.

'Our violent acts should be symbolic,' Mandela tried to explain, but Moses rode over him.

'Symbols! We have no patience with symbolic acts. In Kenya the warriors of Mau Mau took the little children of the white settlers and held them up by their feet and chopped between their legs with razor-sharp pangas and threw the pieces into the pit toilets, and that is bringing the white men to the conference table. That is the type of symbol the white men understand.'

'We will never sink to such barbarism,' Nelson Mandela said firmly, and Moses leaned even closer to him, and their eyes locked. As they stared at each other, Moses was thinking swiftly. He had forced his opponent to make a stand, to commit himself irrevocably in front of the militants on the high command. Word of his refusal to engage in unlimited warfare would be swiftly passed to the Youth Leaguers and the young hawks, to the Buffaloes and the others who

311

made up the foundation of Moses' personal support.

He would not push Mandela further now, that could only lose Moses some of his gains. He would not give Mandela the opportunity to explain that he might be willing to use harder measures in the future. He had made Mandela appear a pacifist in the eyes of the militants, and in contrast had shown them his own fierce heart.

He drew back disdainfully from Nelson Mandela and he gave a soft scornful chuckle, as he glanced at the young men at the end of the table and shook his head as though he had given up on a dull and stubborn child.

Then he sat down, crossed his arms over his chest and let his chin sink forward on his chest. He took no further part in the conference, remaining a massive brooding presence, by his very silence mocking Mandela's proposals for limited acts of sabotage on government property.

He had given them fine words, but Moses Gama knew that they would need deeds before they all accepted him as the true leader.

'I will give them a deed – such a deed that will leave not a doubt in their hearts,' he thought, and his expression was grim and determined.

*　　*　　*

The motorcycle was a gift from his father. It was a huge Harley Davidson with a seat like a cowboy saddle and the gear shift was on the side of the silver tank. Sean was not quite sure why Shasa had given it to him. His final results at Costello's Academy didn't merit such paternal generosity. Perhaps Shasa was relieved that he had managed to scrape through at all, and on the other hand perhaps he felt that encouragement was what Sean needed now, or again it might merely be an expression of Shasa's guilt feelings towards his eldest son. Sean didn't care to consider it too closely. It was a magnificent machine, all chrome and enamel and red glass diamond reflectors, flamboyant enough to catch the eye of any young lady and Sean had wound it up to well over the ton on the straight stretch of road beyond the airport.

Now, however, the engine was burbling softly between his knees, and as they reached the crest of the hill he switched off the headlight and then as gravity took the heavy machine, he cut the engine. They free-wheeled down silently in darkness, and there were no street lights in this elegant suburb. The plots of land around each grand home were the size of small farms.

Near the foot of the hill Sean swung the Harley Davidson off the road. They bumped through a shallow ditch into a clump of trees. They climbed off and Sean pulled the motorcycle up on to its kick stand.

'Okay?' he asked his companion. Rufus was not one of Sean's friends whom he could invite back to Weltevreden to meet the folks. Sean had only met him through their mutual love for motorcycles. He was smaller than Sean by at least four inches, and at first glance appeared to be a skinny runt of a lad with a grey complexion as though road grime and sump oil had soaked into his skin. He had nervously shy mannerisms, hanging his head and avoiding eye contact. It had taken some time for Sean to realize that Rufus's lean body was sinewy hard, that he was as quick and agile as a whippet, and that his whining voice and shifty eyes hid a sharp street-wise intelligence and a caustic and irreverent wit. It had not taken long after that for him to be promoted to the rank of principal lieutenant in Sean's gang.

Since graduating without particular distinction from Costello's Academy, his father had insisted that Sean enter articles with the object of one day becoming a member of the Institute of Chartered Accountants. The auditors of the Courtney Mining and Finance, Messrs Rifkin and Markovitch, had been prevailed upon, not without some misgivings on their part, to accept Sean as an articled clerk. This employment was not as dreary as Sean had at first imagined. He had no compunction in using the family name and his boundless charm to work himself into the plummiest audits, preferably of those companies which employed a large female staff, and none of the senior partners had courage enough to report to Shasa Courtney that his favourite son was on a free ride. The Courtney account was worth almost a quarter of a million pounds annually.

Sean was never more than an hour late for work in the morning, his hangover or his lack of sleep hidden by gold-framed aviator's glasses and his brilliant smile. A little judicious rest during the morning and some light banter with the typists and female clerks would set him up for a lunch at the Mount Nelson or Kelvin Grove which ended just in time for a swift return to the office to hand in an imaginative report to the senior partner, after which he was free for a game of squash or an hour's polo practice at Weltevreden.

He usually took dinner at home, it was cheaper than eating out, and although Shasa added substantially to the miserly salary paid by Messrs Rifkin and Markovitch, Sean was always in a financial crisis. After dinner he was free to shed his dinner jacket and black tie and change into a leather cycling jacket and steel-shod boots and then his other life beckoned, the life so different from his diurnal existence, a life of excitement and danger, full of colourful fascinating beings,

313

of eager women and satisfying companions, of deliberate risks and wild adventures – like the one this evening.

Rufus unzipped his black leather jacket and grinned at him. 'Ready, willing and able, as the actress said to the bishop.' Under the jacket he wore a black roll-neck sweater, black trousers and on his head a black cloth cap.

They didn't have to discuss what they were about to do. They had worked together on the same kind of job four times already, and all the planning had been gone over in detail. However, Rufus's grin was pale and tense in the starlight beneath the trees. This was their most ambitious project yet. Sean felt the delicious blend of fear and excitement like raw spirit in his blood tingling and charging him.

This was what he did it for, this feeling, this indescribable euphoria with which danger always charged him. This was just the first tickle of it, it would grow stronger, more possessing, as the danger increased. He often wondered just how high he could go, there must be a zenith beyond which it was not possible to rise, but unlike the sexual climax which was intense but so fleeting, Sean knew he had not even approached the ultimate thrill of danger. He wondered what it would be like, killing a man with his bare hands? Killing a woman the same way – but doing it as she reached her own climax beneath him? The very idea of that always gave him an aching erection, but until those opportunities presented themselves, he would savour the lesser moments such as these.

'Nail?' Rufus asked, offering him his cigarette tin, but Sean shook his head. He wanted nothing to blunt his enjoyment, not nicotine nor alcohol, he wanted to experience the utmost enjoyment of every instant.

'Smoke half of it and then follow me,' he ordered, and slipped away amongst the trees.

He followed the footpath along the low bank of the stream and then crossed at a shallow place, stepping lightly over the exposed rocks. The high diamond-mesh security fence was on the opposite bank, and he squatted below it. He didn't have to wait long. Within seconds a wolflike shape appeared out of the darkness beyond the fence, and the moment it saw him the German shepherd rushed at him, hurling itself against the heavy-gauge wire fence.

'Hey, Prince,' Sean said quietly, leaning toward the animal, showing not the least sign of fear. 'Come on, boy, you know me.'

The dog recognized him at last. It had only barked once, not creating enough of an uproar to alert the household, and now Sean gently pushed his fingers through the diamond mesh, talking softly and soothingly. The dog sniffed his hand and its long tail began to wave back and forth in friendly salutation. Sean had a way with all living creatures, not only humans. The dog licked his fingers.

Sean whistled softly and Rufus scrambled up the bank behind him. Immediately the German shepherd stiffened and the hair on its back came erect. It growled throatily and Sean whispered, 'Don't be a fool, Prince. Rufus is a friend.'

It took another five minutes for Sean to introduce the two of them, but at last in response to Sean's urging, Rufus gingerly put his fingers through the mesh and the dog sniffed them carefully and wagged his tail.

'I'll go over first,' Sean said, and swarmed up the high fence. There were three strands of barbed wire at the top, but Sean flicked his body over, feet first, arching his back like a gymnast. He dropped lightly to earth and the dog rose on its hind legs and placed its front paws on his chest. Sean fondled his head holding him while Rufus came over the barbed wire with even greater agility than Sean had.

'Let's go,' Sean whispered, and with the guard dog padding along beside them they went up towards the house, crouching as they ran and keeping to the shadow of the ornamental shrubs until they flattened against the wall, shrinking into the leafy ivy that covered the brickwork.

The house was a double-storied mansion, almost as imposing as Weltevreden. It belonged to another leading Cape family, close friends of the Courtneys. Mark Weston had been at school with Shasa and in the same engineering class at university. His wife, Marjorie, was a contemporary of Tara Courtney's. They had two teenage daughters, the elder of which Sean had deprived of her virginity the previous year, and then dropped without another phone call.

The seventeen-year-old child had suffered a nervous breakdown, refusing to eat, threatening suicide and weeping endlessly until she had to be taken out of school. Marjorie Weston had sent for Sean to try to remonstrate with him, and persuade him to let her daughter down gently. She had arranged the meeting without her daughter's knowledge, and while her husband was on one of his regular business trips to Johannesburg.

She took Sean to her sewing room on the ground floor and locked the door. It was Thursday afternoon, the servants' day off, and her younger daughter was at school while the eldest, Veronica, was in her bedroom upstairs palely pining.

Marjorie patted the sofa. 'Please come and sit next to me, Sean.' She was determined to keep the interview friendly. It was only when he was beside her that Marjorie realized how infernally goodlooking he was. Even more so than his father, and Marjorie had always had a strong fancy for Shasa Courtney.

She found that she was becoming a little breathless as she reasoned

315

with Sean, but it was only when she placed her hand on his bare arm and felt the elastic muscle under the smooth young skin that she realized what was happening.

Sean had the philanderer's sure and certain instinct, perhaps he had inherited it from his father. He hadn't really thought about Veronica's mother that way. God! She was as old as his mother. However, since Clare East he had always had a taste for older women, and Marjorie Weston was slim and athletic from swimming and tennis and meticulously tanned to disguise the crow's feet at the corners of her eyes and the first signs of crêping at her throat; and where Veronica was vacuous and simpering, her mother was poised and mature, but with the same mauve-blue eyes that had first attracted him to the daughter and an even more carefully groomed mane of thick tawny hair.

As Sean became aware of her excitement, the flush of blood beneath her tan, the agitated breathing that made her bosom beneath the angora jersey and pearls work like a bellows and the subtle change in her body odour that the average male would not have noticed, but which to Sean was like an invitation on an embossed card, he found his own arousal was spiced by the perversity of the situation.

'A double,' he thought. 'Mother and daughter – now that's something different.'

He didn't have to plot further, he let his infallible instinct guide him.

'You are much more attractive than your daughters could ever be – the main reason I broke off with Ronny was I couldn't bear being near you without being able to do this —' and he leaned over her and kissed her with an open mouth.

Marjorie had believed herself to be in complete control of the situation right up until the moment she tasted his mouth. Neither of them spoke again until he was kneeling in front of her, holding her knees apart with both hands, and she was sprawled across the sofa with her pleated skirt rucked up around her waist. Then she panted brokenly, 'Oh Christ, I can't believe this is happening – I must be crazy.'

Now she sat at the foot of the stairs in her satin bathrobe. She was naked under the robe and every few seconds she shivered in a brief spasm. The night was warm, and the house was in darkness. The girls were asleep upstairs and Mark was away on one of his regular business trips. This was the first chance at an assignation there had been in almost two weeks and she was shivering with anticipation. She had switched off the burglar alarms at nine o'clock as they had arranged – Sean was almost half an hour late. Perhaps something

316

had happened and he wasn't coming after all. She hugged herself and shivered miserably at the thought, then she heard the light tap on the glass of the french windows leading on to the swimming-pool patio, and she leapt to her feet and raced across the darkened room. She found she was panting as she fumbled with the latch.

Sean stepped into the room and seized her. He was so tall and powerful that she turned to putty in his arms. No man had ever kissed her like this, so masterfully and yet so skilfully. She sometimes wondered who had taught him and then was consumed by jealousy at the thought. Her need of him was so intense that waves of giddy vertigo washed over her and without his arms to support her she was certain she would have sagged to the floor. Then he tugged at the knot that secured the belt of her robe. It came undone and he thrust his hand into the opening. She shifted her weight, setting her feet wider apart so he could reach her more easily, and she gave a stifled gasp as she felt him slip his forefinger into her and she pushed hard against his hand.

'Lovely,' Sean chuckled in her ear. 'Like the Zambezi river in flood.'

'Shh,' she whispered. 'You'll wake the girls.' Marjorie liked to think of herself as genteel and refined, yet his crude words increased her excitement to a fever. 'Lock the door,' she ordered him, her voice thick and shaking. 'Let's go upstairs.'

He released her and turned to the door. He pressed it closed until the catch snapped and then turned the key and in the same instant reversed the movement, leaving it unlocked.

'All right.' He turned back to Marjorie. 'All set.'

They kissed again, and she ran her hands frantically down the front of his body, feeling the throbbing hardness through the thin cloth. It was she who broke away at last.

'Oh God, I can't wait any longer.' She took his hand and dragged him up the marble staircase. The girls' bedrooms were in the east wing and Marjorie locked the heavy mahogany door that secured the master suite. They were safe from discovery here, and at last she could let herself go completely.

Marjorie Weston had been married for over twenty years, and she had taken about the same number of lovers in that time. Some of them had merely been mad one-night frolics, others had been longer more permanent liaisons. One had lasted for almost all these twenty years, an erratic on-and-off arrangement, passionate interludes interspersed with long periods of denial. However, none of her other lovers had been able to match this stripling in beauty and performance, in physical endurance and in devilish inventiveness, not even Shasa Courtney who was that other long-term lover. The son had

317

the same intuitive understanding of her needs. He knew when to be rough and cruel and when to be loving and gentle, but in other ways he outstripped his father. She had never been able to exhaust him or even to force him to falter, and he had a streak of genuine brutality and inherent evil in him that could terrify her at times. Added to that was the almost incestuous delight of taking the son after having had the father.

Tonight Sean did not disappoint her. While she was driving hard towards her first climax of the evening he suddenly reached out to the bedside table and lifted the telephone receiver.

'Ring your husband,' he ordered, and thrust the instrument into her hand.

'God, are you mad!' she gasped. 'What would I say to him?'

'Do it!' he said, and she realized that if she refused, he would slap her across the face. He had done that before.

Still holding him between her thighs, she twisted awkwardly and dialled the Carlton Hotel in Johannesburg. When the hotel operator answered, she said, 'I wish to speak to Mr Mark Weston in Suite 1750.'

'You are going through,' the operator said, and Mark answered on the third ring.

'Hello darling,' Marjorie said, and above her Sean began to move again. 'I couldn't sleep, so I thought I'd ring you. Sorry if I woke you.'

It became a contest with Sean trying to force her to gasp or cry out, while she attempted to maintain a casual conversation with Mark. When he succeeded and she gave a little involuntary squeal, Mark asked sharply, 'What was that?'

'I made myself a cup of Milo and it was too hot. I burned my lip.'

She could see how it was exciting Sean also. His face was no longer beautiful but swollen and flushed so that his features seemed coarsened, and in her she felt him swell and harden, filling her to bursting point, until she could control herself no longer, and she broke off the telephone conversation abruptly. 'Goodnight, Mark, sleep well,' and slammed the receiver down on its cradle, just as the first scream came bursting up her throat.

Afterwards they lay still, both of them regaining their breath, but when he tried to roll off her she tightened the grip of her legs and held him hard. She knew that if she could keep him from sliding out, within minutes he would be ready again.

Outside on the front lawn, the dog barked once. 'Is someone there?' she asked.

'No Prince is just being naughty,' Sean murmured, but he was listening intently, even though he knew that Rufus was too good to

318

be heard, and they had planned every detail with care. Both he and Rufus knew exactly what they were after.

To commemorate the first month of their affair, Marjorie had bought Sean a set of Victorian dress studs and links in platinum and onyx and diamonds. She had invited him up to the house on a Thursday afternoon and led him through to Mark Weston's panelled study on the ground floor. While Sean watched, she checked the combination of the wall safe which was discreetly engraved on the corner of the silver-framed photograph of herself and the girls on Mark's desk, and then she had swung aside the false front of the section of the bookcase that concealed the safe and tumbled the combination of the lock.

She left the safe door ajar when she brought the gift to him. Sean had demonstrated his gratitude by pulling her skirts up and her peach-coloured satin bloomers down, then sitting her on the edge of her husband's desk, he lifted her knees and placed her feet on each corner of the leather-bound blotter. Then while he stood in front of her and made love to her, he evaluated the contents of the safe over her shoulders.

Sean had heard his father talk about Mark Weston's collection of British and South African gold coins. It was apparently one of the ten most important in private hands anywhere in the world. In addition to the dozen thick leather-bound albums which contained the collection, the middle shelf of the safe held the ledgers and cash books for the running of the estate and household, and a small gentleman's jewel box, while the top shelf was crammed with wads of pristine banknotes still in the bank wrappers and a large canvas bag stencilled 'Standard Bank Ltd' which obviously contained silver. There could not have been less than £5,000 in notes and coins in the safe.

Sean had explained to Rufus exactly where to look for the safe combination, how to open the false front of the bookcase and what to expect when he did.

The knowledge that Rufus was at work downstairs and the danger of possible discovery stimulated Sean so that at one point Marjorie blurted, 'You aren't human – you are a machine.'

He left her at last, lying in the big bed like a wax doll that had melted in the sun, her limbs soft and plastic, the thick mane of her hair darkened and sodden with her own sweat and her mouth smeared out of shape by exhausted passions. Her sleep was catatonic.

Sean was still pent up and excited. He looked into Mark Weston's study on the way out. The front of the bookcase was open, the safe door wide, the ledgers and cash books tumbled untidily on the floor, and the excitement came on him again in a thick musky wave and he found he was once more fully tumescent.

It was dangerous to remain in the house another minute, and the knowledge made his arousal unbearable. He looked up the marble staircase again and only then did the idea come to him. Veronica's room was the second door down the east wing passage. She might scream if he woke her suddenly, she might hate him so that she would scream when she recognized him, but on the other hand she might not. The risk was lunatic, and Sean grinned in the darkness and started back up the marble staircase.

A silver blade of moonlight pierced the curtains and fell on Veronica's pale hair that swirled across the pillow. Sean leaned over her and covered her mouth with his hand. She came awake struggling and terrified.

'It's me,' he whispered. 'Don't be afraid, Ronny. It's me.'

Her struggles stilled, the fear faded from her huge mauve eyes, and she reached up for him with both arms. He lifted his hand off her mouth and she said, 'Oh, Sean, deep down I knew it. I knew you still loved me.'

Rufus was furious. 'I thought you had been caught,' he whined. 'What happened to you, man?'

'I was doing the hard work.' Sean kicked the Harley Davidson and it roared into life. As he turned back on to the road he felt the weight of the saddle bags pull the machine off balance, but he met her easily and straightened up.

'Slow down, man,' Rufus leaned forward from the pillion to caution him. 'You'll wake the whole valley.' And Sean laughed in the wild rush of wind, drunk with excitement, and they went up over the crest at a hundred miles an hour.

Sean parked the Harley Davidson on the Kraaifontein road and they scrambled down the bank and squatted in the dry culvert beneath the road. By the light of an electric torch they shared the booty.

'You said there would be five grand,' Rufus whined accusingly. 'Man, there isn't more than a hundred.'

'Old man Weston must have paid his slaves.' Sean chuckled carelessly as he split the small bundle of bank notes, and pushed the larger pile towards Rufus. 'You need it more than me, kid.'

The jewel box contained cuff-links and studs, a diamond tie-pin that Sean judged to be fully five carats in weight, masonic medallions, Mark Weston's miniature decorations on a bar – he had won an M.C. at El Alamein and a string of campaign medals – a Pathek Philippe dress watch in gold and a handful of other personal items.

Rufus ran over them with an experienced eye. 'The watch is

engraved, all the other stuff is too hot to move, too dangerous, man. We'll have to dump it.'

They opened the coin albums. Five of them were filled with sovereigns. 'Okay,' Rufus grunted. 'I can move that small stuff, but not these. They are red hot, burn your fingers.' With scorn he discarded the albums of heavy coins, the five-pound and five-guinea issues of Victoria and Elizabeth, Charles and the Georges.

After he dropped Rufus off at the illicit shebeen in the coloured District Six where Rufus had parked his own motorcycle, Sean rode out alone along the high winding road that skirts the sheer massif of Chapman's Peak. He parked the Harley on the edge of the cliff. The green Atlantic crashed against the rock five hundred feet below where he stood. One at a time Sean hurled the heavy gold coins out over the edge. He flicked them underhanded, so that they caught the dawn's uncertain light, and then were lost in the shadows of the cliff face as they fell, so he could not see them strike the surface of the water far below. When the last coin was gone, he tossed the empty albums after them and they fluttered as they caught the wind. Then he flung the gold wristwatch and the diamond pin out into the void. He kept the medals for last. It gave him a vindictive satisfaction to have screwed Mark Weston's wife and daughter, and then to throw his medals into the sea.

When he mounted the Harley Davidson and turned it back down the steep winding road, he pushed the goggles up on to his forehead and let the wind beat into his face and rake his eyes so that the tears streamed back across his cheeks. He rode hard, putting the glistening machine over as he went into the turns so that the footrest struck a shower of sparks from the road surface.

'Not much profit for a night's work,' he told himself, and the wind tore the words from his lips. 'But the thrills, oh, the thrills!'

*   *   *

When all his best efforts to interest Sean and Michael in the planetary system of the Courtney companies had resulted in either lukewarm and deviously feigned enthusiasm or in outright disinterest, Shasa had gone through a series of emotions, beginning with puzzlement.

He tried hard to see how anyone, particularly a young man of superior intellect, and even more particularly a son of his, could find the whole complex interlinking of wealth and opportunity, of challenge and reward, less than fascinating. At first he thought that he was to blame, that he had not explained it sufficiently, that he had somehow taken their response for granted and had through his own omissions, failed to quicken their attention.

321

To Shasa it was the very stuff of life itself. His first waking thought each morning and his last before sleep each night, was for the welfare and sustenance of the company. So he tried again, more patiently, more exhaustively. It was like trying to explain colour to a blind man, and from puzzlement Shasa found himself becoming angry.

'Damn it, Mater,' he exploded, when he and Centaine were alone at her favourite place on the hillside above the Atlantic. 'They just don't seem to care.'

'What about Garry?' Centaine asked quietly.

'Oh Garry!' Shasa chuckled disparagingly. 'Every time I turn around I trip over him. He is like a puppy.'

'I see you have given him his own office on the third floor,' Centaine observed mildly.

'The old broom cupboard,' Shasa said. 'It was a joke really, but the little blighter took it seriously. I didn't have the heart —'

'He takes most things seriously, does young Garrick,' Centaine observed. 'He's the only one who does. He's quite a deep one.'

'Oh, come on, Mater! Garry?'

'He and I had a long chat the other day. You should do the same, it might surprise you. Did you know that he's in the top three in his year?'

'Yes, of course, I knew – but I mean, it's only his first year of business administration. One doesn't take that too seriously.'

'Doesn't one?' Centaine asked innocently, and Shasa was unusually silent for the next few minutes.

The following Friday Shasa looked into the cubbyhole at the end of the passage which served as Garry's office when he was temporarily employed by Courtney Mining during his college vacations. Garry leapt dutifully to his feet when he recognized his father and he pushed his spectacles up on the bridge of his nose.

'Hello, champ, what are you up to?' Shasa asked, glancing down at the forms that covered the desk.

'It's a control,' Garry was caught in a cross-fire – awe at his father's sudden interest in what he was doing and desperation to retain his attention and to obtain his approval.

'Did you know that we spent over a hundred pounds on stationery last month alone?' He was so anxious to impress his father that he stuttered again, something he only did when he was overexcited.

'Take a deep breath, champ.' Shasa eased into the tiny room. There was just room for the two of them. 'Speak slowly, and tell me about it.'

One of Garry's official duties was to order and issue the office stationery. The shelves behind his desk were filled with sheaves of

322

typing paper and boxes of envelopes.

'According to my estimates we should be able to cut that below eighty pounds. We could save twenty pounds a month.'

'Show me.' Shasa perched on the corner of the desk and applied his mind to the problem. He treated it with as much respect as if they were discussing the development of a new gold-mine.

'You are quite right,' Shasa approved his figures. 'You have full authority to put your new control system into practice.' Shasa stood up. 'Well done,' he said, and Garry glowed with gratification. Shasa turned to the door so the lad wouldn't see his expression of amusement, and then he paused and looked back.

'Oh, by the way, I'm flying up to Walvis Bay tomorrow. I'm meeting the architects and the engineers on site to discuss the extensions to the canning factory. Would you like to come along?'

Unable to trust his voice lest he stutter again, Garry nodded emphatically.

*   *   *

Shasa allowed Garry to fly. Garry had been granted his private pilot's licence two months previously, but he still needed a few hours for his twin-engine endorsement. A year older than Garry, Sean had been given his licence immediately he was eligible. Sean flew the way he rode and shot, naturally, gracefully, but carelessly. He was one of those pilots who flew by the grace of God and the seat of his pants. In contrast, Garry was painstaking and meticulous and therefore, Shasa admitted grudgingly, the better pilot. Garry filed a flight plan as though he was submitting a thesis for his doctorate, and his pre-flight checks went on so long that Shasa squirmed in the right-hand seat and only just contained himself from crying out, 'For God's sake, Garry, let's get on with it.'

Yet it was a mark of his trust that he allowed Garry to take the controls of the Mosquito at all. Shasa was prepared to take over at the first sign of trouble, but he was amply rewarded for his forbearance when he saw the sparkle of deep pleasure behind Garry's spectacles as he handled the lovely machine, lifting her up through the silver wreaths of cloud into a blue African sky where Shasa could share with him a rare feeling of total accord.

Once they arrived at Walvis Bay Shasa tended to forget that Garry was with him. He had become accustomed to his middle son's close attendance, and though he did not really think of it, it was becoming familiar and comforting to have him there. Garry seemed to anticipate his smallest need, whether it was a light for his cigarette or a piece of scrap paper and pencil on which to illustrate an idea to the

323

architect. Yet Garry was quiet and unobtrusive, not given to inane questions and bumptious or facetious remarks.

The cannery was fast becoming one of the big winners in the Courtney stable of companies. For three seasons they had captured their full quota of pilchards, and then there had been an unusual development. In a private meeting Manfred De La Rey had suggested to Shasa that if the company were to issue a further ten thousand bonus shares in the name of a nominee in Pretoria, the consequences might be very much to everybody's advantage. Taking Manfred on trust, Shasa had issued the shares as suggested, and within two months there had been a review of their quota by the government Department of Land and Fisheries and that quota had been almost doubled to the two hundred thousand tons of pilchard that they were now permitted to capture annually.

'For three hundred years the Afrikaners have been left out of business,' Shasa smiled cynically as he received the glad tidings. 'But they are catching on fast. They are in the race now, and not too fussy about how they win. The Jews and the English had better look to their business laurels, here come the Nats.' And he set about planning and financing the extension to the cannery.

It was late afternoon before Shasa finished with the architects, but at this season there were still a few hours of daylight remaining.

'How about a swim at Pelican Point?' Shasa suggested to Garry, and they took one of the cannery Land-Rovers and drove along the hard wet sand at the edge of the bay. The waters of the bay stank of sulphur and fish offal, but behind it the high golden dunes and arid mountains rose in desolate grandeur, while out over the protected and silken waters the flamingo flocks were such a brilliant pink as to seem improbable and theatrical. Shasa drove fast around the curve of the bay with the wind ruffling their hair.

'So what, if anything, did you learn today?'

'I learned that if you want other people to talk too freely, you keep quiet and look sceptical,' Garry answered, and Shasa glanced at his son with a startled expression. That had always been a deliberate technique of his, but Shasa had never expected anyone so young and inexperienced to see through it. 'Without saying anything, you made the architect admit that he really hasn't worked out a solution to siting the boiler room yet,' Garry went on. 'And even I could see that his present proposal is an expensive compromise.'

'Is that so?' It had taken Shasa a full day of discussion to reach the same conclusion, but he wasn't going to say so. 'What would you do then?'

'I don't know, Pater, not for sure,' Garry said. He had a pedantic manner of delivering an opinion which had at first irritated Shasa,

324

but which now amused him, particularly as the opinions were usually worth listening to. 'But instead of simply sticking on another boiler, I would explore the possibility of installing the new Patterson process —'

'What do you know about the Patterson process?' Shasa demanded sharply. He had only heard about it himself very recently. Suddenly Shasa found himself arguing as though with an equal. Garry had read all the sales pamphlets and memorized the specifications and figures of the process, and had worked out for himself most of the advantages and disadvantages over the conventional method of preparation and canning.

They were still arguing as they rounded the sandy horn of the bay, and beyond the lighthouse the deserted beach, clean and white, stretched away in dwindling perspective to the horizon. Here the Atlantic waters were wild and green, cold and clean, foamy and effervescent with the rush of the surf.

They stripped off their clothes and, naked, swam out into the tumultuous seas, diving deep beneath each curling wave as it came hissing down upon them. At last they emerged, their bodies tinted blue with the cold, but laughing breathlessly with exhilaration.

As they stood beside the Land-Rover and towelled themselves, Shasa studied his son frankly. Even though sodden with salt water, Garry's hair stuck up in disorderly spikes and without his spectacles he had a bemused myopic look. His torso was massively developed, his chest was like a pickle barrel and he had grown such a coat of dark body hair that it almost obscured the ridges of muscle that covered his belly like chain mail.

'Looking at him, there is no way you would ever suspect that he was a Courtney. If I didn't know better, I would think that Tara had a little fling on the side.' Shasa was certain that Tara might be capable of many things, but never infidelity or promiscuity. 'There is nothing about him of his ancestry,' he thought, and then looked further and grinned suddenly.

'Well at least, Garry, you have inherited one of the Courtney gifts. You've got a wanger on you that would make old General Courtney himself turn in his grave with envy.'

Hurriedly Garry covered himself with his towel and reached into the Land-Rover for his underpants, but secretly he was pleased. Up until now he had always regarded that portion of his anatomy with suspicion. It seemed to be an alien creature with a will and existence of its own, determined to embarrass and humiliate him at the most unexpected or inappropriate moments, like that unforgettable occasion when he was standing in front of the commerce class at business school giving his dissertation and the girls in the front row started

325

giggling, or when he was forced to retreat in confusion from the typing-pool at Centaine House because of the alien's sudden but very apparent interest in the surroundings. However, if his father spoke respectfully of it, and the shade of the legendary general approved, then Garry was prepared to reconsider his own relationship with it and come to terms.

They flew on to the H'ani Mine the next morning. All three of the boys had done their stint at the H'ani. As indeed had Shasa so many years before, they had been required to work their way through every part of the mine's operaton, from the drilling and blasting in the deep amphitheatre of the open pit, to the final separation rooms where at last the precious crystals were recovered from the crushed blue ground.

That forced labour had been more than sufficient for both Sean and Michael and neither of them had ever shown the least desire to return to the H'ani Mine again. Garry was the exception, he seemed to have developed the same love for these remote wild hills as both Shasa and Centaine shared. He asked to accompany his father here whenever Shasa's regular inspection tours were scheduled. In a few short years he had built up an expert knowledge of the mine's operation, and had at one time or another personally performed all of the tasks involved in the process of production. So on their last evening at the mine the two of them, Shasa and Garry, stood on the brink of the great pit and while the sun set over the desert behind them, they stared down into its shadowy depths.

'It's strange to think that it all came out of there,' Garry said softly. 'Everything that you and Nana have built up. It makes one feel somehow humble, like when I am in church.' He was silent for a long moment and then went on. 'I love this place. I wish we could stay longer.'

To hear his own feeling echoed like this, moved Shasa deeply. Of his three sons, this was the only one who understood, who seemed capable of sharing with him the almost religious awe that this massive excavation and the wealth it produced evoked in him. This was the fountainhead, and only Garry had recognized it.

He placed his arm around Garry's shoulders and tried to find words, but after a moment he simply said, 'I know how you feel, champ. But we have to get back home. I have to introduce my budget to the House on Monday.' It was not what he had wanted to say, but he sensed that Garry knew that, and as they picked their way down the rough pathway in the dusk, they were closer in spirit than they had ever been.

*　　*　　*

326

The budget for Shasa's ministry of mines and industry had been almost doubled this year, and he knew that the opposition were planning to give it a rough passage. They had never forgiven him for changing parties. So he was on his mettle as he rose to his feet and sought the Speaker's recognition, and then instinctively glanced up at the galleries.

Centaine was in the middle of the front row of the visitors' gallery. She was always there when she knew that either Shasa or Blaine was going to speak. She wore a small flat hat tilted forward over her eyes with a single yellow bird of paradise feather raked back at a jaunty angle, and she smiled and nodded encouragement as their eyes met.

Beside Centaine sat Tara. Now that was unusual. He couldn't remember when last she had come to listen to him.

'Our bargain doesn't include torture by boredom,' she had told him, but there she was looking surprisingly elegant in a dainty straw basher with a trailing pink ribbon around the crown and elbow-length white gloves. She touched the brim in a mocking salute, and Shasa lifted an eyebrow at her and then turned to the press gallery high above the Speaker's throne. The political correspondents from the English-speaking press were all there, pencils poised eagerly. Shasa was one of their favourite prey, but all their attacks seemed only to consolidate his position in the National Party, and by their pettiness and subjectivity point up the efficiency and effectiveness with which he ran his ministry.

He loved the rough and tumble of parliamentary debate, and his single eye sparkled with battle lust as he took up his familiar slouch, both hands in his pockets, and launched into his presentation.

They were at him immediately, yapping and snapping at his heels, interjecting with expressions of disbelief and outrage, calling out 'Shame on you, sir!' and 'Scandal!' and Shasa's grin infuriated them and goaded them to excesses which he brushed aside with casual contempt, holding his own easily and then gradually overwhelming them and turning their own ridicule back upon them, while around him his colleagues grinned with admiration and encouraged his more devastating sallies with cries of '*Hoor, hoor!* – Hear, hear!'

When the division was called, his party backed him solidly, and his budget was approved by the expected majority. It was a performance which had enhanced his stature and standing. He was no longer the junior member of the cabinet and Dr Verwoerd passed him a note.

'I was right to keep you on the team. Well done.'

In the front of the visitors' gallery Centaine caught his eye, and clasped both hands together in a boxer's victory flourish, yet somehow she made the gesture appear at once regal and ladylike. Shasa's smile faded as he realized that beside her Tara's seat was empty, she had left during the debate, and Shasa was surprised by his own feeling of disappointment. He would have liked her to witness his triumph.

The House was moving on to other business which did not concern him and on an impulse Shasa rose and left the chamber. He went up the wide staircase and down the long panelled passageway to his office suite. As he approached the front entrance to the suite, he checked suddenly and again on impulse turned at the corner of the passage and went down to the unobtrusive and unmarked doorway at the end.

This was the back door to his office, a convenient escape route from unwanted visitors which had been ordered by old Cecil John Rhodes himself as a by-pass of the front waiting-room, a means for special visitors to reach him and leave again unobserved. Shasa found it equally convenient. The prime minister used it occasionally, as did Manfred De La Rey, but the majority of other users were female, and their business with Shasa was seldom political.

Instead of rattling the key in the Yale lock, Shasa slipped it in silently and turned it gently, then pushed the door open sharply. On the inside the door was artfully blended into the panelling of his office and few people knew of its existence.

Tara was standing with her back towards him, bending over the altar chest. She did not know the door existed. Except for the gift of the chest, she had taken little interest in the decoration and furbishment of his office. It was a few seconds before she sensed that she was not alone, and then her reaction was extravagant. She jumped back from the chest and whirled to face him, and as she recognized Shasa, instead of showing relief, she paled with agitation and began to explain breathlessly.

'I was just looking at it – it's such a magnificent piece of work. Quite beautiful, I had forgotten how beautiful —'

One thing Shasa realized immediately, she was as guilty as if she had been caught red-handed in some dreadful crime, but he could not imagine what had made her react that way. She was quite entitled to be in his office, she had her own key to the front door, and she had given him the chest – she could admire it whenever she chose.

He remained silent and fastened his eye upon her accusingly, hoping to trick her into over-explaining, but she left the chest and moved across to the window behind his desk.

'You were doing very well on the floor,' she said. She was still a little breathless, but her colour had returned and she was recovering her composure. 'You always put on such a good show.'

'Is that why you left?' he asked, as he closed the door and pointedly crossed the room to the chest.

'Oh you know how useless I am with figures, you quite lost me towards the end.'

Shasa studied the chest carefully. 'What was she up to?' he asked himself thoughtfully, but he could not see that anything was altered. The Van Wouw bronze sculpture of the Bushman was still in its place, so she could not have opened the lid.

'It's a marvellous piece,' he said, and stroked the effigy of St Luke at the corner.

'I had no idea there was a door in the panel.' Clearly Tara was trying to distract his attention from the chest, and her efforts merely piqued his curiosity. 'You gave me quite a turn.' Shasa refused to be led and ran his fingers over the inlaid lid.

'I should get Dr Findlay from the National Gallery to have a look at it,' Shasa mused. 'He's an expert on medieval and Renaissance religious art.'

'Oh, I promised Tricia I would let her know when you arrived.' Tara sounded almost desperate. 'She's got an important message for you.' She crossed quickly to the interleading door and opened it. 'Tricia, Mr Courtney's here now.' Shasa's secretary popped her head into the inner office.

'Do you know a Colonel Louis Nel?' she asked. 'He's been trying to get hold of you all morning.'

'Nel?' Shasa was still studying the chest. 'Nel? No, I don't think so.'

'He says he knows you, sir. He says you worked together during the war.'

'Oh, good Lord, yes!' She had Shasa's full attention now. 'It was so long ago – but, yes, I know him well. He wasn't a colonel then.'

'He's head of CID for the Cape of Good Hope now,' Tricia told him. 'And he wants you to telephone him as soon as you can. He says it's very urgent, he actually said "life and death".'

'Life and death, hey,' Shasa grinned. 'That probably means he wants to borrow money. Get him on the blower, please Trish.'

He went to his desk, sat down and pulled the telephone towards him. He motioned Tara towards the couch, but she shook her head.

'I'm meeting Sally and Jenny for lunch,' and she sidled towards the door with a relieved expression. But he wasn't looking at her, he was staring out of the window over the oaks to the slopes of Signal Hill beyond, and he didn't even glance round as she slipped out of the room and closed the door quietly behind her.

Louis Nel's call had transported Shasa back almost twenty years in time. 'Was it that long ago?' he wondered. 'Yes, it was. My God, how quickly the years have passed.'

329

Shasa had been a young squadron leader, invalided back from the campaign in Abyssinia where he had lost his eye fighting the Duke of Aosta's army on the drive up to Addis Ababa. At a loose end, certain that his life was ruined and that he was a cripple and a burden on his family and friends, Shasa had gone into seclusion and started drinking heavily and letting himself slip into careless despondency. It had been Blaine Malcomess who had sought him out and given him a scornful and painful tongue-lashing, and then offered him a job helping track down and break up the *Ossewa Brandwag*, the Sentinels of the Wagon Train, a secret society of militant nationalist Afrikaners who were virulently opposed to Field-Marshal Jan Christian Smuts' pro-British war efforts.

Shasa had worked in co-operation with Louis Nel, establishing the identity of the leading members of the pro-Nazi conspiracy and preparing the warrants for their arrest and internment. His investigations of the *Ossewa Brandwag*'s activities had put him in contact with a mysterious informer, a woman who had contacted him only by telephone and who took every precaution to conceal her identity. To this day Shasa did not know who she had been, or indeed if she were still alive.

This informer had revealed to him the *OB* theft of weapons from the government arms and munitions factory in Pretoria, and enabled them to deal a major blow to the subversive organization. Then the same informer had warned Shasa of the White Sword conspiracy. This was an audacious plot to assassinate Field-Marshal Smuts, and in the ensuing confusion to seize control of the armed forces, declare South Africa a republic, and throw in their lot with Adolf Hitler and the Axis powers.

Shasa had been able to foil the plot at the very last minute, but only by the most desperate efforts, and at the cost of his own grandfather's life. Sir Garrick Courtney had been shot by the assassin in mistaken identity, for the old man had physically resembled his good and dear friend, Field-Marshal Smuts.

Shasa had not thought about those dangerous days for many years. Now every detail came back vividly. He lived it all again as he waited for the telephone on his desk to ring; the reckless climb up the sheer side of Table Mountain as he tried to catch his grandfather and the Field-Marshal before they could reach the summit where the killer was waiting for them. He recalled his dreadful sense of helplessness as the rifle shot crashed and echoed against the rocky cliffs and he realized he was too late, the horror of finding his grandfather lying in the track with the ghastly bullet wound which had blown his chest open, and the old Field-Marshal kneeling beside him stricken with grief.

Shasa had chased the killer, using his intimate knowledge of the mountain to cut off his retreat against the top of the cliff. They fought chest to chest, fought for their very lives. White Sword had used his superior strength to break away and escape, but not before Shasa had put a bullet from his 6.5 mm Beretta into his chest. White Sword disappeared and the plot to overthrow Smuts' government collapsed, but the killer had never been brought to justice, and Shasa felt once again the agony of his grandfather's murder. He had loved the old man and named his second son after him.

The telephone rang at last and Shasa snatched it up.

'Louis?' he asked.

'Shasa!' Shasa recognized his voice immediately. 'It's been a long time.'

'It's good to speak to you.'

'Yes, but I wish I was the bearer of better news. I'm sorry.'

'What is it?' Shasa was immediately serious.

'Not on the telephone – can you come down to Caledon Square as soon as possible?'

'Ten minutes,' Shasa said, and hung up.

The headquarters of the CID were only a short walk from the House of Assembly and he stepped it out briskly. The episode with Tara and the chest was put out of his mind as he tried to imagine what bad news Louis Nel had for him.

The sergeant at the front desk had been alerted and he recognized Shasa immediately.

'The colonel is expecting you, Minister. I'll send someone to show you up to his office,' and he beckoned one of the uniformed constables.

Louis Nel was in his shirt-sleeves and he came to the door to welcome Shasa and lead him to one of the easy chairs.

'How about a drink?'

'Still too early for me.' Shasa shook his head, but he accepted the cigarette Louis offered him.

The policeman was lean as ever, but he had lost most of his hair and what remained was ice white. There were dark pouches beneath his eyes and after his welcoming smile his mouth settled back into a thin nervous line. He looked like a man who worried a lot, worked too hard and slept badly at night. He must be past retirement age, Shasa thought.

'How's the family – your wife?' Shasa asked. He had met her only once or twice and could not remember her name or what she looked like.

'We were divorced five years ago.'

'I'm sorry,' Shasa said, and Louis shrugged.

331

'It was bad at the time.' Then he leaned forward. 'Your family – you have three boys and a girl. That's right?'

'Ah! You have been doing a police number on me,' Shasa smiled, but Louis did not respond. His expression remained serious as he went on.

'Your eldest son – his name is Sean. That's right, isn't it?'

Shasa nodded, he was no longer smiling either, and he was seized by a sudden presentiment.

'You want to speak to me about Sean?' he asked softly.

Louis stood up abruptly and crossed to the window. He was looking down into the street as he answered.

'This is off the record, Shasa. Not the way we usually do things, but there are extraordinary factors here. Our past association, your present rank —' He turned back from the window. 'In the usual circumstances this would probably not have been brought to my notice at all, at least not at this stage of the investigation.'

The word 'investigation' startled Shasa, and he wanted Louis to give him the bad news and get it over with but he controlled his agitation and impatience and waited quietly.

'For some time now we have been troubled by a series of house-breakings in the better-class suburbs – you have surely read about them. The press are calling the thief the "Cape Raffles".'

'Of course,' Shasa nodded. 'Some of my friends, good friends, have been the victims – the Simpsons, the Westons. Mark Weston lost his collection of gold coins.'

'And Mrs Simpson lost her emeralds,' Louis Nel agreed. 'Some of those emeralds, the earrings, were recovered when we raided a fence in District Six. We were acting on a tip-off and we recovered an enormous quantity of stolen articles. We arrested the fence – he's a coloured chap who was running an electrical business in the front of his premises and receiving stolen goods through the back door. We have had him locked up for two weeks now, and he is beginning to co-operate. He gave us a list of names, and on it was one lovable little rogue named Rufus Constantine, ever heard of him?'

Shasa shook his head. 'How does this link up with my son?'

'I'm coming to that. This Constantine was apparently the one who passed the emeralds and some of the other booty. We picked him up and brought him in for questioning. He is a tough little monkey, but we found a way to open him up and make him sing to us. Unfortunately the tune wasn't very pretty.'

'Sean?' Shasa asked, and Louis nodded.

'I'm afraid so. Looks as though he was the leader of an organized gang.'

'It doesn't make sense. Not Sean.'

332

'Your son has built up quite a reputation.'

'He was a little wild at one time,' Shasa admitted, 'but he is settling down to his articles now, working hard. And why would he want to get involved in something like that? I mean, he doesn't need the money.'

'Articled clerks are not paid a great fortune.'

'I give him an allowance,' Shasa shook his head again. 'No, I don't believe it. What would he know about house-breaking?'

'Oh, no – he doesn't do it himself. He sets up the job and Rufus and his henchman do the dirty work.'

'Sets it up – what do you mean by that?'

'As a son of yours he is welcome in any home in the city, that is right, isn't it?'

'I suppose so.' Shasa was cautious.

'According to little Rufus, your son studies each prospective victim's home, decides on what valuables there are and pinpoints where they are kept – strong rooms, hidden drawers, wall safes and that sort of thing. Then he begins an affair with one of the family, the mother or a daughter, and uses his opportunities to let his accomplice into the home while he is entertaining the lady of his choice upstairs.'

Shasa stared at him wordlessly.

'By all accounts it works very well, and in more than one case the theft was not even reported to us – the ladies involved were more concerned with their reputations and their husband's wrath than with the loss of their jewellery.'

'Marge Weston?' Shasa asked. 'She was one of the ladies?'

'According to our information – yes, she was.'

Shasa whispered, 'The little bastard.' He was appalled, and totally convinced. It all fitted too neatly not to be true. Marge and Sean, his son and one of his mistresses, it was just not to be tolerated. 'This time he has gone too far.'

'Yes,' Louis agreed. 'Too far by a mile. Even as a first offender, he will probably get five or six years.'

All Shasa's attention snapped back to him. The shock to Shasa's pride and sense of propriety was such that he had not even begun to consider the legal implications, but now his righteous rage was snuffed out at the suggestion of his eldest son standing in the dock and being sentenced to long-term imprisonment.

'Have you prepared a docket yet?' he asked. 'Is there a warrant out?'

'Not yet.' Louis was speaking as carefully. 'We were only given this information a few hours ago.' He crossed to his desk and picked up the blue interrogation folder.

'What can I do?' Shasa asked quietly. 'Is there anything we can do?'

'I've done all I can,' Louis answered. 'I've done too much already. I could never justify holding up this information, nor could I justify informing you of an investigation in progress. I've already stretched my neck way out, Shasa. We go back a long way, and I'll never forget the work you did on White Sword – that's the only reason I took the chance —' he paused to take a deep breath, and Shasa, sensing there was more to come, remained silent. 'There is nothing else I can do. Nothing else anyone can do *at this level*.' He placed peculiar emphasis on the last three words, and then he added seemingly incongruously, 'I'm retiring next month, there'll be someone else in this office after that.'

'How long do I have?' Shasa asked, and he did not have to elaborate. They understood each other.

'I can sit on this file for another few hours, until five o'clock today, and then the investigation will have to go ahead.'

Shasa stood up. 'You are a good friend.'

'I'll walk you down,' Louis said, and they were alone in the lift before they spoke again. It had taken Shasa that long to master his perturbation.

'I hadn't thought about White Sword for years,' he changed the subject easily. 'Not until today. All that seems so far away and long ago, even though it was my own grandfather.'

'I've never forgotten it,' Louis Nel said softly. 'The man was a murderer. If he had succeeded, if you hadn't prevented it, all of us in this land would be a lot worse off than we are today.'

'I wonder what happened to White Sword – who he was and where he is now? Perhaps he is long dead, perhaps —'

'I don't think so – there is something that makes me doubt it. A few years ago I wanted to go over the White Sword file —'

The lift stopped at the ground floor and Louis broke off. He remained silent as they crossed the lobby and went out into the sunlight. On the front steps of the headquarters building, they faced each other.

'Yes?' Shasa asked. 'The file, the White Sword file?'

'There is no file,' Louis said softly.

'I don't understand.'

'No file,' Louis repeated. 'Not in police records or the Justice Department or the central records. Officially, White Sword never existed.'

Shasa stared at him. 'There must be a file – I mean, we worked on it, you and I. It was this thick —' Shasa held his thumb and forefinger apart. 'It can't have disappeared!'

'You can take my word for it. It has.' Louis held out his hand.

'Five o'clock,' he said gently. 'No later, but I will be in my office all day right up to five, if anyone wanted to telephone me there.'

Shasa took his hand. 'I will never forget this.' He glanced at his wristwatch as he turned away. It was a few minutes before noon, and most fortuitously he had a lunch date with Manfred De La Rey. He headed back up Parliament Lane, and the noon-day gun fired just as he went in through the main doors. Everybody in the main lobby, including the ushers, instinctively checked their watches at the distant clap of cannon shot.

Shasa turned towards the members' dining-room, but he was far too early. Except for the white-uniformed waiters, it was deserted. In the members' bar he ordered a pink gin and waited impatiently, glancing every few seconds at his watch, but his appointment with Manfred was for twelve-thirty and it was no good going to search for him. He could be anywhere in the huge rambling building, so Shasa employed the time in cherishing and fanning his anger.

'The bastard!' he thought. 'I've allowed him to fool me all these years. All the signs were there, but I refused to accept them. He's dirty rotten, right to the core —' and then his indignation went off in a new direction. 'Marge Weston is old enough to be his mother, how many of my other women has he been boffing? Is nothing sacred to the little devil?'

Manfred De La Rey was a few minutes early. He came to the members' bar smiling and nodding and shaking hands, playing the genial politician, so that it took him a few minutes to cross the room. Shasa could barely contain his impatience, but he didn't want anyone to suspect his agitation.

Manfred asked for a beer. Shasa had never seen him take hard spirit, and only after he had taken his first sip did Shasa tell him quietly, 'I'm in trouble – serious trouble.'

Manfred's easy smile never faltered, he was too shrewd to betray his emotions to a room full of adversaries and potential rivals, but his eyes went cold and pale as those of a basilisk.

'Not here,' he said, and led Shasa through to the men's room. They stood shoulder to shoulder at the urinal and Shasa spoke softly but urgently, and when he finished, Manfred stood staring at the white ceramic trough for only a few seconds before he roused himself.

'What is the number?'

Shasa slipped him a card with Louis Nel's telephone number at CID headquarters.

'I'll have to use the security line from my office. Give me fifteen minutes. I will meet you back at the bar.' Manfred zipped his fly closed and strode out of the lavatory.

335

He was back in the members' bar within ten minutes, by which time Shasa was entertaining the four other members of the luncheon party, all of them influential back-benchers. When they finished their drinks, Shasa suggested, 'Shall we go through?' As they moved towards the dining-room Manfred took his upper arm in a firm grip, and leaned close to him, smiling as though conveying a pleasantry.

'I've squashed it, but he is to be out of the country within twenty-four hours, and I don't want him back. Is that a bargain?'

'I am grateful,' Shasa nodded, and his anger at his son was compounded by this obligation that had been forced upon him. It was a debt that he would have to repay, with interest.

Sean's Harley was parked down at the sports hall that Shasa had built as a joint Christmas present for all three boys two years previously. It contained a gymnasium and squash court, half Olympic-size indoor swimming-pool and change rooms. As Shasa approached, he heard the explosive echo of the rubber ball from the courts and he went up to the spectators' gallery.

Sean was playing with one of his cronies. He wore white silk shorts but his chest was bare. There was a white sweat band around his forehead, and white tennis shoes on his feet. His body glistened with sweat and was tanned to a golden brown. He was impossibly beautiful, like a romantic painting of himself, and he moved with the unforced grace of a hunting leopard, driving the tiny black ball against the high white wall with such deceptive power that it resounded like a fusillade of rifle fire as it rebounded. He saw Shasa in the gallery and flashed him a dazzle of even white teeth and green eyes, so that despite his anger, Shasa suffered a sudden pang at the idea of having to part from him.

In the change room Shasa dismissed his playing partner curtly: 'I want to speak to Sean – alone,' and as soon as he was gone he turned on his son. 'The police are on to you,' he said. 'They know all about you.' He waited for a reaction, but he was disappointed.

Sean towelled his face and neck. 'Sorry, Pater, you've lost me there. What is it they know?' He was cool and debonair, and Shasa exploded.

'Don't play your games with me, young man. What they know can put you behind bars for ten years.'

Sean lowered the towel and stood up from the bench. He was serious at last. 'How did they find out?'

'Rufus Constantine.'

'The little prick. I'll break his neck.' He wasn't going to deny it and Shasa's last hope that he was innocent faded.

'I'll break any necks that have to be broken,' Shasa snapped.

336

'So what are we going to do?' Sean asked, and Shasa was taken aback by his casual assumption.

'We?' he asked. 'What makes you think that I'm going to save your thieving hide?'

'Family honour,' Sean was matter-of-fact. 'You'll never let me go to court. The family would be on trial with me – you would never allow that.'

'That was part of your calculations?' Shasa asked, and when Sean shrugged, he added, 'You don't understand the words honour or decency.'

'Words,' Sean replied. 'Just words. I prefer actions.'

'God, I wish I could prove you wrong,' Shasa whispered. He was so furious now that he wanted the satisfaction of physical violence. 'I wish I could let you rot in some filthy cell.' His fists were clenched, and before he thought about it, he shifted into balance for the first blow, and instantly Sean was on guard, his hands stiffening into blades crossed before his chest and his eyes were fierce. Shasa had paid hundreds of pounds for his training by the finest instructors in Africa, and all of them had at last admitted that Sean was a natural fighter and that the pupil in each case outstripped the master. Delighted that Sean had at last found something that could hold his interest, Shasa had, before Sean began his articles, sent him to Japan for three months to study under a master of the martial arts.

Now as he confronted his son, Shasa was suddenly aware of every one of his forty-one years, and that Sean was a man in full physical flower, a trained fighter and an athlete in perfect condition. He realized that Sean could toy with him and humiliate him, he could even read in Sean's expression that he was eager to do so. Shasa stepped back and unclenched his fists.

'Pack your bags,' he said quietly. 'You are leaving and you are not coming back.'

They flew north in the Mosquito, landing only to refuel in Johannesburg and then flying on to Messina on the border with Rhodesia. Shasa had a thirty per cent shareholding in the copper mine at Messina, so when he radioed ahead there was a Ford pick-up waiting for him at the airstrip.

Sean tossed his suitcase in the back of the truck and Shasa took the wheel. Shasa could have flown across the border to Salisbury or Lourenço Marques, but he wanted the break to be clean and definite. Sean crossing a border on foot would be symbolic and salutary. As he drove the last few miles through the dry hot bushveld to the bridge over the Limpopo river, Sean slumped down in the seat beside him, hands in his pockets and one foot up on the dashboard.

'I've been thinking,' he spoke in pleasant conversational tones.

337

'I've been thinking what I should do now, and I have decided to join one of the safari companies in Rhodesia or Kenya or Mozambique. Then when I've finished my apprenticeship, I'll apply for a hunting concession of my own. There is a fortune in it and it must be the best life in the world. Imagine hunting every day!'

Shasa had determined to remain withdrawn and stern, and up until now he had succeeded in speaking barely a word since leaving Cape Town, but at last Sean's total lack of remorse and his cheerfully selfish view of the future forced Shasa to abandon his good intentions.

'From what I hear, you wouldn't last a week without a woman,' he snapped, and Sean smiled.

'Don't worry about me, Pater. There will be bags of jig-jig, that's part of the perks – the clients are old and rich and they bring their daughters or their new young wives with them —'

'My God, Sean, you are completely amoral.'

'May I take that as a compliment, sir?'

'Your plans to apply for your own hunting concession and to run your own safari company – what do you intend using in lieu of money?'

Sean looked puzzled. 'You are one of the richest men in Africa. Just think – free hunting whenever you wanted it, Pater. That would be part of our deal.'

Despite himself, Shasa felt a prickle of temptation. In fact, he had already considered starting a safari operation and his estimates showed that Sean was correct. There was a fortune to be made in marketing the African wilderness and its unique wild life. The only thing that had prevented him doing it before was that he had never found a trustworthy man who understood the special requirements of a safari company to run it for him.

'Damn it —' he broke off that line of thought, 'I've spawned a devil's pup. He could sell a secondhand car to the judge who was passing the death sentence on him.' He felt his anger softened by reluctant admiration, but he spoke grimly. 'You don't seem to understand, Sean. This is the end of the road for you and me.'

As he said it they topped the rise. Ahead of them lay the Limpopo river, but despite Mister Rudyard Kipling, it was neither grey green nor greasy and there was not a single fever tree on either bank. This was the dry season and though the river was half a mile wide, the flow was reduced to a thin trickle down the centre of the bed. The long low concrete bridge stretched northwards crossing the orange-coloured sand and straggly clumps of reeds.

They drove over the bridge in silence and Shasa stopped the pick-up at the barrier. The border post was a small square building with a corrugated-iron roof. Shasa kept the engine of the Ford running. Sean climbed out and lifted his suitcase out of the back of the truck, then crossed in front of the bonnet and came to Shasa's open window.

'No, Dad.' He leaned into the window. 'You and I will never reach the end of the road. I am part of you, and I love you too deeply for that ever to happen. You are the only person or thing I have ever loved.'

Shasa studied his face for any trace of insincerity, and when he found none, he reached up impulsively and embraced him. He had not meant this to happen, had been determined that it would not, but now he found himself reaching into the inside pocket of his jacket and bringing out the thick sheaf of banknotes and letters that he had carried with him, despite his best intentions to turn Sean loose without a penny.

'Here are a couple of pounds to tide you over,' he said, and his voice was gruff. 'And there are three letters of introduction to people in Salisbury who may be able to help you.'

Carelessly Sean stuffed them into his pocket and picked up his suitcase.

'Thanks, Pater. I don't deserve it.'

'No,' Shasa agreed. 'You don't – but don't worry too much about it. There won't be any more. That's it, Sean, finished. The first and only instalment of your inheritance.'

As always Sean's smile was a little miracle. It made Shasa doubt, despite all the evidence, that his son was thoroughly bad.

'I'll write, Pater. You'll see, one day we'll laugh about this – when we are together again.'

Lugging his suitcase Sean passed through the barrier, and after he disappeared into the customs hut, Shasa was left with an unbearable sense of futility. Was this how it ended after all the care and love over all the years?

*   *   *

Shasa was amused by the ease with which Isabella was able to overcome her lisp. Within two weeks of enrolling at Rustenberg Girls' Senior School, she was talking, and looking, like a little lady. Apparently the teachers and her fellow pupils had not been impressed by babytalk.

It was only when she was trying to wheedle her father that she still employed the lisp and the pout. She sat on the arm of his chair now and stroked the silver wings of hair above Shasa's ears.

'I have the most beautiful daddy in the world,' she crooned, and

339

indeed the flashes of silver contrasted with the dense darkness of the rest of his hair and the tanned almost unlined skin of his face to enhance Shasa's looks. 'I have the kindest and most loving daddy in the world.'

'And I have the most scheming little vixen in the world for a daughter,' he said, and she laughed with delight, a sound that made his heart contract, and her breath in his face smelled milky and sweet as a newborn kitten, but he shored up his crumbling defences. 'I have a daughter who is only fourteen years old —'

'Fifteen,' she corrected him.

'Fourteen and a half,' he countered.

'Almost fifteen,' she insisted.

'A daughter under fifteen years of age, who is much too precious to allow out of my house after ten o'clock at night.'

'Oh, my big cuddly growly bear,' she whispered in his ear and hugged him hard, and as she rubbed her soft cheek against his, her breasts pressed against his arm.

Tara's breasts had always been large and shapely, he still found them immensely attractive. Isabella had inherited them from her. Over the last few months Shasa had watched with pride and interest their phenomenal growth, and now they were firm and warm against his arm.

'Are there going to be boys there?' he asked, and she sensed the first crack in his defence.

'Oh, I'm not interested in boys, Papa,' and she shut her eyes tight in case a thunderbolt came crashing down on her for such a fib. These days Isabella could think of little else but boys, they even occupied her dreams, and her interest in their anatomy was so intense that both Michael and Garry had forbidden her to come into their rooms while they were changing. Her candid and fascinated examination was too disconcerting.

'How will you get there and back? You don't expect your mother to wait up until midnight, do you? And I'll be in Jo'burg that night,' Shasa asked and she opened her eyes.

'Stephen can take me and bring me back.'

'Stephen?' Shasa asked sharply.

'Mommy's new chauffeur. He's so nice and awfully trustworthy – Mommy says so.'

Shasa wasn't aware that Tara had taken on a chauffeur. She usually drove herself, but that reprehensible old Packard of hers had finally given up the ghost when she was away at Sundi and he had prevailed on her to accept a new Chevvy station wagon. Presumably the chauffeur went with it. She should have consulted him – but they had drifted further and further apart over the last few years and seldom discussed domestic routine.

340

'No,' he said firmly. 'I won't have you driving around on your own at night.'

'I'll be with Stephen,' she pleaded, but he ignored the protest. He knew nothing about Stephen, except that he was male and black.

'I'll tell you what. If you can get a written guarantee from one of the other girls' parents – somebody I know – that they will get you there and back before midnight – well, then, all right, you may go.'

'Oh Daddy! Daddy!' She showered soft warm kisses on his face, and then leapt up and did a little victory pirouette around his study. She had long willowy legs under the flaring skirt and a tight little bottom in lace panties.

'She is probably,' he thought, and then corrected himself, 'she is without doubt the most beautiful child in the entire world.'

Isabella stopped suddenly, and assumed a woebegone expression.

'Oh, Papa!' she cried in anguish.

'What is it now?' Shasa leaned back in his swivel chair and hid his smile.

'Both Patty and Lenora are going to have new dresses, and I shall look an awful frump.'

'A frump, forsooth! We cannot have that now, can we?' And she rushed to him.

'Does that mean I may have a new dress, Daddy darling?' She wound both arms around his neck again. The sound of a motor car coming up the drive interrupted their idyll.

'Here comes Mommy!' Isabella sprang from his lap and seizing his hand dragged him to the window. 'We can tell her about the party and the dress now, can't we, darling Daddy.'

The new Chevrolet with the high tailfins and great chromed grille pulled up at the front steps, and the new chauffeur stepped out. He was an imposing man, tall and broad-shouldered in a dove-grey livery and cap with patent-leather peak. He opened the rear door, and Tara slipped out of her seat. As she passed him she tapped the chauffeur on the arm, an over-friendly gesture so typical of Tara's treatment of the servants which irritated Shasa as much as usual.

Tara came up the front stairs and disappeared from Shasa's view, while the chauffeur went back into the driver's seat and pulled away towards the garages. As he drove below the windows of the study, he glanced up. His face was half obscured by the peak of his cap, but there was something vaguely familiar about his jawline and the way his head was set on that corded neck and those powerful shoulders.

Shasa frowned, trying to place him, but the memory was an ancient one, or erroneous, and then behind him Isabella was calling in her special honeyed voice.

'Oh Mommy, Daddy and I have something to tell you,' and Shasa turned from the window, steeling himself for Tara's familiar accusation of favouritism and indulgence.

*　　*　　*

The hidden door to Shasa's parliamentary suite of offices provided the key to the problem that they had been working on over the weeks that Moses Gama had been in Cape Town.

It was simple enough for Moses to enter the parliament building itself, dressed in chauffeur's livery and carrying an armful of shopping – shoe boxes and hat boxes from the most expensive stores. He merely followed Tara as she swept past the doormen at the front entrance. There was virtually no security in operation, no register to sign, no lapel badges were necessary. A stranger might be asked to show a visitor's pass at the entrance, but as the wife of a cabinet minister, Tara merited a respectful salute, and she made a point of getting to know the doormen. Sometimes she paused to ask after a sick child, or the janitor's arthritis, and with her sunny personality and her concerned condescension, she was soon a favourite of the uniformed staff who guarded the entrance.

She did not take Moses in with her on every occasion, only when she was certain that there was no risk of meeting Shasa. She brought him often enough to establish his presence and his right to be there. When they reached Shasa's suite, Tara would order him to place the parcels in the inner office while she paused to chat with Shasa's secretary. Then, when Moses emerged from the office empty-handed, she would dismiss him lightly.

'Thank you, Stephen. You may go down now. I will need the car at eleven. Please bring it around to the front and wait for me.'

Then Moses would walk down the main staircase, standing respectfully aside for parliamentary messengers and members and cabinet members, once he even passed the prime minister on the stairs, and he had to drop his gaze in case Verwoerd recognized the hatred in his eyes. It gave him a weird feeling of unreality to pass only arm's length from the man who was the author of his people's misery, who more than any other represented all the forces of injustice and oppression. The man who had elevated racial discrimination to a quasi-religious philosophy.

Moses found he was trembling as he went on down the stairs, but he passed the doormen without a glance and the janitor in his cubicle barely lifted his eyes before concentrating once more on his newspaper. It was vital to Moses' plans that he should be able to leave the building unaccompanied, and constant repetition had made that possible. To the doormen he was almost invisible.

342

However, they had still not solved the problem of access to Shasa's inner office. Moses might go in there long enough to deposit the armful of parcels, but he could not risk remaining longer, and especially he could not be in there behind a closed door, or alone with Tara. Tricia, Shasa's secretary, was alert and observant, and obsessively loyal to Shasa; like all Shasa's female employees she was more than just a little in love with him.

The discovery of the concealed rear door to the suite came as a blessing when they were almost desperately considering leaving the final preparation to Tara alone.

'Heavens, it was so simple, after all our worrying!' Tara laughed with relief, and the next time Shasa left for his inspection tour of the H'ani Mine, taking Garry with him as usual, she and Moses made one of their visits to parliament to test their arrangement.

After Moses had left her parcels in the inner office and in front of Tricia, Tara sent him away. 'I won't need the car until much later, Stephen, I'm having lunch with my father in the dining-room.'

Then as he left, closing the outer door behind him, Tara turned back to Tricia.

'I have a few letters to write. I'll use my husband's office. Please see that I'm not disturbed.'

Tricia looked dubious, she knew that Shasa was fussy about his desk and the contents of his drawers, but she could not think of any way to prevent Tara making use of it, and while she hesitated, Tara marched into Shasa's office, closed the door and firmly locked it behind her. Another precedent had been set.

On the outside there was a light tap, and it took her a moment to discover the inside lock, disguised as a light switch. She opened the panelled door a crack, Moses slipped through it into the office. She held her breath against the snap of the lock, and then turned eagerly to Moses.

'Both doors are locked,' she whispered, and she embraced him. 'Oh Moses, Moses – it's been so long.'

Even though they spent so much time in each other's company, the moments of total privacy were rare and precious and she clung to him.

'Not now,' he whispered. 'There is work to do.'

Reluctantly she opened her embrace and let him go. He went to the window first, standing to one side as he drew the drapes so that he could not be seen from outside, and then he switched on the desk lamp and removed his uniform jacket, hanging it on the back of Shasa's chair, before crossing to the altar chest. He paused before it, putting Tara in mind of a worshipper, for his head was bowed and his hands clasped before him reverently. Then he roused himself and

343

lifted the heavy bronze Van Wouw sculpture from the top of the chest. He carried it across the room and placed it on Shasa's desk. He went back and carefully opened the lid, wincing as the antique hinges squeaked.

The interior of the chest had been half-filled with the overflow from Shasa's bookshelves. Piles of old copies of *Hansard*, out-of-date white papers and old parliamentary reports. Moses was annoyed at this unexpected obstacle.

'You must help me,' he whispered to Tara, and between them they began to unpack the chest.

'Keep everything in the same order,' Moses warned, as he passed the piles of publications to her. 'We will have to leave it exactly as it was.'

The chest was so deep that at the end Moses found it easier to climb into it and pass the last of the contents out to her. The carpet was covered with stacks of paper now, but the chest was empty.

'Let me have the tools,' Moses ordered. They were in one of the packets that Moses had carried up from the car, and she handed them to him.

'Don't make any noise,' she pleaded.

The chest was large enough to conceal him completely. She went to the door and listened for a moment. Tricia's typewriter was tapping away reassuringly. Then she went back to the chest and peered into it.

Moses was on his knees working on the floor of the chest with a screwdriver. The screws were authentically antique, taken from another old piece of furniture so that they were not obvious recent additions, and the floor panels of the chest were likewise aged oak and only close examination by an expert would have revealed that they were not original. Once the screws were loose, Moses lifted out the panels to reveal the compartment beneath. This was tightly packed with cotton waste and gently Moses worked it loose, and as he removed the top layer placed it in the package that had contained the tools.

Tara watched with awful fascination as the contents of the first secret compartment came into view. They were small rectangular blocks of some dark amorphous material, like sticky toffee or carpenter's putty, each covered with a translucent greaseproof wrapper and with a label marked in Russian Cyrillic script.

There were ten blocks in the top layer, but Tara knew that there must be two layers below that. Thirty blocks in all, each block weighed two pounds, which made a total of sixty pounds of plastic explosive. It looked mundane and harmless as some kitchen commodity, but Moses had warned her of its lethal power.

'A two-pound brick will destroy the span of a steel bridge, ten pounds would knock down the average house, sixty pounds —' he shrugged. 'It's enough to do the job ten times over.'

Once he had removed the packing and reassured himself of the contents, Moses replaced the panel and screwed it closed. Then he opened the centre panel of the floor. Again it was packed with cotton waste. As he removed it, he explained in a whisper, 'There are four different types of detonators to cover all possible needs. These,' he gingerly lifted a small flat tin the size of a cigarette pack out of its nest of cotton packing, 'these are electrical detonators that can be wired up to a series of batteries or to the mains. These,' he returned the tin to its slot and lifted the loose cotton to reveal a second larger tin, 'these are radio receiver detonators and are set off by a VHF transmission from this miniature transmitter.' It looked to Tara like one of the modern portable radios. Moses lifted it out of its nest. 'It needs only six torch batteries to activate it. Now these are simple acid time-fused detonators, primitive, and the time delay isn't very accurate, but this here is a trembler detonator. Once it is primed, the slightest movement or vibration will set it off. Only an expert will be able to defuse the charge once it is in place.'

Until this moment she had considered only the abstract dialectic of what they were doing, but now she was faced with the actuality. Here before her was the very stuff of violent death and destruction, the innocent appearance no less menacing than the coils of a sleeping mamba, and she found herself wavering.

'Moses,' she whispered. 'Nobody will be hurt. No human life, you said that – didn't you?'

'We have discussed that already.' His expression was cold and scornful, and she felt ashamed.

'Forgive me, please.'

Moses ignored her and unscrewed the third and last panel. This compartment contained an automatic pistol and four clips of ammunition. It took up little space and the rest of the compartment was packed with cotton waste which Moses removed.

'Give me the other packet,' he ordered, and when she passed it to him, he began to pack the contents into the empty recess. Firstly there was a compact tool kit which contained a keyhole saw and hand drill, drill bits and augers, a box of hearing-aid batteries for the detonator and torch batteries for the transmitter, a Penlite torch, a five-hundred-foot roll of thin electrical wire, diamond glass-cutters, putty, staples and tiny one-ounce tins of touch-up paint. Lastly there was a pack of hard rations, dried biscuit and cans of meat and vegetables.

'I wish you had let me give you something more appetizing.'

345

'It will be only two days,' Moses said, and she was reminded how little store he set by creature comforts.

Moses replaced the panel, but he did not tighten the retaining screws fully, so that they could be loosened by hand.

'All right, pass the books to me now.' He repacked the chest, replacing the bundles in the same order as he had found them, so that to a casual glance it would not be apparent that the contents of the chest had been disturbed. Carefully Moses closed the chest and replaced the bronze statue on the lid. Then he stood in front of the desk and surveyed the room carefully.

'I will need a place to hide.'

'The drapes,' Tara suggested, and he nodded.

'Not very original, but effective.' The curtains were embroidered brocade, cut full, and they reached to the floor.

'A key to that door – I'll need one.' He indicated the hidden door in the panelling.

'I will try —' Tara began and then broke off as there was a knock on the interleading door. For a moment he thought she might panic and he squeezed her arm to calm her.

'Who is it?' Tara called in a level voice.

'It's me, Mrs Courtney,' Tricia called respectfully. 'It's one o'clock and I'm going to take my lunch.'

'Go ahead, Tricia. I'll be a little longer, but I'll lock up when I leave.'

They heard the outer door close, and then Moses released her arm. 'Go out and search her desk. See if she has a key to the back door.'

Tara was back within minutes with a small bunch of keys. She tried them in the lock and the third one turned the door in the panelling.

'The serial number is on it.' She scribbled a note of the number on Shasa's noteblock and ripped off the top sheet. 'I'll return the keys to Tricia's desk.'

When she came back, Moses was buttoning his uniform jacket, but she locked the door behind her.

'What I need now is a plan of the building. There must be one in the public works department, and you must get me a copy. Tell Tricia to do it.'

'How?' she asked. 'What excuse can I give?'

'Tell her that you want to change the lighting in here,' he gestured at the chandelier in the roof. 'Tell her you must have an electrical plan of this section, showing the circuits and wall-fittings.'

'Yes, I can do that,' she agreed.

'Good. We are finished here for the time being. We can go now.'

'There is no hurry, Moses. Tricia will not be back for another hour.'

He looked down at her, and for a moment she thought she saw a flash of contempt, even disgust, in those dark brooding eyes, but she would not let herself believe that, and she pressed herself to him, hiding her face against his chest. Within seconds she felt the swelling and hardening of his loins through the cloth that separated their lower bodies, and her doubts were dispelled. She was certain that in his own strange African way he loved her still and she reached down to open his clothing and bring him out.

He was so thick that she could barely encompass him within the circle of her thumb and forefinger, and he was hot and hard as a shaft of black ironstone that had lain in the full glare of the sun at midday.

Tara sank down onto the thick silken rug, drawing him down on top of her.

*　　*　　*

Every day now increased the danger of discovery and both of them were aware of it.

'Will Shasa recognize you?' Tara asked Moses more than once. 'It is becoming more and more difficult to keep you from meeting him face to face. He asked about my new chauffeur a few days ago.'

Isabella had apparently drawn Shasa's attention to the new employee for her own selfish reasons, and Tara could cheerfully have thrashed her for it. But there had been the danger of establishing the importance of her new driver even more clearly in the child's devious mind, so she had let it pass without comment.

'Will he know you?' she insisted, and Moses considered it carefully.

'It was long ago, before the war. He was a child.' Moses shook his head. 'The circumstances were so different, the place so remote – and yet for a short while we were close. I believe we made a deep impression upon each other – if merely because of the unlikelihood of such a relationship, black man and white boy becoming familiar, developing an intimate friendship.' He sighed. 'It is certain, however, that at the time of the trial he must have read the intelligence reports and known of the warrant for my arrest which, by the way, is still in force. Whether he would connect the wanted revolutionary criminal with his childhood friend, I do not know, but we cannot take that chance. We must do what has to be done as soon as possible.'

'It seems that Shasa has been out of town every weekend for the last five years.' Tara bit her lip with frustration. 'But now that I want him gone, he won't leave Weltevreden for a single day. First it's this damned polo business.' The Argentinian polo team was touring the country, and Shasa was hosting their stay in Cape Town, while the polo fields of Weltevreden would be the venue for the first test match of their visit. 'Then immediately after that it will be the British prime minister, Harold Macmillan's visit. Shasa won't be leaving Cape Town before the end of the month at the very earliest.' She watched his face in the driving-mirror as he pondered it.

'There is risk either way,' he said softly. 'To delay is as dangerous as to act hastily. We must choose the exact moment.'

Neither of them spoke again until they reached the bus stop, and Moses parked the Chev on the opposite side of the road. Then he switched off the engine and asked:

'This polo match. When will it take place?'

'The test match is on Friday afternoon.'

'Your husband will be playing?'

'The South African team will be announced in the middle of the week, but Shasa is almost certain to be on the team. He might even be chosen as captain.'

'Even if he is not, he will be the host. He must be there.'

Yes,' Tara agreed.

'Friday – that will give me the whole weekend.' He made up his mind. 'We will do it then.' For a few moments Tara felt the suffocating desperation of somebody trapped in quicksand, sinking slowly, and yet there was an inevitability about it that made fear seem superfluous. There was no escape and she felt instead an enervating sense of acceptance.

'Here is the bus,' Moses said, and she heard the faintest tremor of excitement in his voice. It was one of the very few times that she had ever known his personal feelings to betray him.

As the bus drew up at the halt, she saw the woman and child standing on the platform at the rear. They were both peering eagerly at the parked Chev, and when Tara waved the child hopped down and started across the road. The bus pulled away and Miriam Afrika stayed on the platform at the back of the bus, staring back at them until it turned the next corner.

Benjamin came to meet them, his face bright with anticipation. He was growing into a likely lad, and Miriam always dressed him so well – clean white shirt, grey shorts and polished black shoes. His toffee-coloured skin had a scrubbed look and his crisp dark curls were trimmed into a neat cap.

'Isn't he just too gorgeous?' Tara breathed. 'Our son, Moses, our fine son.'

The boy opened the door and jumped in besides Moses. He looked up at him with a beaming smile and Moses embraced him briefly. Then Tara leaned over the seat and kissed him and gave him a brief but fierce hug. In public she had to limit any show of affection, and as he grew older, their relationship became more difficult and obscure.

The child still believed that Miriam Afrika was his mother, but he was almost six years old now, and a bright intelligent and sensitive boy. She knew that he suspected some special relationship between the three of them. These clandestine meetings were too regular, and emotionally charged, for him not to suspect that something had remained to be fully explained to him.

Benjamin had been told merely that they were good friends of the family, but even at his tender age he would be aware of the social taboos that they were flouting, for his very existence must be permeated by the knowledge that white and black were somehow different and set apart from his own light brown, and sometimes he stared at Tara with a kind of wonder as though she were some fabulous creature from a fairy tale.

There was nothing Tara could think of that could fulfil her more than taking him in her arms and telling him, 'You are my baby, my own true baby, and I love you as much as I love your father.' But she could not even let him sit on the seat beside her in case they were seen together.

They drove out across the Cape Flats towards Somerset West, but before they reached the village, Moses turned off onto a side track, through the dense stands of Port Jackson willow until they came out on to the long deserted curve of beach with the green waters of False Bay before them, and on each side the mountainous ramparts that formed the horns of the wide bay.

Moses parked the Chev and fetched the picnic basket from the boot, and then the three of them followed the footpath along the top of the beach until they reached their favourite spot. From here anyone approaching along the beach would be obvious from half a mile, while inland the exotic growth formed an almost impenetrable jungle. The only persons likely to venture this far along the lonely beach were surf fishermen casting into the tumbling waves for kob and steenbras, or lovers seeking seclusion. Here they felt safe.

Tara helped Benjamin change into his bathing-costume, and then all three of them went hand in hand to the enclosed rock pool where the child splashed and played like a spaniel puppy. When at last he was chilled through and tired, Tara towelled down his shivering body and dressed him again. Then he helped Moses build a fire amongst the dunes and grill the raw sausages and chops upon the coals.

After they had eaten, Benjamin wanted to swim again, but gently Tara forbade him. 'Not on a full stomach, darling.' So he went to

349

search for shells along the tide-mark of the beach, and Tara and Moses sat on the crest of the dune and watched him. Tara was as happy and contented as she could ever remember being until Moses broke the silence.

'This is what we are working for,' he said. 'Dignity and a chance for happiness for all in this land.'

'Yes, Moses,' she whispered.

'It is worth any price.'

'Oh, yes,' she agreed fervently. 'Oh yes!'

'Part of the price is the execution of the architect of our misery,' he said sharply. 'I have kept this from you until now, but Verwoerd must die and all his henchmen with him. Destiny has appointed me his executioner – and his successor.'

Tara paled at his words, but they came as such a shock that she could not speak. Moses took her hand with a strange and unusual gentleness.

'For you, for me and for the child – that he may live with us in the sunshine of freedom.'

She tried to speak, but her voice faltered, and he waited patiently until she was able to enunciate.

'Moses, you promised!'

'No.' He shook his head. 'You persuaded yourself of that, and it was not the time to disillusion you.'

'Oh God, Moses!' The enormity of it crashed in upon her. 'I thought you were going to blow up the empty building as a symbolic gesture, but all along you planned to —' she broke off, unable to complete the sentence, and he did not deny it.

'Moses – my husband Shasa, he will be on the bench beside Verwoerd.'

'Is he your husband?' Moses asked. 'Is he not one of them, one of the enemy?' She lowered her eyes to acknowledge the truth of this, and then suddenly she was agitated again.

'My father – he will be in the House.'

'Your father and your husband are part of your old life. You have left that behind you. Now, Tara, I am both your father and your husband, and the struggle is your new life.'

'Moses, isn't there some way they can be spared?' she pleaded.

He did not speak, but she saw the answer in his eyes and she covered her face with both hands and began to weep. She wept silently, but the spasms of grief shook her whole body. Down on the beach the child's happy cries came to her faintly on the wind, and beside her Moses sat unmoving and without expression. After a while, she lifted her head and wiped the tears from her face with the palms of her hands.

'I'm sorry, Moses,' she whispered. 'I was weak, please forgive me. I was mourning my father, but now I am strong again, and ready to do whatever you require of me.'

* * *

The test match against the visiting Argentinian polo team was the most exciting event that had taken place at Weltevreden in a decade or more.

As mistress of the estate, the planning and organization of the event should have fallen to Tara, but her lack of interest in the sport and her poor organizational skills were too much for Centaine Courtney-Malcomess to abide. She began by giving discreet advice and ended in exasperation by taking all responsibility out of her daughter-in-law's hands. The result was that the occasion was in every respect a towering success. After Centaine had chivvied the coloured greensman, and with Blaine's expert advice, the turf on the field was green and velvety, the going beneath it neither hard enough to jar the legs of the ponies nor soft enough to slow them down. The goalposts were painted in the colours of the teams, the pale blue and white of Argentina, and orange, blue and white of South Africa, and two hundred flags in the same colours flew from the grandstand.

The stand itself was freshly painted, as were the fence pickets and the stables. A fence was erected to keep the general public out of the château's private grounds, but the new facilities designed by Centaine especially for the occasion included an extension to the grandstand, with public toilets below and an open air restaurant that could seat two hundred guests. The extensions to the stables were sufficient for fifty ponies, and there were new quarters for the grooms. The Argentinians had brought their own, and they wore traditional gaucho costume with wide hats and their chaps decorated with silver coins.

Garry tore himself away from his new office at Centaine House which was on the top floor, only three doors down from Shasa, and he spent two days at the stables watching and learning from these masters of horsecraft and the game of polo.

Michael had at last managed to secure an official assignment. He blissfully believed that the *Golden City Mail* in Johannesburg had appointed him their local correspondent on his own merits as a cub-reporter. Centaine, who had made a discreet telephone call to the chairman of Associated Newspapers of South Africa who owned the *Mail*, did nothing to disillusion him. Michael was to be paid five guineas for the day, plus a shilling a word for any copy of his actually printed by the newspaper. He interviewed every member of both

351

teams, including the reserves, all the grooms, the umpire and referees. He drew up a full history and score card of all previous matches played between the two countries going back to the 1936 Olympic Games, and he worked out the pedigrees of all the ponies – but here he showed restraint by limiting the listing to only two generations. Even before the match day he had written enough to make *Gone with the Wind* look like a pamphlet. Then he insisted on telephoning this important copy through to a long-suffering sub at the newspaper offices, and the telephone charges far outstripped his five-guinea salary.

'Anyway, Mickey,' Shasa consoled him, 'if they print everything you have written at a shilling a word, you'll be a millionaire.'

The big disappointment for the family came on the Wednesday when the South African team was announced. Shasa was chosen to play in his usual position at Number Two but he was passed over for the captaincy. This went to Max Theunissen, a flamboyant, hard-riding millionaire farmer from Natal who was a long-time rival of Shasa's, ever since their first meeting on this same field as juniors many years before.

Shasa hid his disappointment behind a rueful grin. 'It means more to Max than it does to me,' he told Blaine, who was one of the selectors, and Blaine nodded.

'Yes,' he agreed. 'That's why we gave it to him, Shasa. Max values it.'

Isabella fell desperately in love with the Argentinian Number Four, a paragon of masculinity with olive skin, dark flashing eyes, thick wavy hair and dazzling white teeth.

She changed her frock three and four times a day, trying out all the most sophisticated of the clothes with which Shasa had filled her wardrobes. She even applied a very light coat of rouge and lipstick, not enough to catch Shasa's attention but just enough, she hoped, to pique José Jesús Goncalves De Santos' interest. She exercised all her ingenuity in waylaying him, hanging around the stables endlessly and practising her most languid poses whenever he hove into view.

The object of her adoration was a man in his early thirties who was convinced that the Argentinian male was the world's greatest lover and that he, José Jesús Goncalves De Santos, was the national champion. There were at least a dozen mature and willing ladies vying for his attention at any one time. He did not even notice the antics of this fourteen-year-old child, but Centaine did.

'You are making an exhibition of yourself, Bella,' she told her. 'From now on you are forbidden to go near the stables, and if I see one speck of make-up on your face again, you may be certain your father will learn about it.'

Nobody went against Nana's orders, not even the boldest and most love-lorn, so Isabella was forced to abandon her fantasy of ambushing José in the hayloft above the stables and presenting him with her virginity. Isabella was not entirely certain what this entailed. Lenora had lent her a forbidden book which referred to it as 'a pearl beyond price'. Whatever it was, José Jesús could have her pearl and anything else he wanted.

However, Nana's strictures reduced her to trailing around after him at a discreet distance, and directing burning but long-range looks at him whenever he glanced in her direction.

Garry intercepted one of these passionate looks and was so alarmed by it that he demanded in a loud voice, and within earshot of her beloved, 'Are you sick, Bella? You keep looking like you are going to throw up.' It was the first time in her life that she truly hated her middle brother.

Centaine had planned for two thousand spectators. Polo was an elite sport with a limited following, and at two pounds each, tickets were expensive, but on the day the gate exceeded five thousand. This guaranteed the club a healthy profit but put a considerable strain on Centaine's logistics. All her reserves, which included Tara, were thrown in to deal with the overflow and to organize the additional food and drink required, and only when the teams rode out on to the field could Tara escape her mother-in-law's all-seeing eye and go up into the stand.

For the first chukka Shasa was riding a bay gelding whose hide was burnished until it shone like a mirror in the sunlight. In his green jersey piped with gold, and his snowy white breeches and glossy black boots, Tara had to admit to herself that Shasa looked magnificent. As he cantered below the stand he looked up and smiled, the black eye-patch gave an intriguing sinister nuance to his otherwise boyish and charming grin, and despite herself Tara responded, waving to him, until she realized that Shasa was not smiling at her but at someone below her in the stand. Feeling a little foolish, she stood on tiptoe and peered down to try and see who it was. The woman was tall with a narrow waist, but her face was obscured by the brim of a garden party hat decorated with roses. However, the arm she lifted to wave at Shasa was slim and tanned with diamond engagement and gold wedding rings on the third finger of her shapely hand.

Tara turned away and removed her hat so that Centaine could not easily pick her out of the crowd, and she worked her way quickly but unobtrusively to the side exit of the stand. As she crossed the carpark and headed around the back of the stables, the first roaring cheer went up from the stand. Nobody would look for her for a couple of hours now, and she began to run. Moses had the Chev parked in the plantation of pines, near the guest cottages and she pulled open the back door and tumbled into the seat.

'Nobody saw me leave,' she panted, and he started the engine and drove sedately down the long driveway and out through the Anreith gateway.

Tara checked her wristwatch; it was a few minutes past three o'clock, but it would take forty minutes to round the mountain and reach the city. They would reach the parliament building at four o'clock when the doormen were thinking about their tea-break. It was a Friday afternoon, and the House was in Committee of Supply, the kind of boring routine business which would leave the members nodding on the benches. In fact, Blaine and Shasa had tactfully arranged this schedule with the whips so that they, and quite a few of their peers, might sneak away to the polo without missing any important debate or division. Many of the other members must have made plans to leave early for the weekend, for the building was quiet and the lobby almost deserted.

Moses parked in the members' carpark and went around to the back of the station wagon to bring out the packages. Then he followed Tara at a respectful distance as she climbed the front staircase. Nobody challenged them, it was all so easy, almost an anti-climax, and they went up to the second floor, past the press gallery entrance, where Tara had a glimpse of three junior reporters slumped dispiritedly on their benches as they listened to the honourable minister of posts and telegraphs droning out his self-congratulations on the exemplary fashion in which he had conducted his department during the previous fiscal year.

Tricia was sitting behind her desk in the outer office painting her fingernails with varnish, and she looked flustered and guilty as Tara walked in.

'Oh, Tricia, that is a pretty colour,' Tara said sweetly, and Tricia tried to look as though her fingers didn't belong to her, but the varnish was wet and she didn't quite know what to do with them.

'I've finished all the letters Mr Courtney left for me,' she tried to excuse herself, 'and it's been so quiet today, and I've got a date tonight – I just thought —' she petered out lamely.

'I've brought up some samples of curtain material,' Tara told her. 'I thought we'd change them when we installed the new light fittings. I would like it to be a surprise for Shasa, so don't mention it to him, if you can avoid it.'

'Of course not, Mrs Courtney.'

'I will be trying to work out the new colour scheme for the curtains, and I'll probably be here until long after five o'clock. If you've

354

finished your work, why don't you go off early? I will take any phone calls.'

'Oh, I'd feel bad about that,' Tricia protested half-heartedly.

'Off you go!' Tara ordered firmly. 'I'll hold the fort. You enjoy your date – I hope you have a lovely evening.'

'It's so kind of you, Mrs Courtney. It really is.'

'Stephen, take those samples through and put them on the couch please,' Tara ordered without looking at Moses, and she lingered while Tricia cleared her desk with alacrity and headed for the door.

'Have a super weekend, Mrs Courtney – and thanks a lot.'

Tara locked the door after her and hurried through to the inner office.

'That was a bit of luck,' she whispered.

'We should give her some time to get clear,' Moses told her, and they sat side by side on the sofa.

Tara looked nervous and unhappy, but she kept silent for many minutes before she blurted out, 'Moses, about my father – and Shasa.'

'Yes?' he asked, but his voice was bleak, and she hesitated, twisting her fingers together nervously.

'Yes?' he insisted.

'No – you are right,' she sighed. 'It has to be done. I must be strong.'

'Yes, you must be strong,' he agreed. 'But now you must go, and leave me to do my work.'

She stood up. 'Kiss me please, Moses,' she whispered, and then after a moment broke from his embrace. 'Good luck,' she said softly.

She locked the outer door of the office and went down the staircase into the main lobby, and half-way down she was suddenly overwhelmed by a sense of doom. It was so strong that she felt the blood drain from her head and an icy sweat broke out on her forehead and upper lip. For a moment she felt dizzy, and had to clutch the banisters to prevent herself from falling. Then she forced herself to go on down and cross the lobby.

The janitor was staring at her strangely. She kept walking. He was leaving his cubicle and coming to intercept her. She felt panic come at her and she wanted to turn and run back up the stairs, to warn Moses that they had been discovered.

'Mrs Courtney.' The janitor stopped in front of her, blocking her path.

'What is it?' she faltered, trying to think up a plausible reply to his demands.

'I've got a small bet on the polo this afternoon, do you know how

355

it's going?' She stared at him, and for a moment it did not make sense. She almost blurted out, 'Polo, what polo?' and then she caught herself and with an enormous effort of will and concentration chatted with the man for almost a minute before she could escape. In the carpark she could no longer control her panic and she ran to the Chev and flung herself behind the wheel sobbing for breath.

*　*　*

When he heard the key turn in the lock of the outer door, Moses went back into Shasa's office and drew the drapes over the windows.

Then he went to the bookshelves and studied the titles. He would not unpack the altar chest until the last moment. Tricia might return for something she had forgotten, there might be a routine check of the offices by the parliamentary staff. Shasa might even come in on the Saturday morning. Although Tara had assured him that Shasa would be fully occupied at Weltevreden with his guests over the whole weekend, Moses would take no chances. He would disturb nothing in the office until it was absolutely necessary.

He smiled as he saw Macaulay's *History of England* on the shelf. It was an expensive leather-bound edition, and it brought back vivid memories of the time when he and the man he was about to kill had been friends – of that time long ago when there had still been hope.

He passed on down the shelves until he reached a section in which Shasa obviously kept all those works with whose principles he differed, works ranging from *Mein Kampf* to Karl Marx with Socialism in between. Moses chose a volume of the collected works of Lenin and took it across to the desk. He settled down to read, confident that any unwanted visitor must give him sufficient time to reach his hiding-place behind the drapes.

He read until the dusk fell and the light failed in the room, then he took the blanket from the package he had brought up from the Chev and settled down on the sofa.

He woke early on Saturday morning, when the rock pigeons began crooning on the ledge outside the window, and let himself out of the panel door. He used the toilets at the end of the passage in the knowledge that it was going to be a long day, and took a cynical pleasure in defying the 'Whites Only' sign on the door.

Although the House did not sit on a Saturday, the main doors were open and there would still be some activity in the building, cleaners and staff, perhaps ministers using their offices. He could do nothing until the Sunday, when Calvinist principles forbade any work or unnecessary activity outside the body of the church. Again he spent the day reading, and at nightfall he ate from the supplies he had brought with him and disposed of the empty cans and wrappers in the rubbish bin in the toilets.

He slept fitfully and was fully awake before dawn on Sunday morning. He ate a frugal breakfast and changed into workman's overalls and tennis shoes from the package before he began a cautious reconnaissance of the House. The building was utterly silent and deserted. Looking down the stairs he saw that the front doors were barred and all the lights were extinguished. He moved about with more confidence, and tried the door to the press gallery. It was unlocked and he stood at the rail and looked down into the chamber where all the laws that had enmeshed and enslaved his people had been enacted and he felt his rage like a captive animal inside his chest, clamouring to be set free.

He left the gallery and went down the staircase into the entrance lobby and approached the high main doors of the chamber. His footsteps echoed from the marble slabs. As he had expected, the doors were locked, but the locks were massive antiques. He knelt in front of them, and from his pocket took the folding wallet of locksmith's picks. His training in Russia had been exhaustively thorough and the lock resisted him for less than a minute. He opened one leaf of the door a crack and slipped through, closing it behind him.

Now he stood in the very cathedral of *apartheid*, and it seemed to him that the evil of it was a palpable thing that pressed in upon him with a physical weight and shortened his breathing. He moved slowly up the aisle towards the Speaker's throne with the massive coat of arms above it, and then he turned to the left, skirting the table on which the mace and despatch boxes would lie, until he stood at the head of the government front benches, at the seat of the prime minister, Dr Hendrik Frensch Verwoerd, and Moses' broad nostrils flared open as though he smelled the odour of the great beast.

With an effort he roused himself, setting aside his feelings and his passions, and became as objective as a workman. He examined the bench carefully, going down on his stomach to peer beneath it. Of course, he had studied every photograph of the chamber that he had been able to obtain, but these had been pathetically inadequate. Now he ran his hands over the green leather; the padding was indented by the weight of the men who had sat upon it, and at this close range it was scuffed and cracked with wear over the years. The bench frame was of massive mahogany, and when he groped up beneath the seat he found the heavy cross members that strengthened it. There were no surprises here, and he grunted with satisfaction.

He returned to Shasa's office, letting himself in through the panel door, and went immediately to unpack the altar chest. Once again he

357

was careful to lay out the contents so that it could be repacked in exactly the same order. Then he climbed into the chest and lifted the floor panels.

The food he set aside for his evening meal, and he piled the blocks of plastic into the blanket. One of the advantages of this explosive was that it was inert and could endure the roughest handling. Without a detonator, it was completely safe.

He picked up the four corners of the blanket and slung it over his shoulder like a tent bag, and then hurriedly went down to the assembly chamber again. He stowed the blanket and its contents under a bench where it would escape casual discovery and went back to the office to fetch the tool kit. The third time he descended to the chamber, he locked the main doors behind him, so as to be able to work in total security.

He could not risk the noise of using an electric drill. He lay on his back beneath the prime minister's bench and began laboriously setting the staples into the mahogany above his face, boring the holes with the hand drill and then screwing in the threaded staples. He worked meticulously, pausing to measure and mark each hole, so it was almost an hour before he was ready to start placing the blocks of plastic. He arranged them in stacks of five, ten pounds of plastic in each stack, and wired them together. Then he wriggled back under the bench and secured each stack of five blocks in place. He threaded each tag end of wire through the loop of a separate staple and twisted them up tightly, then he reached for the next stack of bricks and set that in neatly against the last until the entire underside of the bench was lined with explosive.

Then he crawled out and checked his progress. There was a lip of mahogany below the leather cushion which completely hid the layer of blocks. Even when he squatted down as a person might do to retrieve a pen or fallen order paper from under the bench, he could not see a trace of his handiwork.

'That will do,' he murmured, and started to clean up. Meticulously he brushed up every speck of sawdust from the drilling and the offcuts of wire, then he gathered his tools.

'Now we can test the transmitter,' he told himself and hurried upstairs to Shasa's office.

He inserted the new torch batteries in the transmitter and checked it. The test globe lit up brightly. He switched it off. Next he took the radio detonator from its cardboard box and placed the hearing-aid battery in its compartment. The detonator was the size of a matchbox, made of black bakelite with a small toggle switch at one end. The switch had three positions: 'off', 'test' and 'receive'. A thin twist of wire prevented the switch accidentally being moved to 'on'.

Moses switched it to 'test' and laid it on the sofa, then he went to the transmitter and flipped the 'on' switch. Immediately the tiny globe at one end of the detonator case lit up and there was a loud buzz, like a trapped bee inside the casing. It had received the signal from the transmitter. Moses switched off the transmitter and the buzz ceased and the globe extinguished.

'Now I must check if it will transmit from here to the assembly chamber.'

He left the transmitter on and descended once again to the chamber. Kneeling beside the prime minister's bench, he held the detonator in the palm of his hand and held his breath as he switched it to 'test'.

Nothing happened. He tried it three times more, but it would not receive the signal from the office upstairs. Clearly there was too much brick and reinforced concrete between the two pieces of equipment.

'It was going too easily,' he told himself ruefully. 'There had to be a snag somewhere,' and he sighed as he took the roll of wire from the tool kit. He had wanted to avoid stringing wire from the chamber to the office on the second floor; even though the wire was gossamer thin and the insulating cover was a matt brown, it would infinitely increase the risk of discovery.

'Nothing else for it,' he consoled himself.

He had already studied the electrical wiring plan of the building that Tara had procured from the public works department, but he unrolled it and spread it on the bench beside him to refresh his memory as he worked.

There was a wall plug in the panelling behind the back benches of the government section. From the plan he saw that the conduit was laid behind the panelling and went up the wall into the roof. The diagram also showed the main fuse box in the janitor's office opposite the front door. The office was locked but he picked the lock without difficulty and threw the main switch.

Then he returned to the chamber, located the wall plug and removed the cover, exposing the wiring, and was relieved to find that it was colour-coded. That would make the job a lot easier.

So he left the chamber and went up to the second floor. There was a cleaner's cupboard in the men's toilet that contained a step-ladder. The trap door that gave access to the roof was also in the men's toilet. He found it and set the step-ladder below it. From the top of the ladder he removed the trap door and wriggled up through the square opening.

The space below the roof and the ceiling was dark and smelled of rats. He switched on his Penlite and began to pick his way through the forest of timber joists and roof posts. The dust had been

359

undisturbed for years and rose in a languid cloud around his feet. He sneezed and covered his mouth and nose with a handkerchief as he went forward carefully, stepping from beam to beam, counting each pace to keep himself orientated.

Above the exposed section of wall that was certainly the top of the rear side wall of the chamber, he found the electrical conduits. There were fifteen of them laid side by side. Some had been there a long time, while others were obviously new additions.

It took him a while to isolate the conduit that led down to the chamber below, but when he unscrewed the joint in it, he recognized the coded wiring of the wall-socket that it contained. His relief was intense. He had anticipated a number of problems that he might have encountered at this stage, but now it would be a simple matter to get his own wire into the roof.

He uncoiled the long flexible electrician's spring that he had brought from his tools and fed the end of it into the open conduit tubing until he felt it encounter resistance. Then he began the tedious journey back through the roof, down the step-ladder, along the passage, down the staircase and into the chamber.

He found the end of the electrician's spring protruding from the open wall-socket, and he attached the end of the coil of light detonator wire to it and laid out the rest of the wire so that it would feed smoothly into the conduit when he drew the spring in from the other end.

Back in the roof he recovered the spring and the end of the wire came up with it. Gently he drew in the rest of it, working overhand like a fisherman recovering his handline until it came up firmly against the knot that held the far end to the bench in the chamber below. He coiled the wire neatly and left it, while he returned to the chamber. By this time his overalls were filthy with dust and cob-webs.

He untied the loose end of the wire from the bench and laid it out on the floor, leading it to the pack of plastic explosive under the front bench, making certain he had given himself sufficient slack. Then he worked carefully to conceal the exposed wire from casual detection. He threaded it under the green wall-to-wall carpeting and stapled it securely to the underside of the government benches. He filed a notch in the enamelled metal plate that covered the wall-socket and laid the wire into it while he screwed the cover back into place.

Then he went carefully over the floor and carpet to make certain he had left no trace of his work. Apart from the few inches of un-obtrusive wire protruding from the wall socket, there was nothing to betray his preparations and he sat on Dr Verwoerd's bench to rest for a few minutes before beginning the final phase. He returned upstairs.

The most difficult and frustrating part of the entire job was placing himself in the roof directly above Shasa's office. Three times he had to climb down the ladder into the toilet and then pace out the angles of the passages and the exact location of the office suite before once more climbing back into the ceiling and attempting to follow the same route through the dust and the roof timbers.

Finally he was sure he was in the correct position and gingerly he bored a small hole through the ceiling between his feet. Light came up through the hole, but even when he knelt and placed his eye to the aperture, it was too small to see what lay below. He enlarged it slightly, but he still could see nothing, and yet again he had to make the journey back to the trap door and along the passage to Shasa's office.

Immediately he let himself into the office he saw that he had misjudged. The hole he had bored through the ceiling was directly above the desk, and in enlarging it he had cracked the plaster and dislodged a few fragments which had fallen on to the desk top. He realized that this could be a serious mistake. The hole was not large, but the network of hair cracks around it would be apparent to anyone studying the ceiling.

He thought about trying to cover or repair the damage, but knew that he would only aggravate it. He brushed the white crumbs of plaster off the desk, but this was all he could do. He would have to take comfort in the unlikelihood that anybody would look at the ceiling, and even if they did, that they would think nothing of the minute blemish. Angrily aware of his mistake, he did what he should have done originally and bored the next hole from below, standing on one of the bookshelves to reach the ceiling. Between the window drapes and the edge of the bookshelves, the hole was almost invisible to any but the most painstaking inspection. He went up into the roof and paid the end of the wire down through the second hole. When he returned to the office he found it dangling down the wall, the end of it lying in a tangle on the carpet in the corner.

He gathered and coiled the end and tucked it carefully behind the row of *Encyclopaedia Britannica* on the top shelf and then arranged the window drapes to cover the two or three inches that were visible protruding from the puncture in the ceiling. Once again he cleaned up, going over the shelf and floor for the last speck of plaster, and then, still not satisfied, returning to the desk. Another tiny crumb of white plaster had fallen and he wetted his finger with saliva and picked it up. Then he polished the desk top with his sleeve.

He left the office through the panel door, and went back over

361

everything he had done. He closed the trap door in the roof of the toilet and brushed up the dust that he had dislodged. He replaced the cleaner's ladder in the closet and then returned for the last time to the chamber.

At last he was ready to wire up the detonator. He removed the wire safety device and switched the detonator on. He bored a hole in the soft centre block of explosive and placed the detonator into it. He taped it firmly in place, and then scraped the last inch of insulation from the gleaming copper wire and screwed that into the connector in the end of the black cylindrical detonator and crawled out from under the bench.

He gathered up his tools, made one last thorough check for any tell-tale evidence, and then satisfied at last, he left the chamber, locking the main doors behind him and carefully polishing his sweaty fingerprints from the gleaming brass. Then he let himself into the janitor's office and switched on the current at the mains.

He retreated up the stairs for the last time and locked himself in Shasa's office before he checked his wristwatch. It was almost half past four. It had taken him all day, but he had worked with special care and he was well satisfied as he slumped down on the sofa. The strain on his nerves and the unremitting need for total concentration had been more wearying than any physical endeavour.

He rested awhile before repacking the altar chest. He stuffed his dirty overalls into the empty explosives compartment and placed the transmitter on top of them where he could reach it quickly. It would be a few minutes' work to retrieve it, connect it to the loose wire that was concealed behind the row of encyclopaedia, close the circuit and fire the detonator in the chamber below. He had calculated that Shasa's office was far enough from the centre of the blast, and that there were sufficient walls and cast concrete slabs between to cushion the effects of the explosion and ensure his own survival, but the chamber itself would be totally devastated. A good day's work indeed, and as the light in the room faded, he settled down on the sofa and pulled the blanket up over his shoulders.

At dawn he roused himself and made one last check of the office, glancing ruefully up at the insignificant spider-web of cracks in the ceiling. He gathered up his packages, then he let himself out through the panel door and went to the men's toilet.

He washed and shaved in one of the basins. Tara had provided a razor and hand towel in the packet of food. Then he donned his chauffeur's jacket and cap and locked himself in one of the toilets. He could not wait in Shasa's office for Tricia would come in at nine o'clock, nor could he leave until the House activity was in full swing and he could pass out through the front doors unremarked.

He sat on the toilet seat and waited. At nine o'clock he heard footsteps passing down the passage. Then somebody came in and used the cubicle next to his, grunting and farting noisily. At intervals over the next hour men came in, singly or in groups, to use the basins and urinals. However, in the middle of the morning there was a lull. Moses stood up, gathered his parcels, braced himself, let himself out of the cubicle, and briskly crossed to the door into the passage.

The passageway was empty and he started towards the head of the staircase, and then halfway there he chilled with horror and checked in mid-stride.

Two men came up the stairs, and into the passageway, directly towards Moses. Walking side by side, they were in earnest conversation and the shorter and elder of the two was gesticulating and grimacing with the vehemence of his explanation. The younger taller man beside him was listening intently, and his single eye gleamed with suppressed amusement.

Moses forced himself to walk on to meet them, and his expression fixed into that dumb patient mould with which the African conceals all emotion in the presence of his white master. As they approached each other, Moses stepped respectfully aside to let the two of them pass. He did not look directly at Shasa Courtney's face, but let his eyes slide by without making contact.

As they came level, Shasa burst out laughing at what his companion had told him.

'The silly old ass!' he exclaimed, and he glanced sideways at Moses. His laughter checked and a puzzled frown creased his forehead. Moses thought he was going to stop, but his companion seized his sleeve.

'Wait for the best bit – she wouldn't give him his pants until he —' he led Shasa on towards his own office, and without looking back or quickening his pace, Moses went on down the staircase and out through the front doors.

The Chev was parked in the lot at the top of the lane where he expected it to be. Moses placed his parcels in the back and then went round to the driver's door. As he slid in behind the steering-wheel, Tara leaned forward from the back seat and whispered:

'Oh thank God, I was so worried about you.'

*   *   *

The arrival of Harold Macmillan and his entourage in Cape Town engendered real excitement and anticipation, not only in the mother city but throughout the entire country.

363

The British prime minister was on the final leg of an extensive journey down the length of Africa where he had visited each of the British colonies and members of the Commonwealth on the continent, of which South Africa was the largest and richest and most prosperous.

His arrival meant different things for different sections of the white population. For the English-speaking community it was an affirmation of the close ties and deep commitment that they felt towards the old country. It reinforced the secure sense of being part of the wider body of the Commonwealth, and the certain knowledge that there still existed between their two countries, who had stood solidly beside each other for a century and more through terrible wars and economic crises, a bond of blood and suffering that could never be eroded. It gave them an opportunity to reaffirm their loyal devotion to the queen.

For the Nationalist Afrikaners it meant something entirely different. They had fought two wars against the British crown, and though many Afrikaners had volunteered to fight beside Britain in two other wars – Delville Wood and El Alamein were only part of their battle honours – many others, including most members of the Nationalist cabinet, had vehemently opposed the declarations of war against Kaiser Wilhelm and Adolf Hitler. The Nationalist cabinet included members who had actively fought against the Union of South Africa's war efforts under Jan Smuts, and many now high in government, men like Manfred De La Rey, had been members of the *Ossewa Brandwag*. To these men the British prime minister's visit was an acknowledgement of their sovereign rights and their importance as rulers of the most advanced and prosperous nation on the continent of Africa.

During his stay Harold Macmillan was a guest at Groote Schuur the official residence of the South African prime minister, and the climax of his visit was to be an address to both houses of the legislature of the Union of South Africa, the Senate and the House of Assembly, sitting together. On the evening of his arrival in Cape Town, the British prime minister was to be the guest of honour at a private dinner party to meet the ministers of Dr Verwoerd's cabinet, the leaders of the opposition United Party and other dignitaries.

Tara hated these official functions with a passion, but Shasa was insistent. 'Part of our bargain, my dear. The invitation is specifically for Mr and Mrs, and you promised not to make an ass of me in public.'

In the end she even wore her diamonds, something she had not done in years, and Shasa was appreciative and complimentary.

'You really are a corker when you take the trouble to spruce up 'like that,' he told her, but she was silent and distracted on the drive around the southern slope of Table Mountain to Groote Schuur.

'Something is worrying you,' Shasa said as he steered the Rolls with one hand and lit a cigarette with his gold Ronson lighter.

'No,' she denied quickly. 'Just the prospect of saying the right things to a room full of strangers.'

The true reason for her concern was a long way from that. Three hours previously, while Moses drove her back from a meeting of the executive of the Women's Institute, he had told her quietly, 'The date and the time has been set.' He did not have to elaborate. Since she had picked him up outside the Parliament House just after ten o'clock the previous Monday, Tara had been haunted night and day by her terrible secret knowledge.

'When?' she whispered.

'During the Englishman's speech,' he said simply, and Tara winced. The logic of it was diabolical.

'Both houses sitting together,' Moses went on. 'All of them, all the slave-masters and the Englishman who is their accomplice and their protector. They will die together. It will be an explosion that will be heard in every corner of our world.'

Beside her Shasa snapped the cap of the Ronson and snuffed out the flame. 'It won't be all that unpleasant. I've arranged with protocol that you will be Lord Littleton's dinner partner – you get on rather well with him, don't you?'

'I didn't know he was here,' Tara said vaguely. This conversation seemed so petty and pointless in the face of the holocaust which she knew was coming.

'Special adviser on trade and finance to the British government.' Shasa slowed the Rolls and lowered his side window as he turned into the main gates of Groote Schuur and joined the line of limousines that were moving slowly down the driveway. He showed his invitation to the captain of the guard and received a respectful salute.

'Good evening, Minister. Please go straight on down to the front entrance.'

Groote schuur was high Dutch for 'The Great Barn'. It had once been the home of Cecil John Rhodes, empire builder and adventurer, who had used it as his residence while he was prime minister of the old Cape Colony before the act of Union in 1910 had united the separate provinces into the present Union of South Africa. Rhodes had left the huge house, restored after it was destroyed by fire, to the nation. It was a massive and graceless building, reflecting Rhodes' confessed taste for the barbaric, a mixture of different styles of architecture all of which Tara found offensive.

365

Yet the view from the lower slopes of Table Mountain out over the Cape Flats was spectacular, a field of lights spreading out to the dark silhouette of the mountains that rose against the moon-bright sky. Tonight the bustle and excitement seemed to rejuvenate the ponderous edifice.

Every window blazed with light and the uniformed footmen were meeting the guests as they alighted from their limousines and ushering them up the broad front steps to join the reception line in the entrance lobby. Prime Minister Verwoerd and his wife Betsie were at the head of the line, but Tara was more interested in their guest.

She was surprised by Macmillan's height, almost as tall as Verwoerd, and by the close resemblance he bore to all the cartoons she had seen of him. The tufts of hair above his ears, the horsy teeth and the scrubby moustache. His handshake was firm and dry and his voice as he greeted her was soft and plummy, and then she and Shasa had passed on into the main drawing-room where the other dinner guests were assembling.

There was Lord Littleton coming to her, still wearing the genteelly shabby dinner jacket, the watered silk of the lapels tinged with the verdigris of age, but his smile was alight with genuine pleasure.

'Well, my dear, your presence makes the evening an occasion for me!' He kissed Tara's cheek and then turned to Shasa. 'Must tell you of our recent travels across Africa – fascinating,' and the three of them were chatting animatedly.

Tara's forebodings were for the moment forgotten, as she exclaimed, 'Now, Milord, you cannot hold up the Congo as being typical of emerging Africa. Left to his own devices, Patrice Lumumba would be an example of what a black leader —'

'Lumumba is a rogue, and a convicted felon. Now Tshombe —' Shasa interrupted her and Tara rounded on him, 'Tshombe is a stooge and a Quisling, a puppet of Belgian colonialism.'

'At least he isn't eating the opposition like Lumumba's lads are,' Littleton interjected mildly, and Tara turned back to him with the battle light in her eyes.

'That isn't worthy of somebody —' she broke off with an effort. Her orders were to avoid radical arguments and to maintain her role as a dutiful establishment wife.

'Oh, it's so boring,' she said. 'Let's talk about the London theatre. What is on at the moment?'

'Well, just before I left I saw *The Caretaker*, Pinter's new piece,' Littleton accepted the diversion, and Shasa glanced across the room. Manfred De La Rey was watching him with those intense pale eyes, and as he caught Shasa's eye he inclined his head sharply.

366

'Excuse me a moment,' Shasa murmured, but Littleton and Tara were so occupied with each other that they barely noticed him move away and join Manfred and his statuesque German wife.

Manfred always seemed ill at ease in tails, and the starched wing collar of his dress shirt bit into his thick neck and left a vivid red mark on the skin.

'So, my friend,' he teased Shasa. 'The dagoes from South America thrashed you at your horse games, hey?'

Shasa's smile slipped a fraction. 'Eight to six is hardly a massacre,' he protested, but Manfred was not interested in his defence.

He took Shasa's arm and leaned closer to him, still smiling jovially as he said, 'There is some nasty work going on.'

'Ah!' Shasa smiled easily and nodded encouragement.

'Macmillan has refused to show Doctor Henk a copy of the speech he is going to deliver tomorrow.'

'Ah!' This time Shasa had difficulty in maintaining the smile. If this was a fact, then the British prime minister was guilty of a flagrant breach of etiquette. It was common courtesy for him to allow Verwoerd to study his text so as to be able to prepare a reply.

'It's going to be an important speech,' Manfred went on.

'Yes,' Shasa agreed. 'Maud returned to London to consult with him and help him draw it up, they must have been polishing it up since then.' Sir John Maud was the British high commissioner to South Africa. For him to be summoned to London underlined the gravity of the situation.

'You are friendly with Littleton,' Manfred said quietly. 'See if you can get anything out of him, even a hint as to what Macmillan is going to do.'

'I doubt he knows much,' Shasa was still smiling for the benefit of anybody watching them. 'But I'll let you know if I can find out anything.'

The dinner was served on the magnificent East India Company service, but was the usual bland and tepid offering of the civil service chefs whom Shasa was certain had served their apprenticeship on the railways. The white wines were sweet and insipid, but the red was a 1951 Weltevreden Cabernet Sauvignon. Shasa had influenced the choice by making a gift of his own cru for the banquet, and he judged it the equal of all but the very best Bordeaux. It was a pity that the white was so woefully bad. There was no reason for it, they had the climate and the soil. Weltevreden had always concentrated on the red but he made a resolution to improve his own production of whites, even if it meant bringing in another wine-master from Germany or France and buying another vineyard on the Stellenbosch side of the peninsula.

367

The speeches were mercifully short and inconsequential, a brief welcome from Verwoerd and a short appreciation from Macmillan, and the conversation at Shasa's end of the table never rose above such earth-shaking subjects as their recent defeat by the Argentinians on the polo field, Denis Compton's batting form and Stirling Moss' latest victory in the Mille Miglia. But as soon as the banquet ended Shasa sought out Littleton who was still with Tara, drawing out the pleasure of her company to the last.

'Looking forward to tomorrow,' he told Littleton casually. 'I hear your Super Mac is going to give us some fireworks.'

'Wherever did you hear that?' Littleton asked, but Shasa saw the sudden shift of his gaze and the guarded expression that froze his smile.

'Can we have a word?' Shasa asked quietly, and apologized to Tara. 'Excuse me, my dear.' He took Littleton's elbow and chatting amicably steered him through the glass doors on to the paved stoep under the trellised vines.

'What is going on, Peter?' He lowered his voice. 'Isn't there anything you can tell me?'

Their relationship was intimate and of long standing; such a direct appeal could not be ignored.

'I will be frank with you, Shasa,' Littleton said. 'Mac has something up his sleeve. I don't know what it is, but he is planning on creating a sensation. The press at home have been put on the alert. It's going to be a major policy statement, that is my best guess.'

'Will it alter things between us – preferential trade, for instance?' Shasa demanded.

'Trade?' Littleton chuckled. 'Of course not, nothing alters trade. More than that I can't tell you. We will all have to wait for tomorrow.'

Neither Tara nor Shasa spoke on the drive back to Weltevreden until the Rolls passed beneath the Anreith gateway and then Tara asked, her voice strained and jerky, 'What time is Macmillan making his speech tomorrow?'

'The special session will begin at eleven o'clock,' Shasa replied, but he was still thinking of what Littleton had told him.

'I wanted to be in the visitors' gallery. I asked Tricia to get me a ticket.'

'Oh, the session isn't being held in the chamber – not enough seating. It will be in the dining-room and I don't think they will allow visitors —' he broke off and stared at her. In the reflected light of the headlamps she had gone deathly pale.

'What is it, Tara?'

'The dining-room,' she breathed. 'Are you sure?'

'Of course I am. Is something wrong, my dear?'

'Yes – no! Nothing is wrong. Just a little heartburn, the dinner —'

'Pretty awful,' he agreed, and returned his attention to the road.

'The dining-room,' she thought, in near panic. 'I have to warn Moses. I have to warn him it cannot be tomorrow – all his arrangements will have been made for the escape. I have to let him know.'

Shasa dropped her at the front doors of the château and took the Rolls down to the garages. When he came back, she was in the blue drawing-room and the servants, who had as usual waited up for their return, were serving hot chocolate and biscuits. Shasa's valet helped him change into a maroon velvet smoking-jacket, and the housemaids hovered anxiously until Shasa dismissed them.

Tara had always opposed this custom. 'I could easily warm up the milk myself and you could put on a jacket without having another grown man to help you,' she complained when the servants had left the room. 'It's feudal and cruel to keep them up until all hours.'

'Nonsense, my dear.' Shasa poured himself a cognac to go with his chocolate. 'It's a tradition they value as much as we do – makes them feel indispensable and part of the family. Besides, chef would have a seizure if you were to mess with his kitchen.'

Then he slumped into his favourite armchair and became unusually serious. He began to talk to her as he had at the beginning of their marriage when they had still been in accord.

'There is something afoot that I don't like. Here we stand at the opening of a new decade, the 1960s. We have had nearly twelve years of Nationalist rule and none of my direst predictions have come to pass, but I feel a sense of unease. I have the feeling that our tide has been at full flood, but the turn is coming. I think that tomorrow may be the day when the ebb sets in —' he broke off, and grinned shamefacedly. 'Forgive me. As you know, I don't usually indulge in fantasy,' he said and sipped his chocolate and his cognac in silence.

Tara felt not the least sympathy for him. There was so much she wanted to say, so many recriminations to lay upon him, but she could not trust herself to speak. Once she began, she might lose control and divulge too much. She might not be able to prevent herself gloating on the dreadful retribution that awaited him and all those like him, and she did not want to prolong this *tête-à-tête*, she wanted to be free to go to Moses, to warn him that today was not the day he had planned for. So she rose. 'You know how I feel, we don't have to discuss it. I'm going to bed. Excuse me.'

'Yes, of course.' He stood up courteously. 'I'll be working for the next few hours. I have to go over my notes for my meeting with Littleton and his team tomorrow afternoon, so don't worry about me.'

Tara checked that Isabella was in her room and asleep, before she went to her suite and locked the door. She changed out of her long dress and jewellery into jeans and a dark sweater, then she made a cannabis cigarette and while she smoked it, she waited fifteen minutes by her watch for Shasa to settle down to his work. Then she switched off her lights. She dropped the cigarette butt into the toilet and flushed it away, before she let herself into the passage once again, locking her suite against the unlikely chance that Shasa might come up to look for her. Then she went down the back stairs.

As she crossed the wide stoep, keeping against the wall, staying in the shadows and moving silently, a telephone rang in the library wing and she froze involuntarily, her heart jarring her ribs. Then she realized that the telephone must be Shasa's private line, and she was about to move on, when she heard his voice. Although the curtains were drawn, the windows of his study were open and she could see the shadow of his head against the drapes.

'Kitty!' he said. 'Kitty Godolphin, you little witch. I should have guessed that you'd be here.'

The name startled Tara, and brought back harrowing memories, but she could not resist the temptation to creep closer to the curtained window.

'You always follow the smell of blood, don't you?' Shasa said, and chuckled at her reply.

'Where are you? The Nellie.' The Mount Nelson was simply the best hotel in Cape Town. 'And what are you doing now – I mean right this moment? Yes, I know it's two o'clock in the morning, but any time is a good time – you told me that yourself a long time ago. It will take me half an hour to get there. Whatever else you do, don't start without me.' He hung up and she saw his shadow on the curtain as he stood up from his desk.

She ran to the end of the long stoep and jumped down into the hydrangea bed and crouched in the bushes. Within a few minutes Shasa came out of the side door. He had a dark overcoat over his smoking-jacket. He went down to the garages and drove away in the Jaguar. Even in his haste he drove slowly through the vineyards so as not to blow dust on his precious grapes, and, watching the head-lights disappear, Tara hated him as much as she ever had. She thought that she should have grown accustomed to his philandering, but he was like a tom cat in rut – no woman was safe from him, and his moral outrage against Sean, his own son, for the same behaviour, had been ludicrous.

Kitty Godolphin – she cast her mind back to their first meeting and the television reporter's reaction to the mention of Shasa's name and now the reason for it became clear.

'Oh God, I hate him so. He is totally without conscience or pity. He deserves to die!' She said it aloud, and then clapped her hand over her mouth. 'I shouldn't have said it, but it is true! He deserves to die and I deserve to be free of him – free to go to Moses and my child.'

She rose out of the hydrangea bushes, brushed the clinging soil from her jeans and crossed the lawns quickly. The moon was in its first quarter, but bright enough to throw her shadow in front of her, and she entered the vineyard with relief and hurried down the rows of vines that were heavy with leaf and grape. She skirted the winery and the stables and reached the servants' cottages.

She had placed Moses in the room at the end of the second row of cottages and his window faced out on to the vineyard. She tapped on his window and his response was almost immediate; she knew he slept as lightly as a wild cat.

'It's me,' she whispered.

'Wait,' he said. 'I will open the door.'

He loomed in the doorway, naked except for a pair of white shorts, and his body shone in the moonlight like wet tar.

'You are foolish to come here,' he said, and taking her arm drew her into the single room. 'You are putting everything at risk.'

'Moses, please, listen to me. I had to tell you. It cannot be tomorrow.'

He stared at her contemptuously. 'You were never a true daughter of the revolution.'

'No, no, I am true, and I love you enough to do anything, but they have changed the arrangements. They will not use the chamber where you have set the charge. They will meet in the parliamentary dining-room.'

He stared at her a second longer, then he turned and went to the narrow built-in cupboard at the head of his bed and began to dress in his uniform.

'What are you going to do?' she asked.

'I have to warn the others – they also are in danger.'

'What others?' she asked. 'I did not know there were others.'

'You know only what you have to know,' he told her curtly. 'I must use the Chev – is it safe?'

'Yes, Shasa is not here. He has gone out. Can I come with you?'

'Are you mad?' he asked. 'If the police find a black man and a white woman together at this time of night —' he did not finish the sentence. 'You must go back to the house and make a phone call. Here is the number. A woman will answer, and you will say only "Cheetah is coming – he will be there in thirty minutes." That is all you will say and then you will hang up.'

Moses threaded the Chev through the maze of narrow streets of District Six, the old Malay quarter. During the day this was a colourful and thriving community of small stores and businesses. General dealers and tailors and tinsmiths and *halaal* butcheries occupied the ground-floor shops of the decrepit Victorian buildings, while from the cast-iron fretwork of the open balconies above hung a festival of drying laundry, and the convoluted streets were clamorous with the cries of street vendors, the mournful horns of itinerant fishmongers and the laughter of children.

At nightfall the traders shuttered their premises and left the streets to the street gangs and the pimps and the prostitutes. Some of the more daring white revellers came here late at night, to listen to the jazz players in the crowded shebeens or to look for a pretty coloured girl – more for the thrill of danger and discovery than for any physical gratification.

Moses parked the Chev in a dark side street. On the wall were the graffiti that declared this the territory of the Rude Boys, one of the most notorious of the street gangs, and he waited only a few seconds before the first gang member materialized out of the shadows, an urchin with the body of a child and the face of a vicious old man.

'Look after it well,' Moses flipped him a silver shilling. 'If the tyres are slashed when I come back, I'll do the same for your backside.' The child grinned at him evilly.

He climbed the dark and narrow staircase to the Vortex Club. A couple on the landing were copulating furtively but furiously against the wall as Moses squeezed past. The white man turned his face away but he never missed a beat.

At the door to the club somebody studied him briefly through the peephole and then let him enter. The long crowded room was hazy with tobacco smoke and the sweet smell of cannabis. The clientele included the full spectrum from gang members in zoot suits and wide ties to white men in dinner-jackets. Only the women were all coloured.

Dollar Brand and his Quartet were playing a sweet soulful jazz and everybody was still and attentive. Nobody even looked up as Moses slipped down the side wall to the door at the far end, but the man guarding it recognized Moses and stood aside for him to enter.

In the backroom there was only one man sitting at a round gambling table under a green shaded light. There was a cigarette smouldering between his fingers, and his face was pale as putty, his eyes implacable dark pits.

'You are foolhardy to call a meeting now,' said Joe Cicero, 'without good reason. All the preparations have been made. There is nothing more to discuss.'

372

'I have good reason,' said Moses, and sat down on the empty chair, facing him across the baize-covered table.

Joe Cicero listened without expression, but when Moses finished, he pushed the lank hair off his forehead with the back of his hand. Moses had learned to interpret that gesture as one of agitation.

'We cannot dismantle the escape route and then set it up again later. These things take time to arrange. The aircraft is already in position.'

It was an Aztec chartered from a company in Johannesburg, and the pilot was a lecturer in political philosophy at Witwatersrand University, the holder of a private pilot's licence and a secret member of the South African Communist Party.

'How long can he wait at the rendezvous?' Moses asked, and Cicero thought about it a moment.

'A week at the longest,' he replied.

The rendezvous was an unregistered airstrip on a large drought-stricken ranch in Namaqualand which was lying derelict, abandoned by the discouraged owner. From the airfield it was a four-hour flight to Bechuanaland, the British protectorate that lay against the north-western border of the Union of South Africa. Sanctuary had been arranged for Moses there, the beginning of the pipeline by which most political fugitives were channelled to the north.

'A week must be enough,' Moses said. 'Every hour increases the danger. At the very first occasion that we can be sure Verwoerd will take his seat again, I will do it.'

It was four o'clock in the morning before Moses left the Vortex Club and went down to where he had parked the Chev.

*   *   *

Kitty Godolphin sat in the centre of the bed, naked and cross-legged with all the shameless candour of a child.

In the years Shasa had known her, she had changed very little physically. Her body had matured slightly, her breasts had more weight to them and the tips had darkened. He could no longer make out the rack of her ribs beneath the smooth pale skin, but her but-tocks were still lean as a boy's and her limbs coltishly long and slim. Nor had she lost the air of guileless innocence, that aura of eternal youth which so contrasted with the cynical hardness of her gaze. She was telling him about the Congo. She had been there for the last five months and the material she had filmed would surely put her in line for her third Emmy and confirm her position as the most successful television journalist on the American networks. She was speaking in the breathless voice of an *ingénue*.

373

'They caught these three Simba agents and tried them under the mango trees outside the burnt-out hospital, but by the time they had sentenced them to death, the light was too bad for filming. I gave the commander my Rolex watch, and in return he postponed the executions until the sun was up the next morning so that Hank could film. It was the most incredible footage. The next morning they paraded the condemned men naked through the market-place and the local women bargained for the various parts of their bodies. The Baluba have always been cannibals. When they had sold all three of them, they took them down to the river and shot them, in the head, of course, so as not to damage the meat, and they butchered them there on the river bank and the women queued up to claim their portions.' She was trying to shock him, and it irritated Shasa that she had succeeded.

'Where do you stand, my love?' he asked bitterly. 'One day you are sympathetically interviewing Martin Luther King, and the next you are portraying all the grossest savagery of Africa.'

She laughed, that throaty chuckle that always roused him. 'And the very next day I am recording the British imperialist making bargains with your gang of bully boys while you stand with a foot on the neck of your slaves.'

'Damn it, Kitty. What are you – what are you trying to do?'

'Capture reality,' she told him simply.

'And when reality doesn't conform to your view of it, you bribe somebody with a Rolex watch to alter it.'

'I've made you mad.' She laughed delightedly, and he stood up from the bed and crossed to where he had thrown his clothes over the back of the chair. 'You look like a little boy when you sulk,' she called after him.

'It will be light in an hour. I have to get back home and change,' he said. 'I've got an appointment with my Imperialist slave-masters at eleven.'

'Of course, you've got to be there to hear Supermac tell you how much he wants to buy your gold and diamonds – and he doesn't care whether they are dripping with the sweat and blood —'

'All right, sweetness,' he cut her off. 'That's enough for one night.' He stepped into his trousers, and as he tucked in his shirt, he grinned at her. 'Why do I always pick screaming radical females?'

'You like the stimulation,' she suggested, but he shook his head, and reached for the velvet smoking-jacket.

'I prefer the loving – talking of which, when will I see you again?'

'Why, at eleven o'clock at the houses of parliament, of course. I'll try to get you in the shot, you are so photogenic, darling.'

He went to the bed and stooped over her to kiss that angelic smile on her lips. 'I can never understand what I see in you,' he said.

374

He was still thinking of her as he went down to the hotel carpark and wiped the dew off the windshield of the Jaguar. It was amazing how she had been able so effortlessly to hold his interest over all these years. No other woman, except Tara, had ever done that. It was silly how good he felt when he had been with her. She could still drive him wild with erotic desire, her tricks still worked on him, and afterwards he felt elated and wonderfully alive – and, yes, he enjoyed arguing with her.

'God, I haven't closed my eyes all night, yet I feel like a Derby winner. I wonder if I am still in love with the little bitch.'

He took the Jaguar down the long palm-lined drive from the Mount Nelson Hotel. Considering the proposition and recalling his proposal of marriage and her outright rejection, he went out through the hotel gates and took the main road that skirted the old Malay quarter of District Six. He resisted the temptation to shoot the red of the traffic lights at the foot of Roeland Street. It was highly unlikely there would be other traffic at this time of the morning, but he braked dutifully and was startled when another vehicle shot out of the narrow cross street and turned in front of his bonnet.

It was a sea-green Chevrolet station wagon, and he didn't have to check the number plate to know that it was Tara's. The headlights of the Jaguar shone into the cab of the Chev and for an instant he had a full view of the driver. It was Tara's new chauffeur. He had seen him twice before, once at Weltevreden and once in the House of Assembly, but this time the driver was bare-headed and Shasa could see the full shape of his head.

As he had on both the previous occasions, Shasa had a strong sense of recognition. He had definitely met or known this man before, but the memory was eroded by time and quickly extinguished by his annoyance. The chauffeur was not permitted to use the Chev for his own private purposes, and yet here he was in the small hours of the morning driving around as though the vehicle belonged to him.

The Chev pulled away swiftly. The chauffeur had obviously recognized Shasa and the speed was proof of his guilt. Shasa's first instinct was to give chase and confront the man, but the traffic light was still red against him and while he waited for it to change, he had time to reflect. He was in too good a mood to spoil it with unpleasantness, besides which any confrontation at four in the morning would be undignified, and would inevitably lead to questions about his own presence at the same hour on the fringes of the city's notorious red-light area. There would be a better time and place to deal with the driver, and Shasa let him go, but he had neither forgiven nor forgotten.

Shasa parked the Jaguar in the garage at Weltevreden, and the

375

green Chev was in its place at the end of the line of cars, between Garry's MG and Shasa's customized Land-Rover. As he passed it, he laid his hand on the bonnet of the Chev and it was still hot, the metal ticking softly as it cooled. He nodded with satisfaction and went on up to the house, amused by the necessity to creep up to his own suite like a burglar.

He still felt light and happy at breakfast and he hummed as he loaded his plate with eggs and bacon from the silver chafing dish on the sideboard. He was the first one down but Garry was only a minute behind him.

'The boss should always be the first man on the job, and the last man off it,' he had taught Garry, and the boy had taken it to heart. 'No, no longer boy.' Shasa corrected himself, as he studied Garry. His son was only an inch shorter than he was, but wider across the shoulders and heavier in the chest. Down the full length of the corridor Shasa had often heard him grunting over his body-building weights. Even though he had just shaved, Garry's jaw was blue with beard that by evening would need the razor again, and despite the Brylcreem his hair was already springing up in unruly spikes.

He sat down beside Shasa, took a mouthful of his omelette and immediately began talking shop. 'He just isn't up to the job any more, Pater. We need a younger man in that position, especially with all the extra responsibility of the Silver River Mine coming on stream.'

'He has been with us twenty years, Garry,' Shasa said mildly.

'I'm not suggesting we shoot him, Dad. Just let him take his retirement. He *is* almost seventy.'

'Retirement will kill him.'

'If he stays it will kill us.'

'All right,' Shasa sighed. Garry was right, of course, the man had outlived his usefulness. 'But I will speak to him personally.'

'Thanks, Dad.' Garry's spectacles gleamed victoriously.

'Talking about the Silver River Mine, I have arranged for you to begin your stint up there just as soon as you have written your sup.'

Garry spent more time at Centaine House than in his lecture rooms at business school. As a consequence, he was carrying one subject for his Bachelor's degree in Commerce. He would write the supplementary examination the following week and Shasa was sending him up to work on the Silver River Mine for a year or two.

'After all, it has taken over from the old H'ani now as the Company flagship. I want you to move more and more into the centre of things.' He saw the glow of anticipation behind Garry's spectacles.

'Oh boy, am I looking forward to really starting work, after bashing the books all these dreary years.'

Michael came bursting breathlessly into the dining-room. 'Thank goodness, Pater, I thought I had missed you.'

'Slow down, Mickey,' Shasa cautioned him. 'You'll burst a blood vessel. Have some breakfast.'

'I'm not hungry this morning.' Michael sat down opposite his father. 'I wanted to talk to you.'

'Well, open fire then,' Shasa invited.

'Not here,' Michael demurred. 'I rather hoped we could talk in the gun room,' and all three of them looked grave. The gun room was only used on the most portentous occasions, and a request for a meeting in the gun room was not to be taken lightly.

Shasa glanced at his watch. 'Mickey, Harold Macmillan is addressing both houses —'

'I know, Pater, but this won't take long. Please, sir.' The fact that Michael was calling him 'sir' underlined the seriousness of the request, but Shasa resented the deliberate timing.

Whenever Michael wanted to raise a contentious issue, he did so when Shasa's opportunity to respond was severely curtailed. The lad was as devious as his mother, whose child he indubitably was, spiritually as well as physically.

'Ten minutes, then,' Shasa agreed reluctantly. 'Will you excuse us please, Garry?' Shasa led the way down the passage and locked the gun-room door behind them.

'Very well.' He took his usual place in front of the fireplace. 'What is it, my boy?'

'I've got a job, Dad.' Michael was breathless again.

'A job. Yes, I know you have a part-time job as local stringer for the *Mail*. I enjoyed your report on the polo – in fact you read it to me. Very good it was,' Shasa grinned, 'all five lines of it.'

'No, sir, I've got a full-time job. I spoke to the editor of the *Mail* and they have offered me a job as a cub reporter. I start the first of next month.'

Shasa's grin faded into a scowl. 'Damn it, Mickey. You can't be serious – what about your education? You have two more years to go at university.'

'I am serious, sir. I will get my education on the paper.'

'No,' Shasa raised his voice. 'No, I forbid it. I won't have you leaving university before you are capped.'

'I'm sorry, sir. I've made up my mind.' Michael was pale and trembling, yet he had that obstinate set expression that infuriated Shasa even more than the words – but he controlled himself.

'You know the rules,' Shasa said. 'I've made them clear to all of

377

you. If you do things my way, there is no limit to the help I will give you. If you go your own way, then you are on your own —' he took a breath, and then said it, surprised at how painful it was '— like Sean.' God, how he still missed his eldest son.

'Yes, sir,' Michael nodded. 'I know the rules.'

'Well?'

'I have to do it, sir. There is nothing else I want to do with my life. I want to learn to write. I don't want to go against you, Pater, but I simply have to do it.'

'This is your mother's doing,' Shasa said coldly. 'She has put you up to this,' he accused, and Michael looked sheepish.

'Mater knows about it,' he admitted, 'but it's my decision alone, sir.'

'You understand that you will be forfeiting my support? You'll not receive another penny from me once you leave this house. You'll have to live on the salary of a cub reporter.'

'I understand, sir,' Michael nodded.

'All right, then, Michael. Off you go,' he said, and Michael looked stunned.

'Is that all, sir?'

'Unless you have some other announcement to make.'

'No, sir.' Michael's shoulders slumped. 'Except that I love you very much, Pater, and I appreciate all that you have done for me.'

'You have,' said Shasa, 'a most peculiar way of demonstrating that appreciation, if you don't mind me saying so.' He went to the door.

He was halfway into the city, racing the Jaguar down the new highway between the university and Groote Schuur, before he recovered from his affront at Michael's disloyalty, for that is how Shasa saw his son's decision. Now suddenly he began to think about newspapers again. Publicly he had always disparaged the strange suicidal impulse that gripped so many successful men in their middle years to own their own newspaper. It was notoriously difficult to milk a reasonable profit from a newspaper, but in secret Shasa had felt the sneaking temptation to indulge in the same rich man's folly.

'Not much profit,' he mused aloud, 'but the power! To be able to influence the minds of people!'

In South Africa the English press was hysterically anti-government, while the Afrikaans press was fawningly and abjectly the slave of the National Party. A thinking man could trust neither.

'What about an English-language paper that was aimed at the business community and politically uncommitted,' he wondered, as he had before. 'What if I were to buy one of the smaller weaker papers and build it up? After the Silver River Mine's next dividend is declared, we are going to be sitting on a pile of money.' Then he grinned. 'I must be getting senile, but at least I'll be able to guarantee a job for my drop-out journalist son!' And the idea of Michael as editor of a large influential newspaper had an increasing appeal, the longer he thought about it. 'Still, I wish the little blighter would get himself a decent education first,' he grumbled, but he had almost forgiven him for his treachery by the time he parked the Jaguar in the parking area reserved for cabinet ministers. 'Of course, I'll keep him on a decent allowance,' he decided. 'That threat was just a little bluff.'

A sense of excited expectation gripped the House as Shasa went up the stairs to the front entrance. The lobby was crowded with senators and members of parliament. The knots of dark-suited men formed and dissolved and re-formed, in the intricate play of political cross-currents that fascinated Shasa. As an insider he could read the significance of who was talking to whom and why.

It took him almost twenty minutes to reach the foot of the staircase for as one of the prime actors he was drawn inexorably into the subtle theatre of power and favour. At last he escaped and with only minutes to spare hurried up the stairs and down the passage to his suite.

Tricia was hovering anxiously. 'Oh, Mr Courtney, everybody is looking for you. Lord Littleton telephoned and the prime minister's secretary left a message.' She was reading from her pad as she followed him into the inner office.

'Try to get the PM's secretary first, then Lord Littleton.' Shasa sat at his desk, and frowned as he noticed some chalky white specks on his blotter. He brushed them away irritably, and would have given Tricia an order to speak to the cleaners, but she was still reading from her pad and he had less than an hour to tackle the main items on her list before the joint sitting began.

He dealt with the queries that Verwoerd's secretary had for him. The answers were in his head and he did not have to refer to anybody in his department – and then Littleton was on the line. He wanted to discuss an addition to the agenda for their meeting that afternoon, and once they had agreed that, Shasa asked tactfully, 'Have you found out anything about the speeches this morning?'

'Afraid not, old man. I'm as much in the dark as you are.'

As Shasa reached across the desk to replace the receiver, he noticed another white speck of chalk on his blotter that had not been there a minute before; he was about to brush that away also, when he paused and looked up to see where it had come from. This time he scowled as he saw the small hole in his ceiling and the hair-line cracks around it. He pressed the switch on his intercom.

'Tricia, please come in here a moment.'

When she stood in the doorway, he pointed at the ceiling. 'What do you make of that?'

Tricia looked mystified and came to stand beside his chair. They both peered at the damage.

'Oh, I know,' Tricia looked relieved, 'but I'm not supposed to tell you.'

'Spit it out, woman!' Shasa ordered.

'Your wife, Mrs Courtney, said she was planning some renovations to your office as a surprise. I suppose she has asked Maintenance to do the work for her.'

'Damn!' Shasa didn't like surprises which interfered with the comfortable tenor of his existence. He liked his office the way it was and he didn't want anybody, particularly anyone of Tara's *avant garde* taste, interfering with something that worked extremely well as it was.

'I think she is planning to change the curtains also,' Tricia added innocently. She didn't like Tara Courtney. She considered her shallow, insincere and scheming. She didn't approve of her disrespectful attitude to Shasa, and she wasn't above sowing a few seeds of dissension. If Shasa were free, there was just a chance, a very small and remote chance that he might see her clearly and realize just how much she, Tricia, felt for him, 'And she was talking about altering the light fittings,' she added.

Shasa jumped up from his desk and went to touch his curtains. He and Centaine had studied at least a hundred samples of fabric before choosing this one. Protectively he rearranged the drapes, and then he noticed the second hole in the ceiling and the thin insulated wire that protruded from it. He had difficulty controlling his fury in front of his secretary.

'You get on to Maintenance,' he instructed. 'Talk to Odendaal himself, not one of his workmen, and you tell him I want to know exactly what is going on. Tell him whatever it is, it's damned shoddy workmanship and that there is plaster all over my desk.'

'I'll do that this morning,' Tricia promised, and then, placatingly, 'It's ten minutes to, Mr Courtney – you don't want to be late.'

Manfred De La Rey was just leaving his own office as Shasa came down the passage, and they fell in side by side.

'Have you found out anything?'

'No – have you?'

Manfred shook his head. 'It's too late anyway– nothing we can do now.'

Shasa saw Blaine Malcomess at the door of the dining-room and went to greet him. They filed into the panelled dining-room together.

'How is Mater?'

'Centaine is fine – looking forward to seeing you for dinner tomorrow evening.' Centaine was holding a dinner party in Littleton's honour out at Rhodes Hill. 'I left her giving the chef a nervous breakdown.' They laughed together and then found their seats in the front row of chairs. As minister and deputy leader of the opposition, they both warranted reserved seats.

Shasa swivelled in his seat and looked to the back of the large hall where the press cameras had been set up. He picked out Kitty Godolphin, looking tiny and girlish beside her camera crew, and she winked at him mischievously. Then the two prime ministers were taking their places at the top table and Shasa leaned across to Manfred De La Rey and murmured, 'I hope this isn't all a hoo-ha over nothing – and that Supermac has really got something of interest to tell us.'

Manfred shrugged. 'Let's hope it isn't too exciting either,' he said. 'Sometimes it's safer to be bored —' but he broke off as the Speaker of the House called for silence and rose to introduce the prime minister of Great Britain and the packed room, filled with the most powerful men in the land, settled into attentive and expectant silence.

Even when Macmillan, tall and urbane and strangely benign in expression, rose to his feet, Shasa had no sense of being at the anvil while history was being forged and he crossed his arms over his chest and lowered his chin in the attitude of listening and concentration in which he followed all debate and argument.

Macmillan spoke in an unemotional voice, but with weight and lucidity, and his text had all the indications of having been carefully prepared, meticulously polished and rehearsed.

'The most striking of all the impressions I have formed since I left London a month ago,' he said, 'is the strength of this African national consciousness. In different places it may take different forms, but it is happening everywhere. The wind of change is blowing through the continent. Whether we like it or not, this growth of national consciousness is a political fact. We must all accept it as a fact. Our national policies must take account of it.'

Shasa sat up straight and unfolded his arms, and around him there was a similar stirring of incredulity. It was only then that Shasa realized with a clairvoyant flash that the world he knew had altered its shape, that in the fabric of life that had held together their diverse nation for almost three hundred years, the first rent had been torn by a few simple words, a rent that could never be repaired. While he attempted to grasp the full extent of the damage, Macmillan was going on in those plummy measured tones.

'Of course, you understand this as well as anyone. You are sprung from Europe, the home of nationalism.' Cunningly, Macmillan was including them in his new sweeping view of Africa. 'Indeed, in the history of our times yours will be recorded as the first of the African nationalisms.'

Shasa glanced at Verwoerd beside the British prime minister and he could see that he was agitated and alarmed. He had been caught unawares by Macmillan's stratagem of withholding his text from him.

'As a fellow member of the Commonwealth, it is our earnest desire to give South Africa our support and encouragement, but I hope you won't mind me saying frankly that there are some aspects of your policies which make it impossible for us to do this without being false to our own deep convictions about the political destinies of free men.'

Macmillan was announcing nothing less than a parting of ways and Shasa was devastated by the idea. He wanted to leap to his feet and shout, 'But I am British also – you cannot do this to us.' He looked around him almost pleadingly and saw his own deep distress echoed on the faces of Blaine and most of the other English members of the House.

Macmillan's words had devastated them.

Shasa's mood persisted over the remainder of that day and the next. The atmosphere at the meetings with Littleton and his advisers was one of mourning, and though Littleton himself was apologetic and conciliatory, they all knew that the damage was real and irreparable. The fact was undeniable. Britain was dropping them. She might go on trading with them, but at arm's length. Britain had chosen sides.

Late on the Friday a special session of the House was announced for the following Monday, when Verwoerd would make his accounting to his parliament and his people. They had the weekend to brood over their fate. Macmillan's speech even cast a shadow over Centaine's dinner party on the Friday evening, and Centaine took it as a personal insult.

'The man's timing is atrocious,' she confided to Shasa. 'The day before my party! Perfidious Albion!'

'You French have never trusted the British,' Shasa teased her, his first attempt at humour in forty-eight hours.

'Now I know why,' Centaine retorted. 'Look at the man – typically English. He hides expediency in a cloak of high moral indignation. He does what is best for England and makes himself a saint while he does it.'

It was left for Blaine Malcomess to sum up after the women had

382

left the men to their port and cigars in Rhodes Hill's magnificent dining-room.

'Why are we so incredulous?' he asked. 'Why do we feel it so impossible that Britain would reject us, simply because we fought two wars for her?' He shook his head. 'No, the caravan moves on and so must we. We must ignore the gloating of the London press, we must ignore their delight in this unprecedented rebuke and repudiation of all of us, the Nationalists and those that strenuously oppose them. From now on we will be increasingly alone, and we must learn to stand on our own feet.'

Shasa nodded. 'Macmillan's speech was a huge political gain for Verwoerd. There is only one way for us to go now. The bridge has been chopped down behind us. No retreat is possible. We have to go along with Verwoerd. South Africa will be a republic before the year is out, mark my words, and after that —' Shasa drew on his cigar while he considered '— and after that only God and the Devil know for certain.'

*   *   *

'At times it seems that God and fate take a direct hand in our petty affairs,' Tara said softly. 'But for a tiny detail, the choice of the dining-room rather than the chamber, we might have destroyed the man who had brought us a message of hope.'

'For once it does seem that your Christian God favours us.' Moses watched her in the driving-mirror as he drove the Chevrolet through the Monday rush hour traffic. 'Our timing has been perfect. At the moment when the British Government, supported by the British press and the nation, has recognized our rights, the political destinies of free men, as Macmillan put it, we will deliver our first hard blow for the promised freedom.'

'I am afraid, Moses, afraid for you and for all of us.'

'The time for fear has passed,' he told her. 'Now is the time for courage and resolution, for it is not oppression and slavery that breeds revolution. The lesson is clear. Revolution rises out of the promise of better things. For three hundred years we have borne oppression in weary resignation, but now this Englishman has shown us a glimpse of the future and it is golden with promise. He has given our people hope, and after today, after we have struck down the most evil man in Africa's dark and tormented history, when Verwoerd is dead, the future will at last belong to us.' He had spoken softly, but with that peculiar intensity that made her blood thrill through her veins and pound in her eardrums. She felt the elation, but also the sorrow and the fear.

383

'Many men will die with him,' she whispered. 'My father. Is there no way he can be spared, Moses?'

He did not reply, but she saw the reflection of his gaze in the mirror and she could not bear the scorn. She dropped her own eyes and murmured.

'I'm sorry – I will be strong. I will not speak of it again.' But her mind was racing. There must be some way to keep her father out of the chamber at the fateful moment, but it would have to be compelling. As deputy leader of the opposition, he must attend such solemn business as Verwoerd's speech. Moses disturbed her thoughts.

'I want you to repeat your duties to me,' he said.

'We have gone over it so often,' she protested weakly.

'There must be no misunderstanding.' His tone was fierce. 'Do as I tell you.'

'Once the House is in session – so that we are certain Shasa will not intercept us – we will go up to his suite in the usual way,' she began, and he nodded confirmation as she went over the arrangements, correcting her when she omitted a detail. 'I will leave the office at exactly ten-thirty and go to the visitors' gallery. We must be certain that Verwoerd is there.'

'Do you have your pass?'

'Yes.' Tara opened her handbag and showed him. 'As soon as Verwoerd rises to begin his address, I will return to the office, using the panel door. By that time you will have —' her voice faltered.

'Go on,' he ordered harshly.

'You will have connected the detonator. I will confirm that Verwoerd is in his seat, and you will —' again her voice dried up.

'I will do what has to be done,' he finished for her and then went on, 'After the explosion there will be a period of total panic and confusion – with enormous damage to the ground floor. There will be no control, no organized police or security effort. That period will last sufficiently long for us to go downstairs and leave the building unchallenged, just as most other survivors will be doing.'

'When you leave the country, can I come with you, Moses?' she pleaded.

'No.' He shook his head firmly. 'I must travel swiftly and you would impede us and put us in danger. You will be safer here. It will only be for a short time. After the assassination of the white slave-masters, our people will rise. The young comrades of *Umkhonto we Sizwe* are in position and ready to call the nation to revolution. Millions of our people will spontaneously fill the streets. When they have seized the power, I will return. Then you will have a place of high honour by my side.'

It was amazing how naïvely she accepted his assurances, he

384

thought grimly. Only a besotted woman could doubt that afterwards the security police would take her away, and her interrogation would be brutal. It did not matter. It did not matter if they tried and hanged her. Her husband would be dead with Verwoerd and Tara Courtney's usefulness would be at an end. One day when the people's democratic government of the African National Congress ruled the land, they would name a street or a square after her, the white woman martyr, but now she was expendable.

'Give me your promise, Moses,' she begged him.

His voice was a deep reassuring rumble. 'You have done well, everything I have required of you. You and your son will have a place at my side just as soon as that is possible. I give you my promise.'

'Oh Moses, I love you,' she whispered. 'I shall always love you.' Then she sat back in her seat and adopted the role of cool white madam, as Moses turned the Chevrolet out of Parliament Lane into the members' carpark and the constable at the gate saw the sticker on the windshield and saluted respectfully.

Moses parked in the reserved bay and switched off the engine. They had fifteen minutes to wait before the House went into session.

*   *   *

'Ten minutes to, Mr Courtney,' Tricia called Shasa on the intercom. 'You had better start going down, if you don't want to miss the opening of the PM's speech.'

'Thank you, Tricia.' Shasa had been totally absorbed with his own work. Verwoerd had asked him to draw up a full report on the country's ability to respond to an embargo on sales of military equipment to South Africa by her erstwhile western allies. Apparently Macmillan had hinted at this possibility to Verwoerd, a veiled threat in private conversation just before his departure. Verwoerd wanted the report before the month's end, which was typical of the man, and Shasa would have difficulty meeting that deadline.

'Oh, by the way, Mr Courtney,' Tricia stopped him breaking off the connection. 'I spoke to Odendaal.'

'Odendaal?' It took Shasa a moment to make the mental switch.

'Yes, about the work on your ceiling.'

'Oh, I hope you gave him a flea in the ear. What did he say?'

'He says there has been no work done in your office, and no request from your wife or anybody else for rewiring of any kind.'

'That's decidedly odd,' Shasa looked up at the damage, 'because somebody has definitely been fiddling around in here. If it wasn't Odendaal, then have you any idea who it might be, Tricia?'

'No, Mr Courtney.'

'Nobody been in here to your knowledge?' Shasa insisted.

'Nobody, sir, except of course your wife and her driver.'

'All right, thank you, Tricia.' Shasa stood up and fetched his jacket from the dumb valet in the corner. While he shrugged into it, he studied the hole above his desk and the length of wire that had been drawn out of the corner beside the bookcase and the end tucked behind the row of encyclopaedias. Until Tricia mentioned it, he had forgotten his irritation in the face of other more dire considerations, but now he thought about the little mystery with full attention.

He crossed to the mirror and while he reshaped the knot of his tie and adjusted his black eye-patch, he pondered the additional enigma of Tara's new chauffeur. Tricia's remark had reminded him of it. He still hadn't taken the man to task for his unauthorized private use of the Chev. 'Damn – where have I seen him before?' he wondered, and with one last glance at the ceiling, he left the office. He was still thinking about the driver as he went down the corridor. Manfred De La Rey was waiting for him at the head of the stairs. He was smiling and quietly triumphant, and Shasa realized that he had not spoken to him in private since the shock of Macmillan's speech.

'So,' Manfred greeted him, 'Britannia has cut the apron strings, my friend.'

'Do you remember how once you called me *Soutpiel*?' Shasa asked.

'*Ja.*' Manfred chuckled. '"Salt Prick" – with one foot in Cape Town and the other in London and the best part of you dangling in the Atlantic Ocean. *Ja*, I remember.'

'Well, from now on I will have both feet in Cape Town,' Shasa told him. It was not until that moment, when the fact of Britain's rejection had sunk in, that Shasa realized for the first time that above all other things he was first and foremost a South African.

'Good,' Manfred nodded. 'So at last you understand that although we may not always like each other or agree, circumstances have made us brothers in this land. One cannot survive without the other, and in the end we have only each other to turn to.'

They went down into the chamber and took their seats on the green leather benches, side by side.

When the Assembly rose to pray, to ask God's blessing on their deliberations, Shasa looked across the floor at Blaine Malcomess and felt a familiar rush of affection for him. Silver-haired but tanned and handsome with those protruding ears and big strong nose, Blaine had been a tower in his life for as long as he cared to remember. In his new mood of patriotism – and, yes, of defiance of Britain's rejection – he was glad of the knowledge that this would draw them

386

still closer together. It would narrow the political differences between them, just as it had brought Afrikaner and Englishman closer.

As the prayer ended, he sat down and turned his attention to Dr Hendrik Frensch Verwoerd as he rose to make his address. Verwoerd was a strong articulate speaker and a brilliant debater. His address was sure to be long and carefully reasoned. Shasa knew they were in for fine entertainment and he crossed his arms, leaned against the padded back rest with anticipation and closed his eyes.

Then before Verwoerd could say his first word, Shasa opened his eyes and sat up straight on his bench. In that moment when he had cleared his mind of all recent worry, while he was relaxed and receptive, the ancient memory had flashed in upon him – full blown. He remembered where and when he had last seen Tara's new chauffeur.

'Moses Gama,' he said aloud, but his words were lost in the applause that greeted the prime minister.

*　　*　　*

Tara gave the doorman at the main entrance to parliament a cheery smile, and was surprised at herself. She felt cocooned in a layer of unreality, as though she watched an actress playing her role.

She heard the muffled applause from the chamber as she swept up the stairs with Moses following her at a respectful distance in his chauffeur's uniform and burdened by an armful of parcels. They had done this so often, and Tara smiled again as they passed one of the secretaries in the corridor. She tapped on the door to Shasa's suite and without waiting for an answer swept into the outer office. Tricia rose from her desk.

'Oh, good morning, Mrs Courtney. You'll be late for the PM's address. You'd better hurry.'

'Stephen, you can just leave the parcels.' Tara stopped in front of Tricia as Moses closed the outer door.

'Oh, by the way. Somebody has been working on the ceiling of your husband's office,' Tricia came around the desk, as though to lead the way to Shasa's office. 'We wondered if you knew anything —'

Moses placed the armful of parcels on a chair, and with his hands free turned to Tricia as she came level with him. He whipped one arm around her neck and with his other hand covered her mouth. Tricia was powerless in his grip, but her eyes flew wide with shock.

'There are ropes and a gag in the top packet,' Moses spoke softly to Tara. 'Get them.'

Tara stood paralysed. 'You said nothing about this,' she blurted.

387

'Get them.' His voice was still low, but it crackled with impatience and Tara sprang to obey.

'Tie her hands behind her,' Moses ordered, and while Tara fumbled at the knots, he stuffed a clean, white, folded cloth into the terrified girl's mouth and taped it in place.

'Stay in here,' he ordered Tara, 'in case somebody comes in,' and he bundled Tricia through into the inner office and forced her down on her stomach behind the desk. Swiftly he checked Tara's knots. They were loose and sloppy. He retied them and then bound Tricia's ankles as securely.

'Come in here,' he called, and Tara was flustered and stammering as she rushed in.

'Moses, you haven't hurt her?'

'Stop that!' he told her. 'You have important work to do and you are behaving like a hysterical child.'

She closed her eyes, clenched her fists and took a deep breath. 'I'm sorry.' She opened her eyes. 'I realize that it was necessary. I didn't think. I am all right now.'

Moses had already crossed to the corner of the bookshelf and he reached up and brought down the roll of wire from behind the encyclopaedias. He paid it out across the carpet as he moved back to the desk.

'Good,' he said. 'Now go to your seat in the gallery. Wait five minutes after Verwoerd begins to speak and then come back here. Do not run, do not even hurry. Do everything calmly and deliberately.'

'I understand.' Tara crossed to the mirror and opened her handbag. Quickly she ran a comb through her hair and retouched her lipstick.

Moses had gone to the altar chest and lifted the heavy bronze Bushman statue. He placed it on the carpet and lifted the lid of the chest. Tara hesitated, watching him anxiously.

'Why are you waiting?' he asked. 'Go, woman, and do your duty.'

'Yes, Moses.' She hurried to the door of the outer office.

'Lock both doors behind you,' he ordered.

'Yes, Moses,' she whispered.

As Tara went down the corridor, she was searching in her handbag again, and she found her leather-bound notepad with the miniature gold-plated pencil in the spine loops. At the head of the stairs she paused, and used the banisters to steady the notepad while she scribbled hastily on a blank page.

Daddy,
   Centaine has been seriously injured in a motorcar accident. She is asking for you. Please come quickly.
                                                           Tara

388

She tore the page out of the notebook and folded it. It was the one appeal to which she knew her father would respond and she wrote his name on the folded note.

Instead of going directly to the visitors' gallery, she hurried down the wide staircase into the lobby and ran to one of the uniformed parliamentary messengers who was standing outside the main doors to the chamber.

'You have to get this message to Colonel Malcomess,' she told him.

'I don't like to go in now, Dr Verwoerd is speaking,' the messenger demurred, but she thrust the note into his hand.

'It's terribly urgent,' she pleaded and her distress was evident. 'His wife is dying. Please – please.'

'I'll do what I can.' The messenger accepted the note, and Tara ran back up the stairs. She showed her pass to the doorman at the entrance to the visitors' gallery and squeezed past him.

The gallery was crowded. Somebody had taken Tara's seat, but she edged forward and craned to look down into the chamber. Dr Verwoerd was on his feet, talking in Afrikaans. His silvery curls were neatly cropped and his eyes slitted with concentration as he used both hands to emphasize his words.

'The question that this person from Britain put to us was not addressed to the South African monarchists, nor was it addressed to the South African republicans. It was to all of us that he spoke.' Verwoerd paused. 'The question he asked was simply this. Does the white man survive in Africa or does he perish?'

He had electrified the chamber. There was not a movement nor a shift of eyes from his face – until the uniformed parliamentary messenger slipped unobtrusively down the front row of opposition benches and stopped beside Blaine.

Even then he had to touch Blaine's shoulder to draw his attention, and Blaine accepted the note without seeming to realize what he was doing. He nodded at the messenger, and, with the folded scrap of paper unread in his fingers, once more focused all his attention on Verwoerd where he stood below the Speaker's throne.

'Read it, Daddy!' Tara whispered aloud. 'Please read it.'

*　　*　　*

In all that multitude Shasa was the only one who was not mesmerized by Verwoerd's oratory. His thoughts were a jumbled torrent, one racing after another, overtaking and mingling as they followed without logical sequence.

'*Moses Gama!*' It was scarcely believable that the memory had

389

taken so long to return to him, even over the years and in spite of changes that time had wrought in both of them. They had once been good friends, and the man had made a deep impression on Shasa at a formative period of his life.

Then again, Shasa had heard the name much more recently, it had been on the list of wanted revolutionaries during the 1952 troubles. While the others, Mandela and Sobukwe and the rest, had stood trial, Moses Gama had disappeared, and the warrant for his arrest was outstanding. Moses Gama was still a criminal at large, and a dangerous revolutionary.

'Tara!' His mind darted aside. She had selected Gama as her chauffeur and, given her political leanings, it was impossible that she didn't know who he was. Suddenly Shasa knew that Tara's meek repudiation of her previous left-wing companions and her new conciliatory behaviour had all been a sham. She had not changed at all. This man Moses Gama was more dangerous than all and any of her previous effete companions. Shasa had been hoodwinked. In fact she must have moved even further to the left, crossing the delicate line between legitimate political opposition and criminal involvement. Shasa almost rose to his feet, and then remembered where he was. Verwoerd was speaking already.

'The need to do justice to all, does not mean only that the black men must be nurtured and protected. It means justice and protection for the white men in Africa also —'

Shasa glanced up at the visitors' gallery and there was a stranger sitting in Tara's seat. Where was Tara? She must be in his office – and the association of ideas led him on.

Moses Gama had been in his office. Shasa had seen him in the corridor and Tricia had told him, 'Only Mrs Courtney and her driver.' Moses Gama had been in his office and somebody had drilled the ceiling and laid electrical wires. It had not been Odendaal or Maintenance. It hadn't been anyone who had authority to do so.

'We are not newcomers to Africa. Our forefathers were here before the first black man,' Verwoerd was saying. 'Three hundred years ago, when our ancestors set out into the interior of this land, it was an empty wilderness. The black tribes were still far to the north, making their way slowly southwards. The land was empty and our forefathers claimed it and worked it. Later they built the cities and laid the railways and sank the mine-shafts. Alone, the black man was incapable of doing any of these things. Even more than the black tribes we are men of Africa and our right to be here is as God-given and inalienable as is theirs.'

Shasa heard the words but made no sense of them – Moses Gama, probably with the help and connivance of Tara, had laid electrical wires in his office and – suddenly, he gasped aloud. The altar chest. Tara had placed the chest in his office, like the Trojan horse.

Wild with anxiety now, he swivelled his whole body towards the visitors' gallery, and this time he saw Tara. She was squeezed against one wall and even at this distance Shasa could see that she was pale and distraught. She was watching someone or something on the opposition side of the chamber, and Shasa followed her gaze.

Blaine Malcomess was oblivious of all else as he followed the prime minister's speech. Shasa saw the messenger reach him and hand him the note.

Shasa looked back at the gallery and Tara was still concentrated on her father. After all the years Shasa could read her expression, and he had never seen her so worried and concerned, even when one of the children was gravely ill.

Then her face cleared with patent relief and Shasa glanced back at Blaine. He had unfolded the note and was reading it. Suddenly Blaine leapt to his feet and hurried towards the main doors.

Tara had summoned her father – that much was obvious. Shasa stared at her, trying to divine her purpose. Almost as though she sensed his gaze, Tara looked directly at him, and her relief crumbled into horror and wild guilt. She turned and fled from the visitors' gallery, pushing aside those who stood in her way.

A second longer Shasa stared after her. Tara had enticed her father out of the chamber, and her concern could only have been so intense had she believed he was in some kind of dire danger. This was followed by guilt and horror as she realized that Shasa was watching her. It was clear to Shasa then that something terrible was about to happen. Moses Gama and Tara – there was danger, mortal danger – and Tara was trying to save her father. The danger was pressing and imminent – the wires in his office, the chest, Blaine and Tara and Moses Gama. He knew they were all interwoven and that he had little time in which to act.

Shasa jumped to his feet and strode down the aisle. Verwoerd frowned and checked his speech, watching him, while all around the chamber heads turned. Shasa quickened his stride. Manfred De La Rey reached out to touch him as he passed his bench, but without a glance at him Shasa brushed past his outstretched hand and went on.

As he hurried out into the lobby Shasa saw Blaine Malcomess near the front door talking agitatedly to the janitor. As soon as he saw Shasa he said, 'Thank God!' and came towards him across the chequered marble floor.

391

Shasa turned away from him and looked up the staircase. From the top Tara stared down at him, white-faced and terrified, held by some unnatural passion.

'Tara!' Shasa called and started towards the foot of the staircase, but she whirled and disappeared around the angle of the corridor.

Shasa flew at the stairs, taking them three at a time.

'What's happening, Shasa?' Blaine called after him, but Shasa did not answer.

He came out of the staircase still at a run, and as he rounded the corner Tara was halfway down the corridor ahead of him. He did not waste time by shouting at her, and instead flung himself forward, and sprinted after her. As she ran, Tara glanced over her shoulder and saw him swiftly overtaking her.

'Moses!' she screamed. 'Look out, Moses!'

It was futile, the panelled walls of Shasa's office were too thick and soundproof for her warning to reach him, and her cry confirmed all Shasa's worst suspicions.

Instead of running straight on towards the front door of his suite as Shasa expected, Tara jinked suddenly into the side passage, ducking under Shasa's outstretched arm and he tried to turn with her but he was off balance as she disappeared into his blind spot.

Shasa ran into the corner of the wall, crashing into it head-first, taking it on the brow above his blind eye. The silk patch cushioned the impact slightly, but still the skin split and blood poured down his cheek. Although he was stunned, Shasa managed to keep his feet. He staggered in a full circle, still dazed. Blaine was following him, his face flushed with effort and concern as he ran down the corridor.

'What the hell is going on, Shasa?' he roared.

Shasa turned from him, and saw Tara at the door to the back entrance of his office. She had a key, but she was in such a state that her hands were shaking too wildly to insert it in the lock.

Shasa gathered himself, shaking the darkness out of his head, and the droplets of his blood splattered the wall beside him. Then he launched himself after Tara. She saw him coming and dropped the key, it tinkled at her feet, and she clenched her fists and beat with them on the closed door.

'Moses!' she screamed. 'Moses!'

As Shasa reached her the door was jerked open from the inside, and Moses Gama stood in the threshold. The two men confronted each other over Tara's head until Tara ran forward.

'Moses, I tried to warn you,' she screamed and threw both arms around him.

In that instant Shasa looked beyond the pair and saw that the

392

altar chest stood open, its contents piled on the carpet. The coil of wire that he had found behind the encyclopaedias had been laid across the floor to his desk and connected to some kind of compact electrical apparatus. Shasa had never seen one before, but he knew instinctively that it was a detonation device and that it was ready to fire. On the desk top beside it lay an automatic pistol. As a firearms enthusiast and collector, he recognized it as a Tokarev 7.62 mm, the standard Russian military issue. On the floor behind his desk Tricia lay on her side. She was gagged and bound at wrists and ankles, but she was wriggling desperately and giving little muffled cries.

Shasa lunged forward to tackle Moses Gama, but the black man gathered Tara in his arms and hurled her into Shasa's chest. The two of them reeled backwards against the jamb of the door. Moses spun around and leapt to the desk, as Shasa tried to get free of Tara. She was clinging to him and moaning.

'No! No! He must do it.'

Shasa broke her grip and flung her aside, but across the room Moses was standing over the electrical transmitter. He pressed a switch and a bulb on the panel of the casing glared redly.

Shasa knew that he could not reach Moses across the floor before he fired the device, but his mind was racing ahead of his limbs and body. He saw the wire strung out across the carpet, almost at his feet, and he stooped and took a twist of it around his right hand and heaved back against it with all his strength.

The end of the wire was firmly attached to the transmitter, and as Shasa hauled on it the device was jerked out of Moses' hands and flew off the desk top to clatter across the floor, midway between the two of them.

They both leapt for it at the same instant, but Moses was by a fraction of a second the quickest, and his hands scrabbled on the transmitter. Shasa was in full stride, and he did not check. He leaned forward, and transferred all the weight and power of his body into his hips, swinging his right leg into the kick he aimed at Moses' head.

The kick caught Moses in the side of the temple, and snapped his head over. The transmitter tumbled from his grip and he was flung over backwards, rolling until he crashed into the desk.

Shasa followed him and aimed another flying kick at his head, but Moses caught his foot on his raised forearm and seized his ankle. He twisted violently, lifting the ankle and Shasa was caught on one foot with his weight backwards, and he fell heavily.

Moses pulled himself up the side of the desk and reached out for the Tokarev pistol, and Shasa scrambled after him on hands and knees. As Moses swung the pistol around, Shasa lunged at him again and grabbed his wrist with both hands. They wrestled over the floor, rolling and kicking and grunting, fighting for the Tokarev.

Tara had recovered and now she ran into the room and picked up the fallen transmitter. She stood helplessly with it in her hands.

'Moses, what must I do?' she cried.

Moses grunted with a supreme effort as he rolled on top of Shasa. 'The yellow button. Push the yellow button!'

At that instant Blaine Malcomess ran in through the open door. 'Stop her, Blaine!' Shasa yelled. 'They are going to blow —' Moses' elbow hit him in the mouth and cut off the words.

While the two of them still struggled on the floor, Blaine held out both hands to his daughter.

'Here, give that to me, Tara.'

'Don't touch me, Daddy.' She backed away from him, but she was trying to locate the yellow button, groping for it while she stared at her father. 'Don't try and stop me, Daddy.'

'Blaine,' Shasa gasped, but broke off as Moses attempted once more to wrench his pistol arm out of Shasa's grip. The corded black muscles in Moses' arm bulged and writhed with the effort, and Shasa made a choking sound in his throat as he tried to hold him.

The muzzle blast of the pistol lit the room like a flash bulb and there was the immediate sharp stink of burnt powder.

Blaine Malcomess, his arms outstretched towards Tara, spun around as the bullet hit him and he went reeling into the bookcase. He stood there for a moment with the blood starting to spread in a dark tide down the front of his white shirt and then he sagged slowly on to his knees.

'Daddy!' Tara dropped the transmitter and ran to him. She fell on her knees beside him.

Shock had weakened Shasa's grip for an instant and Moses twisted free and jumped to his feet, but as he lunged for the transmitter, Shasa was after him. He caught Moses from behind as he stooped over the transmitter and with one arm around his throat pulled him away from it. In his efforts to break the throttling grip, Moses dropped the pistol and clawed at Shasa's arm with both hands. They grappled wildly, twisting and grunting, and the transmitter lay at their feet.

Shasa shifted his weight, lifted one foot and drove his heel into the panel of the transmitter, the panel crackled as it was stove in, but the red bulb still burned.

Moses was galvanized to fresh effort by the damage to the transmitter, and he almost tore himself free of Shasa's grip, twisting to face him, but Shasa put out all his strength and they stood chest to chest, gasping and heaving, spittle and sweat and droplets of blood from Shasa's head wound smearing both their faces.

Again Shasa had him off balance for a moment, and he aimed another kick at the transmitter. He landed solidly and it went skidding across the floor and crashed into the wall beyond the desk. The plastic case split open at the impact, the wire tore loose from the terminal and the red bulb flickered and then extinguished.

Moses gave a wild despairing cry and sent Shasa flying backwards over the desk. As he lay sprawled across the desk top, Moses scooped up the pistol from the carpet and staggered to the open doorway. There he turned and raised the Tokarev and aimed at Shasa.

'You!' he gasped. 'You!' but his hands were shaking and the pistol wavered. He fired and the bullet thudded into the desk top beside Shasa's head, tearing up a blur of splinters.

Before Moses could fire again, Manfred De Le Rey bulked in the doorway behind him. He had seen Shasa's agitation and followed him up from the chamber.

He took in the situation at first glance, and he reacted instantly. He swung the big hard fist that had won him an Olympic gold medal, and it crashed into the side of Moses Gama's neck below the ear.

The pistol fell from Moses' hand and he toppled forward unconscious on top of it.

Shasa dragged himself off the desk and tottered across to Blaine. 'Here,' he whispered, as he dropped to his knees beside him. 'Let me have a look.'

Tara was blubbering incoherently. 'Daddy, I'm sorry. I didn't mean this to happen. I only did what I thought was right.'

Shasa tried to pull her away, but she clung to Blaine, blood on her hands and down the front of her dress.

'Let him alone,' Shasa said, but she was hysterical now, and tugged at her father so that his head jerked from side to side loosely. 'Daddy, speak to me, Daddy.'

Shasa leaned back and slapped her hard, knocking her head across.

'Leave him, you murderous bitch,' he hissed at her, and she crawled away from him, her face beginning to redden and swell from the blow. Shasa ignored her and gently opened the jacket of Blaine's dark suit.

Shasa was a hunter, and he recognized the bright clear colour of arterial blood seething with tiny bubbles from the torn lungs.

'No,' he whispered. 'Please, no!'

Only then he realized that Blaine was watching his face, reading in it his own death.

'Your mother —' he said, and the wind of his lungs puffed

395

through the bullet hole in his chest. 'Tell Centaine —' he could not go on.

'Don't talk,' Shasa said. 'We will get a doctor.' He shouted over his shoulder at Manfred who was already on the telephone, 'Hurry, man. Hurry!'

But Blaine gripped his sleeve, tugging it urgently. 'Love —' he choked on his own blood. 'Tell her – love – tell her I love her.' He got it out at last, and panted as the blood gurgled in his chest – and then he gathered himself for his last great effort.

'Shasa,' he said. 'Shasa, my son – my only son.'

The noble silver head fell forward, and Shasa held it to his chest, hugging him as he had never been able to before.

Then still holding him, Shasa wept for the man who had been his friend and his father. The tears squeezed out of his empty eyesocket and trickled from under the silk eye-patch down his face to mingle with his own blood and drip from his chin.

When Tara crawled forward on her knees, and reached out to touch her father's corpse, Shasa lifted his head and looked at her.

'Don't touch him,' he said softly. 'Don't you dare soil him with your touch.' There was such a look in his single eye, such contempt and hatred in his face, that she recoiled from him and covered her face with both hands. Still on her knees, she began to sob hysterically. The sound of it rallied Shasa. Gently he laid Blaine on his back and closed his eyes with his fingertips.

In the doorway Moses groaned and shuddered, and Manfred slammed the telephone back on its cradle and crossed to him. He stood over him, with those huge fists clenched and asked, 'Who is he?'

'Moses Gama.' Shasa stood up, and Manfred grunted.

'So, we have been looking for him for years. What was he doing?'

'I'm not sure.' Shasa went to where Tricia lay and stooped over her. 'But I think he has laid explosives somewhere in the House. That is the transmitter. We'd better clear the place and have the army bomb disposal —' He didn't have to finish, for at that moment there was the sound of running men in the corridor and three of the security guards burst into the suite.

Manfred took over immediately, snapping orders at them. 'Get the handcuffs on that black bastard.' He pointed at Moses. 'And then I want the building cleared.'

Shasa freed Tricia, leaving the gag until last, but the instant her mouth was clear Tricia pointed at Tara where she still knelt sobbing beside Blaine's corpse.

'She —' Shasa did not let her finish. He seized her wrist and jerked Tricia to her feet.

'Quiet!' he snarled at her, and his fury silenced the girl for a moment. He dragged her through into the outer office and closed the door.

'Listen to me, Tricia.' He faced her, still holding both her wrists.

'But she was with him.' Tricia was trembling. 'It was her —'

'Listen to me.' Shasa shook her into silence. 'I know. I know all about it. But I want you to do something for me. Something for which I will always be grateful. Will you do it?'

Tricia sobered and stared at him. She saw the blood and the tears on his face and thought her heart might break for him. Shasa took the handkerchief from his top pocket and wiped his face.

'For me, Tricia. Please,' he repeated and she gulped noisily and nodded.

'If I can,' she agreed.

'Don't say anything about my wife's part in this until the police take a formal statement from you. That won't be until much later. Then you can tell them everything.'

'Why?' she asked.

'For me and for my children. Please Tricia.'

Again she nodded and he kissed her forehead. 'You are a good brave girl,' he said and left her.

He went back into the inner office. The security police were grouped around Moses Gama. He was manacled but he lifted his head and stared at Shasa for a moment. It was a smouldering gaze, dark and filled with outrage. Then they led him away.

The office was crowded and noisy. White-uniformed ambulance attendants were bringing a stretcher through the doorway. A doctor, a member of parliament summoned from the chamber, was working over Blaine as he lay on his back, but now he stood up, shook his head and gestured at the stretcher bearers to take Blaine's body. The uniformed guards, supervised by Manfred De La Rey, were already gathering up the pieces of the smashed transmitter and beginning to trace the wire to its source.

Tara was sitting in the chair behind his desk, weeping silently into her hands. Shasa went past her to the wall safe hidden behind one of the paintings.

He tumbled the combination and swung open the steel door, screening it with his own body. Shasa always kept two or three thousand pounds in banknotes against an emergency. He stuffed the wads into his pockets, and then quickly he sorted through the stack of family passports until he found Tara's. He relocked the safe, went to where she sat and pulled her to her feet.

'Shasa, I didn't —'

'Keep quiet,' he hissed at her, and Manfred De La Rey glanced at him across the office.

397

'She's had a terrible shock,' Shasa said. 'I'm taking her home.'

'Come back here as soon as you can,' Manfred nodded. 'We'll need a statement.'

Still gripping her arm, Shasa marched her out of the office and down the corridor. The fire alarm bells were ringing throughout the building and members and visitors and staff were streaming out through the front doors. Shasa joined them, and as soon as they were out in the sunlight he led Tara to the Jaguar.

'Where are we going?' Tara asked, as they drove away. She sat very small and subdued in her corner of the bucket seat.

'If you talk to me again, I may lose control,' he warned her tightly. 'I may not be able to stop myself strangling you.'

She did not speak again until they reached Youngsfield Airport, and Shasa pushed her up into the cockpit of the silver and blue Mosquito.

'Where are we going?' she repeated, but he ignored her as he went through the start-up procedures and taxied out to the end of the runway. He did not speak until they had climbed to cruise altitude and were flying straight and level.

'The evening flight for London leaves Johannesburg at seven o'clock. As soon as we are in radio contact, I will reserve your seat,' he told her. 'We will get there with an hour or so to spare.'

'I don't understand,' she whispered into her oxygen mask. 'Are you helping me to escape? I don't understand why.'

'For my mother, firstly. I don't want her to know that you murdered her husband – it would destroy her.'

'Shasa, I didn't —' she was weeping again, but he felt no twinge of compassion.

'Shut up,' he said. 'I don't want want to listen to your blubbering. You will never know the depths of my feelings for you. Hatred and contempt are gentle words that do not describe them.' He drew a breath. Then went on, 'After my mother, I am doing it for my children. I don't want them to live their lives with the knowledge of what their mother truly was. That is too much for a young man or woman to be burdened with.'

Then they were both silent, and Shasa allowed the terrible grief of Blaine's death, which up until then he had suppressed, to rise up and engulf him. In the seat beside him Tara was mourning her father also, spasms of weeping shook her shoulders. Her face above the mask was chalky and her eyes were like wounds.

As strong as his grief was Shasa's hatred. After an hour's flying, he spoke again.

'If you ever return to this country again, I will see you hanged. That is my solemn promise. I will be divorcing you for desertion as soon as possible. There will be no question of alimony or maintenance or child custody. You will have no rights nor privileges of any kind. As far as we are concerned, it will be as though you have never existed. I expect you will be able to claim political asylum somewhere, even if it is in Mother Russia.'

Again he was silent, gathering himself, regaining full control.

'You will not even be at your father's funeral, but every minute of every day his memory will stalk you. That is the only punishment I am able to inflict upon you – God grant it is enough. If He is just, your guilt will slowly drive you mad. I pray for that.'

She did not reply, but turned her face away. Later, when they were on approach to Johannesburg, descending through ten thousand feet, with the skyscrapers and the white mine dumps glowing in the late sunlight ahead of them, Shasa asked:

'You were sleeping with him, weren't you?'

Instinctively, she knew it was the last chance she would ever have to inflict pain upon him, and she turned in the seat to watch his face as she replied.

'Yes, I love him – and we are lovers.' She saw him wince, but she wanted to hurt him more and she went on. 'Apart from my father's death, there is nothing I regret. Nothing I have done of which I am ashamed. On the contrary, I am proud to have known and loved a man like Moses Gama – proud of what I have done for him and for my country.'

'Think of him kicking and choking on the rope, and be proud of that also,' Shasa said quietly, and landed. He taxied the Mosquito to the terminal buildings and they climbed down on to the tarmac and faced each other. There was a bruise on her face where he had struck her, and the icy highveld wind pulled at their clothing and ruffled their hair. He handed her the little bundle of bank notes and her passport.

'Your seat on the London flight is reserved. There is enough here to pay for it and to take you where you want to go.' His voice broke as his rage and his sorrow took control of him again. 'To hell or the gallows, if my wish for you comes true. I hope never to see or hear of you again.'

He turned away from her, but she called after him.

'We were always enemies, Shasa Courtney, even in the best times. And we will be enemies to the very end. Despite your wish, you will hear of me again. I promise you that much.'

He climbed into the Mosquito and it was minutes before he had himself sufficiently in hand to start the engines. When he looked out through the windshield again, she was gone.

*   *   *

399

Centaine would not let them bury Blaine. She could not bear the thought of him lying in the earth, swelling and putrefying.

Mathilda Janine, Blaine's younger daughter, came down from Johannesburg with David Abrahams, her husband, in the company Dove, and they sat with the family in the front row of the memorial chapel at the crematorium. Over a thousand mourners attended the service and both Dr Verwoerd and Sir De Villiers Graaff, the leader of the opposition, were amongst them.

Centaine kept the little urn of Blaine's ashes on the table beside her bed for almost a month, before she could get up her courage. Then she summoned Shasa, and the two of them climbed the hill to her favourite rock.

'Blaine and I used to come here so often,' she whispered. 'This will be the place where I shall come when I need to know that he is still close to me.'

She was nearly sixty years old, and when Shasa studied her with compassion, he saw that for the first time she truly looked that old. She was letting the grey grow out in the thick bush of her hair and he saw that soon there would be more of it than the black. Grief had dulled her gaze and weighed down the corners of her mouth, and that clear youthful skin which she so carefully cherished, seemed overnight to have seamed and puckered.

'Do it for me, please Shasa,' she said, and handed him the urn.

Shasa opened it and stepped out of the lee of the rock, into the full force of the south-easter. The wind fluttered his shirt like a trapped bird, and he turned to look back at her.

Centaine nodded encouragement, and he held the urn high and upended it. The ashes streamed away like dust in the wind, and when the urn was empty, Shasa turned to her once more.

'Break it!' she commanded, and he hurled the vessel against the rock face. It shattered, and she gasped and swayed on her feet.

Shasa ran to her and held her in his arms.

'Death is the only adversary I know I shall never overcome. Perhaps that is why I hate it so,' she whispered.

He led her to her seat on the rock and they were silent for a long while, staring out over the wind-speckled Atlantic and then Centaine said, 'I know you have been protecting me. Now tell me about Tara. What was her part in this?'

So he told her, and when he finished Centaine said, 'You have made yourself an accessory to murder. Was it worth it?'

'Yes. I think so,' he answered without hesitation. 'Could any of us have survived her trial if I had allowed her to be arrested and charged?'

'Will there be consequences?'

Shasa shook his head. 'Manfred – he will protect us again. Just as he did with Sean.'

Shasa saw her pain at the mention of Sean's name. Like him she had never recovered from it, but now she said quietly, 'Sean was one thing, but this is murder and treason and attempting to assassinate a head of state. It is fostering bloody revolution and attempting by force to overthrow a government. Can Manfred protect us from that? And if he can, why should he?'

'I don't know the answers to that, Mater.' Shasa looked at her searchingly. 'I thought that perhaps you did.'

'What do you mean?' she asked, and he thought that he might have taken her unawares, for there was fear and confusion in her eyes for an instant. Blaine's death had slowed her and weakened her. Before that, she would never have betrayed herself so readily.

'In protecting us, me in particular, Manfred is protecting himself and his political ambitions,' Shasa reasoned it out carefully. 'For if I am destroyed, then – I am his *protégé* – his own career would be blighted. But there is more than that. More than I can fathom.'

Centaine did not reply, but she turned her head away and looked out to sea.

'It's as though Manfred De La Rey feels some strange loyalty to us, or a debt that he must repay – or even a sense of deep guilt towards our family. Is that possible, Mater? Is there something that I do not know of that would put him under an obligation to us? Have you withheld something from me all these years?'

He watched her struggle with herself, and at one moment it seemed she might burst out with some long-hidden truth, or with a terrible secret that she had carried too long alone. Then he saw her expression firm and it was almost possible to watch the strength and force which had been drained from her since Blaine's death flow back into her.

It was a little miracle. Age seemed to fall away from her. Her eyes brightened and her carriage of head and shoulders was once more erect and perky. Even the lines and creases around her eyes and mouth seemed to smooth away.

'What ever gave you that idea?' she asked crisply, and stood up. 'I've been moping and pining far too long. Blaine would never have approved of that.' She took Shasa's arm. 'Come along. I've still got a life to live and work to do.'

Half-way down the hill, she asked suddenly, 'When does the trial of Moses Gama begin?'

'The tenth of next month.'

'Do you know he once worked for us, this Moses Gama?'

401

'Yes, Mater. I remembered him. That was how I was able to stop him.'

'He was a terrible troublemaker even in those days. We must do all we can to ensure that he pays the extreme penalty. That is the least we can do for Blaine's memory.'

*　　*　　*

'I don't understand why you are saddling me with this little scrubber,' Desmond Blake protested acidly. He had been twenty-two years on the newspaper and before the gin bottle had taken over, he had been the best courtroom and political journalist on the staff of the *Golden City Mail*. The quantities of gin which he absorbed had not only placed a ceiling on his career but had greyed and prematurely lined his face, ruined his liver and soured his disposition without, however, clouding his insight into the criminal mind nor spoiling his political acumen.

'Well, he is a bright lad,' his editor explained reasonably.

'This is the biggest, most sensational trial of our century,' Desmond Blake said, 'and you want me to drag a cub reporter with me, a puking infant who couldn't even cover a local flower show or a mayoral tea party.'

'I think he has a lot of potential – I just want you to take him in hand and show him the ropes.'

'Bullshit!' said Desmond Blake. 'Now tell me the real reason.'

'All right.' The editor showed his exasperation. 'The real reason is that his grandmother is Centaine Courtney and his father is Shasa Courtney, and Courtney Mining and Finance have acquired thirty-five per cent of the shareholding of our parent company over the past months, and if you know nothing else you should know that nobody bucks Centaine Courtney, not if they want to remain in business. Now take the kid with you and stop bitching. I haven't got time to argue any more – I've got a paper to get out.'

Desmond Blake threw up both hands in despair, and as he rose to leave the office his editor added one last unsubtle threat.

'Just look at it this way, Des. It will be good job insurance, especially for an aging newshound who needs the price of a bottle of gin a day. Just think of the kid as the boss's son.'

Desmond wandered lugubriously down the length of the city room. He knew the boy by sight. Somebody had pointed him out as a sprig of the Courtney empire and wondered aloud what the hell he was doing here instead of on the polo field.

Desmond stopped beside the corner desk which Michael was sharing with two other juniors.

402

'Your name is Michael Courtney?' he asked, and the boy leapt to his feet.

'Yes, sir.' Michael was overcome at being directly addressed by somebody who had his own column and by-line.

'Shit!' said Desmond bitterly. 'Nothing is more depressing than the shining face of youth and enthusiasm. Come along, boy.'

'Where are we going?' Michael snatched up his jacket eagerly.

'To the George, boy. I need a double to give me the strength to go through with this little lark.'

At the bar of the George, he studied Michael over the rim of his glass.

'Your first lesson, boy —' he took a swallow of gin and tonic. 'Nothing is ever what it seems to be. Nobody is ever what he says he is. Engrave that on your heart. Your second lesson. Stick to your orange juice. They don't call this stuff mother's ruin for nothing. Your third lesson. Always pay for the drinks with a smile.' He took another swig. 'So you are from Cape Town, are you? Well that's just fine, because that is where we are going, you and me. We are going to see a man condemned to die.'

*   *   *

Vicky Gama took the bus from Baragwanath Hospital to Drake's Farm. It went only as far as the administration building and the new government school. She had to walk the last mile through the narrow dusty lanes between the rows of raw brick cottages. She walked slowly, for although her pregnancy was only four months advanced, she was beginning to tire easily.

Hendrick Tabaka was in the crowded general dealer's shop, watching the tills, but he came to Vicky immediately and she greeted him with the respect due to her husband's eldest brother. He led her through to his office, and called for one of his sons to bring her a comfortable chair.

Vicky recognized Raleigh Tabaka, and smiled at him as he placed her chair. 'You have grown into a fine young man, Raleigh. Have you finished your schooling now?'

'*Yebo, sissie.*' Raleigh returned her greeting with polite reserve, for even though she was the wife of his uncle, she was a Zulu. His father had taught him to distrust all Zulus. 'I help my father now, *sissie*. I learn the business from him and soon I will manage one of the shops on my own.'

Hendrick Tabaka smiled proudly at his favourite son. 'He learns fast, and I have great faith in the boy.' He endorsed what Raleigh had said. 'I am sending him soon to our shop at Sharpeville near Vereeniging to learn the bakery business.'

'Where is your twin brother, Wellington?' Vicky asked, and immediately Hendrick Tabaka frowned heavily and waved at Raleigh to leave the office. As soon as they were alone, he answered her question angrily. 'The white priests have captured Wellington's heart. They have seduced him from the gods of his tribe and his ancestors and taken him to the service of the white man's God. This strange Jesus God with three heads. It grieves me deeply, for I had hoped that Wellington, like Raleigh, would be the son of my old age. Now he studies to be a priest, and I have lost him.'

He sat down at the tiny cluttered table that served him as a desk and studied his own hands for a moment. Then he raised that bald cannonball head, the scalp criss-crossed with ridged scars from old battles.

'So, wife of my brother, we live in a time of great sorrow. Moses Gama has been taken by the white men's police, and we cannot doubt what they will do with him. Even in my sorrow, I must recall that I warned him that this would happen. A wise man does not throw stones at the sleeping lion.'

'Moses Gama did what he knew was his duty. He lived out the deed for which he was born,' Vicky said quietly. 'He struck a blow for all of us – you and me and our children.' She touched her belly where beneath the white nurse's uniform the first bulge of her pregnancy showed. 'And now he needs our help.'

'Tell me how I can help.' Hendrick inclined his head. 'For he was not only my brother, but my chief as well.'

'We need money to hire a lawyer to defend him in the white man's court. I have been to see Marcus Archer and the others of the ANC at the house in Rivonia. They will not help us. They say that Moses acted without their agreement or approval. They say that it was agreed not to endanger human life. They say that if they give us money to help in the defence, the police will trace it to them. They say many other things – everything but the truth.'

'What is the truth, my sister?' Hendrick asked.

And suddenly Vicky's voice was quivering with fury. 'The truth is that they hate him. The truth is that they are afraid of him. The truth is that they are jealous of him. Moses has done what none of them would have dared. He has aimed a spear at the heart of the white tyrant, and though the blow failed, now all the world knows that it was struck. Not only in this land, but beyond the sea, all the world knows now who is the leader of our people.'

'That is true,' Hendrick nodded. 'His name is on every man's lips.'

'We must save him, Hendrick my brother. We must do everything we can to save him.

Hendrick rose and went to the small cupboard in the corner. He

404

dragged it aside to reveal the door of an ancient Chatwood safe built into the wall behind it.

When he opened the green steel door, the safe was packed with wads of banknotes.

'This belongs to Moses. It is his share. Take what you need,' said Hendrick Tabaka.

*   *   *

The Supreme Court of the Cape Province of South Africa stands on one side of the gardens that Jan van Riebeeck, the first governor of the Cape, laid out in the 1650s to provision the ships of the Dutch East India Company. On the opposite side of the beautiful gardens stand the houses of parliament that Moses Gama had attempted to destroy. So he was to be tried within a quarter of a mile of the scene of the crime of which he stood accused.

The case aroused the most intense international interest and the film crews and journalists began flying into Cape Town a week before it was set down to commence.

Vicky Gama arrived by train after the thousand-mile journey down the continent from the Witwatersrand. She travelled with the white lawyer who would defend Moses and more than fifty of the more radical members of the African National Congress, most of them, like herself, under thirty years of age, and many of them secret members of Moses Gama's *Umkhonto we Sizwe* military wing of the party. Amongst these was Vicky's half brother, Joseph Dinizulu, now a young man of almost twenty-one studying to be a lawyer at the black university of Fort Hare. The money given to Vicky by Hendrick Tabaka paid for all of them.

Molly Broadhurst met them at the Cape Town station. Vicky, Joseph and the defence lawyer would be staying at her home in Pinelands during the trial, and she had arranged accommodation for all the others in the black townships of Langa and Guguletu.

Desmond Blake and Michael Courtney flew down together from Johannesburg on the commercial flight, and while Desmond put a severe strain on the bar service, Michael pored over the notebook in which he was roughing out a schedule of all the research into the history of the ANC and the background of Moses Gama and his tribe that he felt they would need.

Centaine Courtney-Malcomess was at the airport to meet the flight. Much to Michael's embarrassment, she had two servants to carry Michael's single valise out to the daffodil-yellow Daimler that, as usual, she was driving herself. Since Tara had left, Centaine had once more taken over the running of Weltevreden.

405

'The paper has booked rooms for us at the Atlantic Hotel, Nana,' Michael protested, after he had dutifully embraced his grandmother. 'It's very convenient for the law courts and the national library.'

'Nonsense,' said Centaine firmly. 'The Atlantic is a bug-run and Weltevreden is your home.'

'Father said I wouldn't be welcome back.'

'Your father has missed you even more than I have.'

Shasa sat Michael beside him at dinner, and even Isabella was almost totally excluded from their conversation. Shasa was so impressed by his youngest son's sudden new maturity that the following morning he instructed his broker to purchase another hundred thousand shares in the holding company that owned the *Golden City Mail*.

Manfred and Heidi dined at Weltevreden the evening before the trial began and while they drank pre-prandial cocktails Manfred expressed the concern that Shasa and Centaine shared.

'What the prosecution and the court must avoid is allowing the proceedings to deteriorate into a trial not of a murderer and a terrorist, but of our social system and our way of life. The vultures of the international press are already assembled, eager to show us in the worst possible light, and as usual to distort and misrepresent our policy of *apartheid*. I only wish we had some control over the courts and the press.'

'You know I can't agree with you on that one.' Shasa shifted in his chair. 'The complete independence of our press and the impartiality of our judicial system gives us credibility in the eyes of the rest of the world.'

'Don't lecture me. I am a lawyer,' Manfred pointed out stiffly.

It was strange how despite their enforced and mutually beneficial relationship, they were never truly friends and antagonism was always ready to surface between them. Now it took some little time for the tension to ease, and for them to adopt once more an outward show of cordiality. Only then could Manfred tell Shasa, 'We have finally agreed with the prosecution not to raise in court the matter of your wife's involvement with the accused. Apart from the difficulty of beginning extradition proceedings with Britain – she would almost certainly ask for political asylum – there is the consideration of her relationship with Gama. Black man and white woman —' Manfred's expression was one of deep disgust. 'It is repugnant to all decent principles. Raising the subject would not further the prosecution, but would simply give the yellow press something more to drool over. No, it will do none of us any good at all.' Manfred put special emphasis on this last sentence. It was all that needed to be said, but Shasa did not let it pass.

'I owe you a great deal – for my son, Sean, and now my wife.'

'*Ja*, you owe me a great deal,' Manfred nodded. 'Perhaps I will ask you for something in return one day.'

'I hope so,' said Shasa. 'I do not like having outstanding debts.'

*   *   *

Outside the Supreme Court both pavements were filled with people. They were standing shoulder to shoulder and overflowing into the street, complicating the efforts of the traffic wardens and impeding the flow of traffic until it was reduced to a crawl.

A newspaper poster, 'GUY FAWKES KILLER TRIAL BEGINS TODAY', hung drunkenly from one of the lampposts until it was knocked down by the push of the crowd and trodden underfoot.

The throng was thickest at the colonnaded entrance to the Supreme Court and each time one of the players in the drama arrived, the journalists and photographers surged forward. The state prosecutor smiled and waved to them like a film star, but most of the others, intimidated by the crowds and the exploding flash bulbs and shouted questions, scurried for the entrance and the protection of the police guards.

Only minutes before the court was due to go into session, a chartered bus turned into the slow-moving stream of traffic and came down towards the entrance. The sound of singing grew louder as it approached, the lovely haunting chorus of African voices rising and sinking and weaving the intricate tapestry of sound that thrilled the ears and raised the gooseflesh on the skins of the listeners.

When the bus finally halted in front of the Supreme Court, a young Zulu woman stepped down into the street. She wore a flowing caftan of green and yellow and black, the colours of the African National Congress, and her head was bound in a turban of the same colours.

Her pregnancy had given Vicky a fullness of body that enhanced her natural fine looks. There was no trace left of the shy little country girl. She carried her head high, and moved with all the confidence and style of an African Evita.

The press cameramen recognized instantly that they were being presented with an unusual opportunity and they rushed forward with their equipment to capture her dark beauty, and the sound of her voice as she sang the thrilling hymn to freedom.

'*Nkosi Sikelel' iAfrika* – God Save Africa.'

Behind her, holding hands, and singing, came all the others, some of them white like Molly Broadhurst and some of them Indians and coloured like Miriam and Ben Afrika, but most of them pure African. They streamed up the steps into the court house to fill the section of

407

the gallery of the courtroom reserved for non-whites and to overflow into the corridors outside.

The rest of the court was packed with the press and the curious, while a separate section had been set aside for observers from the diplomatic corps. Every one of the embassies was represented.

At every entrance to the court were police guards wearing sidearms, and four policemen of warrant officer rank were drawn up around the dock. The prisoner was a killer and a dangerous revolutionary. They were taking no chances.

Yet when he stepped up into the dock, Moses Gama seemed none of these things. He had lost weight during his imprisonment, but this merely enhanced his great height and the wide angularity of his shoulders. His cheeks were hollow, and the bones of his face and forehead were more prominent, but he stood proudly as ever with his chin up and that dark messianic glow in his eyes.

His presence was so overpowering that he seemed to take possession of the room; the gasp and hum of curiosity as he stood before them was subdued by an almost tangible sense of awe. In the back of the gallery Vicky Dinizulu sprang to her feet and began to sing, and those around her came in with the chorus. As he listened to her beautiful ringing voice, Moses Gama inclined his head slightly, but he did not smile or give any other sign of recognition.

Vicky's freedom song was interrupted by a cry of '*Stilte in die hof! Opstaan!* Silence in the court! Stand up!'

The judge-president of the Cape, wearing the scarlet robes which indicated that this was a criminal trial, took his seat on the bench beneath the carved canopy.

Justice André Villiers was a big man with a flamboyant courtroom style. He had a reputation for being a connoisseur of food, good wine and pretty girls. He was also noted for handing down savage sentences for crimes of violence.

Now he slumped massively on the bench and glowered around his court as the charge sheet was read, but his gaze checked momentarily as it reached each female, the length of the pause proportional to the prettiness of the recipient. On Kitty Godolphin he spent at least two seconds and when she smiled her angelic little-girl smile at him, he hooded his eyes slightly before passing on.

There were four main charges on the sheet against Moses Gama, two of attempted murder, and one each of high treason and murder. Every one of these was a capital offence but Moses Gama showed no emotion as he listened to them read out.

Judge Villiers broke the expectant silence that followed the reading. 'How do you plead to these charges?'

Moses leaned forward, both clenched fists on the rail of the dock

408

and his voice was low and full of scorn, but it carried to every corner of the crowded court.

'Verwoerd and his brutal government should be in this dock,' he said. 'I plead not guilty.'

Moses sat down and did not raise his eyes while the judge enquired who appeared for the crown, and the prosecutor introduced himself to the court, but when Mr Justice Villiers asked:

'Who appears for the defence?' before the advocate whom Vicky and Hendrick Tabaka had retained could reply, Moses sprang to his feet again.

'I do,' he cried. 'I am on trial here for the aspirations of the African people. No other can speak for me. I am the leader of my people, I will answer for myself and for them.'

There was such consternation in the court now, such uproar that for a few moments the judge pounded his gavel in vain, demanding silence, and when it was at last obtained, he threatened them.

'If there is another such demonstration of contempt for this court, I will not hesitate to have it cleared.'

He turned back to Moses Gama to reason with him and try to persuade him to accept legal representation, but Moses forestalled him.

'I wish to move immediately that you, Judge Villiers, recuse yourself from this case,' he challenged, and the scarlet-robed judge blinked and was for a moment stunned into silence.

Then he smiled grimly at the prisoner's effrontery and asked, 'On what grounds do you make this application?'

'On the grounds that you, as a white judge, are incapable of being impartial and fair to me, a black man, forced to submit to the immoral laws of a parliament in which I have no representation.'

The judge shook his head, half in exasperation and half in admiration. 'I am going to deny your application for recusal,' he said. 'And I am going to urge you to accept the very able services of the counsel who has been appointed to represent you.'

'I accept neither his services, nor the competence of this court to condemn me. For all the world knows that is what you propose. I accept only the verdict of my poor enslaved people and of the free nations out there. Let them and history decide my innocence or guilt.'

The press were electrified, some of them so enchanted that they made no effort to write down his words. None of them would ever forget them. For Michael Courtney sitting in the back row of the press section, it was a revelation. He had lived with Africans all his life, his family employed them by the tens of thousands, but until this moment he had never met a black man of such dignity and awe-inspiring presence.

Judge Villiers sagged down in his seat. He always maintained his place firmly in the centre-stage of his court, overshadowing everybody in it with the ruthless authority of a born actor. Here he sensed he had met an equal. The entire attention of everybody in the court was captivated by Moses Gama.

'Very well,' Judge Villiers said at last. 'Mr Prosecutor, you may proceed to present the case for the crown.'

The prosecutor was a master of his profession and he had an infallible case. He worked it up with meticulous attention to detail, with logic and with skill.

One at a time he submitted his exhibits to the court. The wiring and the electrical detonator, the Tokarev pistol and spare magazines. Although it was considered too dangerous to allow the blocks of plastic explosives and the detonators into the courtroom, photographs were submitted and accepted. The altar chest was too large to bring into court, and again photographs were accepted by Judge Villiers. Then there were the gruesome photographs of Shasa's office, with Blaine's covered body against the bookcases and his blood splashed over the carpet, and the wreckage of broken furniture and scattered papers. Centaine turned her face away as the photographs were handed in and Shasa squeezed her arm and tried to shield her from the curious glances.

After all the exhibits had been tabled, the prosecutor called his first witness. 'I call the honourable Minister of Mines and Industry, Mr Shasa Courtney.'

Shasa was on the witness stand for the rest of that day and all of the following morning, describing in detail how he had discovered and thwarted the bombing.

The prosecutor took him back to his first childhood meeting with Moses Gama, and as Shasa described their relationship, Moses raised his head and for the first time since he had taken the stand looked directly into Shasa's face. In vain Shasa searched for the slightest trace of that sympathy they had once shared, but there was none. Moses Gama's stare was baleful and unwavering.

When at last the prosecutor had finished with Shasa, he turned to the accused. 'Your witness,' he said, and Justice Villiers roused himself.

'Do you wish to cross-examine the witness?'

Moses shook his head and looked away, but the judge insisted. 'This will be your last opportunity to query or refute the witness's evidence. I urge you to make full use of it.'

Moses crossed his arms over his chest, and closed his eyes as though in sleep, and from the non-white section of the court there were hoots of laughter and the stamping of feet.

Justice Villiers raised his voice, 'I will not warn you again,' and there was silence in the face of his anger.

Over the next four days the prosecutor placed his witnesses on the stand.

Tricia, Shasa's secretary, explained how Moses had gained entrance to the office suite in the guise of a chauffeur and how on the day of the murder Moses had seized and bound her. How she had watched him fire the fatal shot that killed Colonel Malcomess.

'Do you wish to cross-examine the witness?' Judge Villiers asked, and once again Moses shook his head.

Manfred De La Rey gave his evidence and described how he had found Moses Gama with the pistol in his hand and Blaine Malcomess lying on the floor dying. How he had heard him cry, 'You! You!' and saw him deliberately fire the pistol at Shasa Courtney.

'Do you wish to cross-examine the witness?' the judge asked, and this time Moses did not even look up.

An electrical engineer described the captured equipment and identified the transmitter as being of Russian origin. An explosives expert told the court of the destructive power of the plastic explosives placed beneath the government benches.

'In my opinion it would have been sufficient to destroy totally the entire chamber and the adjoining rooms. It would certainly have killed every person in the main chamber, and most of those in the lobby and the surrounding offices.'

After each witness had finished his evidence Moses again refused to cross-examine. At the end of the fourth day the crown had presented its case, and Judge Villiers adjourned the court with one last appeal to the prisoner.

'When the court reconvenes on Monday, you will be required to answer the charges against you. I must once more impress upon you the grave nature of the accusations, and point out to you that your very life is at stake. Yet again I urge you to accept the services of legal counsel.'

Moses Gama smiled at him with contempt.

*　　*　　*

Dinner at Weltevreden that evening was a sombre affair. The only one who was unaffected by the day's events was Garry, who had flown down in the Mosquito from the Silver River Mine for the weekend.

While the rest of the family sat in silence, each of them brooding on the events of these last days and their own particular part in

411

them, Garry was enthusiastically selling to Centaine and Shasa his latest plan for reducing costs at the mine.

'Accidents cost us money in lost production. I'll admit that in the last two years our safety record has been about average for the industry as a whole, but if we could cut down our fatalities to one per hundred thousand shifts or better, we could reduce our overall production costs by over twelve per cent. That is twenty million pounds a year. On top of that we would get the added bonus of worker satisfaction and co-operation. I have put all the figures through the computer.' Garry's eyes behind his spectacles glittered as he mentioned that piece of equipment. Shasa had reports from Dave Abrahams and the general manager of the Silver River that Garry sometimes sat all night at one of the terminals of the new IBM computer that the company had at last installed.

'The lad knows his way around the machine as well, if not better, than any of our full-time operators. He can almost make it sit up and whistle "God Save the Queen".' David Abrahams had not attempted to conceal his admiration and Shasa had remarked deprecatingly, to conceal his paternal pride, 'That will be a redundant accomplishment by next year, when we become a republic.'

'Oh, Garry, you are being an utter bore,' Isabella interrupted him at last. 'All that business about tonnages and penny weights – at the dinner table, what's more. No wonder you can't find a girlfriend.'

'For once I think Bella is right,' Centaine said quietly from the end of the table. 'That's enough for one night, Garry. I just cannot concentrate at the moment. I think this has been one of the worst weeks of my entire life, having to watch that monster, with Blaine's blood on his hands, sitting there defying us and making a mockery of our system of justice. He threatens to tear down the whole structure of government, to plunge us all into anarchy and the same savagery of Africa which rent the land before we whites arrived. Then he smirks at us from the dock. I hate him. I have never hated anything or anybody as much as I hate him. I pray each night that they hang him.'

Unexpectedly it was Michael who replied. 'Yes, we hate him, Nana. We hate him because we are afraid of him, and we are afraid of him because we do not understand him or his people.'

They all stared at him in astonishment.

'Of course we understand him,' Centaine said. 'We have lived in Africa all our lives. We understand them as nobody else does.'

'I don't think so, Nana. I think if we had truly understood and listened to what this man had to say, Blaine would be alive today. I think he could have been an ally and not our deadly enemy. I think Moses Gama could have been a useful and highly respected citizen, and not a prisoner on trial for his life.'

'What strange ideas you have picked up on that newspaper of yours! He murdered your grandfather,' Centaine said, and shot a glance down the table at Shasa. Shasa interpreted it fluently and it meant, 'We have another problem on our hands here,' but Michael was going on obliviously.

'Moses Gama will die on the gallows – I think we all know that. But his words and his ideas will live on. I know now why I had to be a journalist. I know what I have to do. I have to explain those ideas to the people of this land, to show them that they are just and fair, and not dangerous at all. In those ideas are the hopes for our survival as a nation.'

'It is a good thing I sent the servants out,' Centaine interrupted him. 'I never thought to hear words like those spoken in the dining-room of Weltevreden.'

*   *   *

Vicky Gama waited for over an hour in the visitors' room at Roeland Street prison while the warders examined the contents of the package she had brought for Moses and made up their minds whether or not to allow her to hand it to the prisoner.

'It is only clothing,' Vicky pointed out reasonably.

'These aren't ordinary clothes,' the senior warden protested.

'They are the traditional robes of my husband's tribe. He is entitled to wear them.'

In the end the prison governor was called in to arbitrate and when he finally gave his permission, Vicky complained, 'Your men have been deliberately rude and obstructive to me.'

He smiled at her sarcastically. 'I wonder how you will treat us, madam, if you and your brothers in the ANC ever seize power. I wonder if you will allow us even the courtesy of a trial or whether you will slaughter us in the streets, as your husband tried to do.'

When Vicky was at last allowed to hand the parcel to Moses under the watchful eye of four warders, he asked her, 'Whose idea was this?'

'It was mine but Hendrick paid for the skins and his wives sewed them.'

'You are a clever woman,' Moses commended her, 'and a dutiful wife.'

'You, my lord, are a great chief, and it is fitting that you should wear the robes of your office.'

Moses held up the full-length cloak of leopard skins, heavy and glossy golden, studded with the sable rosettes.

'You have understood,' he nodded. 'You have seen the necessity

413

of using the white man's courtroom as a stage from which to shout our craving for freedom to the world.'

Vicky lowered her eyes and her voice. 'My lord, you must not die. If you die, then the great part of our dream of freedom dies with you. Will you not defend yourself, for my sake and for the sake of our people?'

'No, I will not die,' he assured her. 'The great nations of the world will not let that happen. Britain has already made her position clear and America cannot afford to let them execute me. Her own nation is wracked by the struggle of the American coloured people – she cannot afford to let me go to my death.'

'I do not trust the altruism of great nations,' Vicky said softly.

'Then trust in their own self-interest,' Moses Gama told her. 'And trust in me.'

*   *   *

When Moses Gama rose before the court in the golden and black robes of leopard skin, he seemed a reincarnation of one of the ancient black kings. He riveted them.

'I call no witnesses,' Gama told them gravely. 'All I will do is to make a statement from the dock. That is as far as I am prepared to co-operate in this mockery of justice.'

'My lord,' the prosecutor was on his feet immediately. 'I must point out to the court —'

'Thank you!' Judge Villiers interrupted him in frigid tones. 'I do not need to be told how to conduct this trial,' and the prosecutor sank back into his seat, still making inarticulate sounds of protest.

Heavily the scarlet-robed justice turned his attention back to Moses Gama.

'What counsel for the prosecution is trying to tell me is that I should make it clear to you that if you do not enter the witness stand and take the oath, if you do not submit to cross-examination, then what you have to say will have little relevance to the proceedings.'

'An oath to your white man's God, in this courtroom with a white judge and a white prosecutor, with white prosecution witnesses and white policemen at the doors. I do not deign to submit to that kind of justice.'

Judge Villiers shook his head with a woeful expression and turned both his hands palms up. 'Very well, you have been warned of the consequences. Proceed with your statement.'

Moses Gama was silent for a long time, and then he began softly.

'There was once a small boy who wandered with joy through a beautiful land, who drank from the sweet clear rivers, who listened with pleasure to the song of the bird and studied the antics of the springbok and pangolin and all the marvellous wild things, a small boy who tended his father's herds, and sat at night by the fire and listened to the tales of the great heroes of his people, of Bambata and Sekhukhuni and mighty Chaka.

'This boy believed himself to be one of a peaceful people who owned the land on which they lived and were free to move wherever they wished in confidence and joy. Then one day when the boy was nine years of age a curious being came to the kraal at which the boy lived, a creature with a red face and a lordly manner, and the boy saw that the people were afraid, even his father and his grandfather who were chieftains of the tribe, were afraid as the boy had never seen them afraid before.'

There was no sound nor movement in the crowded courtroom as Moses Gama described his loss of innocence and how he had learned the bitter truths of his existence. He described his bewilderment as the universe he knew was proved an illusion. He told them of his first journey into the outside world, where he learned that as a man with a black skin there were places where his existence was circumscribed and limited.

When he went to the white man's towns, he found that he could not walk the streets after curfew without a pass, that he could not live outside the areas that had been set aside for his people on the outskirts of that town, but most important to him he found that he could not attend the white man's schools. He learned that in nearly every public building there was a separate entrance for him to use, that there were skills he was not allowed to acquire, and that in almost every way he was considered different and inferior, condemned by the pigmentation of his skin, always to remain on the bottom rung of existence.

Yet he knew that he was a man like other men, with the same hopes and desires. He knew that his heart beat as fiercely and that his body was as strong, and his brain was as bright and quick as any other. He decided that the way to rise above the station in life that had been allotted him was to use that brain rather than employ his body like a beast of burden as most of his people were forced to do.

He turned to the white man's books and was astonished to find that the heroes of his people were described as savages and cattle-thieves and treacherous rebels. That even the most sympathetic and charitable of the authors he read referred to his people as children, unable to reason or think for themselves, children who must be sternly protected but prevented from taking part in the decisions which governed their lives.

He described to them how at last he had realized that it was all

415

some monstrous lie. That he was not different, that because his skin was black he was not unclean or contaminated or childlike. He knew then for what purpose he had been put upon this earth.

'I came to know that the struggle against injustice was my life,' he said simply. 'I knew that I had to make the white men who ruled me and my people understand.'

He explained how each of his attempts to get the white men to listen had failed. How all his people's efforts had resulted only in more savage and draconian laws, in fiercer oppressions.

'In the end I had to accept that there was only one course left to me. That was to take up arms and to strike at the head of the serpent whose venom was poisoning and destroying my people.'

He was silent and his audience who had listened in complete and rigid silence for most of the morning, sighed and stirred, but as soon as Moses Gama spread his arms they were completely attentive once more.

'Every man has a right and a sacred duty to protect his family and his nation from the tyrant, to fight against injustice and slavery. When he does so he becomes a warrior and not a criminal. I challenge this judge and this white man's court to treat me as a soldier and a prisoner of war. For that is what I am.'

Moses Gama drew his leopard skins about him and sat down, leaving them all shaken and silenced.

Judge Villiers had sat through the entire address with his chin couched in his hand, his eyes hooded with concentration, but now he let his hand drop and he leaned forward to glower at the prisoner.

'You claim to be the leader of your people.'

'I do,' Moses replied.

'A leader is chosen or elected. How were you chosen?'

'When an oppressed people has no voice, then their leaders come forward of their own accord to speak for them,' Moses told him.

'So you are a self-proclaimed leader,' the judge said quietly. 'And your decision to declare war on our society was taken alone. Is that correct?'

'We are involved in a colonial war of liberation,' Moses Gama replied. 'Like our brothers in Algeria and Kenya.'

'You approved of the methods of the Mau Mau then?' Judge Villiers asked.

'Their cause was just – their methods, whatever they might have been, were therefore just.'

'The end justifies the means – any means?'

'The struggle for liberation is all, in the name of liberty any deed is sanctified.'

416

'The slaughter and mutilation of innocents, of women and children. These are also justified?'

'If one innocent should die that a thousand might go free, then it is justified.'

'Tell me, Moses Gama, do you believe in democracy – in the concept of "One man, one vote"?'

'I believe that every man should have one vote to elect the leaders of the nation.'

'And after the leaders are chosen, what should happen?'

'I believe that the people should submit to the wisdom of their chosen leaders.'

'A one-party state – with a president for life?'

'That is the African way,' Moses Gama agreed.

'It is also the way of the Marxists,' Judge Villiers observed drily. 'Tell me, Moses Gama, what makes a black totalitarian government superior to a white totalitarian government?'

'The wishes of the majority of the people.'

'And the sanction of your people, of which only you are aware, makes you a holy crusader – above the laws of civilized man?'

'In this land there are no such laws, for the men who make the laws are barbarians,' said Moses Gama softly, and Judge Villiers had no more questions to put to him.

*   *   *

Twenty-four hours later Mr Justice André Villiers delivered his judgement to a hushed and expectant court.

'The basis of the case brought by the crown against the accused rests upon the consideration of how an individual reacts to what he perceives as an injustice. It raises the question of the individual's right or duty to resist those laws which he considers unjust or evil. I have had to consider what loyalty a person owes to a government, which was elected by a process from which he was totally excluded, a government which has furthermore embarked upon a programme of legislation that will deliberately alienate that person from most of the major rights, privileges and benefits of the society of which he is a member —' For almost an hour Judge Villiers enlarged on and examined this proposition, then he summed up. 'I have therefore reached the conclusion that no duty of loyalty exists towards a state in which the individual is denied the basic democratic right of representation. Accordingly, on the charge of high treason I find the accused not guilty.'

There was a throaty roar from the body of the court and in the non-white section of the gallery they were dancing and singing. For

417

almost a full minute Judge Villiers watched them, and those members of the court who knew him well were amazed by his forbearance. But the judge's features were crumpled with an unusual compassion and terrible sadness as he took up his gavel to quieten them.

In the silence he spoke again. 'I come now to the other charges against the accused. Those of murder and attempted murder. The crown has, with the help of the most eminent and trustworthy witnesses, made out a case which the accused has not attempted to challenge. I accept that the accused placed a large body of explosive in the assembly chamber of the South African parliament with the intention of detonating that charge during a speech by the prime minister and thereby inflicting the greatest possible damage and death. I accept also that when his plot was discovered, he slew Colonel Blaine Malcomess and immediately thereafter attempted to murder Minister Courtney.' The judge paused and turned his head towards Moses Gama who sat impassively in the dock, still wearing his leopard-skin robes of chieftainship.

'The accused has offered the defence that he is a soldier in a war of liberation and is therefore not subject to the civil law. While I have already expressed my sympathy for and understanding of the accused's aspirations and those of the black people whom he claims to represent, I cannot entertain his demand that he be treated as a prisoner of war. He is a private individual who, while fully aware of the consequences of his actions, set out on the dark road of violence, determined to inflict the greatest possible destruction in the most indiscriminate fashion. It is therefore without any hesitation whatsoever that I find the accused guilty of murder and two charges of attempted murder.'

There was no sound in the courtroom as Judge Villiers went on softly, 'The prisoner will rise for sentence.'

Slowly Moses Gama came to his full height and he regarded Judge Villiers with an imperial stare.

'Is there anything you wish to say before sentence is passed upon you?' the judge asked.

'This is not justice. We both know that – and history will record it so.'

'Is there anything further you wish to say?'

When Moses shook his head, Judge Villiers intoned, 'Having found you guilty on the three main charges, I have carefully considered whether any extenuating circumstances exist in your case – and at last having determined that there are none, I have no alternative but to impose upon you the maximum penalty which the law decrees. On all the remaining charges, taken jointly and severally, I sentence you, Moses Gama, to death by hanging.'

418

The silence persisted for a moment longer and then from the rear of the court a woman's voice rose in keening ululation, the harrowing wail of African mourning. It was taken up immediately by all the other black women in the courtroom and Judge Villiers made no attempt to silence it.

In the dock Moses Gama raised a clenched fist above his head.

'*Amandla!*' he roared, and his people answered him with a single voice: '*Ngawethu! Mayibuye! Afrika!*'

*   *   *

Manfred De La Rey sat high in the grandstand, in one of the special boxes reserved for the most important spectators. Every single seat in the stand had been sold weeks before and the standing areas around the field were crammed to capacity. This great concourse of humanity had assembled to watch one of the major events of the sporting calendar, the clash between the Western Province and Northern Transvaal rugby football teams. At stake was the Currie Cup, a trophy for which every province of South Africa competed annually in a knock-out tournament. The fanatical partisanship which this contest evoked went far beyond that of mere sporting competition.

Manfred smiled sardonically as he looked around him. The Englishman Macmillan had said that theirs was the first of the African nationalisms. If that was correct, then this was one of their most important tribal rituals, one that united and reaffirmed the Afrikaners as a cohesive entity. No outsider could grasp the significance of the game of rugby football in their culture. True it had been developed at a British public school almost one hundred and fifty years ago, but then, Manfred thought wryly, it was too good for the *rooinekke* and it took an Afrikaner to understand the game and play it to its full potential.

Then again to call it a game was the same as calling politics or war, a game. It was more, a thousand times more. To sit here amongst his own, to be a part of this immense spirit of Afrikanerdom, gave him the same sort of religious awe that he felt when he stood within the congregation of the Dutch Reformed Church, or when he was part of the throng that gathered before the massive Voortrekker Monument that stood on the hills above the city of Pretoria. On the day of the Covenant with God, his people gathered there each year to celebrate the victory that the Almighty had given them over the Zulu King Dingaan at the battle of Blood River.

As was fitting on such an occasion as this, Manfred wore his green blazer piped in gold with the flying Springbok emblem on the pocket

419

and the legend 'Boxing 1936' below it. No matter that the buttons could no longer fasten across his dignified girth, he wore it with pride.

His pride was infinitely magnified when he looked down on the field. The turf was seared by the frosts of early winter but the highveld sunlight gave everything a lucid quality so that Manfred could make out every detail of his son's beloved features as he stood out near the centre of the field.

Lothar De La Rey's magnificent torso was not obscured by the blue woollen jersey that he wore, rather it was emphasized by the thin stuff, so that the lean hard muscle in his belly and chest stood proud. His bare legs were sturdy, but at the same time long and shapely, and the cap of close-cropped hair, coppery blond, burned like fire in the bright highveld sunshine.

Slowly Lothar bowed his head, as though to pray, and a hush fell over the packed grandstand. There was no breath of sound from even one of the forty thousand throats, and Lothar's dark brows clenched in complete concentration.

Slowly he lifted his arms, spreading them like the wings of a falcon on the edge of flight, until they were at the level of his shoulders, a strangely graceful gesture, and he raised his body on tiptoe so that the great muscles of his thighs tightened and changed shape – and then he began to run.

He ran with the bounding motion of that hunting cat, the cheetah, lifting his knees high and driving his whole body forward. Behind him the turf was scarred by the power of his studded boots, and in the immense silence of the arena his grunting breaths, timed to the long elastic strides, carried to where Manfred sat.

The leather ball, shiny brown and ovate, was balanced on one point, and as Lothar bore down on where it stood on the green turf, his pace quickened yet his body remained in perfect balance. The kick was a continuation of that long driving stride, his right leg whipped straight at the exact instant that his toe struck the ball and his weight was so far forward that his leg swung on up in an arcing parabola until his foot, with his toe extended like that of a ballet dancer, was high above his head, while both his arms were flung forward to maintain that graceful balance. The ball was grossly deformed by the brutal impact of the kick, but in flight it snapped back into shape, and rose in a flat hard trajectory towards the two tall white goalposts at the end of the field. It neither tumbled nor wobbled, but flew with a stable motion, as steady in the air as a flighted arrow.

However, a hoarse and anxious sigh went up from the watchers, as they realized that it was aimed too far to the right. Although the power of that mighty right leg had driven it high above the level of the cross bar, it was going to miss the goalposts on the right and Manfred came to his feet with forty thousand others and groaned in helpless agony.

A miss would mean ignominious defeat, but if the ball passed between the white uprights, it would be victory, sweet and famous, by a single point.

The ball rose higher still, up out of the sheltered arena, and it caught the wind. Lothar had studied the flags on the roof of the grandstand before he began his run, and now the wind swung the ball in gently, but not enough, oh, sweet God, not nearly enough. Then gradually the ball lost impetus and power as it reached the zenith of its trajectory, and as it slowed, so the wind took charge, curving it ever more sharply to the left, and Manfred's groan turned to a roar of delight as it fell through the very centre of the goalposts, grazing the white cross bar, and the referee's shrill long-drawn-out whistle signalled the end of the match.

Beside Manfred, his boyhood friend, Roelf Stander, was pounding his back in congratulation.

'Man, I tell you, he is going to be a Springbok for sure, just like his Pa.'

On the field Lothar was surrounded by his team mates who were fighting for a chance to embrace him, while from the stands a wave of spectators was sweeping across the field to lionize him.

'Come, let's go down to the dressing-room.' Manfred took his companion's arm, but it was not that easy. They were stopped every few paces by the well-wishers and Manfred smiled and shook their hands and accepted their congratulations. Although this was part of his life, and his very soul fed on the adulation and enormous respect which every one of them, even the richest and most famous of them, showed towards him, yet today it irked Manfred to be kept from his son.

When at last they reached the dressing-room, the crowd that filled the corridor outside opened miraculously before them, and where others were turned away, they were respectfully ushered through into the steamy noisy room that stank of sweaty clothing and stale urine and hot masculine bodies.

Lothar was in the centre of the crowd of naked young men, singing and wrestling in rough camaraderie, but when he saw his father he broke away and came to him immediately, dressed only in a pair of grass-stained shorts with his magnificent young body glossy with sweat and a brown beer bottle clutched in one hand. His face was rapturous with pride and the sense of his own achievement.

'My son —' Manfred held out his right hand and Lothar seized it joyously.

421

'My son —' Manfred repeated, but his voice failed him and his vision misted over with pride. He jerked his son's hand, pulling him against his own chest, and held him hard, hugging him unashamedly, even while Lothar's sweat stained his shirt and his team mates howled with delight.

The three of them, Manfred, Roelf Stander and Lothar, drove home in the new ministerial Cadillac. They were happy as schoolboys, grinning and joshing each other and singing the bawdy old rugby songs. When they stopped at the traffic lights before entering the main traffic stream at Jan Smuts Drive that would take them the thirty miles across the grassy undulating highveld to Pretoria, there were two small black urchins darting and dodging perilously amongst the vehicles, and one of them peered through the side window of the Cadillac at Manfred, grinning cockily and holding up a copy of the *Mail* from the bundle of newspapers he carried under his arm.

Manfred was about to dismiss him with an impatient gesture, for the *Mail* was an English rag. Then he saw the headlines: 'Appeal Fails: Guy Fawkes Killer to Hang' and he rolled down his side window and flipped the child a coin.

He passed the paper to Roelf Stander with the terse command, 'Read it to me!' and drove on.

This morning the appeal of Moses Gama against his conviction for murder and attempted murder by the Cape division of the Supreme Court was dismissed by a full bench of the Appellate Division in Bloemfontein and the date set for the execution by hanging was confirmed.

'*Ja, goed.*' Although Manfred scowled with concentration as he listened, his relief was intense. Over the months the media and the public had come to accept the Gama case as something intimately linked to Manfred De La Rey. The fact that he had personally made the arrest and that he was minister of police had combined so that the prosecution of the case had become in the public imagination, a measure of the strength and efficiency of the police force and of Manfred's *kragdadigheid*, his own personal power.

More than any other quality the Afrikaner *Volk* demanded strength and determination in its leaders. This case, with its terrifying message of black peril and bloody revolution, had invoked the most intense feelings of insecurity throughout the land. People wanted to be re-assured that their safety and the security of the state were in strong hands. Manfred, with his sure political instincts, had realized that the dice of his future were being cast.

Unfortunately, there had been a complication in what should have been a straightforward matter of justice and swift retribution. The fact that the judge of the Supreme court had dismissed the charge of

422

high treason and had made some controversial and ill-considered remarks about the individual's duty of loyalty to a state in which he was denied direct representation had been taken up by the foreign press and the case had captured the attention of left-wing liberals and Bolsheviks around the western world. In America the bearded hippies and commie university students had formed 'Save Moses Gama' committees and had picketed the White House and the South African embassy in Washington, while even in England there had been demonstrations in Trafalgar Square outside South Africa House by communist-inspired and -financed gangs of black ex-patriates and some white riff-raff. The British prime minister had summoned the South African high commissioner for consultations and President Eisenhower had instructed his ambassador in Pretoria to call upon Hendrik Verwoerd and appeal for mercy for the con-demned man.

The South African government had stood firm in its rejection of these appeals. Their position was that the matter was one for the judiciary and that they would not interfere with the course of justice. However, their lordships of the Appellate Division were occasionally known to indulge in unwise demonstrations of compassion or obscure legal dialectic, in fits of independent thinking which accorded ill with the hard task of the police and the aspirations of the Afri-kaner *Volk*.

This time, mercifully, they had been spared one of their lordships' quirky decisions and in that little green-painted room in Pretoria Central Prison the noose now waited for Moses Gama, and he would crash through the trap to the eternity into which he had planned to send the leaders of the nation.

'*Ja, goed!* Now read the editorial!' Manfred ordered Roelf Stander. The *Golden City Mail* was one of the English language newspapers, and even for that section of the press the views it held were liberal. Manfred would never have bought it for preference, but having done so he was now prepared to dilute his grim satisfaction at the appeal court's verdict, with the irritation of listening to the left-wing eru-dition of the *Mail's* editorial staff.

Roelf Stander rustled the news sheet and cleared his throat.

'A Martyr is Born,' he read, and Manfred gave a growl of anger.

When Moses Gama dies at the end of the hangman's rope, he will become the most significant martyr in the history of the black African struggle for liberation.

Moses Gama's elevation will not be on account of his moving eloquence nor from the awe-inspiring power of his presence. Rather it will be for the simple reason that he has posed a question so grave and so fateful that by its very nature the answer to it can never be given by a single

423

national court of law. The answer rests instead in the heart of mankind itself. For that question is aimed at the very foundation of man's existence upon this earth. Simply stated, it is this: is a man who is deprived of any peaceful or lawful means of asserting his basic human rights justified in turning, in the last resort, to violence?

Manfred snorted. 'Enough of that. I should not have bothered to have you read it out. It is so predictable. If the black savages cut the throats of our children and eat their raw livers, there would still be those *rooinekke* who would chastize us for not having provided salt for the feast! We will not listen to any more of that. Turn to the sports page. Let us hear what they have to say about Lothie and his *manne*, though I doubt that those *souties* can tell the difference between a stick of biltong and a rugby ball.'

When the Cadillac pulled up the long drive to Manfred's official residence in the elite suburb of Waterkloof, there was a large gathering of family and friends at the swimming-pool at the far end of the wide green lawns and the younger ones came running to meet them and to embrace Lothar as soon as he stepped out of the Cadillac.

'We listened on the radio,' they cried, as they clamoured for a turn to hug and kiss him. 'Oh Lothie, you were wonderful.' Each of his sisters took one of his arms, while their friends and the Stander girls crowded as close as they could to him as they escorted him down to the pool where the older women waited to congratulate him.

Lothar went to his mother first, and while they embraced Manfred watched them with an indulgent smile of pride. What a fine-looking family he had. Heidi was still a magnificent woman and no man could ask for a more dutiful wife. Not once in all the years had he ever regretted his choice.

'My friends, my family, all my loved ones,' Manfred raised his voice, and they turned to him and fell into silent expectation. Manfred was a compelling speaker, and as a nation they were susceptible to oratory and fine words for they were constantly exposed to them, from pulpit and political platform, from the cradle to the grave.

'When I look at this young man who is my son, at this fine young South African, and those of our young people like him, then I know that I need not worry for the future of our *Volk*,' Manfred proclaimed in the sonorous tones to which his listeners responded instinctively, and they applauded and cried '*Hoor, hoor!*' each time he paused.

Amongst the listeners there was one at least who was not entirely captivated by his artistry. Although Sarah Stander smiled and

424

nodded, she could feel her stomach churn and her throat burn with the acid of her rejected love.

Sitting in this lovely garden, watching the man she had loved beyond life itself, the man to whom she would have dedicated every moment of her existence, the man to whom she had given her girlish body and the tender blossom of her virginity, the man whose seed she had taken joyously into her womb, that ancient, now rancid passion changed its shape and texture to become hard and bitter hatred. She listened to Manfred extolling his wife, and she knew that she should have been that woman, those praises should have been for her alone. She should have been at his side to share his triumphs and his achievements.

She watched Manfred embrace Lothar and with his arm around his shoulders, commend his firstborn to them all, smiling with pride as he recited his virtues, and Sarah Stander hated them both, father and son, for Lothar De La Rey was not his firstborn.

She turned her head and saw Jakobus standing on the periphery, shy and self-effacing, but every bit as handsome as the big golden-headed athlete. Jakobus, her own son, had the dark brows and pale topaz-coloured eyes of the De La Reys. If Manfred were not blind, he would see that. Jakobus was as tall as Lothar, but was not possessed of his half-brother's raw-boned frame and layers of rippling muscle. He had an appealing fragility of body, and his features were not so dashingly masculine. Instead, he had the face of a poet, sensitive and gentle.

Sarah's own expression went dreamy and soft as she remembered his conception. She had been little more than a child, but her love had been that of a mature woman, as she crept through the silent old house to the room in which Manfred slept. She had loved him all her life, but in the morning he was leaving, sailing away to a far-off land, to Germany as a member of the Olympic team, and she had been troubled for weeks with a deep premonition of losing him for ever. She had wanted in some way to ensure against that insupportable loss, to try to make certain of his return, so she had given him everything that she had, her heart and her soul and her barely matured body, trusting him to return them to her.

Instead he had met the German woman and had married her. Sarah could still vividly recall the cablegram from Germany that had announced his dreadful betrayal, and her own devastation when she read the fateful words. Part of her had shrivelled and died on that day, part of her soul had been missing ever since.

Manfred De La Rey was still speaking, and he had them laughing now with some silly joke, but he looked towards her and saw that she was serious. Perhaps he read something of her thoughts in her eyes for his own gaze flicked across to where Jakobus stood and then back to her and for an instant she sensed an unusual emotion – regret or guilt – within him.

She wondered not for the first time if he knew about Jakobus. Surely he must at least have suspected it. Her marriage to Roelf had been so hasty, so unheralded, and the birth of Kobus had followed so swiftly. Then the physical resemblance of son to father was so strong, surely Manfred knew it.

Roelf knew, of course. He had loved her without hope until Manfred rejected her, and he had used her pregnancy to gain her consent. Since then he had been a good and dutiful husband and his love and concern for her had never faltered – but he was not Manfred De La Rey. He was not, nor could he ever be, a man as Manfred De La Rey was a man. He had never had Manfred's force and power, his drive and personality and ruthlessness, and she could never love him as she loved Manfred.

Yes, she admitted to herself, I have always loved Manfred, and I will love him to the end of my life, but my hatred of him is as strong as my love and with time it will grow stronger still. It is all that I have to sustain me.

Manfred was ending his speech now, talking about Lothar's promotion. Of course, Sarah thought bitterly, his promotion would not have been so rapid if his father had not been the minister of police and he had not had such skill with a rugby ball. Her own Kobus could expect no such preferment. Everything he achieved would be with his own talent and by his own efforts. She and Roelf could do little for him. Roelf's influence was minimal, and even the university fees for Jakobus' education were a serious drain on their family finances. She had been forced to face the fact that Roelf would never go much further than he was now. His entry into legal practice had been a mistake and a failure. By the time he had accepted that fact and returned to the academic life as a lecturer in law, he had lost so much seniority that it would be many years, if ever, before he was given the chair of law. No there was not much they could do to help Kobus – but then, of course, none of the family, not even Kobus himself, knew what he wanted from life. He was a brilliant student, but he totally lacked direction or purpose, and he had always been a secretive lad. It was so difficult to draw him out. Once or twice Sarah had succeeded in doing so, but she had been frightened by the strange and radical views he expressed. Perhaps it was best not to explore her son's mind too deeply, she thought, and smiled across at him just as, at last, Manfred stopped singing his own son's praises.

Jakobus came to her side now. 'Can I get you another orange juice, Mama? Your glass is empty.'

426

'No, thank you, Kobus. Stay with me for a while. I see so little of you these days.'

The men had charged their beer tankards and led by Manfred trooped towards the barbecue fires on the far side of the pool. Amid laughter and raillery Manfred and Lothar were tying candy-striped aprons around their waists and arming themselves with long-handled forks.

On a side table there was a huge array of platters piled with raw meat, lamb chops and *sosaties* on long skewers, German sausages and great thick steaks, enough to feed an army of starving giants and, Sarah calculated sourly, costing almost her husband's monthly salary.

Since Manfred and his one-armed demented father had mysteriously acquired shares in that fishing company in South West Africa, he had become not only famous and powerful, but enormously rich as well. Heidi had a mink coat now and Manfred had purchased a large farm in the rich maize-producing belt of the Orange Free State. It was every Afrikaner's dream to own a farm, and Sarah felt her envy flare as she thought about it. All that should have been hers. She had been deprived of what was rightly hers by that German whore. The word shocked her, but she repeated it silently – whore!

He was mine, whore, and you stole him from me.

Jakobus was talking to her, but she found it difficult to follow what he was saying. Her attention kept stealing back to Manfred De La Rey. Every time his great laugh boomed out she felt her heart contract and she watched him from the corners of her eyes.

Manfred was holding court; even dressed in that silly apron and with a cooking fork in his hand, he was still the focus of all attention and respect. Every few minutes more guests arrived to join the gathering, most of them important and powerful men, but all of them gathered slavishly around Manfred and deferred to him.

'We should understand why he did it,' Jakobus was saying, and Sarah forced herself to concentrate on her son.

'Who did it, dear?' she asked vaguely.

'Mama, you haven't been listening to a word,' Jakobus smiled gently. 'You really are a little scatterbrain sometimes.' Sarah always felt vaguely uncomfortable when he spoke to her in such a familiar fashion, none of her friends' children would show such disrespect, even in fun.

'I was talking about Moses Gama,' Jakobus went on, and at the mention of that name everybody within earshot turned towards the two of them.

'They are going to hang that black thunder, at last,' somebody said, and everybody agreed immediately.

427

'*Ja*, about time.'

'We have to teach them a lesson – you show mercy to a kaffir and he takes it as weakness.'

'Only one thing they understand —'

'I think it will be a mistake to hang him,' Jakobus said clearly, and there was a stunned silence.

'Kobie! Kobie!' Sarah tugged at her son's arm. 'Not now, darling. People don't like that sort of talk,'

'That is because they never hear it – and they don't understand it,' Jakobus explained reasonably, but some of them turned away deliberately while a middle-aged cousin of Manfred's said truculently,

'Come on, Sarie, can't you stop your brat talking like a commie.'

'Please, Kobie,' she used the diminutive as a special appeal, 'for my sake.'

Manfred De La Rey had become aware of the disturbance and the flare of hostility amongst his guests, and now he looked across the fires on which the steaks were sizzling and he frowned.

'Don't you see, Mama, we have to talk about it. If we don't, people will never hear any other point of view. None of them even read the English newspapers —'

'Kobie, you will anger your uncle Manie,' Sarah pleaded. 'Please stop it now.'

'We Afrikaners are cut off in this little make-believe world of ours. We think that if we make enough laws the black people will cease to exist, except as our servants —'

Manfred had come across from the fires now, and his face was dark with anger.

'Jakobus Stander,' he rumbled softly. 'Your father and your mother are my oldest and dearest friends, but do not trespass on the hospitality of this house. I will not have wild and treasonable ideas bandied about in front of my family and friends. Behave yourself, or leave immediately.'

For a moment it seemed the boy might defy him. Then he dropped his gaze and mumbled, 'I'm sorry, *Oom* Manie.' But when Manfred turned and strode back to the barbecue fire, he said just loud enough for Sarah to hear, 'You see, they won't listen. They don't want to hear. They are afraid of the truth. How can you make a blind man see?'

Manfred De La Rey was still inwardly seething with anger at the youth's ill-manners, but outwardly he was his usual bluff self as he resumed his self-imposed duties over the cooking fires, and led the jovial banter of his male guests. Gradually his irritation subsided, and he had almost put aside Moses Gama and the long shadow that

428

he had thrown over them all, when his youngest daughter came running down from the long low ranch-type house.

'Papa, Papa, there is a telephone call for you.'

'I can't come now, *skatjie*,' Manfred called. 'We don't want our guests to starve. Take a message.'

'It's *Oom* Danie,' his daughter insisted, 'and he says he must talk to you now. It's very important.'

Manfred sighed and grumbled good-naturedly as he untied his apron, and handed his fork to Roelf Stander. 'Don't let them burn!' and he strode up to the house.

'*Ja!*' he barked into the telephone.

'I don't like to disturb you, Manie.'

'Then why do you do it?' Manfred demanded. Danie Leroux was a senior police general, and one of his most able officers.

'It's this man Gama.'

'Let the black bastard hang. That is what he wants.'

'No! He wants to do a deal.'

'Send someone else to speak to him, I do not want to waste my time.'

'He will only talk to you, and we believe he has something important he will be able to tell you.'

Manfred thought for a moment. His instinct was to dismiss the request out of hand, but he let reason dictate to him.

'All right,' he agreed heavily. 'I will meet him.' There would also be a perverse pleasure in confronting a vanquished foe. 'But he is going to hang – nothing will stop that,' he warned quietly.

*   *   *

The prison authority had confiscated the leopard-skin robes of chieftainship, and Moses Gama wore the prison-issue suiting of coarse unbleached calico.

The long unremitting strain of awaiting the outcome of his appeal had told heavily. For the first time Vicky noticed the frosting of white in his cap of dark crinkling hair, and his features were gaunt, his eyes sunken in dark bruised-looking hollows. Her compassion for him threatened to overwhelm her, and she wished that she could reach out and touch him, but the steel mesh screen separated them.

'This is the last time I am allowed to visit you,' she whispered, 'and they will only let me stay for fifteen minutes.'

'That will be long enough, for there is not much to say, now that the sentence has been confirmed.'

'Oh, Moses, we were wrong to believe that the British and the Americans would save you.'

429

'They tried,' he said quietly.

'But they did not try very hard, and now what will I do without you. What will the child I am carrying do without a father?'

'You are a daughter of Zulu, you will be strong.'

'I will try, Moses my husband,' she whispered. 'But what of your people? They are also children without a father. What will become of them?'

She saw the old fierce fire burn in his eyes. She had feared it had been for ever extinguished, and she felt a brief and bitter joy to know it was still alight.

'The others will seek to take your place now. Those of the Congress who hate and envy you. When you die they will use your sacrifice to serve their own ambitions.'

She saw that she had reached him again, and that he was angry. She sought to inflame his anger to give him reason and strength to go on living.

'If you die, your enemies will use your dead body as a stepping-stone to climb to the place you have left empty.'

'Why do you torment me, woman?' he asked.

'Because I do not want you to die, because I want you to live – for me, for our child, and for your people.'

'That cannot be,' he said. 'The hard Boers will not yield, not even to the demands of the great powers. Unless you can find wings for me to fly over these walls, then I must go to my fate. There is no other way.'

'There is a way,' Vicky told him. 'There is a way for you to survive – and for you to put down the enemy who seek to usurp your place as the leader of the black nations.'

He stared at her as she went on.

'When the day comes that we sweep the Boers into the sea, and open the doors of the prisons, you will emerge to take your rightful place at the head of the revolution.'

'What is this way, woman? What is this hope that you hold out to me?'

He listened without expression as she propounded it to him, and when she had finished, he said gravely, 'It is true that the lioness is fiercer and crueller than the lion.'

'Will you do it, my lord – not for your own sake, but for all us weak ones who need you so?'

'I will think on it,' he conceded.

'There is so little time,' she warned.

*　　*　　*

430

The black ministerial Cadillac was delayed only briefly at the gates to the prison for they were expecting Manfred De La Rey. As the steel gates swung open, the driver accelerated through into the main courtyard and turned into the parking slot that had been kept free. The prison commissioner and two of his senior staff were waiting, and they hurried forward as soon as Manfred climbed out of the rear door.

Briefly Manfred shook hands with the commissioner and said, 'I wish to see the prisoner immediately.'

'Of course, Minister, it has been arranged. He is waiting for you.'

'Lead the way.'

Manfred's heavy footfalls echoed along the dreary green-painted corridors, while the senior warders scurried ahead to unlock the interleading doors of each section and relock them as Manfred and the prison commissioner passed through. It was a long walk, but they came at last to the condemned block.

'How many awaiting execution?' Manfred demanded.

'Eleven,' the commissioner replied. The figure was not unusually high, Manfred reflected. Africa is a violent land and the gallows play a central role in the administration of justice.

'I do not want to be overheard, even by those soon to die.'

'It has been arranged,' the commissioner assured him. 'Gama is being kept separate from the others.'

The warders opened one last steel door and at the end of a short passage was a barred cell. Manfred went through but when the commissioner would have followed, Manfred stopped him.

'Wait here!' he ordered. 'Lock the door after me and open it again only when I ring.'

As the door clanged shut Manfred walked on to the end of the passage.

The cell was small, seven foot by seven, and almost bare. There was a toilet bowl against the side wall and a single iron bunk fixed to the opposite wall. Moses Gama sat on the edge of the bunk and he looked up at Manfred. Then slowly he came to his feet and crossed the cell to face him through the green-painted bars.

Neither man spoke. They stared at each other. Though only the bars separated them, they were a universe and an eternity apart. Though their gazes locked, there was no contact between their minds, and the hostility was a barrier between them more obdurate and irreconcilable than the steel bars.

'Yes?' Manfred asked at last. The temptation to gloat over a vanquished adversary was strong, but he withstood it. 'You asked to see me?'

'I have a proposal to put to you,' Moses Gama said.

431

'You wish to bargain for your life?' Manfred corrected him, and when Moses was silent, he smiled. 'So it seems that you are no different from other men, Moses Gama. You are neither a saint nor even the noble martyr that some say you are. You are no better than other men, no better than any of us. In the end your loyalty is to yourself alone. You are weak as other men are weak, and like them, you are afraid.'

'Do you wish to listen to my proposal?' Moses asked, without a sign of having heard the taunts.

'I will hear what you have to say,' Manfred agreed. 'That is why I came here.'

'I will deliver them to you,' Moses said, and Manfred understood immediately.

'By "them" you mean those who also claim to be the leaders of your people? The ones who compete with your own claim to that position?'

Moses nodded and Manfred chuckled and shook his head with admiration.

'I will give you the names and the evidence. I will give you the times and the places.' Moses was still expressionless. 'You have underestimated the threat that they are to you, you have underestimated the support they can muster, here and abroad. I will give you that knowledge.'

'And in return?' Manfred asked.

'My freedom,' said Moses simply.

'*Magtig!*' The blasphemy was a measure of Manfred's astonishment. 'You have the effrontery of a white man.' He turned away so that Moses could not see his face while he considered the magnitude of the offer.

Moses Gama was wrong. Manfred was fully aware of the threat, and he had a broad knowledge of the extent and the ramifications of the conspiracy. He understood that the world he knew was under terrible siege. The Englishman had spoken of the winds of change – they were blowing not only upon the African continent, but across the world. Everything he held dear, from the existence of his family to that of his *Volk* and the safety of the land that God had delivered unto them, was under attack by the forces of darkness.

Here he was being offered the opportunity to deal those forces a telling blow. He knew then what his duty was.

'I cannot give you your freedom,' he said quietly. 'That is too much – but you knew that when you demanded it, didn't you?' Moses did not answer him, and Manfred went on, 'This is the bargain I will offer you. I will give you your life. A reprieve, but you will never leave prison again. That is the best I can do.'

432

The silence went on so long that Manfred thought he had refused and he began to turn away when Moses spoke again.

'I accept.'

Manfred turned back to him, not allowing his triumph to show.

'I will want all the names, all the evidence,' he insisted.

'You will have it all,' Moses assured him. 'When I have my reprieve.'

'No,' Manfred said quietly. 'I set the terms. You will have your reprieve when you have earned it. Until then you will get only a stay of execution. Even for that I will need you to name a name so that I can convince my compatriots of the wisdom of our bargain.'

Moses was silent, glowering at him through the bars.

'Give me a name,' Manfred insisted. 'Give me something to take to the prime minister.'

'I will do better than that,' Moses agreed. 'I will give you two names. Heed them well. They are – Mandela and Rivonia.'

* * *

Michael Courtney was in the city room of the *Mail* when the news that the Appellate Division had denied Moses Gama's appeal and confirmed the date of his execution, came clattering out on the tape. He let the paper strip run through his fingers, reading it with total concentration, and when the message ended, he went to his desk and sat in front of his typewriter.

He lit a cigarette and sat quietly, staring out of the window over the tops of the scraggly trees in Joubert Park. He had a pile of work in his basket and a dozen reference books on his desk. Desmond Blake had slipped out of the office to go down to the George to top up his gin tank and left Michael to finish the article on the American elections. Eisenhower was nearing the end of his final term and the editor wanted a pen portrait of the presidential candidates. Michael was working on his biographical notes of John Kennedy, but having difficulty choosing the salient facts from the vast amount that had been written about the young Democratic candidate, apart from those that everybody knew, that he was a Catholic and a New Dealer and that he had been born in 1917.

America seemed very far away that morning, and the election of an American president inconsequential in comparison with what he had just read on the tape.

As part of his self-education and training, Michael made a practice each day of selecting an item of important news and writing a two-thousand-word mock editorial upon it. These exercises were for his own sake, the results private and jealously guarded. He showed them

433

to no one, especially not Desmond Blake whose biting sarcasm and whose willingness to plagiarize Michael had learned to fear. He kept these articles in a folder in the locked bottom drawer of his desk.

Usually Michael worked on these exercises in his own time, staying on for an hour or so in the evening or sitting up late at night in the little bed-sitter he rented in Hillbrow, pecking them out on his rickety old secondhand Remington.

However, this morning he had been so moved by the failure of Gama's appeal that he could not concentrate on the Kennedy story. The image of the imperial-looking black man in his leopard-skin robes kept recurring before Michael's eyes, and his words kept echoing in Michael's ears.

Suddenly he reached forward and ripped the half-completed page out of his machine. Then he swiftly rolled a clean sheet into it. He didn't have to think, his fingers flew across the keys, and the words sprang up before his eyes: 'A Martyr is Born.'

He rolled the cigarette to the side of his mouth and squinted against the spiral of blue smoke, and the words came in short staccato bursts. He did not have to search for facts or dates or figures. They were all there, crisp and bright in his head. He never paused. He never had to weigh one word against another. The precise word was there on the page almost of its own volition.

When he finished it half an hour later, he knew that it was the best thing he had ever written. He read it through once, shaken by the power of his own words, and then he stood up. He felt restless and nervous. The effort of creation rather than calming or exhausting him had excited him. He had to get outside.

He left the sheet in the typewriter and took his jacket off the back of his chair. The sub glanced up at him enquiringly.

'Going to find Des,' he called. In the newsroom there was a conspiracy to protect Desmond Blake from himself and the gin bottle and the sub nodded agreement and returned to his work.

Once he was out of the building, Michael walked fast, pushing his way through the crowds on the sidewalks, stepping out hard with both hands thrust into his pockets. He didn't look where he was going, but it didn't surprise him when at last he found himself in the main concourse of the Johannesburg railway station.

He fetched a paper cup of coffee from the kiosk near the ticket office and took it to his usual seat on one of the benches. He lit a cigarette and raised his eyes towards the domed glass ceiling. The Pierneef murals were placed so high that very few of the thousands of commuters who passed through the concourse each day ever noticed them.

For Michael they were the essence of the continent, a distillation

434

of all of Africa's immensity and infinite beauty. Like a celestial choir, they sang aloud all that he was trying to convey in clumsy stumbling sentences. He felt at peace when at last he left the massive stone building.

He found Des Blake on his usual stool at the end of the bar counter at the George.

'Are you your brother's keeper?' Des Blake enquired loftily, but his words were slurred. It took a great deal of gin to make Des Blake slur.

'The sub is asking for you,' Michael lied.

He wondered why he felt any concern for the man, or why any of them bothered to protect him – but then one of the other senior journalists had given him the answer to that. 'He was once a great newspaperman, and we have to look after our own.'

Des was having difficulty fitting a cigarette into his ivory holder. Michael did it for him, and as he held a match he said, 'Come on, Mr Blake. They are waiting for you.'

'Courtney, I think I should warn you now. You haven't got what it takes, I'm afraid. You'll never cut the mustard, boy. You are just a poor little rich man's son. You'll never be a newspaperman's anus.'

'Come along, Mr Blake,' said Michael wearily, and took his arm to help him down off the stool.

The first thing Michael noticed when he reached his desk again was that the sheet of paper was missing from his typewriter. It was only in the last few months, since he had been assigned to work with Des Blake, that he had been given his own desk and machine, and he was fiercely jealous and protective of them.

The idea of anyone fiddling with his typewriter, let alone taking work out of it, infuriated him. He looked around him furiously, seeking a target for his anger, but every single person in the long, crowded noisy room was senior to him. The effort it cost him to contain his outrage left him shaking. He lit another cigarette, the last one in his pack, and even in his agitation he realized that that made it twenty since breakfast.

'Courtney!' the sub called across to him, raising his voice above the rattle of typewriters. 'You took your time. Mr Herbstein wants you in his office right away.'

Michael's rage subsided miraculously. He had never been in the editor's office before, Mr Herbstein had once said good morning to him in the lift but that was all.

The walk down the newsroom seemed the longest of his life, and though nobody even glanced up as he passed, Michael was certain that they were secretly sniggering at him and gloating on his dilemma.

435

He knocked on the frosted-glass panel of the editor's door and there was a bellow from inside.

Timidly Michael pushed the door open and peered round it. Leon Herbstein was on the telephone, a burly man in a sloppy hand-knitted cardigan with thick horn-rimmed spectacles and a shock of thick curly hair shot through with strands of grey. Impatiently he waved Michael into the room and then ignored him while he finished his conversation on the telephone.

At last he slammed down the receiver and swivelled his chair to regard the young man who was standing uneasily in front of his desk.

Ten days before, Leon Herbstein had received a quite unexpected invitation to a luncheon in the executive dining-room of the Courtney Mining and Finance Company's new head office building. There had been ten other guests present, all of them leaders of commerce and industry, but Herbstein had found himself in the righthand seat beside his host.

Leon Herbstein had never had any great admiration for Shasa Courtney. He was suspicious of vast wealth, and the two Courtneys – mother and son – had a formidable reputation for shrewd and ruthless business practices. Then again, Shasa Courtney had forsaken the United Party of which Leon Herbstein was an ardent supporter, and had gone across to the Nationalists. Leon Herbstein had never forgotten the violent anti-semitism which had attended the birth of the National Party, and he considered the policy of *apartheid* as simply another manifestation of the same grotesque racial bigotry.

As far as he was concerned, Shasa Courtney was one of the enemy. However, he sat down at his luncheon table quite unprepared for the man's easy and insidious charm and his quick and subtle mind. Shasa devoted most of his attention to Leon Herbstein, and by the end of the meal the editor had considerably moderated his feelings towards the Courtneys. At least he was convinced that Shasa Courtney truly had the best interests of all the people at heart, that he was especially concerned with improving the lot of the black and underprivileged sections, and that he was wielding an important moderating influence in the high councils of the National Party.

In addition, he left the Courtney building with a heightened respect for Shasa Courtney's subtlety. Not once had Shasa mentioned the fact that he and his companies now owned 42 per cent of the stock of Associated Newspapers of South Africa or that his son was employed as a junior journalist on the *Mail*. It hadn't been necessary, both men had been acutely aware of these facts while they talked.

Up to that time Leon Herbstein had felt a natural antagonism towards Michael Courtney. Placing him in the care of Des Blake had been all the preference he had shown to the lad. However, after that luncheon he had begun to study him with more attention. It didn't take an old dog long to attribute the improvement in much of the copy that Des Blake had been turning out recently to the groundwork that Michael Courtney was doing for him. From then onwards whenever he passed Michael's desk, Herbstein made a point of quickly and surreptitiously checking what work was in his machine or in the copy basket.

Herbstein had the journalist's trick of being able to assimilate a full typed sheet at a single glance, and he was grimly amused to notice how often Des Blake's column was based on the draft by his young assistant, and how often the original was better than the final copy.

Now he studied Michael closely as he stood awkwardly before his desk. Despite the fact that he had cropped his hair in one of those appalling brush cuts that the youth were affecting these days and wore a vividly patterned bow tie, he was a likable-looking lad, with a strong determined jawline and clear intelligent eyes. Perhaps he was too thin for his height, and a little gawky, but he had quite noticeably matured and gained in self-assurance during the short period he had been at the *Mail*.

Suddenly Leon realized that he was being cruel, and that his scrutiny was subjecting the lad to unnecessary agony. He picked up the sheet of typescript that lay in front of him, and slid it across his untidy desk.

'Did you write that?' he demanded gruffly, and Michael snatched up the sheet protectively.

'I didn't mean anybody to read it,' he whispered, and then remembered who he was talking to and threw in a lame, 'sir.'

'Strange.' Leon Herbstein shook his head. 'I always believed we were in the business of writing so that others could read.'

'I was just practising.' Michael held the sheet behind his back.

'I made some corrections,' Herbstein told him, and Michael jerked the page out from behind him and scanned it anxiously.

'Your third paragraph is redundant, and "scar" is a better word than "cicatrice" – otherwise we'll run it as you wrote it.'

'I don't understand, sir,' Michael blurted.

'You've saved me the trouble of writing tomorrow's editorial.' Herbstein reached across and took the page from Michael's limp fingers, tossed it into his out basket and then concentrated all his attention on his own work.

Michael stood gaping at the top of his head. It took him ten seconds to realize that he had been dismissed and he backed towards the door and closed it carefully behind him. His legs just carried him to his desk, and then collapsed under him. He sat down heavily in his swivel chair and reached for his cigarette pack. It was empty and he crumpled it and dropped it into his wastepaper basket.

Only then did the full significance of what had happened hit him and he felt cold and slightly nauseated.

'The editorial,' he whispered, and his hands began to tremble.

Across the desk Desmond Blake belched softly and demanded, 'Where are the notes on that American what's-'is-name fellow?'

'I haven't finished it yet, Mr Blake.'

'Listen, kid. I warned you. You'll have to extract your digit from your fundamental orifice if you want to get anywhere around here.'

Michael set his alarm clock for five o'clock the next morning and went downstairs with his raincoat over his pyjamas. He was waiting on the street corner with the newspaper urchins when the bundles of newsprint were tossed on to the pavement from the back of the *Mail*'s delivery van.

He ran back up the stairs clutching a copy of the paper and locked the door to his bed-sitter. It took all his courage to open it at the editorial page. He was actually shaking with terror that Mr Herbstein might have changed his mind, or that it was all some monstrous practical joke.

There under the *Mail*'s crest at the very top of the editorial page was his headline: 'A MARTYR IS BORN'.

He read it through quickly, and then started again and read it aloud, mouthing each word, rolling it over his tongue like a noble and precious wine. He propped the paper, open at the editorial, beside the mirror while he shaved, and then carried it down to the Greek fast-food café where he had his breakfast each morning and showed it to Mr Costa, who called his wife out of the kitchen.

'Hey, Michael, you a big shot now.' Mrs Costa embraced him, smelling of fried bacon and garlic. 'You a big shot newspaperman now.'

She let him use the telephone in the back room and he gave the operator the number at Weltevreden. Centaine answered on the second ring.

'Mickey!' she cried delightedly. 'Where are you? Are you in Cape Town?'

He calmed her down and then read it to her. There was a long silence. 'The editorial, Mickey. You aren't making this up, are you? I'll never forgive you if you are.'

Once he had reassured her, Centaine told him, 'I can't remember ever being so excited about anything in years. I'm going to call your father, you must tell him yourself.'

Shasa came on the line, and Michael read it to him. 'You wrote

438

that?' Shasa asked. 'Pretty hot stuff, Mickey. Of course I don't agree with your conclusions – Gama must hang. However, you almost convinced me otherwise, but we can debate that when next we are together. In the meantime, congratulations, my boy. Perhaps you did make the right decision after all.'

Michael found that he was a minor celebrity in the newsroom, even the sub stopped by his desk to congratulate him and discuss the article for a few moments, and the pretty little blonde on the reception desk who had never before been aware of his existence, smiled and greeted him by name.

'Listen, kid,' said Desmond Blake. 'One little fart doesn't make a whole sewage farm. In future I don't want you pushing copy over my head. Every bit of shit you write comes across my desk, get it?'

'I'm sorry, Mr Blake. I didn't —'

'Yeah! Yeah! I know, you didn't mean it. Just don't go getting a big head. Remember whose assistant you are.'

The news of Moses Gama's reprieve threw the newsroom into a state of pandemonium that didn't subside for almost a week. Michael was drawn in and some of his days ended at midnight when the presses began their run, and began when the first papers hit the streets the next morning.

However, he found that the excitement seemed to release limitless reserves of energy in him and he never felt tired. He learned to work quickly and accurately and his way with words gradually assumed a deftness and polish that was apparent even to himself.

Two weeks after the reprieve the editor called him into his office. He had learned not to knock, any waste of time irritated Leon Herbstein and made him bellow aggressively. Michael went straight on in, but he had not yet entirely mastered the pose of world-weary cynicism which he knew was the hallmark of the veteran journalist, and he was all radiant eagerness as he asked, 'Yes, Mr Herbstein?'

'Okay, Mickey, I've got something for you.' Every time Mr Herbstein used his Christian name, Michael still thrilled with delicious shock.

'We are getting a lot of requests from readers and overseas correspondence. With all the interest in the Gama case, people want to know more about the black political movements. They want to know the difference between the Pan Africanist Congress and the African National Congress, they want to know who's who – who the hell are Tambo and Sisulu, Mandela and Moses Gama and what do they stand for? All that sort of stuff. You seem to be interested in black politics and enjoy digging around in the archives – besides I can't spare one of my top men on this sort of background stuff. So get on with it.' Herbstein switched his attention back to the work on his desk, but Michael by now had sufficient confidence to stand his ground.

'Am I still working under Mr Blake?' he asked. He had learned by this time if you called him 'sir' it just made Leon Herbstein mad.

Herbstein shook his head but did not even look up. 'You are on your own. Send everything to me. No hurry, any time in the next five minutes will do nicely.'

Michael soon discovered that the *Mail*'s archives were inadequate, and served merely to initiate him into the complexity and daunting size of the project he had been set. However, from them he was at least able to draw up a list of the various black political groups and related associations such as the officially unrecognized black trade unions, and from there to compile a list of their own leaders and officials.

He cleared one wall of his bed-sitting room and put up a board on which he pinned all this information, using different-coloured cards for each grouping and press photographs of the principal black leaders. All this achieved was to convince him of how little was known about the black movements by even the most well-informed of the white section of the nation.

The public library added very little to his understanding. Most of the books on the subject had been written ten or more years before and simply traced the African National Congress from those distant days of its inception in 1912 and the names mentioned were all of men now dead or in their dotage.

Then he had his first inspiration. One of the *Mail*'s sister publications under the banner of Associated Newspapers of South Africa was a weekly magazine called *Assegai* after the broad-bladed war spear that the impis of Chaka the Zulu conqueror had wielded. The magazine was aimed at the educated and more affluent section of the black community. Its editorial policy was dictated by the white directors of Associated Newspapers but amongst the articles and photographs of African football stars and torch singers, of black American athletes and film actors, an occasional article slipped through of a fiercely radical slant.

Michael borrowed a company car and went out to see the editor of *Assegai* in the vast black location of Drake's Farm. The editor was a graduate of the black university of Fort Hare, a Xhosa named Solomon Nduli. He was polite but cool, and they had chatted for half an hour before a barbed remark let Michael know that he had been recognized as a spy for the security police, and that he would learn nothing of value.

A week later the *Mail* published the first of Michael's articles in its Saturday magazine edition. It was a comparison of the two leading

African political organizations: the Pan Africanist Congress which was a jealously exclusive body to which only pure-blooded African blacks were admitted and whose views were extremely radical, and the much larger African National Congress which, although predominantly black, also included whites and Asians and mixed blood members such as the Cape coloureds, and whose objectives were essentially conciliatory.

The article was accurate, obviously carefully researched, but, most important, the tone was sympathetic, and it carried the by-line 'by Michael Courtney'.

The following day Solomon Nduli called Michael at the offices of the *Mail*, and suggested another meeting. His first words when they shook hands were, 'I'm sorry. I think I misjudged you. What do you want to know?'

Solomon took Michael into a strange world that he had never realized existed – the world of the black townships. He arranged for him to meet Robert Sobukwe, and Michael was appalled by the depth of the resentment the black leader of the Pan Africanist Congress expressed, particularly for the pass laws, by his enormous impatience to effect an upheaval of the entire society, and by the thinly veiled violence in the man.

'I will try to arrange for you to meet Mandela,' Solomon promised, 'although, as you know, he is underground now, and wanted by the police. But there are others you must talk to.'

He took Michael to Baragwanath Hospital and introduced him to the wife of Moses Gama, the lovely young Zulu woman he had seen at the trial in Cape Town. Victoria was heavily pregnant, but with a calm dignity that impressed Michael deeply until he sensed the same terrible resentment and latent violence in her that he had found in Robert Sobukwe.

The next day Solomon took him back to Drake's Farm to meet a man named Hendrick Tabaka, a man who seemed to own most of the small businesses in the location and looked like a heavyweight wrestler with a head like a cannonball crisscrossed with scars.

He appeared to Michael to represent the opposite end of the black protest consciousness. 'I have my family and my business,' he told Michael, 'and I will protect them from anybody, black or white.' And Michael was reminded of a view that his father had often expressed, but to which Michael had not given much consideration before this. 'We must give the black people a piece of the pie,' Shasa Courtney had said. 'Give them something of their own. The truly dangerous man is one with nothing to lose.'

Michael gave the second article in the series the title 'Rage' and in it he tried to describe the deep and bitter resentment that he had

441

encountered on his journeys into the half-world of the townships. He ended the article with the words:

Despite this deep sense of outrage, I never found the least indication of hatred towards the white person as an individual by any of the black leaders with whom I was able to speak. Their resentment seemed to me to be directed only at the Nationalist government's policy of *apartheid* while the vast treasure of mutual goodwill built up over three hundred years between the races seems to be entirely undiminished by it.

He delivered the article to Leon Herbstein on the Thursday and found himself immediately embroiled in an editorial review of it that lasted until almost eight o'clock that evening. Leon Herbstein called in his assistant and his deputy editor, and their views were divided between publishing with only minor alterations and not publishing at all, for fear of bringing down the wrath of the publications control board, the government censors who had the power to ban the *Mail* and put it out of business.

'But it's all true,' Michael protested. 'I have substantiated every single fact I have quoted. It's true and it's important – that is all that really matters.' And the three older journalists looked at him pityingly.

'All right, Mickey,' Leon Herbstein dismissed him at last. 'You can go on home. I will let you know the final decision in due course.'

As Michael moved dispiritedly towards the door, the deputy editor nodded at him. 'Publish or not, Mickey, it is a damned good effort. You can be proud of it.'

When Michael got back to his apartment he found somebody sitting on a canvas holdall outside his front door. Only when the person stood up did he recognize the massively developed shoulders, the glinting steel-rimmed spectacles and spiky hairstyle.

'Garry,' he shouted joyously, and rushed to embrace his elder brother.

They sat side by side on the bed and talked excitedly, interrupting each other and laughing and exclaiming at each other's news.

'What are you doing in Jo'burg?' Michael demanded at last.

'I've come up from Silver River just for the weekend. I want to get at the new computer main frame in head office, and there are a few things I want to check at the land surveyor's office. So I thought, what the hell – why spend money on a hotel when Mickey has a flat? So I brought my sleeping-bag. Can I doss on your floor?'

'The bed pulls out into a double,' Mickey told him happily. 'You don't have to sleep on the floor.'

They went down to Costa's restaurant and Garry bought a pack of chicken curry and half a dozen Cokes. They ate the food out of the pack, sharing a spoon to save washing up, and they talked until long after midnight. They had always been very close to each other. Even though he was younger, Michael had been a staunch ally during those dreadful childhood years of Garry's bed-wetting and stuttering and Sean's casually savage bullying. Then again Michael had not truly realized how lonely he had been in this strange city until this moment, and now there were so many nostalgic memories and so much unrequited need for affection to assuage, so many subjects of earth-shattering importance to discuss. They sat up into the small hours dealing with money and work and sex and the rest of it.

Garry was stunned to learn that Michael earned thirty-seven pounds ten shillings a month.

'How much does this kennel cost you a month?' he demanded.

'Twenty pounds,' Michael told him.

'That leaves you seventeen pounds ten a month to eat and exist. They should be arrested for slave labour.'

'It's not as bad as that – Pater gives me an allowance to make do. How much do you earn, Garry?' Michael demanded, and Garry looked guilty.

'I get my board and lodging and all my meals at the mine, single quarters, and I am paid a hundred a month as an executive trainee.'

'Son of a gun!' Michael was deeply impressed. 'What do you do with all that?'

It was Garry's turn to look amazed. 'Save it, of course. I've got over two thousand in the bank already.'

'But what are you going to do with all that?' Michael insisted. 'What are you going to spend it on?'

'Money isn't for spending,' Garry explained. 'Money is for saving – that is, if you want to be rich.'

'And you want to be rich?' Michael asked.

'What else is there?' Garry was genuinely puzzled by the question.

'What about doing an important job the best way you can? Isn't that something to strive for, even better than getting rich.'

'Oh sure!' said Garry with vast relief. 'But then, of course, you won't get rich unless you do just that.'

It was almost two in the morning when Michael at last switched off the bedside lamp and they settled down nose to toes, until Garry asked in the darkness the question he had not been able to ask until then.

'Mickey, have you heard from Mater at all?'

Michael was silent for so long that he went on impetuously. 'I have tried to speak to Dad about her, but he just clams up and won't say a word. Same with Nana, except she went a little further. She said "Don't mention that woman's name in Weltevreden again.

443

She was responsible for Blaine's murder." I thought you might know where she is.'

'She's in London,' Michael said softly. 'She writes to me every week.'

'When is she coming back, Mickey?'

'Never,' Michael said. 'She and Pater are getting a divorce.'

'Why, Mickey, what happened that she had to leave like that, without even saying goodbye?'

'I don't know. She won't say. I wrote and asked her, but she wouldn't tell me.'

Garry thought he had gone to sleep, but after a long silence Michael said so softly that he barely caught the words, 'I miss her, Garry. Oh God, how much I miss her.'

'Me too,' said Garry dutifully, but each week that passed was so filled with excitement and new experience that for Garry her memory had already faded and blurred.

The next morning Leon Herbstein called Mickey into his office.

'Okay, Mickey,' he said. 'We are going to run the "Rage" article as you wrote it.' Only then did Michael realize how important that decision had been to him. For the rest of that day his jubilation was tempered by that reflection. Why was his feeling of relief so powerful? Was it the personal achievement, the thought of seeing his name in print again? It was part of that, he was honest with himself, but there was something else even deeper and more substantial. The truth. He had written the truth and the truth had prevailed. He had been exonerated.

Michael went down early the next morning and brought a copy of the *Mail* up to the bed-sitter. He woke Garry up and read the 'Rage' feature to him. Garry had only come in a few hours before dawn. He had spent most of the night in the computer room at the new Courtney Mining building in Diagonal Street. David Abrahams, on Shasa's discreet suggestion, had arranged for him to have a free hand with the equipment when it was not being used on company business. This morning Garry was red-eyed with exhaustion and his jowls were covered with a dense dark pelt of new beard. However, he sat up in his pyjamas and listened with attention while Michael read to him, and when he had finished Garry put on his spectacles and sat solemnly reading it through for himself while Michael brewed coffee on the gas-ring in the corner.

'It's funny, isn't it,' Garry said at last. 'How we just take them for granted. They are there, working the shifts at the Silver River or harvesting the grapes at Weltevreden, or waiting on table. But you never think of them as actually having feelings and desires and thoughts the same as we do – not until you read something like this.'

'Thank you, Garry,' Michael said softly.

'What for?'

'That's the greatest compliment anybody has ever paid me,' Michael said.

He saw very little more of Garry that weekend. Garry spent the Saturday morning at the deeds registry until that office closed at noon and then went on up to the Courtney building to take over the computer as soon as the company programmers went off for their weekend.

He let himself back into the flat at three the next morning and climbed into the bottom end of Michael's bed. When they both awoke late on the Sunday morning, Michael suggested, 'Let's go out to Zoo Lake. It's a hot day and the girls will be out in their sundresses.' He offered the bait deliberately for he was desperate for Garry's company, lonely and suffering from a sense of anti-climax after all the worry and uncertainty previous to the printing of the 'Rage' article and the subsequent apparent lack of any reaction to it.

'Hey, Mickey, I'd love to come with you – but I want to do something on the computer. It's Sunday, I'll have it to myself all day.' Garry looked mysterious and self-satisfied. 'You see, I'm on to something, Mickey. Something incredible, and I can't stop now.'

Alone Michael caught the bus out to Zoo Lake. He spent the day sitting on the lawns reading and watching the girls. It only made him feel even more lonely and insignificant. When he got back to his dreary little flatlet, Garry's bag was gone and there was a message written with soap on his shaving mirror: 'Going back to Silver River. Might see you next weekend. G.'

When Michael walked into the *Mail*'s offices on the Monday morning he found that those members of the newspaper's staff who had arrived ahead of him were gathered in a silent nervous cluster in the middle of the newsroom while half a dozen strangers were going through the filing cabinets and rifling the papers and books on the desks. They had already assembled a dozen large cardboard cartons of various papers, and these were stacked in the aisle between the desks.

'What is happening?' Michael asked innocently, and his sub gave him a warning glance as he explained.

'These are police officers of the security branch.'

'Who are you?' The plain-clothes officer who was in charge of the detail came across to Michael, and when he gave his name the officer checked his list.

'Ah, yes – you are the one we want. Come with me.' He led Michael down to Leon Herbstein's office and went in without knocking.

There was another stranger with Herbstein. 'Yes, what is it?' he snapped, and the security policeman answered diffidently.

445

'This is the one, Captain.'

The stranger frowned at Michael, but before he could speak Leon Herbstein interrupted quickly.

'It's all right, Michael. The police have come to serve a banning order on the Saturday edition with the "Rage" article in it, and they have a warrant to search the offices. They also want to talk to you, but it's nothing to worry about.'

'Don't be too sure of that,' said the police captain heavily. 'Are you the one who wrote that piece of commie propaganda?'

'I wrote the "Rage" article,' Michael said clearly, but Leon Herbstein cut in.

'However, as the editor of the *Golden City Mail* it was my decision to print it, and I accept full responsibility for the article.'

The captain ignored him and studied Michael for a moment before going on. 'Man, you are just a kid. What do you know, anyway?'

'I object to that, Captain,' Herbstein told him angrily. 'Mr Courtney is an accredited journalist —'

'*Ja,*' the captain nodded, 'I expect that he is.' But he went on addressing Michael, 'What about you? Do you object to coming down to Marshall Square police headquarters to help us with our investigations?'

Michael glanced at Herbstein and he said immediately, 'You don't have to go, Michael. They don't have a warrant for your arrest.'

'What do you want from me, Captain?' Michael hedged.

'We want to know who told you all that treasonable stuff you wrote about.'

'I can't disclose my sources,' Michael said quietly.

'I can always get a warrant if you refuse to co-operate,' the captain warned him ominously.

'I'll come with you,' Michael agreed. 'But I won't disclose my sources. That's not ethical.'

'I'll be down there with a lawyer right away, Michael,' Herbstein promised. 'You don't have to worry, the *Mail* will back you all the way.'

'All right. Let's go,' said the police captain.

Leon Herbstein accompanied Michael down the newsroom and as they passed the cartons of impounded literature the captain observed gloatingly, 'Man, you've got a pile of banned stuff there, Karl Marx and Trotsky even – that's really poisonous rubbish.'

'It's research material,' said Leon Herbstein.

'*Ja,* try telling that to the magistrate,' the captain chortled.

As soon as the doors of the elevator closed on the captain and Michael, Herbstein trotted heavily back to his office and snatched up the telephone.

446

'I want an urgent call to Mr Shasa Courtney in Cape Town. Try his home at Weltevreden, his office in Centaine House and his ministerial office at the houses of parliament.'

He got through to Shasa in his parliamentary suite and Shasa listened in silence while Herbstein explained to him what had happened.

'All right,' Shasa said crisply at the end of it. 'You get the Associated Newspapers lawyers down to Marshall Square immediately, then ring David Abrahams at Courtney Mining and tell him what has happened. Tell him I want a massive reaction, everything we have got. Tell him also that I will be flying up immediately in the company jet. I want a limousine at the airport to meet me, and I will go to see the minister of police at the Union Buildings in Pretoria the minute I arrive.'

Even Leon Herbstein, who had seen it all before, was impressed by the mobilization of the vast resources of the Courtney empire.

At ten o'clock that evening Michael Courtney was released from interrogation on the direct orders of the minister of police and when he walked out of the front entrance of Marshall Square headquarters he was flanked by half a dozen lawyers of formidable reputation who had been retained by Courtney Mining and Associated Newspapers.

At the pavement Shasa Courtney was waiting in the back seat of the black Cadillac limousine. As Michael climbed in beside him, he said grimly, 'It is possible, Mickey, to be a bit too bloody clever for your own good. Just what the hell are you trying to do? Burn down everything we have worked for all our lives?'

'What I wrote was the truth. I thought you, of all people, would understand, Pater.'

'What you wrote, my boy, is incitement. Taken by the wrong people and used on simple ignorant black folk, your words could help to open a Pandora's box of horrors. I want no more of that sort of thing from you, do you hear me, Michael?'

'I hear you, Pater,' Michael said softly. 'But I can't promise to obey you. I'm sorry, but I have to live with my own conscience.'

'You are as bad as your bloody mother,' said Shasa. He had sworn twice in as many minutes, the first time in his life that Michael had ever heard his father use coarse language. That and the mention of his mother, also the first time Shasa had done so since she left, silenced Michael completely. They drove without speaking to the Carlton Hotel. Shasa only spoke again when they were in his permanent suite.

'All right, Mickey,' he said with resignation. 'I take that back. I can't demand that you live your life on my terms. Follow your

447

conscience, if you must, but don't expect me to come rushing in to save you from the consequences of your actions every time.'

'I have never expected that, sir,' Michael said carefully. 'And I won't in future either.' He paused and swallowed hard. 'But all the same, sir, I want to thank you for what you did. You have always been so good to me.'

'Oh Mickey, Mickey!' Shasa cried, shaking his head sorrowfully. 'If only I could give you the experience I earned with so much pain. If only you didn't have to make exactly the same mistakes I made at your age.'

'I am always grateful for your advice, Pater,' Michael tried to placate him.

'All right then, here's a piece for nothing,' Shasa told him. 'When you meet an invincible enemy you don't rush headlong at him, swinging with both fists. That way you merely get your head broken. What you do is you sneak around behind him and kick him in the backside, then run like hell.'

'I'll remember that, sir,' Michael grinned, and Shasa put his arm around his shoulders. 'I know you smoke like a bush fire, but can I offer you a drink, my boy?'

'I'll have a beer, sir.'

The next day Michael drove out to visit Solomon Nduli at Drake's Farm. He wanted to have his views on the 'Rage' article, and tell him of the consequences he had suffered at Marshall Square.

That was not necessary. Solomon Nduli somehow knew every detail of his detention and interrogation and Michael found he was a celebrity in the offices of *Assegai* magazine. Nearly every one of the black journalists and magazine staff wanted to shake his hand and congratulate him on the article.

As soon as they were alone in his office, Solomon told him excitedly, 'Nelson Mandela has read your piece and he wants to meet you.'

'But he is wanted by the police – he's on the run.'

'After what you wrote, he trusts you,' Solomon said, 'and so does Robert Sobukwe. He also wants to see you again.' Then he noticed Michael's expression, and the excitement went out of him as he asked quietly, 'Unless you think it's too dangerous for you.'

Michael hesitated only a moment. 'No, of course not. I want to meet them both. Very much.'

Solomon Nduli said nothing. He simply reached across the desk and clasped Michael's shoulder. It was strange what a pleasurable sensation that grip gave Michael, the first comradely gesture he had ever received from a black man.

* * *

448

Shasa banked the HS 125 twin-engined jet to give himself a better view of the Silver River Mine a thousand feet below.

The headgear was of modern design, not the traditional scaffolding of steel girders with the great steel wheels of the haulage exposed. It was instead a graceful unbroken tower of concrete, tall as a ten-storey building, and around it the other buildings of the mine complex, the crushing works and uranium extraction plant and the gold refinery, had been laid out with equal aesthetic consideration. The administration block was surrounded by green lawns and flowering gardens, and beyond that there were an eighteen-hole golf course, a cricket pitch and a rugby field for the white miners. An Olympic-size swimming-pool adjoined the mine club and single quarters. On the opposite side of the property stood the compound for the black mineworkers. Here again Shasa had ordered that the traditional rows of barracks be replaced by neat cottages for the senior black staff and the bachelor quarters were spacious and pleasant, more like motels than institutions to house and feed the five thousand tribesmen who had been recruited from as far afield as Nyasaland in the north and Portuguese Mozambique in the east. There were also soccer fields and cinemas and a shopping complex for the black employees, and between the buildings were green lawns and trees.

The Silver River was a wet mine and each day millions of gallons of water were pumped out of the deep workings and these were used to beautify the property. Shasa had reason to be proud.

Although the main shaft had intersected the gold-bearing reef at great depth – more than a mile below the surface – still the ore was so rich that it could be brought to the surface for enormous profit. What's more, the price could not be pegged at $35 per ounce for much longer. Shasa was convinced that it would double and even treble.

'Our guardian angel,' Shasa smiled to himself as he levelled the wings of the HS 125, and began his preparations for the landing.

'Of all the blessings that have been heaped upon this land, gold is the greatest. It has stood us through the bad times, and made the good times glorious. It is our treasure and more, for when all else fails, when our enemies and the fates conspire to bring us down, gold glows with its bright particular lustre to protect us. A guardian angel indeed.'

Although the company pilot in the right-hand seat watched critically, for Shasa had only converted to jets within the last twelve months, Shasa brought the swift machine in to the long blue tarmac strip with casual ease. The HS 125 was painted in silver and blue with the stylized diamond logo on the fuselage, just as the old Mosquito had been. It was a magnificent machine. With its seating for eight passengers and its blazing speed, it was infinitely more practical than the Mosquito, but Shasa still occasionally mourned her loss. He had flown over five thousand hours in the old Mosquito before at last donating her to the airforce museum, where, restored to her combat camouflage and armaments, she was one of the prime exhibits.

Shasa rolled the glistening new jet down to the hangar at the far end of the strip, and reception committee was out to meet him headed by the general manager of the Silver River, all of them holding their ears against the shrill wail of the engines.

The general manager shook Shasa's hand and said immediately, 'Your son asked me to apologize that he wasn't able to meet you, Mr Courtney. He is underground at the moment, but asked me to tell you he will come up to the guest house as soon as he gets off shift.' The general manager, emboldened by Shasa's smile of paternal approval, risked a pleasantry. 'It must run in the family, but it's difficult to get the little blighter to stop working, we almost have to tie him down.'

There were two guest houses, one for other important visitors to the mine, and this one set aside exclusively for Shasa and Centaine. It was so sybaritic and had cost so much that embarrassing questions had been put to Shasa at the annual general meeting of the company by a group of dissident shareholders. Shasa was totally unrepentant. 'How can I work properly if I'm not allowed at least some basic comforts? A roof over my head – is that too much to ask?'

The guest house had its own squash court and heated indoor pool, cinema, conference room, kitchens and wine cellar. The design was by one of Frank Lloyd Wright's most brilliant pupils and Hicks had come out from London to do the interior. It housed the overflow of Shasa's art collection and Persian carpets from Weltevreden, and the mature trees in the landscaped garden had been selected from all over the country to be replanted here. Shasa felt very much at home in this little *pied-à-terre*.

The underground engineer and the chief electrical engineer were already waiting in the conference room and Shasa went straight in and was at work within ten minutes of landing the jet. By eight o'clock that evening he had exhausted his engineers and he let them go.

Garry was waiting next door in Shasa's private study, filling in the time playing with the computer terminal, but he leapt up as Shasa walked in.

'Dad, I'm so glad I've found you. I've been trying to catch up with you for days – I'm running out of time.' He was stuttering again.

450

These days he only did that when he was wildly over-excited.

'Slow down, Garry. Take a deep breath,' Shasa advised him, but the words kept tumbling out, and Garry seized his father's hand and led him to the computer to illustrate what he was trying to put across.

'You know what Nana has always said, and what you are always telling me about land being the only lasting asset, well —' Garry's powerful spatulate fingers rippled over the computer keys. Shasa watched with curiosity as Garry presented his case, but when he realized what the boy was driving at, he quickly lost interest and concentration.

However, he listened to it all before he asked quietly, 'So you have paid for the option with your own money?'

'I have it signed, here!' Garry brandished the document. 'It cost me all my savings, over two thousand pounds just for a one-week option.'

'Let me recap, then,' Shasa suggested. 'You have spent two thousand pounds to acquire a one-week option on a section of agricultural ground on the northern outskirts of Johannesburg which you intend to develop as a residential township, complete with a shopping complex, theatres, cinemas and all the trimmings —'

'There is at least twenty million pounds of profit in the development – at the very least.' Garry manipulated the computer keyboard and pointed to the rippling green figures. 'Just look at that, Dad!'

'Garry! Garry!' Shasa sighed. 'I think you have just lost your two thousand pounds, but the experience will be worth it in the long run. Of course, there is twenty million profit in it. Everybody knows that, and everybody wants a piece of that action. It's just for that reason that there is such strict control on township development. It takes at least five years to get government approval for a new township, and there are hundreds of pitfalls along the way. It's a highly complex and specialized field of investment, and the outlay is enormous – millions of pounds at risk. Don't you see, Garry? Your piece of land is probably not the best available, there will be a dozen other projects ahead of yours and township development just isn't one of the areas which we deal in —' Shasa broke off and stared at his son. Garry was flapping his hands and stuttering so badly that Shasa had to warn him again, 'Big breath.'

Garry gasped and his barrel chest expanded until his shirt buttons strained. It came out quite clearly.

'I already have approval,' he said.

'That takes years – I've explained.' Shasa was brusque. He began to rise. 'We should change for dinner. Come on.'

451

'Dad, you don't understand,' Garry insisted. 'Approval has already been granted.'

Shasa sat down slowly. 'What did you say?' he asked quietly.

'Township approval was granted in 1891 by the *Volksraad* of the old Transvaal republic. It was signed by President Kruger himself, but it is still perfectly legal and binding. It was just forgotten, that is all.'

'I don't believe it.' Shasa shook his head. 'How on earth did you get on to this, Garry?'

'I was reading a couple of old books about the early days of the Witwatersrand and the gold-mines. I thought that if I was going to learn mining, the very least I could do was bone up on the history of the industry,' Garry explained. 'And in one of the books there was a mention of one of the old Rand lords and his grandiose idea of building a paradise city for the very rich away from the coarse and rowdy centre of Johannesburg. The author mentioned that he had actually bought a six-thousand-acre farm and had it surveyed and that approval had been granted by the *Volksraad*, and then the whole idea had been abandoned.'

'What did you do then?'

'I went to the archives and looked up the proceedings of the *Volksraad* for the years 1889 to 1891 and there it was – the approval. Then I researched the title deeds of the property at the deeds registry and went out to the farm itself. It's called Baviaansfontein and it's owned by two brothers, both in their seventies. Nice old fellows, we got on well and they showed me their horses and cattle, and invited me to lunch. They thought the option was a big joke, but when I showed them my two thousand pounds, they had never seen so much money in one pile in their lives.' Garry grinned. 'Here are copies of the title deeds and the original township approval.' Garry handed them to his father and Shasa read through slowly, even moving his lips like a semi-literate so as to savour every word of the ancient documents.

'When does your option expire?' he asked at last, without looking up.

'Noon on Thursday. We will have to act fast.'

'Did you take out the option in the name of Courtney Mining?' Shasa asked.

'No. In my own name, but of course, I did it for you and the company.'

'You thought this out alone,' Shasa said carefully. 'You researched it yourself, dug up the original approval, negotiated the option with the owners, paid for it with two thousand of your own hard-earned cash. You did all the work and took all the risks and now you want to hand it over to someone else. That isn't very bright, is it?'

'I don't want to hand it over to just anybody – to you, Dad. Everything I do is for you, you know that.'

'Well, that changes as of now,' said Shasa briskly. 'I will personally lend you the two hundred thousand purchase price and we will fly up to Johannesburg first thing tomorrow to clinch the deal. Once you own the land, Courtney Mining will begin negotiating with you the terms of a joint venture to develop it.'

The negotiations started tough, and then as Garry got his first taste of blood, they grew tougher.

'My God, I've sired a monster,' Shasa complained, to hide his pride in his offspring's bargaining technique. 'Come on, son, leave something in it for us.'

To mollify his father a little Garry announced a change in the name of the property. In future it would be known as Shasaville. When they at last signed the final agreement, Shasa opened a bottle of champagne and said, 'Congratulations, my boy.'

That approbation was worth more to Garry than all the townships and every grain of gold on the Witwatersrand.

*　　*　　*

Lothar De La Rey was one of the youngest police captains on the force, and this was not entirely on account of his father's position and influence. From the time he had been awarded the sword of honour at police college, he had distinguished himself in every field that was considered important by the higher command. He had studied for and passed all his promotion examinations with distinction. A great emphasis was placed on athletic endeavour and rugby football was the major sport in the police curriculum. It was now almost certain that Lothar would be chosen as an international during the forthcoming tour by the New Zealand All Blacks. He was well liked both by his senior officers and his peers, and his service record was embellished by an unbroken string of excellent ratings. Added to this he had shown an unusual aptitude for police work. Neither the plodding monotony of investigation nor the routine of patrol wearied him, and in those sudden eruptions of dangerous and violent action, Lothar had displayed resourcefulness and courage.

He had four citations on his service record, all of them for successful confrontation with dangerous criminals. He was also the holder of the police medal for gallantry, which he had been awarded after he had shot and killed two notorious drug dealers during a foot-chase through the black township at night, and a single-handed

453

shoot-out from which he had emerged unscathed.

Added to all this was the assessment by his superiors that while himself amenable to discipline, he had the qualities of command and leadership highly developed. Both these were very much Afrikaner characteristics. During the North African campaign against Rommel, General Montgomery, when told that there was a shortage of officer material, had replied, 'Nonsense, we've got thousands of South Africans. Each of them is a natural leader – from childhood they are accustomed to giving orders to the natives.'

Lothar had been stationed at the Sharpeville police station since graduating from police college and had come to know the area intimately. Gradually he had built up his own network of informers, the basis of all good police work, and through these prostitutes and shebeen owners and petty criminals, he was able to anticipate much of the serious crime and to identify the organizers and perpetrators even before the offence was committed.

The higher command of the police force was well aware that the young police captain with illustrious family connections was in a large measure responsible for the fact that the police in the Sharpeville location had over the past few years built up a reputation of being one of the most vigorous and active units in the heavily populated industrial triangle that lies between Johannesburg, Pretoria and Vereeniging.

In comparison to greater Soweto, Alexandra or even Drake's Farm, Sharpeville was a small black township. It housed a mere forty thousand or so of all ages, and yet the police raids for illicit liquor and pass offenders were almost daily routine, and the lists of arrests and convictions by which the efficiency of any station is judged were out of all proportion to its size. Much of this industry and dedication to duty was quite correctly attributed to the energy of the young second-in-command.

Sharpeville is an adjunct to the town of Vereeniging where in 1902 the British Commander Lord Kitchener and the leaders of the Boer commandos negotiated the peace treaty which brought to an end the long-drawn-out and tragic South African war. Vereeniging is situated on the Vaal river fifty miles south of Johannesburg and its reasons for existing are the coal and iron deposits which are exploited by Iscor, the giant state-owned Iron and Steel Corporation.

At the turn of the century the black workers in the steel industry were originally housed in the Top Location, but as conditions there became totally inadequate and outmoded, a new location was set aside for them in the early 1940s and named after John Sharpe, the mayor for the time being of the town of Vereeniging. As the new dwellings in Sharpeville became available, the population was moved

454

down from Top Location, and although the rents were as high as £2 7s 6d per month, the translocations were effected gradually and peaceably.

Sharpeville was, in fact, a model township, and though the cottages were the usual box shape, they were all serviced with water-borne sewerage and electricity, and there were all the other amenities including a cinema, shopping areas and sports facilities, together with their very own police station.

In the midst of one of the most comprehensive pieces of social engineering of the twentieth century – which was the policy of *apartheid* in practice – Sharpeville was a remarkable area of calm. All around, hundreds of thousands of people were being moved and regimented and reclassified in accordance with those monumental slabs of legislation, the Group Areas Act and the Population Registration Act. All around the fledgeling leaders of black consciousness and liberation were preaching and exhorting and organizing, but Sharpeville seemed untouched by it all. The white city fathers of Vereeniging pointed out with quite justifiable satisfaction that the communist agitators had been given short shrift in the Sharpeville location and that their black people were law-abiding and peaceful. The figures for serious crime were amongst the lowest in the industrialized section of the Transvaal, and offenders were taken care of with commendable expedition. Even the rent-defaulters were evicted from the location in summary fashion, and the local police force was always co-operative and conscientious.

When the law was extended to make it obligatory for black women to carry passes, as well as their menfolk, and when throughout most of the country this innovation was strenuously resisted, the ladies of Sharpeville presented themselves at the police station in such numbers and in such co-operative spirit that most of them had to be turned away with the injunction to 'come back later'.

In early March of 1960 Lothar De La Rey drove his official Land-Rover through this stable and law-abiding community, following the wide road across the open space in front of the police station. The cluster of police buildings, in the same austere and utilitarian design as the others in the location, were surrounded by a wire mesh fence about eight feet high, but the main gates were standing open and unguarded.

Lothar drove through and parked the Land-Rover below the flagpole on which the orange, blue and white national flag floated on a breeze that carried the faint chemical stink of the blast furnaces at the ISCOR plant. In the charge office he was immediately the centre of attention as his men came to congratulate him on the kick that had won the Currie Cup.

455

'Green and gold next,' the duty sergeant predicted as he shook Lothar's hand, referring to the colours of the national rugby team jersey.

Lothar accepted their admiration with just the right degree of modesty, and then put an end to this breach of discipline and routine.

'All right, back to work everybody,' he ordered, and went to check the charge book. Where a charge office in Soweto might expect to have three or four murders and a dozen or so rape cases, there had not been a single 'schedule one' crime committed in Sharpeville during the previous twenty-four hours and Lothar nodded with satisfaction and went through to report to his station commander.

In the doorway he came to attention and saluted, and the older man nodded and indicated the chair opposite him.

'Come in, Lothie. Sit down!'

He rocked his chair on to its back legs and watched Lothar as he removed his uniform cap and gloves.

'*Bakgat* game on Friday,' he congratulated him. 'Thank you for the tickets. Hell, man, that last kick of yours!'

He felt a stab of envy as he examined his number two. *Liewe land!* Beloved Land, but he looked like a soldier, so tall and straight! The commander glanced down at his own slack guts, and then back at the way the lad wore his uniform on those wide shoulders. You had only to look at him to see his class. It had taken the commander until the age of forty to gain the rank of captain, and he was resigned to the fact that he would go on pension at the same rank – but this one. No what! He would probably be a general before he was forty.

'Well, Lothie,' he said heavily. 'I'm going to miss you.' He smiled at the gleam in those alert but strangely pale yellow eyes. '*Ja*, my young friend,' he nodded, 'your transfer – you leave us at the end of May.'

Lothar leaned back in his chair and smiled. He suspected that his own father had been instrumental in keeping him so long on this station, but although it had been increasingly irksome to waste time in this little backwater, his father knew best and Lothar was grateful for the experience he had gained here. He knew that a policeman only really learns his job on the beat, and he had put in his time. He knew he was a good policeman, and he had proved it to them all. Anybody who might be tempted to attribute his future promotions to his father's influence had only to look at his service record. It was all there. He had paid his dues in full, but now it was time to move on.

'Where are they sending me, sir?'

'You lucky young dog.' The commander shook his head with mock envy. 'You are going to CID headquarters at Marshall Square.'

456

It was the plum. The most sought-after, the most prestigious posting that any young officer could hope for. CID headquarters was right at the very nerve centre and heart of the entire force. Lothar knew that from there it would be swift and sure. He would have his general's stars while he was still a young man, and with them the maturity and reputation to make his entry into politics smooth and certain. He could retire from the force on the pension of a general, and devote the rest of his life to his country and his *Volk*. He had it all planned. Each step was clear to Lothar. When Dr Verwoerd went, he knew that his father would be a strong contender to take over the premiership. Perhaps one day there would be a second minister of police with the name of De La Rey, and after that another De La Rey at the head of the nation. He knew what he wanted, what road he had to follow, and he knew also that his feet were securely upon that road.

'You are being given your chance, Lothie,' the commander echoed his own thoughts. 'If you take it, you will go far – very far.'

'However far it is, sir, I will always remember the help and encouragement you have given me here at Sharpeville.'

'Enough of that. You have a couple of months before you go.' The commander was suddenly embarrassed. Neither of them were men who readily displayed their emotions. 'Let's get down to work. What about the raid tonight? How many men are you going to use?'

Lothar had the headlights of the Land-Rover switched off, and he drove slowly for the four-cylinder petrol engine had a distinctive beat that his quarry would pick up at a distance if the vehicle was driven hard.

There was a sergeant beside him, and five constables in the rear of the Land-Rover, all of them armed with riot batons. In addition, the sergeant had an automatic twelve-gauge Greener shotgun and Lothar wore his sidearm on his Sam Browne belt. They were lightly armed, for this was merely a liquor raid.

Sale of alcohol to blacks was strictly controlled, and was restricted to the brewing of the traditional cereal-based beer by state-controlled beer-halls. The consumption of spirits and wines by blacks was forbidden, but this prohibition caused illicit shebeens to flourish. The profits were too high to be passed by. The liquor was either stolen or purchased from white bottle stores or manufactured by the shebeen owners themselves. These home brews were powerful concoctions known generally as *skokiaan*, and according to the recipe of the individual distiller, could contain anything from methylated spirits to the corpses of poisonous snakes and aborted infants. It was not uncommon for the customers of the shebeens to end up permanently blinded, or demented, or occasionally dead.

457

Tonight Lothar's team was setting out to raid a newly established shebeen which had been in business for only a few weeks. Lothar's information was that it was controlled by a black gang called 'The Buffaloes'.

Of course, Lothar was fully aware of the size and scope of the Buffaloes' operations. They were without doubt the largest and most powerful underworld association on the Witwatersrand. It was not known who headed the gang but there had been hints that it was connected to the African Mineworkers' Union and to one of the black political organizations. Certainly it was most active on the gold-mining properties closer to Johannesburg, and in the large black townships such as Soweto and Drake's Farm.

Until now they had not been bothered by the Buffaloes here in Sharpeville, and for this reason the setting up of a controlled shebeen was alarming. It might herald a determined infiltration of the area which would almost certainly be followed by a campaign to politicize the local black population, with the resulting protest rallies and boycotts of the bus line and white-owned businesses, and all the other trouble whipped up by the agitators of the African National Congress and the newly formed Pan Africanist Congress.

Lothar was determined to crush it before it spread like a bush fire through his whole area. Above the soft burble of the engine, out there in the darkness he heard a sharp double fluted whistle and almost immediately it was repeated at a distance, down near the end of the avenue of quiet cottages.

'*Magtig*!' Lothar swore softly but bitterly. 'They've spotted us!' The whistles were the warnings of the shebeen lookouts.

He switched on the headlights and gunned the Land-Rover. They went hurtling down the narrow street.

The shebeen was at the end of the block, in the last cottage hard up against the boundary fence with a stretch of open veld beyond. As the headlights swept across the front of the cottage, he saw half a dozen dark figures pelting away from it, and others were fighting each other to get out of the front door and leaping from the windows.

Lothar swung the Land-Rover up over the pavement, through the tiny garden, and braked it into a deliberate and skilfully executed broadside, blocking the front door.

'Let's go!' he yelled, and his men flung the doors open and sprang out.

They grabbed the bewildered shebeen drinkers who were trapped between the Land-Rover and the cottage wall. As one of them began to resist, he dropped to a practised swing of a riot baton and the limp body was bundled into the back of the vehicle.

458

Lothar sprinted around the side of the cottage, and caught a woman in his arms as she jumped through the window. He turned her upside down in the air and held onto one ankle as he reached out and seized the arm of the next man through the window. In a single swift motion he handcuffed the two of them together, wrist to ankle, and left them floundering and falling over each other like a pair of trussed hens.

Lothar reached the back door of the cottage, and made his first mistake. He seized the handle and jerked the door open. The man had been waiting on the inside, poised and ready, and as the door began to open he hurled his full weight upon it and the edge of it crashed into Lothar's chest. The wind was driven from his lungs, and hissed up his throat as he went over backwards down the steps, sprawling on the hard sun-baked earth, and the man leaped clean over him.

Lothar caught a glimpse of him against the light, and saw that he was young and well built, lithe and quick as a black cat. Then he was racing away into the darkness, heading for the boundary fence that backed up to the cottage.

Lothar rolled over on to his knees and came to his feet. Even with the start the fugitive had, there was nobody who could outrun Lothar in a fair match. He was at the peak of fitness, after months of rigorous training for the Currie Cup match and the national trials, but as he started forward the agony of his empty lungs made him double over and wheeze for breath.

Ahead of him the fleeing figure ducked through a hole in the mesh of the fence, and Lothar fell to his knees and snapped open the holster at his side. Three months before, he had been runner-up in the police pistol championships at Bloemfontein, but now his aim was unsteady with agony and the dark figure was merging with the night, quartering away from him. Lothar fired twice but after each long bright muzzle flash there was no thumping impact of bullet into flesh and the runner was swallowed up by darkness. Lothar slid the weapon back into his holster, and fought to fill his lungs – his humiliation was more painful than his injury. Lothar was unaccustomed to failure.

He forced himself to get to his feet. None of his men should see him grovelling, and after only a minute, and even though his lungs were still on fire, he went back and dragged his two captives to their feet with unnecessary violence. The woman was stark naked. Obviously she had been entertaining a client in the back bedroom, but now she was wailing tragically.

'Shut your mouth, you black cow,' he told her, and shoved her through the back door of the cottage.

459

The kitchen had been used as the bar. There were cases of liquor stacked to the ceiling, and the table was piled with a high pyramid of empty tumblers.

In the front room the floor was covered with broken glass and spilled liquor, evidence of the haste with which it had been vacated, and Lothar wondered how so many customers had fitted into a room that size. He had seen at least twenty escape into the night.

He shoved the naked prostitute towards one of his black constables. 'Take care of her,' he ordered, and the man grinned lasciviously and tweaked one of her tawny melon-round breasts.

'None of that,' Lothar warned him. He was still angry at the one who had got away, and the constable saw his face and sobered. He led the woman through into the bedroom to find her clothing.

Lothar's other men were coming in, each of them leading two or three sorry-looking captives.

'Check their passes,' Lothar ordered, and turned to his sergeant. 'All right, Cronje, let's get rid of this stuff.'

Lothar watched as the cases of liquor were carried out and stacked in front of the cottage. Two of his constables opened them and smashed the bottles against the edge of the kerb. The sweet fruity smell of cheap brandy filled the night and the gutter ran with the amber-brown liquid.

When the last bottle had been destroyed, Lothar nodded at his sergeant. 'Right, Cronje, take them up to the station.' And while the prisoners were loaded into the two police trucks that had followed his Land-Rover, Lothar went back into the cottage to check that his men had not overlooked anything of importance.

In the back room with its tumbled bed and stained sheets, he opened the single cupboard and distastefully used the point of his riot baton to rummage through it.

Beneath the pile of clothing at the bottom of the cupboard was a small cardboard carton. Lothar pulled it out and tore open the lid. It was filled with a neat stack of single-leaf pamphlets, and idly he glanced at the top one until its impact struck him. He snatched up the sheet and turned it to the light from the bare bulb in the ceiling.

'This is the *Poqo* of which it is said, "Take up your spear in your right hand, my beloved people, for the foreigners are looting your land"'

Poqo was the military branch of the Pan Africanist Congress. The word *Poqo* meant pure and untainted, for none other than pureblooded African Bantu could become members, and Lothar knew it for an organization of young fanatics already responsible for a number of vicious and brutal murders. In the little town of Paarl in

460

the Cape, *Poqo* had marched hundreds strong upon the police station and when driven back had vented their fury upon the civilian population, massacring two white women, one a girl of seventeen years. In the Transkei they had attacked a road-party encampment and murdered the white supervisor and his family in the most atrocious manner. Lothar had seen the police photographs and his skin crawled at the memory. *Poqo* was a name to fear and Lothar read the rest of the pamphlet with full attention.

> On Monday we are going to face the police. All the people of Sharpeville will be as one on that day. No man or woman will go to his place of work. No man or woman will leave the township by bus or train or taxi. All the people will gather as one and march to the police station. We are going to protest at the pass law which is a terrible burden, too heavy for us to carry. We will make the white police fear us.
> Any man or woman who does not march with us on Monday will be hunted down. On that day all the people will be as one.
> *Poqo* has said this thing. Hear it and obey it.

Lothar read the crudely printed pamphlet through again, and then he murmured, 'So it has come at last.' He picked out the sentence which had offended him most, 'We will make the white police fear us,' and he read it aloud.

'So! We will see about that!' And he shouted for his sergeant to take the carton of subversive leaflets out to the truck.

*　　*　　*

There was an inevitability in Raleigh Tabaka's life. The great river of his existence carried him along with it so that he was powerless to break free of it or even swim against the current.

His mother, as one of the most adept of the tribal *sangomas* of Xhosa had first instilled in him the deep awareness of his African self. She had showed him the mysteries and the secrets, and read the future for him in the casting of the bones.

'One day you will lead your people, Raleigh Tabaka,' she prophesied. 'You will become one of the great chiefs of Xhosa and your name will be spoken with those of Makana and Ndlame – all these things I see in the bones.'

When his father, Hendrick Tabaka, sent him and his twin brother Wellington across the border to the multi-racial school in Swaziland, his Africanism had been confirmed and underscored, for his fellow pupils had been the sons of chiefs and black leaders from countries like Basutoland and Bechuanaland. These were countries where black tribes ruled themselves, free of the white man's heavy paternal

461

fluences, and he listened with awe as they spoke of how their families lived on equal terms with the whites around them.

This came as a total revelation to Raleigh. In his existence the whites were a breed apart, to be feared and avoided, for they wielded an unchallenged power over him and all his people.

At Waterford he learned that this was not the law of the universe. There were white pupils, and although it was at first strange, he ate at the same table as they did, from the same plates and with the same utensils, and slept in a bed alongside them in the school dormitory, and sat on the toilet seat still warm from a white boy's bottom and vacated it to another little white boy waiting impatiently outside the door for him to finish. In his own country none of these things were allowed, and when he went home for the holidays he read the notices with his eyes wide open – the notices that said 'Whites Only – *Blankes Alleenlik*'. From the windows of the train he saw the beautiful farms and the fat cattle that the white men owned, and the bare eroded earth of the tribal reservations, and when he reached home at Drake's Farm he saw that his father's house, which he remembered as a palace, was in reality a hovel – and the resentment began to gnaw at his soul and the wounds it left festered.

Before Raleigh left to go to school, his Uncle Moses Gama used to visit his father. From infancy he had been in awe of his uncle, for power burned from him like one of those great veld fires which consumed the land and towered into the heavens in a column of dense smoke and ash and sparks.

Even though Moses Gama had been absent from Drake's Farm for so many years, his memory had never been allowed to grow dim, and Hendrick had read aloud to the family the letters that he had received from him in distant lands.

So when at last Raleigh matriculated and left Waterford to return to Drake's Farm and begin work in his father's businesses, he announced that he wanted to take his place in the ranks of the young warriors.

'After you have been to initiation camp,' his father promised him, 'I will introduce you to *Umkhonto we Sizwe*.'

Raleigh's initiation set the final stamp on his special sense of Africanism. With his brother Wellington and six other young men of his initiation class, he left Drake's Farm and travelled by train in the bare third-class carriage to the little magisterial town of Queenstown which was the centre of the Xhosa tribal territories.

It had all been arranged by his mother, and the elders of the tribe met them at Queenstown station. In a rickety old truck they were driven out to a kraal on the banks of the great Fish river and delivered into the care of the tribal custodian, an old man whose duty

462

it was to preserve and safeguard the history and customs of the tribe.

Ndlame, the old man, ordered them to strip off their clothing and to hand over all the possessions they had brought with them. These were thrown on a bonfire on the river bank, as a symbol of childhood left behind them. He took them naked into the river to bathe, and, then still glistening wet, he led them up the far bank to the circumcision hut where the tribal witchdoctors waited.

When the other initiates hung back fearfully, Raleigh went boldly to the head of the column and was the first to stoop through the low entrance to the hut. The interior was thick with smoke from the dung fire and the witchdoctors, in their skins and feathers and fantastic headdresses, were weird and terrifying figures.

Raleigh was smitten with terror, for the pain which he had dreaded all his childhood and for the forces of the supernatural which lurked in the gloomy recesses of the hut, yet he forced himself to run forward and leap over the smouldering fire.

As he landed on the far side the witchdoctors sprang upon him and forced him into a kneeling position, holding his head so he was forced to watch as one of them seized his penis and drew out the rubbery collar of his foreskin to its full length. In ancient times the circumciser would have used a hand-forged blade, but now it was a Gillette razor blade.

As they intoned the invocation to the tribal gods, Raleigh's foreskin was cut away, leaving his glans soft and pink and vulnerable. His blood spattered on to the dung floor between his knees, but he uttered not a sound.

Ndlame helped him rise, and he staggered out into the sunlight and fell upon the river bank, riding the terrible burning pain, but the shrieks of the other boys and the sounds of their wild struggles carried clearly to where he lay. He recognized his brother Wellington's cries of pain as the shrillest and loudest of them all.

Raleigh knew that their foreskins would be gathered up by the witchdoctors, salted and dried and added to the tribal totem. A part of them would remain for ever with the custodians and no matter how far they wandered, the witchdoctors could call them back with the foreskin curse.

When all the other initiates had suffered the circumciser's knife, Ndlame led them down to the water's edge and showed them how to wash and bind their wounds with medicinal leaves and herbs, and to strap their penis against their stomachs. 'For if the Mamba looks down, he will bleed again,' he warned them.

They smeared their bodies with a mixture of clay and ash. Even the hair on their heads was crusted with the dead white ritual paint,

463

so that they looked like albino ghosts. Their only clothing was skirts of grass and they built their huts in the deepest and most secret parts of the forest, for no woman might look upon them. They prepared their own food, plain maize cakes without any relish, and meat was forbidden them during the three moons of the initiation. Their only possession was their food bowl of clay.

One of the boys developed an infection of his circumcision wound, the stinking green pus ran from it like milk from a cow's teat, and the fever consumed him so his skin was almost painfully hot to the touch. The herbs and potions that Ndlame applied were of no avail. He died on the fourth day and they buried him in the forest and Ndlame took his food bowl away. It would be thrown through the front door of his mother's hut by one of the witchdoctors, without a word being spoken, and she would know that her son had not been acceptable to the tribal gods.

Each day from before dawn's light until after sunset, Ndlame gave them instruction and taught them their duties as members of the tribe, as husbands and as fathers. They learned to endure pain and hardship with stoicism. They learned discipline and duty to their tribe, the ways of the wild animals and plants, how to survive in the wilderness, and how to please their wives and raise their children.

When the wounds of the circumcision blade had healed, Ndlame bound up their members each night in the special knot called the Red Dog, to prevent them spilling their seed in the sacred initiation huts. Each morning Ndlame inspected the knots carefully to ensure that they had not been loosened to enjoy the forbidden pleasure of masturbation.

When the three moons had passed, Ndlame led them back to the river and they washed away the white initiation clay and anointed their bodies with a mixture of fat and red ochre, and Ndlame gave them each a red blanket, symbol of manhood, with which they covered themselves. In procession, singing the manhood songs which they had practised, they went to where the tribe waited at the edge of the forest.

Their parents had gifts for them, clothing and new shoes and money, and the girls giggled and ogled them boldly, for they were men now and able at last to take a wife, as many wives as they could afford, for the *lobola*, the marriage fee, was heavy.

The two brothers, accompanied by their mother, journeyed back to Drake's Farm, Wellington to take leave of their father, for he was going on to take holy orders, and Raleigh to remain at his father's side, to learn the multifarious facets of Hendrick Tabaka's business activities and eventually to take the helm and become the comfort and mainstay of Hendrick's old age.

These were fascinating and disturbing months and years for Raleigh. Until this time he had never guessed at his father's wealth and power, but gradually it was revealed to him. The pages in the ledger turned for him one at a time. He learned of his father's general dealer stores, and the butcheries and bakeries in all the black townships spread throughout the great industrial triangle of the Transvaal that was based on the gold-mines and the iron-deposits and the coalfields. Then he went on to learn about the cattle herds and rural general dealer's stores in the tribal reservations owned by his father and cared for by his myriad brothers, about the shebeens and the whores that operated behind the front of legitimate business, and finally he learned about the Buffaloes, that ubiquitous and shadowy association of many men from all the various tribes, whose chief was his own father.

He realized at last just how rich and powerful his father was, and yet how because he was a black man, he could not display his importance and could wield his power only covertly and clandestinely. Raleigh felt his anger stir, as it did whenever he saw those signs 'Whites Only – *Blankes Alleenlik*' and saw the white men pass in their shiny automobiles, or when he stood outside the universities and hospitals which were closed to him.

He spoke to his father about these things that troubled him and Hendrick Tabaka chuckled and shook his head. 'Rage makes a man sick, my son. It spoils his appetite for life and keeps him from sleep at night. We cannot change our world, so we must look for the good things in life and enjoy those to the full. The white man is strong, you cannot imagine how strong, you have not seen even the strength of his little finger. If you take up the spear against him, he will destroy you and all the good things we have – and if the gods and the lightnings intervened and by chance you destroyed the white man, think what would follow him. There would come a darkness and a time without law and protection that would be a hundred times worse than the white man's oppressions. We would be consumed by the rage of our own people, and we would not have even the consolation of these few sweet things. If you open your ears and your eyes, my son, you will hear how the young people call us collaborators and how they talk of a redistribution of wealth, and you will see the envy in their eyes. The dream you have, my son, is a dangerous dream.'

'And yet I must dream it, my father,' said Raleigh, and then, one unforgettable day, his uncle, Moses Gama, returned from foreign lands and took him to meet other young men who shared the same dream.

So, during the day Raleigh worked at his father's business and in the evenings he met with the other young comrades of *Umkhonto we*

465

Sizwe. At first they only talked, but the words were sweeter and headier than the smoke of the *dagga* pipes of the old men.

Then Raleigh joined the comrades who were enforcing the decrees of the African National Congress, the boycotts and the strikes and the work stoppages. He went to Evaton location with a small task force to enforce the bus boycott and they attacked the black workers in the bus queues who were trying to get to their places of employment or who were going to shop for their families, and they beat them with *sjamboks*, the long leather quirts, and with their fighting-sticks.

On the first day of the attacks, Raleigh was determined to demonstrate his zeal to his comrades and he used his fighting-stick with all the skill which he had learned as a child in faction fights with the boys of the other tribes.

There was a woman in the queue for the bus who defied Raleigh's order to go home, and she spat at him and his comrades and called them *tsotsies* and *skelms*, gangsters and rogues. She was a woman in middle age, large and matronly, with cheeks so plump and shiny that they looked as though they had been rubbed up with black shoe polish, and with such a queenly manner that at first the young comrades of *Umkhonto we Sizwe* were abashed by her scorn and might have withdrawn.

Then Raleigh saw that this was his opportunity to prove his ardour and he leaped forward and confronted the women. 'Go home, old woman,' he warned her. 'We are no longer dogs to eat the white man's shit.'

'You are a little uncircumcised boy with filth on your tongue,' she began, but Raleigh would not let her continue. He swung the long supple fighting-stick, and it split her shiny black cheek as cleanly as the cut of an axe, so for an instant Raleigh saw the bone gleam in the depths of the wound before the swift crimson flood obscured it. The big woman screamed and fell to her knees, and Raleigh felt a strange sensation of power and purpose, a euphoria of patriotic duty. For a moment the woman kneeling before him became the focus of all his frustration and his rage.

The woman saw it in his eyes and held up both arms over her head to ward off the next blow. Raleigh struck again, with all his strength and skill, using his wrist so that the fighting-stick whined in the air and the blow landed on the woman's elbow. Her arms were wreathed in layers of deep fat. It hung in dewlaps from her upper arms and in bracelets about her wrists, but it could not cushion the power behind that whistling stick. The joint of her elbow shattered, and her forearm dropped and twisted at an impossible angle as it hung helplessly at her side.

466

The woman screamed again, this time the sound was so filled with outrage and agony that it goaded the other young warriors and they fell upon the bus passengers with such fury that the terminus was strewn with the wailing and sobbing injured and the concrete floor was washed sticky red.

When the ambulances came with sirens wailing to collect the casualties, the comrades of *Umkhonto we Sizwe* pelted them with stones and half bricks and Raleigh led a small group of the bolder ones who ran out into the street and turned one of the stranded ambulances on its side, and when the petrol poured from the tank, Raleigh lit a match and tossed it on to the spread pool.

The explosive ignition singed his eyelashes and burned away the front of his hair, but that evening when they got back to Drake's Farm, Raleigh was the hero of the band of warriors, and they gave him the praise-name of *Cheza* which means 'the burner'.

As Raleigh was accepted into the middle ranks of the Youth League of the ANC and *Umkhonto we Sizwe*, so he gradually understood the cross-currents of power within them and the internal politics of the rival groups of moderates and radicals – those who thought that freedom could be negotiated and those who believed that it must be won with the blade of the spear, those who thought that the treasures so patiently built up over the years – the mines and the factories and the railways – should be preserved and those who believed that it should all be destroyed and rebuilt again in the name of freedom by the pure ones.

Raleigh found himself inclining more and more towards the purists, the hard fighting men, the exclusive Bantu elite, and when he heard the name *Poqo* for the first time, he thrilled to the sound and sense of it. It described exactly his own feelings and desires – the pure, the only ones.

He was present in the house in Drake's Farm when Moses Gama spoke to them and promised them that the long wait was almost at an end.

'I will take this land by its heels and set it upon its head.' Moses Gama told the group of intense loyal young warriors. 'I will give you a deed, a sign that every man and woman will understand instantly. It will bring the tribes into the streets in their millions and their rage will be a beautiful thing, so pure and strong that nobody, not even the hard Boers, will be able to resist.'

Soon Raleigh came to sense in Moses Gama a divinity that set him above all other humans, and he was filled with a religious love for him and a deep and utter commitment. When the news reached Raleigh that Moses Gama had been caught by the white police as he was on the point of blowing up the houses of parliament and

467

destroying all the evil contained in that iniquitous institution, Raleigh was almost prostrated by his grief, and yet set on fire by Moses Gama's courage and example.

Over the weeks and months that followed, Raleigh was exasperated and angered by the calls for moderation from the high councils of the ANC, and by the dispirited and meek acceptance of Moses Gama's imprisonment and trial. He wanted to vent his wrath upon the world, and when the Pan Africanist Congress broke away from the ANC Raleigh followed where his heart led.

Robert Sobukwe, the leader of the Pan Africanist Congress, sent for him. 'I have heard good words of you,' he told Raleigh. 'And I know the man who is your uncle, the father of us all who languishes in the white man's prison. It is our duty – for we are the pure ones – to bring our message to every black man in the land. There is much work to do, and this is the task I have set for you alone, Raleigh Tabaka.' He led Raleigh to a large-scale map of the Transvaal. 'This area has been left untouched by the ANC.' He placed his hand over the sweep of townships and coalfields and industry around the town of Vereeniging. 'This is where I want you to begin the work.'

Within a week Raleigh had conditioned his father to the idea that he should move to the Vereeniging area to take charge of the family interests there, the three stores in Evaton and the butchery and bakery in Sharpeville, and his father liked the idea the more he thought about it, and he agreed.

'I will give you the names of the men who command the Buffaloes down there. We can begin moving the shebeens into the Sharpeville area. So far we have not put our cattle to graze on those pastures, and the grass there is tall and green.'

Raleigh moved slowly at first. He was a stranger in Sharpeville and he had to consolidate his position. However, he was a strong and comely young man, and he spoke fluently all the major languages of the townships. This was not an unusual achievement, there were many who spoke all the four related languages of the Nguni group of peoples, the Zulus, the Xhosas, the Swazi and the Ndebele, which make up almost seventy per cent of the black tribes of South Africa and whose speech is characterized by elaborate clicking and clucking sounds.

Many others, like Raleigh, were also conversant with the other two languages which are spoken by almost the entire remainder of the black population, the Sotho and the Tswana.

Language was no barrier, and Raleigh had the additional advantage of being placed in charge of his father's business interest in the area, and therefore was accorded almost immediate recognition and respect. Sooner or later every single resident of Sharpeville would come to either Tabaka's bakery or butcher shop and be impressed by the articulate and sympathetic young man who listened to their worries and troubles and extended them credit to buy the white bread and fizzy drinks and tobacco; these were the staple diet of the townships where much of the old way of life was abandoned and forgotten, where the soured milk and maize meal were difficult to procure and where rickets made the children lethargic, bent their bones and turned their hair fine and wispy and dyed a peculiar bronze colour.

They told Raleigh their little troubles, like the cost of renting the township houses and the hardship of commuting such distances to their place of work that it was necessary to rise long before the sun. And then they told Raleigh their greater worries, of being evicted from their homes and of the harassment by the police who were always raiding for liquor and pass offences and prostitution and to enforce the influx control laws. But always it came down to the passes, the little booklets that ruled their lives. The police always were there to ask 'Where is your pass? Show me your pass book.' The *dompas*, they called them, 'the damned pass', in which were stamped all their details of birth and residence and right to reside; no black person could get a job unless he or she produced the damned pass book.

From all the people who came to the shops, Raleigh chose the young vital ones, the brave ones with rage in their hearts, and they met discreetly at first in the storeroom at the back of the bakery, sitting on the bread baskets and the piles of flour bags, talking the night through.

Then they moved more openly, speaking to the older people and the children in the schools, going about as disciples to teach and explain. Raleigh used the funds of the butchery to buy a secondhand duplicator, and he typed the pamphlets on the pink wax sheets and ran them off on the machine.

They were crude little pamphlets, with botchy typing errors and obvious corrections and each one began with the salutation, 'This is *Poqo* of which it is said —' and ended with the stern injunction, '*Poqo* has said this thing. Hear it and obey it.' The young men whom Raleigh had recruited distributed these and read them to those who could not read for themselves.

At first Raleigh allowed only men to come to the meetings in the back room of the bakery store, for they were purists and it was the traditional role of the men to herd the cattle and hunt the game and defend the tribe, while the women thatched the huts and tilled the earth for maize and sorghum and carried the children on their backs.

Then the word was passed down from the high command of *Poqo*

469

and PAC that the women were also part of the struggle. So Raleigh spoke with his young men and one evening a girl came to their Friday-night meeting in the bakery storeroom.

She was a Xhosa and she was tall and strong with beautiful swelling buttocks and the round sweet face like one of the wild veld flowers. While Raleigh spoke she listened silently. She did not move or fidget or interrupt and her huge dark eyes never left Raleigh's face.

Raleigh felt that he was inspired that night, and though he never looked directly at the girl and seemed to address himself to the young warriors, it was to her he spoke and his voice was deep and sure and his own words reverberated in his skull and he listened to them with the same wonder as the others did.

When he finished speaking at last, they all sat in silence for a long time and then one of the young men turned to the girl and said, 'Amelia —' that was the first time ever that Raleigh heard her name, 'Amelia, will you sing for us?'

She did not simper or hang her head or make modest protestations. She simply opened her mouth, and sound poured out of her, glorious sound that made the skin on Raleigh's forearms and at the back of his neck tingle.

He watched her mouth while she sang. Her lips were soft and broad, shaped like two leaves of the wild peach tree, with a dark iridescence that shaded to soft pink on the inside of her mouth, and when she reached for an impossibly sweet high note, he saw that her teeth were perfect white as bone that had lain for a season in the veld, polished by the wind and bleached by the African sun.

The words of the song were strange to him, but like the voice that sang them, they thrilled Raleigh:

'When the roll of heroes is called,
Will my name be on it?
I dream of that day when I will
Sit with Moses Gama,
And we will talk of the passing of the Boers.'

She went away with the young men who had brought her, and that night Raleigh dreamed of her. She stood beside the pool in the great Fish river in which he had washed away the white clay paint of his childhood and she wore the short beaded kilt and her breasts and her legs were bare. Her legs were long and her breasts were round and hard as black marble and she smiled at him with those even white teeth, and when Raleigh awoke his seed was splashed upon the blanket which covered him.

Three days later she came to the bakery to buy bread and Raleigh saw her through the peephole above his desk through which he could

470

watch all that was happening in the front of the store and he went through to the counter and greeted her gravely.

'I see you, Amelia.'

She smiled at him and replied, 'I see you also, Raleigh Tabaka,' and it seemed that she sang his name, for she gave it a music that he had never heard in it before.

She purchased two loaves of white bread, but Raleigh lingered over the sale, wrapping each loaf carefully and counting the pennies of her change as though they were gold sovereigns.

'What is your full name?' he asked her.

'I am called Amelia Sigela.'

'Where is your father's kraal, Amelia Sigela?'

'My father is dead, and I live with my father's sister.'

She was a teacher at the Sharpeville primary school and she was twenty years old. When she left with her bread wrapped in newspaper and her buttocks swinging and jostling each other beneath the yellow European-style skirt, Raleigh returned to his desk in the cubicle of his office and sat for a long time staring at the wall.

On Friday Amelia Sigela came again to the meeting in the back room of the bakery and at the end she sang for them once more. This time Raleigh knew the words and he sang with her. He had a good deep baritone but she gilded it and wreathed it in the glory of her startling soprano and when the meeting broke up, Raleigh walked back with her through the dark streets to her aunt's house in the avenue beyond the school.

They lingered at the door and he touched her arm. It was warm and silky beneath his fingers. On the Sunday when he took the train back to Drake's Farm to make his weekly report to his father, he told his mother about Amelia Sigela and the two of them went through to the sacred room where his mother kept the family gods.

His mother sacrificed a black chicken and spoke to the carved idols, particularly to the totem of Raleigh's maternal great-grandfather, and he replied in a voice that only Raleigh's mother could hear. She listened gravely, nodding at what he said, and later while they ate the sacrificial chicken with rice and herbs, she promised, 'I will speak to your father on your behalf.'

The following Friday after the meeting, Raleigh walked home with Amelia again, but this time as they passed the school where she taught, he drew her into the shadow of the buildings and they stood against the wall very close together. She made no attempt to pull away when he stroked her cheek, so he told her:

'My father is sending an emissary to your aunt to agree a marriage price.' Amelia was silent and he went on, 'However, I will ask him not to do so, if you do not wish it.'

471

'I wish it very much,' she whispered, and slowly and voluptuously she rubbed herself against him like a cat.

The *lobola*, the marriage price, was twenty head of cattle, worth a great deal of money, and Hendrick Tabaka told his son, 'You must work for it, just like other young men are forced to do.'

It would take Raleigh three years to accumulate enough to buy the cattle, but when he told Amelia, she smiled and told him, 'Each day will make me want you more. Think then how great will be my want after three years, and think how sweet will be that moment when the wanting is assuaged.'

Every afternoon, when school was out, Amelia came to the bakery and quite naturally she took to working behind the counter selling the bread and the round brown buns. Then when Raleigh closed the shop, she cooked his evening meal for him and when he had eaten, they walked back to her aunt's house together.

Amelia slept in a tiny room hardly bigger than a closet, across the passage from her aunt. They left the interleading doors open and Raleigh lay on Amelia's bed with her and under the blanket they played the sweet games that custom and tribal law sanctioned all engaged couples to play. Raleigh was allowed to explore delicately and with his fingertips hunt for the little pink bud of flesh hidden between soft furry lips that old Ndlame had told him about at initiation camp. The Xhosa girls are not circumcised like the women of some of the other tribes, but they are taught the arts of pleasing men, and when he could stand it no longer, she took him and held him between her crossed thighs, avoiding only the final penetration that was reserved by tribal lore for their wedding night, and skilfully she milked him of his seed. Strangely, it seemed that every time she did this, rather than depleting him, she replenished the well of his love for her until it was overflowing.

Then the time came when Raleigh judged it expedient to begin infiltrating the Buffaloes into the township. With Hendrick Tabaka's blessing and under Raleigh's supervision, they opened their first shebeen in a cottage at the far end of the township, hard up against the boundary fence.

The shebeen was run by two of the Buffaloes from Drake's Farm who had done this type of work for Hendrick Tabaka before. They knew all the little tricks like adulterating the liquor to make it go further and having one or two girls in the back room for the men that liquor had made amorous.

However, Raleigh warned them about the local police force who had an ugly reputation, and about one of the white officers in particular, a man with pale predatory eyes that had given him his nickname 'Ngwi' the leopard. He was a hard cruel man who had

472

shot to death four men in the time he had been in Sharpeville, two of them members of the Buffaloes who had been supplying the township with *dagga*.

At first they were cautious and wary, vetting their customers carefully and placing lookouts on all approaches to the shebeen, but then as the weeks passed, with business improving each night, they relaxed a little. There was very little competition. Other shebeens had been closed down swiftly, and the customers were so thirsty that the Buffaloes could charge three and four times the usual rate.

Raleigh brought the liquor stocks into the township in his little blue Ford pick-up, the crates hidden beneath sacks of flour and sheep carcasses. He spent as little time as possible at the shebeen, for every minute was dangerous. He would drop off the supplies, collect the empty bottles and the cash and be gone within a half an hour. He never drove the pick-up directly to the front door of the cottage, but parked it in the dark veld beyond the boundary fence and the two Buffaloes would come through the hole in the wire mesh and help him carry the crates of cheap brandy.

After a while Raleigh realized that the shebeen offered another good distribution point for the *Poqo* pamphlets that he printed on the duplicator. He usually kept a stock of these in the cottage and the two Buffaloes who ran the shebeen and the girls who worked in the back room had orders to give one to each of their customers.

In early March, not long after the glad tidings of Moses Gama's reprieve and the mitigation of his death sentence to life imprisonment, Sobukwe sent for Raleigh. The rendezvous was in a house in the vast black township of Soweto. It was not one of the boxlike flat-roofed cottages, but was rather a large modern bungalow situated in the elite section of the township known as 'Beverly Hills'. It had a tiled roof, its own swimming-pool, garaging for two vehicles and large plate-glass windows overlooking the pool.

When Raleigh arrived in the blue pick-up, he found that he was not the only invited guest and there were a dozen or so other vehicles parked along the kerb. Sobukwe had invited all his middle-ranking field officers to this briefing and over forty of them crowded into the sitting-room of the bungalow.

'Comrades,' Sobukwe addressed them. 'We are ready to flex our muscles. You have worked hard and it is time to gather in some of the fruits of your labours. In all the places where the Pan Africanist Congress is strong – not only here on the Witwatersrand but across the country – we are going to make the white police fear our power. We are going to hold a mass protest demonstration against the pass laws —'

Listening to Sobukwe speak, Raleigh was reminded of the power

473

and personality of his own imprisoned uncle, Moses Gama, and he was proud to be part of this magnificent company. As Sobukwe unfolded his plans Raleigh made a silent but fervent resolution that at Sharpeville, the area for which he was responsible, the demonstration would be impressive and solid.

He related every detail of the meeting, and every word that Sobukwe had spoken, to Amelia. Her lovely round face seemed to glow with excitement as she listened and she helped him print the sheets announcing the demonstration and to pack them into the old liquor cartons in lots of five hundred.

On the Friday before the planned demonstration, Raleigh ran a shipment of liquor down to the Buffaloes' shebeen, and he took a carton of pamphlets with him. The Buffaloes were waiting for him in the darkness beside the track, and one of them flashed a torch to guide the pick-up into the scraggy patch of black wattle, and they unloaded the liquor and trudged across to the township fence.

In the cottage Raleigh counted the empty bottles and the full ones and checked these figures against the cash in the canvas bank bag. It tallied and he gave a brief word of commendation to the two Buffaloes, and looked into the front room which was packed with cheerful noisy drinkers.

Then when the door to the nearest bedroom opened and a big Basuto iron-worker came out, grinning and buttoning the front of his blue overalls, Raleigh squeezed past him into the back room. The girl was straightening the sheets on the bed. She was bending over with her back to Raleigh and she was naked, but she looked over her shoulder and smiled when she recognized him. Raleigh was popular with all the girls. She had the money ready for him, and Raleigh counted it in front of her. There was no means of checking her, but over the years Hendrick Tabaka had developed an instinct for a cheating girl, and when Raleigh delivered the money to him he would know if she were holding out.

Raleigh gave her a box of pamphlets and she sat beside him on the bed while he read one of them to her.

'I will be there on Monday,' she promised. 'And I will tell all my men these things and give them each a paper.' She placed the box in the bottom of the cupboard and then came back to Raleigh and took his hand.

'Stay a little while,' she invited him. 'I will straighten your back for you.'

She was a pretty plump little thing and Raleigh was tempted. Amelia was a traditional Nguni maiden, and she did not suffer the curse of western-style jealousy. In fact, she had urged him to accept the offers of the other girls. 'If I am not allowed to sharpen your spear, let the joy-girls keep it bright for the time when I am at last allowed to feel its kiss.'

'Come,' the girl urged Raleigh now, and stroked him through the cloth of his trousers. 'See how the cobra awakes,' she laughed. 'Let me wring his neck!'

Raleigh took one step back towards the bed, laughing with her – then suddenly he froze and the laugh was cut off abruptly. Out in the darkness he had heard the whistle of the lookouts.

'Police,' he snapped. 'The leopard —' and there was the sudden distinctive rumble of a Land-Rover being driven hard and headlights flashed across the cheap curtaining that covered the window.

Raleigh sprang to the door. In the front room the drinkers were fighting to escape through the door and windows, and the table, covered with glasses and empty bottles, was overturned and glass shattered. Raleigh shouldered panic-stricken bodies out of his way and reached the kitchen door. It was locked but he opened it with his own key and slipped through, locking it again behind him.

He switched off the lights and stole across to the back door and placed his hand on the door knob. He would not make the mistake of running out into the yard. The leopard was notoriously quick with his pistol. Raleigh waited in the darkness, and he heard the screams and the scuffling, the crack of the riot batons on flesh and bone and the grunting of the men who swung them and he steeled himself.

Just beyond the door, he heard light running footsteps and suddenly the door handle was seized from the far side and violently twisted. As the man on the outside tried to pull the door open, Raleigh held it, and the other man heaved and swore, leaning back on it with all his weight.

Raleigh let the handle go, and reversed his resistance, throwing his body against the cheap pine door so that it burst open. He felt it crash into human flesh and he had a glimpse of the brown-uniformed figure hurtling backwards down the stairs. Then he used his own momentum to leap up and outwards, clearing the police officer like a steeplechaser, and he went bounding away towards the hole in the mesh fence.

As he ducked through it he glanced back and saw the police officer on his knees. Though his features were contracted and swollen with pain and anger, Raleigh recognized him. It was Ngwi, the killer of men, and the blue service revolver glinted in his hand as it cleared the holster at his side.

Fear sped Raleigh's feet as he darted away into the darkness, but he jinked and twisted as he ran. Something passed close to his head with a snapping report that hurt his eardrums and made him flinch

475

his head wildly and he jinked again. Behind him was another thudding report but he did not hear the second bullet and he saw the dark shape of the Ford ahead of him.

He tumbled into the front seat and started the engine. Without switching on the headlights he bumped over the verge on to the track and accelerated away into the darkness.

He found that he still had the canvas bag of money clutched in his left hand, and his relief was intense. His father would be incensed at the loss of the liquor stocks, but his anger would have been multiplied many times if Raleigh had lost the money as well.

*　　*　　*

Solomon Nduli telephoned Michael Courtney at his desk in the newsroom. 'I have something for you,' he told Michael. 'Can you come out to the *Assegai* offices right away.'

'It's after five already,' Michael protested, 'and it's Friday night. I won't be able to get a pass to enter the township.'

'Come,' Solomon insisted. 'I will wait for you at the main gate.'

He was as good as his promise, a tall gangly figure in steel-rimmed glasses, waiting under the street lamp near the main gates, and as soon as he slipped into the front seat of the company car, Michael passed him his cigarette pack.

'Light one for me, as well,' he told Solomon. 'I brought some sardine and onion sandwiches and a couple of bottles of beer. They are on the back seat.' There was no public place in Johannesburg, or in the entire land for that matter, where two men of different colour could sit and drink or eat together. Michael drove slowly and aimlessly through the streets while they ate and talked.

'The PAC are planning their first big act since they broke away from the ANC,' Solomon told Michael through a mouthful of sardine and onion. 'In some areas they have built up strong support. In the Cape and the rural tribal areas, even in some parts of the Transvaal. They have pulled in all the young militants who are unhappy with the pacifism of the old men. They want to follow Moses Gama's example, and take on the Nationalists in a head-on fight.'

'That's crazy,' Michael said. 'You can't fight sten guns and Saracen armoured cars with half bricks.'

'Yes, it's crazy, but then some of the young people would prefer to die on their feet than live on their knees.'

They were together for an hour, talking all that time, and then at last Michael drove him back to the main gates of Drake's Farm.

'So that's it then, my friend.' Solomon opened the car door. 'If

476

you want the best story on Monday, I would suggest you go down to the Vereeniging area. The PAC and *Poqo* have made that their stronghold on the Witwatersrand.'

'Evaton?' Michael asked.

'Yes, Evaton will be one of the places to watch,' Solomon Nduli agreed. 'But the PAC have a new man in Sharpeville.'

'Sharpeville?' Michael asked. 'Where is that? I've never heard of it.'

'Only twelve miles from Evaton.'

'I'll find it on my road map.'

'You might think it worth the trouble to go there,' Solomon encouraged Michael. 'This PAC organizer in Sharpeville is one of the party's young lions. He will put on a good show, you can count on that.'

*   *   *

Manfred De La Rey asked quietly. 'So, how many reinforcements can we spare for the stations in the Vaal area?'

General Danie Leroux shook his head and smoothed back the wings of silver hair at his temples with both hands. 'We have only three days to move in reinforcements from the outlying areas and most of those will be needed in the Cape. It will mean stripping the outlying stations and leaving them very vulnerable.'

'How many?' Manfred insisted.

'Five or six hundred men for the Vaal,' Danie Leroux said with obvious reluctance.

'That will not be enough,' Manfred growled. 'So we will reinforce all stations lightly, but hold most of our forces in mobile reserve and react swiftly to the first hint of trouble.' He turned his full attention to the map that covered the operations table in the control room of police headquarters in Marshall Square. 'Which are the main danger centres on the Vaal?'

'Evaton,' Danie Leroux replied without hesitation. 'It's always one of the trouble spots, and then Van Der Bijl Park.'

'What about Sharpeville?' Manfred asked, and held up the crudely printed pamphlet that he had tightly rolled in his right hand. 'What about this?'

The general did not reply immediately, but he pretended to study the operations map as he composed his reply. He was well aware that the subversive pamphlets had been discovered by Captain Lothar De La Rey, and he knew how the minister felt about his son. Indeed Danie Leroux shared the general high opinion of Lothar, so he did not want to belittle him in any way or to offend his minister.

477

'There may well be disturbances in the Sharpeville area,' he conceded. 'But it is a small township and has always been very peaceful. We can expect our men there to behave well and I do not see any immediate danger. I suggest we send twenty or thirty men to reinforce Sharpeville, and concentrate our main efforts on the larger townships with violent histories of boycotts and strikes.'

'Very well,' Manfred agreed at last. 'But I want you to maintain at least forty per cent of our reinforcements in reserve, so that they can be moved quickly to any area that flares up unexpectedly.'

'What about arms?' Danie Leroux asked. 'I am about to authorize the issue of automatic weapons to all units.' He turned the statement into a query and Manfred nodded.

'*Ja*, we must be ready for the worst. There is a feeling amongst our enemies that we are on the verge of capitulation. Even our own people are becoming frightened and confused.' His voice dropped, but his tone was fiercer and more determined. 'We have to change that. We have to crush these people who wish to tear down and destroy all we stand for and give this land over to bloodshed and anarchy.'

*   *   *

The centres of support for the PAC were widely scattered across the land, from the eastern tribal areas of the Ciskei and the Transkei to the southern part of the great industrial triangle along the Vaal river, and a thousand miles south of that in the black township of Langa and Nyanga that housed the greater part of the migrant worker force that serviced the mother city of Cape Town.

In all these areas Sunday 20 March 1960 was a day of feverish effort and planning, and of a peculiar expectancy. It was as though everybody at last believed that this new decade would be one of immense change.

The radicals were filled with a feeling of infinite hope, however irrational, and with a certainty that the Nationalist government was on the verge of collapse. They felt that the world was with them, that the age of colonialism had blown away on the winds of change, and that after a decade of massive political mobilization by the black leaders, the time of liberation was at last at hand. All it needed now was one last shove, and the walls of *apartheid* would crash to earth, crushing under them the evil architect Verwoerd and his builders who had raised them up.

Raleigh Tabaka felt that marvellous euphoria as he and his men moved through the township, going from cottage to cottage with the same message: 'Tomorrow we will be as one people. No one will go

478

to work. There will be no buses and those who try to walk to the town will be met by the *Poqo* on the road. The names of all who defy the PAC will be taken and they will be punished. Tomorrow we are going to make the white police fear us.'

They worked all that day, and by evening every person, man and woman, in the township had been warned to stay away from work and to assemble in the open space near the new police station early on the Monday morning.

'We are going to make the white police fear us. We want everybody to be there. If you do not come, we will find you.'

Amelia had worked as hard and unremittingly as Raleigh had done, but like him she was still fresh, unwearied and excited as they ate a quick and simple meal in the back room of the bakery.

'Tomorrow we will see the sun of freedom rise,' Raleigh told her as he wiped his bowl with a crust of bread. 'But we cannot afford to sleep. There is still much work to do this night.' Then he took her hand and told her, 'Our children will be born free, and we will live our life together like men, not like animals.' And he led her out into the darkening township to continue the preparations for the great day that lay ahead.

They met in groups on the street corners, all the eager young ones, and Raleigh and Amelia moved amongst them delegating their duties for the morrow, selecting those who would picket the road leading from Sharpeville to Vereeniging.

'You will let no one pass. Nobody must leave the township,' Raleigh told them. 'All the people must be as one when we march on the police station tomorrow morning.'

'You must tell the people not to fear,' Raleigh urged them. 'Tell them that the white police cannot touch them and that there will be a most important speech from the white government concerning the abolition of the pass laws. Tell the people they must be joyful and unafraid and that they must sing the freedom songs that PAC has taught them.'

After midnight Raleigh assembled his most loyal and reliable men, including the two Buffaloes from the shebeen, and they went to the homes of all the black bus drivers and taxi drivers in the township and pulled them from their beds.

'Nobody will leave Sharpeville tomorrow,' they told them. 'But we do not trust you not to obey your white bosses. We will guard you until the march begins. Instead of driving your buses and taxis tomorrow and taking our people away, you will march with them to the police station. We will see to it that you do. Come with us now.'

As the false dawn flushed the eastern sky, Raleigh himself scaled a telephone pole at the boundary fence and cut the wires. When he slid down again he laughed, as he told Amelia, 'Now our friend the leopard will not find it so easy to call in other police to help him.'

* * *

Captain Lothar De La Rey parked his Land-Rover and left it in a sanitary lane in a patch of shadow out of the street lights and he moved quietly to the corner and stood alone.

He listened to the night. In the years he had served at Sharpeville he had learned to judge the pulse and the mood of the township. He let his feelings and his instincts take over from reason, and almost immediately he was aware of the feral excitement and sense of expectation which had the township in its grip. It was quiet until you listened, as Lothar was listening now. He heard the dogs. They were restless, some close, others at a distance, yapping and barking, and there was an urgency in them. They were seeing and scenting groups and single figures in the shadows. Men hurrying on secret errands.

Then he heard the other sounds, soft as insect sounds in the night. The whistle of lookouts on the watch for his patrols and the recognition signals of the street gangs. In one of the dark cottages nearby a man coughed nervously, unable to sleep, and in another a child whimpered fretfully and was instantly hushed by a woman's soft voice.

Lothar moved quietly through the shadows, listening and watching. Even without the warning of the pamphlets, he would have known that tonight the township was awake and strung up.

Lothar was not an imaginative or romantic young man, but as he scouted the dark streets he suddenly had a clear mental picture of his ancestors performing this same dire task. He saw them bearded and dressed in drab homespun, armed with the long muzzle-loaders, leaving the security of the laagered wagons, going out alone into the African night to scout for the enemy, the *swartgevaar*, the black danger. Spying out the bivouac where the black impis lay upon their war shields, waiting for the dawn to rush in upon the wagons. His nerves crawled at those atavistic memories, and he seemed to hear the battle chant of the tribes in the night and the drumming of assegai on rawhide shield, the stamp of bare feet and the crash of war rattles on wrist and ankle as they came in upon the wagons for the dawn attack.

In his imagination the cry of the restless infant in the nearby cottage became the death screams of the little Boer children at Weenen, where the black impis had come sweeping down from the hills to massacre all in the Boer encampment.

He shivered in the night as he realized that though so much had

480

changed, as much had remained the same. The black danger was still there, growing each day stronger and more ominous. He had seen the confident challenging look of the young bucks as they swaggered through the streets and heard the warlike names they had adopted, the Spear of the Nation and the Pure Ones. Tonight, more than ever, he was aware of the danger and he knew where his duty lay.

He went back to the Land-Rover and drove slowly through the streets. Time and again he glimpsed small groups of dark figures, but when he turned the spotlight upon them, they melted away into the night. Everywhere he went he heard the warning whistles out there in the darkness, and his nerves tightened and tingled. When he met his own foot-patrolling constables, they also were nervous and ill-at-ease.

When the dawn turned the eastern sky pale yellow and dimmed out the street lamps, he drove back through the streets. At this time in the morning they should have been filled with hurrying commuters, but now they were empty and silent.

Lothar reached the bus terminus, and it too was almost deserted. Only a few young men in small groups lounged at the railings. There were no buses, and the pickets stared at the police Land-Rover openly and insolently as Lothar drove slowly past.

As he skirted the boundary fence, passing close to the main gates, he exclaimed suddenly and braked the Land-Rover. From one of the telephone poles the cables trailed limply to the earth. Lothar left the vehicle and went to examine the damage. He lifted the loose end of the dangling copper wire, and saw immediately that it had been cut cleanly. He let it drop and walked slowly back to the Land-Rover.

Before he climbed into the driver's seat, he glanced at his wrist-watch. It was ten minutes past five o'clock. Officially he would be off duty at six, but he would not leave his post today. He knew his duty. He knew it would be a long and dangerous day and he steeled himself to meet it.

*   *   *

That Monday morning, 21 March 1960, a thousand miles away in the Cape townships of Langa and Nyanga the crowds began assembling. It was raining. That cold drizzling Cape north-wester blew from the sea, dampening the ardour of the majority, but by 6 a.m. there was a crowd of almost ten thousand gathered outside the Langa bachelor quarters, ready to begin the march on the police station.

The police anticipated them. During the weekend they had been

481

heavily reinforced and all officers and senior warrant officers issued with sten guns. Now a Saracen armoured car in drab green battle paint entered the head of the wide road in which the crowd had assembled, and a police officer addressed them over the loudspeaker system. He told them that all public meetings had been banned and that a march on the police station would be treated as an attack.

The black leaders came forward and negotiated with the police, and at last agreed to disperse the crowd, but warned that nobody would go to work that day and there would be another mass meeting at 6 p.m. that evening. When the evening meeting began to assemble, the police arrived in Saracen armoured cars, and ordered the crowd to disperse. When they stood their ground, the police baton-charged them. The crowd retaliated by stoning the police and in a mass rushed forward to attack them. The police commander gave the command to fire and the sten guns buzzed in automatic fire and the crowd fled, leaving two of their number dead upon the field.

From then on weeks of rioting and stoning and marches racked the Cape peninsula, culminating in a massed march of tens of thousands of blacks. This time they reached the police headquarters at Caledon Square, but dispersed quietly after their leaders had been promised an interview with the minister of justice. When the leaders arrived for this interview, they were arrested on orders of Manfred De La Rey, the minister of police, and because police reserves had by this time been stretched almost to breaking point, soldiers and sailors of the defence force were rushed in to supplement the local police units and within three days the black townships were cordoned off securely.

In the Cape the struggle was over.

*   *   *

In Van Der Bijl Park ten miles from Vereeniging and in Evaton, both notorious centres of radical and violent black political resistance, the crowds began to gather at first light on Monday 21 March.

By nine o'clock the marchers, thousands strong, set out in procession for their local police stations. However, they did not get very far. Here, as in the Cape, the police had been reinforced and the Saracen armoured cars met them on the road and the loud-hailers boomed out the orders to disperse. The orderly columns of marchers bogged down in the quicksands of uncertainty and ineffectual leadership and the police vehicles moved down on them ponderously, forcing them back, and finally broke up their formations with baton charges.

Then abruptly the sky was filled with a terrible rushing sound and every black face was turned upwards. A flight of Sabre jet fighter aircraft of the South African airforce flashed overhead, only a hundred feet above the heads of the crowd. They had never seen modern jet fighters in such low-level flight and the sight and the sound of the mighty engines was unnerving. The crowds began to break up, and their leaders lost heart. The demonstrations were over almost before they had begun.

*　　*　　*

Robert Sobukwe himself marched to Orlando police station in great Soweto. It was five miles from his house in Mofolo, and although small groups of men joined him along the way, they were less than a hundred strong when they reached the police station and offered themselves for arrest under the pass laws.

In most other centres there were no marches, and no arrests. At Hercules police station in Pretoria six men arrived passless and demanded to be arrested. A jocular police officer obligingly took their names and then sent them home.

In most of the Transvaal it was undramatic and anti-climactic – but then there was Sharpeville.

*　　*　　*

Raleigh Tabaka had not slept all night, he had not even lain down to rest but had been on his feet exhorting and encouraging and organizing.

Now at six o'clock in the morning he was at the bus depot. The gates were still locked, and in the yard the long ungainly vehicles stood in silent rows while a group of three anxious-looking supervisors waited inside the gates for the drivers to arrive. The buses should have commenced their first run at 4.30 a.m. and by now there was no possibility that they could honour their schedules.

From the direction of the township a single figure jogged down the deserted road and behind the depot gate the bus company supervisors brightened and moved forward to open the gate for him. The man hurrying towards them wore the brown peaked driver's cap, with the brass insignia of the bus company on the headband.

'Ha,' Raleigh said grimly. 'We have missed one of them,' and he signalled his men to intercept the black-leg driver.

The driver saw the young men ahead of him and he stopped abruptly.

Raleigh sauntered up to him smiling and asked, 'Where are you going, my uncle?'

The man did not reply but glanced around him nervously.

'You were not going to drive your bus, were you?' Raleigh insisted.

483

'You have heard the words of PAC of which all men have taken heed, have you not?'

'I have children to feed,' the man muttered sullenly. 'And I have worked twenty-five years without missing a day.'

Raleigh shook his head sorrowfully. 'You are a fool, old man. I forgive you for that – you cannot be blamed for the worm in your skull that has devoured your brains. But you are also a traitor to your people. For this I cannot forgive you.' And he nodded to his young men. They seized the driver and dragged him into the bushes beside the road.

The driver fought back, but they were young and strong and many in number and he went down screaming under the blows and after a while, when he was quiet, they left him lying in the dusty dry grass. Raleigh felt no pity or remorse as he walked away. The man was a traitor, and he should count himself fortunate if he survived his punishment to tell his children of his treachery.

At the bus terminus Raleigh's pickets assured him that only a few commuters had attempted to defy the boycott, but they had scurried away as soon as they had seen the waiting pickets.

'Besides,' one of them told Raleigh, 'not a single bus has arrived.'

'You have all begun this day well. Now let us move on to greet the sun of our freedom as it dawns.'

They gathered in the other pickets as they marched, and Amelia was waiting with her children and the other school staff at the corner of the school yard. She saw Raleigh and ran laughing to join him. The children giggled and shrieked with excitement, delighted with this unexpected release from the drudgery of the schoolroom, and they skipped behind Raleigh and his young pickets as they went on.

From each cottage they passed the people swarmed out and when they saw the laughing children, they were infected by the gaiety and excitement. Amongst them by now there were grey heads, and young mothers with their infants strapped to their backs, older women in aprons leading a child on each hand, and men in the overalls of the steel company or the more formal attire of clerks and messengers and shop assistants, and the black petty civil servants who assisted in the administration of the *apartheid* laws. Soon the road behind Raleigh and his comrades was a river of humanity.

As they approached the open common ground they saw that there was already a huge concourse of people gathered there, and from every road leading on to the common more came swarming each minute.

'Five thousand?' Raleigh asked Amelia, and she squeezed his hand and danced with excitement.

'More,' she said. 'There must be more, ten thousand – even fifteen

484

thousand. Oh, Raleigh, I am so proud and happy. Look at our people – isn't it a fine sight to see them all here?' She turned and looked up at him adoringly. 'And I am so proud of you, Raleigh. Without you these poor people would never realize their misery, would never have the will to do anything to change their lot, but look at them now.'

As Raleigh moved forward the people recognized him and made way for him, and they shouted his name and called him 'brother' and 'comrade'.

At the end of the open common was a pile of old bricks and builders' rubble and Raleigh made his way towards it, and when he reached it he climbed up on top of it and raised his arms for silence.

'My people, I bring you the word of Robert Sobukwe who is the father of PAC, and he charges you thus – Remember, Moses Gama! Remember all the pain and hardships of your empty lives! Remember the poverty and the oppression!'

A roar went up from them and they raised their clenched fists or gave the thumbs-up sign and they shouted '*Amandla*' and 'Gama'. It was some time before Raleigh could speak again, but he told them, 'We are going to burn our passes.' He brandished his own booklet as he went on. 'We are going to make fires and burn the *dompas*. Then we are going to march as one people to the police station and ask them to arrest us. Then Robert Sobukwe will come to speak for us —' this was a momentary inspiration of Raleigh's, and he went on happily, 'then the police will see that we are men, and they will fear us. Never again will they force us to show the *dompas*, and we will be free men as our ancestors were free men before the white man came to this land.' He almost believed it as he said it. It all seemed so logical and simple.

So they lit the fires, dozens of them across the common, starting them with dry grass and crumpled sheets of newspaper, and then they clustered around them and threw their pass books into the flames. The women began swaying their hips and shuffling their feet, and the men danced with them and the children scampered around between their legs and they all sang the freedom songs.

It was past eight o'clock before the marshals could get them moving, and then the mass of humanity began to uncoil like a huge serpent and crawl away towards the police station.

*   *   *

Michael Courtney had watched the Evaton demonstration fizzle out ignominiously, and from a public telephone booth he phoned the Van Der Bijl Park police station to learn that after a police baton-charge on the marchers, all was now quiet there also. When he tried

485

to telephone the Sharpeville police he could not get through, although he wasted almost ten shillings in the coin slot and spent forty frustrating minutes in the telephone booth. In the end he gave up in disgust and went back to the small Morris station wagon which Nana had given him for his last birthday present.

He set off back towards Johannesburg, steeling himself for Leon Herbstein's sarcasm. 'So you got a fine story of the riot that didn't take place. Congratulations, Mickey, I knew I could rely on you.'

Michael grimaced and lit another cigarette to console himself, but as he reached the junction with the main road he saw the sign 'Vereeniging 10 miles' and a smaller sign below it 'Sharpeville Township', and instead of turning towards Johannesburg, he turned south and the Morris buzzed merrily down the strangely open and uncrowded roadway.

*　　*　　*

Lothar De La Rey kept a toilet kit in his desk, complete with razor and toothbrush. When he got back to the station he washed and shaved in the hand basin in the men's toilet and he felt refreshed, although the sense of ominous disquiet that he had experienced during his night patrol still remained with him.

The sergeant at the charge office saluted him as he entered.

'Good morning, sir, are you signing off duty?' but Lothar shook his head.

'Has the *kommandant* come on duty yet?'

'He came in ten minutes ago.'

'Have you had any telephone calls since midnight, sergeant?'

'Now you come to mention it, sir, no, we haven't. That's funny, isn't it?'

'Not so funny – the lines have been cut. You should have seen that in the station log,' Lothar snapped at him and went through to the station commander's office.

He listened gravely to Lothar's report. '*Ja*, Lothie. You did good work. I'm not happy about this business. I've had a bad feeling ever since you found those damned pamphlets. They should have given us more men here, not just twenty raw recruits. They should have given us experienced men, instead of sending them to Evaton and the other stations.'

'I have called in the foot patrols,' Lothar told him crisply. He did not want to listen to complaints about the decisions of his superiors. He knew there were good reasons for everything. 'I suggest we hold all our men here at the station. Concentrate our forces.'

'*Ja*, I agree,' said the commander.

486

'What about weapons? Should I open the armoury?'

'*Ja*, Lothie. I think you can go ahead.'

'And I'd like to talk to the men before I go out on patrol again.'

'All right, Lothie. You tell them we have everything in hand. They must just obey orders and it will be all right.'

Lothar saluted and strode back into the charge office.

'Sergeant, I want an issue of arms to all white members.'

'Sten guns?' The man looked surprised.

'And four spare magazines per man,' Lothar nodded. 'I will sign the order into the station log.'

The sergeant handed him the keys and together they went through to the strong room, unlocked and swung open the heavy steel Chubb door. The sten guns stood in their racks against the side wall. Cheap little weapons of pressed steel manufacture, they looked like toys, but the 9 mm parabellum cartridges they fired would kill a man as efficiently as the finest crafted Purdey or square-bridged Mauser.

The reinforcements were almost entirely from the police college, fresh-faced and crew-cut, eager boys who looked up at the decorated captain with awe as he told them, 'We are expecting trouble. That's why you are here. You have been issued stens – that alone is a responsibility that each of you must take seriously. Wait for orders, do not act without them. But once you have them, respond swiftly.'

He took one of his constables with him, and drove down to the main township gates with his sten gun on the seat beside him. It was well after six o'clock by then, but the streets were still quiet. He passed fewer than fifty people, all of them hurrying in the same direction. The post office repair truck was waiting at the gate, and Lothar escorted it down to where the telephone wires had been severed. He waited while a linesman scaled the pole and spliced the wires, and then he escorted the truck back to the gates. Before he reached the broad avenue that led up to the station gates, Lothar pulled to the side of the road and switched off the engine.

The constable in the back seat shifted in his seat and began to say something, but Lothar snapped at him, 'Quiet!' and the man froze. They sat in silence for several seconds, before Lothar frowned.

There was a sound like the sea heard from afar, a gentle susurration and he opened the door of the Land-Rover and stepped out. The whisper was like the wind in tall grass, and there was a faint vibration that he seemed to feel in the soles of his feet.

Lothar jumped back into the Land-Rover and drove swiftly to the next road junction, and turned down it towards the open commonage and the school. The sound grew until he could hear it above the beat of the engine. He turned the next corner and tramped so hard on the brakes that the Land-Rover shuddered and skidded to a halt.

Ahead of him from side to side the road was blocked solid with humanity. They were shoulder to shoulder, rank upon rank, thousand upon thousands, and when they saw the police vehicle ahead of them a great shout of *'Amandla'* went up, and they surged forward.

For a moment Lothar was paralysed by shock. He was not one of those unusual creatures who never felt fear. He had known fear intimately, on the clamorous field when standing to meet the concerted rush of muscled bodies across the turf as well as in the silent streets of the township as he hunted dangerous unscrupulous men in the night. He had conquered those fears and found a strange exhilaration in the feat. But this was a new thing.

This was not human, this was a monster he faced now. A creature with ten thousand throats and twenty thousand legs, a sprawling insensate monster that roared a meaningless word and had no ears to hear nor mind to reason. It was the mob and Lothar was afraid. His instinct was to swing the Land-Rover around and race back to the security of the station. In fact, he had already slammed the gear lever into reverse before he had control of himself.

He left the engine running and opened the side door, and the constable in the back seat blasphemed and his voice was thick with terror. 'Sodding Christ, let's get out of here.'

It served to steel Lothar, and he felt contempt for his own weakness. As he had done so many times before, he strangled his fear and climbed onto the bonnet of the Land-Rover.

Deliberately he had left the sten gun on the front seat and he did not even unbutton the holster on his belt. A single firearm was useless against this sprawling monster.

He held up his arms and shouted, 'Stop! You people must go back. That is a police order.' But his words were drowned in the multitudinous voice of the monster, and it came on apace. The men in the front rank started to run towards him and those behind shouted and pressed forward faster.

'Go back,' Lothar roared, but there was not the slightest check in the ranks and they were close now. He could see the expressions on the faces of the men in front, they were grinning, but Lothar knew how swiftly the African mood can change, how close below the smiles lies the violence of the African heart. He knew he could not stop them, they were too close, too excited, and he was aware that his presence had inflamed them, the mere sight of his uniform was enough.

He jumped down and into the cab, reversed the Land-Rover and then accelerated forward, swinging the wheel into a full lock, and he pulled away as the leaders were within arm's reach.

He pushed the accelerator flat against the floorboards. It was almost two miles back to the station. As he made a quick calculation on how long it would take the march to reach it, he was already rehearsing the orders he would give and working out additional precautions to secure the station.

Suddenly there was another vehicle in the road ahead of him. He had not expected that, and as he swerved to avoid it he saw it was a Morris with lacquered wooden struts supporting the station wagon body. The driver was a young white man.

Lothar slowed and pulled his side window open. 'Where the hell do you think you're going?' he shouted, and the driver leaned out of the window and smiled politely.

'Good morning, Captain.'

'Have you got a permit to be here?'

'Yes, do you want to see it?'

'No, hell,' Lothar told him. 'The permit is cancelled. You are ordered to leave the township immediately, do you hear?'

'Yes, Captain, I hear.'

'There might be trouble,' Lothar insisted. 'You are in danger. I order you to leave immediately for your own safety.'

'Right away,' Michael Courtney agreed, and Lothar accelerated away swiftly.

Michael watched him in the rear-view mirror until he was out of sight, and then he lit a cigarette and drove sedately on in the direction from which the police vehicle had come in such desperate haste. The police captain's agitation had confirmed that he was heading in the right direction and Michael smiled with satisfaction as he heard the distant sounds of many voices.

At the end of the avenue he turned towards the sound, and then pulled in to the side of the road and switched off the engine. He sat behind the wheel and stared ahead at the huge crowd that poured down the street towards him. He was unafraid, detached – an observer not a participant – and as the crowd came on he was studying it avidly, anxious not to miss a single detail, already forming the sentences to describe it and scribbling them in his notebook.

'Young people in the vanguard, many children amongst them, all of them smiling and laughing and singing —'

They saw Michael in the parked Morris and they called to him and gave him the thumbs-up signal.

'The good will of these people always amazes me,' he wrote. 'Their cheerfulness and the lack of personal antipathy towards us ruling whites —'

There was a handsome young man in the van of the march, he walked a few paces ahead of the rest. He had a long confident stride so the girl beside him had to skip to keep up with him. She held his hand and her teeth were even and very white in her lovely dark moon face. She smiled at Michael and waved as she passed him.

The crowd split and flowed past on each side of the parked Morris. Some of the children paused to press their faces against the windows, peering in at Michael, and when he grinned and pulled a face at them they shrieked with laughter and scampered on. One or two of the marchers slapped the roof of the Morris with open palms, but it was rather a cheerful greeting than a hostile act and they scarcely paused but marched on after the young leaders.

For many minutes the crowd flowed past and then only the stragglers, the latecomers, cripples and the elderly with stiff hampered gait were going by, and Michael started the engine of the Morris and U-turned across the street.

In low gear he followed the crowd at a walking pace, driving with one hand while he scribbled notes in the open pad on his lap.

'Estimate between six and seven thousand at this stage, but others joining all the time. Old man on crutches with his wife supporting him, a toddler dressed only in a short vest showing his little bum. A woman with a portable radio balanced on her head playing rock 'n' roll music as she dances along. Many peasant types, probably illegals, still wearing blankets and barefooted. The singing is beautifully harmonized. Also many well-dressed and obviously educated types, some wearing government uniforms, postmen and bus drivers, and workers in overalls of the steel and coal companies. For once, a call has gone out that has reached all of them, not just the politicized minority. A sense of excited and naïve expectation that is palpable. Now the song changes – beginning at the head of the march, but the others pick it up swiftly. They are all singing, doleful and tragic, not necessary to understand the words. This is a lament —'

At the head of the march Amelia sang with such fervour that the tears burst spontaneously from her huge dark eyes and glistened down her cheeks:

The road is long
Our burden is heavy
How long must we go on —

The mood of gaiety changed, and the music of many thousand voices soared in a great anguished cry.

How long must we suffer?
How long? How long?

Amelia held hard to Raleigh's hand and sang with all her being and her very soul, and they turned the last corner. Ahead of them at

490

the end of the long avenue was the diamond-meshed fence that surrounded the police station.

Then in the hard china blue of the highveld sky above the corrugated-iron roof of the police station, a cluster of tiny dark specks appeared. At first they seemed to be a flock of birds, but they swelled in size with miraculous speed as they approached, shining in the early rays of the morning sun with a silent menace.

The head of the march stopped and those behind pressed up behind and then halted also. All their faces turned up towards the menacing machines that bore down upon them, with gaping shark mouths and outstretched pinions, so swiftly that they outran their own engine noise.

The leading Sabre jet dropped lower still, skimming the roof of the police station and the rest of the formation followed it down. The singing faltered into silence, and was followed by the first wails of terror and uncertainty. One after another the great airborne machines hurtled over their heads. It seemed they were low enough to reach up and touch, and the ear-splitting whine of their engines was a physical assault that drove the people to their knees. Some of them crouched in the dusty roadway, others threw themselves flat and covered their heads, while still others turned and tried to run back, but they were blocked by the ranks behind them and the march disintegrated into a confused struggling mass. The men were shouting and the women wailed and some of the children were shrieking and weeping with terror.

The silver jets climbed out and banked steeply, coming around in formation for the next pass; their engines screamed and the shock waves of their passing rumbled across the sky.

Raleigh and Amelia were amongst the few who had stood their ground, and now Raleigh shouted, 'Do not be afraid, my friends. They cannot harm you.'

Amelia took her lead from him and she called to her children, 'They will not hurt you, my little ones. They are pretty as birds. Just look how they shine in the sun!' And the children stifled their terror and a few of them giggled uncertainly.

'Here they come again!' Raleigh shouted. 'Wave to them like this.' And he cavorted and laughed, and the other young people quickly imitated him and the people began to laugh with them. This time as the machines thundered over their heads, only a few of the old women fell over and grovelled in the road, but most of them merely cringed and flinched and then laughed uproariously with relief when the machines were past.

Under the urging of Raleigh and his marshals, the march began slowly to disentangle itself and move forward again, and when the jet fighters made their third pass, they looked up and waved at the helmeted heads under the transparent canopies. This time the aircraft did not bank and come around. Instead they winged away into the blue and the terrible sound of their engines dwindled and the people began to sing again and to embrace each other as they marched, celebrating their courage and their victory.

'Today you will all be free,' Raleigh shouted, and those close enough to hear him believed him, and turned to shout to those farther back.

'Today we will all be free!'

Ahead of them the gates of the police station yard were closed and locked, but they saw the ranks of men drawn up beyond the wire. The uniforms were dark khaki and the morning sun sparkled on the badges and on the ugly stubby blue weapons that the white police carried.

*   *   *

Lothar De La Rey stood on the front steps leading up to the charge office, under the lamp with the words 'Police – *Polisie*' engraved upon the blue glass and steeled himself not to duck as the formation of jet fighters flashed low over the station roof.

He watched the distant mob pulse and contract like some giant black amoeba as the aircraft harassed them, and then regain its shape and come on steadily. He heard the singing swell up in chorus and he could make out the features of those in the front ranks.

The sergeant beside him swore softly. 'My God, just look at those black bastards, there must be thousands of them,' and Lothar recognized in the man's tone his own horror and trepidation.

What they were looking upon was the nightmare of the Afrikaner people that had recurred for almost two centuries, ever since their ancestors moving up slowly from the south through a lovely land populated only by wild game had met suddenly upon the banks of the great Fish river the cohorts of this dark multitude.

He felt his nerves crawl like poisonous insects upon his skin as the tribal memories of his people assaulted him. Here they were once more, the tiny handful of white men at the barricades, and there before them was the black barbaric host. It was as it had always been, but the horror of his situation was not in the least diluted by the knowledge that it had all happened before. Rather it was made more poignant, and the natural reaction of defence more compelling.

However, the fear and loathing in the sergeant's voice braced Lothar against his own weakness, and he tore his gaze from the approaching horde and looked to his own men. He saw how pale they were, how deathly still they stood and how very young so many of them were – but then it was the Afrikaner tradition that the boys had always taken their places at the laager barricades even before they were as tall as the long muzzle-loading weapons they carried.

Lothar forced himself to move, to walk slowly down the line in front of his men, making certain that no trace of his own fear was evident in expression or gesture.

'They don't mean trouble,' he said, 'they have their women and children with them. The Bantu always hide the women if they mean to fight.' His voice was level and without emotion. 'The reinforcements are on their way,' he told them. 'We will have three hundred men here within the hour. Just stay calm and obey orders.' He smiled encouragement at a cadet whose eyes were too big for his pale face, whose ears stuck out from under his cap, and who chewed his lower lip nervously as he stared out through the wire. 'You haven't been given orders to load, *Jong*. Get that magazine off your weapon,' he ordered quietly and the boy unclipped the long straight magazine from the side of his sten gun without once taking his eyes from the singing, dancing horde in front of them.

Lothar walked back down the line with a deliberate tread, not once glancing at the oncoming mob, nodding encouragement at each of his men as he came level or distracting them with a quiet word. But once he reached his post on the station steps again he could no longer contain himself and he turned to face the gate and only with difficulty prevented himself exclaiming out loud.

They filled the entire roadway from side to side and end to end and still they came on, more and more of them pouring out of the side road like a Karoo river in flash flood.

'Stay at your posts, men,' he called. 'Do nothing without orders!' And they stood stolidly in the bright morning sunlight while the leaders of the march reached the locked gates and pressed against them, gripping the wire and peering through the mesh, chanting and grinning as behind them the rest of the huge unwieldy column spread out along the perimeter. Like water contained by a dam wall, compressed by their own multitudes, they were building up rank upon rank until they completely surrounded the station yard, hemming in the small party of uniformed men. And still they came on, those at the back joining the dense throng at the main gates until the station was a tiny rectangular island in a noisy restless black sea.

Then the men at the gates called for silence and gradually the chanting and laughter and general uproar died away.

'We want to speak with your officers,' called a young black man in the front rank at the closed gates. He had his fingers hooked through the mesh and the crowd behind him pushed him so hard against the wire that the high gates shook and trembled.

The station commander came out of the charge office, and as he went down the steps Lothar fell in a pace behind him. Together they crossed the yard and halted in front of the gate.

'This is an illegal gathering,' the commander addressed the young man who had called out to them. 'You must disperse immediately.' He was speaking in Afrikaans.

'It is much worse than that, officer,' the young man smiled at him happily. He was replying in English, a calculated provocation. 'You see, none of us are carrying our pass books. We have burned them.'

'What is your name, you?' the commander demanded in Afrikaans.

'My name is Raleigh Tabaka and I am the branch secretary of the Pan Africanist Congress, and I demand that you arrest me and all these others,' Raleigh told him in fluent English. 'Open the gates, policeman, and take us into your prison cells.'

'I am going to give you five minutes to disperse,' the commander told him menacingly.

'Or what?' Raleigh Tabaka asked. 'What will you do if we do not obey you?' and behind him the crowd began to chant.

'Arrest us! We have burned the *dompas*. Arrest us!'

There was an interruption and a burst of ironic cheers and hooted laughter from the rear of the crowd, and Lothar jumped up on the bonnet of the nearest police Land-Rover to see over their heads.

A small convoy of three troop carriers filled with uniformed constables had driven out of the side road and was now slowly forcing its way through the crowd. The densely packed ranks gave way only reluctantly before the tall covered trucks, but Lothar felt a rush of relief.

He jumped down from the Land-Rover and ordered a squad of his men to the gates. As the convoy came on the people beat upon the steel sides of the trucks with their bare fists and jeered and hooted and gave the ANC salute. A fine mist of dust rose around the trucks and the thousands of milling shuffling feet of the crowd.

Lothar's men forced the gates open against the pressure of black bodies and as the trucks drove through, they swung them shut, and hurriedly locked them again as the crowd surged forward against them.

Lothar left the commander to haggle and bluster with the leaders of the crowd and he went to deploy the reinforcements along the perimeter of the yard. The new men were all armed and Lothar posted the older more steady-looking of them on top of trucks from where they had a sweeping field of fire over all four sides of the fence.

'Stay calm,' he kept repeating. 'Everything is under control. Just obey your orders.'

He hurried back to the gateway as soon as he had placed the reinforcements, and the commander was still arguing with the black leaders through the wire.

'We will not leave here until either you arrest us, or the pass laws are abolished.'

'Don't be stupid, man,' the commander snapped. 'You know neither of those things is possible.'

'Then we will stay,' Raleigh Tabaka told him and the crowd behind him chanted:

'Arrest us! Arrest us! Now!'

'I have placed the new men in position,' Lothar reported in a low voice. 'We have nearly two hundred now.'

'God grant it will be enough if they turn nasty,' the commander muttered and glanced uneasily along the line of uniformed men. It seemed puny and insignificant against the mass that confronted them through the wire.

'I have argued with you long enough.' He turned back to the men behind the gate. 'You must take these people away now. That is a police order.'

'We stay,' Raleigh Tabaka told him pleasantly.

As the morning wore on, so the heat increased and Lothar could feel the tension and the fear in his men rising with the heat and the thirst and the dust and the chanting. Every few minutes a disturbance in the crowd made it eddy and push like a whirlpool in the flow of a river, and each time the fence shook and swayed and the white men fingered their guns and fidgeted in the baking sun. Twice more during the morning reinforcements arrived and the crowd let them through until there were almost three hundred armed police in the compound. But instead of dispersing, the crowd continued to grow as every last person who had hidden away in the township cottages, expecting trouble, finally succumbed to curiosity and crept out to join the multitude.

After each new arrival of trucks there was another round of argument and futile orders to disperse, and in the heat and the impatience of waiting, the mood of the crowd gradually changed. There were no more smiles and the singing had a different tone to it as they began to hum the fierce fighting songs. Rumours flashed through the throng – Robert Sobukwe was coming to speak to them, Verwoerd had ordered the passes to be abolished and Moses Gama to be released from jail, and they cheered and sang and then growled and surged back and forth as each rumour was denied.

The sun made its noon, blazing down upon them, and the smell of

495

the crowd was the musky African odour, alien and yet dreadfully familiar.

The white men who had stood to arms all that morning were reaching the point of nervous exhaustion and each time the crowd surged against the frail wire fence they made little jumpy movements and one or two of them without orders loaded their sten guns and lifted them into the high port position. Lothar noticed this and went down the line, ordering them to unload and uncock their weapons.

'We have to do something soon, sir,' he told his commander. 'We can't go on like this – someone or something is going to snap.' It was in the air, strong as the odour of hot African bodies, and Lothar felt it in himself. He had not slept that night, and he was haggard and he felt brittle and jagged as a blade of obsidian.

'What do you suggest, De La Rey?' the commander barked irritably, just as edgy and tense. 'We must do something, you say. *Ja*, I agree – but what?'

'We should take the ringleaders out of the mob.' Lothar pointed at Raleigh Tabaka who was still at the gate. It was almost five hours since he had taken up his station there. 'That black swine there is holding them together. If we pick him and the other ringleaders out, the rest of them will soon lose interest.'

'What is the time?' the commander asked, and although it seemed irrelevant, Lothar glanced at his watch.

'Almost one o'clock.'

'There must be more reinforcements on the way,' the commander said. 'We will wait another fifteen minutes and then we will do as you suggest.'

'Look there,' Lothar snapped and pointed to the left.

Some of the younger men in the crowd had armed themselves with stones and bricks, and from the rear other missiles, chunks of paving slab and rocks, were being passed over the heads of the crowd to those in the front ranks.

'*Ja*, we have to break this up now,' the commander agreed, 'or else there will be serious trouble.'

Lothar turned and called a curt order to the constables nearest him. 'You men, load your weapons and move up to the gate with me.'

He saw that some of the other men further down the line had taken his words as a general order to load, and there was the snicker of metal on metal as the magazines were clamped on to the sten guns and the cocking handles jerked back. Lothar debated with himself for a moment whether he should countermand, but time was vital. He knew he had to get the leaders out of the crowd, for violence was only seconds away. Some of the black youths in front of the crowd were already shaking the mesh and heaving against it.

With his men behind him he marched to the gate and pointed at Raleigh Tabaka. 'You,' he shouted. 'I want to speak to you.' He reached through the square opening beside the gate lock and seized the front of Raleigh's shirt.

'I want you out of there,' he snarled, and Raleigh pulled back against his grip, jostling the men behind him.

Amelia screamed and clawed at Lothar's wrist. 'Leave him! You must not hurt him.'

The young men around them saw what was happening and hurled themselves against the wire.

'Jee!' they cried, that long, deep, drawn-out war cry that no Nguni warrior can resist. It made their blood smoke with the fighting madness, and it was taken up as others echoed them.

'Jee!'

The section of the crowd behind where Raleigh struggled with Lothar De La Rey heaved forward, throwing themselves upon the fence, humming the war cry, and the fence buckled and began to topple.

'Get back!' Lothar shouted at his men, but the back ranks of the crowd surged forward to see what was happening in front – and the fence went.

It came crashing over, and though Lothar jumped back, one of the metal posts hit him a glancing blow and he was knocked to his knees. The crowd was no longer contained, and the ranks behind pushed those in front so they came bursting into the yard, trampling over Lothar as he struggled to get to his feet.

From one side a brick came sailing out of the crowd in a high parabola. It struck the windscreen of one of the parked trucks, and shattered it in a shower of diamond-bright chips.

The women were screaming, and falling under the feet of those who were borne forward by the pressure from behind, and men were fighting to get back behind the wire as others thrust them forward, uttering that murderous war cry *'Jee!'* that brought on the madness.

Lothar was sprawled under the rushing tide, struggling to regain his feet, while a hail of stones and bricks came over the wire. Lothar rolled to his feet, and only because he was a superb athlete he kept his balance as the rush of frenzied bodies carried him backwards.

There was a loud and jarring sound close behind him that Lothar did not at first recognize. It sounded as though a steel rod had been drawn rapidly across a sheet of corrugated iron. Then he heard the other terrible sounds, the multiple impact of bullets into living flesh, like ripe melons bursting open from blows with a heavy club, and he shouted, 'No! Oh good Christ, no!' But the sten guns rushed and tore the air with a sound like sheets of silk being ripped through,

497

drowning out his despairing protest, and he wanted to shout again, 'Cease fire!' but his throat had closed and he was suffocating with horror and terror.

He made another strenuous effort to give the order, and his throat strained to enunciate the words, but no sound came and his hands moved without his conscious volition, lifting the sten gun from his side, jerking back the cocking handle to feed a round into the breech. In front of him the crowd was breaking and turning, the pressure of human bodies against him was relieved, so he could mount the machine pistol to waist height.

He tried to stop himself, but it was all a nightmare over which he had no control, the weapon in his hands shuddered and buzzed like a chain saw. In a few fleeting seconds the magazine of thirty rounds was empty, but Lothar had traversed the sten gun like a reaper swinging a scythe, and now the bloody harvest lay before him in the dust twitching and kicking and moaning.

Only then did he realize fully what he had done, and his voice returned.

'Cease fire!' he screamed and struck out at the men around him to reinforce the order. 'Cease fire! Stop it! Stop it!'

Some of the younger recruits were reloading to fire again, and he ran amongst them striking out with the empty sten to prevent them. A man on the roof of one of the troop carriers lifted his weapon and fired another burst and Lothar leapt on to the cab and knocked up the barrel so that the last spray of bullets went high into the dusty air.

From his vantage point on the cab of the truck, Lothar looked out over the sagging fence across the open ground where the dead and the wounded lay, and his spirit quailed.

'Oh, God forgive me. What have we done?' he choked. 'Oh, what have we done?'

*   *   *

In the middle of the morning Michael Courtney took a chance, for there seemed to be a lull in the activity around the police station. It was, of course, difficult to make out exactly what was happening. He could see only the backs of the rear ranks of the crowd, and over their heads the top of the wire fence and the iron roof of the station. However, the situation seemed for the moment to be quiet and apart from a little desultory singing the crowd was passive and patient.

He jumped into the Morris and drove back down the avenue to the primary school. The buildings were deserted, and without any qualms he tried the door which was marked 'Headmaster' and it was unlocked. There was a telephone on the cheap deal desk. He got through to the *Mail* offices on the first try, and Leon Herbstein was in his office.

'I've got a story,' Michael said, and read out his copy. When he finished he told Leon, 'If I were you, I'd send a staff photographer down here. There is a good chance of some dramatic pictures.'

'Give me the directions how to find you.' Leon acquiesced immediately, and Michael drove back to the police station just as another convoy of police reinforcements pushed through the crowd and entered the station gates.

The morning wore on and Michael ran out of cigarettes, a minor tragedy. He was also hot and thirsty and wondered what it was like standing in that mob out there, hour after hour.

He could sense the mood of the crowd changing. They were no longer cheerful and expectant. There was a sense of frustration, of having been cheated and duped for Sobukwe had not arrived, nor had the white police made the promised announcement to abolish the *dompas*.

The singing started again, but in a harsh and aggressive tone. There were scuffles and disturbances in the crowd, and over their heads Michael saw the armed police take up positions on the cabs of the trucks parked beyond the wire.

The staff photographer from the *Mail* arrived, a young black journalist who was able to enter the township without a permit. He parked his small brown Humber beside the Morris and Michael cadged a cigarette from him and then quickly briefed him on what was happening, and sent him forward to mingle with the back rows of the crowd and get to work.

A little after noon, some of the youths broke away from the crowd and began to search the verges of the road and the nearest gardens for missiles. They pulled up the bricks that bordered the flower-beds and broke chunks off the concrete paving slabs, then hurried back to join the crowd, carrying those crude weapons. This was an ominous development, and Michael climbed up on the bonnet of his beloved Morris, careless of the paintwork which he usually cherished and polished every morning.

Although he was over a hundred and fifty yards from the station gate, he now had a better view over the heads of the crowd, and he watched the growing agitation and restlessness until the police on the vehicle cabs, the only ones he could see, raised and began loading and cocking their weapons. They were obviously responding to an order and Michael felt a peculiar little chill of anxiety.

Suddenly there was a violent disturbance in the densest part of the crowd directly in front of the main gates. The mass of people surged and heaved and there was an uproar of protesting shouts and cries. Those in the rear of the crowd, closest to where Michael stood, pushed forward to see what was going on, and suddenly there was a metallic rending sound.

Michael saw the tops of the gates begin to move, toppling and bending under the strain, and as they went over, there was a scattered volley of thrown rocks and bricks, and then like the waters of a broken dam, the crowd rushed forward.

Michael had never heard the sound of submachine-gun fire before. So he did not recognize it, but he had heard a bullet striking flesh during that childhood safari on which his father had taken the brothers.

The sound was unmistakable, a meaty thumping, almost like a housewife beating a dusty carpet. However, he couldn't believe it, not until he saw the policemen on the cabs of the vehicles. Even in his horror he noticed how the weapons they held jumped and spurted tiny petals of fire an instant before the sound reached him.

The crowd broke and ran at the first buzzing bursts of fire. They spread out like ripples across a pond, streaming back past where Michael stood, and incredibly some of them were laughing, as though they had not realized what was happening, as though it were all some silly game.

In front of the broken gates the bodies were strewn most thickly, nearly all of them face down and with their heads pointing outwards, in the direction they were running as they were struck down, but there were others farther out and the guns were still clamouring and people were still falling right beside where Michael stood, and the area around the police station was clear, so that through the dust he could see the figures of the uniformed police beyond the sagging wire. Some of them were reloading and others were still firing.

Michael heard the flitting sound of bullets passing close beside his head, but he was too mesmerized and shocked to duck or even to flinch.

Twenty paces away a young couple ran back past him. He recognized them as the pair who had headed the procession earlier, the tall good-looking lad and the pretty moon-faced girl. They were still holding hands, the boy dragging the girl along with him, but as they passed Michael the girl broke free and doubled back to where a child was standing bewildered and lost amongst the carnage.

As the girl stooped to pick up the child, the bullets hit her. She was thrown back abruptly as though she had reached the end of an invisible leash, but she stayed on her feet for a few seconds longer, and Michael saw the bullets come out through her back at the level of her lowest ribs. For a brief moment they raised little tented peaks in the cloth of her blouse, and then erupted in pink smoky puffs of blood and tissue.

The girl pirouetted and began to sag. As she turned, Michael saw the two entry wounds in her chest, dark studs on the white cloth, and she collapsed on to her knees.

Her companion ran back to try and support her, but she slipped through his hands and fell forward on her face. The boy dropped down beside her and lifted her in his arms, and Michael saw his expression. He had never before seen such desolation and human suffering in another being.

*   *   *

Raleigh held Amelia in his arms. Her head drooped against his shoulder like that of a sleepy child and he could feel her blood soaking into his clothing. It was hot as spilled coffee and it smelled sickly sweet in the heat.

Raleigh groped in his pocket and found his handkerchief. Gently he wiped the dust from her cheeks and from the corners of her mouth, for she had fallen with her face against the earth.

He was crooning to her softly, 'Wake up, my little moon. Let me hear your sweet voice —'

Her eyes were open and he turned her head slightly to look into them. 'It is me, Amelia, it is Raleigh – don't you see me?' But even as he stared into her widely distended pupils a milky sheen spread over them, dulling out their dark beauty.

He hugged her harder, pressing her unresisting head against his chest and he began to rock her, humming softly to her as though she were an infant, and he looked out across the field.

The bodies were strewn about like overripe fruit fallen from the bough. Some of them were moving, an arm straightened or a hand unclenched, an old man began to crawl past where Raleigh knelt, dragging a shattered leg behind him.

Then the police officers were coming out through the sagging gates. They wandered about the field in a dazed uncertain manner, still carrying their empty weapons dangling from limp hands, stopping to kneel briefly beside one of the bodies, and then standing again and walking on.

One of them approached. As he came closer Raleigh recognized the blond captain who had seized him at the gate. He had lost his cap and the top button was missing from his tunic. His crew-cut hair was darkened with sweat, and droplets of sweat stood on his waxen pale forehead. He stopped a few paces off and looked at Raleigh. Although his hair was blond, his eyebrows were dark and thick and his eyes were yellow as those of a leopard. Raleigh knew then how he had earned his nickname. Those pale eyes were underscored with smudges of fatigue and horror, dark as old bruises, and his lips were dry and cracked.

They stared at each other – the black man kneeling in the dust with the dead woman in his arms and the uniformed white man with the empty sten gun in his hands.

'I didn't mean it to happen —' said Lothar De La Rey and his voice croaked, 'I'm sorry.'

Raleigh did not answer, gave no sign of having heard or understood and Lothar turned away and walked back, picking his way amongst the dead and the maimed, back into the laager of wire mesh.

The blood on Raleigh's clothing began to cool, and when he touched Amelia's cheek again he felt the warmth going out of it also. Gently he closed her eyelids, and then he unbuttoned the front of her blouse. There was very little bleeding from the two entry wounds. They were just below her pointed virgin breasts, small dark mouths in her smooth amber-coloured skin, set only inches apart. Raleigh ran two fingers of his right hand into those bloody mouths, and there was residual warmth in her torn flesh.

'With my fingers in your dead body,' he whispered. 'With the fingers of my right hand in your wounds, I swear an oath, my love. You will be avenged. I swear it on our love, upon my life and upon your death. You will be avenged.'

*   *   *

In the days of anxiety and turmoil following the massacre of Sharpeville, Verwoerd and his minister of police acted with resolution and strength.

A state of emergency was declared in almost half of South Africa's magisterial districts. Both the PAC and ANC were banned and those of their supporters suspected of incitement and intimidation were arrested and detained under the emergency regulations. Some estimates put the figure of detainees as high as eighteen thousand.

In early April at the meeting of the full cabinet to discuss the emergency, Shasa Courtney risked his political future by rising to address a plea to Dr Verwoerd for the abolition of the pass book system. He had prepared his speech with care, and the genuine concern he felt for the importance of the subject made him even more than usually eloquent. As he spoke he became gradually aware that he was winning the support of some of the other senior members of the cabinet.

502

'In a single stroke we will be removing the main cause of black dissatisfaction, and depriving the revolutionary agitators of their most valuable weapon,' he pointed out.

Three other senior ministers followed Shasa, each voicing their support for the abolition of the *dompas*, but from the top of the long table Verwoerd glowered at them, becoming every minute more angry until at last he jumped to his feet.

'The idea is completely out of the question. The reference books are there for an essential purpose: to control the influx of blacks into the urban areas.'

Within a few minutes he had brutally bludgeoned the proposal to death, and made it clear that to try to resurrect it would be political suicide for any member of the cabinet, no matter how senior.

Within days Dr Hendrik Verwoerd was himself on the brink of the chasm. He visited Johannesburg to open the Rand Easter Show. He made a reassuring speech to the huge audience that filled the arena of the country's largest agricultural and industrial show, and as he sat down to thunderous applause, a white man of insignificant appearance made his way between the tiers of seats and in full view of everybody drew a pistol and holding it to Dr Verwoerd's head fired two shots.

With blood pouring down his face Verwoerd collapsed, and security guards overpowered his assailant. Both bullets, fired at point-blank range, had penetrated the prime minister's skull, and yet his most remarkable tenacity and will to survive combined with the expert medical attention he received, saved him.

In little more than a month he had left hospital and had once more taken up his duties as the head of state. The assassination attempt seemed to have been without motive or reason, and the assailant was judged insane and placed in an asylum. By the time Dr Verwoerd had fully recovered from the attempt on his life calm had been restored to the country as a whole, and Manfred De La Rey's police were in total control once more.

Naturally the reaction of the international community towards the slaughter and the subsequent measures to regain control was heavily critical. America led the rest in her condemnations, and within months had instituted an embargo on the sale of arms to South Africa. More damaging than the reaction of foreign governments was the crash on the Johannesburg stock exchange, the collapse of property values and the attempted flight of capital out of the country. Strict exchange-control regulations were swiftly imposed to forestall this.

Manfred De La Rey had come out of it all with his power and position greatly enhanced. He had acted the way his people expected

503

him to, with strength and forthright determination. There was no doubt at all now that he was one of the senior members of the cabinet and in the direct line of succession to Hendrik Verwoerd. He had smashed the Pan Africanist Congress and the ANC. Their leaders were in total disarray and all of them were in hiding or had fled the country.

With the safety of the state secured, Dr Verwoerd could at last turn his full attention to the momentous business of realizing the golden dream of Afrikanerdom – the Republic.

The referendum was held in October 1960, and so great were the feelings, for and against, engendered by the prospect of breaking with the British crown that there was a ninety per cent poll. Cunningly, Verwoerd had decreed that a simple majority, and not the usual two-thirds majority, would suffice, and on the day he got his majority: 850,000 to 775,000. The Afrikaner response was an hysteria of joy, of speeches and wild rejoicing.

In March the following year Verwoerd and his entourage went to London to attend the conference of the Commonwealth prime ministers. He came out of the meeting to tell the world, 'In the light of opinions expressed by other member governments of the Commonwealth regarding South Africa's race policies, and in the light of future plans regarding the race policies of the South African government, I told the other prime ministers that I was withdrawing my country's application for continued membership of the Commonwealth after attaining the status of a republic.'

From Pretoria Manfred De La Rey cabled Verwoerd, 'You have preserved the dignity and pride of your country, and the nation owes you eternal gratitude.'

Verwoerd returned home to the adulation and hero worship of his people. In the heady euphoria, very few, even amongst the English-speaking opposition, realized just how many doors Verwoerd had locked and barred behind him and just how cold and bleak the winds that Macmillan had predicted would blow across the southern tip of Africa in the coming years.

*   *   *

With the Republic safely launched Verwoerd could at last select his praetorian guard to protect it and hold it strong. Erasmus, the erstwhile minister of justice who had acted neither as ruthlessly nor as resolutely as was expected during the emergency, was packed off as the ambassador of the new Republic to Rome, and Verwoerd presented two new ministers to his cabinet.

The new minister of defence was the member for the constituency of George in the Cape, P. W. Botha, while Erasmus's replacement as minister of justice was Balthazar Johannes Vorster. Shasa Courtney knew Vorster well, and as he listened to him make his first address to the cabinet, he reflected how much like Manfred De La Rey the man was.

They were almost the same age and, like Manfred, Vorster had been a member of the extreme right-wing anti-Smuts pro-Nazi *Ossewa Brandwag* during the war. Whereas it was generally accepted that Manfred had remained in Germany during the war years – although he was very mysterious and secretive about that period of his life – John Vorster had been interned in Smuts' Koffiefontein concentration camp for the duration.

Both Vorster and De La Rey had been educated at Stellenbosch University, the citadel of Afrikanerdom, and their political careers had run closely parallel courses. Although Manfred had won his seat in parliament in the historic 1948 elections, John Vorster in the same elections had gained the distinction of being the only candidate in South African history to lose by a mere two votes. Later, in 1953, he vindicated himself by winning the same Brakpan seat with a majority of seven hundred.

Now that the two of them were seated at the long table in the cabinet room, their physical resemblance was striking. They were both heavy rugged-looking men, with bulldog features, both obdurate, unflinching and tough, the epitome of the hard Boer.

Vorster confirmed this for Shasa as he began to speak, leaning forward aggressively, confident and articulate. 'I believe we are in a fight to the death with the forces of communism, and that we cannot defeat subversion or thwart revolution by closely observing the Queensberry rules. We have to put aside the old precepts of *habeas corpus*, and arm ourselves with new legislation that will enable us to preempt the enemy, to pick out their leaders and put them away where they can do little harm. This is not a new concept, gentlemen.'

Vorster smiled down the table and Shasa was struck by the way in which his dour features lit up with that impish smile.

'You all know where I spent the war years, without the benefit of trial. Let me tell you right now – it worked. It kept me out of mischief and that's what I intend to do with those who would destroy this land – keep them out of mischief. I want power to detain any person whom I know to be an enemy of the state, without trial, for a period of up to ninety days.'

It was a masterly performance and Shasa felt some trepidation in having to follow it, especially when he could not be so sanguine in his own view of the future.

'At the moment I have two major concerns,' he told his colleagues seriously. 'The first is the arms embargo placed upon us by the Americans. I believe that other countries are soon going to bow to American pressure and extend the embargo. One day we might even have the ridiculous situation where Great Britain will refuse to sell us the arms we need for our own defence.' Some of the others at the table fidgeted and looked incredulous. Shasa assured them: 'We cannot afford to underestimate this hysteria of America for what they call civil rights. Remember that they sent troops to help force blacks into white schools.' The memory of that appalled them all and there were no further signs of disbelief as Shasa went on. 'A nation who can do that will do anything. My aim is to make this country totally self-sufficient in conventional armaments within five years.'

'Is that possible?' Verwoerd asked sharply.

'I believe so.' Shasa nodded. 'Fortunately, this eventuality has been anticipated. You yourself warned me of the possibility of an arms embargo when you appointed me, Prime Minister.'

Verwoerd nodded and Shasa repeated, 'This is my aim; self-sufficient in conventional weapons in five years —' Shasa paused dramatically. 'And nuclear capable in ten years.'

This was stretching their credulity and there were interjections and sharp questions, so that Shasa held up his hands and spoke firmly.

'I am deadly serious, gentlemen. We can do it! Given certain circumstances.'

'Money,' said Hendrik Verwoerd, and Shasa nodded.

'Yes, Prime Minister, money. Which brings me to my second major consideration.' Shasa drew a deep breath, and steeled himself to broach an unpalatable truth. 'Since the Sharpeville shootings, we have had a crippling flight of capital from the country. Cecil Rhodes was wont to say that the Jews were his birds of good omen. When the Jews came, an enterprise or a country was assured of success, and when the Jews left you could expect the worst. Well the sad truth, gentlemen, is that our Jews are leaving. We have to entice them to stay and bring back those who have already left.'

Again there was restlessness around the table. The National Party had been conceived on that wave of anti-semitism between the world wars, and although it had abated since then, traces of it still existed.

'These are the facts, gentlemen.' Shasa ignored their discomfort. 'Since Sharpeville, the value of property has collapsed to half what it was before the shooting, and the stock market is at its lowest since the dark days of Dunkirk. The businessmen and investors of the world are convinced that this government is tottering and on the point of capitulating to the forces of communism and darkness. They see us as being engulfed in despondency and anarchy, with black

506

mobs burning and looting and white civilization about to go up in flames.' They laughed derisively and John Vorster made a bitter interjection.

'I have just explained what steps we will take.'

'Yes.' Shasa cut him off quickly. 'We know that the foreign view is distorted. We know that we still have a strong and stable government, that the country is prosperous and productive and that the vast majority of our people, both black and white, are law-abiding and content. We know that we have our guardian angel, gold, to protect us. But we have to convince the rest of the world.'

'Do you think that's possible, man?' Manfred asked quickly.

'Yes, with a full-scale and concerted campaign to give the truth of the situation to the businessmen of the world,' Shasa said. 'I have recruited most of our own leaders in industry and commerce to assist. We will go out at our own expense to explain the truth. We will invite them here – journalists, businessmen and friends – to see for themselves how tranquil and how under control the country truly is, and just how rich are the opportunities.'

Shasa spoke for another thirty minutes and when he ended, his own fervour and sincerity had exhausted him; but then he saw how he had finally convinced his colleagues and he knew the results were worth the effort. He was convinced that from the horror of Sharpeville he could mount a fresh endeavour that would carry them to greater heights of prosperity and strength.

Shasa had always been resilient, with extraordinary recuperative powers. Even in his airforce days, when he brought the squadron in from a sortie over the Italian lines and the others had sat around the mess, stunned and shattered by the experience, he had been the first to recover and to start the repartee and boisterous horse-play. Shasa left the cabinet room drained and exhausted but by the time he had driven the vintage SS Jaguar around the mountain and through the Anreith gate of Weltevreden, he was sitting up straight in the bucket seat, feeling confident and jaunty again.

The harvest was long past and the labourers were in the vineyards pruning the vines. Shasa parked the Jaguar and went down between the rows of bare leafless plants to talk to them and give them encouragement. Many of these men and women had been on Weltevreden since Shasa had been a child, and the younger ones had been born here. Shasa looked upon them as an extension of his family and they in turn regarded him as their patriarch. He spent half an hour with them listening to their small problems and worries, and settling most with a few words of assurance, then he broke off and left them abruptly as a figure on horseback came down the far side of the vineyard at full gallop.

507

From the corner of the stone wall Shasa watched Isabella gather her mount, and he stiffened as he realized what she was going to do. The mare was not yet fully schooled and Shasa had never trusted her temperament. The wall was of yellow Table Mountain sandstone, five foot high.

'No, Bella!' he whispered. 'No, baby!'

But she turned the mare and drove her at the wall, and the horse reacted gamely. Her quarters bunched and the great muscles rippled below the glossy hide. Isabella lifted her and they went up.

Shasa held his breath, but even in his suspense he could appreciate what a magnificent sight they made, horse and rider, thoroughbreds both – the mare with her forelegs folded up under her chest and her ears pricked forward, soaring away from the earth, and Isabella leaning back in the saddle, her back arched and her young body supple and lovely, long legs and fine thrusting breasts, red mouth laughing and her hair flying free, sparkling with ruby lights in the late yellow sunlight.

Then they were over and Shasa exhaled sharply. Isabella swung the mare down to where he stood at the corner.

'You promised to ride with me, Pater,' she scolded him. Shasa's instinct was to reprimand her for that jump, but he prevented himself. He knew she would probably respond by pulling the mare's head around and taking the jump again from this side. He wondered just when he had lost control of her, and then grinned ruefully as he answered himself.

'About ten minutes after she was born.'

The mare was dancing in a circle and Isabella flung her hair back with a toss of her head.

'I waited almost an hour for you,' she said.

'Affairs of state —' Shasa began.

'That's no excuse, Pater. A promise is a promise.'

'It's still not too late,' he pointed out, and she laughed as she challenged him.

'I'll race that old banger of yours down to the stables!' And she booted the mare into a gallop.

'Not fair,' he called after her. 'You have too much start,' but she turned in the saddle and stuck her tongue out at him. He ran to the Jag, but she cut across north field and was dismounted by the time he drove into the stableyard.

She tossed her reins to a groom and ran to embrace him. Isabella had a variety of kisses, but this type, lingering and loving, with a little bit of ear-nuzzling at the end, was reserved for when she badly wanted something from him, something that she knew he was going to try to refuse.

While he pulled on his riding boots she sat close beside him on the bench and told him a funny story about her sociology professor at varsity.

'This huge shaggy St Bernard wandered into the lecture theatre and Prof. Jacobs was quick as a flash. Better that the dogs should come to learning, he said, than learning should go to the dogs.' She was a natural mimic. As they left the saddle room, she hugged his arm.

'Oh, Daddy, if only I could find a boy like you, but they're all so utterly dreary.'

'Long may they remain that way,' he wished fervently.

He made a cup with his hands for her to mount, but she laughed at him and sprang to the saddle easily on those long lovely legs.

'Come on, slowcoach. It'll be dark soon.'

Shasa enjoyed being alone with her. She enchanted him with her mercurial changes of mood and subject. She had a quick mind and quirky sense of humour, to go with her extraordinary face and body, but she alarmed him when she showed flashes of that restless refusal to concentrate for long on a single topic. Sean had been like that, needing constant stimulation to hold his interest, easily bored by anything that could not keep the same breathless pace that he set. Shasa was amazed that Isabella had lasted out a year of university studies, but he was resigned to the fact that she wasn't going to graduate. Every time they discussed it, she was more disparaging of the academic life. Make-believe, she called it. Kids' stuff. And when he replied, 'Well, Bella, you are still a kid', she bridled at him.

'Oh, Daddy, you don't understand!'

'Don't I? Don't you think I was your age once?'

'I suppose so – but that was in biblical times, for God's sake.'

'Ladies don't swear,' he remonstrated automatically.

She attracted admirers in slavish droves, and treated them with callous indifference for a while and then dropped them with almost feline cruelty, and all the time the restlessness in her was more apparent.

'I should have been stricter with her right from the beginning,' he decided grimly, and then grinned. 'What the hell, she's my only indulgence – and she'll be gone soon enough.'

'Do you know that when you smile like that you are the sexiest man in the world?' she interrupted his thoughts.

'What do you know about sexiness, young lady?' he demanded gruffly to cover his gratification, and she tossed her head at him.

'Wouldn't you like to know?'

'No thank you,' he refused hastily. 'I'd probably have a hernia on the spot.'

509

'My poor old Daddy.' She edged the mare over until their knees touched and she leaned across to hug him.

'All right, Bella,' he smiled. 'You'd better tell me what you want. Your heavy artillery has demolished my defences entirely.'

'Oh, Daddy, you make me seem so scheming. I'll race you down to the polo grounds.'

He let her lead, holding his stallion's nose just behind her stirrup all the way down the hill. Nonetheless, she was flushed with triumph as she pulled in the mare and turned back to him.

'I had a letter from Mater,' she said.

For a moment Shasa didn't realize what she had said, then his smile iced over and he glanced at his gold Rolex wristwatch.

'We'd better be getting back.'

'I want to talk about my mother. We haven't talked about her since the divorce.'

'There isn't anything to discuss. She's out of our lives.'

'No.' Isabella shook her head. 'She wants to see me – me and Mickey. She wants us to go to London and visit her.'

'No,' he said fiercely.

'She's my mother.'

'She signed away all claim to that title.'

'I want to see her – she wants to see me.'

'We'll talk about it some other time.'

'I want to talk about it now. Why won't you let me go?'

'Your mother did things which put her beyond the pale. She would exert an influence of evil upon you.'

'Nobody influences me – unless I want them to,' she said. 'And what did mother do anyway? Nobody has ever explained that.'

'She committed an act of calculated treachery. She betrayed us all – her husband, her father, her family, her children and her country.'

'I don't believe it.' Isabella shook her head. 'Mater was always so concerned for everybody.'

'I cannot, and will not, give you all the details, Bella. Just believe me when I tell you that if I had not spirited her out of the country, she would have stood trial as an accessory to the murder of her own father and for the crime of high treason.'

They rode up to the stables in silence, but as they entered the yard and dismounted, Isabella said quietly, 'She should have the chance to explain it to me herself.'

'I can forbid you to go, Bella, you are still a minor. But you know I won't do that. I'll simply ask you not to go to London to see that woman.'

'I'm sorry, Daddy. Mickey is going, and I am going with him.'

She saw his expression, and went to him quickly. 'Please try to understand. I love you, but I love her too. I have to go.'

They drove up to the house in the Jaguar without speaking again, but as he parked the car and switched off the ignition, Shasa asked, 'When?'

'We haven't decided yet.'

'I tell you what. We'll go together some time and perhaps we could go on to Switzerland for a week's skiing or Italy to do some sight-seeing. We might even stop in Paris to get you a new frock. Lord knows, you are short of clothes.'

'My dear father, you are a crafty old dog, aren't you?'

They were still laughing as they went arm in arm up the front steps of Weltevreden. Centaine came out of her study door across the lobby. When she saw them she snatched the gold-rimmed reading glasses off her nose – she hated even the family to see her wearing them – and she demanded, 'What are you two so merry about? Bella is wearing her triumphant expression. What has she talked you into this time?'

Centaine didn't wait for an answer, but pointed to the huge banana-shaped package almost ten foot long, wrapped in thick layers of brown hessian, that lay in the middle of the chequered marble floor.

'Shasa, this arrived for you this morning and it has been cluttering up the house all day. Please get rid of it, whatever it is.'

Centaine had lived on alone at Rhodes Hill for almost a year after Blaine's death before Shasa had been able to persuade her to close the house up and return to Weltevreden. Now she ran a strict routine to which they were all expected to conform.

'Now what on earth is this?' Shasa tentatively attempted to lift one end of the long package, and then grunted. 'It's made of lead, whatever it is.'

'Hold on, Pater,' Garry called from the top of the staircase. 'You'll bust something.' He came bounding down the stairs, three at a time. 'I'll do that for you – where do you want it?'

'The gun room will do. Thanks, Garry.'

Garry enjoyed showing off his strength and he lifted the heavy package easily, and manoeuvred it down the passageway, then through the gun-room door and laid it on the lion skin in front of the fireplace.

'Do you want me to open it?' he asked, and without waiting for an answer went to work on it.

Isabella perched on the desk, determined not to miss anything, and none of them spoke until Garry had stripped away the last sheet of hessian and stood back.

'It's magnificent,' Shasa breathed. 'I have never seen anything quite like that in my life before.' It was a single tusk of curved ivory, almost ten foot long, as thick as a pretty girl's waist at one end and tapering to a blunt point at the other.

'It must weigh almost a hundred and fifty pounds,' Garry said. 'But just look at the workmanship.'

Shasa knew that the ivory workers of Zanzibar were the only ones who could do something like this. The entire length of the tusk had been carved with hunting scenes of exquisite detail and the finest execution.

'It's beautiful.' Even Isabella was impressed. 'Who sent it to you?'

'There is an envelope —' Shasa pointed to the litter of discarded wrappings, and Garry picked it out and passed it to him.

The envelope contained a single sheet of notepaper.

In camp on the Tana river
Kenya.

Dear Dad,
Happy birthday – I'll be thinking of you on the day. This is my best jumbo to date – 146 lbs. before the carving.
Why don't you come hunting with me?

Love,
Sean

With the note in one hand, Shasa squatted beside the tusk and stroked the creamy smooth surface. The carvings depicted a herd of elephant, hundreds of them in a single herd. From old bulls and breeding cows to tiny calves, they fled in a long spiral frieze around the ivory shaft, diminishing in elegant perspective towards the point. The herd was harassed and attacked by hunters along its length, beginning with men in lionskins armed with bows and poisoned arrows, or with broad-bladed elephant spears; towards the end of this primeval cavalcade the hunters were on horseback and wielding modern firearms. The path of the herd was strewn with great fallen carcasses, and it was beautiful and real and tragic.

However, it was neither the beauty nor the tragedy that thickened Shasa's voice as he said, 'Will you two leave me alone, please.' He did not look around at them, he did not want them to see his face.

For once Isabella did not argue, but took Garry's hand and led him from the room.

'He hasn't forgotten my birthday,' Shasa murmured, as he stroked the ivory. 'Not once since he left.' He coughed and stood up abruptly, jerked the handkerchief from his breast pocket and blew his nose loudly and then wiped his eyes.

'And I haven't even written to him, I haven't even replied to one of his letters.' He stuffed the handkerchief back into his pocket and went to stand at the window, staring out over the lawns where the peacocks strutted. 'The stupid cruel thing is that he has always been my favourite of the three of them. Oh God, I'd give anything to see him again.'

*   *   *

The rain was icy grey, drifting like smoke over the thick forests of bamboo that cloaked the crests of the Aberdare Mountains.

The four of them moved in single file with the Ndorobo tracker on the point, following the spoor in the forest earth that beneath the litter of fallen bamboo leaves was the colour and consistency of molten chocolate.

Sean Courtney took the second position, covering the tracker and poised to make any quick decision. He was the youngest of the three white men but command had quite naturally devolved upon him. Nobody had contested it.

The third man in the line, Alistair Sparks, was the youngest son of a Kenyan settler family. Although he possessed enormous powers of endurance, was a fine natural shot and a consummate bushman, he was lazy and evasive and needed to be pushed to exercise all his skills to the full.

Raymond Harris was on the drag at number four. He was almost fifty years old, full of malaria and gin, but in his time had been one of the legendary white hunters of East Africa. He had taught Sean everything he knew, until the pupil had excelled the master. Now Raymond was content to bring up the rear and let Sean and Matatu, the tracker, get them into position for the kill.

Matatu was naked except for his filthy tattered loincloth and the rain made tiny rivulets down his glossy black hide. He worked the spoor with the same instinct and superhuman sense of sight, smell and hearing, as one of the wild animals of the forest. They had been following these tracks for two days already, stopping only when the light failed completely each night, and taking up the chase again with the first flush of dawn.

The spoor was running sweet and hot. Sean was probably as good a tracker as a white man could be and he judged that they were only four or five hours behind and gaining swiftly. The quarry had angled up the steep slope of this nameless peak, heading to cross the ridge just below the main crest. Sean caught glimpses of the top through the dense vault of bamboo over their heads and the blown streamers of misty rain.

Suddenly Matatu stopped dead, and Sean popped his tongue to

warn the others and froze with his thumb on the safety-catch of the big double-barrelled Gibbs.

After a moment Matatu turned abruptly aside, dropping the spoor, and went sliding as swiftly and silently as a dark serpent down the slope, away from the line and direction of the quarry.

Five years before, when Sean had first taken Matatu into his service, he might have protested and tried to force him to stay with the run of the spoor, but now he followed without argument, and although he was going at his best hunting speed, he just managed to hold the tracker in sight.

Sean was dressed in a cloak of colobus monkey skins and he wore Somali sandals of elephant hide on his feet and a shaggy cap of monkey skin covered his obviously Caucasian hair. His arms, legs and face were blackened with a mixture of rancid hippo fat and soot, and he had not bathed in two weeks. He looked and smelled like the men he was hunting.

There were five Mau Mau in the band that they were pursuing, all of them members of the notorious gang run by the self-styled General Kimathi. Five days previously they had attacked one of the coffee shambas near Nyeri in the foothills of the mountain range. They had disembowelled the white overseer and stuffed his severed genitals into his mouth, and they had chopped off his wife's limbs with the heavy-bladed pangas, beginning at wrist and ankle and working gradually towards the trunk of her body, until they hacked through the great joints in her shoulders and groin.

Sean and his group of scouts had reached the shamba almost twelve hours after the gang had fled. They had left the Land-Rover and taken the spoor on foot.

Matatu took them directly down the slope. The narrow river at the bottom was a tumultuous silver torrent. Sean stripped off his furs and sandals and went into it naked. The cold chilled his bones until they ached and the roaring waters swirled over his head but he carried the line across and then brought the others safely over.

Matatu was the last across, carrying Sean's clothing and his rifle, and immediately he was off again, like a wraith of the forest. Sean followed him with the agony of cold shuddering through his body and the sodden furs a heavy burden to add to the rifle and his pack.

A herd of buffalo crashed away through the forest ahead of them, and the bovine stink lingered in their nostrils long after they were gone. Once Sean had a glimpse of a huge antelope, ginger red with vertical white stripes down its heavy body and a head of magnificent spiral horns. It was a bongo. He would have charged one of his rich American clients $1000 for a shot at that rarest and most elusive of all antelopes, but it ghosted away into the bamboo and Matatu led them on without apparent purpose or direction, the spoor three hours cold behind them.

Then Matatu skirted one of the rare forest clearings and stopped again. He glanced back over his naked shoulder and grinned at Sean with the patent adoration of a hunting dog who acknowledges the most important being in its universe.

Sean stepped up beside him and looked down at the spoor. He would never know how Matatu did it. He had tried to make him explain, but the wizened little gnome had merely laughed with embarrassment and hung his head. It was a kind of magic that went beyond the mere art of observation and deduction. What Matatu had just done was to drop the spoor when it was sweet and hot, and go off at an improbable tangent, running blind through trackless bamboo and over wild peaks, to meet the spoor again with the unerring instinct of a migrating swallow, having cut the corner and gained three hours on the quarry.

Sean squeezed his shoulder and little Ndorobo wriggled his whole body with pleasure.

They were less than an hour behind the gang now, but the rain and the mist were bringing on the night prematurely. Sean signalled Matatu on. Not one of them had spoken a single word all that day.

The men they were chasing were becoming careless. In the beginning they had anti-tracked and covered spoor, doubled and jinked so cunningly that even Matatu had puzzled to unravel the sign and get away on the run of it – but now they were feeling confident and secure. They had broken off the succulent bamboo shoots to chew as they marched, leaving glaring wounds on the plants, and they had trodden deeply, heeling with fatigue, leaving sign that Matatu could follow like a tarmac road. One of the fugitives had even defecated on the track, not bothering to cover his faeces, and they were still steaming with his body warmth. Matatu grinned at Sean over his shoulder and made the fluttery hand signal which said 'Very close'.

Sean eased open the action of the double-barrelled Gibbs, without allowing the sidelock to click. He slid the brass-cased cartridges out of the breeches, and replaced them with two others from the leather ammunition pouch beneath his monkey-skin cape. The .577 cartridges were thicker than a man's thumb and the clumsy, blunt-nosed bullet heads were jacketed in copper and capped with soft blue lead so they could mushroom through living tissue, tearing open a wide channel and inflicting terrible damage. This little ritual of changing his cartridges was one of Sean's superstitions – he always did it just before he closed with dangerous game. He closed the rifle as gently and silently as he had opened it and glanced back at the two men behind him.

515

The whites of Alistair's eyes gleamed in his blackened face. He carried the Bren gun. Sean had not been able to wean him from it. Despite its unwieldy long barrel and great weight, Alistair loved the automatic weapon. 'When I'm after Mickey Mouse I like to be able to turn the air blue with lead,' he explained with that lazy grin. 'Nobody is going to get a chance to stuff my knackers down my throat, matey!'

At the rear Ray Harris gave Sean the thumbs-up signal, but the sweat and rain had cut pale runnels through the soot and fat on his face, and even through the camouflage Sean could see how haggard he was with fear and fatigue. 'The old man is getting past it,' Sean thought dispassionately. 'Have to put him out to grass soon.'

Ray carried the Stirling sub-machine-gun. Sean suspected it was because he could no longer manage the weight of a more substantial weapon. 'In the bamboo it's point blank.' Ray excused his choice, and Sean had not bothered to argue or to point out that the tiny 9 mm bullets would be deflected by the frailest twig, and smothered in the dense vegetation of the Aberdares – while the big .600 grain slug from his own Gibbs would plough straight through branch and stem and still blow the guts out of the Mickey Mouse on the other side, while the stubby 20-inch barrels were perfect for close work in the bamboo, and he could swing them without risking hooking up in the brush.

Sean clicked his tongue softly and Matatu went away on the spoor in that soft-footed, ungainly lope which he could keep up day and night without tiring. They crossed another heavily bambooed ridge and in the valley beyond Matatu stopped again. It was so dark by now that Sean had to move up beside him, and go down on one knee to examine the sign. It took him almost a minute to make sense of it, even after Matatu had pointed out the other set of tracks coming in from the right.

Sean gestured Ray to move up and laid his lips to his ear. 'They have joined another party of Mickey Mice – probably from the base camp. Eight of them, three women, so we have thirteen in a bunch now. A lovely lucky number.'

But as he spoke the light was going, and the rain started again, spilling softly out of the purple-black sky. Within five hundred yards Matatu stopped for the last time and Sean could just make out the pale palm of his right hand as he made the wash-out signal. Night had blanketed the spoor.

The white men each found a treetrunk to prop themselves against, spreading out in a defensive circle facing outwards. Sean took Matatu under the monkey-skin cloak with him as though he were a tired gun dog. The little man's skinny body was as cold and wet as a trout

516

taken from a mountain stream and he smelled of herbs and leaf mould and wild things. They ate the hard salted dry buffalo meat and cold maize cakes from their belt pouches and slept fitfully in each other's warmth while the raindrops pattered down on the fur over their heads.

Matatu touched Sean's cheek and he was instantly awake in the utter darkness, slipping the safety-catch of the Gibbs that lay across his lap. He sat rigid, listening and alert.

Beside him Matatu snuffled the air and after a moment Sean did the same. 'Woodsmoke?' he whispered, and both of them came to their feet. In the darkness, Sean moved to where Alistair and Ray were lying and got them up. They went forward in the night, holding the belt of the man ahead to keep in contact. The whiffs of smoke were intermittent but stronger.

It took almost two hours for Matatu to locate the Mau Mau encampment precisely, using his sense of smell and hearing, and at the end the faint glow of a patch of camp-fire coals. Although the bamboo dripped all around, they could hear them – a soft cough, a strangled snore, the gabble of a woman in a nightmare – and Sean and Matatu moved them into position.

It took another hour; but in the utter darkness before the true dawn, Alistair was lying up the slope, forty feet from the dying camp fire. Raymond was amongst the rocks on the bank of the stream on the far side, and Sean lay with Matatu in the dense scrub beside the path that led into the camp.

Sean had the barrel of the Gibbs across his left forearm and his right hand on the pistol grip with the safety-catch under his thumb. He had spread the fur cloak over both himself and Matatu, but neither of them even drowsed. They were keyed up to the finest pitch. Sean could feel the little Ndorobo trembling with eagerness where their bodies touched. He was like a bird dog with the scent of the grouse in his nostrils.

The dawn came stealthily. First Sean realized that he could see his own hand on the rifle in front of his face, and then the short thick barrels appeared before his eyes. He looked beyond them and made out a tendril of smoke from the fire rising out of the Stygian forest towards the lighter pitch of darkness that was the sky through the canopy of bamboo.

The light came on more swiftly, and he saw that there were two crude shelters, one on each side of the fire, low lean-tos not more than waist high, and he thought he saw a movement in one of them, perhaps a recumbent figure rolling over and pulling up a skin blanket over his head.

Again somebody coughed, a thick phlegmy sound. The camp was

517

waking. Sean glanced up the slope and then down into the stream bed. He could see the soft sheen of the water-polished boulders – but nothing of the other two hunters.

The light hardened. Sean closed his eyes for a moment and then opened them again. He could see sharply the support of the roof of the nearest shelter, and dimly beyond it a human shape wrapped in a fur blanket.

'Shooting light in two minutes,' he thought. The others would know it also. All three of them had waited like this in countless dawns beside the rotting carcass of pig or antelope for the leopard to come to the bait. They could judge that magical moment when the sights were crisp enough to make the sure killing shot. This dawn they would wait for Sean before they came in with the Bren and the Stirling.

Again Sean closed his eyes and when he opened them again the figure in the nearest shelter was sitting up and looking towards him. For a gut-swooping instant he thought he had been spotted and he almost fired. Then he checked himself as the head turned away from him.

Abruptly the figure threw the fur blanket aside and stood up, crouching under the low roof of the shelter.

Sean saw it was a woman, one of the Mau Mau camp followers, but for Sean just as cruel and depraved as any of her menfolk. She stepped out into the open beside the dead fire wearing only a short kilt of some pale material. Her breasts were high and pointed and her skin smooth and glossy as newly mined anthracite in the soft dawn light.

She came directly towards where Sean lay, and though her gait was still clumsy and unsteady with sleep, he saw that she was young and comely. A few more paces and she would stumble over him, but then she stopped again and yawned and her teeth were very white, gleaming in the soft grey light.

She lifted her kilt around her waist and squatted facing Sean, spreading her knees and bowing her head slightly to watch herself as she began to urinate. Her water splashed noisily and the sharp ammoniacal tang of it made Sean's nostrils flare.

She was so close that he did not have to lift the Gibbs to his shoulder. He shot her in the stomach. The heavy rifle bounded in his grip and the bullet picked the girl up and while she was in the air it broke her in half, blowing a hole through her spine into which her own head would have fitted, and she folded up, loose and floppy as a suit of discarded clothing as she fell back onto the muddy forest floor.

Sean fired the second barrel as one of the other Mau Mau bolted out of the nearest shelter. The Gibbs made a sound like the slamming of a great steel door, and the man was hurled back into the shelter with half his chest torn away.

Sean had two more cartridges held between the fingers of his left hand, and as he opened the breech of the Gibbs the spent brass cases pinged away over his shoulder and he slid the fresh cartridges into the empty breeches and closed the rifle again in the same movement.

The Bren and the Stirling were firing now. Their muzzle flashes were bright and pretty as fairy lights in the gloom, twinkling and sparkling, and the bullets went *frip! frip! frip!* amongst the leaves and sang shrilly as they ricocheted into the forest.

Sean shot again and the Gibbs cannoned down another naked figure, knocking him flat against the soft earth as though he had been run down by a locomotive. And again he shot, but this one was a snap shot and the Mau Mau jinked just as the Gibbs thundered. The bullet hit him in the shoulder joint and blew his right arm off so it hung by a tatter of torn flesh and flapped against his side as he spun around. Raymond's Stirling buzzed and cut him down.

Sean reloaded and shot left and right, clean kills with each barrel and by the time he had reloaded again the camp was silent, and the Bren and the Stirling had ceased firing.

Nothing moved. All three men were deadly natural shots, and the range was point blank. Sean waited a full five minutes. Only a fool walked directly up to dangerous game no matter how dead it appeared to be. Then he rose cautiously to his knees with the rifle at high port across his chest.

The last Mau Mau broke. He had been feigning dead in the far shelter, and he had judged his moment finely, waiting until the attackers relaxed and began to move. He flushed like a jack rabbit and shot into the bamboo on the far side of the clearing. Alistair's Bren was blanketed by the wall of the nearest shelter but he fired nevertheless and the bullets futilely thrashed the hut. From the river bank Ray had a clearer shot, but he was a fraction of a second slow, the cold had brought out the malaria in his blood and his hand shook. The bamboo absorbed the light 9 mm bullets as though he had fired into a haystack.

For the first ten paces the running Mau Mau was screened from Sean's view by the wall of the nearest hut, and then Sean caught only a flickering glimpse of him as he dived into the bamboo, but already Sean was on him, swinging the stubby double barrels as though he were taking a right-hand passing shot on a driven francolin. Although he could no longer see his quarry in the dense bamboo, he continued his swing on the line of the man's run, instinctively leading him. The Gibbs gave its angry bellow and red flame blazed from the muzzle.

519

The huge bullet smashed into the wall of bamboo, and at Sean's side Matatu shouted gleefully, '*Piga!* Hit!' as he heard the bullet tell distinctly on living flesh.

'Take the blood spoor!' Sean commanded and the little Ndorobo loped across the clearing. But it was not necessary: the Mau Mau lay where he had dropped. The bullet had ploughed through bamboo, leaf and stem, without being deflected an inch from its track.

Ray and Alistair came into the camp, weapons ready, and picked over the bodies. One of the other Mau Mau women was still breathing, though bloody bubbles seethed on her lips, and Ray shot her in the temple with the Sten.

'Make sure none of them got away,' Sean ordered Matatu in Swahili.

The little Ndorobo made a quick circuit of the encampment to check for out-going spoor, and then came back grinning. 'All here.' He gloated. 'All dead.' Sean tossed the Gibbs to him and drew the ivory-handled hunting-knife from the sheath on his belt.

'Damn it, laddie,' Ray Harris protested as Sean walked back to where the body of the first girl lay. 'You are the bloody end, man.' He had seen Sean do this before and although Ray Harris was a hard, callous man who for thirty years had made his living out of blood and gunfire, still he gagged as Sean squatted over the corpse and stropped the blade on the palm of his hand.

'You are getting soft, old man.' Sean grinned at him. 'You know they make beautiful tobacco pouches,' he said, and took the dead girl's breast in his hand, pulling the skin taut for the stroke of the knife blade.

*　　*　　*

Shasa found Garry in the boardroom. He was always there twenty minutes before any of the other directors arrived, arranging his piles of computer print-out sheets and other notes around him and going over his facts and figures for one last time before the meeting began. Shasa and Centaine had argued before appointing Garry to the board of Courtney Mining.

'You can ruin a pony by pushing him too hard too soon.'

'We aren't talking about a polo pony,' Centaine had replied tartly. 'And it's not a case of pushing. He's got the bit between his teeth, to continue your chosen metaphor, Shasa, and if we try and hold him back we will either discourage him or drive him out on his own. Now is the time to give him a bit of slack rein.'

'But you made me wait much longer.'

'You were a late-blooming rose, and the war and all that business held you up. At Garry's age you were still flying Hurricanes and chasing around Abyssinia.'

So Garry had gone on the board, and like everything else in his life he had taken it very seriously indeed. Now he looked up as his father confronted him down the length of the boardroom.

'I heard you have been borrowing money on your own bat,' Shasa accused.

Garry removed his spectacles, polished them diligently, held them up to the light and then replaced them on his large Courtney nose, all to gain time in which to compose his reply.

'Only one person knows about that. The manager of the Adderly Street branch of Standard Bank. He could lose his job if he blabbed about my personal business.'

'You forget that both Nana and I are on the board of the Standard Bank. All loans of over a million pounds come up before us for approval.'

'Rand,' Garry corrected his father pedantically. 'Two million rand – the pound is history.'

'Thanks,' Shasa said grimly. 'I'll try to move with the times. Now how about this two million rand you have borrowed?'

'A straightforward transaction, Dad. I put up my shares in the Shasaville township as collateral, and the bank lent me two million rand.'

'What are you going to do with it? That's a small fortune.' Shasa was one of the few men in the country who would qualify that amount with that particular adjective, and Garry looked mildly relieved.

'As a matter of fact, I have used half a million to buy up fifty-one per cent of the issued shareholding of Alpha Centauri Estates, and loaned the company another half million to get it out of trouble.'

'Alpha Centauri?' Shasa looked mystified.

'The company owns some of the prime property on the Witwatersrand and here in the Cape Peninsula. It was worth almost twenty-six million before the crash at Sharpeville.'

'And now it's worth zero,' Shasa suggested, and before Garry could protest. 'What have you done with the other million?'

'Gold shares – Anglos and Vaal Reefs. At the fire sale prices I paid for them they are returning almost twenty-six per cent. The dividends will pay the interest on the entire bank loan.'

Shasa sat down in his seat at the head of the boardroom table and studied his son carefully. He should have been conditioned by now, but Garry still managed to surprise Shasa. It was an imaginative but neatly logical coup, and if it had not been his own son, Shasa would have been impressed. As it was, he felt duty bound to find flaws in it.

'What about your Shasaville shares – you are taking an awful chance.'

Garry looked puzzled. 'I don't have to explain it to you, Pater. You taught me. Shasaville is tied up. We can't sell or develop aggressively until land values recover, so I've used my shares to take full advantage of the crash.'

'What if land values never recover?' Shasa demanded relentlessly.

'If they don't, it will mean the country is finished anyway. I will lose my share of nothing which is nothing. If they do recover, I will be in profit twenty or thirty million.'

Shasa picked at that for a while and then changed his angle of attack. 'Why didn't you come to me to borrow the money, instead of going behind my back?'

Garry grinned at him and tried to smooth down the crest of wiry black hair that stuck up on his crown. 'Because you would have given me a list of five hundred reasons why not, just as you are doing now. Besides, I wanted to do this one on my own. I wanted to prove to you that I'm not a kid any more.'

Shasa twiddled the gold pen on the pad in front of him and when he could think of no other criticism, he grumbled, 'You don't want to get too damned clever for your own good. There is a line between good business sense and outright gambling.'

'How do you tell the difference?' Garry asked. For a moment Shasa thought he was being facetious and then he realized that as usual Garry was deadly serious. He was leaning forward eagerly waiting for his father to explain, and he really wanted to know.

Shasa was saved by the entry of the other senior directors: Centaine on the arm of Dr Twentyman-Jones and David Abrahams arguing amiably but respectfully with his father, and thankfully he let the subject drop. Once or twice during the meeting he glanced down the table at Garry, who was following all the discussion with a rapt expression, the light from the picture window reflecting a miniature image of the crest of Table Mountain in the lenses of his spectacles. When all the business on the agenda had been completed and Centaine had started to rise to lead them through to the executive dining-room, Shasa arrested them.

'Madame Courtney and gentlemen, one additional piece of business. Mr Garry Courtney and I have been discussing the general state of the property market. We both feel that property and equities are very much undervalued at the moment and that the company should take advantage of this fact, but I'd like him to tell you in his own words and to put forward certain proposals. Would you oblige us please, Mr Courtney?'

It was Shasa's own way of giving the lad a jolt and cutting him back a little. In the six months since his elevation, Garry had never been called upon to address the full board and now Shasa dropped it on him without warning and sat back with vindictive relish in his wing-backed leather chairman's throne and folded his arms.

At the bottom of the table Garry blushed furiously, and glanced longingly at the stinkwood door, his only escape, before giving the traditional salutation to his fellow directors.

'Ma-Ma-dame Courtney and ge-ge-gentlemen.' He stopped and threw his father a pitiful look of appeal, but when he received a stern uncompromising frown in return, he took a deep breath and launched into it. He stumbled once or twice, but when first Abe Abrahams and then Centaine shot cutting questions at him, he forgot about his stutter and talked for forty-five minutes.

At the end they were silent for a while, and then David Abrahams said, 'I should like to propose that we appoint Mr Garrick Courtney to prepare a list of specific proposals to follow up the presentation that he has just made to this meeting, and to report back to us at an extraordinary meeting early next week, at a time convenient to all members of the board.'

Centaine seconded, and it was adopted unanimously, and then David Abrahams ended, 'I should like the minutes to record the board's gratitude to Mr Courtney for his lucid address and to thank him for bringing these considerations to the board's attention.'

The glow of achievement and recognition lasted Garry all the way down in the elevator to the basement garage where his MG stood in his private parking bay beside Shasa's Jaguar. It stayed with him all the way down Adderley Street to the lonely skyscraper of the Sanlam building which stood on the open ground of the foreshore that had been reclaimed from the sea. Even going up in the lift to the twentieth floor of the Sanlam building he still felt tall and important and decisive. Only when he entered the reception area of Gantry, Carmichael and Associates did the vital glow begin to fade, and his stiff van Heusen collar bit painfully into the corded muscles of his bull neck.

The two pretty young girls at the desk showed him the full amount of deference due to one of the partnership's important clients, but by this time Garry was too nervous to take advantage of the chair he was offered and he wandered around the lobby pretending to admire the tall vases of proteas while surreptitiously checking his image in the floor-to-ceiling mirrors behind the floral display.

He had paid forty guineas off the peg for the double-breasted suit in his favourite Prince of Wales check, but the swell of his chest muscles made the lapels flare unevenly and the material rucked up around his biceps. He yanked at the cuffs in an attempt to smooth the sleeves, and then abandoned that effort and instead concentrated on trying to press his hair flat with the heel of his palm. He started guiltily as he saw in the mirror the door to the partners' sanctum open and Holly Carmichael come striding into the reception lobby.

As Garry turned to face her, all his recent bravado and confidence collapsed around him and he gawked at her. It was impossible but she was even more poised and chic than the vivid image of her he had carried with him since their last meeting.

Today she was wearing a blue and white striped Chanel suit with a pleated skirt that swirled around her calves, allowing just a flash of her perfect rounded knees as she came towards him. Her lightly tanned legs in sheer nylon had the patina of polished ivory, and her ankles and her wrists in the cuffs of the Chanel suit were elegantly turned, her feet and hands narrow and yet perfectly proportioned to her long willowy limbs.

She was smiling and Garry felt the same sensuous vertigo that he sometimes experienced after bench pressing five times his own body-weight of iron. Her teeth were opalescent, and as her mouth formed his name and smiled, he watched it with breathless fascination.

She was as tall as he was, but he knew he could lift her with one hand and he quivered at the almost sacrilegious thought of taking this divine creature in his hands.

'Mr Courtney, I hope we haven't kept you waiting.' She took his arm, and led him towards her office. He felt like a performing bear on a chain beside her grace and lightness. The light touch of her fingers on his arm burned like a branding iron.

Her hair was streaked with a shading of all the colours of blond from platinum to dark burnt honey, and it fell in a lustrous cascade to just above the padded shoulders of the Chanel suit, and every time she moved her head he caught the perfume of those shining tresses and his stomach muscles contracted.

Her fingers were still on his biceps and she was talking directly into his face, still smiling. Her breath smelled like a flower and her mouth was so beautiful and soft and red that he felt guilty looking at it, as though he were spying on some secret and intimate part of her body. He tore his eyes from her mouth and raised them to her eyes. His heart jumped against his ribs like a maniac in a padded cell for one eye was sky blue and the other violet flecked with gold. It gave her face a striking asymmetry, not exactly a squint but a disconcerting myopic imbalance and Garry's legs felt as weak as if he had run ten miles.

'I have something for you at last,' Holly Carmichael said, and led him into her office.

The long room reflected her own extraordinary style, which had attracted Garry to her work long before he had met her. He had first seen an example of it in the *Institute of Architects Year-book*. Holly Carmichael had won the 1961 award of the Institute for a beach house on the dunes overlooking Plettenburg Bay that she had designed as a holiday home for one of the Witwatersrand insurance magnates. She used wood and stone and material in a blend that was at the same time modern and classical, that married space and shape in a natural harmony that excited the eye and yet gave solace to the soul.

Her office was decorated in soft mulberry and ethereal blue, functional and yet both restful and unmistakably feminine. The delicate pastel drawings on all four walls were her own work.

In the centre of the floor on a low table stood a miniature-scale reproduction of the Shasaville estate, as she visualized it after development was complete. Holly led Garry to it and stood back while he circled it slowly, studying it from every angle.

She watched the change come over him.

All the gawkiness was gone. Even the shape of his body seemed to change. It was imbued with the same kind of massive grace as that of the bull in the arena tensing for the charge.

Holly researched the background of all her clients, in order to better anticipate their requirements. With this one she had taken special care. The word in the marketplace was that, despite appearances, Garrick Courtney was a formidable presence and had already demonstrated his acumen and courage by procuring the Shasaville title and a controlling interest in Alpha Centauri Estates.

Her accountant had drawn up an approximate list of his assets which included, along with his property interests, considerable equity in blue chip gold companies and the Courtney mining shares which he had acquired from his family when he was appointed to the board of that company.

More significant was the prevailing view that both Centaine and Shasa Courtney had given up on his brothers, and decided that Garrick Courtney was their hope for the future. He was the heir apparent to the Courtney millions and nobody knew the sum total of those – two hundred million, five hundred million – not inconceivably a billion rand. Holly Carmichael shivered slightly at the thought.

As she watched him now she saw not a large bumbling young man in steel-rimmed spectacles, who made an expensive suit of fine wool look like a bag of laundry, and whose hair stood up in a startled tuft at the crown. She saw power.

Power fascinated Holly Carmichael, power in all its forms – wealth,

525

reputation, influence and physical power. She shivered slightly as she recalled the feel of the muscle under his sleeve.

Holly was thirty-two years of age, almost ten years senior to him, and her divorce would count heavily against her. Both Centaine and Shasa Courtney were conservative and old-fashioned.

'They'll have to be good to stop me,' she told herself. 'I get what I want – and this is what I want, but it's not going to be a push-over.'

Then she considered the effect she had on Garry Courtney. She knew he was besotted with her. The first part would be easy. Without any effort at all she had already enmeshed him, she could enslave him as readily. After that would come the difficult part. She thought of Centaine Courtney and all she had heard about her, and she shivered again, this time with neither pleasure nor excitement.

Garry stopped in front of her. Although their eyes were on a level, he now seemed to tower over her as he glowered at her. A moment before she had felt herself perfectly in control, now suddenly she was uncertain.

'I've seen what you can do when you really try,' he said. 'I want you to try for me. I don't want second best. I don't want this.'

Holly stared at him in amazement. She had not even contemplated his rejection, certainly not in such brutal terms. Her shock persisted a moment longer and then was replaced with anger.

'If that is your estimate of my work, Mr Courtney, I suggest you find yourself another architect,' she told him in a cold fury and he didn't even flinch.

'Come here,' he ordered. 'Look at it from this angle. You've stuck that roof on the shopping centre without any regard to the view from the houses on this slope of the hill. And look here. You could have used the fairways of the golf course to enhance the aspect of these flagship properties instead of shutting them off the way you have.'

He had taken hold of her arm, and though she knew he was not extending even a small part of his strength, still the potential she could feel in his fingers frightened her a little. She no longer felt confident and patronizing as he pointed out the flaws in her design. While he spoke she knew that he was right. Instinctively she had been aware of the defects he was now exposing, but she had not taken the trouble to find the solutions to them. She had not ex-pected somebody so young and inexperienced to be so discriminat-ing – she had treated him like a doting boy who would accept any-thing she offered. Her anger was directed at herself as much as at him.

He finished his criticism at last and she said softly, 'I'll return

526

your deposit and we can tear up the contract.'

'You signed the contract and accepted the deposit, Mrs Carmichael. Now I want you to deliver. I want something beautiful and startling and right. I want something that only you can give me.'

She had no answer, and his manner changed, he became peculiarly gentle and solicitous.

'I didn't mean to insult you. I think at the least you are the very best, and I want you to prove me right – please.'

She turned away from him and went to her drawing-board at the end of the room, slipped out of her jacket and tossed it over the desk and picked up one of her pencils.

With the pencil poised over the blank sheet, she said, 'It seems that I've got a lot of lost ground to make up. Here we go —' and she drew the first bold decisive line across the sheet. 'At least we know now what we don't want. Let's find out what we do want. Let's start with the shopping centre.'

He came to stand behind her and watched in silence for almost twenty minutes before she glanced back at him with the violet eye glinting through the veil of shining blond hair. She didn't have to ask the question.

'Yes,' he nodded.

'Don't go away,' she said. 'When you are near I can feel your mood and judge your response.'

He took off his jacket and threw it beside hers over the desk top, and he stood beside her in his shirtsleeves with his hands thrust into his trouser pockets and his shoulders hunched. He remained absolutely still, his concentration monumental, and yet his presence seemed to inspire her to tap the mystical springs of her talent. At last she saw in her mind how it should have been and she began to rough it out, her pencil flying and flicking over the sheet.

When the day faded, he went to close the curtains and switch on the overhead lights. It was after eight when she at last threw down her pencil and turned to him. 'That's the feeling I want to give it. You were right – the first attempt wasn't worthy.'

'Yes, I was right in one other respect. You are the very best.' He picked up his jacket and shrugged it over his massive shoulders, and she felt a tingle of dismay. She didn't want him to go yet, she knew when he did she would feel exhausted and spent. The effort of creation had drained her resources.

'You can't send me home to begin cooking at this hour,' she said. 'That would be the sadistic act of a truly cruel taskmaster.'

Suddenly all his confidence evaporated, and he blushed and mumbled something inaudible. She knew she would have to take charge from here.

527

'The least you can do is feed the slave. How about offering me dinner, Mr Courtney?'

She created her usual stir of masculine interest as she preceded Garry into the restaurant, and she was glad he had noticed. She was surprised by the aplomb with which he discussed the wine list with the *maître* until she remembered that Weltevreden was one of the leading wineries of the Cape of Good Hope.

During dinner their conversation was serious, and she was relieved not to have to endure the usual banalities of a first date. They discussed the Sharpeville crisis and its implications, social and economic, and she was amazed at the depth of his political insight until she remembered that his father was a minister in Verwoerd's cabinet. He had a ringside seat.

'If it wasn't for that Prince of Wales check suit and those ghastly steel-framed spectacles,' she thought, 'and the crest of hair that makes him look like Woody Woodpecker —'

When he asked her to dance she had misgivings. They were the only couple on the tiny circular floor, and there were a dozen people in the room she knew. However, the moment he put his arm around her waist she relaxed. Despite his bulk he was agile and light on his feet with an excellent sense of timing, and she began to enjoy herself, until abruptly his dancing style changed and he held her differently. For a while she was puzzled. She attempted to maintain the close contact of hips which had enabled her to anticipate his moves, and only then she became aware of his arousal. She was at first amused and then despite herself intrigued. Like the rest of him it was massive and hard. She played a little game of brushing lightly against him and withdrawing, all the while chatting casually and feigning total ignorance of his predicament. Afterwards he drove her in the MG to where her own car was parked. She hadn't ridden in an open sports car since her varsity days and the wind in her hair gave her a nostalgic thrill.

He insisted on following her Mercedes back to Bantry Bay to see her safely home and they said goodnight on the pavement outside her apartment block. She considered inviting him up for coffee, but her sure instinct warned her to protect the shining image of her that he so obviously had conceived.

Instead she told him, 'I'll have some more drawings for you to look at by the end of next week.'

This time she put everything of her talent into the preliminary sketches, and she knew they were good. He came to her office again and they worked over them until late and then dined together. It was Thursday night and the restaurant was half empty. They had the dance floor to themselves and this time she worked her hips lightly and cunningly against him as they moved.

When she said goodnight outside her apartment block, she asked, 'I suppose you will be at the Met on Saturday?'

The Metropolitan Handicap was the premier race on the Cape turf calendar.

'I don't race,' Garry replied reluctantly. 'We are polo people, and Nana, my grandmother, doesn't approve of me —' he stopped himself as he realized how callow that sounded, and he ended, '— well, somehow I've just never got around to racing.'

'Well, it's about time you did,' she said firmly. 'And I need a partner for Saturday – that's if you don't object.'

Garry sang all the way home to Weltevreden, bellowing happily into the rushing night air as he drove the MG through the curves and dips of the mountain road.

It took Garry a while to understand that the actual racing was not the main attraction of the meeting. It was secondary to the fashion show and the complicated social interaction of the racegoers.

Amongst the bizarre and outrageous creations that some of the women wore, Holly's floating blue silk and the wide-brimmed hat with a single real pink rose on the brim were elegant and understated, but drew envious glances from the other women. Garry discovered that he knew nearly everybody in the members' enclosure; many of them were friends of his family, and Holly introduced him to those he did not know. They all reacted to the Courtney name, and Holly was subtly attentive, drawing him into conversation with these strangers until he felt at ease.

They made a remarkable couple, 'Beauty and the Beast', as one of the unkind wags suggested, and a buzz of gossip followed them around the ring: 'Holly has been out cradle-snatching', and 'Centaine will have her burned at the stake'.

Garry was totally oblivious to the stir they were creating, and once the horses were brought into the ring for the first race, he was in his element. Horses were part of the life at Weltevreden. Shasa had carried him on the saddle before he could walk, and he had a natural eye for horseflesh.

The first race was a maiden handicap, and the betting was wide open as none of these two-year-olds had raced before. Garry singled out a black colt in the parade. 'I like his chest and legs,' he told Holly and she checked his number on the card.

'Rhapsody,' she said. 'There has never been a good horse with an ugly name – and he's trained by Miller and ridden by Tiger Wright.'

'I don't know about that, but I do know that he is in peak condition and he wants to work,' Garry told her. 'Just look at him sweating already.'

'Let's have a bet on him,' Holly suggested, and Garry looked dubious. The family strictures against gambling echoed in his ears, but he didn't want to offend Holly or appear childish in her eyes.

'What do I do?' he asked.

'You see those gangsters standing up there?' She pointed at the line of bookmakers. 'You pick any one of them, give him your money and say, "Rhapsody to win." ' She handed Gerry a ten-rand note. 'Let's dib ten each.'

Garry was appalled. Ten rand was a great deal of money. It was one thing to borrow two million on a legitimate business scheme, but quite another thing to hand ten to a stranger in a loud suit with a cigar. Reluctantly he produced his wallet.

Rhapsody was in the ruck at the turn, but as they came clear of the bend, Tiger Wright steered him wide and then asked him to run. The colt jumped away and caught the leaders in front of the stand where Holly was hopping up and down and holding her hat on with one hand. He was two lengths clear at the post and Holly threw both arms around Garry's neck and kissed him in front of ten thousand beady eyes.

As Garry handed over her share of their winnings, she said, 'Oh, wouldn't it be fun to own one's very own racehorse.'

He phoned her apartment at six o'clock the following morning.

'Garry?' she mumbled. 'It's Sunday. You can't do this to me – not at six o'clock.'

'This time I've got something to show you,' he said, and his enthusiasm was so infectious that she agreed weakly.

'Give me an hour to wake up properly.'

He drove her down to the curving beach of False Bay beyond Muizenberg and parked at the top of the dunes. Forty horses with their apprentice jockeys and grooms were cantering along the edge of soft white sand or wading bareback in the curling green surf. Garry led her down to the group of four men who were supervising the training and introduced her.

'This is Mr Miller.' The trainer and his assistants looked at Holly approvingly. She wore a pink scarf around her forehead but her thick blond hair fell freely down the back of her neck and the short marine peajacket emphasized the length and shape of her legs in the ski pants and calf boots.

The trainer whistled to one of his apprentices and only when he turned the colt out of the circle of horses did Holly recognize it.

'Rhapsody,' she cried.

'Congratulations, Mrs Carmichael,' the trainer said. 'He's going to do us all proud.'

'I don't understand.' She was bewildered.

530

'Well,' Garry explained, 'you said it would be fun to own your own horse, and it is your birthday on the twelfth of next month. Happy birthday.'

She stared at him in confusion, wondering how he knew that date and how she was going to tell him that she couldn't possibly accept such an extravagant gift. But Garry was so rosy with self-satisfaction, waiting to be thanked and applauded, that she thought, 'And why not – just this once! The hell with conventions!'

She kissed him for the second time, while the others stood around and grinned knowingly.

In the MG on the way home she told him. 'Garry, I cannot possibly accept Rhapsody. It's much too generous of you.' His disappointment was transparent and pathetic. 'But,' she went on, 'I could accept half of him. You keep the other half and we will race him together, as partners. We could even register our own racing colours.' She was amazed at her own genius. A living creature owned jointly would cement the bond between them. 'Let all the Courtneys rant and rave. This one is mine,' she promised herself.

When they reached her apartment, she told him, 'Park there, next to the Mercedes.' And she took his arm and led him to the elevator.

Like her office, the apartment was an expression of her artistry and sense of form and colour. The balcony was high above the rocks, and the surf crashed and sucked back and forth below them so that it seemed they stood on the prow of an ocean liner.

Holly brought a bottle of champagne and two tulip glasses from the kitchen. 'Open it!' she ordered and held the glasses while he spilled the creaming wine into them.

'Here's to Rhapsody,' she gave him the toast.

While she made a huge bowl of salad for their brunch, she instructed him in the art of mixing a dressing for it.

They drank the rest of the champagne with the salad and then sprawled on the thick carpet of her living-room floor, surrounded by books of silk samples as they discussed their racing colours, and finally decided on a vivid fuchsia pink.

'It will look beautiful against Rhapsody's glossy black skin.' She looked up at him. He was kneeling beside her, and her instinct told her that this was the precise moment.

She rolled slowly on to her back and hooded those bi-coloured eyes invitingly, but still he hesitated and she had to reach up with one hand and draw his head down to hers, and then his strength shocked her.

She felt helpless as an infant in his embrace, but after a while when she was certain that he would not hurt her, she began to enjoy the sensation of physical helplessness in the storm of his kisses and

531

let him take control for a while until she sensed that he needed guidance once again.

She bit him on the cheek and when he released her and started back in surprise and consternation, she broke from his grip and darted to the bedroom door. As she looked back he was still kneeling in the centre of the floor, staring after her in confusion, and she laughed and left the door open.

He came in like a bull at the cape, but she stopped him dead with another kiss and, holding his mouth with hers, unbuttoned his shirt and slipped her hand into the opening. She was unprepared for the thick pelt of springing dark hair that covered his chest, and her own reaction to it. All her other men had been smooth and soft. She believed that was her preference, but now her sexual arousal was instantaneous and her loins swam with excitement.

She dominated him with her lips and fingertips, not allowing him to move while she undressed him and then, as the last of his clothing fell around his ankles, she exclaimed aloud, 'Oh dear God!' and then caught his wrist to prevent him covering himself with his hands.

None of her other men had been like this, and for a moment she felt uncertain of her ability to cope with him. Then her wanting overwhelmed any doubts and she led him to the bed. She made him lie there while she undressed in front of him, and every time he tried to cover himself she ordered him. 'No! I like to look at you.'

He was so different, all muscle and hair: his concave belly was rippled with muscle like the sand on a wind-swept beach and his limbs were clad in muscle. She wanted to begin, but she wanted even more to ensure that this would be something that he would never forget, that would make him hers for all his life.

'Don't move,' she whispered, and naked she stooped over him. She let her breasts swing forward and her nipples just brush the curls on his chest, and she touched the tip of her tongue to the corner of his eye and then ran it down slowly to his mouth.

'I have never done this before,' he whispered hoarsely. 'I don't know how.'

'Shh, my darling, don't talk,' she whispered into his mouth, but the idea of his virginity elated her.

'He's mine,' she told herself triumphantly. 'After today he will be mine for ever!' And she ran her tongue down across his chin, down over his throat, until she felt him thrust up hard and thick between her dangling breasts and then she reached down and took him in both hands.

It was darkening in the room when at last they lay exhausted. Outside the sun had sunk into the Atlantic and left the evening sky infuriated by its going. Garry lay with his cheek cushioned on her

532

breasts. Like an unweaned child he could not get enough of them. Holly was proud of her bosom and his fascination with it amused and flattered her. She smiled contentedly as he nuzzled against her.

His spectacles lay on the bedside table and she studied his face in the half light. She liked the big virile nose and the determined line of his jaw, but the steel-framed spectacles had to go, she decided, those and the Prince of Wales checks which emphasized the squatness of his body. On Monday her first concern would be to find out from Ian Gantry, her partner, the name of his personal tailor. She had already chosen the pattern – crisp grey or distinguished blue, with a vertical chalk stripe that would make him taller and slimmer. His reconstruction would be one of her most challenging and rewarding projects and she looked forward to it.

'You are wonderful,' Garry murmured. 'I've never met anybody like you in my life.' Holly smiled again and stroked his thick dark hair. It sprang up under her fingers.

'You've got a double crown,' she told him softly. 'That means you are lucky and brave.'

'I didn't know that,' he said, which was not surprising, as Holly had invented it as she said it.

'Oh yes,' she assured him. 'But it also means that we have to grow our hair a little fuller over the crown, otherwise it will stand up in a tuft like this.'

'I didn't know that either.' Garry reached up and felt his tuft. 'I'll try that, but you'll have to tell me how long to let it grow – I don't want to look like a hippy.'

'Of course.'

'You are wonderful,' he repeated. 'I mean, totally wonderful.'

*　　*　　*

'The woman is obviously a gold-digger,' Centaine said firmly.

'We can't be sure of that, Mater,' Shasa demurred. 'I have heard that she is a damned good architect.'

'That has absolutely nothing to do with it. She is old enough to be his mother. She is after one thing, and one thing only. We'll have to put a stop to this immediately. Otherwise it could get out of hand. It's the talk of the town, all my friends are gloating. They were at Kelvin Grove on Saturday, smooching all over the dance floor.'

'Oh, I think it will blow over,' Shasa suggested. 'Just so long as we take no notice.'

'Garry hasn't slept at Weltevreden for a week. The woman is as blatant and shameless —' Centaine broke off and shook her head. 'You'll have to speak to her.'

533

'Me?' Shasa raised an eyebrow.

'You are good with females. I'd be sure to lose my temper with the hussy.'

Shasa sighed, although secretly he welcomed the excuse to have a look at this Holly Carmichael. He couldn't imagine what Garry's taste in women would be. The lad had never given any indications before. Shasa imagined sensible shoes and horn-rimmed glasses, fat and fortyish, serious and erudite – and he shuddered. 'All right, Mater, I'll warn her off, and if that doesn't work we can always send Garry down to the vet to be fixed.'

'I wish you wouldn't joke about something as worrying as this,' said Centaine severely.

Although Holly had been expecting it for almost a month, when the call finally came the shock of it was unmitigated. Shasa Courtney had addressed the Businesswomen's Club the previous year, so she recognized his voice instantly, and was glad that it was he rather than Centaine Courtney she had to content with.

'Mrs Carmichael, my son Garry has shown me some of your preliminary sketches for the Shasaville township. As you know, Courtney Mining and Finance are considerable shareholders in the project. Although Garry is responsible for the development, I hoped we could meet to exchange a few ideas.'

She had suggested her own office, but Shasa neatly thwarted her attempt to choose the field of battle and sent a chauffeur to bring her out to Weltevreden in the Rolls. She realized that she was being deliberately placed in surroundings which were intended to overpower her, and show her up in the splendour of a world in which there was no place for her. So she went to endless pains with her dress and appearance, and as she was ushered into Shasa Courtney's study she saw him start and knew that first blood was hers. She made the room with all its treasures seem as though it had been designed around her, and Shasa Courtney's cool supercilious smile faded as he came to take her hand.

'What a magnificent Turner,' she said. 'I always think he must have been an early riser. The sunlight only has that golden lustre in the early morning.' His expression changed again as he realized there was depth below her striking exterior.

They circled the room, ostensibly admiring the other paintings, fencing elegantly, testing each other for weakness and finding none, until Shasa deliberately broke the pattern with a direct personal compliment to fluster her.

'You have the most remarkable eyes,' he said, and watched her keenly to see how she would react. She counter-attacked instantly.

'Garry calls them amethyst and sapphire.' She had wrongfooted him neatly. He had expected her to avoid that name until he raised it.

534

'Yes, I understand the two of you have been working closely.'

He went to the ivory-inlaid table on which glasses and decanters had been set out.

'May I offer you one of our sherries? We are very proud of them.'

He brought her the glass and looked into those extraordinary eyes. 'The little devil,' he thought ruefully. 'He has done it again. Who would have expected Garry to come up with something like this!'

She sipped the wine. 'I like it,' she said. 'It's dry as flint without any astringency.'

He inclined his head slightly to acknowledge the accuracy of her judgment.

'I can see that it would be fruitless to attempt to obfuscate. I didn't ask you here to discuss the Shasaville project.'

'That's good,' she said. 'Because I didn't even bother to bring the latest drawings.'

He laughed delightedly. 'Let's sit down and get comfortable.'

She chose the Louis Quatorze chair with Aubusson embroidered upholstery because she had seen the twin to it in the Victoria and Albert Museum, and she crossed one ankle over the other and watched him struggle to get his eyes back up again.

'I had fully intended to buy you off,' he said. 'I realize, after having met you, that would have been a mistake.'

She said nothing, but watched him over the rim of the glass, and her foot swung like a metronome, with the same ominous rhythm.

'I wondered what price to set,' he went on. 'And the figure of one hundred thousand came to mind.'

The foot kept swinging and despite himself Shasa glanced down at her calf and exquisitely turned ankle.

'Of course, that was ludicrous,' he went on, still watching her foot in the Italian leather court shoe. 'I realize now that I should have considered at least half a million.'

He was trying to find her price, and he looked back at her face, searching for the first glint of avarice, but it was hard to concentrate. Sapphire and amethyst, forsooth, Garry's hormones must be boiling out of his ears – and Shasa felt a stab of envy.

'Naturally, I was thinking in pounds sterling. I haven't adjusted to this rand business yet.'

'How fortunate, Mr Courtney,' she said, 'that you decided not to insult us both. This way we can be friends. I'd prefer that.'

All right, that didn't work out the way he had planned. He set down his sherry glass. 'Garry is still a child,' he changed tack.

She shook her head. 'He's a man. It just needed somebody to convince him of that. It wasn't difficult to do.'

'He doesn't know his own mind.'

'He is one of the most definite and determined men I have ever

535

met. He knows exactly what he wants and he will do anything to get it.' She waited a moment to let the challenge contained in those words become clearer, then she repeated softly, 'Anything.'

'Yes,' he agreed softly. 'That's a Courtney family trait. We will do anything to get what we want – or to destroy anything that stands in our way.' He paused, just as she had done and then repeated quietly, 'Anything.'

'You had three sons, Shasa Courtney. You have one left. Are you willing to take that chance?'

He reared back in his chair and stared at her. She was unprepared for the agony that she saw in his expression and for a moment she thought she had gone too far. Then he subsided slowly.

'You fight hard and dirty,' he acknowledged sadly.

'When it is worthwhile.' She knew it was dangerous with an opponent of this calibre, but she felt sorry for him. 'And for me this is worthwhile.'

'For you, yes, I can see that – but for Garry?'

'I think I owe you complete honesty. At the beginning it was a little bit of daring. I was intrigued by his youth – that in itself can be devastatingly appealing. And by the other obvious attractions which you have hinted at.'

'The Courtney empire and his place in it.'

'Yes. I would have been less than human if that hadn't interested me. That's the way it started, but almost immediately it began to change.'

'In what way?'

'I began to understand his enormous potential, and my own influence in developing it fully. Haven't you noticed any change in him in the three months since we have been together? Can you truly tell me my influence on him has been detrimental?'

Despite himself Shasa smiled. 'The pinstripe suits and the horn-rimmed glasses. They are a vast improvement, I'll admit.'

'Those are only the unimportant outward signs of the important inward changes. In three months Garry has become a mature and confident man, he has discovered many of his own strengths and talents and virtues, not the least of which is a warm and loving disposition. With my help he will discover all the others.'

'So you see yourself in the role of architect still, building a marble palace out of clay bricks.'

'Don't mock him.' She was angry, protective and defensive as a lioness. 'He is probably the best of all the Courtneys and I am probably the best thing that will ever happen to him in his life.'

He stared at her, and exclaimed with wonder as it dawned upon him. 'You love him – you really love him.'

'So you understand at last.'

She stood up and turned towards the door.

'Holly,' he said, and the unexpected use of her first name arrested her. She wavered, still pale with anger, and he went on softly, 'I didn't understand, forgive me. I think Garry is a fortunate young man to have found you.' He held out his hand. 'You said we might be friends – is that still possible?'

*　　*　　*

Table Bay is wide open to the north-westerly gales that bore in off the wintry grey Atlantic. The ferry took the short steep seas on her bows and lurched over the crests, throwing the spray as high as the stubby masthead.

It was the first time Vicky had ever been at sea and the motion terrified her as nothing on earth had ever done. She clutched the child to her, and stared straight ahead, but it was difficult to maintain her balance on the hard wooden bench, and thick spray dashed against the porthole and poured over the glass in a wavering mirage that distorted her view. The island looked like some dreadful creature swimming to meet them, and she recalled all the legends of her tribe of the monsters that came out of the sea and devoured any human being found upon the shore.

She was glad that Joseph was with her. Her half-brother had grown into a fine young man. He reminded her of the faded photograph of her grandfather, Mbejane Dinizulu, that her mother kept on the wall of her hut. Joseph had the same broad forehead and wide-spread eyes, and although his nose was not flattened but high-bridged, his clean-shaven chin was rounded and full.

He had just completed his law degree at the black University of Fort Hare, but before he underwent his consecration into the hereditary role of Zulu chieftainship, Vicky had prevailed upon him to accompany her upon the long journey down the length of the sub-continent. As soon as he returned to the district of Ladyburg in Zululand, he would begin his training for the chieftainship. This was not the initiation to which the young men of the Xhosa and the other tribes were forced to submit. Joseph would not suffer the brutal mutilation of ritual circumcision. King Chaka had abolished that custom. He had not tolerated the time that his young warriors wasted in recuperation, which could better be spent in military training.

Joseph stood beside Vicky, balancing easily to the ferry's agitated plunges, and he placed his hand upon her shoulder to reassure her. 'Not much longer,' he murmured. 'We will soon be there.'

Vicky shook her head vehemently, and clutched her son more

537

securely to her bosom. The cold sweat broke out upon her forehead, and waves of nausea assailed her, but she fought them back.

'I am the daughter of a chief,' she told herself. 'And the wife of a king. I will not surrender to womanly weakness.'

The ferry ran out of the gale into the calm waters in the lee of the island, and Vicky drew a long ragged breath and stood up. Her legs were unsteady, and Joseph helped her to the rail.

They stood side by side and stared at the bleak and infamous silhouette of Robben Island. The name derived from the Dutch word for seal, and the colonies of these animals that the first explorers had discovered upon its barren rocks.

When the fishing and sealing industries based upon the island failed, it was used as a leper colony and a place of banishment for political prisoners, most of them black. Even Makana, the prophet and warrior, who had led the first Xhosa onslaughts against the white settlers cross the great Fish river had been sent here after his capture, and here he had died in 1820, drowned in the roaring seas that beat upon the island as he tried to escape. For fifty years his people had refused to believe he was dead, and to this day his name was a rallying cry for the tribe.

One hundred and forty-three years later, there was another prophet and warrior imprisoned upon the island, and Vicky stared out across the narrowing strip of water at the low square unlovely structure, the new high-security prison for dangerous political prisoners where Moses Gama was now incarcerated. After his stay of execution, Moses had remained on death row at Pretoria Central Prison for almost two years, until finally mitigation of the death sentence to life imprisonment at hard labour had been officially granted by the state president and he had been transferred to the island. Moses was allowed one visit every six months, and Vicky was bringing his son to see him.

The journey had not been easy, for Vicky herself was the subject of a banning order. She had shown herself an enemy of the state by her appearances at Moses' trial, dressed in the colours of the African National Congress, and her inflammatory utterances which were widely reported by the news media.

Even to leave the township of Drake's Farm to which the banning order confined her, she had to obtain a travel permit from the local magistrate. This document set out precisely the terms upon which she was allowed to travel, the exact time which she was required to leave her cottage, the route and means of transport she must take, the duration of her visit to her husband and the route she must take upon her return journey.

The ferry manoeuvred in towards the jetty and there were uniformed warders to seize the mooring ropes as they were thrown across. Joseph took the boy's hand from her and with his free hand helped Vicky across the narrow gap. They stood together on the wooden boards of the jetty and looked around uncertainly. The warders ignored them as they went on with the business of docking and unloading the ferry.

It was ten minutes before one of them called across to them, 'All right, come this way,' and they followed him up the paved road towards the security block.

The first glimpse that Vicky had of her husband after six months appalled her.

'You are so thin,' she cried.

'I have not been eating very well.' He sat down on the stool facing her through the mesh of the screen. They had developed a cryptic code during the four visits she had been allowed at Pretoria Central, and not eating well meant that he was on another hunger strike.

He smiled at her and his face was skull-like so that his lips had retracted and his teeth were too big for his face. When he placed his hands on the shelf in front of him his wrists protruded from the cuffs of his khaki prison uniform and they were bone covered with a thin layer of skin.

'Let me see my son,' he said, and she drew Matthew to her.

'Greet your father,' she told the boy, and he stared solemnly at Moses through the grille. The gaunt stranger on the other side of the wire had never picked him up or held him on his lap, had never kissed or fondled him, had never even touched him. The mesh was always between them.

A warder sat beside Moses to see that the visiting rules were strictly observed. The time allowed was one hour, sixty minutes exactly, and only family matters could be discussed – no news of the day, no discussion of prison conditions and especially nothing with a political flavour to it.

One hour of family matters, but they used their code. 'I am sure that my appetite will return once I have news of the family,' Moses told her, 'on paper.' So she knew that he was hunger-striking to be allowed to read the newspapers. Therefore he would not have heard the news about Nelson Mandela.

'The elders have asked *Gundwane* to visit them,' she told him. *Gundwane* was their code name for Mandela. It meant 'cane rat' and the elders were the authorities. He nodded to show that he understood that Mandela had at last been arrested, and he smiled tautly. The information he had given to Manfred De La Rey had been used effectively.

'How are the family members on the farm?' he asked.

539

'All is well, and they are planting their crops,' Vicky told him, and he understood that the *Umkhonto we Sizwe* teams working out of Puck's Hill had begun their campaign of terror bombings. 'Perhaps you will all be reunited sooner than we think,' she suggested.

'Let us hope so,' Moses agreed. A reunion would mean that the Puck's Hill team would join him here on the island, or take the shorter road to the gallows.

The hour passed too swiftly, and the warder was standing up. 'Time up. Say your goodbyes.'

'I leave my heart with you, my husband,' Vicky told him, and watched the warder lead him away. He did not look back at her, and his gait dragged like that of an exhausted old man.

'It is only the starvation,' she told Joseph as they walked back to the ferry. 'He is still courageous as a lion, but weak from lack of food.'

'He is finished,' Joseph contradicted her quietly. 'The Boers have beaten him. He will never breathe the air of freedom again. He will never see the outside of his prison again.'

'For all of us, born black, this whole country is a prison,' Vicky said fiercely, and Joseph did not reply until they were once more aboard the ferry and running back before the gale, towards the flat-topped mountain whose lower slopes were flecked with white walls and shining glass.

'Moses Gama chose the wrong road,' Joseph said. 'He tried to assault the walls of the white fortress. He tried to burn it down, not realizing that even if he had succeeded all he would have inherited would have been ashes.'

'And you, Joseph Dinizulu,' Vicky flashed at him scornfully, 'you are wiser?'

'Perhaps not, but at least I will learn from the mistakes of Moses Gama and Nelson Mandela. I will not spend my life rotting in a white man's prison.'

'How will you assault the white man's fortress, my clever little brother?'

'I will cross the lowered drawbridge,' he said. 'I will go in through the open gates, and one day the castle and its treasures will be mine, even if I have to share a little of them with the white man. No, my angry little sister, I will not destroy those treasures with bombs and flames. I will inherit them.'

'You are mad, Joseph Dinizulu.' She stared at him, and he smiled complacently at her.

'We shall see who is mad and who is sane,' he said. 'But remember this, little sister, that without the white man we would still be living in grass huts. Look to the north and see the misery of those countries which have driven out the whites. No, my sister, I will keep the white man here – but one day he will work for me, not I for him.'

*   *   *

'Forget your anger, my son.' Hendrick Tabaka leaned forward and placed his right hand on Raleigh's shoulder. 'Your anger will destroy you. Your enemy is too strong. See what has happened to Moses Gama, my own brother. See what is the fate of Nelson Mandela. They went out to fight the lion with bare hands.'

'Others are still fighting,' Raleigh pointed out. 'The warriors of *Umkhonto we Sizwe* are still fighting. Every day we hear of their brave deeds. Every day their bombs explode.'

'They are throwing pebbles at a mountain,' Hendrick said sadly. 'Every time they explode a little bomb against the pylon of a power line, Vorster and De La Rey arm another thousand police and write another hundred banning orders.' Hendrick shook his head. 'Forget your anger, my son, there is a fine life for you at my side. If you follow Moses Gama and Mandela, you will end the way they have ended – but I can offer you wealth and power. Take a wife, Raleigh, a good fat wife and give her many sons, forget the madness and take your place at my side.'

'I had a wife, my father, and I left her at Sharpeville,' Raleigh said. 'But before I left her, I made a vow. With my fingers deep in her bloody wounds, I made a vow.'

'Vows are easy to make,' Hendrick whispered, and Raleigh saw how age had played like a blowtorch across his features, withering and searing and melting the bold lines of his cheekbones and jaw. 'But vows are difficult to live with. Your brother Wellington has also made a vow to the white man's god. He will live like a eunuch for the rest of his life, without ever knowing the comfort of a woman's body. I fear for you, Raleigh, fruit of my loins. I fear that your own vow will be a heavy burden for all your life.' He sighed again. 'But since I cannot persuade you, what can I do to ease the rocky pathway for you?'

'You know that many of the young people are leaving this country?' Raleigh asked.

'Not only the young ones,' Hendrick nodded. 'Some of the high command have gone also. Oliver Tambo has fled and Mbeki and Joe Modise with many others.'

'They have gone to set the first phase of the revolution afoot.' Raleigh's eyes began to shine with excitement. 'Lenin himself taught us that we cannot move immediately to the communist revolution. We must achieve the phase of national liberation first. We have to

541

create a broad front of liberals and churchmen and students and workers under the leadership of the vanguard party. Oliver Tambo has gone to create that vanguard party – the anti-*apartheid* movement in exile – and I want to be part of that spearhead of the revolution.'

'You wish to leave the country of your birth?' Hendrick stared at him in bewilderment. 'You wish to leave me and your family?'

'It is my duty, Father. If the evils of this system are ever to be destroyed, we will need the help of that world out there, of all the united nations of the world.'

'You are dreaming, my son,' Hendrick told him. 'Already that world, in which you place so much trust and hope, has forgotten Sharpeville. Once again money from the foreign nations, from America and Britain and France, is pouring into this country. Every day the country prospers —'

'America has refused to supply arms.'

'Yes,' Hendrick chuckled ruefully. 'And the Boers are making their own. You cannot win, my son, so stay with me.'

'I must go, my Father. Forgive me, but I have no choice. I must go, but I need your help.'

'What do you want me to do?'

'There is a man, a white man, who is helping the young ones to escape.'

Hendrick nodded. 'Joe Cicero.'

'I want to meet him, Father.'

'It will take a little time, for he is a secret man, this Joe Cicero.'

It took almost two weeks. They met on a municipal bus that Raleigh boarded at the central depot in Vereeniging. He wore a blue beret, as he had been instructed, and sat in the second row of seats from the back.

The man who took the seat directly behind him lit a cigarette and as the bus pulled away, said softly, 'Raleigh Tabaka.'

Raleigh turned to look into a pair of eyes like puddles of spilled engine oil.

'Do not look at me,' Joe Cicero said. 'But listen carefully to what I tell you —'

Three weeks later Raleigh Tabaka, carrying a duffel bag and authentic seaman's papers, went up the gangplank of a Dutch freighter that was carrying a cargo of wool to the port of Liverpool. He never saw the continent disappear below the watery horizon for he was already below decks at work in the ship's engine room.

* * *

Sean did the deal at breakfast on the last day of the safari. The client

542

owned seventeen large leather tanneries in as many different states and half the real estate in Tucson, Arizona. His name was Ed Liner and he was seventy-two years of age.

'Son, I don't know why I want to buy myself a safari company. I'm getting a little long in the tooth for this big game stuff,' he grumbled.

'That's bullshit, Ed,' Sean told him. 'You nearly walked me off my feet after that big jumbo, and the trackers all call you *Bwana One-Shot*.'

Ed Liner looked pleased with himself. He was a wiry little man with a ruff of snowy hair around his brown-freckled pate.

'Give me the facts again,' he invited. 'One last time.'

Sean had been working on him for three weeks, since the first day of the safari, and he knew Ed had the figures by heart, but he repeated them now.

'The concession is five hundred square miles, with a forty-mile frontage on the south bank of Lake Kariba —' As he listened, Ed Liner stroked his wife as though he were caressing a pet kitten.

She was his third wife and she was just two years younger than Sean, but fifty years younger than her husband. She had been a dancer at the Golden Egg in Vegas, and she had a dancer's legs and carriage, with big innocent blue eyes and a curling cloud of blond hair.

She watched Sean with a vicious little curl to her cupid-bow lips as he made his pitch. Sean had been working on her just as assiduously as he had on her husband, thus far with as little success.

'All you've got, honey,' she had told Sean, 'is a pretty face and a hungry dick. The woods are full of those. Daddy Eddie has got fifty million bucks. It's no contest, sonny boy.'

The camp table was set under a magnificent wild fig tree on the banks of the Mara river. It was a bright African morning. The plain beyond the river was golden with winter grass, and studded with flat-topped acacia trees. The herds of wildebeest were dark shadows on the gold and a giraffe was feeding from the upper branches of the nearest acacia, his long graceful neck swaying against the brittle blue of the sky, his hide paved with bold rectangles of red brown. From up-river there came the bellowing sardonic laughter of a bull hippo, while from the branches of the fig tree above them the golden weaver birds dangled upside down from their woven basket nests, fluttering and shrilling to entice the drab brown females to move in and take up residence. Legend had it that both Hemingway and Ruark had camped at this very spot and breakfasted beneath this same wild fig.

'What do you think, Sugar Sticks?' Ed Liner ran his bony brown fingers down the inside of his wife's thigh. She wore wide-legged

543

khaki culottes and from where Sean sat he could see a little red blond pubic curl peeking out from under the elastic of her panties. 'Do you think we should give old Sean here a half million bucks to set up our very own safari outfit down in the Zambezi valley of Rhodesia?'

'You know best, Daddy Eddie,' she affected a cute little-girl voice, and she batted her long eyelashes at him and turned so that her bosom strained the buttons of her khaki shirt.

'Just think of it,' Sean invited. 'Your very own hunting concession, to do with as you want.' He watched her carefully as he went on. 'You could shoot the full quota all yourself if you wanted, as many animals as you wanted.' Despite her curls and pouting lips, Lana Liner had as vicious a sadistic streak as any man Sean had ever hunted with. While Ed had chosen only to take the lion and elephant that he had paid for, Lana had killed every single animal she was entitled to, and then had killed those her husband had refused.

She was a passable shot, and derived as much pleasure from cutting down one of the dainty little Thompson's gazelle with her .300 Weatherby magnum as she had when she dropped her black-maned Masai lion with a perfect heart shot. He had seen the sexual radiance in her immediately after each kill, heard her rapid breathing and seen the pulse beat in her throat with excitement, and his philanderer's instinct had assured him that Lana Liner was vulnerable to him only in those few minutes after she had seen the bullet strike and the blood flash.

'As much hunting as you want, whenever you want it,' Sean tempted her, and saw the excitement in her baby blue eyes.

She ran the tip of her tongue over her scarlet lips and said in her breathless little-girl voice, 'Why don't you buy it for my birthday, Daddy Eddie.'

'Goddamm!' Ed laughed. 'Why not! Okay, son, you've got yourself a deal. We'll call it Lana Safaris. I'll get my lawyers to draw up the papers soon as we get home to Tucson.'

Sean clapped his hands, and shouted at the kitchen tent. 'Maramba! *Letta* champagne *hapa*. *Pacey*! *Pacey*!' and the camp waiter in his long white kanza and red pill-box fez brought the green bottle on its silver tray, dewed with cold from the refrigerator.

They drank the wine and laughed in the morning sunlight, and shook hands and discussed the new venture until the gunbearer brought the hunting car around with the rifles in the racks and Matatu, the Ndorobo tracker, perched up on the back and grinning like a monkey.

'I've had enough,' Ed said. 'Guess I'll get packed up and ready to meet the charter plane when it comes in this afternoon.' Then he saw

544

the pout of disappointment on Lana's red lips. 'You go off with Sean, Sugar Sticks,' he told her. 'Have a good hunt, but don't be late back. The charter flight is due to arrive at three, and we must get back to Nairobi before dark.'

Sean drove with Lana in the seat beside him. He had cut the sleeves out of his shirt to leave his upper arms bare, and they were sleek and glossy with muscle. Dark chest hair curled out of the vee neck of the shirt, and he wore his shining dark hair in a page-boy almost to his shoulders, but bound up around the forehead with a patterned silk bandana to keep it out of his eyes.

When he grinned at her, he was almost impossibly handsome, but there was a vindictive twist to his smile as he said, 'Ready for a bit of sport, sport?' And she said. 'Just as long as I get to do the shooting, sonny boy.'

They followed the track along the river bank, heading back towards the hills. The Land-Rover was stripped and the windshield removed, and Matatu and the gunbearer in the raised back seat scanned the edges of the riverine bush and searched the track for sign of passage during the night.

Alarmed by the engine beat, a bushbuck family came dancing up the bank from the river, heading for the dense cover with the ewe and the lamb leading, and the ram, striped and spotted with cream on a dark chocolate ground, his corkscrew horns held high.

'I want him,' Lana cried and reached over her shoulder for the Weatherby.

'Leave him,' Sean snapped. 'He won't go fifteen inches and you've got a better trophy already.'

She pouted at him sulkily, and he ignored her as the bushbuck scampered into the bush. Sean hit four-wheel drive and angled the Land-Rover down the bank of one of the Mara's tributaries, splashed and jolted through water as deep as the hubs and then roared up the far bank.

A small herd of Burchell's zebra cantered away ahead of them, stiff black manes erect, their vivid stripes shaded to nondescript grey at a distance, uttering their abrupt honking bark. Lana eyed them hungrily, but she had already shot the twenty zebra allowed on both her and Ed's licences.

The track swung back towards the river and through trees they had a view across the wide plains. The Masai Mara, which meant the great spotted place of the Masai, and the grassland were blotched with herds of game and clumps of acacia.

'*Bwana*,' Matatu cried, and at the same instant Sean saw the sign. He braked the Land-Rover and with Matatu beside him went to examine the splashes of khaki-green dung and the huge round bovine prints in the soft earth of the track. The dung was loose and wet, and Matatu thrust his forefinger into one of the pats to test for body heat.

'They drank at the river an hour before dawn,' he said.

Sean walked back to the Land-Rover and stood close to Lana, almost touching her as he said, 'Three old bulls. They crossed three hours ago, but they are feeding and we could catch them within an hour. I think they are the same three we saw the day before yesterday.' They had spotted the dark shapes in the dusk, from the opposite bank of the wide Mara river, but with insufficient daylight left for them to circle upstream to the ford and take up the chase. 'If they are the same old mud bulls, one of them is a fifty-incher, and there aren't many of them that size around any more. Do you want to have a go?'

She jumped down from the Land-Rover, and reached for the Weatherby in the gun rack.

'Not that popgun, Sugar Sticks,' Sean warned her. 'Those are big mean old buff out there. Take Ed's Winchester.' The .458 threw a bullet more than twice as heavy as the 200-grain Nosler that the Weatherby fired.

'I shoot better with my own piece than with Ed's cannon,' Lana said. 'And only Ed is allowed to call me Sugar Sticks.'

'Ed is paying me a thousand dollars a day for the best advice on Harley Street. Take the .458, and is it all right if I call you Treacle Pins, then?'

'You can go screw, sonny boy,' Lana said and her baby voice gave the obscenity a strangely lascivious twist.

'That's exactly what I had in mind, Treacle Pins, but let's go kill a buff first.'

She tossed the Weatherby to her gunbearer, and strode away from him with her hard round buttocks oscillating in the khaki culottes. 'Just like the cheeks of a squirrel chewing a nut,' Sean thought happily, and took the big double-barrelled Gibbs down from the rack.

The spoor was gross, three big bull buffalo weighing over a ton each and scarring the earth with brazen hooves and grazing as they went. Matatu wanted to run away with it, but Sean checked him. He didn't want to bring Lana up to the chase shaking and panting with fatigue, so they went out on it at an extended walk, going hard but keeping within the girl's capabilities.

In the open acacia forest they reached the spot where the bulls had ceased feeding and bunched up, then struck determinedly towards the blue silhouette of distant hills, and Sean explained to Lana in a whisper, 'This is where they were when the sun rose. As soon as it was light, they headed for the thick stuff. I know where they will lie up, we'll catch them with another half hour.'

Around them the forest closed in, and acacia gave way to the dense claustrophobic thorn and green jess. Visibility ahead dropped to a hundred and then fifty feet, and they had to crouch beneath the interlacing branches. The heat built up, and the dappled light was deceptive, filling the forest with strange shapes and menacing shadow. The stink of the buffalo seemed to steam around them in the heat, a rank gamy smell, and they found the flattened beds and smeared yellow dung where the bulls had lain down for the first time, and then stood up and moved on.

Ahead of them Matatu made the open-handed sign for 'Very close', and Sean opened the breech of the Gibbs and changed the big brass .577 Kynoch cartridges for two others from his bullet pouch. He kept the original pair between the fingers of his left hand, ready for an instant reload. He could fire those four cartridges in half the time it would take even the most skilled rifleman to fire four from a magazine rifle. It was so silent and still in the jess that they could hear each other breathe, and the blood pounding in their own ears.

Suddenly there was a clatter, and they all froze. Sean recognized the sound. Somewhere just ahead of them a buffalo had shaken his great black head to drive away the plaguing flies, and one of his curved horns had struck a branch. Sean sank on to his knees signalling Lana to come up beside him, and together they crawled forward.

Suddenly and unexpectedly they came to a hole in the jess, a tiny clearing twenty paces across, and the earth was trodden like a cattle kraal and littered with pancakes of old black dung.

They lay on the edge of the clearing and peered across into the tangled vegetation on the far side. The sunlight into the clearing dazzled them, and the shadow beyond it was confused and obscure.

Then the bull shook his head again, and Sean saw them. They were lying in a bunch, a mountainous mass of blackness in the shadows, and their heads overlapped so that the heavy bosses and curls of horn formed an inextricable puzzle. Though they were less than thirty paces away, it was impossible to separate one animal from the others, or one set of horns from the bunch.

Slowly Sean turned his head and laid his lips against Lana's ear. 'I am going to get them up,' he whispered. 'Be ready to take the shot as I call it.'

She was sweating and trembling. He could smell her fear and excitement, and it excited him also. He felt his loins thicken and stiffen, and for a moment he savoured the sensation, pressing his hips against the earth as though he had her body under him. Then deliberately he

547

knocked the brass cartridges in his left hand against the steel barrels of the Gibbs. The sharp metallic sound was shocking in the silence.

Across the clearing the three bulls lumbered to their feet, and faced the sound. Their heads were lifted, drooling wet muzzles held high and the bosses of rough horn, black as ironstone, joined above their vicious piggy little eyes, the tips curving down and up again to the wide points, and their ears flared like trumpets.

'The middle one,' Sean said softly. 'Rake him through the chest.'

He stiffened in anticipation of her shot, and then glanced sideways. The barrel of the Weatherby was describing small erratic circles as Lana tried to hold her aim, and it flashed upon Sean that she had forgotten to change the power of her variable telescopic sight. She was looking at a bull buffalo from thirty paces through a lens of ten multiplications. It was like looking at a battleship through a microscope: all she was seeing was a black shapeless mass.

'Don't shoot!' he whispered urgently but the Weatherby erupted in a long blazing muzzle-flash across the clearing, and the big bull lurched and tossed his head, grunting to the strike of shot. Sean saw the dried mud puff from his scabby black skin, low down in the joint of his right shoulder, and as the bull spun away into the jess, Sean swung the Gibbs on him to take the back-up shot. But one of the other buffalo turned across the wounded animal, screening him for the instant that it took for him to crash away into the jess, and Sean lifted the Gibbs without firing.

They lay side by side and listened to the thunderous rush of bodies dwindle into the jess.

'I couldn't see clearly,' Lana said in her childish piping treble.

'You had the scope on full power, you dilly bitch.'

'But I hit him!'

'Yes, Treacle Breeches, you hit him – more's the pity. You broke his right front leg.' Sean stood up and whistled for Matatu. In a few quick words of Swahili he explained the predicament, and the little Ndorobo looked at Lana reproachfully.

'Stay here with your gunbearer,' Sean ordered Lana. 'We'll go and finish the business.'

'I'm going with you.' Lana shook her head.

'This is what I'm paid for,' Sean told her. 'Cleaning up the mess. Stay here and let me do my job.'

'No,' she said. 'It's my buff. I'll finish it.'

'I haven't got time to argue,' Sean said bitterly. 'Come on then, but do as you are told.' And he waved Matatu forward to pick up the blood spoor.

There were bone splinters and hair where the bull had stood.

'You smashed the big bone,' Sean told her. 'It's a racing certainty that the bullet broke up. At that range it was probably still going 3500 foot per second when it hit – even a Nosler bullet can't stand that.'

The bull was bleeding profusely. Bright blood had sprayed the jess as he blundered through, and blood had formed a dark gelatinous puddle where he stood for the first time to listen for his pursuers. The other two bulls had deserted him and Sean grunted with satisfaction. That would prevent confusion, shooting at the wrong animal in the mix-up.

Lana kept close beside him. She had removed the scope from the Weatherby and left it with the gunbearer, and now she carried the rifle at high port across her chest.

Abruptly they stepped into another narrow clearing, and Matatu squeaked and bolted back between Sean and the girl as the bull broke from the far side of the clearing and came down on them in a bizarre crabbing sideways gait. His nose was up, and the long mournful droop of his horns gave him a funereal menace. His broken leg flapped loosely, hampering his gait, so he rocked and plunged, and bright blood was forced in a spurting stream from the wound by the movement.

'Shoot!' said Sean. 'Aim at his nose!' But without looking at her he sensed her terror, and her first movement as she turned to run.

'Come on, you yellow bitch. Stand and shoot it out,' he snarled at her. 'This is what you wanted – now do it.'

The Weatherby whiplashed, and flame and thunder tore across the clearing. The buffalo flinched to the shot, and black flinty chips flew from the boss of his horns.

'High!' Sean called. 'Shoot him on the nose. 'And she shot again, and hit the horn a second time and the bull kept coming.

'Shoot!' Sean called, watching the great armoured head over the express sights of the Gibbs. 'Come on, bitch, kill him!'

'I can't,' she screamed. 'He's too close!' The bull filled all their existence, a mountain of black hide and muscle and lethal horn, so close that at last he dropped his head to toss and gore them, to rip and trample and crush them under the anvil of his crenellated boss.

As the massive horns went down, Sean shot him through the brain and the bull rolled forward over his own head. Sean pulled Lana out from under the flying hooves as the bull somersaulted. She had dropped the rifle and now she clung to him helplessly, shaking, her red mouth slack and smeared with terror.

'Matatu!' Sean called quietly, holding her to his chest, and the little Ndorobo reappeared at his side like a genie. 'Take the gunbearer with you,' Sean ordered. 'Go back to the Land-Rover and bring it back here, but do not hurry.'

549

Matatu grinned lewdly and ducked his head. He had an enormous respect for his *Bwana*'s virility and he knew what Sean was going to do. He only wondered that it had taken so long for the *Bwana* to straighten this pale albino creature's back for her. He disappeared into the jess like a black shadow and Sean turned the girl's face up to his own and thrust his tongue deeply into the wet red wound of her mouth.

She moaned and clung to him, and with his free hand he unbuckled her belt and jerked down the culottes. They fell in a tangle around her ankles and she kicked them away. He hooked his thumbs into the waistband of her panties and tore them off her, then he pushed her down on top of the hot and bleeding carcass of the buffalo. She fell with her legs sprawled open and the muscles of the dead animal were still twitching and contracting from the brain shot, and the sweet coppery smell of blood mingled with the rank wild stink of game and dust.

Sean stood over her and tore open the front of his breeches and she looked up at him with the terror still clouding her eyes.

'Oh you bastard,' she sobbed. 'You filthy rotten bastard.'

Sean dropped on his knees between her long loose limbs and cupped his hands under her hard little buttocks. As he lifted her lower body he saw that her fluffy blond mount was already as sodden as the fur of a drowned kitten.

They drove back to camp with the body of the dead bull crammed into the back of the Land-Rover, the great horned head dangling over the side, and Matatu and the gunbearer perched upon it, singing the hunter's song.

Lana never said a word all the way back. Ed Liner was waiting for them under the dining tent, but his welcoming grin faded as Lana threw her torn panties on the table in front of him and piped in her little-girl voice, 'You know what naughty old Sean did, Daddy Eddie? He raped your little girl, that's what he did – he held her down and stuck his big dirty thing into her.'

Sean saw the fury and the hatred in the old man's faded eyes, and he groaned inwardly. 'The bitch,' he thought. 'The sneaky little bitch. You loved it. You screamed for more.'

Half an hour later Lana and Ed were in the red and silver Beechcraft Baron when it took off from the narrow bush strip. As it banked away on course for Nairobi, Sean glanced down at his own trouser front.

'Well okay, King Kong,' he murmured. 'I hope you are satisfied, that just cost us fifty thousand dollars an inch.' He turned back to the Land-Rover still shaking his head sadly as he picked up the bundle of mail that the pilot of the Beechcraft had brought down

550

from the office in Nairobi. There was a yellow cable envelope on top of the pile and he opened it first.

'I am marrying Holly Carmichael on 5th August. Please be my best man. Love. Garry.'

Sean read it through twice, and Lana and Ed Liner were forgotten.

'I'd love to see what kind of bag would marry Garry,' he chuckled. 'Pity I can't go home —' he broke off and thought about it. 'But why not! Why the hell not! Living dangerously is half the fun.'

* * *

Shasa Courtney sat at his desk in the study at Weltevreden, studying the Turner on the opposite wall as he composed the next paragraph in his mind.

He was drafting his Chairman's Report for the cabinet select committee of Armscor. The armaments company had been set up by special act of parliament, and the strict secrecy of its operations was ensured by that act.

When President Eisenhower had initiated the arms embargo against South Africa as a punitive reaction to the Sharpeville massacre and the racial policies of the Verwoerd government, the country's annual expenditure on weapons manufacture had been a mere £300,000. Four years later they had an annual budget of half a billion.

'Dear old Ike did us a big favour.' Shasa smiled now. 'The law of unforeseen consequences in action again, sanctions always backfire. Now our biggest worry is to find a testing ground for our own atomic bomb.'

He addressed himself once more to that section of his report, and wrote:

> Taking into consideration the foregoing, I am of the opinion that we should adopt the third option, i.e. underground testing. With this in view, the corporation has already conducted investigations to determine the most suitable geological areas. (See attached geological survey reports.)
>
> The shot holes will be drilled by a commercial diamond drilling company to a depth of four thousand feet to obviate contamination of the underground water supplies.

There was a knock on the door and Shasa looked up in angry disbelief. The entire household knew that he was not to be disturbed, and there was no reason nor excuse for this intrusion.

'Who is it?' he barked, and the door was opened without his permission.

For a moment he did not recognize the person who stepped into the study. The long hair and deep tan, the flamboyant costume – the gilet of kudu skin, and the bright silk scarf knotted at the throat, the mosquito boots and cartridge belt were all unfamiliar. Shasa stood up uncertainly.

'Sean?' he asked. 'No, I don't believe this is happening.' He wanted to be angry and outraged. 'Damn it, Sean, I warned you never —' but he could not go on, his joy was too intense and his voice petered out.

'Hello Dad.' Sean came striding towards him, and he was taller and more handsome and self-assured than Shasa remembered. Shasa abhorred all manner of theatrics and affectation of dress, but Sean wore his costume with such panache that it appeared natural and correct.

'What the hell are you doing here?' Shasa found his voice at last, but there was no rancour in his question.

'I came as soon as I got Garry's cable.'

'Garry cabled you?'

'Best man – he wanted me to be his best man, and I didn't even have a chance to change.' He stopped in front of Shasa, and for a moment they studied each other.

'You are looking good, Pater,' Sean smiled, and his teeth were white as bone against the tan.

'Sean, my boy.' Shasa lifted his hands, and Sean seized him in a bear hug.

'I thought about you every single day —' Sean's voice was tight and his cheek was pressed to Shasa's cheek. 'God, how I missed you, Dad.'

Shasa knew instinctively that it was a lie, but he was delighted that Sean had bothered to tell the lie.

'I've missed you, too, my boy,' he whispered. 'Not every day, but often enough to hurt like hell. Welcome back to Weltevreden.' And Sean kissed him. They had not kissed since Sean was a child, that sort of sentimental display was not Shasa's usual style, but now the pleasure of it was almost unbearable.

Sean sat at Centaine's right hand at dinner that evening. His dinner jacket was a little tight around the chest and smelled of moth balls, but the servants, overjoyed to have him home, had pressed razor edges into the crease of his trousers and steamed out the silk lapels. He had shampooed his hair, and oddly the thick glossy locks seemed to enhance rather than detract from his over-powering masculinity.

Isabella, taken by surprise like everybody else, had come drifting downstairs, dressed for dinner with her shoulders and back bare, but her cool and distant poise had evaporated as she saw Sean. She squealed and rushed at him.

'It's been so boring since you went away!'

She wouldn't let go of his arm until they went in to dinner, and even now she leaned forward to watch his lips as he talked, her forgotten soup cooling, avid to take in every word. When Shasa at the end of the table made a remark about Kenyan barbers and Sean's hair style, she rushed to her eldest brother's defence.

'I love his hair like that. You are so antediluvian sometimes, Papa. He's beautiful. I swear if Sean ever cuts a single hair on his beautiful head, I will take vows of silence and chastity on the spot.'

'A consummation devoutly to be prayed for,' murmured her father.

Centaine, although less effusive, was as delighted as any of them to have Sean home again. Of course, she knew every detail of the circumstances in which he had left. She and Shasa were the only ones in the family who did, but that had been almost six years ago, and things could change in that time. It was difficult to believe that anybody who looked like that, even more beautiful than her own beloved Shasa, and who was possessed of such charm and natural grace, could be entirely bad. She consoled herself that although he had made a few mistakes when he was a child, he was now a man. Centaine had seldom seen more of a man, and she listened as attentively as the rest of them to his stories and laughed as merrily at his sallies.

Garry kept repeating, 'I didn't really believe you'd come. I sent that cable on an impulse. I wasn't even sure of your address.' And then to Holly, who was sitting beside Sean at the long table, 'Isn't he wonderful, Holly – isn't he everything I told you?'

Holly smiled and murmured polite agreement, and twisted slightly in her chair to prevent Sean pointing up the story he was telling by placing his hand on her thigh again. She glanced around the table, and caught Michael's eye. He was the only one who was not following Sean's tale with total concentration. Holly had only met Michael for the first time the previous day, when he arrived from Johannesburg for the wedding, but the two of them had found an immediate *rapport*, which had swiftly deepened as Holly had discovered Michael's protective concern and affection for Garry.

Now Michael raised an eyebrow at Holly, and smiled an apology at her. He had seen his elder brother looking at her, he had seen through Sean's devices to attract her attention, and had even seen her start and pale as Sean touched her beneath the table. He would talk to Sean after dinner, and quietly warn him off, for Garry himself would never see what was happening. He was too besotted by his elder brother's return. It was up to Michael – it had always been his

553

duty to protect Garry from Sean. In the meantime he smiled reassurance at Holly, and Sean intercepted the look and interpreted it accurately. He showed no reaction. His expression was frank and open and his voice sparkling and full of humour as he finished the story and the others all laughed, all except Michael and Holly.

'You are so funny,' Isabella sang. 'I just hate you for being my brother. If only I could find another boy who looked like you.'

'There's not one of them good enough for you, Bella,' Sean said, but he was watching Michael, and as the laughter subsided, he asked lightly, 'And so, Mickey, how is life on that commie newspaper of yours? Is it true that you are going to change its name to the *ANC Times*, or is it the *Mandela Mail* or the *Moses Gama Gazette*?'

Michael laid down his knife and fork and met Sean's gaze squarely.

'The policy of the *Golden City Mail* is to defend the helpless, to attempt to secure a decent dignified existence for all, and to tell the truth as we see it – at any cost.'

'I don't know about that, Mickey,' Sean grinned at him. 'But a couple of times out there in the bush I've wished that I had a copy of the *Golden City Mail* with me – yes, sir, every time I run out of toilet paper, I wish I had your column right there.'

'Sean!' Shasa said sharply, and his indulgent expression faded for the first time since Sean's arrival. 'There are ladies present.'

'Nana.' Sean turned to Centaine. 'You have read Mickey's column, haven't you? Don't tell me you agree with those bright pink sentiments of his?'

'That's enough,' Shasa said sternly. 'This is a reunion and a celebration.'

'I'm sorry, Pater.' Sean was mock contrite. 'You are right. Let's talk about fun things. Let me tell Mickey about the Mau Mau in Kenya, and what they did to the white kids. Then he can tell me about his commie ANC friends here, and what he wants them to do to our kids.'

'Sean, that's not fair,' Michael said softly. 'I am not a communist, and I have never advocated communism or the use of force —'

'That's not what you wrote in yesterday's edition. I had the great and glorious privilege of reading your column on the plane down from Jo'burg.'

'What I actually wrote, Sean, was that Vorster and De La Rey between them are making the mistake of labelling as communist everything that our black population sees as desirable – civil rights, universal franchise, trade unions and black political organizations such as the ANC. By naming these as communist-inspired they are making the idea of communism highly attractive to our blacks.'

'We've just got a black government in Kenya, with a convicted terrorist and murderer as the new head of state. That's why I'm getting out and moving to Rhodesia. And here is my own beloved brother paving the way for another black Marxist government of rabble-rousers and bomb-throwers right here in the good old Republic. Tell me, which of the terrorists do you fancy for president, Mickey, Mandela or Moses Gama?'

'I won't warn either of you again,' Shasa told them ominously. 'I will not abide politics at the dinner table.'

'Daddy is right,' Isabella joined in. 'You are both being so utterly dreary – and just when I was beginning to really enjoy myself.'

'And that's enough from the peanut gallery also,' Centaine picked out Isabella. 'Eat your food please, Mademoiselle, you are all skin and bones as it is.' But she was studying Sean.

'He has been home six hours and already we are all at each other's throats,' she thought. 'He still has a talent for controversy. We must be wary of him – I wonder why he really came home.'

She found out very soon after dinner, when Sean asked to see her and Shasa in the gun room.

After Shasa had poured a tiny glass of Chartreuse for her, and balloon snifters of Hennessy for Sean and himself, they all settled down in the leather chairs. The men went through the ritual of preparing their cigars, cutting the tips and warming and finally lighting them with the cedarwood tapers.

'All right, Sean,' Shasa said. 'What did you want to talk to us about?'

'You know how we discussed the safari business, Pater, just before I left?' Shasa noticed how he showed no contrition as he mentioned his enforced departure. 'Well, I've had six years of experience now, and I won't offend you with false modesty. I'm one of the top hunters in the business. I've a list of over fifty clients who want to hunt with me again. I have their telephone numbers, you can ring them and ask them.'

'All right, I will,' Shasa said. 'But go on.'

'Ian Smith's government in Rhodesia is developing the safari business there. One of the concessions they are putting up for auction in two months' time is a plum.' Shasa and Centaine listened in attentive silence, and when Sean finished almost an hour later, they exchanged a significant glance. They understood each other perfectly after thirty years of working so closely, and they did not have to speak to agree that Sean had made a virtuoso performance. He was a good salesman, and his figures added up to the promise of rich profits, but Shasa saw the little shadow at the back of his mother's dark eyes.

'Just one thing perturbs me a little, Sean. After all these years you

555

come breezing in again – and the first thing you do is ask for half a million dollars.'

Sean stood up and strolled across the gun room. The carved tusk hung above the stone fireplace, the central position in the room, pride of place amongst all Shasa's own hunting trophies.

Sean studied it for a moment, and then turned back slowly to face them.

'You never wrote to me once in all those years, Pater. That's all right, I understand why. But don't accuse me of not caring. I thought about you and Nana every day I was away.' It was cleverly done. He did not mention the tusk on the wall, and Centaine could have sworn there were genuine tears just at the back of his marvellously green clear eyes. She felt her doubts soften and begin to dissolve.

'My God, how can any woman resist him,' she thought. 'Even his own grandmother!' She looked across at Shasa and was amazed to see that Sean had shamed him. Neatly and adroitly he had shifted guilt and Shasa had to cough and clear his throat before he could speak.

'I must admit it sounds interesting,' he said gruffly. 'But you'll have to speak to Garry.'

'Garry?' Sean asked in surprise.

'Garry is the director in charge of new projects and investments,' Shasa told him and Sean smiled.

He had just knocked together two of the toughest, shrewdest heads in the business. Garry would be a piece of cake.

*　　*　　*

Holly Carmichael's father was the Presbyterian minister of a small parish in Scotland, and he and his wife flew out to Africa quite determined to see their daughter decently married, and to pay for the privilege.

Centaine took him for a ride around the estate and explained kindly that only by being very selective could she restrict her guest list to under a thousand. 'Those are just family friends, and our most important business and political associates. Of course it does not include the workers here on Weltevreden or the employees of Courtney Mining and Finance who will be accorded their own separate festivities.'

The Reverend Carmichael looked stricken.

'Madam, I love my daughter – but a clergyman's stipend—'

'I don't really like to mention it,' Centaine went on smoothly, 'but it is Holly's second marriage – and you have already done your duty with the first. I would be grateful if you would consent to perform

556

the ceremony, and let me take care of the other small details.' With one deft stroke Centaine had procured a clergyman to marry her grandson, for despite veiled offers to install stained-glass windows and restore church roofs, both the local Church of England and Anglican priests had refused to perform the offices. At the same time she had achieved a free hand with the wedding arrangements.

'It will be,' she promised herself, 'the wedding of the decade.'

The old slave church on the estate had been rethatched and restored for the occasion, and the bougainvillaea blossom of exactly the shade that Holly had chosen for her dress was flown down from the eastern Transvaal in the company aircraft to decorate it. The rest of the ceremony and the following celebrations were arranged on the same scale and with similar attention to detail with all the resources of Weltevreden and the Courtney group of companies to carry them through.

The church could seat only 150, and twenty of those were the coloured family retainers from the estate who had known and cared for Garry since the day of his birth. The other thousand guests waited in the marquee on the polo field and the ceremony was relayed to them over the public address system.

The road down the hill from the church to the polo field was lined with the other estate workers whose seniority and length of service were insufficient to procure them a seat in the church. They had stripped Centaine's rose garden of blooms and they showered Garry and his new bride with rose petals as they led the procession down the hill in the open carriage, and the women danced and sang and tried to touch Holly for luck as she went by.

In his grey topper Garry stood taller than Holly and his bulk of shoulder and chest made her seem light as a cloud of pink mist beside him, so lovely that the guests gasped and hummed with admiration as he brought her into the marquee on his arm.

The best man's speech was one of the highlights of the afternoon. Sean had them roaring and squealing with laughter and clapping his most amusing sallies, although Holly frowned and reached for Garry's hand under the table when Sean made oblique references to Garry's stutter and his Charles Atlas course.

Sean was the first to dance with Holly after she and Garry had circled the floor in the wedding waltz. He held her close as they turned together and murmured, 'Silly girl, you could have had the pick of the litter, but, never fear, it's still not too late.'

'I did and it is,' she replied, and her smile was cold and thorny. 'Now why don't you go off and give my bridesmaids the benefit of your charms. The poor things are panting like puppy dogs.'

Sean turned the rebuff with a light laugh and handed her over to

Michael for the rest of the dance. While he snapped his fingers at one of the waiters to bring him another glass of champagne, he surveyed the tent from the vantage point of the raised dais, picking out the interesting females, making his selections not only on the basis of their looks but on their apparent availability. Those who sensed his scrutiny and blushed or simpered or boldly returned his regard went immediately to the head of his list.

In passing he noticed that Isabella had finally got around Nana, and was wearing one of those mini-skirts that were all the rage. The hem finished just below the creases of her cheeky little buttocks, and with the impartial eye of the connoisseur he saw that her legs were quite extraordinary, and that every man, no matter what his age, glanced down at them as she circled the dance floor.

Thinking of Nana, he looked around for her quickly. Her seat at the high table was empty. Then he found her. She was near the back of the tent, sitting at a table with a big burly man who had his back turned to Sean. They were in earnest conversation, and his grandmother's intensity interested him. He knew that Centaine never wasted effort on the trivialities. The man must be important. As he thought that, the man turned slighty and Sean recognized him. His heart skipped guiltily. It was the minister of police, Manfred De La Rey. He was the one who had quashed the charges against Sean, in return for his guarantee to leave the country and never return.

Sean's instinct was to slip away without drawing De La Rey's attention to himself and then he grinned at his own stupidity. He had just stood up and made a dashing speech in front of them all. 'How's that for drawing attention?' he thought, and then grinned again at his own daring. 'Living dangerously is half the fun,' he reminded himself, and jumped down off the dais without spilling a drop of champagne and deliberately sauntered across the tent towards his grandmother and her companion.

Centaine saw him coming and placed her hand on Manfred's sleeve. 'Careful, here he comes now.' It had just taken all her influence, a recital of all the debts and secrets between them, to protect Sean, and now here was the impudent young devil flaunting himself in front of Manfred.

She tried to warn him off with a frown, but Sean stooped and kissed her cheek. 'You are a genius, Nana, there has never been a party like this. The planning and the eye to detail – we are all proud of you!'

He hugged her and though she pushed him off haughtily saying, 'Now don't be a big booby,' her frown was displaced by the ghost of a smile. 'Damn it, he's got the cheek of all the Courtneys,' she thought proudly, and then turned to Manfred.

'You don't know my grandson. Sean, this is Minister De La Rey.'

'I've heard of you,' Manfred growled without offering to shake hands. 'I've heard a great deal about you.' And with relief Centaine turned to the couple who were returning to the table from the dance floor. 'And this is Mrs De La Rey and her son Lothar – all old friends of the family. Heidi, may I present my grandson Sean.'

Sean bowed over her hand, and Heidi considered him thoughtfully and said in her lisping German accent. 'He is the only one of your grandchildren I have not met, Centaine. A fine boy.'

Sean turned to Lothar and held out his hand. 'Hello. I'm Sean – and if I didn't know who you were, I'd be the only one in the country. Your play against the Lions on the last tour was magical, that boot of yours is worth a million rand.'

The two young men sat down on a pair of empty chairs and were immediately engrossed in a discussion of rugby football and the recent visit of the British team. Although she continued her conversation with Manfred, Centaine watched her two grandsons covertly. Apart from their youth and self-assurance, they were so different in appearance, one blond and Germanic, the other dark and romantic, yet she sensed that they were in other ways very similar. Strong men, untroubled by unnecessary scruples, men who knew what they wanted and how to go about getting it. Perhaps they inherited that from her, she smiled to herself, and perhaps like her they were hard and unrelenting adversaries, prepared to destroy anything that stood in their way.

Centaine had the trick of listening to two conversations at once and she heard Lothar De La Rey say, 'Mind you, I've heard about you also and what you did in Kenya. Didn't you get a citation for the George Cross for cleaning up the last of the Mau Mau gangs?'

Sean laughed. 'My timing was wrong. The Brits couldn't give me a gong for shooting Mickey Mice at the same time as they were handing the country over to Kenyatta. Not really cricket, you know, old boy. But how did you find out about that?'

'It's my job to know these things,' Lothar told him, and Sean nodded.

'Yes, of course, you are in the police. Aren't you a major or something?'

'As of last week, a colonel in the bureau for state security.'

'Congratulations.'

'You know, anything you could tell us about Mau Mau will be useful. I mean the real first-hand stuff about anti-terrorist work. You see, I think we might have the same problem here one of these days.'

'Well, the worst was over by the time I got there, but yes, of

559

course – anything I can do. I'm going back up north in a few weeks, to Rhodesia. But if I can help —'

'Rhodesia.' Lothar dropped his voice so that Centaine could no longer hear. 'That's interesting. We'd like to know what's going on there also. Yes, I think it is vital that we get together before you leave. A man like you in place could be of really crucial help to us —' Lothar broke off. His expression changed and he stood up hurriedly, looking over Sean's shoulders.

Following his gaze Sean looked around and Isabella stood close behind him. She draped one hand languidly over Sean's shoulder, and leaned one hip against him, but she was watching Lothar.

'This is Bella, my baby sister,' Sean told Lothar, and Isabella murmured, 'Not such a baby any more, big brother.' She had not taken her eyes off Lothar's face.

She had first noticed him in the church during the ceremony and recognized him immediately. He was one of the most famous athletes in the country, a national heart-throb. Sean's conversation with him had given her the opportunity she had been waiting for.

Despite the fact that her voice was cool and her manner aloof and distant, Sean felt her tremble against him and he grinned inwardly, 'Your ovaries are going off like fire crackers, little sister.' But he said, 'Why don't you sit down and bring a little sunlight into our drab existence, Bella?'

She ignored him and spoke directly to Lothar. 'Do you spend all your time dressed up in a rugby jersey, pushing people around in scrums and kicking little balls? Or somewhere along the line did you learn to dance, Lothar De La Rey?'

'Ouch!' Sean murmured. Even for a Courtney, that was pretty direct. And Lothar inclined his head and asked gravely,

'May I have the pleasure of this dance, Isabella Courtney?'

They made one circuit of the floor without speaking and then Lothar said, 'If you were my woman, I would not allow you to wear a skirt like that.'

'Why? Don't you like my legs?' she asked.

'I like your legs very much indeed,' he replied. 'But if you were my woman, I would not like other men to look at them the way they are doing now.'

'You are a prude, Lothar De La Rey.'

'Perhaps, Isabella Courtney, but I believe there is a time and a place for everything.'

She pushed a little closer to him and thought happily to herself, 'So let's find that time and place, you big gorgeous hunk of brawn.'

*　　*　　*

Morosely Manfred watched his son on the dance floor and his wife leaned across and echoed his thoughts.

'That hussy is throwing herself at Lothie. Just look at her, showing everything she has. I wish I could go and pull her away from him.'

'I wouldn't do that, *skat*,' Manfred advised soberly. 'Nothing could make her more attractive to him than our disapproval. But don't worry, Heidi. We have brought him up the right way. He might have a little man's sport with her, but that's not the kind of girl he will bring home.' He stood up heavily. 'Trust our boy, Heidi. But now you must forgive me. I must talk to Shasa Courtney – it's very important.'

Shasa in full morning dress, a white carnation in his buttonhole, the black patch over one eye and a long black cheroot between his teeth was in deep conversation with the groom, but when he saw Manfred approaching and recognized the seriousness of his mien, he slapped Garry's shoulder lightly and said, 'I think it's a good bet, but you listen to what Sean has to say. Make up your own mind, then come and discuss it with me,' and then he left Garry and came to meet Manfred.

'We must talk – privately,' Manfred greeted him.

'Now?' Shasa looked incredulous, but Manfred insisted.

'It will not take long.'

'Let's go up to the house.' Shasa took his arm, and chatting amiably led him to the exit, as though they were going off to the men's room together. As soon as they were outside the marquee, they headed for the carpark behind the grandstand.

Manfred prowled around Shasa's gun room, restlessly peering at the framed photographs of hunting safaris, at the mounted animal heads and the racks of sporting rifles and shotguns in their glass-fronted cabinet, while Shasa slouched in one of the armchairs and watched him patiently, letting him take his time, puffing on the black cheroot.

'Is this room secure? We cannot be overheard?' Manfred asked, and Shasa nodded.

'Perfectly secure. I do much of my private business here – besides which, the house is deserted. Every last servant is down at the polo field.'

'*Ja, nee, goed!*' Manfred came to take the armchair facing Shasa.

'You cannot go off to England as you planned,' he said, and Shasa laughed.

'Why on earth not?'

'I will tell you why.' Manfred assured him, but made no attempt to do so. Instead he asked, 'Did you ever see a film called *The Manchurian Candidate*?' He pronounced it in the Afrikaans fashion 'fi-lim'.

561

For a moment Shasa was surprised by the irrelevance of the question. Then he replied, 'No, I didn't get around to the movie, but I did read the book by Richard Condon. Rather enjoyed it, to tell the truth.'

'Do you remember the story-line?'

'Yes. It was about a plot to assassinate one of the American presidential candidates.'

'That's right,' Manfred nodded. 'The assassin was hypnotized and programmed to respond to the sight of a playing card, one of the aces, I think.'

'Ace of spades,' Shasa agreed. 'The death card. He would respond like an automaton to any command he received after he had seen the ace. In a hypnotic trance he was ordered to carry out the assassination.'

'Do you think the idea was credible? Do you think a man could be completely subjected to the hypnotic suggestion of another?'

'I don't know,' Shasa admitted. 'The Koreans and the Russians are supposed to have perfected the technique of brainwashing. Perhaps it is possible, in special circumstances, with a particularly susceptible subject – I don't know.'

Manfred sat in silence for so long that Shasa began to fidget. Then he spoke curtly, 'Our jobs are in danger,' he said, and Shasa went very still. '*Ja.*' Manfred nodded heavily. 'Verwoerd is thinking of reshuffling the cabinet. You and I will be sacked.'

'You have done a difficult job,' Shasa said softly. 'And you have done it as well as was humanly possible. The storm is over, the country is calm and stable.'

Manfred sighed. '*Ja*, you also. In a few short years since Sharpeville, you have helped rally the economy. Foreign investment is pouring in, thanks to your efforts. The value of property is higher than it was before the crisis. You have done an excellent job building up the armaments industry. Very soon our own atomic bomb – but we are going to be sacked. My information is always reliable.'

'Why?' Shasa asked, and Manfred shrugged.

'Verwoerd took two bullets in the head. Who knows what damage that caused.'

'He shows no signs of any permanent damage. He is just as logical, rational and decisive after the operation to remove the bullets.'

'Do you think so?' Manfred asked. 'Do you think his obsession with race is logical and rational?'

'Verwoerd was always obsessed with racial matters.'

'No, my friend, that is not so,' Manfred contradicted him. 'He didn't want the ministry of Bantu affairs when Malan first offered it to him. Race meant nothing to him. He was concerned only with the growth and survival of Afrikaner nationalism.'

'He certainly threw himself into it body and soul, when he did take the job,' Shasa smiled.

'*Ja*, that's true, but then he saw *apartheid* as uplifting to the blacks, a chance to conduct their own affairs, and become masters of their own destiny. He saw it as exactly similar to the partition of India and Pakistan. He was concerned with racial differences, but he was not a racist. Not in the beginning.'

'Perhaps.' Shasa was dubious.

'Since those bullets in the head he has changed,' Manfred said. 'Before that he was strong-willed and certain of his own infallibility, but since then he will brook not the slightest criticism or even a hint that anything he says or does might be wrong. Race has become an obsession, to the point of lunacy – this business with the coloured English cricketer, what is his name again?'

'Basil D'Oliveira – and he is South African. He plays for England because he can't play for South Africa.'

'*Ja*, it's madness. Now Verwoerd even refuses to have a black servant to tend him. He would not attend the film version of *Othello* because Laurence Olivier had painted his face black. He has lost all sense of proportion. He is going to undo all the hard painstaking work we have done to restore calm and prosperity. He is going to destroy this country – and he is going to destroy us personally, you and me, because we have stood up to some of his wilder excesses in cabinet. You even suggested he permanently abolish the pass laws – he has never forgiven you for that. He calls you a liberal.'

'All right, but I can't believe he would take the ministry of police away from you.'

'That is what he plans. He wants to give it all to John Vorster – combine justice and police into a single portfolio and call it "Law and Order", or some such other title.'

Shasa stood up and went to the cabinet at the end of the room. He poured two large cognacs and Manfred did not protest when he placed one of them on the table at his elbow.

'You know, Shasa, for a long time now I have had a dream. I've never told anybody about it, not even Heidi, but I will tell you. I dreamed that one day I would be the prime minister, and that you, Shasa Courtney, would be the state president of this country of ours. The two of us, Englishman and Afrikaner, side by side as South Africans.'

They sat quietly and thought about it, and Shasa found himself becoming angry at being cheated of that honour. Then Manfred went off at another tangent.

'Do you know that even though the Americans are refusing to sell

563

us arms, we still co-operate very closely with their CIA on all matters of intelligence that affect our mutual interests in southern Africa?' Manfred asked, and although Shasa could not fathom this new change of direction, he nodded.

'Yes, of course, I know that.'

'The Americans have just interrogated a Russian defector in west Berlin. They passed on some of the intelligence to us. There is a Manchurian Candidate in place, and his target is Verwoerd.'

Shasa gaped at him. 'Who is the assassin?'

'No.' Manfred held up his hands. 'They don't know. Even though the Russian was highly placed, he did not know. All he could tell the Americans was that the assassin has access to the prime minister, and he will be used soon, very soon.' He picked up the cognac glass, and swirled the oily brown liquid around the crystal bowl. 'There was one other small clue. The assassin has a history of mental illness, and he is a foreigner, not born in this country.'

'With that information it should be possible to identify him,' Shasa mused. 'You could check every single person who has access to the PM.'

'Perhaps,' Manfred agreed. 'But what we must decide – here in secret, just the two of us – is do we really want to find the Manchurian Candidate and stop him. Would it be in the best interest of our country to prevent the assassination?'

Shasa spilled the cognac down the lapels of his morning jacket, but he did not seem to notice. Aghast, he was staring at Manfred. After a long pause, he set down his glass, drew a silk handkerchief from his inner pocket and began to mop the spilled liquor.

'Who else knows about this?' he asked, concentrating on his cleaning, not looking up.

'One of my senior officers. He is the liaison with the military attaché at the American embassy, who is the CIA man here.'

'No one else?'

'Only me – and now you.'

'Your officer is trustworthy?'

'Completely.'

At last Shasa looked up. 'Yes, now I see why I should cancel my trip to London. If something should happen to Verwoerd, it would be essential for me to be here when his successor is chosen.'

He lifted his glass in a salute, and after a moment Manfred returned the gesture. They drank the silent toast, watching each other's eyes over the rims of the crystal glasses.

*   *   *

There were only two couples left on the dance floor, and except for the band and the servants who were cleaning up and stacking the chairs, the marquee was empty.

At last the coloured band-master descended from the stand and approached Sean diffidently. 'Master, it's after two o'clock already.' Sean glared at him over the head of the girl he was dancing with, and the man quailed. 'Please, Master, we've been playing since lunchtime, nearly fourteen hours.'

Sean's thunderous expression changed dramatically into that radiant boyish smile of his. 'Off you go then! You have been just great – and this is for you and your boys.' He tucked a crumpled wad of banknotes into the band-leader's top pocket, and called to the other couple.

'Come on, gang. We are off to Navvies.'

Isabella had her face pressed to Lothar's shirt front, but she looked up brightly.

'Oh goody!' she cried. 'I've never been there. Nana says it's sordid and disreputable. Let's go!'

Sean had borrowed Garry's MG and Isabella raced him in her new Alfa Romeo, and managed to keep up with him through the curves of the mountain drive. They were neck and neck as they tore down Buitenkant Street to the notorious Navigator's Den in the Bo-kaap area near the docks.

Sean had purloined two bottles of whisky from the bar in the marquee, and his partner was draped around his neck.

'Let's carouse,' he suggested, and pushed his way through the cluster of seamen and prostitutes who crowded the entrance to the nightclub.

The interior was so dark that they could only barely make out the band, and the music was so loud that they had to sit close and yell at each other.

'You are a marvellous brother,' Isabella shouted and leaned across to kiss Sean. 'You don't preach to me.'

'It's your life, Bella baby, you enjoy it – and call me if anybody tries to stop you.'

She perched on Lothar's knee and nuzzled his neck. Sean's partner had collapsed, and he laid her out full length on the padded bench, with her head in his lap, while he and Lothar sat with their shoulders touching and talked seriously. The music blanketed their voices, so that from farther than a few feet nobody could overhear them.

'Do you know that you still have a rather prominent billing in the police files?' Lothar asked.

'It does not come as any great surprise,' Sean admitted.

'You don't mind taking a chance, do you?' Lothar smiled. 'I like your nerve.'

565

'From what I know and see, I'd say that you are a fairly nerveless customer yourself,' Sean grinned back at him.

'I could make sure that your file disappeared,' Lothar offered.

'In exchange for a little something or other, no doubt?'

'Naturally,' Lothar agreed. 'You get nothing for nothing.'

'And all you get for a pinch of dung is a cloud of flies,' Sean laughed, and refilled the whisky glasses. 'What do you want from me?'

'If you were to act as an intelligence agent for the bureau for state security – our man in Rhodesia – we might forget about your little indiscretions.'

'Why not?' Sean agreed instantly. 'Anything for a laugh and living dangerously is half the fun.'

'Do stop being so boring, you two,' Isabella cried, stroking Lothar's cheek. 'Come and dance with me.'

Sean's partner sat up groggily and blurted, 'I'm going to be sick.'

'Emergency,' said Sean. He hauled her to her feet and hustled her through to the tiny women's room.

There were two other females fussing over the single wash hand basin, and they squealed demurely.

'Don't worry about us, ladies.' Sean pushed his partner into the cubicle and aimed her at the toilet bowl. Noisily she got shot of what was troubling her and then straightened up and grinned at him shakily. Tenderly he wiped her mouth with a wad of toilet paper.

'How are you feeling?'

'I feel better now.'

'Good, let's go somewhere and ball.'

'Okay,' she said, perking up miraculously. 'That's what I've been waiting for the whole evening.'

Sean stopped beside Lothar and Isabella on the crowded floor.

'We are cutting out of here – something just came up, if you will pardon the expression.'

'I'll call you at Weltevreden some time tomorrow,' Lothar said. 'Just to arrange the details.'

'Don't make it too early,' Sean advised and grinned at his sister. 'See you later, Bella Bunny.'

'For God's sake, don't say "Be good!"' Isabella pleaded.

'Perish the thought.' Sean picked up his partner and carried her down the stairs.

Isabella made one more circuit of the floor, just to let Sean get clear, then she murmured, 'That's enough dancing for one night – let's go.'

Lothar had never seen a woman drive with Isabella's skill and flair. He relaxed in the passenger seat and watched her. Despite the long day and its excesses, she was still dewy fresh as a rosepetal and her eyes were clear and sparkling.

She was the first English girl he had ever been with, and her free and forthright manner at once appalled and intrigued him. With their strict Calvinist upbringing Afrikaner girls would never make themselves so available or behave with such abandon. Yet although she shocked him more than a little, she was without any doubt the most strikingly lovely girl he had ever met.

Isabella drove straight through the intersection of Paradise Road and Rhodes Drive.

'You've missed the turn to Weltevreden,' he pointed out, and she gave him a brief impish grin.

'That's not where we are going. From here you are in my hands, Lothar De La Rey.'

They followed the coastal road from Muizenberg around the bay, through the deserted streets of Simonstown, the British naval base, and then on towards the tip of the continent.

Where the road skirted a high cliff above the sea, Isabella pulled the Alfa off the road and cut the engine.

'Come on,' she ordered, took his hand and led him to the edge of the cliff. The dawn was turning the eastern sky to lemon and orange, and far beneath them the cliffs were folded upon themselves to form a sheltered bay. 'It's so beautiful here,' Isabella whispered. 'One of my favourite places.'

'Where are we?' Lothar asked.

'It's called Smitswinkel Bay,' she told him, and led him by the hand to the start of the steep pathway that descended the cliff.

At the bottom a narrow horse-shoe of silver sand surrounded the bay, and above the beach a few locked and shuttered shacks were crammed against the foot of the cliff. The dawn light filtered down, soft and pearly, and the waters of the bay glowed with the misty sheen of moonstones.

Isabella kicked off her shoes and walked down to the water's edge, and then without looking round at him she slipped her dress off her shoulders and let it drop to the sand. Beneath it she wore only a pair of silk and lace panties. For a long moment she stood staring out across the bay and her back was long and shaped like the neck of a lovely vase, the beads of her spine just showed beneath skin that was pale and lustrous as mother-of-pearl. Then she stooped to pull the panties down to her ankles, and stepped out of them.

She was naked and Lothar's breathing caught in his throat as he watched her walk slowly down to the water's edge, her hips rolling in time to the lazy pulse of the ocean. She walked out until she was waist-deep and she lowered herself until only her head was above the surface. Then she turned and looked back at him. The challenge and the invitation were as clear as if she had called them aloud.

Lothar undressed as unhurriedly as she had done. Naked, he walked into the bay and she rose to meet him, the waters streaming from her bare shoulders down her breasts, and she lifted her arms and placed them around his neck.

She teased him with her tongue, letting him explore the warmth and softness of her mouth, and she gave a little purring chuckle as she felt how much he wanted her.

The sound goaded him and he lifted her in his arms and carried her out beyond her depth. She was forced to cling to him, and her body was weightless. He handled her like a doll and she offered no resistance. His strength seemed limitless – it made her feel helpless and vulnerable, but she was grateful for his patience. To hurry now would spoil it all. She wanted this to be something far beyond the frenzied groping and often painful thrusting that was all she had been offered by the three or four college lads she had allowed this far.

She learned quickly that he could tease as well as she could, and he let her float around him, light as the buoyant kelp in the gentle swell of the ocean while he stood foursquare and refused to make the final assault. In the end it was she who succumbed to impatience.

In contrast to the cool water that eddied around her, he was like a flaming brand buried deep in her body. She could not believe the hardness and the heat, and she cried aloud with incredible delight. None of the others had been anything like this. From now on this was all that counted, this was what she had been searching for all along.

Still clinging together they waded ashore, and by now it was full morning. They bundled up their clothes and still naked she led him to the last shack in the row. While she searched for the key in her purse, he asked, 'Who does this belong to?'

'It's one of Daddy's hiding places. I only discovered it quite by chance and he doesn't know that I have a key.'

She got the door open and led him into the single room.

'Towels,' she said, and opened one of the cupboards. They made a game out of drying each other, but the light-hearted mood changed quickly to serious intent, and she dragged him to the bunk against the wall.

'Where I come from the man does the asking,' he chuckled.

'You are an old-fashioned chauvinist prude,' she told him.

As she clambered up onto the bunk he saw that her bottom was still bright pink from the cold waters of the bay; he found that peculiarly endearing and he was suddenly overwhelmed by a sense of tenderness towards her.

'You are so gentle,' she whispered. 'So strong and yet so gentle.'

It was mid-morning before they felt hungry, and dressed only in one of her father's old fishing jerseys, Isabella raided the larder for their breakfast.

'How do you fancy smoked oysters and asparagus with your baked beans?'

'Won't your father miss you?' he asked as he opened the cans.

'Oh, Daddy is a push-over. He will believe anything I tell him. It's my grandmother we have to watch out for, but I've arranged with one of my girlfriends to cover for us.'

'Ah, so you knew where we were going to end up?' he asked.

'Of course.' She rolled her eyes at him. 'Didn't you?'

They sat cross-legged on the bunk with the plates on their laps and Isabella tasted the mixture. 'It's ghastly,' she gave her opinion, 'if I wasn't starving I wouldn't touch it.'

'Of course, you will see your mother while you are in London?' he asked, and the loaded spoon stopped half-way to Isabella's mouth.

'How did you know I was going to London – and how did you know my mother was there?'

'I probably know more about your mother than you do,' Lothar told her, and she replaced the spoon on her plate and stared at him.

'For instance?' she challenged.

'Well, for instance, your mother is a rabid enemy of this country. She is a member of the banned ANC and of the anti-*apartheid* group. She associates regularly with members of the South African Communist Party. In London she runs a safe house for political refugees and escaped terrorists.'

'My mother?' Isabella shook her head.

'Your mother was deeply implicated in the plot to blow up the houses of parliament and assassinate most of the members of the House, including the prime minister – and your father and my father.'

Isabella was still shaking her head, but he went on expressionlessly, watching her with those golden leopard eyes.

'She was directly responsible for the death of her own father, your grandfather, Colonel Blaine Malcomess. She was an accomplice of Moses Gama who is now serving a life sentence for terrorism and murder, and if she had not escaped she would probably be in jail with him.'

'No,' said Isabella softly. 'I don't believe it.'

She was amazed and distressed by the change in him. Minutes before he had been so gentle, now he was hard and cruel, wounding her with words as he went on, 'For instance, did you know that your mother was Moses Gama's lover, and that she bore him a son? Your half-brother is an attractive coffee colour.'

'No!' Isabella recoiled, shaking her head in disbelief. 'How do you know all this?'

'From the signed confession of Moses Gama, the man himself. I can arrange for you to see a copy, but that is not really necessary. You will almost certainly meet your bastard half-brother in London. He is living there with your mother. His name is Benjamin Afrika.'

Isabella jumped up and carried her plate to the kitchenette. She dumped the food into the garbage bin and without looking around, she asked, 'Why are you telling me all this?'

'So that you will know your duty.'

'I don't understand.' She still would not look at him.

'We believe your mother and her associates are planning some sort of violent action against this country. We are not sure what it is. Any information on their activities would be invaluable.'

Isabella turned slowly and stared at him. Her face was pale and stricken.

'You want me to spy on my own mother?'

'We simply would like to know the names of the people you meet in her company while you are in London.'

She was not listening. She cut in on what he was saying.

'You planned this. You picked me out, not because you thought I was attractive or sweet or desirable. You deliberately set out to seduce me, just for this.'

'You are beautiful, not attractive. You are magnificent, not sweet,' he said.

'And you are a bastard, a ruthless heartless bastard.'

He stood up and went to where his clothes hung behind the door.

'What are you going to do?' she demanded.

'Get dressed and go,' he told her.

'Why?'

'You called me a bastard.'

'You are.' Her eyes were glutted with tears. 'An irresistible bastard. Don't go, Lothar, please don't go.'

*   *   *

Isabella was relieved when her father told her that he was unable to fly to London with her and Michael. Meeting her mother again after all these years, and after what Lothar had told her, would be difficult enough, without her father there to complicate matters and confuse her feelings. She had, indeed, tried to beg off going to London herself. She wanted to be close to Lothar, but he had been the one who insisted she make the trip.

'I will be back in Johannesburg and we wouldn't see much of each other anyway,' he told her. 'And besides that you have your duty and you have given me your word.'

'I know Daddy would give me a PR job with the company in Jo'burg. I could get a flat and we could see lots of each other, I mean lots and lots!'

'When you come back from London,' he promised.

*   *   *

There were representatives from South Africa House and the London office of Courtney Mining to meet Isabella and Michael at Heathrow and a company limousine to take them to the Dorchester.

'Pater always overdoes it by a mile,' Michael remarked, embarrassed by the reception. 'We could have taken a taxi.'

'No point in being a Courtney, unless you get to enjoy it,' Isabella disagreed.

When Isabella was shown up to her suite which looked out over Hyde Park, there was an enormous bouquet of flowers waiting for her with a note:

Sorry I can't be with you, darling. Next time we will paint the town bright scarlet together.

Your old Dad.

Even before the porter had brought her bags up, Isabella dialled the number that Tara had given her and she was answered on the third ring.

'This is the Lord Kitchener Hotel, may I help you?'

It was strangely nostalgic to be greeted by an African accent in a strange city.

'May I speak to Mrs Malcomess, please?'

In her letter Tara had warned her that she had reverted to her maiden name after the divorce.

'Hello, Mater.' Isabella tried to sound natural when Tara came on the line, but Tara's delight was unrestrained.

'Oh Bella darling, where are you? Is Mickey with you? How soon can you get here? You have got the address, haven't you? It's so easy to find.'

Isabella tried to match Michael's enthusiasm and excitement as they drove through the streets of London and the taxi-driver pointed out the landmarks they passed, but she was in a funk at the prospect of seeing her mother again.

It was one of those rather seedy little tourist hotels in a side street off the Cromwell Road. Only part of the neon sign was lit. 'The Ord

Kitch', it flashed in electric blue, and on the glass of the front door were plastered the emblems of the AA and *Routiers* and a blaze of credit card stickers.

Tara rushed out through the glass doors while they were still paying off the taxi. She embraced Michael first, which gave Isabella a few moments to study her mother.

She had put on weight, her backside in the faded blue jeans was huge, and her bosom hung shapelessly in the baggy man's sweater.

'She's an old bag.' Isabella was appalled. Even though Tara had never gone to any pains with her appearance, she had always had an air of freshness and neatness. But now her hair had turned grey, and she had obviously made a half-hearted attempt to henna it back to its original colour, and then given up. The grey was streaked brassy ginger and violent mulberry red, and it was twisted up into a careless bun at the nape of her neck from which parti-coloured wisps had escaped.

Her features had sagged almost to obscure the bone structure which had been one of her most striking assets, and though her eyes were still large and bright the skin around them had creased and bagged.

At last she released Michael, and turned to Isabella.

'My darling little girl, I would hardly have recognized you. What a lovely young woman you have become.'

They embraced. Isabella recalled how her mother had smelled, it was one of her pleasant childhood memories, but this woman smelled of some cheap and flowery perfume, of cigarette smoke and boiled cabbage, and – Isabella could barely credit her own senses – of underclothing that had been worn too long without changing.

She broke off the embrace, but Tara kept hold of her arm, and with Michael on the other side of her led them into the Lord Kitchener Hotel. The receptionist was a black lad, and Isabella recognized his voice as the one who had answered her phone call.

'Phineas is from Cape Town also,' Tara introduced them. 'He is one of our other runaways. He left after the troubles in sixty-one and, like the rest of us, he won't be going home yet. Now let me show you around the Lordy —' she laughed. 'That's what my permanent guests call it, the Lordy. I thought of changing the name, it's so colonial and Empire —'

Tara chattered on happily, as she led them around the hotel. The carpets in the passages were threadbare, and the rooms had washbasins, but shared the toilet and bathroom at the end of each passage.

Tara introduced them to any of her guests they met in the corridors or public rooms. 'These are my son and daughter from Cape Town,' and they shook hands with German and French tourists who spoke no English, Pakistanis and Chinese, black Kenyans and coloured South Africans.

'Where are you staying?' Tara wanted to know.

'At the Dorchester.'

'Of course.' Tara rolled her eyes. 'Fifty guineas a day, paid for by the sweat of the workers in the Courtney mines. That is what your father would have chosen. Why don't you and Mickey move in here? I have two nice rooms on the top floor free at the moment. You would meet so many interesing people, and we'd see so much more of each other.'

Isabella shuddered at the thought of sharing the toilet at the end of the passage and jumped in before Michael could agree.

'Daddy would be furious, he has prepaid for us – and now we know our way, it's only a short taxi ride.'

'Taxis,' Tara sniffed. 'Why not take the bus or the underground like any ordinary person?'

Isabella stared at her speechlessly. Didn't she understand that they weren't ordinary people? They were Courtneys. She was about to say so, when Michael sensed her intention and intervened smoothly.

'Of course you are quite right. You'll have to tell us what number bus to take and where to get off, Mater.'

'Mickey darling, please don't call me Mater any longer. It's so terribly *bourgeois*. Call me either Mummy or Tara, but not that.'

'All right. It will be a little bit strange at first, but okay. I'll call you Tara.'

'It's almost lunch time,' Tara announced blithely. 'I asked cook to make a bread and butter pudding, I know it's one of your favourites, Mickey.'

'I'm not awfully hungry, Mater – Tara,' Isabella announced. 'And it must be jet-lag or something, but —'

Michael pinched her sharply. 'That's lovely, Tara. We'd love to stay for lunch.'

'I just have to look into the kitchen – make sure it's all under control – come along.'

As they entered the kitchen a child came running to Tara. He must have been helping the Irish cook, for his hands were white with flour to the elbows. Tara hugged him, happily heedless of the flour that rubbed off on her sweater.

A mat of short woolly curls covered his pate, and his skin was a clear light toffee colour. His eyes were huge and dark, and he had appealing gamine features. He reminded Isabella of any one of the dozens of children of the estate workers on Weltevreden. She smiled at him, and he gave back a cocky but friendly grin.

'This is Benjamin,' Tara said. 'And these, Benjamin, are your

573

brother and sister – Mickey and Isabella.'

Isabella stared at the child. She had tried to discount and forget all that Lothar had told her, and in some measure she had succeeded. But now it all came rushing back, the words roaring in her ears like flood waters.

'Your half brother is an attractive coffee colour,' Lothar had told her and she wanted to scream, 'How could you, Mater, how could you do this to us?' But Michael had recovered from his obvious surprise, and now he held out his hand towards the child and said,

'Hi there, Ben. It's fine that we are brothers – but how about you and me being friends also?'

'Hey, man – I like that,' Benjamin agreed instantly. To add to Isabella's dismay and confusion, he spoke in a broad south London accent.

Isabella spoke barely a dozen words during lunch. The pea soup was thickened with flour that had not cooked through and it stuck to the roof of her mouth. The boiled silverside lay limply in its own watery gravy, and the cabbage was cooked pink.

They sat at the table with Phineas, the receptionist, and five other of Tara's guests, all black South African expatriates, and the boisterous conversation was almost entirely conducted in left-wing jargon. The government of which Isabella's beloved father was a minister was always referred to as the 'racist regime' and Michael joined cheerfully in the discussion about the redistribution of wealth and the return of the land to those who worked it after the revolution had succeeded and the People's Democratic Republic of Azania had been established. Isabella wanted to scream at him, 'Damn you, Mickey, they are talking about Weltevreden and the Silver River Mine. These are terrorists and revolutionaries – and their sole purpose is to destroy us and our world.'

When the bread-and-butter pudding was served, she could take it no longer.

'I'm sorry, Tara,' she whispered. 'I have a splitting headache, and I simply have to get back to the Dorchester and lie down.' She was so pale and discomforted that Tara made only a token protest and genuine noises of concern. Isabella refused to let Michael escort her. 'I won't spoil your fun. You haven't seen Mater – Tara – in ages. I'll just grab a taxi.'

Perhaps it really was fatigue that had weakened her, but in the cab she found herself weeping with chagrin and shame and fury.

'Damn her! Damn her to hell,' she whispered. 'She has disgraced and dishonoured all of us, Daddy and Nana and me and all the family.'

As soon as she reached her room she locked her door, threw herself

574

on the bed and reached for the telephone.

'Exchange, I want to put a call through to Johannesburg in South Africa —' She read the number out of her address book.

The delay was less than half an hour and then a marvellously homey Afrikaans accent said, 'This is police headquarters, bureau for state security.'

'I want to speak to Colonel Lothar De La Rey.'

'De La Rey.'

Despite the thousands of miles that separated them, his voice was crisp and clear, and in her imagination she saw him again naked on the beach in the dawn, like a statue of a Greek athlete but with those glowing golden eyes, and she whispered, 'Oh God Lothie, I've missed you. I want to come home. I hate it here.'

He spoke quietly, reassuring and consoling her, and when she had calmed he ordered her, 'Tell me about it.'

'You were right. Everything you said was true – even to her little brown bastard, and the people are all revolutionaries and terrorists. What do you want me to do, Lothie? I'll do anything you tell me.'

'I want you to stay there, and stick it out for the full two weeks. You can telephone me every day, but you must stay on. Promise me, Bella.'

'All right – but, God, I miss you and home.'

'Listen, Bella. I want you to go to South Africa House the first opportunity you have. Don't let anybody know, not even your brother Michael. Ask for Colonel Van Vuuren, the military attaché. He will show you photographs and ask you to identify the people you meet.'

'All right, Lothie – but I've told you twice already how much I miss you, while you, you swine, haven't said a word.'

'I have thought about you every day since you left,' Lothar said. 'You're beautiful and funny and you make me laugh.'

'Don't stop,' Isabella pleaded. 'Just keep talking like that.'

Adrian Van Vuuren was a burly avuncular man, who looked more like a friendly Free State farmer than a secret service man. He took her up to the ambassador's office and introduced her to His Excellency who knew Shasa well and they chatted for a few minutes. His Excellency invited Isabella to the races at Ascot the coming Saturday but Colonel Van Vuuren intervened apologetically.

'Miss Courtney is doing a little job for us at present, Your Excellency. It might not be wise to make too much public display of her connections to the embassy.'

'Very well,' the ambassador agreed reluctantly, 'But you will come to lunch with us, Miss Courtney – not often we have such a pretty girl at our gatherings.'

Van Vuuren gave her the short tour of the embassy and its art treasures, which ended in his office on the third floor.

'Now, my dear, we have some work for you.'

A pile of albums was stacked on his desk, each full of head-and-shoulder photographs of men and women. They sat side by side and Van Vuuren flicked through the pages, picking out the mug shots of the people she had met at the Lord Kitchener Hotel.

'You make it easier for us by knowing their names,' Van Vuuren remarked, and turned to a photograph of Phineas, the hotel receptionist.

'Yes, that's him,' Isabella confirmed, and Van Vuuren looked up his details in a separate ledger. 'Phineas Mophoso. Born 1941. Member of PAC. Convicted of public violence 16 May 1961. Violated bail conditions. Illegal emigration late 1961. Present location believed U.K.'

'Small fry,' Van Vuuren grunted, 'but small fry often shoal with big fish.' He offered to provide an embassy car to drive Isabella back to the Dorchester.

'Thank you, but I'll walk.'

She had tea alone at Fortnum & Masons and when she got back to the hotel Michael was frantic with worry.

'For heaven's sake, Mickey. I'm not a baby. I can look after myself. I just felt like exploring on my own.'

'Mater is giving a party for us at the Lord Kitchener this evening. She wants us there before six.'

'You mean Tara, not Mater – and the Lordy, not the Lord Kitchener. Don't be so *bourgeois* and colonial, Mickey darling.'

At least fifty people crowded into the residents' lounge of the Lordy for Tara's party, and she provided unlimited quantities of draught bitter and Spanish red wine to wash down the Irish cook's unforgettable snacks. Michael entered into the spirit of the occasion. He was at all times the centre of an arguing gesticulating group. Isabella backed herself into a corner of the lounge and with a remote and icy *hauteur* discouraged any familiar approach from the other guests, while at the same time memorizing their names and faces as Tara introduced them.

After the first hour the smoky claustrophobic atmosphere, and the volume of conversation lubricated by Tara's Spanish plonk, became oppressive and Isabella's eyes felt gritty and a dull ache started in her temples. Tara had disappeared and Michael was still enjoying himself.

'That's my patriotic duty for tonight,' she decided, and sidled towards the door taking care not to alert Michael to her departure.

As she passed the deserted reception desk, she heard voices from

576

behind the frosted glass door of Tara's tiny office, and she had an attack of conscience.

'I can't just go off without thanking Mater,' she decided. 'It was an awful party, but she went to a lot of trouble and I am one of the guests of honour.'

She slipped behind the desk, and was about to tap on the panel of the door when she heard her mother say, 'But, comrade, I didn't expect you to arrive tonight.' The words were commonplace, but the tone in which Tara said them was not. She was more than agitated – she was afraid, deadly afraid.

A man's voice replied, but it was so low and hoarse that Isabella could not catch the words, and then Tara said, 'But they are my own children. It's perfectly safe.'

This time the man's reply was sharper. 'Nothing is ever safe,' he said. 'They are also your husband's children, and your husband is a member of the fascist racist regime. We will leave now and return later after they have gone.'

Isabella acted instinctively. She darted back into the lobby and out through the glass front doors of the hotel. The narrow street was lined with parked vehicles, one of them a dark delivery van tall enough to screen her. She hid behind it.

After a few minutes, two men followed her out of the front entrance of the hotel. They both wore dark raincoats but their heads were bare. They set off briskly, walking side by side towards the Cromwell Road and as they came level with where she leaned against the side of the van, the street light lit their faces.

The man nearest to her was black, with a strong, resolute face, broad nose and thick African lips. His companion was white and much older. His flesh was pale as putty and had the same soft amorphous look. His hair was black and lank and lifeless. It hung on to his forehead, and his eyes were dark and fathomless as pools of coal tar – and Isabella understood why her mother had been afraid. This was a man who inspired fear.

Colonel Van Vuuren sat beside her at his desk with the pile of albums in front of them. 'He is a white man. That makes life a lot easier for all of us,' he said as he selected one of the albums.

'These are all white,' he explained. 'We have got them all in here. Even the ones safely behind bars, like Bram Fischer.'

She found his photograph on the third page.

'That's the one.'

'Are you sure?' Van Vuuren asked. 'It's not a very good photo.'

It must have been taken as he was climbing into a vehicle, for the background was a city street. He was glancing back, most of his body obscured by the open door of the vehicle, and movement had blurred his features slightly.

'Yes. That's him all right,' Isabella repeated. 'I could never mistake those eyes.'

Van Vuuren referred to the separate ledger. 'The photograph was taken in East Berlin by the American CIA two years ago. He is a wily bird, that's the only picture we have. His name is Joe Cicero. He is the secretary general of the South African Communist Party and a colonel in the Russian KGB. He is a chief of staff of the military wing of the banned ANC, the *Umkhonto we Sizwe*.' Van Vuuren smiled. 'And so, my dear, the big fish has arrived. Now we must try and identify his companion. That will not be so easy.'

It took almost two hours. Isabella paged through the albums slowly. When she finished one pile, Van Vuuren's assistent brought in another armful of albums and she began again. Van Vuuren sat patiently beside her, sending out for coffee and encouraging her with a smile and a word when she flagged.

'Yes.' Isabella straightened up at last. 'This is the one.'

'You have been wonderful. Thank you.' Van Vuuren reached for the ledger and turned to the *curriculum vitae* of the man in the photograph.

'Raleigh Tabaka,' he read out. 'Secretary of the Vaal branch of PAC and member of *Poqo*. Organizer of the attack on the Sharpeville police station. Disappeared three years ago, before he could be detained. Since then there have been rumours that he was seen in training camps in Morocco and East Germany. He is rated as a trained and dangerous terrorist. Two big fish together. Now, if we could just find what they are up to!'

*   *   *

Tara Courtney waited up long after her party had broken up. The last guests had staggered through the glass doors, and Michael had kissed her goodnight and gone off to try and pick up a late cruising taxi in the Cromwell Road.

Since first she had met him, Joe Cicero had been associated with danger and suffering and loss. There was always an aura of mystery and a passionless evil surrounding him. He terrified her. The man with him she had met for the first time that night. Joe Cicero had introduced him only as Raleigh, but Tara's heart had gone out to him immediately. Although he was much younger, he reminded her so strongly of her own Moses. He had the same smouldering intensity and compelling presence, the same dark majesty of bearing and command.

They came back a little after two in the morning, and Tara let them in and led them through to her own bedroom in the back area of the hotel.

'Raleigh will stay with you for the next two or three weeks. Then he will return to South Africa. You will provide everything he asks for, particularly the information.'

'Yes, comrade,' Tara whispered. Although she was the registered owner and licensed proprietress of the hotel, the money for the purchase had been provided by Joe Cicero and she took her orders directly from him.

'Raleigh is the nephew of Moses Gama,' Joe said, watching her carefully with those expressionless black eyes as she turned to the younger man.

'Oh Raleigh, I didn't realize. It is almost as though we are one family. Moses is the father of my son, Benjamin.'

'Yes,' Raleigh answered. 'I know that. This is the reason that I am able to give you the object of my mission to South Africa. Your dedication is proven and unquestioned. I am going back to Africa to free your husband and my uncle, Moses Gama, from the prison of the fascist racist Verwoerd regime to lead the democratic revolution of our people.'

Her joy dawned slowly with her understanding. Then she went to Raleigh Tabaka and as she embraced him she was weeping with happiness.

'I will give anything to help you succeed,' she whispered through her tears. 'Even my life.'

*　　*　　*

Jakobus Stander had only two classes on a Friday morning, and the last one ended at 11.30. He left the grounds of the University of the Witwatersrand immediately afterwards and caught the bus down to Hillbrow. It was a ride of only fifteen minutes and he reached his flat a little after midday.

The suitcase was still on the low coffee table where he had placed it the night before, after he had finished working on it. It was a cheap brown case made of imitation leather with a pressed metal lock.

He stood staring at it with pale topaz-coloured eyes. Except for the eyes, he was an unremarkable young man. Although he was tall, he was too thin and the grey flannel trousers hung loosely around his waist. His hair was long, flecked with dandruff, hanging over the back of his collar, and the elbows of his baggy brown corduroy jacket were patched with leather. Rather than a tie he wore a turtle-neck jersey with the collar rolled over. It was the self-consciously shabby uniform of the left-wing intellectual, adopted by even the Professor of the Department of Sociology in which Jakobus was a senior lecturer.

Without removing the jacket, he sat down on the narrow bed and stared at the suitcase.

'I am one of the only ones left,' he thought. 'It's all up to me now. They have taken Baruch and Randy and Berny – I am all alone.'

There had been less than fifty of them even in the best times. A small band of true patriots, champions of the proletariat, almost all of them white and young, members of the young liberals or students and faculty members involved in radical student politics at the English-speaking universities of Cape Town and the Witwatersrand. Kobus had been the only Afrikaner in their ranks.

At first they had called themselves the National Committee of Liberation, and their methods had been more sophisticated than *Umkhonto we Sizwe* and the Rivonia group. They had used dynamite and electrical timing devices, and their successes had been many and heartening. They had destroyed power substations and railway switching systems, even a reservoir dam, and in the triumphant mood of those early days they had restyled themselves the African Resistance Movement.

In the end they had been destroyed in exactly the same manner as Mandela and his Rivonia group, by the inefficiency of their own security and the inability of the members who were captured by the security police to withstand interrogation.

He was one of the only ones left, but he knew that his hours of freedom were numbered. The security police had taken Berny two days ago and by now he would have talked. Berny was not made of heroic stuff, a small pale and nervous creature, too soft-hearted for the cause. Jakobus had argued against his recruitment, but that was too late now. The bureau for state security had Berny, and Berny knew his name. There was very little time left, but still he procrastinated. He looked at his wristwatch. It was almost one o'clock. His mother would be home by now, preparing his father's lunch. He lifted the telephone.

Sarah Stander stood over the kitchen stove. She felt tired and dispirited, but she seemed always to be tired these days. The telephone rang and she turned down the hot plate of the stove, and wiped her hands on her apron as she went through to her husband's study.

The room was lined with shelves of dusty law books that had once been a promise of hope to her, a symbol of success and advancement, but now seemed rather to be the fetters that bound Roelf and her in penury and mediocrity.

580

She lifted the phone. 'Hello. This is Mevrou Stander.'

'Mama,' Jakobus replied, and she gave a little coo of joy.

'My boy – where are you?' But at his reply her spirits plunged again.

'In the flat in Johannesburg, Mama.' That was a thousand miles away, and her longing to see him devastated her.

'I hoped you were —'

'Mama,' he cut her off. 'I had to speak to you. I had to explain. Something terrible is going to happen. I wanted to tell you – I don't want you to be angry with me, I don't want you to hate me.'

'Never!' she cried. 'I love you too much, my boy —'

'I don't want Papa and you to feel bad. What I do is not your fault. Please understand and forgive me.'

'Kobus, my son, what is it? I don't understand what you are saying.'

'I can't tell you, Mama. Soon you will understand. I love you and Papa – please remember that.'

'Kobus,' she cried. 'Kobus!' but the earpiece clicked and then there was only the hum of a broken connection.

Frantically she rang the exchange and asked to be reconnected but it took fifteen minutes before the operator called her back.

'There is no reply from your Johannesburg number.'

Sarah was distraught. She roamed around her kitchen, the midday meal forgotten, twisting her apron in her fingers, trying desperately to think of some way of reaching her son. When her husband came in through the front door she rushed down the passageway and threw her arms around his neck, and she gabbled out her fears.

'Manie!' Roelf said. 'I will telephone him. He can send one of his men around to Kobus's flat.'

'Why didn't I think of that?' Sarah sobbed.

The secretary in Manfred's ministry told them he was not available and would not be in again until Monday morning.

'What will we do now?' Roelf was as worried as she was.

'Lothie.' Sarah brightened. 'He is in the police in Johannesburg. Ring Lothie, he will know what to do.'

*   *   *

Jakobus Stander broke the connection to his mother, and jumped to his feet. He knew he must act quickly and decisively now. Already he had wasted too much time, they would be coming for him soon.

He picked up the suitcase and left the flat, locking the door behind him. He rode down in the lift, still holding the heavy suitcase, even though the handle cut into his fingers. There were two girls in the lift with him. They ignored him and chattered to each other all the way down. He watched them surreptitiously. 'It may be you, he thought. 'It could be anybody.'

The girls barged out of the lift ahead of him, and he followed slowly, walking lopsidedly because of the weight of the brown suitcase.

He caught the bus at the corner and took the seat nearest the door, placing the suitcase on the seat beside him, but retaining his grip on the handle all the way.

The bus stopped outside the side entrance of the Johannesburg railway station, and Jakobus was the first passenger to alight. Lugging the suitcase, he started towards the station entrance, and then his steps began to drag and his mouth went dry with terror. There was a constable of the railway police at the entrance, and as Jakobus hesitated he looked directly at him. Jakobus wanted to drop the suitcase and run back to the bus which was pulling away behind him, but the press of other passengers bore him forward like a dead leaf in a stream.

He did not want to catch the constable's eye. He trudged forward head bowed, concentrating on the heels of the fat woman in white shoes just ahead of him. He looked up as he came level with the station portals, and the constable was walking away from him, his hands clasped lightly behind his back. Jakobus's legs felt rubbery and his relief was so intense that he thought he was going to be ill. He fought down his nausea and kept on going with the stream of commuters.

At the centre of the concourse under the high arched skylight of glass there was a goldfish pond surrounded by wooden benches. Although most of the benches were crowded with travellers snatching a few minutes' rest between trains or awaiting the arrival of friends, there was room for Jakobus at the end of one of them.

He sat down and placed the suitcase between his feet. He was sweating heavily and he had difficulty in breathing. Waves of nausea kept welling up from the pit of his guts and there was a bitter sick taste at the back of his throat.

He wiped his face with his handkerchief and kept swallowing hard until gradually he had control of himself again. Then he looked around him. The other benches were still crowded. In the centre of the one facing him there was a mother with two daughters. The youngest one was still in napkins, she sat on her mother's lap with a dummy in her mouth. The elder girl had skinny sun-browned legs and arms and frilly petticoats under her short skirt. She leaned against her mother's side and sucked a lollipop on a stick. Her mouth was dyed bright red by the sticky candy.

All around Jakobus passed a continual stream of humanity, coming and going down the broad staircase that led up to the street. Like columns of ants, they spread out to reach the separate platforms, and the loudspeakers boomed out information on arriving and departing trains, and the hiss and huff of escaping steam from the locomotives echoed against the high arches of glass above where Jakobus sat.

He looked down at the suitcase between his feet. He had drilled a needle hole through the imitation leather. A strand of piano wire emerged from the aperture, and he had fixed a brass curtain ring to the end of it, and taped the ring to the brown leather beside the handle.

Now he picked at the tape with his fingernail and peeled it away. He stuck his forefinger through the brass ring and gently pulled the wire taut. There was a muted click from the interior of the suitcase and he started guiltily and looked around him again. The little girl with the lollipop stuck in her cheek had been watching him. She gave him a sticky smile and shyly cuddled closer to her mother's side.

Using his heels and the back of his legs, Jakobus pushed the suitcase slowly under the bench on which he was seated. Then he stood up and walked briskly across to the men's toilets on the far side of the concourse. He stood in front of one of the porcelain urinals and checked his wristwatch. It was ten minutes after two. He zipped up his fly and walked out of the men's room.

The mother and the two little girls were still sitting where he had left them, and the brown suitcase lay under the bench opposite. As he passed the child recognized him and smiled again. He did not return the smile but went up the staircase into the street. He walked down to the Langham Hotel at the corner and went into the men's bar. He ordered a cold Castle beer and drank it slowly, standing at the bar, checking his wristwatch every few minutes. He wondered if the mother and the two little girls had left, or if they were still sitting on the bench.

The ferocity of the explosion shocked him. He was almost a block away but it knocked over his glass and the dregs of the beer ran across the bar top. There was consternation throughout the bar room. Men were swearing with surprise and astonishment and rushing to the door.

Jakobus followed them out into the street. The traffic had stopped, and people were swarming out of the buildings to block the pavements. From the station entrance a cloud of dust and smoke billowed and through it staggered vague shadowy figures, powdered with dust, their clothing hanging off them in rags. Somewhere a woman began to scream, and all around him there were shouted questions.

583

'What is it? What happened?'

Jakobus turned and walked away. He heard the sirens of the police cars and the fire engines coming closer, but he did not look back.

* * *

'No, *Tannie* Sarie, I haven't seen Kobus since we last met at Waterkloof.' Lothar De La Rey tried to be patient. The Standers were old friends of his parents, and he had spent many happy childhood holidays at the cottage on the Stander farm at the seaside. That was before *Oom* Roelf Stander had been forced to sell the farm. 'Yes, yes *Tannie*. I know, but Kobus and I live in different worlds now – I know how worried you must be. Yes, of course.'

Lothar was taking the call in his private office in the headquarters complex of Marshall Square, and he glanced at his wristwatch as he listened to Sarah Stander's plaintive voice. It was just before two o'clock.

'What time was it when he telephoned you?' Lothar asked, and listened to her reply. 'That was an hour ago. Where did he say he was speaking from? All right, *Tannie*, what is his address in Hillbrow?' He scribbled it on the pad in front of him. 'Now tell me, *Tannie*, what was it exactly he said. Something terrible and you must forgive him? Yes, that doesn't sound very good, I agree. Suicide? No, *Tannie* Sarie, I'm sure he didn't mean that, but I will send one of my men to check his flat, why don't you ring the university in the meantime?'

One of the other telephones on his desk squealed and he ignored it. 'What did they say at the university?' he asked. 'All right, *Tannie*, I will telephone you and *Oom* Roelf just as soon as I have any news.' By now all three of his telephones were shrilling, and Captain Lourens, his assistant, was signalling him frantically from the door of his office.

'Yes, I understand, *Tannie* Sarie. Yes, I promise I will telephone you. But I must ring off now.' Lothar replaced the receiver and looked up at Lourens.

'*Ja*, what is it, man?'

'An explosion at the main railway station. It looks like another bomb.'

Lothar jumped to his feet and snatched up his jacket. 'Casualties?' he demanded.

'There are bodies and blood all over the place.'

'The bloody swines,' Lothar said bitterly.

The street was cordoned off. They left the police car at the barrier and Lothar, who was in plain clothes, showed his identification and the sergeant saluted him. There were five ambulances parked outside the station entrance with their lights flashing.

At the head of the staircase leading down into the main concourse Lothar paused. The damage was terrible. The glass in the arched skylights had been blown out and it coated the marble floors, glittering like a field of ice crystals.

The restaurant had been turned into a first-aid station and the white-jacketed doctors and ambulance crews were at work. The stretcher-bearers were carrying their grisly loads up the staircase to the waiting vehicles.

The officer in charge of the investigation was a major from Marshall Square. He had his men searching the wreckage already, working methodically in an extended line across the concourse. He recognized Lothar and beckoned to him. The glass crunched under Lothar's feet as he crossed to join him.

'How many dead?' he asked without any preamble.

'We have been incredibly lucky, Colonel. About forty injured, mostly by flying glass, but only one dead.'

He reached down and pulled back the plastic sheet that was spread at his feet.

Under it lay a little girl in a short dress with a frilly lace petticoat. Both her legs and one arm had been blown away, and the dress was soaked with her blood.

'Her mother lost both eyes, and her little sister will lose one arm,' the major said, and Lothar saw that the child's face was miraculously unscathed. She seemed to be sleeping. Her mouth was bright red with sticky sugar and in her remaining hand she still clutched the stick of a half-eaten lollipop.

'Lourens,' Lothar said quietly to his assistant. 'Ring Records. Use the telephone in the restaurant. Tell them I want a computer run on my desk when I get back to the square. I want the name of every known white radical on the list. It had to be a white man in this section of the station.'

He watched Lourens cross the concourse and then he looked down at the tiny body under the plastic sheet.

'I'm going to get the bastard who did this,' he whispered. 'This one isn't going to get away.'

His staff were waiting for him when he got back to the office forty minutes later. They had already vetted the computerized list and checked the names of those in detention, in exile or those whose whereabouts could be assumed to be outside the Witwatersrand area.

There remained 396 suspects unaccounted for. They were listed in alphabetical order and it was almost four o'clock before they had worked down to the 'S' section. As Lothar folded over the last sheet of the print-out the name seemed to leap from the page at him:

STANDER, JAKOBUS PETRUS

In the same moment Sarah Stander's plaintive voice echoed in his ears.

'Stander,' he said crisply. 'This one is a new addition.' He had last checked the list twenty-four hours before. It was one of the most important tools of his trade, the names upon it so familiar that he could conjure up each face clearly in his mind's eye. Kobus' name had not been there on his last reading.

Captain Lourens picked up the internal telephone to Records, and spoke to the files clerk on the section, then he turned back to Lothar as he hung up the receiver.

'Stander's name comes from the interrogation of a member of the African Resistance Movement. Bernard Fisher. He was arrested on the fifth, two days ago. Stander is a lecturer at Wits University.'

'I know who he is.' Lothar strode out of the operations room into his private office and ripped the top sheet off his notepad. 'And I know where he is.' He drew the .38 police special from his shoulder holster and checked the load as he gave his orders. 'I want four units of the flying squad and a break-in team with flak jackets and shot-guns – and I want photographs of the bomb victims, the girl —'

The flat was on the fifth floor at the end of a long open gallery. Lothar placed men on every stairwell and both fire escapes, at the lift station and in the main lobby. He and Lourens went up with the break-in team, and they all moved stealthily into position.

With the police special cocked in his right hand, his back against the wall, clear of the door, he reached out and rang the bell.

There was no reply. He rang again, and they waited tensely. The silence drew out. Lothar reached out to ring a third time, when there were light hesitant footsteps beyond the glass panel door.

'Who is it?' a breathless voice called.

'Kobus – it's me, Lothie.'

'*Liewe Here!* Sweet God!' and the sound of running footsteps receded into the flat.

'Go!' said Lothar and the hammer man from the break-in team stepped up to the door with the ten-pound sledgehammer. The lock burst open at the first stroke and the door crashed back against its hinges.

Lothar was the first one in. The lounge was deserted and he ran straight through into the bedroom.

Behind him Lourens shouted, '*Pasop!* Look out! He might be armed,' But Lothar wanted to stop him reaching a window and jumping.

586

The bathroom door was locked and he heard running water beyond it. He took the door with his shoulder, and the panel splintered. His own momentum carried him on into the bathroom.

Jakobus was leaning over the wash basin, shaking tablets from a bottle into the palm of his hand and cramming them into his mouth. His cheeks bulged, and he was gagging and swallowing.

Lothar brought the barrel of the revolver down on the wrist that held the bottle, and the bottle shattered into the basin. He caught Jakobus by his long hair and forced him to his knees. He wedged open his jaws with thumb and forefinger and with the fingers of his other hand hooked the crushed damp porridge of tablets out of his mouth.

'I want an ambulance team with a stomach pump up here,' he yelled at Lourens. 'And get an analysis of that bottle – its label and contents.'

Jakobus was struggling and Lothar hit him open-handed, back and across the face. Jakobus whimpered and subsided, and Lothar thrust his forefinger deeply down his throat.

Gasping and choking and retching, Jakobus started struggling again, but Lothar held him easily. He worked his forefinger around in his throat, keeping on even when hot vomit spurted up over his hand. Satisfied at last he let Jakobus lie in a puddle of his own vomit while he rinsed his hands in the basin.

He dried his hands and seized Jakobus by the back of his shirt. He hauled him to his feet, dragged him through into the lounge and flung him into one of the armchairs.

Lourens and the forensic team were already working over the apartment.

'Did you get the photographs?' Lothar asked, and Lourens handed him a buff envelope.

Jakobus sat huddled in the chair. His shirt was fouled with vomit, and his nose and eyes were red and running. The corner of his mouth was torn where Lothar had forced it open, and he was trembling violently.

Lothar sorted through the contents of the envelope and then he laid a glossy black and white print on the coffee table in front of Jakobus.

Jakobus stared at it. It was a photograph of the truncated body of the child, nestled in a pool of her own blood with the lollipop in her hand. He began to weep. He sobbed and choked and turned his head away. Lothar moved around behind his chair and caught the back of his neck, forced his head back.

'Look at it!' he ordered.

'I didn't mean it,' Jakobus whispered brokenly. 'I didn't mean it to happen.'

587

The cold white fury faded from Lothar's brain, and he released Jakobus's head and stepped back from him uncertainly. Those were the words he had used. 'I didn't mean it to happen.' The exact words he had used as he had stood over the black boy with the dead girl's head cradled in his lap and the raw wounds running red into the dust of Sharpeville.

Suddenly Lothar felt weary and sickened. He wanted to go away by himself. Lourens could take over from here, but he braced himself to fight off the despair.

He laid his hand on Jakobus's shoulder, and the touch was strangely gentle and compassionate.

'*Ja*, Kobus, we never mean it to happen – but still they die. Now it is your turn, Kobus, your turn to die. Come, let's go.'

*   *   *

The arrest was made six hours after the bomb blast, and even the English press was fulsome in its praise of the efficiency of the police investigation. Every front page across the nation carried photographs of Colonel Lothar De La Rey.

Six weeks later in the Johannesburg Supreme Court, Jakobus Stander pleaded guilty to the charge of murder and was sentenced to death. Two weeks later his appeal was denied by the Appellate Division in Bloemfontein and sentence of death was confirmed. Lothar De La Rey's promotion to brigadier was announced within days of the Appellate Division's decision.

*   *   *

Raleigh Tabaka arrived in Cape Town while the Stander trial was still in progress. He came back the way he had left, as a crewman on a Liberian-registered tramp steamer.

His papers, although issued in the name of Goodwill Mhlazini, were genuine and he passed quickly through customs and immigration and with his bag over his shoulder walked up the foreshore to the main Cape Town railway station.

When he reached the Witwatersrand the following evening, he caught the bus out to Drake's Farm and went to the cottage where Victoria Gama was staying. Vicky opened the door and she had the child by the hand. There was the smell of cooking from the little kitchenette in the back.

She started violently as she saw him. 'Raleigh, come in quickly.' She drew him into the cottage and bolted the door.

'You shouldn't have come here. You know that I am banned.

588

They watch this place,' she told him as she went quickly to the windows and drew the curtains. Then she came back to where he stood in the centre of the room and studied him.

'You have changed,' she said softly. 'You are a man now.' The training and the discipline of the camps had left their mark. He stood straight and alert, and he seemed to exude an intensity and a force that reminded her of Moses Gama.

'He has become one of the lions,' she thought, and she asked, 'Why have you come here, Raleigh, and how can I help you?'

'I have come to free Moses Gama from the prison of the Boers – and I will tell you how you can help me.'

Victoria gave a little cry of joy, and clutched the child closer to her. 'Tell me what to do,' she pleaded.

He would not stay to eat the evening meal with Victoria, would not even sit down on one of the cheap deal chairs.

'When is your next visit to Moses?' he asked in a low but powerful voice.

'In eight days' time,' Victoria told him, and he nodded.

'Yes, I knew it was soon. That was part of our planning. Now, here is what you must do —'

When the prison launch ran out from Cape Town harbour, carrying Victoria and the child to exercise their six-monthly visiting rights, Raleigh Tabaka was on the deck of one of the crayfish trawlers that was moored alongside the repair wharf in the outer harbour. Raleigh was dressed like one of the trawlermen in a blue jersey, yellow plastic overalls and sea boots. He pretended to be working on the pile of crayfish pots on the foredeck, but he studied the ferry as it passed close alongside before it made the turn out through the entrance to the breakwater. He made out Victoria's regal figure in the stern. She was wearing her caftan in yellow, green and black, the colours of the ANC which always infuriated the jailers.

When the ferry had cleared the harbour and was set on course towards the low whale-backed profile of Robben Island far out in the bay, Raleigh walked back along the deck of the eighty-foot trawler to the wheelhouse.

The skipper of the trawler was a burly coloured man, dressed like Raleigh in jersey and waterproofs. Raleigh had met his son at the Lord Kitchener Hotel in London, an activist who had taken part in the Langa uprising and had fled the country immediately afterwards.

'Thank you, comrade,' Raleigh said, and the skipper came to the door of the wheelhouse and took the black pipe from between his even white teeth.

'Did you find out what you wanted?'

'Yes, comrade.'

'When will you need me for the next part?'

'Within ten days.' Raleigh replied.

'You must give me at least twenty-four hours' warning. I have to get a permit from the fisheries department to work in the bay.'

Raleigh nodded. 'I have planned for that.' He turned his head to look forward towards the trawler's bows. 'Is your boat strong enough?' he asked.

'You let me worry about that,' the skipper chuckled. 'A boat that can live in the South Atlantic winter gales is strong enough for anything.' He handed Raleigh the small canvas airline bag that contained his street clothes. 'We will meet again soon then, my friend?'

'You can be sure of that, comrade,' Raleigh said quietly and went up the gangplank on to the wharf.

Raleigh changed out of his trawlerman's gear in the public toilet near the harbour gates, and then went across to the carpark behind the customs house. Ramsami's old Toyota was parked up against the fence, and Raleigh climbed into the back seat.

Sammy Ramsami looked up from the copy of *The Cape Times* he was reading. He was a good-looking young Hindu lawyer who specialized in political cases. For the previous four years he had represented Vicky Gama in her never-ending legal battle with authority, and he had accompanied her from the Transvaal on this visit to her husband.

'Did you get what you wanted?' he asked, and Raleigh grunted noncommittally.

'I don't want to know what this is all about,' Sammy Ramsami said, and Raleigh smiled coldly.

'Don't worry, comrade, you will not be burdened with that knowledge.'

They did not speak again, not for the next four hours while they waited for Vicky to return from the island. She came at last, tall and stately in her brilliant caftan and turban, the child beside her, and the coloured stevedores working on the dock recognized her and cheered her as she passed.

She came to the Toyota and climbed into the front seat with the child on her lap.

'He is on another hunger strike,' she said. 'He has lost so much weight he looks like a skeleton.'

'That will make our work a lot easier,' said Sammy Ramsami and started the Toyota.

At nine o'clock the next morning Ramsami presented an urgent application to the Supreme Court for an order that a private physician be allowed access to the prisoner Moses Gama, and as grounds to support his application he presented the sworn affidavits of Victoria Dinizulu Gama and the local representative of the International Red Cross as to the deterioration in the prisoner's physical and mental condition.

The judge in chambers issued an order calling on the minister of justice to show cause within twenty-four hours why the access order should not be granted. The state attorney general opposed the application strenuously, but after listening to Mr Samuel Ramsami's submission, the judge granted the order.

The physician named in the order was Dr Chetty Abrahamji, the same man who had delivered Tara Courtney's son. He was a consulting physician at Groote Schuur Hospital. In company with the government district physician, Dr Abrahamji made the ferry trip out to Robben Island where for three hours he examined the prisoner in the prison clinic.

At the end of the examination he told the State doctor, 'I don't like this at all. The patient is very much under weight, complaining of indigestion and chronic constipation. I don't have to spell out what those presentations suggest.'

'Those symptoms have been caused by the fact that the prisoner has been on a hunger strike. In fact I have been considering attempting to force-feed.'

'No, Doctor,' Abrahamji interrupted him. 'I see the symptoms as much more significant. I am ordering a Cat Scan.'

'There are no facilities available for a Cat Scan on the island.'

'Then he will have to be moved to Groote Schuur for the examination.'

Once again the state attorney general opposed the order for the prisoner to be moved from Robben Island to Groote Schuur Hospital, but the judge was influenced by Dr Abrahamji's written report and impressed by his verbal evidence and once again granted the order.

Moses Gama was brought to the mainland amid the strictest conditions of secrecy and security. No previous warning of the move was given to any person outside those directly involved, to prevent the organization of any form of demonstration by liberal political bodies, and to frustrate the intense desire of the press to obtain a photograph of this patriarch of black aspirations.

It was necessary, however, to give Dr Abrahamji twenty-four hours' advance notice to enable him to reserve the use of the test equipment at the hospital, and the police moved into the area of the hospital the evening before the transfer. They cleared the corridors and rooms through which the prisoner would move of all but essential hospital staff, and searched them for explosives or any indication of illegal preparations.

From the public telephone booth in the main hospital administration block Dr Abrahamji rang Raleigh Tabaka at Molly Broadhurst's house in Pinelands.

'I am expecting company at two o'clock tomorrow afternoon,' he said simply.

'Your guest must not leave you until after nightfall,' Raleigh replied.

'That can be arranged,' Abrahamji agreed, and hung up.

The prison ferry came in through the harbour entrance at one o'clock in the afternoon. The deadlights of the cabin portholes were closed, and there were armed prison warders on deck, fore and aft, and their vigilance was apparent, even from where Raleigh was working on the foredeck of the trawler.

The ferry sailed across the harbour to 'A' berth, its usual mooring. There was an armoured prison van waiting on the dock, with four motor-cycle police in uniform and a grey police Land-Rover. Through the riot screens on the cab of the Land-Rover Raleigh could make out the shape of helmets and the short thick barrels of automatic shotguns held at port arms.

As the ferry touched the wharf, the prison van reversed up and the rear doors swung open. The armed warders seated on the padded benches in the body of the truck jumped down to meet the prisoner. Raleigh had just a glimpse of a tall gaunt figure in plain prison khaki uniform as he was hustled up the gangplank and into the waiting van, but even across the width of the harbour basin he could see that Moses Gama's hair was now pure silvery white, and that he was manacled at the wrists and that heavy leg-irons hampered his gait.

The doors of the van slammed shut. The motor-cycle escort closed in formation around it and the Land-Rover followed closely behind it as it sped away towards the main dock gates.

Raleigh left the trawler and Molly Broadhurst was waiting for him beyond the main gates. They drove up the lower slopes of Table Mountain to where the hospital stood, a massive complex of white walls and red clay tiles below the stone pines and open meadows of Rhodes Estate and the tall grey rock buttresses of the mountain itself. Raleigh made a careful note of the time required for the journey from the docks to the hospital.

They drove slowly up the busy road to the main entrance of the hospital. The police Land-Rover, motor-cycles and armoured van were lined up in the public carpark beyond the entrance to the out-patients section. The warders had doffed their riot helmets and were standing around the vehicles in relaxed attitudes.

'How will Abrahamji keep him there until dark?' Molly wanted to know.

'I did not ask,' Raleigh replied. 'I expect he will keep on demanding further tests, or will deliberately sabotage the machinery – I don't know.'

Raleigh turned the car in a circle in front of the main entrance and they drove back down the hill.

'You are sure there is no other way to leave the hospital grounds?' Raleigh asked.

'Quite sure,' Molly replied. 'The van must pass here. Drop me at the bus stop. It will be a long wait and at least I will have a bench to sit on.'

Raleigh pulled into the kerb. 'You have the number of the telephone on the dock, and coins?' She nodded.

'Where is your nearest telephone from here?' he insisted.

'I have checked it all carefully. There is a public phone booth at the corner.' She pointed. 'It will take two minutes for me to reach it, and if it is out of order or occupied, there is another telephone in the café across the street. I have already made friends with the proprietor.'

Raleigh left her at the bus stop and drove back to the centre of town. He left Molly's car in the side street they had agreed upon so that it would not be found at the docks or anywhere in the vicinity and he walked back down the Heerengracht showing his seaman's papers at the gate.

The skipper of the trawler was in the wheelhouse and he handed Raleigh a mug of heavily sweetened coffee which he sipped as they went over the final arrangements.

'Are my men ready?' Raleigh asked as he stood up, and the skipper shrugged. 'That is your business, not mine.'

They were in the bottom of the trawler's deep hold where the heat in the unventilated space was oppressive. Robert and Changi were stripped to vests and jogging shorts. They jumped up as Raleigh came down the ladder.

'So far it goes well,' Raleigh assured them. They were old companions from the PAC *Poqo* days, and Changi had been at Sharpeville on the terrible day that Amelia died.

'Are you ready?' Raleigh asked him.

'We can check,' Changi suggested. 'Once more will not hurt us.'

The inflatable Zodiac boat that stood on the floor of the hold was the 17-foot 6-inch model that could carry ten adults with ease. The fifty-horsepower Evinrude outboard motor could push it at thirty knots. The cover of the engine had been painted matt black.

The rig had been stolen by Robert and Changi working together from the yard of a boat dealer two days before, and could not be traced back to any of them.

593

'The engine?' Raleigh demanded.

'Robert has checked and serviced it.'

'I even changed the gear-box oil,' Robert agreed. 'She runs beautifully.'

'Tanks?'

'Both full,' Robert said. 'We have a range of a hundred miles or better.'

'Wet suits?'

'Check,' Changi said. 'And thermal blankets for the leader.'

'Tools?' Raleigh asked, and Changi opened the padded flotation bag and laid out the tools on the deck, checking each as Raleigh called them from his list.

'Good,' Raleigh agreed at last. 'You can rest now. Nothing more to do.'

Raleigh climbed up out of the hold. It was still too early. He glanced at his wristwatch. Not yet four o'clock, but he left the trawler and went down the dock to the public telephone booth at the end.

He telephoned directory enquiries and asked for a fictitious number in Johannesburg, just to make certain the line was in order. Then he sat on the edge of the wharf with his legs dangling and watched the seagulls squabbling over the offal and refuse that floated on the harbour waters.

It was fully dark by seven-forty but it was another twenty minutes before the telephone in the booth rang and Raleigh jumped up.

'They are on their way.' Molly's voice was soft and muffled.

'Thank you, comrade,' Raleigh said. 'Go home now.'

He hurried back down the wharf and the trawler skipper had seen him coming. As Raleigh jumped down on to the dock the two deckhands threw off the lines. The big caterpillar motor blustered and the trawler surged away from the dock and headed out through the entrance.

Raleigh swarmed down into the hold where Robert and Changi were already in their wet suits. They had Raleigh's suit laid out for him and they helped him into it.

'Ready?' one of the deckhands called down from above.

'Send it down,' Raleigh shouted back, and they watched the arm of the derrick swing out over the hold, silhouetted against the stars, and the line came down from the boom.

The three of them worked swiftly, hooking the Zodiac on, but before they had finished, the beat of the trawler's engine died away and the motion of the hull in the water changed as the vessel's way died and she began to drift.

Raleigh led them up the ladder on to the deck. The night was moonless, but the stars were bright and clear. The light breeze was from the south-east, so there was unlikely to be a change in this fair weather. All the trawler's navigational lights and the lights in the wheelhouse were extinguished.

Cape Town was ablaze with lights. The mountain was floodlit, a great ghostly silver hulk under the stars, while behind them the lights on Robben Island twinkled low on the black sea. Raleigh judged that they were about half-way between the city and the island.

The skipper was waiting for him on deck.

'We must move fast now,' he said.

Robert and Changi climbed into the Zodiac. Their wet suits were black, the rubber sides of the boat were black and the engine cover of the Evinrude was black. They would be almost invisible on the black waters.

'Thank you, comrade,' Raleigh said and offered the skipper his hand.

'*Amandla!*' said the skipper as he gripped it. 'Power!' and Raleigh took his place in the bows of the Zodiac.

The winch clattered and the Zodiac rose swaying, swung out over the side, and then fell swiftly to the surface of the water.

'Start up,' Raleigh instructed, and Robert whipped the starter cord and the engine fired and caught with the first pull.

'Cast off,' Raleigh ordered, and Changi unhooked the line from the boom, while Robert manoeuvred the Zodiac alongside the trawler and tied on to the light line from the rail. He let the engine idle for five minutes to warm it thoroughly and then cut it.

The two vessels lay silently linked together and the minutes passed torturously.

Suddenly the skipper called down. 'I have them in sight.'

'Are you certain?' Raleigh cupped his hands around his mouth to reply.

'I've seen that ferry every day of my life.' The skipper was leaning over the rail. 'Start your motor and cast off.'

The Evinrude roared into life and the Zodiac dropped back astern of the trawler. Now Raleigh could make out the ferry. It was coming almost directly towards them, both the green and red navigational lights showed.

The trawler moved forward, a wash of white water churning out from under her stern. She was still completely blacked out, and her speed built up rapidly. The skipper had assured Raleigh that she was capable of fourteen knots. She turned in a wide arc across the black surface and headed straight for the approaching ferry at speed.

Robert ran the Zodiac out to one side, and dropped back slightly, shearing off two hundred feet from the larger vessel.

The ferry held its course. Clearly it hadn't spotted the darkened ship bearing down out of the night. Raleigh stood up in the bows of the Zodiac steadying himself with two turns of the painter around his wrist and he watched the two vessels come together. The ferry was half the length of the steel-hulled trawler and it lay much lower in the water.

At the very last moment somebody on board the ferry shouted and then the bows of the trawler crashed into her, taking her just forward of the beam. Raleigh had warned the skipper not to damage the cabin and risk harming the occupants.

The trawler checked and the bows rose high as she trod the smaller vessel down, and then the ferry rolled over in a flurry of foam and breaking water. The trawler drove over her, broke free of her swamped hull, and went dashing away into the darkness. Within a hundred yards she had disappeared.

'The chains will pull him under,' Raleigh shouted. 'Work quickly!' He fitted his face plate over his mouth and nose.

Robert sent the Zodiac roaring alongside the sinking ferry. She had turned turtle and her bottom was painted with orange anti-fouling. Her lights were still burning beneath the water and there were three or four swimming warders thrashing around, trying to get a grip on the sides.

Raleigh and Changi, each carrying a short jemmy bar, slid over the side and dived under the trawler's submerged transom.

Raleigh jammed the point of the jemmy into the lock of the cabin door and with a single heave tore it away. The door slid back and a burst of trapped air exploded in silver bubbles around his head.

The cabin was flooded, but the lights were still burning, lighting the interior like a goldfish bowl, and a confusion of bodies, clad in the serge uniform of the prison service, were struggling and kicking and swirling around the cabin. Amongst them Raleigh picked out the khaki cotton drill tunic of a prisoner. He seized a handful of it and pulled Moses Gama clear.

Changi took Moses Gama's other arm and they swam him between them out from under the heaving transom and up to the surface. It had taken less than sixty seconds since the trawler had rammed, and Robert gunned the Zodiac up to them the moment they surfaced. He reached down and caught hold of Moses Gama's arm, the two men in the water heaved from under him and he rolled over the side of the Zodiac on to the floor boards.

Raleigh and Changi seized the loops of rope on the Zodiac's side to pull themselves up and the moment they were on board Robert gunned the Evinrude and they shot away from the foundering vessel. The splashing and cries of distress faded behind them as Robert turned the Zodiac back towards the shore. The long deserted stretch of Woodstock beach showed as a pale line of sand and surf in the starlight ahead.

Raleigh stripped off his face plate and leaned solicitously over the figure on the deck. He lifted him into a sitting position, and Moses Gama coughed painfully.

'I see you, my uncle,' Raleigh said softly.

'Raleigh?' Moses' voice was rough with the salt water he had swallowed. 'Is it you, Raleigh?'

'We will be ashore in ten minutes, my uncle.' Raleigh tucked one of the thermal blankets around Moses' shoulders. 'All the plans for your escape have been carefully laid. Everything's ready for you, my uncle. Soon now you will be where nobody can touch you.'

Robert ran the rubber inflatable in through the surf at full throttle and they shot up the sand, clear of the water. As they came to a standstill, they lifted Moses Gama out of the Zodiac and ran with him up the beach, carrying him between them so his chained feet barely touched the sand.

There was a small closed van parked amongst the dunes and Raleigh jerked the rear doors open and they lifted Moses into the back and laid him on the mattress that covered the floorboards. Changi jumped in beside him and Raleigh slammed the rear doors closed. Robert would take the Zodiac out and sink it.

Raleigh stripped off the jacket of his wet suit. The key to the van was on a loop of nylon line around his neck. He opened the driver's door and slid behind the wheel. The van was facing back along the track. The track joined the road that skirted the industrial area of Paarden Eiland and Raleigh drove sedately along it, towards the black township of Langa.

*   *   *

The official Cape Town residence of the minister of police was one of those clustered around the prime minister's residence at Groote Schuur. The cumbersome physical division of the legislative and executive arms of government between the cities of Cape Town and Pretoria made for costly duplications. During the annual session of parliament in Cape Town all the ministers and the entire diplomatic corps were forced to move down from Pretoria a thousand miles to the north, and official residences had to be maintained in both cities at enormous expense.

Manfred De La Rey's ministerial residence was an elegant Edwardian mansion set in acres of its own private lawns and gardens. As Roelf Stander parked his shabby little secondhand Morris in front of this imposing building, it seemed oddly out of place.

597

Sarah Stander had been desperately trying to arrange a private meeting with Manfred ever since her son had been convicted and sentenced to death. However, Manfred had been in Pretoria, or at his ranch in the Free State or opening a memorial to the women who had died in the British concentration camps during the Boer war, or addressing the National Party caucus, and therefore unable to see her.

Sarah had persisted, telephoning his office at parliament every day, telephoning Heidi at home and pleading with her, until at last Manfred had agreed to see her at seven o'clock in the morning before he left for parliament.

Sarah and Roelf had driven in the Morris from Stellenbosch, leaving before sun-up so as not to be late for the appointment. When the coloured butler showed them through to the dining-room, Manfred and Heidi were seated at the breakfast table.

Heidi sprang up and came to kiss Sarah's cheek.

'I am sorry we have not seen you for so long, Sarie.'

'Yes,' Sarah agreed bitterly. 'I also am sorry – but as you explained to me, Manie has been too busy for us.'

Manfred stood up from the head of the table. He was in his shirt-sleeves and the linen table napkin was tucked into the top of his dark suit trousers.

'Roelf,' he smiled, and they shook hands like old friends.

'Thank you for agreeing to see us, Manie,' Roelf said humbly. 'I know how busy you are these days.' The years had not been kind to Roelf Stander, he had greyed and shrunk and Manfred felt a secret satisfaction as he studied him.

'Sit down, Roelf.' Manfred led him to a place at the breakfast table. 'Heidi has ordered breakfast for you – will you start with porridge?'

He seated Roelf and then reluctantly turned back to Sarah. She was still standing beside Heidi.

'Hello Sarie,' he said. She had been such a pretty little thing. They had grown from childhood together. There were still the remains of that girlhood beauty in her eyes and the shape of her face. The memory of the love they had once shared rushed back to him, and he felt the sweet nostalgic yearning for his youth. He had a vivid image of her lying naked on a bed of pine needles in the forest high up on the slopes of the Hottentots Holland mountains on the day that they had become lovers.

He searched in his heart for a vestige of what he had felt for her then, but he found none. Any love that once had flowered between them had been smothered by the knowledge of her treachery. For more than two decades he had delayed his revenge, contenting himself with slowly undermining and reducing this woman to her present state, waiting for exactly the right moment to extract the final retribution. It had come – and he savoured the moment.

'Hello, Manie,' she whispered, and she thought, 'He has been so cruel. He has filled my life with pain that has been difficult to bear. Now all I ask from him is my son's life – surely he will not deny me that also.'

'So, why have you come to see me?' Manie asked, and Heidi led Sarah to a seat at the table. She took the silver tea-pot from the coloured servant and told him, 'Thank you, Gamat, you can leave us now. Please close the door.' And she poured steaming coffee into Sarah's cup.

'Yes, Sarie,' she agreed. 'Tell us why you have come to see us.'

'You know why I have come to you,' Sarah said. 'It is Kobus.'

A deathly stillness held them all over the slow passage of the seconds, and then Manfred sighed.

'*Ja,*' he said. 'Kobus. Why do you come to me about Kobus?'

'I want you to help him, Manie.'

'Kobus has been tried and convicted of a sickening act of senseless brutality,' Manfred said slowly. 'The highest court in the land has decreed that he must die on the gallows. How can I help Kobus?'

'The same way you helped that black terrorist, Moses Gama.' Sarah was pale and the coffee cup clattered as she tried to set it down on the saucer. 'You saved his life – now save the life of my son.'

'The state president exercised leniency in Gama's case —'

'No, Manie,' Sarah interrupted. 'It was you that changed it. I know – you have the power to save Kobus.'

'No.' He shook his head. 'I haven't got that sort of power. Kobus is a murderer. The worst kind of killer – one without compassion or remorse. I cannot help him.'

'You can. I know you can, Manie. Please, I beg of you, save my son.'

'I cannot.' Manfred's expression set. His mouth hardened into a straight unrelenting line. 'I will not.'

'You must, Manie. You have no choice – you must save him.'

'Why do you say that?' He was becoming angry. 'There is nothing I *must* do.'

'You must save him, Manie, because he is your son also. He is the child of our love, Manie, you have no choice. You must save him.'

Manfred sprang to his feet and placed his hand protectively on Heidi's shoulder. 'You come into my house and insult me and my wife.' His voice shook with the force of his anger. 'You come here with wild stories and accusations.'

599

Roelf Stander had sat quietly through it all, but now he lifted his head and spoke softly. 'It is true, Manie. Every word she tells you is true. I knew she was carrying your child when I married her. She told me frankly. You had deserted her – you had married Heidi and I loved her.'

'You know it is true,' Sarah whispered. 'You have always known, Manie. You cannot have looked into Kobus's eyes without knowing. Both your sons have your yellow eyes, Manie, Lothar and Kobus – both of them. You know he is your son.'

Manfred sank back on to his chair. In the silence Heidi reached across and deliberately took his hand. That reassuring touch seemed to rally him.

'Even if that were true, there is nothing I would do. No matter whose son he is, justice must run its course. A life for a life. He must pay the penalty for his deed.'

'Manie, please. You must help us —' Sarah was weeping now, and the tears at last spilled down her pale cheeks. She tried to throw herself at Manfred's feet, but Roelf caught her and held her. She struggled weakly in his arms, but he held her and looked at Manfred.

'In the name of our friendship, Manie, everything we have done and shared – won't you help us?' he pleaded.

'I am sorry for you, Roelf.' Manfred stood up again. 'You must take your wife home now.'

Roelf drew Sarah gently towards the door, but before they reached it Sarah pulled out of his hands and faced Manfred again.

'Why?' she cried in anguish. 'I know you can – why will you not help us?'

'Because of you White Sword failed,' he said softly. 'That is why I will not help you.'

She was struck dumb by the words, and Manfred turned to Roelf. 'Take her away now,' he ordered. 'I have finished with her at last.'

During the long journey back to Stellenbosch Sarah huddled in the passenger seat and sobbed brokenly. Only when Roelf parked the Morris outside their cottage did she straighten up, and her voice and her face were ruined with grief.

'I hate him,' she repeated. 'Oh God, how I hate him.'

*   *   *

'I spoke to David Abrahams this morning,' Isabella said, leaning forward in the saddle to pat the mare's neck so that her father couldn't see her face. 'He offered me a job at the Johannesburg office.'

600

'Correction,' said Shasa. 'You telephoned David and told him that Johannesburg needed a PRO at a salary of two thousand a month plus dress allowance plus five-day week and a company car – and I believe you even stipulated the make, Porsche 911, wasn't it? David called me the minute you hung up.'

'Oh Daddy, don't be so technical.' Isabella tossed her head defiantly. 'You wouldn't want me to dress in rags and starve up there would you?'

'What I would want is for you to stay here where I can keep an eye on you.' Shasa felt the leaden weight of impending loss in his chest as he looked at her. She was the spice of his life, and she had only been back from London a month or so. Now she wanted to be off again. His instinct was to fight to keep her, but Centaine had advised, 'Let them go gently, and there is a chance they will come back to you.'

'It isn't Siberia or the Outer Hebrides, Daddy. Do be practical. It's just up the road.'

'A thousand miles up the road,' Shasa agreed. 'And much closer to the rugby stadium at Loftus Versveld.'

'I don't know what you mean.' It was very seldom Shasa could catch her off-balance, and vindictively he relished her agitation.

'Rugby football,' he explained. 'Great sweaty oafs beating their bony heads together.'

She recovered splendidly. 'Pater, if this has anything to do with Lothar De La Rey, I would just like to point out that he is one of the greatest athletes of our time and the youngest brigadier in the history of the police force – and that he means absolutely nothing to me at all.'

'Your indifference is monumental. I am greatly relieved.'

'Does that mean I can accept David's job offer?'

Shasa sighed and the loneliness descended upon him like a winter's evening. 'How can I stop you, Bella?'

She let out a triumphant squeal and leaned out of the saddle to wrap those long tanned arms around his neck, and Shasa's stallion danced under him with aristocratic affront.

Isabella chattered merrily all the way back to the château.

'One thing I forgot to mention to David was a housing allowance. Flats are so awfully expensive in Joey's. I couldn't find anything suitable on the pittance he is paying me.' Shasa shook his head with admiration.

The grooms were waiting in the kitchen yard to take the horses, and still in their jodhpurs and riding boots they went through to the breakfast room with Isabella hanging lovingly on her father's arm.

Centaine was at the sideboard, helping herself to scrambled eggs

601

from the chafing dish. She was still in her gardening clothes and had been amongst her roses since dawn. Now she looked at Isabella inquiringly – and Isabella gave her a happy wink.

'Damn it,' Shasa intercepted the exchange. 'I've been set up. It's a conspiracy.'

'Of course, I told Nana first.' Isabella hugged his arm. 'I always start at the top.'

'When she was little I always threatened to hand her over to a policeman if she was naughty,' Centaine said complacently as she carried her plate to the breakfast table. 'I hope this policeman can cope with her.'

'He's not a policeman,' Isabella protested. 'He's a brigadier.'

Shasa ladled eggs and fried tomato on to his plate and went to his place at the head of the table. The morning paper was folded neatly on his side plate, and he shook it open at the front page as he sat down. The main news was the proposed meeting between the British prime minister, Harold Wilson, and Ian Smith to settle the Rhodesian issue. Now he saw that the suggested venue was a British warship at sea. Israel and Jordan were still disputing the Hebron Valley, and closer to home the Robben Island ferry had capsized during the night with the certain loss of at least two lives, while eight others were missing.

The telephone on the sideboard rang and Centaine looked up from buttering her toast. 'That will be Garry,' she said. 'He rang twice while you were out riding.'

'It's only eight o'clock in the morning,' Shasa protested, but he went to answer the telephone. 'Hello, Garry, where are you?'

Garry sounded surprised. 'At the office, of course.'

'What's the problem?'

'Swimming-pools,' Garry answered. 'I have a chance to get the franchise for a new process of making cheap swimming-pools. It's called Gunite. Holly and I saw it when we were on honeymoon in the States.'

'Good Lord, only the very rich can afford private swimming-pools,' Shasa protested.

'Everybody will buy my swimming-pools – every home in the country will have one by the time I'm finished.'

Garry's enthusiasm was infectious.

'It works, Pater. I've seen it, and the figures add up perfectly. Only trouble is I have to give an answer by noon today. Someone else is interested.'

'How much?' Shasa asked.

'Four million initially – that's for the franchise and plant. Another four million over two years for running costs, then we will be into profit.'

'All right,' Shasa said. 'Go ahead.'

'Thanks, Pater. Thanks for trusting me.'

'Well you haven't let me down yet. How is Holly?'

'She's fine. She's right here with me.'

'At the office at eight in the morning?' Shasa laughed.

'Of course.' Again Garry sounded surprised. 'We are a team. The swimming-pools were her idea.'

'Give her my love,' Shasa said and hung up.

As he went back to his seat, Centaine said, 'It's the prime minister's budget vote this afternoon. I thought I'd drop in.'

'It should be interesting,' Shasa agreed. 'I think Verwoerd is going to make a major policy speech about the country's international position. I have a committee meeting on armaments this morning, but why don't you meet me for lunch and you can listen to Doctor Henk's speech from the public gallery afterwards. I'll ask Tricia to get you a ticket.'

Tricia was waiting for him anxiously when an hour later Shasa walked into his parliamentary suite.

'The minister of police wants to see you most urgently, Mr Courtney. He asked me to let him know the moment you arrived. He said he'd come to your office.'

'Very well.' Shasa glanced at his appointment book on her desk. 'Let him know I'm here and then get a ticket for my mother for the public gallery this afternoon. Is there anything else?'

'Nothing important.' Tricia picked up the in-house telephone to ring the minister of police's office and then paused. 'There has been a strange woman ringing you this morning. She called three times. She wouldn't give her name and she asked for Squadron Leader Courtney. Funny, isn't it?'

'All right, let me know if she calls again.' Shasa was frowning as he went through to his own office. The use of his old airforce rank was strangely disquieting. He went to his desk and began work on the mail and the memoranda that Tricia had placed on his blotter, but almost immediately the buzzer rang on his intercom.

'Minister De La Rey is here, sir.'

'Ask him to come right in, Tricia.'

Shasa rose and went to meet Manfred, but as they shook hands he could see that Manfred was a worried man.

'Did you read the news report about the sinking of the ferry?' Manfred did not even return his greeting but came immediately to business.

'I noticed it, but didn't read it all.'

'Moses Gama was on the boat when it sank,' Manfred said.

'Good Lord.' Shasa glanced involuntarily at the ivory and gold-leaf altar chest which still stood against the wall of his office. 'Is he safe?'

'He is missing,' Manfred said. 'He may have drowned, or he may be alive. Either way we are in a very serious predicament.'

'Escaped?' Shasa asked.

'One of the survivors, a prison officer, says that there were two vessels at the accident scene, a large ship without lights that collided with the ferry and another smaller craft that arrived seconds after the ferry capsized. In the darkness it was impossible to see any details. It is a distinct possibility that Gama was spirited away.'

'If he drowned, we will be accused of murdering him,' Shasa said softly, 'with disastrous international repercussions.'

'And if he is at large, we will face the possibility of a popular uprising of the blacks similar to Langa and Sharpeville.'

'What are you doing about it?' Shasa asked.

'The entire police force is on full alert. One of our best men, my own son Lothar, is flying down from the Witwatersrand in an air-force jet to take charge of the investigation. He will land within the next few minutes. Navy divers are already attempting to salvage the wreckage of the ferry.'

For another ten minutes they discussed all the implications of the wreck, and then Manfred moved to the door.

'I will keep you informed as we get further news.'

Shasa followed him into the outer office, and as they passed Tricia's desk she stood up.

'Oh, Mr Courtney, that woman called again while you were with Minister De La Rey.' Manfred and Shasa both paused, and Tricia went on, 'She asked for Squadron Leader Courtney again, sir, and when I told her you were in conference, she said she had news for you about White Sword. She said you'd understand.'

'White Sword!' Shasa froze and stared at her. 'Did she leave a number?'

'No, sir, but she said that you must meet her at the Cape Town railway station at five-thirty this afternoon. Platform four.'

'How will I know who she is?'

'She says she knows you by sight. You are merely to wait on the platform, she will come to you.'

Shasa was so preoccupied with the message that he did not notice Manfred De La Rey's reaction to the code name 'White Sword'. All colour had drained from Manfred's craggy features, and his upper lip and jowls were covered by a sheen of perspiration. Without another word he turned and strode out into the corridor.

The name 'White Sword' kept plaguing Shasa all though the Armscor meeting. They were discussing the new air-to-ground missiles for the airforce but Shasa found it difficult to concentrate. He was

604

plagued by the memory of his grandfather, that good and gentle man whom Shasa had loved and who had been murdered by White Sword. His death had been one of the fiercest tragedies of his young life, and the rage that he had felt at the brutal killing came back to him afresh.

'White Sword,' he thought. 'If I can find out who you are, even after all these years, you will pay, and the interest will be more onerous for the time the debt has stood.'

* * *

Manfred De La Rey went directly to his office at the end of the corridor after he had left Shasa. His secretary spoke to him as he passed her desk but he did not seem to hear her.

He locked the door to his own office, but did not sit at the massive mahogany desk. He prowled the floor restlessly, his eyes unseeing and his heavy jaws chewing like a bulldog with a bone. He took the handkerchief from his jacket pocket and wiped his chin and then paused to examine his face in the wall mirror behind his desk. He was so pale that his cheeks had a bluish sheen, and his eyes were savage as those of a wounded leopard caught in a trap.

'White Sword,' he whispered aloud. It was twenty-five years since he had used that code name, but he remembered standing on the bridge of the German U-boat, coming in towards the land in darkness, with his hair and great bushy beard dyed black, staring out at the signal fires on the beach where Roelf Stander waited for him.

Roelf Stander had been with him through all the dangerous days and the wild endeavours. They had planned many of their operations in the kitchen of the Stander cottage in the little village of Stellenbosch. It was there in that kitchen that he had given them the details of the action that would be the signal for the glorious uprising of Afrikaner patriots. And at all those meetings Sarah Stander had been present, a quiet unobtrusive presence, serving coffee and food, never speaking – but listening. It was only many years later that Manfred had been able to guess at how well she had listened.

In 1948, when the Afrikaners had at last won at the ballot box the power which they had failed to seize at the point of the sword, Manfred's hard and loyal work had been rewarded with a deputy minister's post in the department of justice.

One of his first acts had been to send for the files of the unsolved attempt on the life of Jan Smuts, and the murder of Sir Garrick Courtney. Before he destroyed the files he read them through carefully, and he learned that they had been betrayed. There had been a traitor in their gallant band of patriots – a woman who had tele-

605

phoned the Smuts police officers to warn them of the assassination.

He had guessed at the woman's identity, but had never extracted his full retribution, waiting for the moment to ripen, savouring the thought of revenge over the decades, watching the traitor's misery, watching her growing old and bitter, while frustrating her husband's efforts to succeed in law and politics, in the guise of mentor and adviser, steering him into folly and disaster until Roelf Stander had lost all his sustenance, his property and his will to carry on. All that time Manfred had waited for the perfect moment for the final revenge stroke – and at last it had arrived. Sarah Stander had come to him to plead for the life of the bastard he had placed in her womb – and he had denied her. The pleasure of it had been exquisite, made more poignant by the years he had waited for it.

Now the woman had turned vindictive. He had not anticipated that. He had expected the blow to break and destroy her. Only the greatest good fortune had given him forewarning of this new betrayal she planned.

He turned from the mirror and sat down at his desk. He reached determinedly for the telephone and told his secretary, 'I want Colonel Bester in the bureau for state security.'

Bester was one of his most trusted officers.

'Bester,' he barked. 'I want a detention order drawn up urgently. I will sign it myself, and I want it executed immediately.'

'Yes, Minister. Can you give me the name of the detainee?'

'Sarah Stander,' Manfred said. 'Her address is 16 Eike Laan, Stellenbosch. If the arresting officers cannot find her there, she should be on platform four of the Cape Town railway station at five-thirty p.m. this afternoon. The woman must speak to no one before she is arrested – your men must make certain of that.'

As Manfred hung up he smiled grimly. Under the law he had the power to arrest and detain any persons for ninety days, and to hold that person completely *incommunicado*. A great deal could happen in ninety days. Things could change, a person might even die. It was all taken care of. The woman could cause no further trouble.

The telephone on his desk rang, and Manfred snatched it up, expecting it to be Bester again.

'Yes, what is it?'

'Pa, it's me – Lothie.'

'Yes, Lothie. Where are you?'

'Caledon Square. I landed twenty minutes ago, and I have taken over the investigation. There is news, Pa. The divers have found the ferry. There is no sign of the prisoner's body but the cabin door has been forced open. We must assume that he escaped. Worse than that, somebody engineered his escape.'

'Find him,' Manfred said softly. 'You must find Moses Gama. If we don't, the consequences could be disastrous.'

'I know,' Lothar said. 'We will find him. We have to find him.'

*   *   *

Centaine refused to eat the food in the parliamentary dining-room. 'It's not that I am fussy, *chéri*, in the desert I ate live locusts and meat that had lain four days in the sun, but —' She and Shasa walked down through the gardens, across the top end of town to the Café Royal on Greenmarket Square, where the first oysters of the season had arrived from Knysna lagoon.

Centaine sprinkled lemon juice and tabasco sauce, scooped a gently pulsating mouthful from the half shell and sighed with pleasure.

'And now, *chéri*,' she dabbed the juice from her lips, 'tell me why you are so far away that you do not laugh at even my best efforts.'

'I'm sorry, Mater.' Shasa signalled to the waiter to top up his champagne glass. 'I had a strange phone call this morning – and I haven't been able to concentrate on anything else. Do you remember White Sword?'

'How can you ask?' Centaine laid down her fork. 'Sir Garry was more dear to me than my own father. Tell me all about it.'

They spoke of nothing else for the rest of the lunch, exploring together ancient memories of that terrible day on which a noble and generous man had died, a man who had been precious to them both.

At last Shasa called for the bill. 'It's half past one already. We will have to hurry to reach the House before it begins. I don't want to miss any part of Verwoerd's speech.'

At sixty-six years of age Centaine was still active and agile, and Shasa was not forced to moderate his stride for her. They were still talking animatedly as they passed St George's Cathedral and turned into the gardens.

Ahead of them two men sat on one of the park benches, and there was something about them that caught Shasa's attention even at a distance of a hundred yards. The taller of the pair was a swarthy-complexioned man who wore the uniform of a parliamentary messenger. He sat very stiffly upright and stared straight ahead of him with a fixed expression.

The man beside him was also dark-haired but his face was colour-less as putty, the dead black hair fell forward on to his forehead. He was leaning close to the parliamentary messenger, speaking into his ear as though imparting a secret, but the messenger's face was ex-pressionless and he showed not the least reaction to the other man's words.

As they came level with the bench, Shasa leaned forward to see

607

past Centaine, and at less than five paces looked directly into the pale face of the smaller of the men. His eyes were black and implacable as pools of liquid tar, but as Shasa studied him, the man deliberately turned his face away. Yet his lips kept moving, talking so softly to the man in the parliamentary uniform that Shasa could not catch even a murmur of his voice.

Centaine tugged at his sleeve. '*Chéri*, you are not listening to me.'

'I'm sorry, Mater,' Shasa apologized absentmindedly.

'I wonder why this woman chose the railway station,' Centaine repeated.

'I suppose she feels safer in a public place,' Shasa hazarded, and glanced back over his shoulder. The two men were still on the bench, but even in his preoccupation with other things, the passionless malevolence that Shasa had seen in that tar-black gaze made him shiver as though an icy wind had blown upon the back of his neck.

As they turned into the lane that led to the massive edifice of parliament, Shasa felt suddenly confused and uncertain. There was too much happening all around him over which he had no control. It was a sensation to which he was not accustomed.

*   *   *

Joe Cicero whispered the formula softly, 'You can feel the worm in your belly.'

'Yes,' the man beside him replied, staring straight ahead. Only his lips moved as he made the reply, 'I can feel the worm.'

'The worm asks if you have the knife.'

'Yes, I have the knife,' said the man. His father had been a Greek and he had been born illegitimate in Portuguese Mozambique of a Mulatto woman. His mixed blood was not apparent. It seemed merely as though he was of Mediterranean extraction. Only Europeans were employed as messengers in the South African parliament.

'You can feel the worm in your belly,' Joe Cicero reinforced the man's conditioning.

'Yes, I can feel the worm.'

Eight times in the past few years he had been in mental institutions. It was while he was in the last of these that he had been selected and the conditioning of his mind accomplished.

'The worm asks if you know where to find the devil,' Joe Cicero told him. The man's name was Demetrio Tsafendas and he had been introduced into South Africa the previous year, once his conditioning was completed.

'Yes,' said Tsafendas. 'I know where to find the devil.'

'The worm in your belly orders you to go straight to where the devil is,' Joe Cicero said softly. 'The worm in your belly orders you

608

to kill the devil.' Tsafendas stood up. He moved like an automaton. 'The worm orders you to go now!'

Tsafendas started towards the parliament building with an even unhurried tread.

Joe Cicero watched him go. It was done. All the pieces had been placed with great care. At last the first boulder had started to roll down the hillside. It would gather others as it built up speed and momentum. Soon it would be a mighty avalanche and the shape of the mountain would be changed for ever.

Joe Cicero stood up and walked away.

* * *

The first person Shasa saw as he and Centaine walked up the front steps to the parliament entrance was Kitty Godolphin and his heart surged with excitement and unexpected pleasure. He hadn't seen her since that illicit interlude in the south of France eighteen months before. Shasa had chartered a luxury yacht and they had cruised as far as Capri. When they parted, she had promised to write – but she never kept her promises, and here she was again with no warning, smiling that sweet girlish smile with the devilment in her eyes, coming to greet him as innocently and naturally as though their last kiss had been hours before.

'What are you doing here?' he demanded without any preliminaries, and Kitty said to Centaine,

'Hello, Mrs Courtney. How did such a nice cultured lady ever end up with such an ill-mannered son?'

Centaine laughed, she liked Kitty. Shasa thought that it was a case of kindred spirits. Kitty explained, 'I was in Rhodesia to get a profile on Ian Smithy before he meets Harold Wilson, and I made a side trip for the speech that Verwoerd is giving today, and of course to visit with you.'

They chatted for a few minutes, then Centaine excused herself. 'I must get a good seat in the gallery.'

As she moved away Shasa asked Kitty softly, 'When can I see you?'

'This evening?' Kitty suggested.

'Yes – oh no, damn it.' He remembered his rendezvous with the White Sword informer. 'Where are you staying?'

'The Nellie as usual.'

'Can I call you there later?'

'Sure,' she smiled. 'Unless I get any better offers.'

'You little bitch! Why don't you marry me?'

'I'm too good for you, buster.' It had become one of their stock jokes. 'But I don't mind an order of small beer and chips on the side. See you later.'

Shasa watched her climb the staircase towards the press gallery. Over all the years he had known her, she seemed not to have aged a day. She still had the body of a girl, and the light spring of youth in her step. He pushed back the sudden cold gloom of loneliness that threatened to engulf him and walked into the chamber.

The benches were filling. Shasa saw that the prime minister was in his seat at the head of the government benches. He was talking to Frank Waring, the minister of sport, and the only other Englishman in the cabinet.

Verwoerd looked fit and vigorous. It seemed impossible that he had taken two revolver bullets through his skull and had come back with such power to dominate his own party and the entire chamber this way. He seemed to have an infinite capacity for survival and, of course, Shasa grinned cynically, the luck of the devil himself.

Shasa started towards his own seat, and Manfred De La Rey jumped up and came to intercept him.

He seized Shasa's arm and leaned close to him. 'The divers have raised the ferry. Gama's body is not in it and the door to the cabin has been forced. It looks as though the bastard has got clean away. But we have every exit from the country guarded and my men will get him. He cannot get away. I think the prime minister is going to make the announcement of his disappearance during his speech this afternoon.'

Shasa and Manfred began walking towards their seats on the front bench, when somebody bumped so roughly against Shasa that he exclaimed and glanced around. It was the uniformed messenger that Shasa had noticed on the park bench.

'Be careful, fellow,' Shasa snapped at him as he recovered his balance, but the man did not seem to hear.

Although his expression was vacant and his eyes staring and unseeing, the messenger walked with a quick determined step, brushing past Manfred and heading towards the opposition benches on the left side of the Speaker's throne.

'Damned rude,' Shasa said, pausing to watch him.

Suddenly the messenger seemed to change his mind, he veered across the chamber and hurried towards where Dr Verwoerd was sitting. The prime minister saw him coming and looked up expectantly, supposing that the man had a message for him. Nobody else in the chamber seemed to be taking any notice of the messenger's erratic behaviour, but Shasa was watching with puzzlement.

As the messenger stood over Dr Verwoerd, he swept his dark uniform jacket open and Shasa saw the silver flash of steel.

'Good Christ!' he exclaimed. 'He's got a knife.'

The messenger lifted the blade and struck once, and strangely the

610

prime minister was smiling, as though he did not realize what was happening. The blade came free and the silver was misted pink with blood.

Shasa started forward, but Manfred still had hold of his arm. 'The Manchurian Candidate,' he hissed and Shasa froze.

Standing over the prime minister, the assassin struck again and then again. With each blow the blood spurted down his white shirt front and Dr Verwoerd lifted his hands in a pathetic gesture of appeal.

At last the men closest to him realized what was happening and they leapt upon the assailant. A knot of struggling men swarmed over him, but the man was fighting back with a kind of demonic strength.

'Where is the Devil?' he shouted wildly. 'I'll get the Devil.'

They bore him to the green carpet and pinned him there.

Dr Verwoerd still sat in his seat staring down at his own chest from which the bright flood poured. Then he pulled the lapels of his jacket closed as though to hide the terrible sight of his own blood, and with a sigh slid forward and crumpled on to the carpeted floor of the chamber.

Shasa and Manfred De La Rey were in Shasa's parliamentary office when Tricia brought the news through.

'Gentlemen, the party whip has just telephoned. Dr Verwoerd has been declared dead on arrival at the Volks Hospital.'

Shasa went to the liquor cabinet behind his desk and poured two glasses of cognac.

They watched each other's eyes as they drank silently, and then Shasa lowered his glass and said, 'We must start at once to draw up a list of those we can rely on to support you. I think John Vorster is the man you will have to beat for the premiership, and his people will already be busy.'

They worked together through the afternoon preparing their lists, placing ticks and crosses and queries against the names. Telephoning, wheedling and extorting, arranging meetings, making promises and commitments, trading and compromising, and as the afternoon wore on a stream of important visitors, allies and potential allies, passed through Shasa's suite.

While they worked, Shasa watched Manfred, and wondered again how fate had chosen such strange travelling companions as they were. It seemed that they had nothing in common except that one most vital trait – burning unrelenting ambition and hunger for power.

Well, it was at their fingertips now, almost within their grasp, and Manfred was a man possessed. The effect of his enormous force of character was apparent on the men who came up to Shasa's office suite. One by one they were swept along by it, and one by one they swore their allegiance to him.

Slowly it dawned upon Shasa that it was no longer a possibility – or even a probability. They were going to win. He knew in his guts and his heart. It was theirs – the premiership and the presidency between them. They were going to win.

In the heady excitement of it all the afternoon passed swiftly, the grandfather clock in the corner of Shasa's office chimed the hours softly, such a familiar sound that he hardly noticed it until it struck five and he started and jumped to his feet, confirming the time with his wristwatch.

'It's five o'clock.' He started towards the door.

'Where are you going? I need you here,' Manfred called after him. 'Come back, Shasa.'

'I'll be back,' Shasa answered, and ran into the outer office.

There were men waiting there, important men. They stood up to greet him, and Tricia called, 'Mr Courtney —'

'Not now.' Shasa ran past them. 'I'll be back soon.'

It would be quicker on foot than trying to take the Jaguar through the five o'clock rush-hour traffic, and Shasa began to run.

He realized that the woman informer was so nervous and afraid that she would probably not linger at the rendezvous. He had to get there before the appointed time. As he ran he reviled himself for having forgotten such an important appointment, but it was all confusion and uncertainty.

He raced down the sidewalk, crowded with office workers relieved of the tedium of their day who poured out of the buildings. Shasa pushed and shoved, and weaved and ducked. Some of those he barged into shouted angrily after him.

He sprinted through the columns of slowly moving vehicles, and ran into the Adderley Street entrance of the railway station. The clock above the main concourse stood at five thirty-seven. He was already late, and platform four was at the far end of the building.

Wildly he raced down the concourse, and barged on to the quay. He slowed to a hurried walk, and made his way down the platform, examining the faces of the commuters waiting there. They stared back at him incuriously, and he glanced up at the platform clock: five-forty. Ten minutes late. She had come and gone. He had missed her.

He stood in the centre of the platform and looked despairingly around him, not certain what to do next. Overhead the public address system squawked, 'Train from Stellenbosch and the Cape Flats arriving Platform Four.'

That was it, of course. Shasa felt a vast relief. The train was late.

She must be on the train, that was why she had chosen this place and time.

Shasa craned his head anxiously as the carriages rumbled slowly into the platform and, with a squeal and hiss of vacuum brakes, came to a halt. The doors were thrown open and passengers spewed out of them, beginning to move in a solid column towards the platform exit.

Shasa jumped up on the nearest bench, the better to see and to be seen.

'Mr Courtney.' A woman's voice. Her voice – he recognized it, even after all the years. 'Mr Courtney.'

He stood on tiptoe, trying to see over the heads of the passengers.

'Mr Courtney!' There she was, caught up in the crowd, trying to push her way through to him, and waving frantically to attract his attention.

He recognized her instantly. The shock immobilized him for a few seconds as he stared at her. It was the Stander woman, the one he had met briefly at Manfred's holiday cottage when he had flown there to make the cannery deal with him. That was years ago, but he remembered that she had called him Squadron Leader. He should have pieced it together at that time. How foolish and unperceptive he had been. Shasa was still standing on the bench staring at her, when suddenly something else caught his attention.

Two men were roughly pushing their way through the crowds of passengers. Two big men in dark ill-fitting suits and the fedora hats that were somehow the mark of the plain-clothes security police. Clearly they were making for the Stander woman.

At the same moment as Shasa, she saw the two detectives and her face went white with terror.

'Mr Courtney!' she screamed. 'Quickly – they are after me.' She broke out of the crowd and began to run towards Shasa. 'Hurry, please hurry.'

Shasa jumped down from the bench and ran to meet her, but there was an old woman carrying an armful of parcels in his way. He almost knocked her down, and in the moments it took to untangle himself, the two detectives had caught up with Sarah Stander, and seized her from either side.

'Please!' She gave a despairing scream, then with wild, improbable strength broke free of her captors, and ran the last few paces to Shasa.

'Here!' She thrust an envelope into Shasa's hand. 'Here it is.'

The two security officers had recovered swiftly and bounded after her. One of them seized both her arms from behind and dragged her away. The other came to confront Shasa.

'We are police officers. We have a warrant for the arrest of the woman.' He was panting with his efforts. 'She gave something to you. I saw it. You must hand it over to me.'

'My good man!' Shasa drew himself up and gave the detective his most haughty stare. 'Do you have any idea just who you are speaking to?'

'Minister Courtney!' The man recognized him then, and his confusion was comic. 'I'm sorry, sir. I didn't know —'

'What is your name, rank and serial number?' Shasa snapped.

'Lieutenant Van Outshoorn No. 138643.' Instinctively the man stood to attention.

'You can be sure you will hear more of this, Lieutenant,' Shasa warned him frostily. 'Now carry on with your other duties.' Shasa turned on his heel and strode away down the platform, tucking the envelope into his inner pocket, leaving the detective staring after him in dismay.

He did not open the envelope until he reached his office again. Tricia was still waiting for him.

'I was so worried when you ran out like that,' she cried. Good, loyal Tricia.

'It's all right,' he reassured her. 'It all worked out fine. Where is Minister De La Rey?'

'He left soon after you, sir. He said he would be at home at Groote Schuur. You could reach him there if you needed him.'

'Thank you, Tricia. You may go home now.'

Shasa went through to his own office and locked the door. He went to his desk and sat down in his studded leather chair. He took the envelope from his inner pocket and laid it in front of him on the desk blotter, and he studied it.

It was of cheap coarse paper, and his name was written in a round girlish hand. The ink had smeared and run.

'Meneer Courtney.'

Shasa was suddenly reluctant to touch it again. He had a premonition of some terrible revelation which would turn the even tenor of his existence into strife and turmoil.

He picked up the Georgian silver paper knife from his desk set and tested the point with his thumb. He turned the envelope over and slid the point of the knife under the flap. The envelope contained a sheet of ruled notepaper with a single line of writing in the same girlish script.

Shasa stared at it. There was no sense of shock. Deep in his subconscious he must have known the truth all along. It was the eyes, of course, the yellow topaz eyes of White Sword that had stared into his own on the day his grandfather died.

There was not even a moment of doubt, no twinge of incredulity.

614

He had even seen the scar, the ancient gun-shot wound in Manfred's body, the mark of the bullet he had fired at White Sword and every other detail fitted perfectly.

'Manfred De La Rey is White Sword.'

From the moment they had first met that childhood day upon the fishing jetty at Walvis Bay, the fates had stalked them, driving them inexorably towards their destiny.

'We were born to destroy each other,' Shasa said softly, and reached for the telephone.

It rang three times before it was answered.

'De La Rey.'

'It's me,' Shasa said.

'*Ja*. I have been waiting.' Manfred's voice was weary and resigned, in bitter contrast to the powerful tones in which he had exhorted and rallied his supporters just a short while before. 'The woman reached you. My men have informed me.'

'The woman must be set free,' Shasa told him.

'It has been done already. On my orders.'

'We must meet.'

'*Ja*. It is necessary.'

'Where?' Shasa asked. 'When?'

'I will come to Weltevreden,' Manfred said, and Shasa was taken too much by surprise to respond. 'But there is one condition.'

'What is your condition?' Shasa asked warily.

'Your mother must be there when we meet.'

'My mother?' This time Shasa could not contain his amazement.

'Yes, your mother – Centaine Courtney.'

'I don't understand – what has my mother got to do with this business?'

'Everything,' said Manfred heavily. 'She has everything to do with it.'

*   *   *

When Kitty Godolphin got back to her suite that evening, she was in a mood of jubilation. Under her direction, Hank's camera had captured the dramatic moments as the blood-stained body of Dr Verwoerd was carried from the chamber to the waiting ambulance, and she had recorded the panic and confusion, the spontaneous unrehearsed words and expressions of his friends and his bitter enemies.

The moment she entered the suite, she booked a call through to her news editor at NABS in New York to warn him of the priceless footage she had obtained. Then she poured herself a gin and tonic and sat impatiently beside the telephone waiting for her call to come through.

She lifted it as it rang.

'Kitty Godolphin,' she said.

'Miss Godolphin.' A strange voice, speaking with a deep melodious African accent, greeted her. 'Moses Gama sends you his greetings.'

'Moses Gama is serving a life sentence in a high security prison,' Kitty replied brusquely. 'Don't waste my time, please.'

'Last night Moses Gama was rescued by warriors of the *Umkhonto we Sizwe* from the Robben Island prison ferry,' said the voice, and Kitty felt the flesh of her cheeks and lips go numb with the shock of it. She had read the reports of the ferry sinking. 'Moses Gama is in a safe place. He wishes to speak to the world through you. If you agree to meet him, you will be allowed to use your camera to record his message.'

For a full three seconds she could not answer. Her voice had failed her but her mind was racing. 'This is the big one,' she thought. 'This is the one that comes only once in a lifetime of work and striving.' She cleared her throat and said, 'I will come.'

'A dark blue van will arrive at the ballroom entrance to the hotel in ten minutes from now. The driver will flick his lights twice. You are to enter the rear doors of the van immediately, without speaking to any person.'

The vehicle was a small Toyota delivery van, and Kitty and Hank with the sound and camera equipment were cramped in the interior so that it was difficult to move, but Kitty crawled forward until she could speak to the driver.

'Where are we going?'

The driver glanced at her in the rear-view mirror. He was a young black man of striking appearance, not handsome but with a powerful African face.

'We are going into the townships. There will be police patrols and road-blocks. The police are everywhere searching for Moses Gama. It will be dangerous, so you must do exactly as I tell you.'

For almost an hour they were in the van, driving through darkened back streets, sometimes stopping and waiting in silence until a shadowy figure came out of the night to whisper a few words to the driver of the van, then going on again until at last they parked for the last time.

'From here we walk,' their guide told them, and led them down the alleys and secret routes of the gangs and comrades, slipping past the rows of township cottages, twice hiding while police Land-Rovers cruised past, and finally entering the back door of one of the thousands of identical undistinguished cottages.

616

Moses Gama sat at a table in the tiny back kitchen. Kitty recognized him instantly although his hair was now almost completely silver and his great frame was skeletally wasted. He wore a white open-neck shirt and dark blue slacks, and as he rose to greet her, she saw that though he had aged and his body was ravaged, the commanding presence and his messianic dark gaze were as powerful as when she had first met him.

'I am grateful that you have come,' he told her gravely. 'But we have very little time. The fascist police follow closely as a pack of wolves. I have to leave here within a short while.'

Hank was already at work, setting up his camera and lights, and he nodded to Kitty. She saw that the gritty reality of the surroundings, the bare walls and plain unadorned wooden furniture would add drama to the setting, and Moses' silver hair and enfeebled condition would touch the hearts of her audience.

She had prepared a few questions in her mind, but they were unnecessary. Moses Gama looked at the camera and spoke with a sincerity and depth that was devastating.

'There are no prison walls thick enough to hold the longing of my people for freedom,' he said. 'There is no grave deep enough to keep the truth from you.'

He spoke for ten minutes and Kitty Godolphin who was old in experience and hardened in the ways of a naughty world was weeping unashamedly as he ended, 'The struggle is my life. The battle belongs to us. We will prevail, my people. *Amandla! Ngawethu!*'

Kitty went to him and embraced him. 'You make me feel very humble,' she said.

'You are a friend,' he replied. 'Go in peace, my daughter.'

'Come.' Raleigh Tabaka took Kitty's arm and led her away. 'You have stayed too long already. You must leave now. This man's name is Robert. He will lead you.'

Robert was waiting at the kitchen door of the cottage.

'Follow me,' he ordered, and led them across the bare dusty backyard, through the shadows to the corner of the road. There he stopped unexpectedly.

'What happens now?' Kitty asked in a whisper. 'Why are we waiting here?'

'Be patient,' Robert said. 'You will learn the reason soon.'

Suddenly Kitty was aware that they were not alone. There were others waiting like them in the shadows. She could hear them now, the murmur of voices, quiet but expectant. She could see them as her eyes adjusted to the night, many figures, in small groups, huddled beside the hedges or in the shelter of the buildings.

Dozens, no hundreds of people, men and women, and every

moment their numbers increased as more came out of the night shadows, gathering round the cottage that contained Moses Gama, as though his presence was a beacon, a flame that, like moths, they could not resist.

'What is happening?' Kitty asked softly.

'You will see,' Robert replied. 'Have your camera ready.'

The people were beginning to leave the shadows, creeping closer to the cottage, and a voice called out

'*Baba!* Your children are here. Speak to us, Father.'

And another cried. 'Moses Gama, we are ready. Lead us!'

And then they began to sing, softly at first, '*Nkosi Sikelel' iAfrika* – God save Africa!' and the voices joined and began to harmonize, those beautiful African voices, thrilling and wonderful.

Then there was another sound, distant at first, but swiftly growing closer, the sobbing undulating wail of police sirens.

'Have your camera ready,' said Robert again.

*   *   *

As soon as the American woman and her cameraman had left the cottage, Moses Gama began to rise from the table.

'It is done,' he said. 'Now we can leave.'

'Not yet, my uncle,' Raleigh Tabaka stopped him. 'There is something else that we must do first.'

'It is dangerous to delay,' Moses insisted. 'We have been in this place too long. The police have informers everywhere.'

'Yes, my uncle. The police informers are everywhere.' Raleigh put a peculiar emphasis on his agreement. 'But before you go on to the place where the police cannot touch you, we must talk.'

Raleigh came to stand at the front of the table facing his uncle.

'This was planned with great care. This afternoon the white monster Verwoerd was assassinated in the racist parliament.'

Moses started. 'You did not tell me this,' he protested, but Raleigh went on quietly.

'The plan was that in the confusion after Verwoerd's assassination you would emerge to lead a spontaneous rising of our people.'

'Why was I not told of this?' Moses asked fiercely.

'Patience, my uncle. Hear me out. The men who planned this are from a cold bleak land in the north, they do not understand the African soul. They do not understand that our people will not rise until their mood is ready, until their rage is ripe. That time is not yet. It will take many more years of patient work to bring their rage to full fruit. Only then can we gather the harvest. The white police are still too strong. They would crush us by raising their little finger and

618

the world would stand by and watch us die as they watched the rebellion in Hungary die.'

'I do not understand,' Moses said. 'Why have you gone this far if you did not intend to travel to the end of the road?'

'The revolution needs martyrs as well as leaders. The mood and temper of the world must be roused, for without them we can never succeed. Martyrs and leaders, my uncle.'

'I am the chosen leader of our people,' Moses Gama said simply.

'No, my uncle.' Raleigh shook his head. 'You have proved unworthy. You have sold out your people. In exchange for your life, you delivered the revolution into the hands of the enemy. You gave Nelson Mandela and the heroes of Rivonia to the foe. Once I believed you were a god, but now I know that you are a traitor.'

Moses Gama stared at him silently.

'I am glad you do not deny this, my uncle. Your guilt is proven beyond any doubt. By your action you have forfeited any claim to the leadership. Nelson Mandela alone has the greatness for that role. However, my uncle, the revolution needs martyrs.'

From the pocket of his jacket Raleigh Tabaka took something wrapped in a clean white cloth. He laid it on the table. Slowly he opened the bundle, taking care not to touch what it contained.

They both stared at the revolver.

'This pistol is police issue. Only hours ago it was stolen from a local police arsenal. The serial number is still on the police register. It is loaded with police-issue ammunition.'

Raleigh folded the cloth around the grip of the pistol. 'It still has the fingerprints of the police officers upon it,' he said.

Carrying the pistol he went round the table to stand behind Moses Gama's chair and placed the muzzle of the pistol at the back of his neck.

From outside the cottage they heard the singing begin.

'God save Africa.' Raleigh repeated the words. 'You are fortunate, my uncle. You have a chance to redeem yourself. You are going to a place where nobody can ever touch you again, and your name will live for ever, pure and unsullied. "The great martyr of Africa who died for his people."'

Moses Gama did not move or speak, and Raleigh went on softly, 'The people have been told you are here. They are gathered outside in their hundreds. They will bear witness to your greatness. Your name will live for ever.'

Then above the singing they heard the police sirens coming closer, wailing and sobbing.

'The brutal fascist police have also been told that you are here,' Raleigh said softly.

The sound of the sirens built up and then there were the roar of engines, the squeal of brakes, the slamming of Land-Rover doors, the shouted commands, the pounding footsteps, and the crash of the front door being smashed in with sledgehammers.

As Brigadier Lothar De La Rey led his men in through the front door of the cottage, Raleigh Tabaka said softly, 'Go in peace, my uncle,' and he shot Moses Gama in the back of the head.

The heavy bullet threw Moses forward, his shattered head slammed face down upon the table, the contents of his skull and chips of white bone splattered against the wall and over the kitchen floor.

Raleigh dropped the police pistol onto the table and slipped out into the dark yard. He joined the watching throng in the street outside, mingling with them, waiting with them until the covered body was carried out of the front door of the cottage on a stretcher. Then he shouted in a strong clear voice, 'The police have murdered our leader. They have killed Moses Gama.'

As the cry was taken up by a hundred other voices, and the women began the haunting ululation of mourning, Raleigh Tabaka turned and walked away into the darkness.

* * *

A servant opened the front door of Weltevreden to Manfred De La Rey.

'The master is expecting you,' he said respectfully. 'Please come with me.'

He led Manfred to the gun room and closed the double mahogany doors behind him.

Manfred stood on the threshold. There was a log fire burning in the hearth of the stone fireplace and Shasa Courtney stood before it. He was wearing a dinner-jacket and black tie and a new black silk patch over his eye. He was tall and debonair with silver wings of hair at his temples, but his expression was merciless.

Centaine Courtney sat at the desk below the gun racks. She also wore evening dress, a brocaded Chinese silk in her favourite shade of yellow with a necklace of magnificent yellow diamonds from the H'ani Mine. Her arms and shoulders were bare and in the muted light her skin seemed flawless and smooth as a young girl's.

'White Sword,' Shasa greeted him softly.

'*Ja*,' Manfred nodded. 'But that was long ago – in another war.'

'You killed an innocent man. A noble old man.'

'The bullet was intended for another – for a traitor, an Afrikaner who had delivered his people to the British yoke.'

'You were a terrorist then, as Gama and Mandela are terrorists

620

now. Why should your punishment be any different from theirs?'

'Our cause was just – and God was on our side,' Manfred replied.

'How many innocents have died for what other men call "just causes"? How many atrocities have been committed in God's name?'

'You cannot provoke me.' Manfred shook his head. 'What I attempted was right and proper.'

'We shall see whether or not the courts of this land agree with you,' Shasa said, and looked across the room to Centaine. 'Please ring the number on the pad in front of you, Mater. Ask for Colonel Bothma of CID. I have already asked him to be available to come here.'

Centaine made no move, and her expression, as she studied Manfred De La Rey, was tragic.

'Please do it, Mater,' Shasa insisted.

'No,' Manfred intervened. 'She cannot do it – and nor can you.'

'Why do you believe that?'

'Tell him, Mother,' said Manfred.

Shasa frowned quickly and angrily, but Centaine held up her hand to stop him speaking.

'It is true,' she whispered. 'Manfred is as much my son as you are, Shasa. I gave birth to him in the desert. Although his father took him still wet and blind from my child bed, although I did not see him again for almost thirteen years, he is still my son.'

In the silence one of the logs in the fireplace fell in a soft shower of ash and it sounded like an avalanche.

'Your grandfather has been dead for twenty years and more, Shasa. Do you want to break my heart by sending your brother to the gallows?'

'My duty – my honour,' Shasa faltered.

'Manfred was as merciful once. He had it in his power to destroy your political career before it began. At my request and in the knowledge that you were brothers, he spared you.' Centaine was speaking softly, but remorselessly. 'Can you do less?'

'But – he is only your bastard,' Shasa blurted.

'You are my bastard also, Shasa. Your father was killed on our wedding day, before the ceremony. That was the fact that Manfred could have used to destroy you. He had you in his power – as he is now in your power. What will you do, Shasa?'

Shasa turned away from her, and stood with his head bowed staring into the fireplace. When he spoke at last, his voice was racked with pain.

'The friendship – the brotherhood even – all of it is an illusion,' he said. 'It is you, Mater, whom I must honour.'

No one replied to him, and he turned back to Manfred.

'You will inform the caucus of the National Party that you are not available for the premiership and you will retire from public life,' he said quietly, and saw Manfred flinch and the ruination of his dreams in the agony of his expression. 'That is the only punishment I can inflict upon you, but perhaps it is more painful and lingering than the gallows. Do you accept it?'

'You are destroying yourself at the same time,' Manfred told him. 'Without me the presidency is beyond your grasp.'

'That is my punishment,' Shasa agreed. 'I accept it. Do you accept yours?'

'I accept,' said Manfred De La Rey. He turned to the double mahogany doors, flung them open and strode from the room.

Shasa stared after him. Only when they heard his car pull away down the long driveway did he turn back to Centaine. She was weeping as she had wept on the day that he brought her the news of Blaine Malcomess' death.

'My son,' she whispered. 'My sons.' And he went to comfort her.

*   *   *

A week after the death of Dr Hendrik Verwoerd, the caucus of the National Party elected Balthazar Johannes Vorster to the premiership of South Africa.

He owed his elevation to the awe-inspiring reputation that he had built for himself while he was minister of justice. He was a strong man in the mould of his predecessor and in his acceptance speech he stated boldly, 'My role is to walk fearlessly along the road already pointed out by Hendrik Verwoerd.'

Three days after his election he sent for Shasa Courtney.

'I wanted personally to thank you for your hard work and loyalty over the years, but now I think it is time for you to take a well-earned rest. I would like you to go as the South African ambassador to the Court of St James in London. I know that with you there South Africa House will be in good hands.'

It was the classic dismissal, but Shasa knew that the golden rule for politicians is never to refuse office.

'Thank you, Prime Minister,' he replied.

*   *   *

Thirty thousand mourners attended the funeral of Moses Gama in Drake's Farm township.

Raleigh Tabaka organized the funeral and was the captain of the honour guard of *Umkhonto we Sizwe* that stood at the graveside and gave the ANC salute as the coffin was lowered into the earth.

Vicky Dinizulu Gama, dressed in her flowing caftan of yellow and green and black, defied her banning order to make a speech to the mourners.

Fierce and strikingly beautiful, she told them, 'We must devise a death for the collaborators and sell-outs, that is so grotesquely horrible that not one of our people will ever dare to turn traitor upon us.'

The sorrow of the multitudes was so terrible that when a young woman amongst them was pointed out as a police informer, they stripped her naked and whipped and beat her until she fell unconscious. Then they doused her with petrol and set her alight and kicked her while she burned. Afterwards the children urinated on her charred corpse. The police dispersed the mourners with tear gas and baton-charges.

Kitty Godolphin filmed it all, and when the footage was cut in with the Moses Gama interview and the graphic footage from the scene of his brutal slaying by the police, it was amongst the most gripping and horrifying ever shown on American television.

When Kitty Godolphin was promoted to head of NABS news, she became the highest-paid female editor in American television.

*   *   *

Before taking up his post as ambassador in London, Shasa went on a four-week safari in the Zambezi valley with his eldest son. The Courtney Safaris hunting concession covered five hundred square miles of wonderful game-rich wilderness, and Matatu led Shasa to lion and buffalo and a magnificent old bull elephant.

The Rhodesian bush war was becoming deadly earnest. Sean had been awarded the Silver Cross of Rhodesia for gallantry and around the camp fire he described how he had won it.

'Matatu and I were following a big bull jumbo when we cut the spoor of twelve ZANU gooks. We dropped the jumbo and tracked the terrs. It was pissing with rain and the cloud was on the treetops so the fire force couldn't get in to back us up. The terrs were getting close to the Zambezi so we pushed up on them. The first warning we had that they had set an ambush for us was when we saw the fairy lights in the grass just ahead of us.

'Matatu was leading and he took the first burst in the belly. That made me fairly bitter and I went after the gooks with the old .577. It was five miles to the river and they ran like the clappers of hell, but I polished off the last two in the water before they could reach the Zambian side. When I turned around, there was Matatu standing right behind me. The little bugger had backed me up for five miles with his tripes hanging out of the hole in his guts.'

Across the camp fire the little Ndorobo's face had brightened as he heard his name mentioned, and Sean told him in Swahili, 'Show the *Bwana Makuba* your new belly button.'

Obligingly Matatu hoisted his tattered shirt tails and displayed for Shasa the fearsome scars the AK 47 bullets had left on his stomach.

'You are a stupid little bugger,' Sean told him severely, 'running around with a hole in your guts, instead of lying down and dying like you should have. You are bloody stupid, Matatu.'

Matatu's whole body wriggled with pleasure. 'Bleddy stupid bugger,' he agreed proudly. He knew that this was the highest accolade to which he could possibly aspire, uttered as it was by the godhead of his entire firmament.

*　　*　　*

While Shasa was still packing his books and paintings for the journey to London, Garry and Holly moved into Weltevreden.

'I'll be over there for at least three years,' Shasa said. 'And when I come back we can talk again, but I shall probably get myself a flat in town. On my own the old place is just too big for me.'

Holly was pregnant, and prevailed on Centaine to stay on to help her 'just until the baby is born'.

'Holly is the only woman that Mater can stand within half a mile of her on a permanent basis,' Shasa remarked to Garry as the two ladies of Weltevreden began planning the redecoration of the nursery wing together.

*　　*　　*

Isabella's love affair with Lothar De La Rey survived in stormy seas and wild winds during the months of the enquiry into the death of Moses Gama.

The commission of enquiry exonerated Brigadier Lothar De La Rey with a verdict of 'No Guilt'. The local English-language as well as the international press jeered cynically at this verdict and an emergency meeting of the General Assembly of the United Nations passed a resolution calling for comprehensive mandatory sanctions on South Africa, which was predictably vetoed in the Security Council. However, amongst his own people, Lothar's reputation was greatly enhanced and the Afrikaans press lauded him as its chosen hero.

Not a week after the commission made its findings public, Isabella woke in the bedroom of her luxurious Sandton flat to find Lothar

624

already fully dressed, standing over the bed and watching her with an expression of such deep regret that she sat up quickly, fully awake, and let the pink satin sheets fall to her waist.

'What is it, Lothie?' she cried. 'Why are you leaving so early? Why are you looking at me like that?'

'There will be a by-election in the Doornberg constituency. It's one of our safe seats. The party organizers have offered it to me, and I have accepted. I'm resigning my police commission and going into politics.'

'Oh, that's wonderful,' Isabella cried, and reached out to him with both arms. 'I was reared on politics. We will make a great team, Lothie. I'll be an amazing help to you – you'll see!'

Lothar lifted his eyes from her naked breasts, but made no move to touch her, and she let her arms drop.

'What is it?' Her expression changed.

'I'm going back to my own people, Bella,' he said quietly. 'Back to my *Volk* and my God. I know what I want. I want one day to succeed where my father failed. I want the position he almost achieved, but I need a wife who is one of my own people. A good Afrikaner girl. I have already chosen her. I am going to her now. So we must say goodbye, Bella. Thank you. I will never forget you, but it is over now.'

'Get out,' she said. 'Get out – and don't come back.'

He hesitated and her voice rose to a scream, 'Get out, you bastard. Get out!'

He went to the bedroom door and closed it softly behind him, and Isabella snatched the water jug from the bedside table and hurled it at the door. It shattered and she threw herself face down on the bed and began to weep.

She cried all that day, and at nightfall went into the bathroom and filled the bath with hot water. Lothar had left a packet of razor blades on the shelf next to her douche bag, and she unwrapped one of them slowly and held it up in front of her eyes. It looked terrifyingly evil, and the light glinted on the edge, but she lowered it until it touched the skin of her wrist. It stung like a scorpion and she jerked her wrist away.

'No, Lothar De La Rey, I won't give you the satisfaction,' she said angrily, and dropped the blade into the toilet bowl and went back into the bedroom. She picked up the phone.

When she heard her father's voice, Isabella trembled with the shock of what she had almost done.

'I want to come home, Daddy,' she whispered.

'I'll send the jet for you,' Shasa said without hesitation. 'No, hell, I'll fly up to fetch you myself.'

She was waiting on the tarmac and she ran into his arms. Half-way back to Cape Town he touched her cheek and said, 'I'll need an

625

official hostess at "Highveld".' That was the ambassador's residence in London. 'I'm even prepared to renegotiate your salary.'

'Oh Daddy,' she said. 'Why aren't all the men in the world like you!'

*　　*　　*

Jakobus Stander was hanged in the Pretoria Central prison. Sarah Stander and her husband were waiting outside when the death notice was posted on the main gates of the prison.

The night that they returned to the cottage in Stellenbosch Sarah rose once Roelf was asleep and in the bathroom she took a massive overdose of barbiturates.

She was dead in the bed beside him when Roelf Stander woke the following morning.

*　　*　　*

Manfred and Heidi went to live on their farm in the Free State where Manfred raised pedigree merino sheep.

At the agricultural show in Bloemfontein Manfred won a blue ribbon for the champion ram on show three years in succession.

Always fleshy, Manfred put on a great deal of weight, eating out of boredom more than appetite. Only Heidi knew how he chaffed at inactivity, how much he longed to walk once again the corridors of power, and how pointless and frustrating he felt his existence had become.

He suffered his heart attack while wandering alone in the veld and shepherds found his body the next morning lying where he had fallen. Centaine flew up in the company jet to his funeral. She was the only member of the Courtney family present when Manfred was buried with full honours in Heroes Acre, surrounded by the graves of many other outstanding Afrikaners, including Dr Hendrik Verwoerd.

*　　*　　*

When Shasa Courtney was driven back from Buckingham Palace in the ambassadorial limousine after presenting his credentials to Her Majesty Queen Elizabeth II, the streets were wet with the grey London drizzle.

Despite the weather, the demonstrators were waiting for him in Trafalgar Square with their placards: 'The spirit of Moses Gama lives on' and '*Apartheid* is a crime against humanity.'

As Shasa alighted from the limousine in front of the embassy, the

626

demonstrators tried to push forward, but a line of blue-uniformed London bobbies linked arms to hold them back.

'Shasa Courtney!' Half-way across the sidewalk Shasa stopped dead in his tracks at the familiar voice, and he looked around.

He did not recognize her at first, then he saw her in the front rank of the demonstration and he turned back. He struck a tall elegant figure in his court dress and top hat. He stopped in front of her and spoke to one of the constables.

'Thank you, officer, but I know this lady, you may let her through.' Then, as she ducked under the constable's outstretched arm, he greeted her, 'Hello, Tara.'

He found it difficult to believe how she had changed. She was a blowsy middle-aged drab, only her eyes were still beautiful as they blazed at him.

'Moses Gama lives on. The monsters of *apartheid* can murder our heroes, but the battle is ours. In the end we will inherit the earth.' Her voice was a screech.

'Yes, Tara,' he replied. 'There are heroes and there are monsters, but most of us are ordinary mortals caught up in events too turbulent for any of us. Perhaps when the battle is over, all we will inherit will be the ashes of a once beautiful land.'

He turned away from her and walked into the entrance of the embassy without looking back.

Author's Note

Once again I have taken some small liberties with the timetables of history, in particular the dates on which the *Umkhonto we Sizwe* and *Poqo* movements began, Nelson Mandela was acquitted in his first treason trial, and Harold Macmillan made his 'Winds of Change' speech.

I hope that you, the reader, will forgive me for the sake of the narrative.

Wilbur Smith

The Courtney Novels:

WHEN THE LION FEEDS

'Mr Smith is a natural story-teller . . .'
(*The Scotsman*)

THE SOUND OF THUNDER

'A violent sage-type story set in Boer War Africa and told with vigour and enthusiasm.'
(*The London Standard*)

A SPARROW FALLS

'He packs humanity into a bag already overflowing with adventure, excitement, and realism.'
(*Yorkshire Post*)

THE BURNING SHORE

'. . . Courage, drama, love and revenge on land, sea and in the air towards the end of the first world war are blended in fine style. Mr Smith's research into events and places is spot-on, as usual.'
(*Bolton Evening News*)

POWER OF THE SWORD

'. . . A stupendous story, written in the grand old manner, from the master of thoroughgoing adventure.'
(David Hughes, *The Mail on Sunday*)

The Ballantyne Novels:

A FALCON FLIES

'There is throughout *Falcon Flies* a genuine sense of excitement and wonder.' (*Sunday Telegraph*)

MEN OF MEN

'A splendid read.' (*Financial Times*)

THE ANGELS WEEP

'. . . action, adventure and romance . . .' (*Yorkshire Post*)

THE LEOPARD HUNTS IN DARKNESS

'. . . big, bold and bloody' (*The Scotsman*)

Also by Wilbur Smith:

THE DARK OF THE SUN

'If the phrase "a man's book" has any meaning, it describes this powerful savage story.'
(*Books & Bookmen*)

SHOUT AT THE DEVIL

'A fast and thrilling adventure.'   (*Northern Echo*)

GOLD MINE

'. . . violent action and informed technical detail . . . Mr Smith is at his liveliest and best.'
(*The London Standard*)

THE DIAMOND HUNTERS

'A gem of a suspense/adventure novel.'   (*Mirror*)

THE SUNBIRD

'A splendid panoramic piece of writing, with colourful characters woven into an enthralling plot.'
(*Oxford Times*)

EAGLE IN THE SKY

'Wilbur Smith . . . rarely misses a trick . . . Terribly competent.'   (*Sunday Times*)

THE EYE OF THE TIGER

'... Supreme professionalism, vividness, and attention to detail.'

(Sunday Express)

CRY WOLF

'A rattling good adventure yarn ...'

(The London Standard)

HUNGRY AS THE SEA

'Hardly time to draw a breath. You can see at once why this is a bestseller.'

(The London Standard)

WILD JUSTICE

'... a gold-plated guarantee of pace, tension, and a thoroughly satisfying plot.'

(Morning Telegraph)